ROGUE ELEMENT

He seemed to hear all the noises at once. The smash of the hammerhead and the splintering of wood, the tinkling of shattered glass and the thud of heavy boots. They intruded rudely into the velvet nothingness of his sleep, a distant alarm bell deep within him starting to ring out urgently. He ignored it, rolled over, snuggling against the warmth of Evie's back. That was over, his life as a soldier in the African bush all finished. Even in the restless twilight between sleep and wakefulness, he reminded himself that his days of perpetual danger were over. Go back to sleep . . .

The bedroom door exploded under the impact.

Terence Strong is a freelance journalist and writer. He has a keen interest in international politics and military affairs and special forces in particular. This specialist knowledge has been used extensively in his bestselling thrillers which include *Whisper Who Dares*, *The Tick Tock Man*, and *White Viper*. His latest novel, *Deadwater Deep*, is also published in Arrow.

Also by Terence Strong

Whisper Who Dares
The Fifth Hostage
Conflict of Lions
Dragonplague
That Last Mountain
Sons of Heaven
This Angry Land
Stalking Horse
The Tick Tock Man
White Viper
Deadwater Deep

The Terence Strong web page is at:

http://www.totalweb.co.uk/tangled web/authors/tstrong.html

ROGUE ELEMENT

Terence Strong

ARROW

Published in the United Kingdom in 1998 by
Arrow Books

3 5 7 9 10 8 6 4 2

Copyright © Terence Strong 1997

The right of Terence Strong to be identified as the author
of this work has been asserted by him in accordance
with the Copyright, Designs and Patents Act, 1988

First published in the United Kingdom in 1997 by William Heinemann

Arrow Books
The Random House Group Limited
20 Vauxhall Bridge Road, London SW1V 2SA

Random House Australia (Pty) Limited
20 Alfred Street, Milsons Point, Sydney
New South Wales 2061, Australia

Random House New Zealand Limited
18 Poland Road, Glenfield
Auckland 10, New Zealand

Random House South Africa (Pty) Limited
Endulini, 5a Jubilee Road, Parktown 2193, South Africa

The Random House Group Limited Reg. No. 954009

www.randomhouse.co.uk

A CIP catalogue record for this book
is available from the British Library

Papers used by Random House are natural, recyclable
products made from wood grown in sustainable forests. The
manufacturing processes conform to the environmental
regulations of the country of origin.

Phototypeset by Intype London Ltd
Printed and bound in the United Kingdom by
Cox & Wyman Ltd, Reading, Berks

ISBN 0 7493 2159 8

For Princess
with love

Author's Note

The background to this fictional story includes part of Northern Ireland's secret history that has never been previously revealed.

It was written in response to the increasingly common policy of betrayal and abandonment by government agencies of those who have loyally served the Crown, sometimes at great personal risk.

A raft of examples have come to light in recent years, ranging from those involved in the murky clandestine war in Ulster to company directors doing business with pariah regimes around the world with the connivance and encouragement of intelligence agencies.

Yet when such operations come unstuck, as inevitably some do, instead of being protected, co-opted civilian helpers have been thrown to the wolves – left to carry the can whilst those ultimately responsible remain answerable to no one. And it has all been done with transparent deceit or with the breath-taking pomposity and arrogance of government agencies and ministers who consider themselves beyond the law.

Defence of the realm is one thing, but whose narrow realm of self-interest are we talking about?

Despite recent window-dressing, the intelligence agencies remain largely unaccountable. They would argue, probably rightly, that they cannot operate effectively any other way. But as every adult in the real world knows, the price demanded of individuals in a free society is a sense of personal honour, self-discipline and responsibility. And the awesome freedom afforded the security services demands those qualities in equally awesome measure.

Issuing gagging orders and otherwise preventing innocent parties from defending themselves in law hardly squares with this. Society without honour and responsibility is anarchy. So what happens when such anarchy is allowed to run unchecked by those who rule society?

In the interests of authenticity, the background and chronological details of some characters in this book have been inspired by real people. However, my creations are purely fictional and their personalities and activities subject to wide-ranging artistic licence in the weaving of the tale. Therefore, it would be totally incorrect to assume any reliable or meaningful connection between my characters and real people or their activities and actions, either in the past or in the future. Try to, and you'd be wrong.

That said, it is primarily a story of action and legal drama to be enjoyed. In the process, it may enlighten the reader to what has been done in his or her name. Only you can decide whether or not that meets with your approval.

Terence Strong
London 1997

Many friends, acquaintances and contacts in Northern Ireland have made it possible to piece together the fascinating facts within this story. Sadly, it would be unwise to name them here. But they know who they are, and the debt of thanks I owe them.

Obviously the fictional organisations I have mentioned should not be taken to imply any association whatsoever with genuine commercial businesses of the same or similar names.

Less controversially, I must thank my personal 'legal' team of solicitor Bill Webb of Sherwood Wheatley (Kingston), who now packs a tablecloth in his briefcase, and barrister Christopher Sutton-Mattocks for so enthusiastically agreeing to 'take on my case' despite their already heavy workloads. Any technical errors that remain are down to me alone. No doubt, neither Bill nor Chris will thank PR diva Beth Macdougall of MCA for having introduced me, so I will do that with pleasure. Likewise senior clerk at chambers, Robin Driscoll, for making me feel like one of the family.

Additionally, I am indebted to Michael Mansfield QC for his words of wisdom and the wealth of thought-provoking material within his book Presumed Guilty (Mandarin, 1994); Gerald James, who has been through it all, and the stunningly creative songwriting duo, Rozi and Rob Morris, for kindly allowing me to borrow lyrics from one of their songs, 'Colours', and use them in a very different context.

Staffordshire owes as much gratitude as I do to my dear friend Pat Hudson of GEC Alstrom for selling me on Cannock Chase. Prison Governor Richard Feeney helped immensely and took my descriptions on the chin with good humour; Officer Dave Hoskins was my cheerful and patient guide and Mark ('Better luck in the future, mate'), Gary and Trev told me the other side of the coin.

Head Ranger of Cannock Chase, John Quigley, will never forgive me for being inaccurately immortalised within these pages, while my kind guide to this relatively little-known wildlife haven, Mick Payne, escapes unscathed. Meanwhile my manhunt and dragnet over their territory was kindly orchestrated by Chief Superintendent Ray Woolridge (Retd) and Detective Superintendent Alec Salt.

Old friends Neil and John Carter came up trumps again with their contributions, as has my tireless typist Judy Coombes.

And a very personal note of thanks goes to two charming ladies, one who lent her name and the other a celebrity actress who unwittingly inspired the character of Sam Browne.

Prologue

'So tell me,' she said.

He was standing at the window, holding the yellowing net curtain to one side, staring out at the warm, wet night. It had grown dark while they'd talked and now the soft August rain fell like sparkling grains of amber around the sodium streetlight.

Just like that, he thought, tell me. As if it was that goddamn easy. If it were that simple he'd have told them months ago. Chosen any one of the tabloid hacks who were trying to track him down, cheque-books out and pens poised. Name your price, Roddy Littlechild, just name it.

Perhaps he should have done. Taken the money and run. Let them splash their grotesque headlines between the bingo promotion and a picture of some semi-naked model. Let them run to a three-page spread, picking the juicy bits from his story, making up the parts he had deliberately left out, barely bothering to check the facts. Not that such facts were easily checked. No one would ever admit to anything.

But he hadn't wanted that. If it was going to be told at all, he wanted it at least to be accurate. The cold hard truth.

She spoke again, her voice now edged with impatience. 'It's gone ten, Roddy. I've got to get home.'

'Sure,' he said, dropping the curtain and turning to face back into the kitchenette of the seedy little flat.

Lisa Hardcastle. Well-named. Hard-nosed, hard bitch, he thought. Pushy, thirtysomething director on the *Fifth Amendment* series for Channel Four. Working for Double Vision Productions, freelance documentary makers who appreciated her impeccable left-wing credentials. Journalistic teeth cut on the *New Statesman* and the *Guardian*, she was desperate for recognition and a media award before plunging into belated motherhood.

His face was in shadow so she couldn't see how he glared at

her, sitting there in her Levi jeans and jacket, her long marma-
lade hair a frizzed mess. All carrot cake, non-fat yoghurts and
spritzers, he thought unkindly. She was not happy with the glass
of cheap Tesco plonk he'd poured her. He lit a cigarette and
could sense rather than see her recoil at the spiral of grey smoke
drifting in her direction.

Unfair, Littlechild chided himself. She was just doing her job
and he knew he wasn't making it any easier for her.

And she had good reason to be annoyed. He had dragged
her out here, to his temporary home in Southall, the dowdy
western suburb of London. His bolt hole, his sanctuary. To talk,
while his wife of two years worked the wine-bar shift, because
he didn't want Evie to witness this. Didn't want her to see his
act of betrayal. Because that was what it felt like.

He said: 'What do you want to know?' His Ulster accent had
long since been softened by an easy South African drawl that
wasn't unattractive to the ear.

Lisa sighed, tapping her pencil on the blank sheet of her
notepad. 'This is what – our third meeting? And for the past two
hours you've been chuntering on. Bits and pieces. Nothing
coherent.'

He drew himself up to his full height, several inches over six
feet. 'I can't give you details until we've agreed the money,' he
said.

Money. Christ, that sounded awful, not like him at all. But
that's how it was now, how it had to be, and they'd driven him
to it.

'Chicken and egg,' Lisa replied with quiet exasperation. 'I've
sold my producer on the general idea. He's taken soundings and
the reaction was positive. *Panorama* and *World in Action* want
you, not to mention several of the broadsheets. There's quite a
buzz in the office that this could be big. We might even kick off
the new series with you.'

Fifth Amendment – allowing the famous and infamous to give
their version of negatively reported events, to defend themselves against unpopular public opinion on a platform free from
rival bias. The opportunity to put records straight.

'So how much?' he asked.

'Say a grand per big shock horror revelation,' she replied, allowing it to sound like an auction for scandal. She smiled tightly and her voice was low as she added: 'I'm sorry, Roddy, but that's the bottom line. So tell me, when you were working for the South Africans in the late 1980s, *did* you help sell arms to Protestant Loyalists in Ulster?'

'NO,' he replied emphatically. 'That's the whole point.'

She leaned back in her chair. 'So what *is* the point? What *are* the exclusive, earth-shattering revelations I can tell my bosses to expect?'

Littlechild lit a fresh cigarette from the stub of the last. Security lamps from the car-breaker's yard opposite sent elongated shadows across the room, casting Lisa Hardcastle into darkness. He felt safer in the gloom, more secure. And the muted sound of traffic beyond the grimy glass of the window created a sense of forced, airless intimacy.

At last he said: 'You can tell your boss two things. But no details, not yet. Not until we've agreed figures and a contract's been signed. Okay?'

He was aware of her nodding, saw the glistening whites of her eyes, wide and intent in the deep shadow and thought how little she knew. Even this supposedly tough and cynical journalist was really just like the rest of them, taking everything at face value.

But then he realised he couldn't blame her for not understanding. It had all begun so long ago, over twenty years. A generation. Lisa Hardcastle would have been in the fifth form, all ponytail and navy schoolgirl knickers, into Pink Floyd and maybe just attended her first CND rally.

Twenty years, he thought. How the time had flown, because to him it seemed like only yesterday.

Patiently he said: 'I doubt you remember 1969 and the Catholic civil rights marches. Protesting against discrimination in jobs and housing. Against gerrymandering by the Unionists, and the brutality of the old B Specials. It wasn't a record for Britain to be proud of, the politicians had ignored the province for too long. Some people had a rough deal before the government sent in the troops to stop Protestant mobs firebombing Catholics out of their homes.'

Lisa nodded. 'I've done my homework, Roddy, believe me.'

'Well, there's something your homework won't have told you. At that time, the Dublin Government was seriously contemplating a military incursion into the North.'

That stunned her; he heard her sharp intake of breath. 'Intervention? You're not serious?'

'They certainly were.' He moved across to the cheap kitchen cabinet and opened one of the sliding plastic doors, extracting two tumblers and a half-empty bottle of Bushmills. Perhaps she'd prefer this; he certainly felt the need of something stronger. 'The plan was to seize key installations and protect the Catholic enclaves. They'd gamble that the British Government wouldn't want the embarrassment of a fight. Dublin would risk an odd skirmish, knowing full well that the UN or the Americans would step in to mediate and that Britain would be forced out in the end. You have to remember the uncertainty of those times. Nightly riots, burning barricades, entire fleets of buses hijacked and torched, shootings and bombings. And all on the streets of British towns. Imagine those things happening on the mainland, in Glasgow or Cardiff – but with the additional threat of intervention by an adjoining foreign country. Thousands of Irish troops assembled on the border on the pretext of setting up first-aid stations for Catholic refugees from Ulster.'

She accepted the offered glass, aware that her hand had developed a slight tremor. 'Would you mind if we had the light on? This is spooky enough as it is.' As he obliged, she asked: 'So why didn't the Irish Army intervene?'

He shrugged. 'I don't know. But anyway, wiser counsels prevailed, probably when British troop reinforcements arrived from the mainland. But that incursion option has never been removed from the Dublin agenda. That threat has not gone away.'

She pulled a face, clearly not believing.

Littlechild said: 'The Irish Army has a fully prepared battle plan and they've rehearsed it regularly on at least two occasions in the past ten years. Their last exercise was Operation Autumn

4

Gold and that was mounted just prior to the Downing Street Declaration which triggered the current peace process.'

'But that was only – what? – two years ago. I can hardly believe it.'

'It was a way of putting extra pressure on the Major Government to co-operate. Dublin dressed the troop movements up as a hunt for Provo arms caches along the Irish border, but that didn't fool anyone in the know. You don't need armoured cars and artillery for a weapons search.'

'Did they find any?'

'What?'

'Weapons.'

'What do you think?'

Lisa looked up at him, unblinking. 'Don't fuck with me, Roddy. This is dangerous stuff you're saying.'

'Don't I know it, lady. That's why we're talking.' He knew he should have eaten something. The Bushmills had hit the mark and his head was starting to swim. His pent-up anger began to swell, filling his brain to bursting.

At that point the telephone rang. The sudden intrusive noise made Lisa Hardcastle jump as it shattered the hushed and secretive atmosphere of the kitchenette. He made no move.

'Aren't you going to . . . ?'

There was a click as the answerphone cut in, then the tape began to whir. 'I always call back nowadays, in case it's someone from the press. I'll see to it later.'

She gave a tightly sympathetic smile. For a moment she felt guilty, sorry for him. Sorry she'd been one of those hounding him, contributing to that haunted look in his eyes. 'What was the other thing?' she asked, squinting down to read her notes. 'You said there were two things you'd tell me now.'

Littlechild swirled the remains of the whiskey round his glass and studied it intently.

'After backing down from the incursion idea at the start of the troubles, Dublin changed tactics. It went for the covert approach. And in 1970 the Provisional IRA was born. The splintering away of the Provos from the Stickies – sorry, that's the old Official IRA – was actively encouraged by the members of the Irish administration.'

'What exactly are you saying, Roddy?'

'I'm telling you it was Dublin that organised, then funded and armed the Provos. They provided a black account and secretly arranged with dealers in Belgium to provide arms and plastic explosive.'

Lisa had recovered from her initial shock. 'This *is* true, Roddy? You're not winding me up – or setting me up?'

'Oh, it's true all right, lady. How else do you suppose those unemployed thickos on the Lower Falls so easily got hold of an arsenal of weapons and became experts in making bombs almost overnight? They were trained by Irish military intelligence at Fortnaree in Donegal.'

'Can you actually prove any of this, Roddy?'

Now she could see his wry smile. 'Ah, proof is it you're after? Well, I doubt such things were ever committed to paper.'

'These accusations have to implicate some important political figures or civil servants of the time.' At least she sounded as though she believed him.

'The problem is knowing who knew what was going on and turned a blind eye.'

'Can anyone corroborate what you're saying?'

He was silent for a moment. 'There was some media coverage at the time, but nothing that showed the true extent of what went on. I've seen documents, though. Not from their side, of course, from ours. Classified stuff. Intelligence reports.'

'You mean MI5?'

'MI5, yes, and MI6 – they operate in the Irish Republic. A foreign land, you see.'

She completely missed the subtle point he was making. That, to him, Dublin represented a sovereign alien state. But Lisa's mind was elsewhere, racing ahead to explore the possibilities and problems of making her documentary. 'You don't have copies of these reports?'

'Of course not.'

'Then it would just be your word.'

'Others have seen them too.'

6

'Who?'

He swallowed hard on the whiskey before answering. 'Several people who've been connected with various Loyalist paramilitaries. And, of course, people in MI5 itself.'

'Retired, you mean?'

He nodded. 'No one currently serving would talk. Nor would ex-members unless it was strictly non-attributable.'

'Can you think of anyone who would talk on camera? You know, back-lit? An anonymous silhouette?' Now she could hardly keep the excitement from her voice.

'I don't know. Some of the paramilitaries might. Many feel cheated by the concessions being made to the Provos in this so-called peace process. Some might be willing to confirm what I've told you.' He knew she was testing him. 'All I know, Lisa, is that both the Loyalists and the British Government were fighting the PIRA terrorists by the only effective methods available to them short of provoking all-out war with the Irish Republic. It's been a messy, dirty battle, but at least it kept the lid on the terrorists for over twenty years.'

'So what part *did* you play in this dirty war, Roddy?'

He took a deep breath. 'I've been working with MI5 since the beginning.'

'You're an agent?'

'I think the term they use is an "alongsider". An agent of sympathy, if you like. Not for money or any reward – just doing my duty to the Crown and helping protect my homeland from those set on destroying it.'

'Very noble.'

'I thought so,' he retorted quietly.

'How exactly did you help, Roddy?'

He sensed he'd already said enough. 'That's for later. When we've agreed a deal. You've enough there to go on.'

'And you never arranged arms shipments to the Loyalists when you were in South Africa?' she pressed.

His anger flared. 'No, dammit. You'll get all that after we've a deal, not before.'

She began gabbling then, clearly excited by what she'd learned. Talking enthusiastically about talking heads and

7

dramatic reconstructions. He smiled politely, but inside he felt like Judas. To Lisa Hardcastle it was all a game. Shock horror revelations to get the TV ratings up.

'I'll get back to you as soon as I can,' Lisa said, picking up her bag. On the dingy landing she hesitated and looked back at the big Ulsterman. 'Thank you for telling me, Roddy, it can't have been easy. What I don't understand is why you've decided to talk now?'

He leaned against the door jamb, feeling strangely relieved the deed was done. 'Because I've got no choice. It's the only way I can clear my name.'

'You mean the rumours?'

He nodded, running a large hand through the thick mass of curled brown hair in a gesture of exasperation. 'They've all but ruined me. Just look at this place! I've no job and I'm forced into hiding with my wife.'

Lisa was puzzled. 'So who do you think is behind these rumours?'

He seemed surprised she didn't realise. 'MI5, of course. Didn't you know?'

She shook her head. 'But you've just told me you've been helping them for over twenty years?'

'Yes, well, that's true enough. But in the end they started putting on me, and I refused to help. That's when they turned nasty.'

'Just because you stopped helping?'

He nodded. 'In their eyes I could no longer be trusted. If I wasn't with them, I must be against them. As far as they were concerned I knew too much, could do too much damage. They wouldn't have minded if I'd stayed abroad, tucked away safely somewhere. But not back here in London in the middle of this peace process.'

'MI5 told you that?'

' "Get out of the country or we'll drive you out." ' He gave a wry smile. 'I've even been head-hunted by a firm in Singapore. A totally unsuitable job I know nothing about, but great pay. I knew who was behind it.'

She was seeing him differently now, glimpsing what lay

8

behind the tense and haunted features. 'So why didn't you take it?'

He stared at her as though she were mad. 'Because this is my country, Lisa. I've come home. This is where I want to live with my wife and raise a family. And if the peace holds, I might even persuade Evie to move to Belfast, maybe one of the quiet suburbs . . .'

Lisa Hardcastle smiled awkwardly. 'Sorry, Roddy. Stupid question.'

When she was gone, he closed the door and returned to the kitchenette. He realised his hands were trembling. Too late now, old son, he told himself. You've done it. He stared at the bottle of Bushmills. He knew it wasn't the answer, but poured another one anyway.

What had he told Lisa Hardcastle before she'd left? All that stuff about going back to Belfast. He drained half his glass in a single gulp. If only. Dream on, old son.

The door opened then. It was Evie. She looked tired as she slipped off her damp raincoat and hung it behind the door. 'Who was that woman I passed on the stairs?'

Littlechild sat down on the threadbare sofa and regarded his wife over the rim of his glass. Thirty-three with pale good looks and fetching in the plain black waitress dress despite the four-month swell of her belly.

He hated lying, especially to Evie. 'That was Lisa Hardcastle.'

'The Channel Four woman? But I thought you'd decided . . .'

'I changed my mind. We can't go on living like this. Look at you, you're all in. It's no life for you and how are we going to manage when the wee one arrives?'

Evie poured herself a small measure of the whiskey, sat down by his side and eased off her shoes. 'You could have told me you were going to see her.'

'It wasn't something I was proud of. I felt like a traitor.'

She gave a short laugh of derision. 'You, a traitor? Ha, that's a good one. You don't owe those people anything. They owe you. If there are any traitors around, it's them. You know how I feel about it. Shout from the rooftops.'

He looked again at his glass, studying it as though some answer lurked within the golden liquid. It was good to have Evie on his side. But still— 'Your brother wouldn't agree. He told me it wasn't a good idea.'

She touched his wrist and gently moved his hand so it rested on the curve of her stomach; it was a comfort to her. 'Chris is very sweet and very concerned about his kid sister. And you, ever since you saved his life that time . . .'

Littlechild shook his head dismissively. 'It was nothing. I only did what any other soldier would do for his oppo.'

'Perhaps. But where you and I are concerned, Chris is hardly impartial. If someone else was in the trouble you're in, I'm sure he'd say to hell with it and tell the media exactly what's been going on.'

But Littlechild wasn't convinced. 'Chris has been in the SAS, right? He's worked with these people – MI5 and the rest. He knows what they're capable of.'

'Yes, darling, but he hasn't had to go through what we're going through. It's not his decision to make. For what it's worth, I think you've done the right thing.'

He grinned at her. She had the knack of always making him believe that everything would be all right, like a mother's healing kiss. That short ash-blonde hair and those baby-blue eyes with their pale lashes that always lifted his spirits when he felt the world crushing down on him. He was so thankful he'd married her two years earlier and wondered why the hell he hadn't asked her fifteen years earlier when they'd first met.

'I love you,' he said.

Her eyes glittered with mischief. 'Let's make love. Here. Now.'

'Aren't you exhausted?'

'Yes.' She patted the large hand that rested on her stomach. 'But we ought to make the most of it while we can. And I think we both need cheering up.' As she placed her glass on the telephone table beside her, she noticed the red light blinking on the answerphone. 'Did you know there was a message?'

'I'd clean forgotten. It rang when that journalist was here.'

Evie pressed the replay button and turned up the volume. A

metallic computerised voice said: '*Message One. Ten-o-five p.m.*' A click, then a pause. '*Hello, Roddy. This is Donny Fitzpatrick. Long time, no see. Did Billy Baker tell you I'd call? No, look, it's okay. No need to be alarmed, but I need to see you urgently. Please ring me back as soon as you get in. It doesn't matter what the time is. Okay?*' He gave his number and the tape clicked off.

Littlechild felt his blood chill. He wasn't aware that his jaw had dropped, wasn't aware that he was staring, unseeing, into space. For a couple of seconds he was aware of nothing in the room.

His head was filled with the image of the wet playground in south-west Belfast. Finaghy Primary. Grey skies and black tarmac. The shriek of children ringing in his ears. Grey flannel shorts, threadbare blazer. Skinny white legs, knees scabbed and grey woollen socks collapsed around his ankles. Conkers. His oncer, soaked in vinegar until it was as hard as stone. Invincible.

Donny Fitzpatrick, the Taig boy from the next street beating him. From the street that he and his Protestant pals never ventured into even then. Smashing his oncer to smithereens. Little Roddy, not feeling the pain where Fitzpatrick's conker had ricocheted and taken the skin off his knuckles. No pain, just shock and crushed pride. To be beaten was bad enough, but to be beaten by a Taig! That was something little Roddy would never tell his father. The stern-faced Presbyterian had warned him enough times not to play with them, not to mix with the Papist scum for fear of his very soul. It was a defeat he would have to suffer in silence.

'Who is he?' Evie asked. 'You look as if you've seen a ghost.'

Her voice came through to him at last. 'What?'

'Donny Fitzpatrick. Who is he?'

Who indeed? Donny Fitzpatrick, the wee Taig boy who had once smashed his prized oncer, had gone on to become Chief of Staff of the Provisional IRA.

'Just someone I used to know. We were at the same school.'

Evie frowned. Since she'd known him she'd learned the Ulster habit of analysing names, to establish whether they had Catholic or Protestant roots. 'Is he connected? Is he IRA?'

'I think so,' he said; knew so, he meant. Couldn't be more

11

connected than being a former Chief of Staff, but he didn't want to worry Evie. And he never told her of the last time they'd met, when the British Government was making one of its spasmodic attempts to put out feelers for peace. His controller at MI5 had remembered Littlechild's schooldays' anecdote and had asked him to front the contact. He'd obliged as he usually did, flying back specially from South Africa. But in the end, the talks had come to nothing.

It had been strange, though, seeing Fitzpatrick again. How he had changed. As a grubby little schoolboy he'd always had a cheeky grin on his face, but now he never smiled. The happy child had grown into a hard and angry man. Yet, for a while they had talked without rancour or bitterness, recalling shared memories of better times, not discussing their differences but remembering all they had in common. A childhood on the streets of Belfast.

'Were you expecting him to call?' Evie asked.

He drained his drink. 'Not really. I had a telephone call from someone I know the other day.'

'Was that the Billy Baker he mentioned?'

Littlechild nodded. 'King Billy. One of the Loyalist gang leaders. Said that he knew Fitzpatrick wanted to contact me, that it would be a good idea for me to meet him. He was smoothing the way. Said there'd be no danger.'

'You didn't mention it.'

'There was no point. Billy was persistent, but I told him I wasn't interested.'

'So Billy Baker's a Loyalist and Fitzpatrick is IRA. At least they're talking to each other, not shooting. Why does he want to meet you?'

He shrugged. 'I've no idea.'

'Did you give this Billy Baker our number here?'

'Certainly not.'

'Then how did he get it?'

'I don't know.' He did, of course. Baker had been playing along with MI5 for some time now; they'd have given it to him. But he didn't want to worry Evie on that score.

'Perhaps you should find out what Fitzpatrick wants.'

Maybe to kill me, Littlechild thought, despite Billy's reassurance. But he didn't say that to his wife, just: 'Perhaps I should.'

'I mean, if Fitzpatrick's got our number he can get our address. It wouldn't be difficult. So it wouldn't hurt to find out what he wants.'

'You want me to?'

She smiled tightly. 'If this Fitzpatrick's IRA, then I'd rather like to know he's not going to be calling round here on the off chance.'

Littlechild nodded. 'He sounded friendly enough.'

'And there is a ceasefire going on,' she thought aloud.

He made his decision. Evie was right. There was a peace of sorts and while he and Fitzpatrick had their political differences, they'd never exactly been sworn enemies. Besides, he was intrigued. He stood and walked to the telephone table and dialled the number, realising for the first time that it was a London exchange.

Almost immediately the receiver was snatched up at the other end. As though Fitzpatrick had been waiting for it to ring.

'Donny?'

'Yeah?'

'Roddy Littlechild.'

'Thank God for that. How y'doing? I was afraid you'd decide not to get back to me. But I'm really glad you have. I need to speak with you.'

'I'm here.'

'Not over the phone. I need to talk face to face. It's very urgent. And in our mutual best interest.'

'Look, I'm out of all that.'

Fitzpatrick sensed him slipping away. 'Please, Roddy, I must speak with you. There's no danger and this is no set up if that's what you're thinking. As you can see, I'm in London.'

Littlechild hesitated. 'How about lunchtime tomorrow, somewhere central?'

'I had more in mind now, tonight. As I said, it's just a wee bit urgent.'

'It's gone ten,' he protested, taken aback.

13

'Look, if you grab a taxi you could be with me in thirty minutes. I'll pay. It won't take long.'

Littlechild looked at Evie as she attempted to follow the one-sided conversation. She shrugged, bemused. He said: 'Okay, Donny, where are you?'

Fitzpatrick told him.

'No,' Littlechild decided. 'If we're going to meet, make it somewhere public.'

Fitzpatrick understood. 'There's a pub around the corner. The Duke's Head, you can't miss it. Do a nice drop of Beamish. If you hurry, we should get a couple in before they close.'

Littlechild hung up. 'This is crazy.'

Evie smiled. 'I can tell you're dying to see him. You're as curious as I am.'

'You don't mind?'

She shook her head. 'Only that we were just about to make mad passionate love, Rodney Littlechild. So you'd better make it up to me tomorrow night. With accumulated interested.'

The rain had eased up slightly which was probably why he'd scarcely stepped onto the pavement when a black cab came along with its hire light on.

He flagged it down and climbed aboard. For the entire twenty-minute journey he stared out of the window, deep in thought and not registering a thing he saw. His mind was else-where, deeply engrossed in what Donny Fitzpatrick could possibly want with him. Despite his and Evie's reassurance to each other that he was in no danger, still he felt unnerved. The war in Ulster might be over, temporarily at least, but there were still plenty of people with old scores to settle. So it didn't do to drop your guard.

'Here's the Duke's Head, chief,' the cabby said.

Littlechild leaned forward in his seat as the illuminated sign approached on their offside. Up ahead he saw another pub, its lighted windows reflecting on the rain-lacquered pavement.

'I've changed my mind,' he said. 'Drive on and drop me on the corner, will you?'

'You're the boss.' The driver changed down and accelerated.

Littlechild noted the call box as they passed, then dug in his pocket for his wallet before the taxi pulled up. He thrust a note through the glass hatch. 'Keep the change.'

Then he was out, moving back along the pavement in the direction from which the taxi had just come, until he reached the call box. Through its rain-streaked glass, he could see the Duke's Head across the street. Dialling 192, he asked for the pub's telephone number, memorised it and entered it into the keypad as soon as the computerised voice had come to an end.

The publican's voice was gruff and disinterested, obviously irritated by the interruption.

'Sorry to trouble you,' Littlechild said, 'but a friend of mine's drinking in your bar – we are due to meet and I can't make it. I wonder if I could have a word.'

A grunt. 'What you think this is? Bloody lonely hearts?'

'I'm really sorry. His name's Fitzpatrick.'

The man didn't answer. For a moment the earpiece was filled with the background noise of pub chatter and the thud of jukebox music. Then Fitzpatrick was on the line. 'Roddy? What is this?'

'A change of plan. Have you got a mobile phone?'

'What? Er – no, I haven't.'

'Good. Then leave immediately. Turn right and you'll find there's a pub two hundred yards up the road. I'll meet you there.'

Now Fitzpatrick understood; a last-minute switch of venue, just in case Littlechild was being set up after all. 'I've a lovely tankard of Beamish smiling at me.'

'Leave it, Donny. Exit this instant or it's off.'

Littlechild hung up and stared across the street. If Fitzpatrick left within a few seconds, he'd keep the appointment. Any longer delay and the man might have time to make a call, warn others of the change of plan. It wasn't foolproof, of course, but it was a wise precaution.

Suddenly, Littlechild realised that his heart was thumping, the blood pulsing in his temples. Then the door of the saloon bar opposite opened and he saw the figure emerge. Old habits died hard, he mused. Fitzpatrick was hunched against the drizzle, wearing Northern Ireland's unofficial uniform for civilians: a hooded waterproof top, blue jeans and trainers. He walked swiftly, not looking up or around, hands thrust deep in his trouser pockets.

No one followed him. There were parked cars around, but as far as Littlechild could tell, none was occupied. He waited until he saw his quarry disappear into the Mortar and Pestle, before he left the call box and went after him.

He found Fitzpatrick at the bar, waiting for the head of the second Guinness to be topped up. The two men shook hands briefly.

'Rotten night,' the Republican ventured.

A smile twitched on Littlechild's face. 'Home from home. Let's grab a seat.'

They sat at a table in the window alcove, away from the boisterous chatter of the group of locals clustered around the bar. Fitzpatrick had put on weight, Littlechild thought. Probably because he was no longer living on the edge, his nerves were beginning to heal after a year or more of peace. His face was fuller and he was smiling more than when they'd last met. Maybe he had more to smile about. But then maybe not, because his eyes remained as dark and angry as ever.

'Where'd you get my telephone number, Donny?'

A shrug. 'Does it matter?'

'It matters.'

Fitzpatrick wiped the tideline of froth from his upper lip with the back of his hand. 'We're getting a lot of unofficial help during these negotiations with the Brit Government.'

'What sort of help?'

'Expert help. People who can show us the way around certain obstacles to agreement.'

Littlechild was already fairly certain who had given his number, for the simple reason that no one knew it. Not even friends and family. Evie hadn't even let her brother know when they'd last moved home a few weeks earlier. They were determined to cover their tracks.

16

He said: 'This expert help – you mean security people?'

Fitzpatrick's face remained a mask. 'Probably. They don't exactly say.'

'And they gave you my number?'

'A woman who calls herself White, Mrs Tabitha White. Claims to be something in the Northern Ireland Office.'

Littlechild felt the muscles tighten in his neck. Tabitha White. He might have known. Of all the controllers and handlers or whatever else they called themselves at MI5, he had good reason to remember her. Fortyish, upright with twinset and pearls and highlighted grey hair drawn severely back from her forehead to form a perfect bun at the back. Peering over the top of her spectacles like a headmistress, she had given it to him straight. Get out of the UK or we'll drive you out. Not in those precise words, but she didn't exactly dress it up either.

Fitzpatrick saw the recognition in his eyes. 'I can see you've met the lady. Quite formidable, eh?' A dry chuckle. 'And not unsympathetic to the Republican cause. She suggested you could be the one to speak to.'

'Before we continue this conversation,' Littlechild said suddenly, 'I'm going to the gents. If you still want to talk, come with me.'

For a second fear flickered in Fitzpatrick's eyes. Had the tables been turned? Had Littlechild arranged for a hastily gathered group of friends to be lurking in wait for him?

The bigger Ulsterman rose from the table and ambled through the door marked by a brass plaque. Fitzpatrick followed a few moments later.

No one stood at the chipped urinal bowls and a cursory check confirmed that the stalls were empty. Littlechild turned to Fitzpatrick. 'Sorry, Donny, but if you've been dealing with that woman, I've got to check you're not wired.'

The man raised his arms, a smile on his face. 'I can see she really got to you, Roddy. Be my guest.'

He was clean and when they returned to the bar, the tension had noticeably lessened.

A couple had come in while they'd been gone and had taken a nearby table. So when Fitzpatrick spoke he kept his voice low.

'I'll not beat about the bush, Roddy. These peace talks have reached a stalemate. The Brits are saying no all-party conference until we start talking about decommissioning of weapons. There's a fudge on offer by entering a twin-track process. That is, we agree to talk hypothetically about handing over arms and how we'd do it in return for all-party talks. Maybe Adams would go with that, probably McGuinness too. The big bananas at Sinn Fein just fancy themselves as feted politicians and stuff the rest of us. But I'm against it as are the hardline boys down in Armagh and the South. We see it as capitulation and we haven't fought all these years just to snatch defeat from the jaws of victory.'

Littlechild regarded the other man carefully. 'Forgive me if I say I don't really give a stuff about the Provos' hand-wringing. You said you wanted to talk in our mutual best interest.'

Fitzpatrick leaned forward conspiratorially, his voice low. 'Am I right in thinking you're against the way this whole business is going? You believe the Brit Government is selling the Unionists down the river?'

Instinctively Littlechild pulled back. 'I'm out of all that, Donny. I haven't lived there for over twenty years. I just hope the peace gets established so my family can go back.'

'Peace at any price, eh?' Fitzpatrick was deliberately goading.

'No. But if the British Government sticks to its position on IRA weapons, then it won't be a sell-out.'

Fitzpatrick chuckled without mirth. 'Don't really think they'll willingly risk a return to violence, do you? They'll play the devolution card through the European Union, pass the problem to Brussels. Then the Eurocrats'll bow to pressure from the White House. You know that.'

Littlechild was very aware of the likelihood. He knew it was exactly what most of his Loyalist friends in Ulster believed would happen, sooner or later. Whitehall couldn't wait to wash its hands of the province, everyone was sure of that. Non-committally he said: 'Only time will tell.'

The other man smiled gently. 'I don't believe you mean that, and by then it would be too late. I think you're as opposed to this peace process as my people are – but for different reasons.

18

You can't stop a boxing match before the twelfth round without a knockout. It can't be done.'

'So what do you want from me?'

'We're under severe pressure – I mean severe – to start handing over weapons. Yet we know you know that the Loyalists have a vast secret armoury of weapons. Maybe even more than we have. Don't deny it,' he challenged.

Littlechild said nothing.

'I want you to confirm that fact,' Fitzpatrick said, 'swear an affidavit just confirming the existence and true extent of the Loyalist armoury. Something we can wave in the face of the Brit Government and wipe the smug smile off the bastards' faces! Loyalist arms along with our arms or none at all. The arms they've always denied you have.'

'Was this Tabitha White's bright idea?'

Fitzpatrick took another swallow of his Guinness. 'It doesn't matter. It makes good sense.'

'Not to me, it doesn't. I know nothing about Loyalist arms.'

'Maybe you do and maybe you don't, Roddy. The point is everyone's seen that documentary and read the press reports. True or not, you've got a reputation. If you speak up, the Brits will have to listen. We'll have called their bluff, because they already *know* it's true. Then the pressure's off and we keep our guns and Semtex and no one sells you out.'

'You mean the war resumes?'

'Maybe and maybe not, but we keep the status quo. We've clearly not beaten the British Government into submission yet, and that's what it's going to take to get what we want.'

'The full twelve rounds?'

'Sure. Let's not stop it in the tenth. None of us likes it the way it is now.'

The landlord called time. Littlechild emptied his glass and rose to his feet. 'I'll think about it.'

'Not for too long, eh? You've got my number.' He extended his hand. Littlechild hesitated before taking it. 'Maybe some day, Roddy, our kids or maybe our grandchildren will play conkers together, eh? Like in the good old days.'

Rodney Littlechild turned and walked out into the mild

damp night. He was thankful to be away from Fitzpatrick, away from a world he thought he had finally left behind.

He walked for a while, mindlessly wandering along the quiet backstreets, his mind in turmoil. Just what game was Tabitha White – or whatever her real name was – playing at? He'd always felt she had a sneaking sympathy for the Republicans' aims, although she'd never come out and said so to him. But would she really go this far off her own bat? Sabotage everything the ceasefire had achieved so far? He couldn't believe that. There had to be another agenda, but for the life of him he couldn't think what it could be.

After half an hour he found he'd hit a mental blank wall, his brain refusing to function any more. He waved down a passing taxi and gave his address.

Well, to hell with Donny Fitzpatrick. If he rang again, it would be screened by the answerphone and his call just wouldn't be returned. It had been a mistake ever to have agreed to meet him.

When he climbed up the creaking stairs to their flat, he found Evie fast asleep. He was thankful in a way; he really didn't relish telling her what he had been asked to do. In the dark he stripped to his boxer shorts and slid beneath the duvet beside her. Gently he kissed the back of her neck before turning over and falling into a deep and dreamless sleep.

He seemed to hear all the noises at once. The smash of the hammerhead and the splintering of wood, the tinkling of shattered glass and the thud of heavy boots. They intruded rudely into the velvet nothingness of his sleep, a distant alarm bell deep within him starting to ring out urgently. He ignored it, rolled over, snuggling against the warmth of Evie's back. That was over, his life as a soldier in the African bush all finished. Even in the restless twilight between sleep and wakefulness, he reminded himself that his days of perpetual danger were over. Go back to sleep . . .

The bedroom door exploded under the impact.

'Christ!' He sat up in bed with a start, his heart thudding. The pale dawn light seemed blinding in its intensity, obscuring the menacing dark shapes moving all around him.

'ARMED POLICE! ARMED POLICE!' The voice was bellowing, deafening, filling his head. 'DO NOT MOVE! ARMED POLICE!'

His mouth dropped as he recognised the uniforms, the flak vests and blue NATO helmets of the firearms team as they jostled for position. Tight, pale faces and intense, excited eyes behind the lowered visors, arms extended and half a dozen guns held in double-handed grips.

Someone grabbed the duvet, ripped it off the bed. Evie screamed, suddenly awake, naked and exposed to the gazing eyes of the intruders.

'Check the pillows!' a voice ordered.

Littlechild reached for Evie as she began to shake and cry hysterically, waking from a dream into an inexplicable nightmare of reality.

'Leave her!' another voice said. 'Keep your hands in sight at all times – stretch out your arms, palms up!'

'What the hell?' he protested.

'Shut it!'

Bewildered, he obeyed as Evie was told to leave the bed. She was given her dressing gown and told to face the wall. Handcuffs were snapped around her wrists and she was led out to the living room.

'Now you,' the officer said to Littlechild. 'Swing your legs over the side. Stand – slow now – and step to the wall.'

Then he was ordered to kneel before he, too, was handcuffed.

He heard the voice in his ear, smelt the spearmint on the breath. 'Rodney Albert Littlechild, I am Detective Chief Inspector Millman of the Anti-Terrorist Branch. I am arresting you on suspicion of being involved in the murder last night of one Donal Fitzpatrick.' There was a short intake of breath. 'You do not have to say anything. But it may harm your defence if you do not mention, when questioned, something which you later rely on in court. Anything you do say may be given in evidence. Do you understand?'

Already reeling with shock, it took a moment for Littlechild to register what was being said. Fitzpatrick – murdered – last night? He couldn't believe his ears. It was crazy.

The hands on Littlechild's arms and shoulders lifted him to his feet and two officers bundled him into the living room.

Evie was waiting, trembling in the half-hearted hug of reassurance from a plump WPC who looked almost young enough to be her daughter.

'This is ridiculous,' Littlechild protested. 'I only met Fitz-patrick for a drink . . .'

'Save all that for the interview,' Millman said. 'But first I want you present while we conduct a search. Do you have any lawfully held weapons or drugs on the premises?'

As soon as Evie's identity was confirmed, her handcuffs were removed and the WPC took her to the kitchenette to make tea. Meanwhile, all curtains were closed as the SO19 search teams began their thorough and methodical work in pairs. They looked at, into, under and over everything, one hunting while the second nagged and reminded in case anything was over-looked. Furniture was moved, cupboards emptied, drawers taken out, carpets lifted, light-switch plates removed and plugs dismantled. Whenever anything of remotest interest was found, Littlechild was asked what it was and if it was his? All questions and answers were entered religiously in the search book.

When one search team finally began examining the answer-phone, a sudden thought occurred to Evie. 'Wait!' she shouted. 'I can prove Roddy didn't go out to kill anyone! That man called Roddy, begging for a meeting. His message is on the answerphone.'

Millman appeared irritated. He gestured impatiently to one of the other detectives to play the tape.

Oh, bless you, Evie, Littlechild thought, relief flooding through him. Why hadn't I thought of that?

'There's only one message,' Evie said breathlessly. 'The first one.'

The officer pressed the replay button. Nothing. He looked up. 'The tape's clear.'

Littlechild felt sick, like dropping in a lift in a shaft. He was slipping into an abyss and could see no way out. This was all a terrible, terrible mistake. He'd been caught up in some deadly coincidence, seen the wrong man at the wrong time.

Then, inexplicably, a picture of Fitzpatrick's acned face was floating before his eyes, laughing and mouthing the words: 'I can see you've met the lady. Quite formidable, eh?'

Tabitha White.

Christ! Perhaps this wasn't just coincidence and mistaken identity after all. Was she somehow involved? And if she was, then he was so deep in the shit he'd never crawl out.

He struggled against the restraining officer. 'I *must* speak to a solicitor.'

'All in good time,' Millman replied flatly and Littlechild felt his only lifeline slip through his fingers.

The SO19 team leader approached them. 'We're all finished here now, sir.'

Millman turned to his prisoner. 'Right, let's get you out of here.'

'Where are you taking him?' Evie demanded.

'To the station for questioning.'

'Which station?'

'You'll be informed later.'

'No-o-o-o!' Evie squealed in anguish as two officers moved to her husband's side.

Littlechild resisted, dug his heels into the carpet, forcing against the muscle power of those trying to propel him forward. Gasping for breath, he managed to half-turn his head until he could just see his wife. She looked pale and shocked.

'Get a lawyer, Evie! Quickly!'

She couldn't think, didn't know any lawyers, didn't even have a family solicitor.

Littlechild was losing his battle of strength, the carpet sliding and rucking beneath his feet. His mind was spinning, panicking. He'd need someone good, very good. Then an inspiration. The solicitor who had defended his friend in Ulster six years earlier. God, what was the name? A blank, nothing.

His resistance crumbled, his body sagging, its weight held by the arresting officers and his feet dragging the carpet behind him. The name, the name, the goddamn name? Something to do with a uniform. That was it, an army uniform – that was it, like the army belt.

'Sam Browne!' he yelled breathlessly. 'Browne with an e. In Belfast!' Belfast was the last word she heard before he was bundled down the stairs, past the gawping faces of the other residents gathered on the landing below.

One

It was dark and he was frightened. Really frightened.

And cold. Why hadn't he realised that the Iraqi desert would be this cold at night? Even in the scrape hewn into the shale – his gopher hole – with thermals and fibre pile and feather sleeping bag, he was still shivering.

Not Arctic cold, but a damp cold that gnawed into his bones. Or perhaps it wasn't the cold at all. Maybe it was just the fear. Fear despite the Armalite's reassuring feel in his fingers.

The fear and the dark and the noise. A slow irregular chime of a goat's bell. Nearer, ever nearer. Knowing that where there is a goat, there is a herdsman never far behind. And when the herdsman passed his hide, one of two things would happen. The herdsman would either not see him and pass by. Or he would see him and still pass by, pretending that he hadn't.

And then the decision would have to be made – how to respond? To accept that he had not been compromised and pray that he was right. Or he would have to creep out after the innocent old peasant or young boy and slit his throat. Quickly and silently, so as not to alert the Iraqi mobile patrol that was camped in the nearby wadi.

He peered out over the rim of the hole. It was pitch black – no moon, no stars. He felt very alone, still finding it hard to accept he'd become separated from the rest of the team. But the chime of the bell had receded now, and the immediate danger had passed. He must preserve his energy, get some kip. So cold, so tired.

The hand was on his shoulder, startling him. 'Get up!'

He tried to turn, to twist away and bring the Armalite into the firing position, but his body was paralysed. He stared at the blackness, heart tripping and the icy sweat drenching his body. Still he could see nothing. It was so dark that he thought he'd gone blind. Again he felt the goatherd's bony fingers on his shoulder shaking him. Imagined the wizened face.

'Dad, for goodness' sake get up!'

Lomax awoke with a jolt. He was lying, shirt unbuttoned, on the sofa and a chill August breeze was jigging the curtains at the open French windows.

'Come on, Dad, do you *know* what time it is?' Manda demanded. 'It's nearly eleven and the place is a tip. And it stinks of stale cigarette smoke. God, you'd never have got away with this if Mum was still living here. It's disgusting!'

God, his head hurt. The deep pulsing throb began at the back of his head and spread across his skull until it ended in red raw pain behind his eyeballs. He tried to move. Christ!

'Do you want an Alka-Seltzer?' Impatient.

He moved his mouth to speak. It was as parched as the Iraqi desert of his dream. 'I'd like – a little peace and quiet.' He looked up at his nineteen-year-old daughter. Techno college sweat shirt, blue jeans and a beguilingly pretty face had it not been for the sternly disapproving eyes behind those awful steel-rimmed Trotsky specs. 'And a ton of aspirin.'

'I'll get you some Codeine.'

Ah, she cares really, he thought, and watched her walk briskly towards the kitchen. Her mother's walk, purposeful with a sort of unselfconscious flick of the hips with each stride. Careful not to jerk his head, he looked around the living room. Party-popper streamers still hung from the light fittings and battalions of dead men lined the drinks cabinet. CDs and old vinyl 45s were strewn over the dining table, testament to their raucous singalong down memory lane.

And there had been a lot of memories to recall, he thought, and not a few ghosts to lay to rest. Friends and foes alike, but thankfully more foes. For some at the party those foes had been Communist terrorists in Malaya, Indonesian guerrillas in Borneo and Yemeni infiltrators in Oman. For Chris Lomax it had been Argentinians, Provo gunmen in Ulster, Bosnian Serb militiamen and Iraqi conscripts. Not to mention a lonely goatherd in the wrong place at the wrong time.

No, he decided savagely, definitely *not* to mention him.

And friends who hadn't made it, who had failed to 'beat the clock' that stood in tribute to their memory at the Stirling Lines barracks of 22 Special Air Service Regiment in Hereford. Scottie, Jatna, Mike Ash. Some Lomax had known personally, some not. All gone. They'd toasted them all.

Was it really twelve years since he'd first passed selection from the Parachute Regiment, already a 'mature' entrant of thirty-two years? It seemed like only yesterday. No, it *was* only yesterday. And here he was, unwanted, yet with still so much more to give. Rejected. Compulsory retirement they called it, but that wasn't how it felt. He felt as young today – well, perhaps not *today* exactly – as the day he'd stormed across the wind-ragged spine of Pen-y-Fan to establish a record time for the Regiment's 'fan dance' that was yet to be broken.

Manda returned with a glass of water, the tablets already dissolving. 'I'm cooking breakfast. D'you want some?'

He managed to hold down his bile at the very thought, and gulped the disgusting bitter liquid. 'I'll pass, thanks.'

'You look dreadful. I'd hate to be your liver.'

'And I'd hate to be your sense of humour. Or your compassion for that matter.'

'You've given me compassion fatigue, Dad. I'd feel sorry for you, only you're so busy feeling sorry for yourself there's no room left.'

A lop-sided grin cracked his face. 'Out of the mouths of babes . . .'

She laughed, smiling for the first time. 'It's a good job I love you.'

'You have a funny way of showing it.'

'It's for your own good.'

He handed back the glass. 'Now, don't I remember your mother using those self-same words?' He could focus more clearly on her now. 'Has everyone gone?'

'Tig, Bill, Gypsy Pete and Toothbrush got a taxi back to Hereford at seven. Most of the others went about half an hour ago, including Jerry Tucker – he wanted to catch the midday Belfast shuttle. But Ran's sleeping it off in the spare room – if anything, he's in a worse state than you.'

27

He pounced on that. 'See? The youngsters haven't got the stamina of us old-timers.'

'No, Dad, but he had flown halfway round the world to be at your farewell bash. He was zonked with jet lag before he even got here.'

'Mmm.' Grudging.

'Len Pope's running down to the newsagent's to get a paper . . .'

Ah, not so good. Pope was his own age and had left the Regiment a month earlier. And the newsagent's shop was three miles away.

'And Joe's waiting for his breakfast.'

Well, 'Big Joe' Monk would be, wouldn't he? He'd retired on the same day as Pope and had never been one to run when he could walk. Or better still, hitch a lift.

'It was a good turnout,' he thought aloud. 'And your cake was a great surprise. Thanks.'

Only a few crumbs remained of the shield-shaped rich fruit mix with its sand-coloured icing and skilfully piped winged danger and motto on a scroll.

'It's a pity most of it ended on the wall.'

'Ah.' His memory of that bit was foggy. 'Big Joe started that. Threw it at that officer he never could stand. Said he'd always wanted to frag him and this was his chance. Then everyone seemed to take sides.'

Manda looked at the wallpaper. 'So I see. Still, you've plenty of time now for redecorating, haven't you, Dad?'

He groaned as she returned to the kitchen.

Still, as he'd said to her, it had been a good turnout.

Shame Rob D'Arcy had to leave at midnight. Lucky the man managed to make it at all really because he was a big fish now out there in the civilian pond, running a multimillion-pound security company. High-powered stuff with worldwide government contracts. He might yet find himself beating a path to D'Arcy's door like so many before him.

But a greater shame was the fact that Roddy hadn't been there.

In fact, the big friendly Ulsterman wasn't *anywhere*, that was the trouble. Lomax's sister and Roddy Littlechild had upped and disappeared just four weeks earlier. And they'd left no forwarding address.

Lomax wasn't unduly concerned. He knew the reason why, because Roddy had hinted heavily at what he might do the last time they'd met.

Since his late teens, Roddy had spent all but two years out of twenty-three in Africa. He had first gone to Rhodesia where he served in the army, returning to Britain only after the collapse of the white Smith regime when the country's name was changed to Zimbabwe.

That was when he had joined the Parachute Regiment, meeting Lomax – and his little sister Evie, just eighteen – for the first time.

After two years, during which both men had served together in the Falklands campaign, Roddy had gone back to the continent with which he was besotted and joined the South African security police. Foreseeing black majority rule and the country's likely collapse into chaos, he'd returned to England again in late 1992.

Within eighteen months he'd established himself in a job as senior vehicle mechanic, had bought a small house and had married Evie.

Then the TV documentary had been shown, hinting that Roddy had been involved in smuggling arms to Loyalist terrorists in Northern Ireland. Press stories followed.

He was sacked from his job. Just when he thought he'd secured another one, the offer would be withdrawn at the eleventh hour. In desperation, he'd set up his own small vehicle repair business, despite being badly undercapitalised. But the media stories of his Loyalist terrorist connections persisted and his customers deserted him. He and Evie were at their wits' end about what to do and were teetering on the edge of bankruptcy.

During a long and sombre night's drinking with his old friend, he had confided to Lomax that he'd long been associated with Britain's Security Service, but now they had fallen out. It was they, he claimed, who were behind the smear campaign in an effort to drive him from the country.

In truth, Lomax wondered if his friend wasn't becoming just a little paranoid. Nevertheless, it was hardly any wonder that Roddy and Evie had gone into hiding to escape the tabloid newshounds and attempt to start a new life.

Lomax knew they'd contact him again when the dust had settled over their tracks. It was just a shame it hadn't been before last night. Because whatever Lomax owed his oppos in the Regiment, past and present, he owed no one more than his old comrade in the Paras.

He owed Roddy Littlechild his life and you couldn't owe more than that.

Easing himself from the sofa, he walked unsteadily to the mirror above the sideboard. A monster with bloodshot grey eyes and tangled fair hair like a bird's nest stared back at him. He hardly recognised himself – only the determined sandpaper chin and straight nose looked familiar.

Monk appeared at the door. 'Shit, Chris, you look awful.'

Lomax looked over. The huge moustachioed man with the tombstone teeth was clutching a tumbler of gooey yellow liquid. 'You don't look so clever yourself. What's that?'

'Bombay oyster. Raw egg, brandy . . .'

'I know, I know.'

'Never fails.'

The thick smell of bacon and eggs was wafting from the kitchen. 'Serving up!' Manda called.

'She's a dream, that girl,' Monk said. 'I should divorce Marsha and marry her.'

'Don't even fantasise about it,' Lomax warned.

'Come and watch me eat.'

Monk amassed a mountain of sausages and mushrooms to go with his egg and bacon, taking Len Pope's share on the basis he was 'late for mess breakfast', a cardinal sin in army life.

'So how are you finding civvy street?' Lomax asked.

'Great, like being on permanent R and R,' Monk replied through a mouthful of food. 'Nice lie-in till it's time to stroll down to the boozer for a liquid lunch.'

Lomax knew his old friend well enough to read between the

30

lines: he was bored out of his skull. 'Don't think Manda would let me get away with that.'

She dumped the toast rack on the table. 'You seem to be making a good start, if you ask me.'

'I'm not asking you, sweet child.' He looked back at Monk and his true feelings, his suppressed anger, bubbled to the surface. 'It's all such a bloody waste, Joe! I ask you, forty-five, that's all. Years of practical experience, all dumped because of some edict from paper-pushers in Whitehall who've never seen a shot fired in anger.'

Monk regarded his friend through the steam of the coffee mug he nursed between his enormous hands. 'Was a time, Chris, when you and me would have been running down to the newsagent's with Len. When we reckoned a fifteen-klick run was the only cure for a hangover. Maybe them pen-pushers aren't so much green as cabbage-looking.'

Lomax grinned. Monk had a point, maybe they had slowed up. A bit. 'What's on the job front?'

'Bugger all. But I bent Rob D'Arcy's ear last night. Plenty on if I don't mind a divorce and ten months a year in Moscow or Kazakhstan. Marsha won't put up with that, but I don't see I've an option.' For a second, his cheerful expression appeared to fade. 'And what about you? How's that book of yours coming along?'

Chris Lomax's account of his harrowing exploits in the Gulf War had been a major talking point and source of good-humoured ridicule in the Squadron for the past six months. Jokes about how he'd be a millionaire if he followed in the footsteps of *Bravo Two Zero* and *The One That Got Away*.

'I've spoken to a couple of publishers,' Lomax said, 'but they both reckoned it would be a book too many on the subject. Said the market's been saturated.'

At least its writing had been a sort of therapy. There'd been a sense of relief in spilling out his fears and emotions on paper, baring his soul about the mission that had damned near turned him into a nervous wreck and had driven Fran out of his life after twenty-one happy years of marriage. That must have taken some doing, he realised now, and all because he couldn't face

31

up to the fact that his bottle had gone. Couldn't accept that he'd become a coward overnight, that he jumped every time he heard a car backfire, and froze in action because all he could see in his mind's eye was the enemy's rounds whistling directly towards him. Only him. Each with his name clearly engraved on it. But at least now the bad dreams were less frequent.

Manda said: 'Maybe your appalling spelling and bad grammar had something to do with it.'

Lomax frowned. 'That's unfair. It's not that bad.'

'What about a book on tracking and survival?' Monk asked. 'You're the best I've ever known.'

'A compliment from Joe Monk – I'll treasure this moment.' They shared a laugh. 'Thanks anyway, but old Lofty got there first.'

'You're better than he ever was!'

'Makes no difference, Joe, no one's interested.' His daughter had removed her apron and joined them at the table. 'Manda thinks I should set up a business of some sort.'

'What sort?'

'No idea.'

Manda said: 'Trouble is, Dad hasn't got a clue about the commercial world.'

Lomax laughed: 'A vote of confidence from the Business Student of the Year.'

The telephone rang in the hall.

His immediate thought was Hereford. The adjutant at Stirling Lines, calling him in for an emergency. But then he remembered and the thrill of anticipation died before he even lifted the receiver. Probably a cold canvas call from a double-glazing firm.

'Lomax speaking.'

'Oh, Chris, thank God you're home!'

'Evie? How are you? Sorry you missed the party.'

'Chris, something awful's happened,' she gabbled. 'They've taken Roddy away.'

He realised something was wrong, badly wrong. His sister was almost hysterical and making no sense. 'What d'you mean, sis? Calm down. Who's taken him away?'

'The police, this morning. They just smashed their way into our bedroom. It scared the life out of me. It was awful.'

'Why, Evie?' This was madness, he thought, as he tried to sound reassuring. 'What did the police want?'

She was starting to sob now, her words almost incomprehensible. 'They arrested him, Chris. They accused him of murdering a man he met last night. It's not true, Chris, it's just NOT true!' She was almost screaming.

'Of course it's not, Evie,' he consoled, still bewildered. Murder? God, had Evie really got this right? It was too improbable for words. 'Where are you now?'

'I'm calling from our new flat in Southall.'

'Have they taken him to the local nick?'

'I don't know where, they refused to say. Oh, Chris, it's awful! The police seemed to think he was some kind of terrorist.'

'You're joking!'

'No. Maybe that's just because of the man they say he murdered. Someone called Donny Fitzpatrick.'

The small hairs sprang up on the back of his neck. He really wasn't hearing this. If it was the same man, Donny Fitzpatrick was a former Chief of Staff of the Provisional IRA.

'He hasn't even got a lawyer. Chris, he must have a lawyer, mustn't he? I mean this is a *murder* charge.'

'Er – lawyer? Yes, yes, of course.'

'He told me to get this solicitor in Belfast. A man called Sam Browne. With an e. I've tried Directory Enquiries, but they haven't got a number for him and I've no idea which firm he works for . . .'

'Look, don't worry, sis, I'm on my way. I'll sort it out. Don't fret.' He glanced at his watch. 'I'll be with you around two. Give me your address.'

She told him, his words of calm authority like a balm, and her blubbering sobs reduced to an occasional sniff as she fought back the tears.

He hung up and returned to the kitchen. Monk and Manda were staring at him, sensing something was wrong.

'What is it, Dad?'

'Roddy's been arrested for murder.'

33

Monk's mouth dropped. 'Your mate, Roddy? Your sister's bloke?'

'And it gets worse. If I understand it right, he's supposed to have murdered someone in the Provos. In London last night.'

Manda looked stunned, the blood draining from her face. 'Roddy wouldn't? . . .'

Lomax shook his head. 'I don't know. But I can't stop to discuss it now. I've got to get down to London.' He turned to his daughter. 'A chance to put your business management training to use – I want you to get onto the Law Society in London and find the current whereabouts of a solicitor called Sam or Samuel Browne, with an e. Used to work for a practice in Belfast. Roddy's in deep shit, so don't take no for an answer. Call me on the mobile as soon as you've got a number for him.'

'Solicitor called Sam Browne,' Monk repeated thoughtfully. 'Rings a vague bell.'

Lomax nodded as he picked up his car keys from the rack by the door. 'I think Browne was the name of the solicitor who defended Peter Keegan in Belfast about six years back.'

'I remember Keegan. An agent the army was running in the Ulster Defenders, that Loyalist paramilitary lot. Overstepped the mark and got done for conspiracy to murder.'

Lomax said: 'I was backup to Keegan's army handler for a while. Point is that Keegan and Roddy knew each other from way back, went to the same school. I guess that's why Roddy thought of this bloke Browne.'

Manda said: 'So this man Keegan was found guilty?'

'Yes,' Lomax replied. 'It was a stitch-up. He went down for twenty years.'

'Then are you sure this solicitor Sam Browne is a good choice?'

Lomax's and Monk's eyes met across the table. There was no answer to that.

Rodney Littlechild stared up at the fluorescent tube that cast its stark light around the bare walls of the interview room. There was only a burly and untalkative uniformed officer by the door.

They were letting him stew, he knew. For maybe half an

hour now they'd gone to the canteen for a break. Millman had promised him a cup of tea. It hadn't yet materialised.

Littlechild wasn't surprised. He'd sat in on enough police interviews in South Africa, when they'd had a suspected ANC terrorist in, to know all the tricks, all the wrinkles. Some of those Afrikaner slopeheads could get the Pope to confess to devil worship and they'd been none too fussed about how they extracted their information. Resorting to physical force wasn't unknown and mental torture quite common. Even his protests when they went too far were unheeded. Not a few suspects had hurled themselves to their deaths through windows rather than face another bout of questions.

Thank God this was Britain, he thought, where things like that didn't happen. And he was grateful now for the hours of horrific anti-interrogation training he had endured both in South Africa and in Rhodesia before that. In those days it wasn't mild-mannered English cops they were expected to be up against, but thumbscrews from Cuba backing up terrorist guerrilla forces in Angola and Mozambique.

He glanced at his wrist. Just a pale strip of skin where the strap had been. Bastards! No window in the airless room with its closed-circuit TV cameras and wall-mounted pad mikes. Nothing to tell him if it was night or day. Around noon, he guessed, but in a few hours he'd start to lose all track of time.

Without warning the door opened. Detective Chief Inspector Millman was back, big with broad shoulders encased in a slightly crumpled charcoal suit, hair dark and wavy with flecks of silver at the temple, and blunt unsmiling features that might have been chiselled out of a lump of rock.

With him was the slim, ginger-haired DS Henwick whose slight harelip gave him a quite sinister look when he smiled, which he did a lot. Mostly he played 'soft man' to Millman's 'hard man', although already they'd swapped roles too often to be convincing.

Millman gave a wintry smile. 'Sorry, Rodney, the tea machine's out of order. Still, a service engineer's due in later. Won't be long.'

'No problem,' Littlechild lied. His throat was parched and he knew damned well you didn't run a nick the size of Paddington Green without a constant flow of hot liquid. But he wasn't going to let such a crude tactic get to him.

Millman seated himself on the opposite side of the interview desk next to Henwick who reached for the twin-deck tape recorder and snapped it on.

Millman said boredly: 'Interview with Rodney Albert Littlechild resumed at 12.30 hours. Present: DCI Millman and DS Henwick of the Anti-Terrorist Branch.'

'I demand a solicitor,' Littlechild said. 'You're not holding me under the Prevention of Terrorism Act. This isn't right.'

'Don't be obtuse, Rodney,' Millman replied in an even tone. 'The custody sergeant explained it to you and you said you understood.'

'It's still not right.' Worth pushing it, he thought.

Millman sighed. 'You're being held under the Police and Criminal Evidence Act 1984, Section 58, as authorised by Detective Superintendent Dymock. That means that for a serious arrestable offence I can refuse you permission to consult a solicitor for up to thirty-six hours.'

'Look, Roddy, a little co-operation and we can all get some rest,' Henwick added amiably. 'It's not nice being without representation and we don't like doing it, but it serves a purpose. We know you've had accomplices in this murder and we want them too. Someone must have tipped you off about when and where Fitzpatrick would be. And someone else probably supplied you with the murder weapon.'

'That's nonsense,' Littlechild replied.

'And we want those people too,' Henwick persisted. 'You're known to associate with members of Loyalist terror gangs – no point denying it, Special Branch has confirmed as much – and therefore witnesses to your crime could be in serious danger from your associates.'

Littlechild shook his head. 'Even if it were true, what difference would it make if I had proper legal advice?'

'Because a lawyer could deliberately or unwittingly tip off the rest of the gang,' Millman interjected. 'So to my mind, it justifies the precaution in this case.'

'So tell us who else was involved,' Henwick said with that well-intentioned smile of his.

Littlechild sighed. 'I had no accomplices for the simple reason I haven't murdered *anyone*!'

'You're not making things any easier for yourself, Roddy. So okay, let's go over your version of events again, starting with what you were doing yesterday evening. You say you had a visitor at your flat. A television director–journalist called Lisa Hardcastle, right? And you were discussing the making of a programme that denies your alleged involvement with shipping arms to Loyalist paramilitaries in Northern Ireland?'

'Correct.' He'd earlier considered hedging, but no doubt the police would be interviewing her anyway. 'The phone rang while we were talking, so I let the answerphone pick it up.'

'So when did Miss Hardcastle leave you?' Henwick asked.

'About ten fifteen. At the same time my wife came home. She noticed the answerphone light was on.'

'Ah, the mysterious vanishing message,' Millman said.

'It was Donny Fitzpatrick asking to meet me. Ask Evie, she heard it.'

'Had your wife ever met Mr Fitzpatrick?' Millman asked.

'No.'

'So she'd never heard his voice?'

'No.'

'Therefore, this person could have been anyone impersonating him?'

Littlechild shook his head. 'That's crazy. Who'd want to do that?'

'An accomplice perhaps? If you or your wife hadn't accidentally wiped the tape, it might've given some credence to your story that Fitzpatrick asked to see you. I mean, we are aware that your wife has no criminal record, is of good character and has never even set foot in Northern Ireland. *If* she heard such a message, she'd believe it and you. A jury might find her testimony quite convincing.'

'I phoned him back. She heard that too.'

'But your wife only heard one side of the conversation, right? Your side?'

'Yes.'

'So again, it could have been anyone.'

'But it *wasn't*!' Littlechild protested.

Millman persisted. 'It could have been your accomplice again. Tipping you off where Fitzpatrick could be found, or perhaps just confirming?'

'It was Fitzpatrick who answered.'

'Fine. We will check your telephone records.'

Littlechild felt a sudden flood of relief. He'd never thought of that; the phone company's records would back his story.

'Fitzpatrick's address was written on the pad by your phone,' Henwick pointed out mildly, 'yet you say you never went there.'

'I wrote it down, then changed my mind. Thought it could be a trap. I arranged to meet him at a pub.'

'The Duke's Head?'

Littlechild agreed.

Millman said: 'You are seriously asking us to believe that you, who have friends in the Loyalist paramilitaries and have been alleged to have supplied them with arms, went voluntarily and unarmed to meet a former IRA Chief of Staff alone?'

It sounded lame, he knew, and he wished to hell he'd never even considered it. 'We were at school together as kids. There was never any personal animosity between us. And he sounded genuine on the phone, as if he needed my help. He said a meeting would be to our mutual benefit.'

'Only such a meeting never took place, did it?' Millman challenged. 'You see, we've traced the taxi driver who picked you up outside your home and took you to the Duke's Head. He says when you got there, you told him to drive on. You alighted several hundred yards away. I suggest it was so that you could watch and stalk Fitzpatrick back to his apartment where you shot . . .'

'NO!'

'We've spoken to the landlord of the Duke's Head. He recognised a photograph of Fitzpatrick. Says he was drinking alone, having arrived about ten thirty. He remembers particularly because Fitzpatrick received a call from someone to say he couldn't make the meeting.'

38

'I know,' Littlechild hissed. 'That was me!'

Millman looked perplexed. 'But you'd just been dropped across the road. If it was you, how come you couldn't make it? Bunions playing you up?'

'I've already told you. I phoned from a call box to change the venue. To the Mortar and Pestle just down the road. I wanted to see Fitzpatrick leave *alone*, to be sure there was no one with him. To be sure it wasn't a trap.'

'So despite once being schoolboy chums, you didn't trust him after all?'

Littlechild fell back in his chair, drained. Even in his exhausted state he knew it sounded contradictory. But why does anyone do anything? Not all actions and decisions are based on sound logic or reason, we just do them.

'I can look at this one of two ways,' Millman continued. 'Either that call was made by the man Fitzpatrick was really meeting there and who genuinely cancelled their rendezvous. Or I can believe your story so far, except that you phoned to cancel the meeting – to enable you to avoid being seen by witnesses, having safely established his whereabouts so you could stalk him to a place where it would be safe to murder him.'

'For Christ's sake, I phoned him to change the venue, not cancel the rendezvous.'

'That's not what you told the landlord. Why should you lie to him?'

Littlechild felt his exasperation rising and fought to hold it in check. 'I just wanted to speak to Donny. The landlord didn't want my whole life history. Anyway, I did speak to Donny and we met at the Mortar and Pestle about ten minutes later.'

'What time?'

'I don't know. About ten to eleven. I think they'd already called last orders. You can check it out, the barman will have seen us and probably the crowd at the bar – I think they were regulars. Oh, and a couple – a middle-aged man and a younger woman – who came in just after us. Looked like a husband and wife, didn't say much, just shared a packet of pork scratchings.'

The wan smile on Millman's face looked curiously out of

place as he extracted a notebook from his inside pocket. 'While I was on my break, I called the investigating officer who has been to the Mortar and Pestle and I have to tell you informally that the landlord does not recall seeing anyone resembling either you or Donny just before closing time. Nor your colourful description of the married couple. Maybe one of the regulars will remember you. We haven't traced them all yet.'

Littlechild sat stony-faced. He remembered the group, standing around laughing and joking, celebrating someone's birthday, all eyes on some wag who thought he was a comedian. He wouldn't be surprised if none of them had noticed him or Fitzpatrick.

Henwick spoke next. 'What did you do after this meeting you allege you had with Fitzpatrick?'

'I went home.'

'How? By public transport or taxi?'

'Taxi.'

'Straightaway?'

'No, I walked for a bit.'

'How long?'

'I don't know, thirty minutes, maybe forty. I wanted to think.'

'Are you aware,' Millman added, 'that we are able to pinpoint the time of death to eleven forty-five? Where were you then?'

'Walking.'

'I see. Well, unfortunately for you, Mr Littlechild, we know otherwise. What you will not have been aware of is that, because Mr Fitzpatrick was a leading IRA figure involved in the peace negotiations, he was being kept under discreet surveillance. He was watched entering the Duke's Head alone and leaving alone. I understand he took a short stroll before returning to his flat. Shortly afterwards a man was seen in the grounds and entering the premises. Moments later one of the team realised where they'd seen that face before. Your face, Mr Littlechild.'

The Ulsterman gave a snort of derision. 'Your people wouldn't know me from Adam!'

'My people – no, perhaps not. But this was an MI5 surveillance team and one of them had seen your picture on file.

40

Apparently, you keep contact with some pretty unsavoury friends in Belfast.'

Littlechild stared at the man opposite. Any doubts he had were dispelled. Now he knew and he felt the clammy hand of fear run its fingers down his spine.

'Sorry, Roddy,' Henwick said cheerfully, 'but it looks like you walked straight into it. When the MI5 officer finally put a name to the face, you were followed inside. It was an unfortunate delay. Barely a minute later, Fitzpatrick was found dead.'

'How was he killed?'

'Why don't you tell us?'

'Because I don't frigging *know*!'

Millman said: 'Then let me remind you. A silenced .45 automatic. Six rounds, fired through the front door. Four hit him. A nasty mess.'

Henwick couldn't bear to be 'Mr Nice Guy' any longer. 'Looks like you could be facing a life sentence, Roddy.'

The blood drained from Littlechild's face. This was no coincidence, this was far, far more than just being in the wrong place at the wrong time.

Two

Barney winced as the enormous padded red glove thudded into the punchbag.

He really didn't fancy being on the receiving end of that. Packed a hefty straight-armed jab. And a pretty mean left hook, for a girl.

She was light on her feet, dancing all the time, the pink silk shorts sighing as she moved on the balls of her feet, emphasising the long tanned legs. Tall, but shoulders hunched now to present a smaller target to the imaginary opponent. Just the eyes peering over the top of the gloves, hard and bright as sapphires, waiting for her chance. Fair hair pinned tight back from her face, drops of perspiration glistening on her high cheekbones.

Thwack! Lean muscles rippling along her arm. *Thwack, thwack!*

God, she was so quick he almost missed it. Two low body blows to the nonexistent torso, then a straight to the head as the nonexistent arms dropped their defence.

'Good!' he called. 'Now keep your guard up!'

Had he said 'girl'? Well, he wished she had been because he wouldn't have minded her in his ladies' team. But at forty-something, he'd never get her into a licensed bout. Shame that.

Beautifully preserved, he thought. More his sort than the aggressive teenage butch types who came in from the nearby high-rise estate. She had maybe passed the first flush of youth, but he noticed how blokes half her age slowed what they were doing when she walked in. Funny how they all came to a natural break in their sparring or finished their dumb-bell reps in record time.

'Okay, sweetheart, take a break.' He grinned. 'Before I have to invest in a new punchbag.'

THWACK!

'Christ!'

'One for luck,' she said.

'Who was that – your ex?'

She laughed huskily. 'No, I got him out of my system in my first week here. That was the beak at Bow Street Magistrates.'

'Rather him than me.'

He handed her a towel. She was out of breath, he noticed, as he tried not to let his eyes linger on the green cutaway vest and the dark stain of sweat between her breasts. Not big, how he liked them, but they had a nice way of moving beneath the thin material. And he found the telltale button imprints quite arousing

Her eyes met his and they both knew. He was annoyed with himself because he didn't want her to think of him like that. And he really didn't want to feel her fist in his face. But more than that, after five years, he really didn't want her to stop coming to Barney's Boxing Gym. She was a regular every morning before work, or lunchtime like today, when she had an early court appearance. It might be unrequited love, but Barney was content with that. Really quite preferred it.

She thrust her gloved hands out to him and her expression, with its slightly mocking half-smile, said she had forgiven him.

He unwrapped the velcro straps at her wrists. 'You still smokin'?'

'Afraid so.'

'Thought so, you sound like a steam train.'

'Liar,' she replied. 'I'm down to twenty-five – on a good day.'

'And the booze?'

Her eyes were wide, provoking. 'Can't get enough of it.'

He cared. He said: 'I think you get plenty. No good running three times a week and comin' here most days, then undoin' all that with cigs and Scotch and microwave suppers.'

She leaned forward and kissed his whiskery leather cheek. 'I do my best, Barney. But cigs go with the stress of the job and microwave meals with the hours. I keep off the booze till ten o'clock, but hell, when you're working to past midnight on a big case for the next day . . .'

He frowned. 'And you're a workaholic.'

She dumped the leather gloves in his upturned palms. 'That's what my ex always said.'

'He should know.'

The mobile began its irritating little bleep from the locker room. 'Oh, bugger,' she murmured. 'Excuse me, Barney.' And he watched her go, pink silk twitching to the sway of her hips.

She picked up the handset from her shoulder bag. 'Hello, Browne speaking.'

'Ernie.' Her senior partner Eisner announced himself without preamble. 'Got a hot one for you, babe. Had a good mind to turn it down out of hand – sounds like another big one on miserable Legal Aid rates. At least it's not another of your waifs and strays.'

Browne laughed. 'Justice has its price, Ernie.'

'I know, babe, I just think it's the client who should pay it, not me. Or am I being old-fashioned?'

'Probably. What's this about?'

'Homicide rap apparently and our man's being denied representation.' Eisner was a devotee of American crime fiction, anything from Chandler to Elmore Leonard, and peppered his conversation with its slang, which sounded very odd from a crusty old Jewish solicitor. 'Just had the guy's brother-in-law on the phone. He and the man's wife are scorching their way here even as we speak.'

Browne felt an involuntary thrill of expectation rush through her. 'What did the brother-in-law tell you?'

'He sounded like an army type, retired major or something, perhaps. Appears our prospective client is a Protestant from Northern Ireland and used to be a friend of a certain Peter Keegan . . .'

God! Now her heart really was pumping. Keegan. Probably the biggest case she'd ever had and certainly the biggest one she'd ever lost. Well, that wasn't strictly true, because Keegan had ignored her advice to fight, but it had certainly felt like a personal failure at the time.

She said: 'How long has our prospective been held?'

'About eight hours.'

Long enough, she thought. Long enough without a lawyer or

any other friendly face to put on the squeeze, to persuade the unwary or unwitting to agree anything to end the pressure, to stop the questions.

'Has he been charged yet?'

'We don't think so.'

That was something. 'When will the brother-in-law and wife be here?'

'They spoke to me as they left the wife's home in Southall, so I reckon another thirty minutes.'

'I'm on my way.' An afterthought: 'And thanks, Ernie, for not turning them down.'

She just knew he was grinning, pleased to have made her day. '*Ciao*,' he said and hung up.

Bless you, Ernie, she thought as she half-walked and half-skipped to the shower cubicle and stripped off.

She and Ernie had developed an instant rapport the moment she'd entered the shabby Balham offices to apply for the position of junior partner in the hectic, but not unprofitable practice. Other applicants had more money to invest and arguably more years of experience, but the truth was Eisner was bored and tired of conveyancing and divorce and defending petty criminals from the local estate. He had romantic notions of running a dynamic firm of 'attorneys', an Anglicised version of *LA Law*, with himself as a sort of Perry Mason figurehead.

Browne had come straight from Belfast, still licking her wounds after what she regarded as the Keegan fiasco. After five years of defending alleged criminals, IRA and Loyalist terrorists, fighting in the front line of justice or injustice, depending how you looked at it, she felt that the system had finally beaten her.

Yet it wasn't long before she was up and running again in south London.

And she looked far from beaten to Ernie Eisner. This was what he had been looking for, a sort of female knight in shining armour, a gladiator who saw the courtroom as an arena and was not afraid to spill blood. Her own rare appearances before the bench were impressive and Eisner half-wished she had opted to become a barrister herself, but she was by nature a backroom girl, a street fighter who knew how to bend the rules. And soon she'd assessed and made a selection of the finest and most able barristers from the Inns of Court.

Eisner admired her as an unflagging champion of the underdog, especially where bureaucracy was concerned, and she'd made her mark with a number of major criminal appeals, steering her barristers to victory in overturning verdicts reckoned to be 'unsafe'. Her fellow partners would sometimes become exasperated at her ceaseless tilting at windmills and for taking on seemingly hopeless cases. Yet there was also a grudging pride, because as often as not she won.

The only problem was that many such cases proved to be long and arduous and had to be fought within the parsimonious restrictions of the Legal Aid system. Often an immense amount of additional work had to be undertaken to ensure even a chance of success. That increased the workload of the other partners and inevitably meant that more mundane, but more lucrative commercial work didn't get the attention it deserved. As a result, some long-term clients of Eisner, Pollock and Browne had upped and walked.

Browne might have proved good for the firm's profile and reputation, but not always for business. Nevertheless, old Ernie would not have a word said against her. In his eyes she could do no wrong; it was almost as though he regarded her as the daughter he never had.

And that, she reflected as she lathered and rinsed, was probably exactly what he did.

After a brisk rub down with a towel she dressed in a cream blouse and pale coffee business suit, stuffed her tights into her shoulder bag and headed for the door. Lighting a cigarette, she waved to Barney as she left.

He watched and shook his head sadly. Incorrigible, a hopeless case. And he'd seen that look in her eyes before. Something big was brewing.

More twenty-hour days, more cigs, more booze and more microwave dinners. He had a feeling he wouldn't be seeing much of her for a while.

Lomax slowed his C-reg Cavalier so that Evie could read the numbers above the tatty shop fronts. Electrical repairers, fly-blown cafes, second-hand furniture and a DIY store, and an open-all-hours corner grocer's shop. It was an unprepossessing part of south London, no estate agents or building societies here.

'Are you sure this is right?' she asked.

'You were navigating, sis, and the sign did say The Broadway.'

'God, I do hope we're not making a mistake. I suppose it is the same Sam Browne.'

'Manda seemed certain it was him.'

Evie wasn't sure. 'She's just a kid.'

'But a smart one. Business Student of the Year.'

'This isn't funny, Chris. If we've got the wrong Browne, we'll have lost a whole day.'

Lomax pointed suddenly. 'Got it! Number thirty-five. Over there. Above that Chinese takeaway.'

Evie groaned. Nightmare upon nightmare.

The bare wooden staircase up to Eisner, Pollock and Browne's office was stacked on one side with obsolete legal papers going back two decades. A stripped-pine door led to an office with two large sashcord windows and another mountain range of document bundles. Somewhere amid the precarious paper pillars they'd managed to cram filing cabinets, a Xerox copier and three desks, one of which doubled as reception.

A blowsy blonde in her early twenties looked up from her PC and grinned cheerfully at them. ''Allo, I'm Totty, 'ow may I 'elp you?'

Lomax was taken aback; under other circumstances he might have found it difficult not to smile. 'I've an appointment with Mr Browne. My name's . . .'

Totty's grubby little fingernail, bitten to the quick, was already on the appointments book. 'Mr Lomax. And this will be Mrs Littlechild.' She was on her feet, extending her hand whilst managing a sort of bobbing curtsy at the same time. 'So pleased t'meet you. We'll go straight in because this is very urgent, innit?'

A young, acne-faced male clerk in shirtsleeves looked up from his desk by the window. 'You'd better warn them, Tots, otherwise they'll think he's a TV.' The eyes were laughing behind the old-fashioned swot's spectacles.

'TV?' Evie asked. She was lost.

''E means transvestite,' Totty said with an air of exasperation. 'Never mind Wayne, Mrs Littlechild. Wayne the Pain we girls call 'im, but he's okay really. Just won't grow up.'

Evie frowned. 'But what did he mean?'

Totty smiled. 'Mr Browne's a woman. A lot of people make that mistake. Sam for Samantha, see, not Samuel. Do follow me.'

'The gorgon awaits,' Wayne called after them. Then added: 'Don't worry, sir, the boss is on *your* side.'

They followed the plump little figure in its white blouse, dark tights and a puppy-fat rump squeezed optimistically into a pencil skirt. She led the way into a long bare corridor lined with more documents bound in pink legal ribbon.

'Unusual name,' Lomax commented conversationally.

Totty giggled. 'Me real name's Samantha – like Miss Browne, but she said we couldn't 'ave two in the same firm. So she gave me a nickname. Sweet, innit?'

Lomax caught Evie's eye. At least someone had a sense of humour.

'You must be gaspin' for a cuppa, I'll get one for you PDQ,' she said and opened the end door without knocking. 'Mr Lomax and Mrs Littlechild, boss.'

'Oh, shit,' Browne said, hitting the PC keyboard as they entered. The screen went blank.

Evie looked uncertainly round the office. Obviously it had once been someone's living room, but a long time ago because the faded Regency paper was peeling with damp in the corners. Not that much of the decor could be seen behind the rows of filing cabinets topped with leather-bound law books. It looked similarly chaotic to the outer office except for a small expanse of threadbare carpet and only one desk which was littered with empty mineral water bottles and an overflowing ashtray.

The solicitor was taken by surprise, turning her back on the

48

PC and peering up over the top of her half-moon reading glasses. 'Oh, I'm so sorry. What must you think?' She rose to greet them. 'I'm Sam Browne.'

Lomax wasn't quite sure what he was expecting. But after driving through this squalid part of the city and being taken aback by the mayhem of the outer office, he certainly wasn't expecting anyone as smart and stunning as the woman who stood before him now. And most definitely not the beautifully articulated voice that spoke with a sort of soft and breathless urgency. 'Mrs Littlechild, Mr Lomax, I'm so pleased you found us quickly. You must be worried sick. Do take a seat, both of you.' She waved a hand absently round the office. 'And please don't judge by appearances. We are quite efficient really. They've been trying to get decorators in since before I came here five years ago, but it's never the right moment. It would be such an upheaval and we're always so busy.'

But Lomax wasn't convinced, suddenly feeling it was a mistake to be here. He said: 'Not *too* busy, I hope.'

Browne stopped what she was saying and for a second their eyes locked. There was a brittle silence before she spoke, this time in a very measured tone: 'I always have time for justice, Mr Lomax. Why else would you have come to see me?'

Evie said: 'My husband asked me to find you. It was the last thing he said before they dragged him off.'

'I think it was because of your work on the Keegan trial in Belfast,' Lomax said. 'Roddy – that's Mr Littlechild – and he were friends. Or at least acquaintances.'

'Yes, Ernie Eisner mentioned you'd said that,' Browne replied. 'At least it explains why you're here. Now, in view of the fact your husband's accused of murdering a member of the IRA,' she addressed Evie, 'I'm making a working assumption he's being held at Paddington Green. That's the top-security police station.'

Evie looked aghast. 'Isn't that where they take terrorists? Is that why he's not being allowed a solicitor?'

'They won't be holding him under the Prevention of Terrorism Act for murder,' Browne said. 'No point. They'll be using paragraphs 6 and 8 under a Section 58. That means

49

they're entitled to withhold legal access for up to thirty-six hours if they think there are accomplices to a serious crime or that witnesses could be placed in danger.'

'So what happens next?' Lomax asked.

'I'm trying to confirm that your husband is at Paddington Green, but I'm hitting a brick wall at the moment. No one's admitting anything and they've promised someone will get back to me – but I'm not holding my breath. Meanwhile, young Totty is chasing them up every fifteen minutes.' A tight reassuring smile. 'She may not look it, but Totty can be very tenacious. Now, I suppose you didn't catch the name of the arresting officers?'

Evie said: 'I was so shocked and half-asleep I can hardly remember anything.'

'I can imagine. It must have been awful for you.'

'There was an inspector, a big man. I think his name was Mill-something. Maybe it was Milton, or perhaps Millford.'

Browne scribbled it down. 'Well, that's something. I've also been trying to call up my old files on the Keegan trial, just in case there was some cross-reference to your husband.' She grimaced and jabbed a thumb at the blank screen of her PC. 'Trouble is we've just installed Windows 95 and it seems to have buggered everything up – excuse my French. So that'll have to wait, I'm afraid.' She redirected her gaze at her new clients. 'Before we run through what happened, I'd like to call in Mr Eisner; he's our senior partner. The thing is, on the face of it, this could be a big case for a company of our size and we'll have to give it everything we've got.'

'I understand,' Evie replied.

'If your husband is charged with murder of a leading figure in the IRA, then I'm going to have to be on it full time for weeks with full backup, and we might have to hire in more staff for our routine business . . .' She reached for the telephone, noticed Evie staring at the overfull ashtray and emptied it into her bin with an embarrassed smile before dialling the senior partner's extension.

Ernie Eisner arrived a few minutes later and immediately put his company's new clients at their ease with his warm handshake and crinkled smiling eyes. Short and stocky with thinning curly hair and a face like lumpy porridge, he for some reason reminded Lomax of a theatrical agent. Perhaps it was the prominent, squashy and unmistakably Jewish nose. Or the American bootlace tie and fancy waistcoat worn beneath the conventional dark suit.

After Totty dispensed a tray of biscuits and tea in unmatching cups and saucers, Browne patiently took Evie twice through events of the previous night. She took down notes while Lomax's sister spoke and occasionally she asked a question. Eisner watched and listened, paddling his tea with a spoon but leaving it otherwise untouched.

When Evie finished talking, an ominous silence hung over the gathering until Browne finally spoke: 'Your husband wasn't afraid to go alone to meet this IRA man, this Fitzpatrick?'

Evie hesitated, remembering how, stupidly, she'd encouraged her husband and even now she didn't really know why she had. 'He was wary, I think, but not afraid. They'd known each other since school, you see, and I thought with there having been peace for over a year . . .' Tears began to well in her eyes.

Browne glanced at her notes: 'I've got to ask you what he was going to tell this Lisa Hardcastle? That your current financial predicament is as a direct result of pressure from – let's say – MI5, to drive him out of the country?'

Evie dabbed at her eyes with a handkerchief Lomax gave her. 'Yes. One of their people actually told him so.'

'Why should they want to do that?'

'Because Roddy knows a lot about what MI5 has been doing in Northern Ireland over the years. They're afraid he might talk, I suppose.'

'But,' Browne hesitated, selecting her words with care, 'if I understand correctly, your husband has helped them – MI5, the British Government if you like – for a number of years.'

A sniff, wiping her nose on the white linen. 'He says he always did what he could. He loves Northern Ireland, always has – until they asked him to do things and he refused.'

'What sort of things?'

'I don't know exactly. Roddy didn't tell me everything. But that's when they turned against him.'

Ernie Eisner spoke for the first time, his voice a soft croak. 'How did your husband help MI5 during all this time, Mrs Littlechild?'

She shook her head. 'I'm sorry. Roddy never discussed the details with me. But before we married he said there was something I ought to know, that he had helped MI5 in its fight against the IRA. I think it was just something he wanted to get off his chest. He said it was better that he didn't go into detail and I accepted that.'

'Of course,' Eisner said, understanding.

'And this answerphone tape?' Browne asked. 'How do you explain why it was blank?'

Evie opened her mouth to speak but the words stuck in her throat, and the tears began again. 'I – I don't – know. I was sure I hadn't touched the machine, but I must have wiped it without thinking. I'd had a drink at the wine bar where I work and a – a drop of Bushmills when I got home. I just don't know.'

Browne nodded. She recognised that late-night-one-drink-too-many amnesia all too well herself. 'There's one final question I must ask. Please forgive me, because there's really no easy way to put it. In your deepest heart of hearts, do you think your husband could have killed this man?'

Evie's answer was instantaneous. 'NO!' she blurted. 'Roddy would never hurt a fly! He's a big, lovely, gentle giant! I could never marry someone who – who . . .' She broke down in a racking sob, the dam finally bursting under an unremitting flood of tears. 'I – I'm sorry,' she blubbed.

Eisner rose to his feet and put his arm round her shoulders. 'Perhaps you'd like some fresh air, honey. There's a small park round the corner. We could go sit there for a while?'

Sam Browne smiled tightly. 'Good idea, Ernie, it's been a traumatic time. Mrs Littlechild must be exhausted.' As Lomax also started to rise, she said: 'Would you mind staying while they're gone? Just a few questions, you know.'

Lomax shrugged. 'Sure.'

As Evie left with Eisner, Browne asked: 'How well do you know your sister, Mr Lomax?'

That was a curious question. 'How well does any boy know his kid sister? Same family but, like all women, from a different planet.'

It was the first time he noticed her mad eye. Browne's right eyebrow rose and the eye itself seemed to enlarge, the pupil and glittering sky-blue iris fixing him with a mesmeric power. He would learn to read it as a warning signal as time went on. 'Different planet, Mr Lomax. Is that what you think?'

He shifted uncomfortably, thinking maybe this solicitor was exactly that – from another planet. 'Just a joke. Can't live with them, can't live without them, sort of thing,' he said lamely.

'Are you married, Mr Lomax?' she asked evenly.

God, why did she make him feel so awkward? 'Er – not exactly, not any more. Why d'you ask?'

'I just wondered. It's a question we always ask on Planet Zeus.'

He grinned, unsure whether she was annoyed or just having a joke at his expense. He cleared his throat. 'In fact, Evie and I have always got on rather well. Once we were over the age difference. I was about eleven when she was born.'

'And all this stuff about MI5, she could be – er, well, let's say, letting her imagination run away with her?'

'I don't think so. Roddy told me the same thing himself.'

'And her view that her husband would be incapable of murder?'

Lomax smiled. 'Well, Evie usually sees the best in people, I must admit. Maybe she's a little bit gullible in that respect, but she's sharp enough. If she says Roddy really wasn't keen to go last night, I believe her.'

Browne didn't return his smile. 'You mean that intuition we aliens tend to have?'

'Er – something like that.'

She leaned back in her chair. 'And how well do *you* know your brother-in-law?'

'Well enough. It was through me that the two of them first met. Roddy came back from Rhodesia in 1980 and joined the

Paras. We served together in the Falklands.' He felt compelled to add: 'He saved my life.'

That mad eye again. 'Really? So you are very close.'

He nodded.

'Yet he never told you any details about his involvement in MI5? Either then or since?'

'No, but then he was a very private man. And I only saw him occasionally after '83 when he went to South Africa. When we met it was always for a few bevvies and to reminisce about old times. The first I heard any rumour that he'd been tied up with anything dubious was that TV documentary and I didn't believe a word of it. An MI5 connection was mentioned in that, but it was obviously pure speculation.'

She placed her elbows on the arms of her chair and laced her fingers together across her chest. 'Do *you* think Roddy is capable of murder?'

He avoided her eyes; to his own ears this was going to sound like a betrayal, but he felt it ought to be said. 'Roddy was a soldier, just like me. We both fought in the Falklands, so I can't deny he's *capable* of killing someone. Evie described him as a gentle giant and that's fairly accurate. I met people far more capable and *likely* to murder later when I served with the Regiment.'

'Which regiment?' She looked perplexed. 'I'm sorry.'

'The SAS. In fact I did some minding work with Peter Keegan and his army handlers. Followed his trial with some interest.'

'Oh, really, you know Peter Keegan?' Browne seemed genuinely intrigued. 'How long were you with the SAS?'

'Twelve years. Until yesterday. I was recovering from the party when I got Evie's call this morning.'

She tilted her head to one side. 'Goodness me. So should I really be addressing you as – what? – Captain, or would it be Major Lomax?'

He laughed. 'Staff Sergeant. Not a rank that carries into civvy street. I specialised in escape and evasion, tracking, that sort of thing. I ran a special training cadre.'

Browne was taken aback. 'But you sound . . .' She stopped herself in time.

'Like an officer?' He was perversely pleased to see her look embarrassed now. 'Just ten O-levels, I'm afraid – couldn't bear the thought of university; I was too keen to see the world. Don't worry; even SAS troopers are often mistaken for officers.'

She recovered quickly. 'I wasn't exactly apologising, Mr Lomax. I'm sure if I asked, you'd swear the army was run by senior NCOs.'

'You said it.'

Again their eyes locked for a silent moment, the atmosphere of mutual antagonism palpable in the small office. Christ, Lomax thought, I bet that's it. Samantha Browne is an officer's daughter. She's got it stamped right through her like a stick of Brighton rock.

'So,' she said, 'your friend Roddy is innocent, you'd say, from what you know of his personality?'

Lomax forced his concentration back on track. 'Well, he could get pretty heated on some subjects. Like what he was fighting for in Rhodesia and South Africa.'

'And Northern Ireland? The IRA?'

A pause. 'I honestly don't know. But if this man Fitzpatrick wanted to see him under a flag of truce, then I know Roddy would have respected that. I'd stake my life on it.'

'Thank goodness you won't need to do that.'

Her telephone rang from beneath a pile of papers. Browne located it and snatched up the handset. 'Hello, Totty. Yes. Who? Custody sergeant? Okay, put him through.'

She covered the mouthpiece. 'Paddington Green.' With her free hand she shook out a cigarette from the pack on her desk. Lomax leaned forward and offered her a flame from his lighter. She exhaled gratefully as the policeman came on the line. 'Ah, hello, Custody Sergeant. I understand you are holding my client, Mr Rodney Littlechild. I'm his solicitor, Sam Browne.'

Lomax watched fascinated as she listened and studied the smoke coiling from her cigarette. Her cheeks began to flush.

'Listen, Mr Custody Sergeant, I know you can't confirm such matters to complete strangers over the phone. I'm not stupid.

I'm not asking you to confirm it, I *know* you're holding my client and I've been waiting nearly two hours for someone to return my call. Now please get the senior arresting officer on the line immediately. Inspector Millford.' Her eyes blazed. 'Yes, yes, Millman – whatever.'

Another icy silence as she listened.

Then her tone lightened perceptibly. 'Yes, I know he's engaged. He's engaged in interrogating *my* client. How many other murder inquiries has he got on today? At this moment he is trying to squeeze a false confession out of my client who has not even been granted his rightful access to a solicitor. I expect your DCI Millman is pulling out his fingernails even as we speak.'

Lomax overheard the sound of male laughter from the receiver.

'I'm glad you think it's funny. Ah, right. Thirty-six hours under PACE. Well, thank you for confirming that to a complete stranger. Now get Millman to call me back in five minutes or I'm straight down there. And I'll scream and bloody scream until I see DCI Millman. Gottit?' She listened and a slow smile of satisfaction started to spread across her face. She gave Lomax a thumbs-up sign. 'Right, Sergeant, you know where to reach me and I *expect* a call. Now your name and number, if you please? In the next ten minutes, right? This conversation has been recorded. Thank you.' She replaced the receiver abruptly. Then noticed the suction-pad cup of the tape deck's microphone wire lying on top of her desk. 'Well, it would have been if I'd remembered to plug it in.'

Lomax said: 'That was some performance.' He didn't bother hiding his tone of disapproval.

She eyed him frostily. 'That wasn't a performance, Mr Lomax, that was for real.'

She wasn't taking this seriously, Lomax was sure of that. To her it was just a game. He said sternly: 'I'm not sure it's the way to get results.'

Her mad eye widened a fraction. 'An expert are you? You'd prefer the – what is it you SAS supermen call it – the winning hearts-and-minds approach? If I'd tried that with the police, your friend Mr Littlechild would have confessed to being Mary Poppins by the time I got to see him.'

He retreated grudgingly. 'I'm sure you know best.'

She leaned forward, stubbing out her cigarette end as she did so. 'I tell you what I do know. The thirty-six hour rule is real sledgehammer stuff. Usually it's reserved for major drug traffickers or big-time villains with bent solicitors who might tip off others involved.' She gave a jerky little smile at that. 'Somebody's obviously given the police the idea that your brother-in-law has Loyalist terrorist connections, maybe even co-conspirators in Fitzpatrick's murder. Something that would justify denying legal access.'

'Who'd have done that?'

'One guess, if it's true MI5 have been playing fast and loose with the Littlechilds and making threats. So maybe I should read more into the use of denial of access in this case.'

'Like what?'

'Like they're using it quite legally to get your brother-in-law on his own without representation for as long as possible. Let's assume, as both you and Evie believe, that Roddy is innocent. They'd be aware that it will take a lot of pressure and persuasion to make him admit to it.'

Lomax frowned. 'You're suggesting the police *know* he's innocent?'

She smiled uneasily. 'I hope to God our legal system isn't that corrupt. No, I'm sure the arresting officers think they've got their man. But maybe higher up . . .'

'MI5?'

'Nowadays the Security Service is working very closely with the regular police, pushing for a new role for themselves, even though they're politically unaccountable – despite the public window dressing. If they, or someone, know or knows that Roddy is innocent, they'd obviously say the opposite to the police who would have no reason to disbelieve confidential MI5 intelligence. They'd easily persuade the police quite legally to deny access and let them innocently do their dirty work.'

It was a frightening proposition, Lomax thought, and one that left a nasty taste in his mouth. Over the years in the SAS he had rubbed shoulders with MI5 members and had brief snapshot glimpses of some of their operations. He and others in the Regiment had rather to take it on trust that what they were doing was for the greater good. But sometimes, particularly in Northern Ireland, it had left him wanting to ask questions. Questions to which he knew he would be given no answers. He'd witnessed some fairly dark deeds being done; there was no doubt in his mind of the extreme lengths to which the service, unaccountable in its secret domain, was capable of going. And if Roddy was in its sights, he could be in deep, deep trouble.

'But why should they want to frame him?' Lomax asked himself aloud.

Browne sucked on the end of her pen for a moment. 'Perhaps they were afraid of what he might reveal to Lisa Hardcastle.'

The telephone rang again and he jumped. God, perhaps he really should take something for his nerves.

'Yes? Right, put him on,' Browne said, covering the mouthpiece. 'They've obviously had a discussion and decided speaking to me is a job for the big white chief. Stand by for pomp and arrogance and intimidation of a humble suburban solicitor by a higher authority.' She indicated another telephone on a small table next to Lomax's chair. 'Do listen in on the extension. You might learn something.'

He'd just picked up the handset when Superintendent Eric Dymock came on the line, his voice deep, resonant and full of gravitas. 'Is that Miss Browne? I don't believe we've had the pleasure, but I've read your name in the papers. Your reputation goes before you.'

And that's why I've been put on to handle you, Lomax read between the lines.

Sam Browne's voice had dropped an octave and sounded seductively husky with the hint of a laugh. 'You shouldn't believe all you read, Superintendent, you know how the papers exaggerate. Anyway, thank you for coming back to me so promptly.' So silky, so genuine.

'My pleasure. So what can I do for you?' Playing games.

'You're holding my client, Mr Rodney Littlechild, on suspicion of murder and he requires immediate access to legal advice as, of course, you are well aware is his right.'

'Oh dear, Miss Browne, I do believe someone at this end has fallen down. You should have been advised that Mr Littlechild is being quite legally denied access to a solicitor in accordance with PACE. You understand what that means?'

'Fully,' Browne replied evenly. 'And it is totally inappropriate in this case. My client is neither a drug trafficker nor a master criminal.'

An intake of breath, steeling himself. 'You may think what you like, Miss Browne, but with due respect it is not up to you to tell the police how to conduct their investigation. I personally gave authority in writing for Mr Littlechild to be held without legal access for up to the permitted thirty-six hours.'

'Then perhaps you'd be kind enough to indicate the strength of evidence you have to entitle you to take this exceptional step?'

'I am not prepared to discuss this over the phone.' Uncompromising.

'In person. I'll be with you in thirty minutes.'

'Not possible, Miss Browne.'

'Then I'm afraid it's not good enough. You cannot hold someone without access on a whim. You need strength of evidence, you know that, or we'll have your case thrown out in pretrial argument.'

A sigh. 'Very well. We are advised that Mr Littlechild has Loyalist terrorist connections and most certainly had accomplices who we also wish to apprehend.'

'That's a nonsense, Detective Superintendent. My client is not a terrorist.'

'Again with respect, Miss Browne. We do not know that.'

'Since when are terrorists regular agents of the Security Service?'

He wasn't expecting that. 'Er – I wouldn't know what your client claims to have been. It is anyway irrelevant. He is arrested on suspicion of murder under common law. It's as simple as that.'

'If it's that simple,' she retorted, 'then I should be granted access. In one breath you assume him to be a terrorist – highly improbable as he's spent most of the past twenty years abroad – and in the next you dismiss as unimportant his claim to have been a loyal servant of MI5. You're being rather selective in your decisions about what might or might not be relevant to this case, aren't you?'

Impatience crept into his voice. 'Miss Browne, I am a very busy man. I cannot spend time arguing semantics with you. Mr Littlechild will continue to be held without access on my personal authority. What is more, I am informed that he has not yet been offered the opportunity to ask for legal advice. Therefore, strictly speaking, you do not even represent him.'

Lomax saw the blood colouring Browne's cheeks, saw her mad eye widen a fraction and the sinews tighten in her neck. 'Wrong, Detective Superintendent. He made his request at the point of arrest – a request for *me* personally – and it was witnessed by his wife who will testify to such in court. Furthermore, I am preparing a formal complaint of misuse of police powers in this case.'

'Your privilege,' he responded blandly. He knew and knew that she knew such a complaint would get nowhere. Now, irritation was plain as he spoke. 'I have nothing further to say on the matter. When your – when the senior interviewing officer sees fit, legal access will be offered.'

Browne's eyes met Lomax's across the table and she gave an almost imperceptible shake of her head. It wasn't looking good; their only chance was slipping away.

Her voice softened. 'Are you aware that Mr Littlechild had a meeting with a woman called Lisa Hardcastle yesterday evening? She works for a TV documentary company.'

Dymock hesitated, obviously wondering where Browne's question was leading. 'I believe so.'

'Do you know what Mr Littlechild was going to tell her?'

'Is that relevant?'

'Well, you seem to be making all the decisions in that department. I suggest you ask your colleagues in the Security Service.'

'What do you mean?'

'Because I am about to arrange a press conference for Mr

Littlechild's wife. She is going to tell the media exactly what Mr Littlechild was going to tell Lisa Hardcastle. I suggest you buy all the papers on the way in tomorrow. It'll be making quite a splash.'

Lomax stared at her. He just wasn't believing this.

Dymock's voice was low and harsh. 'Miss Browne, this is outrageous. Even overlooking the overtone of blackmail, I shall remind you that this case is *sub judice*.'

She grinned now, knowing she had him. 'I think the tabloids may consider that borderline until my client is charged, don't you, Detective Superintendent? And *when* he is, I'm entitled to *immediate* access. Now, please excuse me, I have a lot to organise!' The receiver slammed down. She reached for her cigarettes. 'You know, Mr Lomax, I rather enjoyed that.'

He didn't understand. 'Evie doesn't know what Roddy was going to tell that journalist – and you certainly don't.'

Browne smiled, allowing the smoke to escape past her even white teeth. 'But Detective Super Dymock doesn't know that. The police get paranoid about the press. My guess is he'll go running straight to MI5 and they'll have apoplexy. We've called their bluff.'

They talked about the case and her previous experience in the Peter Keegan trial in Belfast for some ten minutes before the call came through.

It wasn't Dymock this time, but Chief Inspector Millman. 'Miss Browne? I have officially to inform you that we are holding a Mr Littlechild on suspicion of murder. It looks likely we'll have enough to charge him by tomorrow morning. He has requested legal representation and I will then be prepared to grant this. Say, nine o'clock? Do you know how to get to Paddington Green?'

'Oh, yes, Chief Inspector, I do believe I can find my way.' Slowly she replaced the receiver. 'Just enough of a compromise, you see, Mr Lomax, to persuade me not to carry out our threat. I just hope your brother-in-law can hold out. He has to be allowed eight hours undisturbed overnight, so their interview time is running out. But the fact is the police rarely need the full thirty-six hours. Most prisoners break down within twenty-four. And if he does sign a confession, then I'm afraid there'll be little I can realistically do for him.'

'I wish there was something I could do for him. He saved my life once, and now when he needs help . . .'

'There is one thing you can do.' She gave a tight little smile and arched her eyebrow.

'What's that?'

'Pray.'

Detective Chief Inspector Millman drew himself up to his full height. He was unshaven and looked as exhausted as the big man who sat before him, shoulders hunched over the interview table. They'd finished their questioning at ten o'clock the previous night, and had begun again at six that morning. It had been a long verbal duel.

Henwick glanced pointedly at his wristwatch. A quarter to nine. They were running out of time; this was their last chance.

Millman cleared his throat: 'Is there anything you'd like to say?'

Littlechild glowered up at him. 'Like what? A confession?'

'Anything that would make your future easier for you. Anything you may later want to rely on in court.'

The shaggy head of unkempt hair shook slowly. 'I've nothing more to add.' Littlechild stared at his own hands stretched out on the desk before him, but gave no indication that he was listening. He'd cracked it, beaten them. But it hardly felt like a victory.

The detective sighed. 'Right, let's get you charged. Your solicitor's waiting outside.'

The prisoner looked up; it was the first he'd heard of it. 'Solicitor?'

'The one you asked for. Samantha Browne.' Millman's face bore a strange expression. 'As if you didn't have enough problems.'

Without further delay, Littlechild was escorted out of the custody suite to the front desk where the custody sergeant was laughing and sharing a joke with a tall and strikingly attractive middle-aged blonde in an emerald-coloured business suit.

'Rodney Littlechild for charging,' Millman announced.

The smile died on the sergeant's face as he swallowed what he was eating and threw a foil wrapper surreptitiously into his bin. 'Prisoner's brief's just arrived, sir. Miss Browne,' he said, quickly adopting a sombre tone.

Littlechild only knew her by name and reputation and certainly hadn't anticipated the warm and dazzling smile. 'Hello, Roddy, nice to meet you.' Without waiting for his tongue-tied reply, she added: 'You, too, Detective Chief Inspector.'

Millman was immediately irked that he felt distracted by her obvious charm and he tried to cover it with a moody and noncommittal grunt of acknowledgement.

'Rodney Albert Littlechild,' the custody sergeant began solemnly, 'you are charged that on the night of August 15 you did murder Donal Padraig Fitzpatrick, which is against the peace . . .'

When the formalities were complete, Browne followed Millman, Henwick and the prisoner to the consultation room.

'I've brought a few home comforts,' she told Littlechild and extracted a small blue gingham cloth from the large plastic bag she carried and proceeded to spread it over the interview table. Littlechild and the detectives watched bemused as she produced hot bacon rolls and croissants wrapped in foil and two plastic mugs containing sachets of Colombian coffee. And, lastly, a small framed family snap of Evie.

'Your wife sends her love. She's thinking of you.'

Millman could stand it no more. 'Miss Browne, this is most irregular . . .'

She gave him her most disarming smile. 'Yes, it's amazing what a custody sergeant will allow in return for a bacon roll, isn't it? Don't worry, he's already checked everything. No containers to hide explosives and no files hidden in the fruitcake. It may be irregular, but then he had to concede there are no rules exactly forbidding it either. So let's humanise this process a little, shall we?'

Browne knew how helpless and abandoned a newly arrested prisoner felt, especially after being broken down by hour after hour of intense interrogation. Littlechild would be at a low ebb, feeling degraded and humiliated, and police canteen food was hardly likely to raise his spirits. She thrust the two mugs at Millman with a wide smile. 'I suppose I couldn't ask you to be a sweet and fill these with hot water?'

The inspector had taken them on reflex before he realised what he was doing. He stared down at them with contempt.

'Only sachets of coffee,' she assured him, 'not coke.'

In disgust, he passed the mugs to DS Henwick. 'Get these filled,' he ordered and marched from the room without another word.

'So you've been charged,' Browne said later as she watched Littlechild tuck into the bacon roll like a starving man. 'And you haven't made any form of confession?'

He swallowed and washed the food down with the sweet black coffee. 'No way, although I came pretty close at times. The anti-interrogation training helped.'

She nodded. 'South African Army?'

He looked surprised. 'You're well briefed.'

'I spent all yesterday afternoon and part of the evening with your wife.'

'How is she?'

'Better now. Over the initial shock. Her brother's been looking after her.'

'Chris is a pal.'

'You're wearing overalls, I see.'

'What? Oh, yeah, I think they took my entire wardrobe away for tests.'

'Of course. But to be on the safe side we must verify exactly what you were wearing the night before last.'

'Sure.'

'Look, Roddy, if you can bear it, I'd like you to go over the background of events leading to the night of the murder. I'm sorry to be a pain, but it really is necessary.'

Inwardly he groaned, but knew she was right. He ran briefly through his life history, then explained the recent pressure he had been placed under by MI5, and finally recounted what had happened on the night he'd met with Fitzpatrick.

Browne listened intently without interruption, just sipping her coffee and smoking to aid her concentration. She believed that first impressions of a client always counted, and she already found herself admiring Littlechild's resilience.

He was a large-boned man, weighing maybe sixteen stone and standing several inches over six feet tall. His large blunt features prevented him from being exactly handsome, but his rather serious eyes came alive when he spoke about subjects close to his heart. Southern Africa, Northern Ireland, Evie. He didn't smile much – he had little to smile about, she realised – but when he did, it was charming and quite infectious. A quiet and thoughtful man, she decided, who probably needed a beer or two to help him drop his guard and become the affable and good-humoured companion that Lomax had described. 'Upright' and 'intensely loyal' were two terms that stuck in Browne's mind and she made a mental note to write them down after the interview.

His voice was low and his words carefully chosen. Holding back, she knew, like they always did until she could coax them into giving her their trust.

When he had finished, Browne said: 'The prosecution will be looking for a motive, Roddy. My guess is they'll say: "Look, this man has a staunch Protestant background with old childhood friends who are in the paramilitaries. He's gained military experience abroad with vilified racist regimes. He hates blacks like he hates the Roman Catholic Church in general and the IRA in particular. Like all hard-line Loyalists he thinks the current peace process is a sellout to terrorism. What better motive to kill Fitzpatrick and cause the cease-fire to collapse?" What would you say to that?'

A ghost of a smile passed across Littlechild's lips. 'Well, Fitzpatrick's dead and the ceasefire lives. He wouldn't have been the one to kill anyway, because he was against it himself. Besides, it would take more than the death of one man to bring it down – there's quite a large clique who are holding sway in the IRA at the moment.'

She considered that. 'The prosecution will say you're now being wise after the event. That you saw killing as the only solution to stop a sellout, handing your beloved country over to Dublin.'

Littlechild shook his head. 'Not as long as the British Government keeps its word – that the majority in Ulster will have the final say through the ballot box.' He leaned forward and for the first time she saw those serious grey eyes dancing with the light of passion. 'I want to take Evie home, to raise our kid there. I can't do that if we're plunged back into bloody carnage for another generation. No, while London keeps its word, then I personally would stay my hand.'

For a moment she was tempted to ask, but if London didn't? But somehow she thought she knew the answer to that.

Instead, she said: 'You didn't kill Fitzpatrick, Roddy, but someone did. Have you any idea who that might have been?'

He looked at her steadily and she saw the worry in his eyes. 'I've thought of nothing else – that's when I wasn't being questioned by Millman and his sidekick. I haven't slept, couldn't, just kept churning it over and over.'

'Any conclusions?'

He looked uncomfortable and glanced round the deserted interview cell. Browne realised suddenly she'd seen this before, the same fear, the same paranoia. Back in Belfast when she'd been with Peter Keegan before his trial. At last he said, almost casually: 'I don't know. Some shadowy force.' But the fierce burning look in his eyes belied the throwaway phrase.

He meant MI5, Her Majesty's Security Service. They both knew it.

She said: 'But why would they kill or have Fitzpatrick killed?'

'As I've already said, he was head of a faction of the Provos that's dead opposed to the peace process. And they want to get rid of anyone standing against progress.'

'These people,' she said, trying not to sound too sceptical, 'I know they bend a lot of rules, fight dirty. I know that from defending Peter Keegan. But a murder like this is a bit hard to believe.'

'For you maybe, but I *know*. Before they turned against me, I had a visit from one of them. She wanted me to set up an old friend of mine – Stevie Gavin – because he too is resolutely against the peace process as a complete sellout.'

'Who is this Stevie Gavin?'

'A leading Loyalist paramilitary. Known as "Rattler", short for Rattlesnake. He runs a hard-line splinter group called the Ulster Defenders.' He indicated her cigarettes. 'Would you mind if I scrounged one of them, Miss Browne?'

She handed him the pack and then gave him a light. 'I think you'd better call me Sam. More informal, because we're going to be seeing a lot of each other over the next few months.'

'Sure.' His eyes softened. 'Sam.'

At last she sensed she was breaking through the barrier. 'So tell me more about Stevie Gavin?'

He allowed a trail of smoke to escape his lips. 'Well, I've known Stevie since school, like I had Fitzpatrick. As you've probably gathered, Stevie Gavin is no angel. No, in fact, Stevie Gavin is a murderin' little shite. He was always wild at school, so he'd probably have become a gangster of some sort if the Troubles hadn't come along when they did. But it was the Troubles and the existence of the IRA that turned him into a killer. He passionately believes that what he's done is right. He's told me he'll happily stand and give an account of his actions before God when his day comes. And he means it.'

Browne smiled awkwardly. 'He sounds charming.'

'Fact is, Sam, he is. In other circumstances you'd probably call him a lovable rogue. Bet you've defended a few of them in your time? He's got a bit hard now, mind. Hard and cynical, beginning to realise how the Brits have used him.'

'How?'

'In the past, MI5 were content for Gavin to kill Provos on their behalf. They'd give him a name, an address and he'd always be happy to oblige. Then, when it suited them, they wanted me to betray him.'

'They wanted you to help get him arrested?'

Littlechild gave a short, dry laugh without humour. 'No, Sam, they wanted me to kill him.'

Three

Sam Browne spent most of her journey to Southall with her mobile tucked under her chin and wreaking minor havoc in the dense urban traffic as she juggled handset and *A-Z* atlas with the steering wheel while changing gear.

After briefing Ernie Eisner on the urgent letters she wanted sent to Paddington Green, she spoke to Totty to resolve any problems that had arisen in her absence. Then she put a call through to Tristram Meyrick QC's chambers in the Temple and arranged a preliminary meeting for that evening.

Two more wrong turns and an altercation with a reversing delivery lorry and she found herself in Evie Littlechild's street. Immediately she felt sorry for the woman. It was a sadly rundown neighbourhood with many of the houses boarded up, rubbish-strewn pavements, and the crushing machine of a nearby breaker's yard providing constant background noise.

The vertical row of bell-buttons confirmed that the once proud Victorian residence had been divided up into flatlets. There was no name beside the top button. Roddy and his wife being ultracautious, she decided as she rang.

Lomax's voice came over the intercom, but it was another few minutes before he descended the stairs to let her in. 'All a bit primitive, I'm afraid,' he apologised. 'No automatic opening.'

She was taken aback to see that his trousers and sweater were covered in dust and cobwebs, his face smudged with dirt. 'I see you've been doing some housework,' she said. 'A belated spring clean?'

He smiled. 'Not quite. I've been up in the loft.'

The hallway tiles were chipped and a pram and a mountain bike obstructed the passage to the bottom of the wooden staircase, the air smelling of cooking cabbage.

'Hope you're feeling fit,' Lomax said. 'It's a long haul.'

He wasn't exaggerating. By the time they reached the top

floor, she was slightly out of breath, although Lomax seemed totally unaffected. The low ceilings and sloping walls suggested that this had once been the servants' quarters, so these partitioned flatlets would be the cheapest in the building. Two front doors stood side by side on the top landing and above them a trapdoor hung open. 'A communal loft,' he explained as he closed the trap and folded the stepladder. 'I was checking if that's how they did it.'

She didn't follow, still trying to regain her breath. 'Did what?'

'Bugged the place. A microphone in a ceiling-light rose.'

'Pardon me?'

Lomax extracted a thin strand of cobweb dangling from his hair. 'If Roddy's telling the truth, and I'm sure he is, anyone trying to set him up would have to get their timing right. That means they'd have to know exactly what Roddy planned to do and when. It follows.'

'Er – yes, I suppose it does.' She glanced up at the trapdoor. 'Did you find anything?'

'Nothing conclusive, but then there wouldn't be, would there?'

'What do you mean?'

'They'd be professionals; Sector One of A Branch if this is official.'

'But there was nothing actually there?'

'Not now.' He pushed open the door to Evie's flat. 'Anyway, come on in. I'll put a brew on.'

The place was a mess. All the furniture in the living room had been stacked to one side and the carpet rolled back to reveal bare boards. Drawers from the sideboard and wall units were stacked separately and various ornaments lay on the dining table with their bases removed. 'What's been happening?' she asked.

'All part of the bug hunt,' he replied from the kitchen where he was filling the kettle. 'Evie's getting some sleep, but she's due up soon.'

'The wine-bar job? God, surely she's not up to that today?'

He returned to the living room. 'Desperate for the money,

I'm afraid. I'll take her in some tea in a minute. How was Roddy?'

'Well enough, but feeling pretty down.'

'I'm not surprised,' Lomax answered and rolled the carpet back into position.

'You seem to know a lot about bugs,' she observed, 'and where to look for them.'

He gave a sheepish grin, rather boyish, she thought. 'I've planted a few in my time. But mostly providing backup while Box did the dirty deed.'

'Box?'

'Sorry. Slang for the Security Service. MI5's postal address used to be Box 500, Whitehall. Maybe it still is. Anyway, the name stuck.' He began repositioning the furniture. 'I've gone through all the favourite places, like behind drawers and hidden in the base of ornaments and lamps or fixed to curtains. I've removed all the plug sockets . . .'

'What about the telephone?'

'Clean, but then I thought it would be. Roddy was on his guard and knew Box were making a nuisance of themselves. I've no doubt he checked the phone himself. There's a communal junction box downstairs, but no unexplained wires. Anyway, they'd probably do that at one of the street boxes in the district or at the main exchange. We'd never know.'

The thought made her feel quite uneasy. 'At least you didn't actually find anything in the loft.'

He was now replacing the drawers. 'There is something else.' Next to the sofa and telephone table a pair of small double doors were set into a dormer. Lomax opened them, ducked his head and stepped out onto the flat roof of an extension at the back of the house.

Browne followed and found herself looking down onto the leafy trees and back gardens of the neighbouring houses.

'There's an iron fire-escape ladder down to the garden,' Lomax explained. 'It's easily accessible once you've scaled the perimeter wall.'

'I see,' she said, and in her imagination could see a black-clad figure climbing stealthily in the dark.

Lomax turned back to the double doors and pointed to the rotting timber frame. 'D'you see this?' He jabbed his forefinger at the tiny hole. 'That's one very lonely woodworm, or else it was made for some type of probe mike.'

'You're kidding?'

He demonstrated with a straight length of fuse wire. It went right through to the interior. Straightening his back, he said: 'It's a popular method if you don't want to access the property and they'd have been aware that Roddy would know what to look out for.' He rattled the handle. 'The paintwork's flaked here and you can see very slight indentations in the wood. Fresh, not weathered.'

'Forced entry? But you said . . .'

'Maybe the night before last, ahead of the police raid.' He indicated the scattering of paint scrapings underfoot.

'Very recent. And I found footprints in the garden, through the shrub beds from the fence. Trainers, probably a common pattern. It was a wet night and the intruder left earth deposits on the rungs of the fire-escape ladder. Male, about ten stone.'

'You can tell that?'

He nodded. 'From the footprints. It used to be my job.'

'Of course, tracking. I'd forgotten.' Suddenly she thought of the answerphone tape wiped clean and shivered despite the mild sunshine. 'Do you mind if we go back inside?'

Lomax poured the tea and took a mug in to Evie. She emerged a few minutes later wearing a dressing gown, her face waxy and drawn. 'God, I must look awful,' she said, running a hand through her hair. It was matted and stringy. 'I really ought to wash it.'

'Did you sleep?' Lomax asked.

She nursed the mug in her hands. 'A bit. Not much.' She looked at Browne. 'How's Roddy?'

'Fine. He sends his love.'

She recounted her meeting at Paddington Green, deliberately trying to sound more optimistic than she felt. 'Look, Evie, the simple fact is that Roddy did not murder Fitzpatrick. Therefore it's logical that any evidence cannot be more than circumstantial. If we can expose that to a judge and jury, the

71

case may well collapse.' She turned to Lomax. 'I think it's vital that we establish that Roddy was a loyal and dedicated servant of the Crown, an MI5 agent. And that they turned against him and made very serious threats.'

'Won't they deny that?' Evie asked.

'I expect so. Although it's not our job to prove who did kill Fitzpatrick, I think it'll be essential to open the judge and jury's minds to the likely possibilities – whatever they might be.'

Evie was listening to the solicitor carefully. 'How can we do that?'

'I don't know yet. But we can start with Peter Keegan. As you know, I defended him in Belfast in 1989. He and Roddy knew each other. If anyone can confirm that your husband worked for MI5, he can.'

'But he's serving twenty years,' Lomax pointed out.

'Exactly,' Browne replied. 'He's doing time for multiple murder conspiracies. But it doesn't prevent him appearing as a defence witness and, in a way, a highly credible one who really knows about that murky world.'

'Why should he agree to give evidence?' Evie asked.

'Because he was a friend of Roddy's and an ally. Keegan was an army informer and your husband was run by MI5 – ' Browne hesitated, turning to Lomax. 'You said that you knew Keegan, Chris?'

He nodded. 'Vaguely. We exchanged a few words when I took him to meet his controller. A sort of minder role.'

'Then he might appreciate a friendly face.'

Lomax wasn't so sure. 'He's as likely to think of me as the enemy. I was working for the men who deserted him when things got rough.'

'But he'll realise that was nothing to do with you, won't he?'

'We'll see.'

'Does that mean you'll come with me to see Keegan? I'd be most grateful.'

He glanced at Evie, who shrugged. Why not, what harm would it do? 'Okay, unless I've got a job interview.'

Browne blinked, forgetting this soldier was now unemployed. 'Oh, yes, of course. Anyway, I'll have to get permission from the prison authorities and agreement from Peter Keegan himself.' She glanced at her watch. 'My God, is that the time? I'm due to see a barrister at six in central London. His name is Meyrick, Tristram Meyrick. He's very good and I hope to persuade him to take the case. I suppose the two of you wouldn't like to join me? You're more familiar with the details than I am yet.'

Evie gave a plaintive smile. 'The wine bar, I'm afraid. I can't afford the sack.'

Lomax said: 'I'd be happy to come.'

Browne smiled. 'That's good. Perhaps we can drop Evie on the way.'

'Standard rates, I suppose?' Keith Billbury asked.

It was almost the first question asked by the senior clerk of Tristram Meyrick QC's chambers at 10 Paper Buildings.

He had greeted Browne in his usual ebullient fashion, kissing her cheek and unashamedly addressing her as Cruella, the wicked and aristocratic dog-snatcher from the Disney film. Things were just winding down from the hectic rush as Billbury and his team sorted all the briefs arriving from solicitors for the next day's trials, criminal and civil, at courts the length and breadth of the land.

It was Billbury's job to be mother hen to the forty barristers of varying ages, experience and abilities, who worked from the chambers of Sir Neville Grant-Montague QC. He had to keep even the most junior – and sometimes useless – advocate as gainfully employed as possible, juggle fees and availability amongst his solicitor clients and, with uncanny clairvoyance, sort out the nightmare of trial calendars. But his most important task of all was to make sure they all got paid for their work. For, despite the fact that much of solicitors' income resulted from chasing bad debtors and defaulters, Billbury knew from long experience that they themselves were always the last ones to put their hands in their pockets. Or, sometimes, even to buy a round of drinks.

Eisner, Pollock and Browne were no exception.

'I do believe our fees on Regina v. Willis are still outstanding.'

Browne gave one of her best pouty smiles. 'I'll speak to Ernie about it. The cheque's as good as in the post.'

'I hope so,' Billbury said, 'cos we're obviously not goin' to get very fat and rich on this Littlechild thing. No question it's Legal Aid?'

'No question, Keith. We signed up this morning.'

'From what you told me on the blower this afternoon, you'll get nothing but obstruction from the Board if the spooks are involved. Pity this killer of terrorists hasn't got loads of family dosh to spend on his defence, cos that's what he's gonna need.'

Browne coughed. 'Sorry, I should have explained. Chris Lomax is Roddy Littlechild's brother-in-law.'

For a moment Billbury looked suitably abashed, but only for a moment. 'Sorry, Mr Lomax spoke a bit out of turn there.'

Lomax fixed the man with a hard stare. 'My brother-in-law isn't a killer of terrorists, as you put it. That's the whole point.'

Billbury grinned and shrugged, perching himself on the edge of a cluttered desk beside an ashtray piled high with cigarette ends. The Italian floral silk tie, which matched his braces, was open at the throat and he had a can of lager in his hand. Clearly this was unwind time. It could have been an office at Hereford after a hazardous but successful mission. 'If this Roddy Littlechild *had* topped the bloke, though, they should be giving him a bloody medal. That's what most people would think. Trouble is Legal Aid's always a double-edged sword. Everyone gets paid – even if we have to wait a year – but the Board is very tight-fisted in what it allows.'

'Keith's right,' Browne agreed. 'The system works all right for barristers, to a point, but it's hardly profitable for the solicitor who has to do all the legwork.'

Lomax found himself thinking, barristers doing alright, narrow margins for solicitors, what about the poor bloody defendant? This was just a game to them. What's in it for me? Who cares whether a man is innocent or guilty? Billbury clearly didn't give a toss whether Roddy had killed a man or not. Just pay us the money and we'll sing your tune.

Perhaps the senior clerk read it in Lomax's eyes. 'Sorry, all this probably sounds a bit cynical. 'Tis, I suppose, but we see it every day. Every defendant reckons he's innocent, then we find later he's the biggest villain under the sun. And anyway, Britain's famous legal system is just about as fair as a lottery. Mostly we can tell if we'll win or lose a case straightaway – just from experience. But we have to go through the motions, play the charade anyway. Because at the end of the day, we've got mortgages to pay and wives and kids to feed.'

'Not a very rosy picture you're painting, Keith,' Browne chided.

Billbury grinned, but he was unrepentant. 'If it's roses you want, try a florist, not a lawyer. It's as well that everyone knows the bottom line. We do what we do because we get paid for it. And the better we are the more work we get. Lucky for your brother-in-law, we just happen to be the best.'

Perversely Lomax found himself warming to the man. Proud of his team, a pro. Worked hard, probably played hard too, and no bullshit.

'We've no room for bleeding hearts,' the clerk added. 'Like doctors and police, we can't allow ourselves to get emotionally involved. Not when you see the tragedies, the heartbreak and the bloody injustice of it all. Take that road and you'll end up topping yourself every time you lose a case.'

'Hope you're not talking for me, dear heart.'

Lomax turned. Two barristers had appeared at the door behind him; one was young and black with a set of grinning white teeth and incongruously was plugged into a Sony Walkman which emitted a faint and irritating reggae beat.

The man who had spoken was tall, slim and pale-faced with a prematurely balding crown. About my age, Lomax thought, and with a certain presence despite his rather thin and regular features. This man was no Rumpole, his face unmemorable except for an intensity in the dark and intelligent eyes.

It was the voice, Lomax realised. The voice was everything. Pitched fairly lightly now, it still carried natural authority. It would not have sounded amiss on stage at the Royal Shakespeare Company.

'Tristram,' Browne said, 'how lovely to see you.'

'And you, dear heart.' He turned to the smiling black

barrister. 'This is young Ronnie Rock. New generation, God help us, but he *has* just won his first major case!'

'Won?' Billbury echoed in disbelief. 'Those two were guiltier than sin itself!'

'Rape case,' Tristram Meyrick explained. 'Not particularly nasty. Ronnie here persuaded the jury it was high spirits that got out of hand and the girl sending out the wrong signals.'

Ronnie Rock didn't like that bland interpretation. 'And that's what it was, Tristram. She was drunk, both blokes were former lovers, they watched a blue movie together, got randy, then the next day she regrets it . . .'

Meyrick raised his hand. 'Okay, okay. Far be it from me to cast aspersions, young Ronald. God, I'm getting hoarse. Going to lose my voice, I think. Now, Sam, dear heart, Keith's been telling me about this tasty little case.'

Browne introduced Lomax. 'This is Chris, the defendant's brother-in-law. Former SAS.'

Meyrick's eyebrows raised. 'Really? Good grief, a comrade-in-arms. I served in 21 back in the eighties. I know you real men don't think we part-timers count, but – anyway, delighted to meet you.'

Afterwards, Lomax considered how his impression of Meyrick had changed at that moment. Suddenly the slightly cynical and effete manner of the stereotypical thespian could be seen in a different light, imagined as an officer, maybe captain, who enjoyed sending himself up, playing the role. 21 SAS might be one of the two part-time regiments, but they went through the same arduous training with none of the rewards of active service at the end of it. Well, none which were officially admitted.

'Look,' Meyrick said, 'we've got to go and celebrate Ronnie's victory. Join us for a pint. Somewhere quiet where we can have a chat.'

The barrister was a good listener. While Ronnie Rock and Keith Billbury stood laughing and chatting at the bar with other clerks and barristers, Meyrick had led the way to a corner table. For the best part of an hour Browne and Lomax talked while Meyrick sipped at his beer and gave them his full attention.

From time to time he jotted down points in his pocket notebook.

'So there it is,' Browne said finally.

At length, Meyrick replied, addressing himself to Lomax. 'Listen, Chris, from what you've both just told me, you are a potential witness. That means I'm not allowed to discuss the case with you. Certainly not the details.' He glanced around, ensuring that no one was within earshot. 'But we're up against people who will readily bend the rules and therefore we may have to do the same ourselves. You know more about this sort of thing than I do, so I'd appreciate your views. However . . .'

Lomax saw it coming. 'This conversation isn't taking place, right?'

'Exactly, it's just a social chat.' He then cut straight to the heart of the issue. 'I'm sure you both realise the serious implications of this case – fascinating as it is? There are only three possibilities as I see it. One is that the defendant committed the crime, which, of course, we know he did not. The second is that our client was unfortunately in the vicinity when a person or persons unknown murdered Mr Fitzpatrick. Not impossible, given the victim's position in the IRA and likely enemies.'

'Another member of the Provos?' Lomax suggested.

That made sense to Browne. 'Roddy said Fitzpatrick was opposed to the peace process. That would put him at loggerheads with some of the IRA leadership.'

'I'm sure that wouldn't be allowed to happen,' Lomax thought aloud. 'Not while he was under MI5 protection.'

Meyrick looked grim. 'Which brings me to the third possibility. That the crime was done at the behest of MI5.'

'Roddy suggested something similar,' Browne confirmed, 'but I find that impossible to believe.'

Lomax agreed. 'It would never get sanctioned. For a start, the timing. The process is at a critical stage and it wouldn't be in the government's interest to blow it off course. And Fitzpatrick was high profile, at least to people in the know. It would raise suspicions.'

'Unless,' Meyrick said slowly, 'there was a ready-made culprit. If MI5 learned that Roddy Littlechild was going to make shock horror revelations in a TV documentary, there would be a strong incentive to shut him up, and jail's a good place for that. Couple it to the fact that Fitzpatrick was dead set against the peace process. It's rather convenient the way things are turning out. Fitzpatrick eliminated and his supposed killer, another thorn in their side, shut away for life.'

That was a sobering thought that Lomax would have preferred not to hear.

'MI5 wouldn't kill someone just like that?' Browne's eyes were wide and glistening.

Very beautiful, Lomax thought. He said: 'You know from the evidence in the Keegan case that they can and do, Sam. Although they'd virtually always use someone else, someone unconnected. A deniable op. If they're involved themselves, then harassment is more their style. Applying untraceable pressure, pulling strings, like they've been doing with Roddy and Evie.'

Meyrick agreed. 'There's no shortage of people willing to do it. I came across enough hard cases down on their luck through 21. More than a couple would do a wet job if the money was right and they thought it had unofficial MI5 approval.'

Lomax couldn't disagree there. 'It would still be unlikely to get sanction from the top.'

Meyrick nodded. 'You're right. No government minister would know, or rather would want to know about it. All nod and a wink stuff. We're talking about a rogue element here, I'm sure of it. But one that nevertheless has to be high up the command chain to make such decisions. Below Director General in MI5, maybe a deputy department head.'

'And the political sanction?' Browne asked.

'I'm guessing,' Meyrick replied. 'Obviously below Home Secretary, but probably someone in his office. Maybe others in the Northern Ireland Office or the MOD.'

Browne felt a sensation like the palm of a cold hand on her back. 'This is sick.'

'The point is, Sam, we should assume the worst. If we're right, we'll be faced with obstruction at every turn, and we'll be up against an omnipotent adversary, the secret state. It also means that security must be paramount. Establish safe communications and as little as possible committed to paper. Anything that is should be triplicated and not kept in my chambers or at your offices.'

Browne paled. 'You really think . . .?'

Lomax said: 'Tristram's right. I've seen those guys at work. They could steal the pyjamas off you while you sleep.'

She whistled softly, then smiled in an attempt to lighten the mood. 'Then it's just as well I don't wear any.'

Lomax and Meyrick exchanged glances. There really was no answer to that.

The next morning, Rodney Littlechild appeared before Belmarsh Magistrates Court and stood stone-faced and ramrod-backed while he was remanded in custody. Only as he turned did he smile thinly while he searched for and found Evie's face amongst those in the public gallery. She had a handkerchief pressed to her cheek, but lifted her hand to wave. Lomax was by her side; at least she was in safe hands.

Sam Browne saw the prisoner briefly in the cell below the courtroom where she gave him as much optimistic news as she could. Tristram Meyrick QC had agreed to take the case, and on the face of it thought his chances of acquittal were good, and she'd written a letter to Peter Keegan requesting an interview. And it wasn't raining. Not a lot really, and they both knew it.

She stood and watched as he was taken off in handcuffs to the underground passage which led directly to Belmarsh High Security Prison. It was a place as bleak as it sounded, a soulless and modern purpose-built fortress on the desolate mud flats beside the Thames estuary. And her heart went out to him.

Three weeks later, Sam Browne still had received no response to her written request to the Anti-Terrorist Branch to visit the scene of crime or to have access to witness statements and the forensic evidence. Millman and Henwick were always out of the office or engaged in interviews and failed to return her calls while Detective Superintendent Dymock's office simply referred her back to the arresting officers. Every approach was blocked.

The only bright note was from Peter Keegan. On Meyrick's advice she had bypassed the prison authorities and hand-written a letter direct to Keegan telling him that a friend of his was in trouble and she would like to meet him as discreetly as possible. If Keegan agreed, he should formerly request that he see his former solicitor, Samantha Browne, to discuss an application for early release. It was not something the authorities could refuse.

A telephone call came through from HM Prison Stafford, not Ulster. Apparently Keegan had been transferred to the mainland to be closer to his elderly mother.

'I'll come at the usual visiting time,' she told the duty officer, 'and no need for a closed visit.' No need to be private.

The man had laughed. 'It's more comfortable in the visitors' lounge here, that's for sure. If you can stand the screaming kids.'

'That's what I thought,' she lied. Private interview rooms can be more easily bugged, she thought.

Boots scraped outside Peter Keegan's segregation cell and the key turned. 'Get your kit together. Back to your old cell. Five minutes to smarten up, then the governor wants to see you. Look sharp.'

Through the interminable steel doors and barred gates, unlock and lock again, down passages and along gantries, up steps and down, back to his cell. A nod from Hutch who shared it with him, the screw waiting while Keegan sluiced his face and ran a comb through his hair. Then more doors and gates, unlocked and relocked, back to the governor's dark-panelled office.

A brisk knock, a command to enter. March in, almost like a bloody soldier, Keegan standing by his escort while Rook finished what he was writing before even looking up. A mournful face, deeply lined and the sunless colour of putty, receding hair and sober suit.

There was never any preamble with Rook. 'You're a fool, Keegan.'

'Sir.'

'Hope your time in CC and four weeks' lost remission has cooled your temper.'

'Yes, sir. It was a very stupid thing for me to have done.'

Rook's eyes were dark, fathomless; he'd have made a good poker player. 'Yes, very stupid. I wanted to help you, Keegan. Wanted to move you to D Wing, give you an easier time.'

'I know, sir. May I ask how Girton is, now?'

The governor watched, cautious before answering. 'He's back on the wing. Sutures in his forehead, his nose broken and nasty bruising.'

'I'm glad he's recovering, sir,' Keegan said, but meant, then I should have hit the bastard harder.

'I'm pleased to hear your remorse, Keegan,' Rook said, 'but it's all too late. I can hardly allow your transfer to D after this, can I? No soft option for you now. You know my rules.'

'No, sir. I suppose not, sir.'

The governor was unblinking. 'The question is, should I send you back to F? Make you start all over again?'

Meaning back to the bottom of Rook's snakes-and-ladders game, where everyone had to start. Pitched into overcrowded F Wing with the tossers and losers who stayed there because they didn't have the savvy to behave and acquiesce for the three weeks it took to move on to B, C or G. For you to get four days' 'association' with the other cons, watch the telly, receive visitors and use the phone.

Keegan didn't answer, held his jaw firm.

Rook regarded the prisoner in front of him. Not a big man, maybe five-ten in his socks and around eleven stone, but with a wiry strength. Black hair and sable-coloured eyes, almost gypsy with a dark intensity that gave just a hint of his inner resilience. How many years under cover for Army Intelligence? Rook asked himself. Six years, if he remembered correctly. Six years on the edge and all he had to show for it was a twenty-year sentence, a broken marriage and financial ruin.

The governor said: 'I've taken your obvious remorse into consideration and the fact that Mr Girton provoked you. I'm fully aware of his little games and the powerbase he's built for himself on G Wing. But I have a feeling he'll steer well clear of you now. Therefore your presence may have a balancing effect, so I've decided to let you return to your present cell. Not for your sake, Keegan, but for the sake of harmony on G Wing, right?'

Yeah! Keegan thought, but struggled to keep the grin off his face. Still on G, still with a view of Crookedbridge Road. Still with Gaza and Hutch, the team intact. All three ex-soldiers who looked after their own. So everything still on track.

'Put one foot wrong, Keegan, and you'll serve out the rest of your time back in F,' Rook was saying. 'Understood? Now, there's a gentleman here from the Home Office who wants a word with you.'

For the first time, Keegan became aware of the man sitting on the leather sofa behind him, had missed the dark-suited figure as the escorting screw had wheeled him in, hard-right to face Rook's desk.

'Mr Prendergast,' Rook added.

The man didn't rise from the sofa. Mid-forties, Keegan guessed, tall and thin with a sallow complexion and light brown hair that had been carefully trimmed. His dark suit was expensively tailored with hand-stitched lapels and the shine on the Church's brogues would have done a guardsman proud.

'Really just a routine visit, Mr Keegan,' he said in a bored-sounding voice. 'The legal department is aware that you are being considered as a material witness in a pending murder trial.'

Keegan raised an eyebrow. 'Just a request to explore the possibilities.'

'From your former solicitor, I notice.'

'Sure, Miss Browne defended my case in Belfast. I feel I at least owe her the courtesy of listening to what she has to say. Nothing wrong with that.'

Prendergast nodded, but he hardly looked satisfied with the answer. 'You realise that to give evidence in someone else's trial might not be in your own best interest?'

Keegan said: 'Is that free advice? Personally, I think it's a matter between me and my brief.'

'Just being helpful,' Prendergast replied. 'Remember, Keegan, when the Parole Board meets it takes into consideration a prisoner's remorse for his crime. And his actions will be considered more relevant than his words.'

'Meaning?'

'Meaning giving evidence for the defence at a former Loyalist gang member's trial may not be seen as the action of a remorseful prisoner.'

'I'll remember that, sir.'

Rook coughed pointedly. 'If you've no more questions, Mr Prendergast?' He looked at Keegan. 'Now, I'm afraid I've some news for you – not good. Your mother's been taken into hospital, pneumonia. She's not at all well.'

Keegan stared. It had happened, as he knew it would. His widowed mother had suffered chronic bronchitis for years and had been virtually bedridden for the past nine months. The whole family had known it was just a matter of time. He'd been banking on it, laying plans. Not wishing it, but also afraid that when it finally came it would be too late. Dear old Mum, you've never let me down. The timing's perfect.

'Has she got long?' he asked.

'A slow decline, they said. A week, ten days. She's in Birmingham Royal Infirmary.'

'Can I visit her?'

Rook consulted the file on his desk. 'I'm considering having you sent to Winson Green for a month. It would be easier to arrange visits from there.'

'I'd be grateful.' Rook not quite the complete bastard after all.

'I'll confirm it with Winson Green and arrange for you to go tomorrow after breakfast. Okay?'

'Thank you, sir.'

'Right, now visiting is in half an hour and your Miss Browne is listed. Remember what I said earlier and don't let me down again.'

Keegan straightened his back. 'Sir.' And the prison officer marched him out.

Rook turned to Prendergast. 'If you still want to watch, I suggest you go to the observation room before visiting starts.'

*

Lomax hated prisons. He'd seen the inside of several during anti-riot exercises when the SAS was expected to go in ahead of the warders to restore order, take out the most dangerous ringleaders. Just the thought of it brought on an uncommon sense of claustrophobia. To be locked in every night with people you probably didn't even like; the snoring and the farting; to see proper daylight for only an hour a day; the grinding, mind-numbing routine; the congealed and lukewarm institutionalised food and even being subjected to other people's choice of television. Outsiders had no conception of what even an 'easy regime' was like.

HM Prison Stafford on Gaol Road had been rebuilt in 1793 and modernised since. He and Sam Browne entered through the towering granite face of the gate lodge and joined the congregating mass of visitors: some men, but mostly wives and girlfriends with kids and babies in tow. Everyone was searched, clothing, bags and even the nappies young mums brought in case a change was needed. Drugs, Lomax knew, was what they were looking for, now a major problem in every prison.

The visitors' lounge was lushly carpeted, bright and airy with a high-vaulted ceiling and canary-yellow walls. They were allocated one of the groups of chairs, each gathered around a low coffee table which made it impossible to pass contraband beneath. Lomax and Browne took the blue padded chairs, the single red one left vacant for the prisoner.

When everyone was settled, the cons started coming in one by one. There was much hugging and kissing and tears, a lot of children shrieking with delight as they recognised their fathers.

Keegan looked older than Lomax remembered, but then *he* probably did too. People changed more than they realised in – how many must it be? – eight years. But the man looked well, pale but fit. Certainly better than when Lomax had last seen him. That haunted expression had gone, the nervous mannerisms of the undercover agent replaced with a quiet confidence.

'Hello, Peter,' Browne said, extending her hand.

'Sam.' He ignored Lomax. 'You still look stunning.'

She blushed slightly. 'That's the make-up. It gets thicker every year.'

'I don't believe that.'

'I think you know Mr Lomax.'

Keegan turned his head, eyes narrowing. 'Do I?'

'By sight,' Lomax said. 'You just knew me as Chris.'

Recognition dawned. 'God, my minder. It's been a long time. Don't think I ever saw you properly.' A laugh at the memory. 'We were always creeping about in shadows.'

'How you doing, Peter?'

'As well as can be expected in this shit hole. You still with the mob?'

'No, I'm out.'

Keegan turned to Browne. 'What's this all about, Sam?'

Browne told him.

He listened intently for twenty minutes without interruption. When she'd finished he turned to Lomax. 'So you're Roddy's brother-in-law? Small world.'

Lomax said: 'He needs your help.'

'What do you want me to do?'

'Give evidence,' Browne replied. 'MI5 have made it clear they're going to deny he was ever an agent of theirs.'

'All the main Loyalist players have worked for them at one time or another,' Keegan said. He added: 'Wittingly or otherwise.'

'You can start by testifying to that,' Browne replied. 'Tell the jury how it was, how it is. Everyone running their own shadow show – the RUC, Army Intelligence and MI5. No one knows better than you.'

'True enough,' Keegan conceded. 'At the time the army was running me, MI5 was running Roddy. Neither of us knew. They played us like pawns, expendable.'

'But you discovered that Roddy was an agent in the end?'

Keegan nodded. 'It was confirmed by my army controller. It came as quite a shock, but it shouldn't have done.'

'Why?' Browne asked.

'Like I said, we'd all volunteered or been used at one time or another. Trying to help them screw the Provos.'

'When you were undercover for Army Intelligence in the Ulster Defenders, before you were unearthed by the Penny Inquiry, who else might have known that Roddy was on MI5's payroll in South Africa?'

85

'Not the Defenders' leader Rattler, that's for sure. Stevie Gavin was as surprised as I was – especially at being double-shafted by me and Roddy at the same time. Between them, the army and MI5 had the Defenders well stitched up.'

'No one else knew?' Browne pressed.

'It's just a guess.'

'Who?'

'King Billy. That's what they call him. Billy Baker. Runs a drinking club off the Shankill Road. Calls himself a Loyalist paramilitary, but he's hardly that. Has a gang of thugs to manage various criminal activities, then shoots the occasional Catholic for good measure.'

'That's the name,' Browne murmured. 'The man Roddy said called to tell him that Fitzpatrick was going to make contact. Roddy said Baker could only have got his new number from MI5.'

'That would make sense. King Billy always kept well in with MI5. Suited them both, especially in the old days. It would have been typical of Baker to have known Roddy was with MI5 and keep quiet. Just enjoy the pleasure of seeing Stevie Gavin and the Defenders fucked about. There was never any love lost between them.'

'Perhaps I could get to see this Billy Baker,' Browne thought aloud.

'He'd only see you if it was in his interest, and he won't be easy to find.' Keegan's eyes became fierce slits. 'And I wouldn't try too hard if I were you. He can't be trusted an inch.'

'Then it's down to you to help Roddy. Tell the jury what you've just told me, but with all the details. If he knows you're on his side, he'll know he has a chance. I'm sure later there'll be heavy pressure put on Roddy to plead guilty. Inducements offered. You know the form, Peter, you pleaded guilty in a plea bargain so MI5 could keep its dirty linen locked away.'

Keegan gave a wry smile. 'Against your advice, Sam.'

'Against my advice,' Browne repeated. 'But Roddy might accept it if he knows you'll back him. And if I can prove he was a loyal and trusted MI5 agent I stand a better chance of prising apart the prosecution case, creating doubt. There can be no forensic evidence, and any eye-witness identification by MI5 would become highly suspect . . .'

'Get real, Sam. Don't you realise what you're up against?'

'Of course. I've been here before, remember?'

'They're already on to you.'

'What d'you mean? Who are?'

'The spooks, the government. I saw the governor half an hour ago and there was someone from the Home Office, someone called Prendergast, advising me not to co-operate with you. Said I wouldn't be doing myself any favours.'

Browne's anger boiled. 'They've no right to say that. From the Home Office, you say? What was his name again?'

'Prendergast. Does the name mean anything to you?' Keegan asked.

'Not yet, but I intend to find out who he damn well is,' Browne replied.

'They'll just give you some cock-and-bull story, but I know a spook when I see one,' Keegan said. 'That's what you're up against. You can't win and neither can Roddy or me. We're just casualties amongst the foot soldiers of someone's turf war.'

'What d'you mean?'

'Have you asked yourself why? Why I was abandoned when my undercover role was discovered? Why no one in government pulled any strings to help me? Why Roddy's been set up by the very people he's always served?'

'Roddy turned his back on them.'

Keegan was dismissive. 'That's no reason. An excuse perhaps, but no reason. Once upon a time that would never have happened.'

'So what do you think the reason is?' Lomax pressed.

'I *know* what the reason is.' The prisoner made no attempt to hide his bitterness, his disgust. 'The playing field has gradually been changing over the past ten years, only I was too blind to see it. But then I *was* an early victim. You can trace it back to the Brighton bomb when the Provos damn near wiped out Maggie Thatcher and the entire British Cabinet. That was the start of the rot.'

'It concentrated a few minds,' Lomax agreed.

'And heralded a lot of changes, especially in the Security Service and government departments. Quite a few new faces appeared, people with new ways of doing things. The old Cold War warriors were on their way out, and when they went, old loyalties went with them. Funny how quickly the Anglo-Irish Agreement followed Brighton, opening the door for Dublin to have a say in running Ulster.' He looked at Lomax. 'Your friends in Army Intelligence were okay, but the relationship with MI5 cooled with the Loyalists. Chilled, more like. Groups like ours, the UDA, UVF or the Ulster Defenders could always be relied on to help them out. Claim responsibility for a body in a field, get them off the hook.'

Browne glanced at Lomax for confirmation. 'Did that happen?'

Lomax nodded. 'Not with us, but we heard the stories. The Regiment was on the inside track. There was definitely collusion with some of the Loyalist factions, but not all. They were seen as allies, but a bit crazy and unpredictable.'

Keegan said: 'This new generation of spooks and Whitehall mandarins were quickly taking over as the old-timers were put out to grass.'

'Different values?' Browne guessed.

'Some might say no values at all,' Keegan retorted. 'Pragmatists, schemers, too clever by half. They could see no benefit in prolonging the Irish Troubles by keeping Ulster within the United Kingdom. And as the Communist bloc started to collapse, the province began losing its strategic military importance. Suddenly it was a new game, new rules. I couldn't believe some of those redbrick graduate bastards in MI5. I met a few of them when they pulled the rug out from under me. Full of self-righteous morality about the so-called dirty tactics their predecessors had used. Conveniently forgot those guys had experience from the last war and when the Berlin Wall went up, through the terror wars in Kenya, Israel, Cyprus, Aden, Malaya . . . Conveniently forgot those guys who had stopped the Ulster situation from exploding for nearly twenty years.'

'They hadn't stopped it, though,' Browne pointed out.

Keegan smiled. 'Now you sound just like them.'

Lomax said: 'It was the politicians who prevented it. Left to their own devices, the army and MI5 would have sorted out the Provos. Just like they had elsewhere.'

Keegan agreed. 'The politicians put them in a straitjacket. Because this was too close to home, our own soil. And they were scared of American reaction. They've always been scared of that.' He shrugged. 'So this new policy developed, to get peace at any price, to get Ulster united with Dublin in all but name. Looking back, you can see it clearly now. And people like me and Roddy are embarrassments to be got rid of, along with any evidence of MI5's dubious behaviour in the past. In retrospect it's decided those activities were politically incorrect.'

'Roddy would have done best to have stayed in South Africa,' Lomax said.

'You're not wrong there,' Keegan replied. 'I wish to hell I'd stayed.'

'You were in South Africa?'

'For a while. Back in 1985 for a couple of years. I'd been working as an informer and then an agent for the army on and off since the mid-seventies and I was at the end of my tether. A nervous wreck. I talked to Army Intelligence and then someone in MI5 suggested I went to South Africa with my family. MI5 were always keen for Loyalists to get some proper military training, and that was the ideal place.'

'Why should MI5 want you to have military training?' This was something Browne hadn't been told before. Not why he'd chosen to go there.

'In case of intervention in Ulster by the Irish Army. It's always been a serious concern since the late sixties. If it had happened, there'd have been a popular uprising – but you can't hope to win in guerrilla warfare without proper training.'

He said it so matter-of-factly, as if everyone knew. Repeating exactly what the television journalist Lisa Hardcastle had said Roddy Littlechild told her when Browne had interviewed her a week earlier as a possible defence witness. At the time, she wasn't sure Hardcastle had got it right, it had sounded too fanciful, and she'd yet to ask Littlechild himself about it. Now here was confirmation.

Keegan noticed her reaction. 'So Roddy never told you?'

'Told me what?'

'The reason why he first went to Rhodesia. He was a teenager then, keen to do his bit in the fight against the Provos. He didn't just go to Rhodesia in search of excitement; it was suggested that he go.'

'By MI5?'

'Sure, their people. They pushed the idea hard, encouraged lots of youngsters to go, not just Roddy. Arranged introductions with the Rhodesian Army and provided money for the air fares. At the time, of course, no one knew these people were MI5. Most were just naive wee kids then, but Roddy's learned since.' He fixed Browne's gaze. 'No one's going to risk that stuff getting out in open court – and certainly not in the middle of the peace process. That's why you're up against it.'

'Does that mean you won't help?'

'I didn't say that, Sam. Just don't get your hopes up, or Roddy's.' He sat back in his chair and looked up at the light fitting high above his head. 'See that? There's a security camera up there. They watch your every move. One of the screws let it slip once, heard them joking how they can zoom in up the wives' and girlfriends' skirts if they've got the angle right.'

Instinctively Browne glanced up and closed her knees.

Keegan added: 'Those they're really interested in get put right underneath the camera. That means they're interested in us. So don't produce any paperwork or anything sensitive.'

Lomax leaned forward. 'Listen, Peter, I owe Roddy for the time he saved my life at Goose Green. I don't know if you feel you owe him anything, but you do owe me. That time, the rendezvous on the Ballygowan Road, you'd have walked straight into that stakeout . . .'

'Calling in the favours, Chris?'

'If you like.'

Keegan smiled. 'You don't have to.' He looked across at Browne. 'You were right, Sam, back at my Diplock trial in Belfast. I should have fought them then, recognised their betrayal for what it was. But I was broken, a burnt-out case. I'm eleven and a half stone now; then I was just over nine.'

'You'll give evidence?' she pressed.

'Sure.'

Browne looked relieved, but there was something about the way he said it that made Lomax wonder. As if the man was just saying it to please, to get them off his back.

Prendergast looked at the VDU more closely in the observation room. 'Can you get a close-up of the man?'

'Sure,' said the prison officer at the control, and the camera zoomed in until the face almost filled the screen.

Clean-shaven, mid-forties. The features too craggy, too unfinished to be handsome, just reprieved by a ready lazy smile. Some silvery strands in the fair hair that was slightly too long to be neat. And the eyes, grey and warm, humorous but alert. Once or twice Prendergast saw the pupils dilate and the light die in them, saw the other side of the man.

'Want a print-out?' the warder asked.

'Could you?'

'No problem.'

Another prison officer glanced at his list. 'Name's Lomax. Christopher Lomax. Listed as solicitor's clerk.'

Naughty, Prendergast thought, but said nothing. So that was Lomax. He recognised the name from Rodney Littlechild's file. The man's friend and brother-in-law. Former SAS.

What he wouldn't have given to have listened to what they were saying to Keegan, to have had a radio mike secreted in one of the armchairs. But this was low-key, just covering bets. No need to get tongues wagging.

Keegan was history, had been locked away with his secrets and still another good five years to serve. Keegan had known Littlechild and vice versa, so that was the obvious connection. It was tenuous stuff nevertheless. It told him that Samantha Browne was desperate. That she was just trawling, was on a fishing expedition.

Nothing to worry about, just keep an eye on them.

Then all three had looked up, their faces staring at him through the monitor.

Prendergast took an instinctive backward step, for a moment imagining they could see him. One of the warders noticed and grinned. Stupid, an unspoken shared joke, but it left Prendergast with an uneasy feeling.

After that he couldn't fully believe anything he saw on the screen, couldn't take it at face value. They could be three actors on a TV screen. Any of the expressions, the gestures, could have been for his benefit. Keegan had shaken his head, quite vehemently, and then all three had shaken hands, Keegan kissing the solicitor on the cheek before they went.

All the visitors left first, followed by the prisoners. Only then did Prendergast leave the observation room with the prison officer and wonder if maybe he should increase Keegan's insurance premiums a little, just for safety's sake. When he reached the chief warder's office, he asked to see the governor again.

Rook wasn't pleased at another interruption. 'What is it, Mr Prendergast?'

'I've been thinking about Keegan. In retrospect, I think you were rather lenient with him.'

The governor pursed his lips, wondered what was coming next.

'Might not look too good in my report. And I'd hate it to reflect badly on you. Perhaps if the transfer to Winson Green were to be cancelled . . .'

'I can't do that. There are genuine compassionate grounds and Keegan has been a model prisoner until now.'

'Maybe that – was it Ginger Girton – could be persuaded to press a charge of grievous bodily harm?'

Rook's patience was running thin. 'I doubt it. Cons don't work like that. It's tantamount to grassing. He'd sort it his own way, or more likely just respect Keegan in future.'

Prendergast shrugged. 'Then I'm sorry, Governor, I'll have to file my report as it stands.'

Rook made a decision, and immediately regretted it. But the words were already out. 'When he returns from Winson Green, after his month's transfer, I could put him back in F for a spell.' Break my word, he thought.

'That's more like it, Governor. I'm sure that'll seem more

appropriate to my superiors. There's a lot of public and political pressure to be harder on the criminal fraternity nowadays.'

Don't I know it, Rook thought acidly.

'One small favour, Governor. When you tell Mr Keegan of your decision, drop my name into the conversation. Let him know we're still interested in him.'

Four

Hutch looked up as the key turned and Keegan re-entered his cell.

'How you doin', Pete? How was seg?'

The door slammed shut. 'Fine. Enjoyed the peace and quiet.'

Their joke. Ken Hutchinson, gabby Scouser, armed robber, former child delinquent, former soldier with the Cheshires, just like Keegan. Regimental ties, although they'd never served together.

Keegan moved away from the door and lowered his voice. 'I saw Rook. I'm getting a transfer to Winson Green.'

Hutch's eyes widened. 'It's on?'

'Yes.'

'Why the transfer?'

'My mum's in the infirmary at Brum. They don't give her long.'

'I'm sorry, mate.' Hutch handed him a roll-up.

'Don't be. It was on the cards. Truth is, I think she'll be pleased when her time comes. Life's not been much fun.'

'When do you go?'

'Tomorrow. After breakfast.'

'Christ, that doesn't give you long.'

'Long enough – if we've planned it right.' And they should have, he thought, because he'd spent hours on the card-phone over the past six months. And recently hours at the window overlooking Crookedbridge Road. If it wasn't right now, it never would be.

As soon as the cell door was opened for the association period that evening, Hutch went looking for Gaza on the floor below. John Gascoigne, another former Cheshire, shared his friend's excitement at the news. No time to drop their guard, they decided. Watch Keegan's back for him, just in case Ginger Girton hadn't learned his lesson and was planning his revenge.

The two men went back to Keegan's cell and walked, one each side of him, down to where the card-phones were in the main hall between the gantries and the cells.

Keegan made the call. 'It's on. Tomorrow.'

Hutch and Gaza stayed by his side until lights out and they were locked back in their cells.

Then Keegan stood on a chair to reach the barred window and used a smuggled torch to give the recognition signal. Over the wall in Crookedbridge Road, the answering flash came from the bedroom window of the rented bedsit.

The conversation in Morse went on for twenty minutes before the bedsit curtains were closed and Keegan climbed off the chair and sat on his bunk.

'You meant everything you said?' Hutch asked, still not quite believing.

'Every word – if I can pull it off. You and Gaza have been good mates and I won't let you down. I know what it is to be let down.' He grinned at his friend; a nervous grin, because the time had come. 'One favour. I'll write my mum a letter. See she gets it.'

'No problem.'

Keegan knew he wouldn't sleep anyway and writing pages of things he'd always wanted to say but never had, helped pass the time. There were tears in his eyes when he wrote the final words: Goodbye, Mum. Love Pete.

And the bastards were even stealing his last farewell. Because of them he had to do what he had to do.

It was going to be another scorcher of a day.

Nesbit leaned against the wheel of his artic's tractor unit in his denim shorts and black Def Leppard T-shirt and drained the last drops from the can of Lilt. Eight thirty.

He felt nervous and took out his aggression on the can, crushing it in his huge palm and tossing it into the long grass beside the lay-by. Felt stronger for that, tougher, ready for the job. He swaggered rather than walked around the trailer, checking that he'd loosened enough knots and slipped sufficient ropes from the brass eyelets of the tarpaulin for the slipstream to do its job.

Satisfied, he hauled himself up into the cab and started the diesel. The town of Stafford behind him and ahead Junction 13 onto the M6 motorway and the thirty plus-mile run to Birmingham.

Anywhere will do, the caller had said last night, but sooner rather than later, nearer Stafford than Birmingham.

In truth Nesbit had been surprised to get the call from the man he knew only as Tim. They'd first met two months earlier, Tim approaching him at his local pub. Said he was a friend of Hutch and Nesbit knew Hutch from way back.

'Sometime soon, in the next few weeks or months, we'll need to cause a traffic hold-up on the M6.' Meaning you're an independent, run your own rig. 'Are you interested? A grand in it for you and another to cover costs if you're fined.' Which they both knew was unlikely. 'Half up front, half after.'

Nesbit was always interested in easy money. Hutch was in Stafford nick and therefore maybe he was planning a heist from the inside.

Tim had read his mind. 'Better for you not to know. There'll be nothing to connect you. I'll ring you when it's about to happen.'

And it had happened last night, a motorcycle courier delivering the package to Nesbit's home an hour later. Five hundred in used notes.

This morning Nesbit had put the alarm on for five and had driven to the yard and spent an hour loading a suitable cargo. Alloy tubing, he decided, because once the first ones went off the tail, there'd be nothing to stop the rest. And alloy was light, shouldn't cause any serious damage to the cars or drivers behind him; he really wouldn't want that on his conscience.

Once they were stacked, he placed four cardboard boxes across the rear end of the trailer. When the tubes began to roll, they'd take the boxes with them. The boxes would split on impact with the tarmac and spread their contents. The contents were brittle plastic containers full of galvanised roofing tacks.

All set, everything covered.

Nesbit kept his speed down as he approached the sliproad to the M6, watched the tarpaulin in his wing mirrors. Didn't want the cops pulling him over for an unsafe load until he was in position, until he'd done the job.

He settled down at fifty, the tarpaulin beginning to flap, the crosswind beginning to stir. One mile, two – The flapping getting wilder, a length of loose rope twitching, lengthening like a snake. Nesbit's eye on the mirror, watching for the white paintwork and flashing blue strobe of a patrol car.

A passing sales rep in a Peugeot flashed him a warning.

Eight miles, still flapping but still firm. Sod. He'd warned the man called Tim this was no precise science. Nesbit stepped on the gas, felt the load begin to rock slightly, the slipstream combining with the crosswind.

Sixty, sixty-five.

A clear stretch behind him now. A good time for it to happen, clear of vehicles. His foot went down again, the sun hot in the cab, the sweat staining his T-shirt.

Seventy and pushing it. The tarpaulin like a mad thing now, a giant blue plastic sail hauled aloft.

'C'mon, you bastard!'

Suddenly a coach, gaining fast. National Express, it had to be. Those buggers always in a hurry.

He felt the load shift, sensing rather than hearing the clink and clank of rolling alloy. Cardboard boxes exploding their shrapnel in his wake, tubes spinning and bouncing across all three lanes.

And suddenly the tarpaulin lifting free, like a paraglider wrenched from its mountings by the slipstream, airborne, flying like a kite.

'Oh, Christ!'

Nesbit watched in horror in his mirror as the tarpaulin wrapped itself around the front of the overtaking coach.

The blue Sierra from Cannock Cabs pulled up inside the prison yard and waited as the escort party approached.

Keegan wore uniform denims and was handcuffed between two officers in short-sleeve order.

'Nice day,' said the driver as they climbed into the back seat.

The officer called Mark was a sun freak; always the Med in summer and the UV lamp in winter. 'Another stinker, can't last.'

'Always a nice day to be getting out of this place,' the other officer said. Grumps, as he was nicknamed, was a Yorkshireman.

The Security PO peered through the window to check, the two officers lifted their wrists to show the cuffs. Mark smiled in acknowledgement; Grumps didn't.

As the driver turned left into Gaol Road, the gates swung closed. 'Have you heard about the smash on the M6?'

'No,' Mark replied.

'Came over the radio ten minutes ago. Sounds nasty. Southbound lane closed. Thought I'd take the A34.'

Grumps grunted. 'All right.' It was the obvious choice.

'Take your time,' Mark said. 'No hurry.' And nice scenery, he thought.

Fifty yards behind them a white Astra hatchback pulled out of a side street and began to follow, keeping two cars between itself and the vehicle in front. The driver wore a woollen hat and spoke into a CB. 'Tango Alpha to Tango Oscar. Footballer has left stadium. Also confirmed on scanner, taxi company has advised on diversion. Acknowledge. Over.'

The radio set wheezed with static. '*Roger, Alpha. Keep informed. Out.*'

In the taxi it was becoming unbearably hot, the outside temperature already in the seventies. The radio pumped out Classic Rock's version of 'Paint It Black', Grumps staring straight ahead and Mark watching the pedestrians on the pavements. A lot of young mothers wearing skimpy shorts and tank tops, pushing prams or with toddlers in tow. Lots of lovely brown legs, he thought dreamily, as they began clearing the south-east suburbs of Stafford.

The red Renault Safrane, stolen two months earlier, resprayed, registration plates changed, and garaged ever since, waited a few miles down the road. It was stationary in the entrance to the car park beside the Chetwynd Arms public house, just south of the Brocton Crossroads, the engine running.

Like the driver of the Astra, the man behind the wheel wore a woollen hat and held a CB to his ear. The voice was saying: '*Footballer clearing Walton-on-the-Hill. Traffic steady at forty-five mph. I've just overtaken. Am in position behind taxi. ETA two minutes . . .*'

The man in the Safrane felt the muscles clenching in his stomach and reached across to the bolt-cutters on the passenger seat.

Again the set crackled, the voice higher this time, excited. '*Passing Seven Stars pub NOW!*' Just over a mile to go. '*Looking good, looking good! Over.*'

'Roger,' the Safrane's driver acknowledged. Nothing more to say now. Just the job to do. 'Out.'

The taxi driver drummed a little tattoo on the steering wheel. He was not an impatient man but the estate in front was dawdling, no more than forty-five. He could see it was fully loaded: Mum and Dad in the front and the kids making faces at him over the baggage in the back. Sodding holiday-makers, they assumed the whole friggin' world was on vacation just because they were. That was the trouble living near a place like Cannock Chase, which they were just coming up to now. What was the posh name for it? An Area of Outstanding Natural Beauty. Ten thousand acres of wild heath and woodlands. And come summer the tourists swarmed like bees round a honey pot, rarely walking but always driving and clogging the roads for miles. Locals could only call the place their own in the depths of winter.

He caught sight of the white Astra in his mirror. That hadn't been there a minute before. Hadn't seen it overtake. Still, couldn't blame the man for wanting to get a move on.

His eyes shifted in the mirror, the younger prison officer with his eyes closed, smiling, enjoying the warmth. The older man asleep, mouth slack. And the poor sod in between looking nervous, edgy. Wonder what he's doing time for?

Up ahead Brocton Crossroads. Bungalows on the left, a splash of colour in the front gardens, a farmhouse coming up on his right. The dawdler in front down to forty. Typical! Thumb in bum, mind in neutral.

The flash of the blue strobe caught his eye in the rearview mirror. The white vehicle behind a police car, hadn't realised that. An Astra, didn't know they used them. Must be getting old, must sharpen up.

Crossroads passing and the vehicle alongside, squeezing by. No police insignia and the strobe a single magnetic clamp-on type. That's why he hadn't spotted it. Must be going after the estate. Book him for dawdling. That would be a turn-up for the book, he thought gleefully. That would teach the bastard! Spoil his friggin' holiday!

Pulling in. HEY, WATCH IT! The police Astra carving in front of him, their wings almost touching. The taximan stamped on his brakes, felt the wheels lock on the road, the skid starting. His reaction not quick enough, the shriek of metal engaging as the sparks flew.

Now the Astra pulled ahead, edging in front. He could see the nearside indicator blinking, signalling him to pull over.

God, I'm for it, he thought. Hitting a cop car. Can't argue with them, the local magistrates always took their side.

He edged into the grass verge and stopped opposite a pub car park, the Astra just inches from his bonnet and the officer climbing out. In the back, Mark had his eyes open and Grumps was coming to.

The cab driver couldn't believe his eyes. It wasn't a policeman coming towards him. It was a man in black overalls with a balaclava down over his face. Another man crossing the road from a Safrane parked beside the pub opposite. Dressed the same, bolt-cutters in his hands.

Wrenching open the taxi driver's door, the first man shoved the muzzle of a gun against his cheek. The weapon seemed odd, long and unbalanced. 'You, keep your hands on the wheel! Don't anyone move!' He reached across the driver's lap and tore the radio mike from its mountings.

Now the nearside rear door was opened by the second man. 'Out!' he ordered. Mark obeyed, struggling to untangle his legs, the man pulling him, shouting 'C'MON! C'MON!' Still awkward, one hand remaining attached to the prisoner who was shuffling his way along the seat. Grumps now wide awake and wishing he was still asleep, almost wondering if he still was.

Mark and the prisoner standing side by side, the prisoner stooped because he was still handcuffed to the second prison officer.

'Who the hell are you?' Keegan demanded. He sounded scared.

'You know who the fuck we are! Fuckin' bastard!' Mark paled as he recognised the harsh accent he'd heard a hundred times on the television news. Northern Ireland. 'Now hold your hands up!'

The jaws of the bolt-cutters snapped over the cuffs and they fell to the ground.

'Stay where you are!' the man ordered Grumps. 'Keep your hand still!' A second snap of the cutters, Grumps still crouched, half in and half out of the car. 'Back inside, you two.'

Grumps slid back across the seat and Mark scrambled after him, the door slamming behind.

Now the two men and their prize moved towards the Safrane. Then one gunman turned, lifted up the weapon.

'Oh, Christ!' breathed the taxi driver.

It wasn't the loud report he'd expected as he shut his eyes, anticipating the windscreen crystallising and the round slamming into him.

Just a soft *phut, phut* sound and he felt the vehicle lurch forward and down as the front tyres blew.

As the men in the taxi recovered their senses and breathed in relief, Grumps said: 'Oh fuck, who's shit themselves?'

'Sorry,' the driver muttered, his head pressed against the wheel. He was sobbing.

The Safrane shrieked out onto the A34 in a cloud of dust and swung south in the direction the taxi had been travelling.

In the back, the first gunman was sitting beside Keegan. He yanked off his balaclava, the fringe of blond hair sweat-slicked to his forehead and his blue eyes on fire with excitement. 'Hi, Da, we must stop meeting like this!'

Keegan grinned. 'You're a right chip off the old block and no mistake.'

'Hello, Peter,' the driver of the Safrane said, not taking his eyes off the road. His voice had an unmistakable South African drawl. 'I never dreamed I'd see you again in such bizarre circumstances.'

'You remember Johan van Niekerk?' Keegan's son asked.

'How could I ever forget, old friend?' He reached forward and slapped the man on the shoulder. A gesture of thanks. 'And I liked the Ulster accent. Very convincing.'

And they all laughed. It was the first time Keegan had felt like laughing in six long years.

Within minutes of the prison officer known as Grumps making an emergency 999 call from the Chetwynd Arms on the A34, the control room of Staffordshire Police Force headquarters had swung into action.

The first patrol car diverted to the scene of the abduction had set up an immediate incident post. Because the use of firearms had been confirmed, the duty officer alerted the detective superintendent as well as the inspector who would normally be in overall command of the police reaction.

Barely five minutes after the alert being given, patrol cars were forming a ring of roadblocks in a fifteen-mile radius around the ambush point. An 'all-cars' had been issued to adjoining constabularies in the search for the Renault Safrane and the armed Tactical Support Unit was called up.

Of the twelve members initially available, one each was allocated to the vehicle checkpoints, leaving four men in reserve.

It was almost certain that the – assumed – 'armed terrorists' who had abducted the prisoner would be planning to swap vehicles; the question was where? It might be logical for them to attempt to clear the area and lose themselves in the dense urban sprawls of Wolverhampton or Walsall.

On the other hand Cannock Chase offered numerous secluded car parks in the area of Brindley Heath or the Country Park that were perfect to make the switch. In which case it could be hours before the police knew what car they were looking for, by which time Peter Keegan could have been executed and his killers have got clean away.

'We'll have to go public,' Detective Superintendent Bill Johnson told his inspector. 'Call up local radio, then the BBC. We'd better go national, on the assumption they're out of the area already. On no account should anyone approach these people.'

'Consider it done, sir.'

A duty WPC on the control-room radio console swivelled in her chair and interrupted: 'Sir, the missing Safrane has been located. Barely a mile from the SOC, in woods beside the A34. Looks like it crashed. No occupants, but there appears to have been some sort of struggle. There's blood all over the place. SOCO's going straight there.'

'Are there any signs of another vehicle having been present?'

The WPC relayed the question. 'No, sir. No sign of a switch.'

Bill Johnson groaned inwardly. The abductors were still plainly on his patch. There went the round of golf he'd promised himself later that afternoon. 'Thanks, Fiona. Tell them I'm on my way.'

In fact, one of the earliest vehicles stopped at the A34 checkpoint outside the Chetwynd Arms was an ancient dark green camper van heading north towards Stafford.

An officer waved it down. 'Excuse me, sir, may I ask where you've come from?'

'Cannock. I'm touring. Been to Warwick Castle. Now I'm on my way to the Peak District.'

'On your own? No passengers?'

'That's right.'

'Mind if I check?' The policeman peered in the windows and seemed satisfied. 'What's that accent?'

'South African.'

'Thought so. Expect you know why we've got the road blocked?'

Clever question, van Niekerk thought. It was now thirty minutes since the ambush and he guessed the police had reacted fast to seal off the area.

'Something about an escaped prisoner? That's what the policeman said at the other roadblock.'

'That's right. We're looking for a red Renault Safrane, probably being driven in a hurry. Three men.'

Van Niekerk shook his head. 'I wouldn't know a Safrane if it jumped out and bit me. Sorry, Officer.'

'I'll just take your details and you can get on.'

His old passport and international driving licence under the name of Steyn, courtesy of the former South African Directorate of Covert Collection, genuine logbook and insurance. No problem. He grinned as he handed them over. A piece of piss.

Lomax had an appointment with an executive recruitment agency in London which specialised in the security field. It was while he was driving in that he heard on the car radio the news of Keegan's abduction by masked gunmen.

Still shocked and distracted by it, he felt he made a complete hash of the interview, barely able to wait for it to end. When it did, he drove straight to the offices of Eisner, Pollock and Browne.

In fact, Browne had just returned from spending the morning in court and none of her colleagues had heard the news either.

She was stunned. 'God, this is *terrible* news for Roddy.'

'It's even worse for Keegan if the police are right.'

'That they were terrorists? Do you think it's the IRA?'

'God knows, Sam. I hope not, for his sake.'

She sounded glum. 'Still, I suppose there's a good chance they'll be caught soon.'

'Let's hope it's before they get a chance to top Keegan.'

She winced. 'Don't even think that, Chris. I'll make sure the prison lets me know the moment they have any news.'

'How are things going otherwise?' he asked.

'Not good,' she sighed, 'but then no worse than expected. The trouble is the police tend to have tunnel vision once they have a suspect. Try to make everything fit their theory of how a crime was committed and who committed it. They won't even consider the possibility that someone other than Roddy murdered Fitzpatrick. That's what we're really up against.'

'I'm not sure I follow.'

'They'll have interviewed dozens of people, but in the end will only select witness statements that fit the preconceived police view of what happened. Unused statements that may support Roddy's story will only turn up in the pre-committal bundle months from now. In other words the prosecution will be on the home straight while the defence is just leaving the starting gate.'

'That doesn't sound very fair.'

'It isn't, but that's the way it works.' She looked weary. 'The police don't see it as their job to help us build a defence against them.'

Lomax considered for a moment. 'Understandable, I suppose. But what can you do about it?'

'Well, I've requested a list of names and details of people who've been interviewed, but I'm getting no response as yet. Problem is I'm not supposed to interview prosecution witnesses without approval from the Crown Prosecution Service. And they'll insist on a police presence – probably DS Henwick who interviewed them in the first place.'

'That could be a bit intimidating, couldn't it?'

'You said it, Chris.' She lit a cigarette to calm her anger. 'Rather runs in the face of the old principle of there being no property in a witness.' Then she offered him the pack. 'Sorry, forgetting my manners.'

He declined. 'I'm giving up, again. Two days into cold turkey.'

She gave a knowing little half-smile at that. 'Poor you. Anyway, I've no intention of waiting months before interviewing witnesses for us. I'll keep pestering. It's the same with my request to visit the scene of crime.'

'Surely you can do that?'

'I've never had a problem before. Trying to deny access must be something of a precedent – and it's an outrageous one.'

'Is that what they've done? Why?'

'Dymock told me this morning that it's because Fitzpatrick was killed in an MI5 safe house.'

Lomax gave a cynical smile. 'Not a good advertisement for MI5.'

'The Crown Property Agency has refused permission, citing interests of national security and all that.'

'You're not letting them get away . . .?'

Her eyes blazed. 'No, I am not. I've told Dymock we're going to court to enforce our right. I'm hoping for a hearing tomorrow. I'm just afraid it'll be too late.'

'Why should it be?'

'Because they must know we'll win right of access. Therefore, it's a delaying tactic, unless they're hoping I'll not pursue it. I just can't really think *why*. That's the puzzle.'

Lomax said thoughtfully: 'It sounds to me that someone's got something to hide. Something that could support Roddy's case.'

Browne sighed. 'I won't know that until I see the place. But in general it's looking more and more as if he's being well and truly stitched up.'

'Is there anything you can do about it?'

'I'm thinking of hiring a private investigator for backup. I'll need written advice from Ronnie Rock to get approval from the Legal Aid Board and they're not known for their generosity. Totty and Wayne will have to put in most of the legwork. I'll be lucky if the firm breaks even in the end.'

The thought flashed through Lomax's mind that he could contribute his modest savings. Then he immediately envisaged his daughter Manda lambasting him for doing so. He could hear her pointing out he'd need every penny to survive until he landed a job or else get a business of his own up and running.

He said: 'All I can offer is time.' Again he was hearing his daughter's words rather than his own, but then she was Business Student of the Year, bless her.

'I beg your pardon?' Browne was confused.

'Sorry, thinking aloud. Could I help in any way? Do some of the things that a private investigator might?'

There was a slightly dismissive look in her eyes. 'That's sweet of you, Chris, but I don't think so.'

He felt affronted by that. 'Look, Sam, I've plenty of experience in debriefing soldiers and civilians during and after hostage situations and the like, and I've plenty of experience in covert ops, surveillance and the like.'

'I'm not sure that's the same. Good private investigators are usually former policemen with plenty of personal contacts still on the force.'

'Okay,' he countered with rising irritation, 'I'm not ideal, but I'm available.'

She frowned, unsure. 'You wouldn't be paid much.'

'I'm not in this for the money, Sam.' He considered for a moment. 'So what's your first priority? The safe house?'

She frowned. 'What are you thinking of doing?'

'Taking a look.'

'You're not breaking in,' she said, clearly horrified. 'You'd get me struck off.'

He grinned at her. 'Nothing illegal, I promise. Just see what's what. Have you got the address?'

Browne nodded. 'Bascombe Court. Number Thirty-two.'

'Then I'll go round.'

'What, now?'

'No time like the present. Want to come?'

The apartment block was stylish and fairly modern and set in well-maintained grounds.

Lomax parked beneath a discreetly placed estate agent's sign that read: Luxury apartments for lease. He and Browne approached the beige marble portico with its plate-glass security doors and keypad entryphone. First he pressed Thirty-two, but there was no response. The bottom button was marked Caretaker. 'Try that,' Browne suggested.

Moments later a middle-aged man appeared in the lobby, hastily pulling a grey uniform blazer over his cardigan and stuffing a piece of toast in his mouth.

'Sorry,' Lomax began as the caretaker opened the door. 'I didn't mean to disturb you.'

The man swallowed the last of his toast and gave a friendly smile. ''S what I'm paid for. How can I help?'

'My wife and I are looking for a flat in this area. We were just passing and saw the sign.'

'Oh, that! Yes, well it's a permanent fixture really. There's always someone moving in or moving out.'

'Are there any for sale at the moment?'

He beckoned them in and over to the desk where he opened his notebook. 'Three at the moment. Number Nine, Number Forty-seven and Number Thirty-two.'

Lomax checked his smile. The MI5 safe house was compromised and hardly safe any more. So sell it, was the obvious answer. 'Could we have a look at them?'

'Well, I've only got permission to show people Number Nine without an appointment.'

'That's on the ground floor, I suppose?' Browne said. 'I wouldn't like that.'

The caretaker nodded his understanding. 'And it's north-facing, a bit gloomy. Forty-seven faces north too, but it's brighter.'

Lomax and Browne virtually said it in unison. 'We'd like south-facing.'

'That would be Thirty-two. It's being redecorated and you'll have to go through the estate agents, an accompanied visit, the owner insists.'

'Who's the owner?' Lomax asked.

'A Mrs White. Only seen her once or twice. She sublets it.'

'Look,' Browne said, 'I really like the look of this place, but the two of us are frantically busy. We'll go through the estate agent tomorrow, if only I could have a teensy peep at Thirty-two. I really can't afford to waste the time if it's no good.' She gave one of her most heart-melting smiles. 'Just a peek?'

'Well, I really don't know.' The man shifted uncomfortably.

Lomax produced his wallet and took out a twenty. 'It wouldn't do any harm, would it? I mean it *is* for sale. In fact it'd do the owner Mrs White a favour if we like it, because we're cash buyers.'

'Well, I suppose. But you mustn't let on you've already seen it.'

'I promise,' Browne said.

'And be careful not to spoil your clothes, because the painters are in.'

He led them to the elevator and they jetted smoothly to the third floor. The corridor was lush grey carpet and lemon walls with expensive concealed lighting and the apartment doors were pale oak. That of Number Thirty-two was patched with a sheet of plywood, presumably to cover the bullet holes.

'Bit of an accident,' the caretaker said. 'We're getting a replacement, but it has to be specially made.' He inserted the key and stepped aside to allow them in.

From the small square hallway they could see straight through the open doorway to the lounge. The floor was covered in white dust sheets and a paint-splattered ladder stood by the bare whitewashed picture window. All the carpeting and underlay had been removed leaving just the gripper rails nailed into the concrete.

'They're making a thorough job,' Lomax murmured.

They wandered around for five minutes, looking casually. It had a large double bedroom where no doubt Donny Fitzpatrick had slept, now devoid of all furniture like all the other rooms. There was a second, smaller bedroom which would have been for any MI5 minder, a combined bathroom and WC and an elaborate fitted kitchen.

Browne took a genuine and wistful interest in this. While she discussed it with the caretaker, Lomax strolled back into the lounge. He gave the picture window a tap with his forefinger and tried to peer out, but the limewash had been laid on too thickly. Then on impulse he stooped and lifted the edge of the dust sheet on the floor. Bare concrete fire-floor again. He stooped and folded it back several feet. Then he saw the dark brown smudge ingrained in the surface. His heart tripped for a second. He pulled it back some more. The mark was nearly three feet in diameter and looked old and faded. He ran his fingers over the coarse surface, then glanced up at the walls to his left and right. There, some two feet above the skirting board were several patches of filler. The decorators had already worked halfway around the room; by the end of the following day the secrets of the wall would be hidden for good.

He dropped the dust sheet back as Browne and the caretaker entered. 'Nice dimensions,' Lomax said. 'I'm impressed.'

'And I've *always* wanted a kitchen like this one.'

The caretaker seemed pleased with their enthusiasm. 'You'll like it here, I promise you.'

They followed him back out to the corridor, Lomax lingering for a moment by the front door. From the inside the six bullet holes were clearly visible. So were the tiny drill holes running all the way around. He made a note of the make of the lock as the caretaker shut the door. 'And please, not a word that I showed you round.'

Browne smiled. 'I think you can rely on us about that.' She looked at Lomax, slightly differently, he thought. 'Don't you, darling?'

Lomax had never experienced anger like it before. It enveloped him like a black cloud, pressing in on his skull until it felt as though it was about to burst. He took it out on his battered Cavalier, accelerating hard, aware of but not properly noticing other traffic.

'And you think I'm a bad driver,' Sam Browne said. 'What's got into you?'

'Seeing that apartment, that's what's got into me!'

'I don't understand. Do you want to pull over and we can talk about it?'

It made sense, before he killed them both. 'Good idea, let's grab a drink at the next greasy spoon.',

Minutes later they pulled in at a cafe. Lomax ordered a pot of tea and a couple of disgusting jam doughnuts.

He said: 'I don't know what I thought before. I mean, I believed Roddy, but I couldn't fully accept that Box would set him up. Not like this. Box is government, when all's said and done. The buck stops at Number Ten. And this is the government I've risked my bloody life for on more than one occasion.'

She drank some of the stewed tea and pulled a face. 'What's

got you in this mood? The apartment seemed ordinary enough to me – apart from the bullet holes in the door.'

'The whole thing stinks,' Lomax said. 'I knew something didn't add up before and now I know why.' Browne was fishing in her bag for cigarettes. 'Could I have one of those?'

'I thought you were giving up.'

He laughed bitterly. 'That was yesterday. And if it's the same government behind this that keeps telling me to quit them, then I'll bloody well start again.'

'Fighting talk,' she quipped, giving him a light.

'Listen, Sam, if you put someone in a safe house, you don't put a surveillance team outside. You put a minder in the apartment with him, whether he likes it or not, and turn the place into a fortress.'

'That didn't look like much of a fortress.'

'Not now, but it was. For a start, the windows are bullet-proof glass and the front door had been reinforced with either steel or a sheet of Kevlar armour.'

She frowned. 'It can't have been, Chris; you saw the bullet holes. They went right through. Fitzpatrick was killed in the hall.'

Lomax shook his head. 'No. The back of the front door had screw holes all over it where the armoured sheet was fixed. It was probably removed *after* the killing, along with extra security bolts and chains. You could see the pattern of holes quite clearly. *Then* someone pumped rounds through the door.'

'Why?'

'Because, if Roddy *had* stalked Fitzpatrick and got in to ring his bell, neither Fitzpatrick nor his minder would have let him in. They'd have been straight on the radio for backup. Fitzpatrick was killed in the lounge by someone he knew, someone who was already in there.'

'How can you be sure?'

'I looked under the dust sheet. There was a bloodstain. Someone had bleached it and scoured it with a wire brush, but getting stains out of concrete ain't easy.'

'Couldn't it have been from – I don't know – something else?'

'I know bloodstains when I see them. If that wasn't where

111

Fitzpatrick was murdered, then someone had one hell of a haemorrhage there once upon a time.' He shoved away the plate with the half-eaten doughnut. 'And there was no sign of any blood on the floor by the front door.'

She stared at him. 'But we can't be certain, Chris, because they've already taken away the carpets.'

'Exactly. The place has been sanitised. MI5's bin men have been hard at work. That's why they're keeping you away. If a replacement door hadn't had to be specially made, my guess is that would have gone by now.'

Browne shivered. 'This is getting more sinister by the minute, Chris. Any remaining evidence is going to have vanished.'

Lomax thought for a moment. 'Would photographs help?'

'The police SOCO will have taken pictures.'

'But not necessarily of the things that count.'

'I suppose so. But how . . .?'

An idea was forming in his mind. 'Best you don't know.'

Five

By the time he'd dropped Browne back at her office, Lomax had settled on a course of action. Deciding against phoning from Evie's flat, he used a street corner call box to ring Joe Monk, the former SAS colleague whom he'd last seen the day after his farewell party.

'Glad I caught you in.'

Monk sounded morose. 'Easy enough to catch me in nowadays, old son. My life revolves around the Job Centre, the pub and the bookie's. Just one light on the horizon, I've been short-listed for a job as lavatory attendant in a shopping centre along with five hundred others.'

'You're overqualified.'

'Tell me about it.' A heavy sniff of resignation. 'So what d'you want, Chris?'

'I need a favour. A little job needs doing in London at sparrow's fart tomorrow.'

Monk perked up immediately. 'Is it legal?'

'No, and it's unpaid too. But I'll cover your exes.'

His friend didn't hesitate. 'Well, it beats being bored for a living.'

'Still got your locksmith's kit?' It was standard issue with Regiment soldiers and Monk had always been one of the best at using it.

'Oh, that sort of job! What are we up against?'

'With luck someone will let you in. But anyway, it's nothing exotic, a five-lever Chubb.'

'Piece of piss.'

'And can you make yourself look like a decorator?'

'I'll stick a paintbrush up my arse if it'll make you happy.'

'And call in at my place tonight. I'll get Manda to look out my Leica and flash unit.'

'You want to take pictures of me, too?'

'Piss off, Joe.'

They arranged to rendezvous at six the next morning at the Heston service station on the M4 into London, then Lomax hung up and called Manda.

'Managing without me, sweetheart?'

'Are you joking? For once the place is tidy, there's food in the fridge and the house doesn't stink of tobacco.'

'Yes, I'm missing you too,' Lomax replied with a chuckle before asking her to get his photographic case down from the loft. 'Someone will call round for it.'

'Someone?' She was sharp all right, and he felt proud of her.

'Not on an open line. You'll recognise him when you see him.'

'Dad? What are you up to?'

'Nothing, sweetheart, just indulge your old man, please.'

'Well, Dad, if you're doing nothing, you might be pleased to hear the adjutant from Stirling Lines rang.'

Lomax raised an eyebrow. 'What did he want?'

'He's had Staffordshire Police on to him. They want to enlist the help of an army tracker for some escaped prisoner.'

'Peter Keegan?'

'I think that was the name.'

'Are you winding me up?'

'No.' Indignant – obviously she was unaware of Keegan's involvement with her uncle's predicament. 'He said their top trackers are tied up on training cadres and a murder hunt in Kenya right now. He suggested you. Says will you call. I've got the policeman's number.'

Lomax had run out of change so waited until he returned to Evie's before he rang the detective superintendent at Stafford. Although it was gone eight, Bill Johnson was still in his office. He sounded weary, but cheerful.

'I'm glad you called. This one's proving a bit tricky for our boys. The Regiment recommended you, said you were the best. Hope you're interested. Between you and me you can virtually name your price. A lot of flapping going on way above my head, if you get my drift.'

After a moment's consideration, Lomax thought of a fee and

doubled it; Manda would have approved. Johnson didn't baulk, just sounded relieved. 'And you can be here by lunchtime tomorrow?'

'Let's say two in the afternoon.'

'Not a moment too soon,' Johnson replied.

The next day broke warm, moist and drizzling. Monk was already parked in his ancient Escort at the Heston service station when Lomax arrived.

Monk was dressed in a woollen hand-knitted hat and paint-stained overalls; he had a flask of coffee open and was demolishing a bacon wedge with those familiar tombstone teeth.

'This is about Roddy, isn't it?' he asked with his mouth full.

Lomax nodded. 'I want to get pictures of the apartment where he's supposed to have killed Fitzpatrick.'

'Is that all?'

'It was an MI5 safe house, Joe, and the whole thing was a stitch-up. Someone in Box is running their own agenda, but I can't work out what it is.'

'So what's new?' Monk licked his fingers. 'I read the newspaper report. Didn't sound like Roddy – and he wouldn't have been daft enough to get caught.'

'The thing is, they've got decorators in.' Lomax explained what he had seen the previous evening with Browne. 'I want a record of it. Assuming the workmen will turn up at eight or half past, I reckon you should go in at seven thirty.'

'Me? On my jack?'

'The caretaker's seen me. Don't worry, you can hack it without me holding your hand.' He grinned. 'You get a big kiss after.'

'Promises, promises.'

Monk followed in his car as Lomax drove south and across the Thames to Bascombe Court. They parked and Lomax watched Monk's overalled bulk saunter up to the portico, a can of Dulux swinging from each huge fist. Moments later the caretaker opened the door.

'Supplies for Thirty-two, squire.'

'You're early.'

'Got lucky with the traffic. If you have a key, I'll let myself in.'

As the apartment was empty, it was not a problem. Monk entered, shut the door and took the Leica from the bellows pocket in his overalls. Memorising the rough layout Lomax had sketched for him, he photographed the front door and hallway, the bloodstain and wall repairs in the lounge. Ten minutes later he was done.

He met the caretaker again in the lobby. The man indicated the two cans of Dulux Magnolia. 'Takin' them back?'

'Wrong colour, innit? Some cockup at the yard.'

Dulux Magnolia didn't come cheap, and Monk had promised Marsha he'd repaint their lounge.

On the way out, he passed two men carrying in a replacement front door and a glazier's van was now parked outside loaded with sheets of standard units to replace the bullet-proof glass in the apartment.

Lomax watched Monk enter his Escort, then followed until they arrived at a pub car park two miles away.

'I'll process 'em for you,' Monk offered.

'You're a pal.'

For once, Monk looked serious. 'You're right about what you said, Chris. Seen it with my own eyes now. Our friend Roddy's got himself in some pretty deep shit.'

'Don't I know it?'

'Yeah well, just don't get yourself dragged into it. Whatever's going down, these people are seriously bad news.' He looked at his friend closely. 'If you need any help, anything, you know where I am.'

'Sure, scrubbing lavatories.'

Both men grinned.

'Joe will bring the photographs round personally,' Lomax told Browne. He'd decided to visit her at her office before setting off north to Stafford.

He wondered why he'd taken the trouble to call round and not just telephoned. It was a mild shock to find her looking so haggard, drawn and without make-up and her hair a mess.

'I wasn't expecting visitors, Chris.' She stubbed out her

cigarette in the overflowing ashtray. 'I've been working through the night on Roddy's defence.'

He nodded towards the tumbler and empty whisky bottle in the waste bin. 'Sure it wasn't a party?'

She gave a weary smile. 'I wish. That stuff helps keep the brain cells ticking in the wee small hours.'

'You'll kill yourself if you keep working like this.'

'My life, my choice,' she replied, her eyes hardening. Then she forced a smile. 'Sorry, I'm a bit tetchy. But Roddy's case is a big one for us to handle, and I can't let the other work slip. Solicitors can go bust too, you know.'

'Better bust than dead.'

'I'll get an early night tonight. Skip the all-night rave.'

Lomax said suddenly, on impulse: 'I'd have liked to take you out to dinner tonight. Make sure you relax properly.'

She leaned back in her chair and tapped her teeth with her pen as she regarded him over the top of her reading spectacles. 'Is that a proposition, Mr Lomax?'

He wasn't sure whether she was offended or not. 'It might have been, but it isn't. The Staffordshire police have been on to me. They want my help in tracking down Keegan. They reckon he and his abductors have gone to ground in Cannock Chase.'

Her mouth dropped in surprise. 'That's *some* coincidence!'

He shrugged. 'Not really, it's a small world and not many trackers. At least in a roundabout way it'll be helping Roddy if I can find Keegan.' He added pointedly: 'And I'm getting well paid for it.'

'It does help, doesn't it,' she laughed. 'When do you start?'

'As soon as I can get there.'

'Then why are you standing here gossiping with me?'

There was a lop-sided grin on his face. 'I really don't know.'

But suddenly he did. Suddenly he knew perfectly well. And so did Browne as she watched him move towards the door. 'That proposition,' she said, 'I hope it will keep.'

Then she abruptly turned back to the papers on her desk.

He made good time up the M40 to Birmingham. The early rain had surrendered to a clear sky and he had sunshine all the way.

Something had lifted his spirits. It may have been the weather, it may have been the tape cassette of pastoral symphonies he was playing, or it may have been his encounter with Sam Browne.

It was difficult to make her out. She had an awesome reputation and he didn't always approve of the way she dealt with figures of authority. Surely it could be counterproductive? But then, he realised, his job had always been to work alongside those people. People like the police and the intelligence services. He was sure that his own hackles would have been up if he'd ever encountered the redoubtable Sam Browne.

Yet her fearless disregard for conventional authority was somehow stirring, as was her almost evangelical belief in justice for anyone she considered innocent. And, thankfully, that included his friend and brother-in-law.

He had the feeling there was currently no man in her life, yet he didn't feel inclined to question her about it. Although her sense of humour flared from time to time, she never encouraged familiarity. So why had he made that clumsy suggestion? He'd half-expected her to savage him like a Rottweiler on the spot. Perhaps she was just tired and he'd been lucky. Then he remembered her last remark, and thought maybe not.

At least he was glad Roddy had Sam Browne on *his* side.

The mental picture flashed through his mind then. Roddy incarcerated at Belmarsh. Just the name of the place created the image of despair. The big Ulsterman, the man who had saved his life at Goose Green, sitting slumped on the edge of his prison cot. Head in his hands, seeing no way out. Seeing only the mountain of evidence stacked against him and the shadow cast over the rest of his life. His life and Evie's, and even that of their unborn child.

Suddenly Lomax felt guilty for enjoying the drive, the sunshine and the music. Guilty for watching Sam Browne's legs after she'd surrendered a night's sleep without complaint to fight for his friend.

Around Birmingham the journey slowed. The bypassing M42 was clogged with traffic and he'd lost time before he broke clear again on the M6 to the north of the city.

Following Detective Superintendent Bill Johnson's directions, he left the motorway at Junction 11 for the market town of Cannock, then picked up the A34 running towards Stafford.

It was there that he encountered the police vehicle checkpoint, all traffic leaving and entering the area still being stopped and searched. A young constable directed Lomax to the site where the abandoned Renault Safrane had been found. A man in a crumpled fawn raincoat noticed his arrival and detached himself from the group of police officers behind the tape cordon.

'Mr Lomax, I presume.' His handshake was firm and dry and the seen-it-all eyes had a disconcertingly penetrating gaze.

'At your service.'

'Bill Johnson. Pleased to have you aboard.' In his late forties, Lomax decided, and a regular career copper. Straight and hard-working, the once handsome face now lined and the dark gelled hair beginning to thin. 'I've booked you in at the Hatherton Country Hotel in Penkridge. A bit smart but we've got a special rate.' Definitely a regular copper, Lomax thought, as the man added: 'Would you like to check in and freshen up?'

'No, let's crack on. Plenty of time when the light fades.' He could tell that pleased Johnson. 'So what have we got?'

The superintendent explained. Barely a mile to the north on the same road, the taxi carrying the prisoner Peter Keegan and two prison officers had been forced to pull over by the Safrane, now abandoned. Two armed men in balaclavas had emerged, talking with distinct Northern Ireland accents. Almost certainly Provisional IRA. Keegan had been bundled into the Safrane which had driven off at speed. Twenty minutes after the incident, the Safrane had been found crashed in a grass track in these roadside woods. There were signs of a scuffle and empty cartridge cases had been found. Ominously, the seats of the car were heavily bloodstained.

'What's your reading of what happened?' Lomax asked.

Johnson sucked on his teeth. 'Clearly they came here to switch vehicles, there's no other explanation, although we've found no sign of another car. It seems Keegan fought back and made a run for it. The blood on the seats isn't his. There were

119

9mm cartridge cases on the ground by the back door and we've found two of the rounds embedded in trees to the west.'

'So that's the way Keegan started running presumably? Let's take a look.'

The scene-of-crime officer had identified three sets of footprints around the abandoned car and had isolated those belonging to Keegan's prison-issue footwear; he produced photographs and diagrams of the three different heel and sole patterns.

'The only fingerprints we've found belong to Keegan. Obviously the other two wore gloves.'

Lomax spent an hour rummaging through the undergrowth in the direction in which the 9mm rounds had been fired. But the only footprints he found belonged to size ten police boots.

'Any luck?' Johnson asked.

Lomax shook his head. 'The earth's quite dry. Not good for prints.'

'That's what the SOCO said. Any thoughts?'

'How sure are you the abductors were IRA? What exactly did they say to the prison officers?'

Johnson consulted his notebook. 'As far as the officers recall, when Keegan asked them who the hell they were, one answered: "You know who we are!" then said, "Fucking bastard!" or similar, seemingly addressed to Keegan.'

Lomax frowned. 'And that was all?'

'The accents, the guns, the balaclavas – it's a pretty sound assumption.'

'Maybe,' Lomax said noncommittally and stood, looking along the grassy firebreak to the track. 'Now, if Keegan ran away into the trees, then these two wounded Provos will have presumably hurried off to the switch vehicle.'

'Of which we've found no sign. So what's happened to the gunmen? Did they get away or are they still around?'

'Any switch vehicle must have had access to the track in order to reach the road. Shall we walk back?'

Together they strolled along the firebreak, where the grass had been badly trampled by the police outside the immediate cordon around the Safrane.

Johnson was saying: 'This is a major headache, Chris. I've got Keegan and possibly two armed IRA men on the loose in the Chase. While we can seal it off with armed police, I'm loath to send in unarmed search teams. For the minute all we can do is contain the area and run armed perimeter patrols. We're watching from various vantage points and we've got a chopper up with a thermal imager. But all we can actively do is wait for something or someone to show up. It's an absolute nightmare. We're trying to let residents only through the checkpoints and that's causing serious disruption and a lot of resentment from locals. And you just try telling the English they can't take their dogs for a walk! I'm terrified someone will stumble onto one of these characters and then we'll have a murder on our hands.'

They had reached the track which led to the A34, and now Lomax could see that the firebreak continued on the other side through more woodland.

'Have your lads searched on the other side of the track?'

Johnson nodded. 'Just to make sure no one was hiding there, but we've been concentrating on the area around the car.'

They crossed the track and proceeded along the firebreak. Here, Lomax noticed, the grass was relatively untrampled. At one point he stopped and knelt by a strip of bruised grass. He ran his fingers over the earth beneath it.

'What is it?' Johnson asked.

'Have any police vehicles been down here?'

'No, we've kept everything back on the main road.'

'If you use a blowtorch to clear this patch, I think you'll find a tyre print underneath. The earth still feels soft, so it's been recently disturbed. It could be your missing switch vehicle.'

That pleased Johnson. He turned and beckoned a constable on the track to call the SOCO over pronto.

Lomax stood and squinted down the firebreak, following the twin lines of bruised grass which was now recovering and making it near impossible to detect with an untrained eye. He studied the arc of the trail to the place he thought it disappeared into the treeline, then lifted his gaze. Now that he knew what he was looking for, it was quite distinct. Bright yellow-white scars against blackish bark where twigs and branches had been snapped. To quite a height he noticed, much higher than a car.

'Over here,' he said, 'and please follow in my footsteps.'

Crossing to the edge of the wood, he peered in at the dense foliage of a holly tree. At his feet the grass had given way to earth. Tracks and footprints.

'Your thoughts?' Johnson pressed.

'It was a van or small truck, not a car. Wider than a car, see? And deep, considering how dry it is. Therefore heavy.' He took the SOCO's photographs from his pocket. 'And Keegan's footprints. No doubt about it.'

Another hour passed before Lomax finished studying the area around the holly tree, working alongside the SOCO. Finally he retraced his footsteps back to the track where Bill Johnson waited and poured him coffee from his vacuum flask.

Lomax gulped it down with relish.

'Well?' the superintendent asked, unable to conceal his impatience.

'Bill, I'm afraid you're going to have to do a rethink.'

'Yes?'

'Back at the car – when it crashed, presumably when Keegan fought back and took his abductors by surprise – it wasn't Keegan who was injured, as we know from the blood samples. In the aftermath, it wasn't them shooting at Keegan. It was Keegan shooting at them. Somehow he managed to get a gun off one of them.'

'How d'you figure that out?'

'Because these prints were obviously made after the crash and they're coming from the direction of the abandoned car.'

Johnson couldn't quite follow. 'Run me through it again, would you?'

'They pull over in the Safrane to make the switch. Probably told Keegan what was happening, where the van was hidden as they arrived. There's a struggle, Keegan gets a gun and the two men are injured. They rush off into the woods and Keegan shoots after them.'

'Then what?'

Lomax shrugged. 'My guess is, after the initial shock, he

122

realises the situation he's in. Hey, I'm free! He walks back to the van to see if he can use it. But, of course, it's locked and he hasn't got a key, and time is running out. He's aware the police are just up the road and will be looking for the Renault Safrane. So he makes a snap decision and heads off into the wilds.'

'How can you be sure?'

'Because his footprint pattern crosses the firebreak and into that fringe of trees beside the A34. I haven't checked it out yet, but my guess is he crossed the main road and into Cannock Chase. It offers him perfect country to go to ground and sort himself out.'

'Are you really certain?' Johnson pressed. 'I mean the van has gone now.'

'I'm certain, Bill. I should think the two Provos, if that's who they were, circled round in the woods, came back to their vehicle and scarpered. Two very nervous and embarrassed bunnies. The only thing I can't explain is the presence of a bicycle tyre mark. Heavy tread, probably a mountain bike.'

'That's still brilliant, Chris,' Johnson said, nodding in slow agreement as he visualised the likely scenario. 'Well done! But, if you're right in every detail, it means Keegan is now loose, armed and desperate in the Chase.'

Lomax gave a half-smile. 'Better that than two IRA gunmen. Keegan will evade and threaten if cornered, but he'd never shoot to kill unless it was to save his own life. Just not the type.'

'The adjutant at Hereford said you'd had dealings with him in the past, but he wasn't specific.'

'I worked with him in Northern Ireland for a bit, mostly on protection duties.'

Johnson nodded his understanding. 'Quite a character, I see, reading his file. Must have had nerves of steel working under-cover all that time.'

'But not a natural born killer, at least in my judgment.'

'Had a few men sent to their deaths though, didn't he? That's why he's serving time.'

Lomax nodded. 'I can't deny that. But some might say he had to let some killings go ahead to preserve his own cover.'

'The judge didn't think that was an excuse.'

123

A grim smile passed over Lomax's lips. 'But then I doubt the judge had ever been in deep cover inside a terrorist organisation.'

The policeman thought about that for a moment. 'So your assessment would be I could send in search-and-sweep parties without risk to life.'

'I believe so, as long as it's planned and methodical. Obviously there has to be a risk if he's panicked. But if we close the net slowly, I reckon he'll see sense and give himself up. He's a staunch Loyalist. It would go against the grain to shoot English policemen or members of the public. Keegan's biggest problem has always been the buzz he got from the undercover game.'

Johnson shook his head, not understanding that at all.

Lomax smiled. 'There's nothing like it, believe me.' He glanced up at the sky, the sun now hovering in the west. 'Not much more I can do today, Bill. What say we adjourn to my hotel. We could go over maps of the area and discuss the best way to handle things tomorrow.'

'Splendid idea. I'll see if I can get the head ranger of Cannock Chase to join us. Knows the area inside out.'

As the late summer twilight settled over the country, Lord Moffat stepped unnoticed onto a hot and dusty Horse Guards Parade in Whitehall.

Although a big man, over six feet tall with his corpulent belly disguised by the artful cut of his suit, he had the knack of anonymity. The florid and heavily jowled face was unremarkable. His walk was purposeful, but never rushed. Newspaper folded neatly beneath his left arm, his right swung the furled umbrella at a steady rate. And he never raised his booming baritone voice, even to hail a passing cab. He didn't draw attention to himself, never had. In the environs of power, in Whitehall and Westminster, he simply blended in.

'One of those grey men in grey suits the *Guardian* is always prattling on about,' he would sometimes joke to his few close friends, 'that's me. I ask you, do I really look that sinister?' And he'd laugh and pour another port or another brandy.

In private, in his own tight clique, Lord Moffat was known for

124

his good company and ready wit. That rare commodity, a *bon vivant* and raconteur who was also a good listener and who could be trusted with your darkest secret. Lord Moffat knew a lot of secrets, collecting and hoarding them as others did postage stamps or tins of food. Because you never knew when secrets might be useful. But not his own; he kept them to himself. Sometimes, he thought, even from himself.

He slipped quietly across the road to St James's Park. Not a head would turn amongst the tourists and lovers lounging on the lawns to enjoy the balmy evening as he walked the pathway towards the Mall and London's gentlemen's clubland beyond. Under other circumstances, he might have met Roger Pinfold at the Morpeth Arms pub, the favourite watering hole of MI5 officers near their new Thames House headquarters beside the river; after all, Moffat was as at home with a pint of Young's bitter as he was with a bottle of Leoville-Barton.

But he wanted his hastily requested meeting to be away from prying eyes and alert ears of the intelligence community, so the Reform Club and the Travellers were out. Instead, he'd opted for a light supper at the Ritz in Piccadilly.

It was a pleasant evening for the walk. Moffat enjoyed walking, rarely using any form of transport in central London; it was the only exercise he had. What he liked about it most was that it enabled him to think, allowed his mind to wander as he strode the familiar streets.

This evening, his thoughts naturally drifted back over the years and he realised, not for the first time, that his whole life had been preparing him for what lay ahead. The past ten years had been momentous, but the best was yet to come.

An hereditary peer, Lord Anthony Patrick Moffat had been born in 1932. His father had inherited a rundown family estate in the Wirral and had married Mary Meagher, the eldest daughter of a wealthy family of Irish aristocracy just in time to save his stately home from financial ruin. A marriage of convenience – at least that was what Moffat concluded with the benefit of hindsight.

His parents had always squabbled. Mostly over his father's drinking and gambling debts, but also over the future of their young son Anthony. Both were Catholic so there was no argument as to their offspring's religious upbringing, but his education was quite another affair. Never very impressed with the English system, when war broke out in 1939, his mother had the very excuse she wanted for her son to be educated in Ireland.

Eventually, to everyone's surprise, not least his own, he'd earned a place at University College, Dublin. At first he had hated the changes to his life, the enforced independence. Had felt desperately alone and almost suicidal.

Then he met Fergal. The moment the gregarious Fergal, a fellow undergraduate a year older than himself arrived on the scene, everything changed. For the first time in his life the young Lord Moffat had found a true friend; more than that, a soul mate. They shared a love of jazz and folksongs, of history and literature. And good food and drink. Seldom were they out of each other's company.

It was to be a lifelong friendship, although they had lost touch while Moffat embarked on his diplomatic career with lowly appointments in far-flung places around the world until, in 1965, he was posted to Dublin as head of Chancery. And he loved it. Aged just thirty-three, it was as if he had come home. He enjoyed the company of the Irish, their love of music and the arts, their carefree lifestyle and their sense of fun.

Then one evening Moffat had dropped in at his regular bar on the way home, when who should he find standing next to him? Fergal hadn't changed. It was as though their ten-year separation had never been and it seemed they picked up their conversation almost exactly where they'd left off. He learned that Fergal worked for some obscure Irish Government department and was resigned to plodding his way towards eventual retirement and a handsome pension.

For the next four years they were to see each other regularly, but with one difference from the old days. Now they often talked about politics, especially the worsening situation in Ulster. They found they both had a strong empathy with the Republican cause, for the reuniting of the Six Counties with Eire.

Looking back now, he wondered why it had taken so long for him to realise that Fergal worked for the foreign intelligence arm of the Irish Special Branch.

For the next ten years, Moffat's career evolved around senior advisory postings to the United Nations in New York, the British Embassy in Washington, the Foreign Office in London and back again to Dublin. He never did make ambassador.

When the Thatcher Government swept to power in 1979, it came as a complete surprise to him to be invited to become a special adviser to the Northern Ireland Office, in recognition of his knowledge of Irish affairs and his priceless contacts in both Dublin and the pro-Irish lobby in American politics.

After the Brighton bombing, when the Provisional IRA had come close to wiping out the Prime Minister and her entire Cabinet, Lord Moffat had been invited to sit in as adviser on the ultrasecret Cabinet Intelligence Unit.

He had never forgotten the moment when a very senior permanent undersecretary had taken him to lunch at Whites.

Over a pudding of syrup sponge and custard, he had been told: 'Look, Anthony, you ought to be aware that there is a consensus of private opinion amongst senior civil servants within the Cabinet Office, the Foreign Office and the Home Office, that it is no longer in Britain's long-term best interests for Northern Ireland to remain within the Union. No one will tell you this outright, of course, and anyone who did would deny it.'

'As you would deny it, Sir Charles?'

A wintry smile and another mouthful of sponge. 'Can't be in our interests to have terrorists blowing up our elected politicians, can it? Ulster is a millstone round our necks. I mean it's a financial liability. Costs us millions in security and compensation and no one ever goes there. Given a referendum, the great British public would have had our troops out years ago. They don't understand the situation over there, and frankly don't care.'

But Moffat knew there were other considerations. The Soviet Union had a high diplomatic presence in Dublin and an active

127

interest in Eire. 'What about Ulster's strategic importance? The North Atlantic anti-submarine screen, etc?'

'Yes, yes, you're right, of course. I'm talking medium to long term here. There's every sign of a slow thaw in the Cold War. If it continues, our strategic interest in Northern Ireland will gradually diminish to the point of no return. Brussels already regards Ulster as naturally part of Eire and has little time for notions of national sovereignty.'

'So what are you saying?'

'In your new position you will be advising ministers over the next few years. Some will have strong feelings about Ulster remaining part of Britain, others will not. I'm not telling you what to say, but you should be aware of the ultimate *realpolitik* of the situation.'

And so there it was, even then. He had been shown the inside track and given the bottom line. Ulster was surplus to requirements, unwanted baggage on the journey into the future, the new federal Europe and the next millennium.

He'd been made welcome by ministers and senior civil servants in the Cabinet Intelligence Unit and they listened to his views and advice with respect. He never pushed a particular line, was never passionate or stubborn, just answered the questions he was asked in polite and almost diplomatic language.

Within a year, the concept of the Anglo-Irish Agreement had been formed and signed, permitting Dublin a modest say in the way that Northern Ireland should be run. Yet it was the biggest constitutional breakthrough since partition in 1921.

Of course, the following ten years had had ups and downs, negotiations between Dublin, the Provisional IRA and the Ulster Unionists never easy. But Lord Moffat's personal influence had grown continuously as he was accepted into the various inner circles of power. He became well known to all the intelligence agencies and had a full-time seat on the CIU as well as the Permanent Secretaries' Committee on the Intelligence Services. In addition he served on other select and joint committees, plus some highly confidential subcommittees within the Cabinet Office.

Yet he was still mainly unknown to the world at large and the media in particular. Most newspaper editors would have been hard-pressed to expand much beyond the minimal seven-line entry in *Who's Who*. And that was the way he liked it. It was also the way Fergal liked it.

Moffat was beginning to tire in the languid warmth of the city evening and the cool of the Ritz lobby was particularly welcome. Roger Pinfold was already waiting for him in the restaurant. Moffat joined him and ordered a Pimms. He didn't particularly like the MI5 officer, but he was his man. Private school and Sussex University, new wave and eager to get to the top. If the political drift from the Cabinet Office and the permanent undersecretaries was that they wanted to get rid of the Ulster millstone, then Pinfold would comply in every way he could.

'I gather the American's been on, sir?' Pinfold said.

Nowadays there was only one 'American' that featured in their regular conversations.

In many ways, Curtis Manning was Moffat's opposite number in Washington. Holding a high-powered position within the upper echelons of the CIA, he was personal adviser to the Oval Office on matters concerning Northern Ireland. President Clinton was keen for the Ulster peace to hold so he could claim it as a personal achievement on the world stage to add to Palestine and the still shaky Bosnian ceasefire.

'Yes, he's keeping a close watching brief, Roger. He didn't like the way we handled Fitzpatrick and Littlechild and now someone's alerted him about Keegan's escape. It's unsettled him.'

'What's wrong with the man?'

'He'd like Ulster to be fully sanitised.'

Pinfold sighed. 'You can't sanitise twenty-five years of urban guerrilla warfare. Those sorts of stains don't ever come out. Besides, he and his friends have thrown their share of shit into the pot.'

'Eloquently put,' Moffat observed. 'But then I think Curtis Manning is all too aware of that. Indeed, that's *why* he's unsettled. Of course, he was quite happy to hear that Fitzpatrick had met with an accident and would have been happier still if Littlechild had met with the same fate. He has no conception of the furore *that* would have caused over here.'

'So he doesn't appreciate the neat solution?' Pinfold was choosing his words with care, not letting Moffat be told what he knew the man would already have read between the lines. 'Doesn't appreciate the fortunate circumstances that have placed Littlechild in the frame for murder.'

Moffat fiddled with his tie. 'Curtis is afraid Littlechild will fight it in court and wash all our dirty linen in public.'

'You've assured him that won't happen?'

'Of course, but I don't think Curtis is too familiar with the legal niceties of it all.'

Pinfold shook his head slowly. 'Whatever happens, the poor bastard's going to go down for ten to fifteen years, and all he's ever done is help us when we asked. Us and Curtis Manning.'

Lord Moffat studied the other man over the menu. Perhaps he'd misjudged him slightly. There was just a little humanity in him, just a hint of conscience. If, of course, you overlooked that it was Pinfold himself who'd decided that the decks had to be cleared, that Littlechild had to go. That the man knew too much that could damage them and should be put out of harm's way for a decade or so. And all because he was no longer co-operative. Because he wouldn't co-operate in the assassination of an old friend. In Pinfold's book, anyone who wasn't with you was against you. So Littlechild was against him and Littlechild was now a liability.

'What about Peter Keegan?' Moffat asked, changing tack. 'Have you been in touch with Staffordshire police?'

'One of my people has. They're confident he's still in the area, reckon they've got him confined to Cannock Chase.'

'What's all this about him being abducted by the IRA?'

Pinfold shrugged. 'It seemed a logical assumption. Anyway, the latest is he got away from them, grabbed a gun and ran off. The police reckon he'll be caught within the next forty-eight hours.'

'I do hope so. Maybe then Curtis Manning will get off my back.'

Pinfold actually showed sympathy, or a hint of it. 'Keegan's on the run, what does the American think he's going to do? Be interviewed on *News at Ten*?'

'Probably.' A shared but unsmiling joke.

'Well, he won't get the chance. The police have got a top ex-SAS tracker on the job.'

'Ah, yes,' Moffat said and lifted the late edition of the London *Evening Standard* from the table and unfolded the front page. 'SAS Gulf Hero Tracks Escaped Terrorist,' he read and raised one eyebrow. 'The same Lomax?'

'Yes, sir. Unfortunate that. But the police arranged it before any of our people realised. There's nothing sinister in it. The police asked Hereford for a tracker and Lomax's name came up.'

'Rather a visible link between Keegan and Littlechild, don't you think?'

'With respect, sir, only we know that. The press hasn't mentioned he's Littlechild's brother-in-law or that the two are friends. Trouble is it *would* look a bit odd if we had him kicked off the case now. That really would get the tabloids asking questions. Anyway, I've got people keeping an eye on Lomax.'

'And the Browne woman?'

'Of course.'

'I hope we haven't underestimated her. I'm not happy she went to see Keegan. Smells to me she's planning for defence in depth.'

Pinfold smiled at the military term coming from a man of such unmilitary bearing. 'She's good, sir. You'd expect her to explore all avenues. But hopefully she's good enough to recognise that her client just can't win. What we have on him is totally conclusive. We'll keep them guessing for as long as possible, unnerve them. Then let them see there's no way out. Then he'll opt to take the offer, even if she doesn't want him to.'

'I'm sure you're right, Roger. Then I can tell Curtis Manning to relax, that everything's under control?'

Pinfold gave one of his enigmatic little smiles. He didn't see the need to mention that the previous evening he'd learned that two people answering to the description of Lomax and Browne had managed to gain access to 32 Bascombe Court. Lord

Moffat didn't need to be worried with that. Best anyway to keep everything boxed and separate, that was the rule.

'Good,' Moffat said. 'Then we can relax and enjoy our meal. I thought I'd start with the salmon mousse. Your tab, I believe?'

Six

Lomax was up by five and nursing a thick head.

The previous evening had gone well, Bill Johnson and his police team meeting at the hotel with the head ranger of Cannock Chase. Armed with large-scale maps, he'd explained that the area was a very rough and thick crescent shape. The western half was mostly open heathland or deciduous woods, comprising the Country Park to the north and Brindley Heath to the south. An exception to this was the densely planted conifer forest abutting the A34 road. It was into this that Keegan was thought to have disappeared.

The inner, western half of the crescent was almost entirely made up of evergreen plantation, crisscrossed by tracks and a few public roads which were now sealed off by police VCPs.

'I could tell you the best places to disappear,' the head ranger had offered, 'but then this bloke has always lived in Northern Ireland, right? So he wouldn't know them anyway.'

Lomax had agreed. 'Better to arrange the best general coverage rather than specific areas – unless we get a sighting. He's had enough time to get to almost any part of the Chase by now and we've got limited resources. If we can man observation posts and mounted patrols during the day, then put up the helicopter with the thermal imager for an hour or two each night . . .' Johnson winced as he visualised the rising bill. 'Then we'll soon get a lead,' Lomax concluded.

By late evening the plan had been finalised. All minor roads across the Chase would remain sealed, the exception being the A460 which dissected the crescent, linking Rugeley with Hednesford and Cannock; nevertheless there'd be a VCP at each end and police vehicles would patrol that stretch of road regularly. Warnings of an armed escaped prisoner at large would continue on local radio and television and be reinforced by posters put up all over the Chase.

Police control was to be set up at the ranger's Visitor Centre which would provide basic comforts and endless cups of tea. The Chase would be divided into seven distinct operational areas, all of which would be subjected to regular patrols. These would be run by police vehicles or one of the Ranger Service's five Land-Rovers. By calling in other rangers from the north and the Works Unit, the total strength would be boosted to seventeen four-wheel-drive vehicles and personnel to man them.

The southern loop of the Chase came under the Forestry Commission who would provide two of their own rangers and vehicles. All had walkie-talkie radio communications.

Where the terrain was suitable, observation posts would be established at various vantage points, using fire-watch towers, radio transmitter masts and water towers. For patrolling really difficult ground, police officers on scrambler bikes would be deployed or 'The Jockeys', members of the Mounted Branch whose headquarters was a short distance away.

With their master plan finalised, the drinks had begun to flow thick and fast from the hotel bar as police and rangers unwound after the pressures of a long day.

Now Lomax was paying the price for an enjoyable three hours and the nightcap malts at midnight. He downed three cups of strong, sweet black coffee in his room, shaved, showered and left without calling down for a breakfast tray. It was still dark as he drove over the motorway bridge and into the Chase, heading for the Visitor Centre.

There were already several police vehicles and Ranger Service Land-Rovers in the car park when he arrived and uniformed officers manning the radio caravan outside. The head ranger called Ned, a jovial man with a ginger beard, was distributing coffee, aspirin and whisky tots to anyone who had the need or the stamina.

Superintendent Johnson arrived a few minutes later. To Lomax's mild irritation he bustled in brightly, apparently none the worse for the previous night's excesses. Without preamble he accepted coffee from Ned and addressed his audience. 'Right now, we've had a few encouraging developments. Over-

134

night, our colleagues have been sifting through statements taken from motorists at VCPs since the ambush. It appears one driver saw a figure crossing the A34 on foot from the woods where the Safrane was found. Having checked the times, it would appear to have been about twenty minutes after the ambush.'

There was a low murmur of interest around the room. 'Unfortunately,' Johnson added, 'he doesn't sound like our man. The witness is sure he was wearing an anorak and camouflage trousers, or similar, and was carrying a rucksack.'

'Probably a poacher,' someone quipped.

'More than likely,' Johnson agreed with good humour. 'We'll know for certain when we've found him, because although there's no way Keegan would have been dressed like that or had a rucksack, this backpacker *was* in the vicinity at the same time as our man. He could be an important witness and we're putting out an appeal for him to come forward.

'Likewise a mountain biker was seen on the Chase at around the same time. A family out for a walk thought it might have been Keegan when they saw the TV news. Again, obviously it wasn't our man, but we're putting out an appeal for the cyclist to make himself known to us. Either of these two could provide a vital lead.'

'Any news from the chopper, sir?' another policeman asked, noticing the sheaf of prints Johnson was holding.

'I'm just coming to that.' He turned to Lomax. 'The helicopter went up twice. The thermal imager picked up something on its first flight around eleven fifteen last night. Looks distinctly like a human form in the area around Anson's Bank.'

'Where's that?' Lomax asked, moving to the wall map.

'Here,' Ned replied, jabbing a ruler at a location in the southwest of the Country Park. It was just over a mile in a direct line from where the Safrane had been abandoned. 'Arguably a good spot to hole up. It's covered with trenches used for training during the First World War – used to be a couple of massive army camps nearby. 'Course the trenches are well overgrown which can make it pretty hazardous for the unwary.'

Lomax nodded thoughtfully and turned to Johnson. 'What happened on the second flight?'

'That was between two and three this morning. Obviously, the pilot concentrated on Anson's Bank again. But this time there was no sign.'

Lomax accepted the photograph of the thermal image. The hunched shape of the human form was unmistakable, white against varying shades of grey and black representing the heavy summer foliage of bracken, brush and trees. Different prints showed the man's progress across a line of trenches. 'Presumably we can pinpoint the spot?'

'We've got an exact location,' Johnson confirmed.

'How deep can one of these imagers penetrate underground?'

'Depends on the ambient temperature of the earth or rubble. So at night in this country when it gets quite chill, down to several feet. Why?'

'So if he was digging himself some sort of foxhole, he'd have to go pretty deep.'

'And he doesn't have a spade,' Johnson reminded.

'Wouldn't need to here,' Ned said. 'He's got trenches already dug. If he put some branches over the top and covered them in leaves he'd be quite snug – until it rained.'

Lomax nodded. 'But he'd also show up on a thermal imager.'

'So he's definitely moved on,' Johnson thought aloud.

'About my poacher,' said the police officer who'd made the earlier quip. 'Maybe it's him. What I mean is, it just might not be Keegan.'

'Do you get poacher trouble?' Lomax asked Ned.

'Sure. We've got fallow deer on the Chase an' there's always someone willing to take a pop at them. So it could be a poacher you've picked up. Pretty daft one to try it with all the area sealed off with police.'

Johnson smiled. 'You'd be surprised. There are plenty of daft villains – our prisons are full of them.'

Lomax intervened. 'I'd like to get down there by first light anyway. Tracking's best done while the sun's at a low angle.'

Johnson drained his coffee. 'Right then, let's go.'

By six thirty Ned's Land-Rover was pulling into the Anson's Bank car park as the morning sun broke clear of the horizon. Deciduous woodland of oak and beech and younger birch. Nevertheless, it was fairly open and didn't offer especially good cover. Despite the network of hidden trenches, Lomax couldn't imagine a former soldier like Peter Keegan choosing to go to ground here.

He followed Ned and Johnson forward into the yellowing, waist-high bracken; the only other man with them was an armed escort from the Tactical Support Unit.

'Quite a popular area is this,' Ned was saying, pointing out one of the trenches now completely concealed by the previous season's layer of dried and brittle fern detritus. 'Step on that and you'd drop up to three or four feet into a trench and guarantee yourself a broken leg. Kids love to play here. Then you get visitors from the Katyn Memorial, or the war cemeteries at the lower end of the park, tending to wander up this way.'

'Not a place I'd choose,' Lomax said.

'*If* you knew the area,' Johnson reminded. He consulted his marked map and handed it to Ned. 'Anyway, I think this is the place the helicopter spotted our mystery man, whoever he is.'

The three men sat on a wayside log and opened a flask of coffee, while Lomax quietly went about his business. After ten minutes he found what he was looking for – a faint footprint in the dusty earth beside a trench. Using a soft-focus torch to give additional side light and a magnifying glass, he was able to verify it was Keegan's imprint.

He marked it with a lolly stick from the bundle he kept wrapped in an elastic band in his windproof pocket and began hunting for the next print. It took a long time to find it because the grass was thick and only the edge of a heel had imprinted in the earth underneath. Adding another lolly stick, he measured the footprint length and then the stride with the markers on his tracking stick before going in search of the next.

When he couldn't find a print, he merely put the first marker over the toe of the last impression and rotated the tracking stick. He then knew the next missing heel print would be under the point of the stick. It was an agonisingly slow business that totally absorbed him. While the armed officer stayed nearby, Johnson and Ned soon became bored. They returned to the Land-Rover, promising to return later.

The sun strengthened on Lomax's back and the stillness closed in around him until he felt utterly alone, slowly tuning in to the sounds of nature and its secrets. Breeze rustling the bracken, the movement of beetles and grasshoppers, and once, the sudden slithering of a disturbed snake.

Patiently Lomax followed his trail of meagre clues. Bruised grass, turned leaves and broken spider's webs, stones disturbed to leave their darker undersides exposed, grains of sand scattered onto pebbles from the soles of Keegan's boots.

At last Lomax stopped. In front of him the sandy track was heavily disturbed where his quarry had left the track. To his right the bracken stems had been snapped, oozing stringy sap. He prodded with his stick, opening up a tunnel through the ferns and the void of one of the old training trenches.

Silently he stood and beckoned over the armed officer. It looked to Lomax as though Keegan had veered off the track, most probably to find somewhere to sleep. The last thing he wanted was to stumble in and wake the man in panic. It would be a shame for such a pleasant morning to be spoiled with a bullet between the eyes.

As the officer steadied himself and thumbed off the safety catch of his Heckler and Koch, Lomax called out quietly: 'Hey, Peter! It's Chris Lomax here! Remember me? I'm with armed police! Don't worry, you're quite safe! Just come out slowly with your hands up and without the gun. I repeat, I'm with armed police.'

There was no response; they tried again.

'Okay,' Lomax told the policeman, 'I'm going in.'

He wriggled a few feet through the dense stalks of bracken before he found the sandy edge of the trench. Then he smelt it, a sooty charcoal odour. The beam of his torch played into the four-foot trench where dead bracken had been drawn into a mound to form a rough mattress. Beside it was a little mound of charred twigs.

138

While Johnson was called up on the radio, Lomax completed his search of the little subterranean den. The man had left only one clue behind, the wrapper from an Opal Fruit sweet. An accumulation of black and brown chippings were collected on a flat shelf of stone; it took Lomax a moment to realise what they were. Insect legs and beetle shells. Keegan was getting hungry and obviously hadn't forgotten his survival training.

'So what can you tell me?' Johnson asked, clearly pleased with the result.

'Chummy obviously spent part of yesterday here, down in the trench. And he's started to feel hungry, because he's been eating insects.'

Johnson pulled a face.

Lomax grinned. 'They're not so bad when cooked. You should try my worm omelette sometime.'

'I hope that's not a chat-up line you use on the girls.' Johnson stared around at the wild bracken scrub that hid the network of trenches. 'So what will he do next? Put down traps for birds or animals?'

'I doubt it. You need tools to build traps and it's a long-term project. He probably tried the insects to stave off his hunger and see if he *could* do it. Having decided how foul they are, he'll try stealing food.'

'There are plenty of houses around the Chase, on the out-skirts,' Johnson confirmed.

'Water's going to be an even bigger problem, Bill, especially if the weather stays dry.'

'There are a couple of pools up near Brocton to the north. 'Bout a mile away. One in a quarry and one in a nature reserve.'

Lomax said: 'He'll want fresh running water if possible.'

'Plenty of streams,' Ned interrupted. 'One across the way there along Sherbrook Valley at the edge of the Country Park. That's the nearest.'

'I expect he's resting up in the day, so it might be worth putting an observation post over there tonight,' Lomax suggested.

Johnson liked that idea. 'I'll have a radio link established between them and the helicopter.'

'Ideally we should get a fix on his whereabouts as near dawn as possible.'

'Right,' the superintendent agreed. 'In the meantime, can you pick up his trail from here?'

Lomax nodded. 'Yes, but it'll be a long process. Bear in mind this is where he was seen at eleven fifteen last night. Given he's had five hours on the move since then, I'll be a long way behind.'

'I could bring in the dog teams. They'd be quicker.'

Lomax laughed gently. 'Being replaced by a computer, Bill, is one thing but by a dog!'

'I'm under pressure to get Keegan back. I dread to think what this operation's costing.'

'Trouble is that dogs and handlers tend to make a mess of the trail and they can be easily duped by someone who knows what he's doing.'

Johnson considered for a moment. 'Well, Keegan should know what he's doing. I've checked with army records. When he was with the Cheshires back in the sixties, he did a two-day survival course. Nevertheless, dogs are still quicker.'

Lomax wasn't going to argue. Dogs worked on one sense while human beings worked on four, rarely using smell. But human beings also had that mysterious sixth sense and could think into the mind of a quarry. 'If it makes you feel happier, Bill, fine. Then tomorrow I can start fresh on anything we pick up tonight.'

'Good idea,' Johnson agreed, pleased that his tracker wasn't going to sulk. 'That's settled. Meanwhile, this afternoon I'm planning to visit Keegan's wife, wondered if you might like to come along.'

'Me?'

'Purely selfish reason. You knew Keegan and his world so you might well pick up on something that I miss.'

'You think he might make contact with her?'

'Possible, although they're apparently separated. But you know what some women are like. Too soft for their own good. Women who love too much and all that stuff. Can't help themselves. Show them the hardest, meanest bastard in the world and they see a little boy who needs mothering.'

Keegan's wife had reverted to her maiden name. Heather Andrews now lived in Derby, Johnson explained as they sped along in the white police Rover.

She had been born in Banbridge, Northern Ireland, and after her husband had been sentenced, had moved to Derby when he was transferred to the mainland so that she could continue to visit him regularly. But the strain had been too much and the marriage had crumbled. Now there was a For Sale sign outside the modest maisonette.

Although she'd been expecting them, she clearly wasn't relishing the visit. Her offer of tea and biscuits was polite ritual rather than a gesture of welcome. She was in her mid-forties with a thickening waist and heavy arms. Her face was pale as though it had been drained of all emotion, as if she was just waiting for life's next blow to her happiness and self-esteem. The eyes were dull, no longer caring about anyone or anything, and her short hair as colourless as the skirt and jumper she wore.

'I see you're selling up,' Johnson said, accepting the cheap china cup and saucer. 'Just the one lump, please.'

Heather smiled mirthlessly. 'I've been selling up, as you put it, for two years. No buyers, not unless you give it away.'

'Going back to Ulster?'

She nodded. 'There's nothing left for me here. Peter got transferred here so his mother could visit – his parents moved over here early in the Troubles. His family's always had connections in this area, Stafford and Derby.'

'So you came too?'

That bitter sad smile again. 'Daft, aren't I? It seemed a good idea at the time. Also safer. Some idiot in the Ulster Defenders might think it was a good idea to have me targeted. You know how warped some of their thinking can be. If they couldn't get Pete for his betrayal, they'd as likely go for me.'

'But not now?'

Her eyes didn't reflect hurt, more an inner bruising. 'Now I just don't care any more. Besides, this peace seems to be holding. Well, at least I'd thought . . .'

'Until your husband was snatched?' Lomax intervened.

Heather appeared to notice him properly for the first time. 'You're not police, are you? I didn't catch the name.'

'Lomax. Chris Lomax. At one time I worked with your husband.'

Her nostrils flared. 'Not one of those bloody spooks?'

'No, I was with the army. I've retired now.'

'Army Intelligence,' she said, her voice softer now. 'They were all right. They stood by Pete, spoke up for him at his trial. It was those other bastards. MI5 or Group or whatever they called themselves.'

'I was Regiment,' Lomax said. 'I was backup to Peter on occasions, bodyguard, minder, you know.'

She nodded, remembering. 'I used to warn him. Told him you could never trust those slippery bastards. How one day they'd stab him in the back when it suited. When they abandoned him after his arrest, he cried like a baby. It was like his own parents had rejected him. He couldn't believe it.'

'I've been called in by the police to help track him down,' Lomax explained.

'I'm anxious to get to him before the IRA come back for another try,' Johnson added. 'That's my real anxiety.'

Heather said: 'I don't know why he just doesn't give himself up. I mean, he's already served over half his sentence. It doesn't seem like him. I mean, he wasn't expecting to be – well, freed like this, I suppose.'

'He might try to make contact with you,' Johnson said gently.

'I doubt it. We've been washed up for a good three years, ever since . . .' Her voice trailed off and she bit her tongue.

'Yes?' Johnson pressed.

She shrugged. What the hell. 'Ever since I found out he'd had some slag. A lover, I suppose he'd call her. Some slag he'd been knocking around with for years. She was something to do with the Defenders, someone's sister. All that anguish, all that heartbreak I went through. Wondering why he was later home than he said. The missing nights, the missing weekends. Expecting the RUC at the door to tell me he'd been found in some ditch with a bullet in his head. And all the time he'd been – been with her.'

'Her?'

'Ferguson.' She whispered the name as though not wanting it to pass her lips. 'Susie Ferguson.'

'Where is she now?'

'I don't know.' Heather paused and stared at Johnson. 'And I don't care.'

'Where did she live when you last knew?'

'Portadown.' She gave the address.

Johnson said: 'Will you let us know if Peter makes contact with you?'

She shook her head. 'No. He's still my husband and I think he's been betrayed enough, don't you?' She stared at the reproduction print on the opposite wall. 'We got out of all this once, you know? Pete started helping MI5 way back at the start of the Troubles. Small things at first until he was so deep in they wouldn't let him get out. Said he was too valuable. Pete liked that, liked to feel wanted. And all the time our wee son was growing up.'

'That's Tim?' Johnson asked.

Heather nodded. 'Finally, in 1985, I persuaded Pete to give it all up and change our life. His controllers didn't like it – even threatened to expose him to the Loyalist gangs. But, anyway, we went to live in Durban. For two glorious years. Tim was fourteen then, and *loved* it.'

'But then you went back to Belfast,' Lomax said.

'They appealed to Pete's vanity. Army Intelligence or MI5, whoever. Said they desperately needed him. The Loyalist terror gangs were out of control, running riot. They needed him to rein them in.' She gave a forlorn shake of her head, still not quite believing. 'In truth, I think Pete was missing the buzz. So we all traipsed back to wet and miserable Belfast.'

Johnson completed the story. 'And two years later he was arrested.'

'And only one person spoke up for him. The rest, those who had pleaded with him to come back, never lifted a finger to help him.' Her eyes seemed to refocus; she was back in the present, her moment of self-pity over. 'So don't ask me to betray him. No doubt you'll have this house watched and tap the phone? Fine, so long as you do your own dirty work.'

'And your son, Tim?' Johnson asked gently. 'Where is he now?'

'What d'you want with him?' Heather returned sharply.

'Same as you. In case your husband tries to make contact?'

Her laugh was harsh. 'He'll have a job. Tim joined the Legion. The Foreign Legion.'

'When was that?'

'Three years ago, when Pete and I broke up. He blamed me. He left the Parachute Regiment and went to France. I haven't heard from him since.'

'I'm sorry.'

Lomax said: 'You mentioned Peter had family ties in this area, relatives?'

'Well, his dad's dead now, of course. And you know his mother's in hospital?'

Johnson said: 'Yes, that's the reason Peter was being transferred, so he could visit.'

'Used to be an uncle and a couple of aunts. But the aunts have passed over now and the uncle is senile. In some home at Morecambe.'

'Did Peter ever spend time with them over here as a child?'

Heather nodded. 'The maiden aunt used to live in Cannock. He'd spend holidays with her.'

Lomax frowned. 'Wasn't a keen walker by any chance, was she?'

A look of surprise crossed Heather's face. 'How did you know?'

'Just a hunch.'

'Aunt Betsy was a rambler and bird-watcher. In fact, I think that's why she never married. Mad keen on natural history and wildlife.'

'She knew the Chase then?'

'Knew it? She practically lived there.'

★

'Does that make a difference?' Johnson asked Lomax as they headed back to the Chase in the squad car.

'It could mean Keegan would feel quite at home there. Once he's reorientated himself. Takes a while to familiarise yourself again with old childhood haunts, even if they haven't changed.'

Johnson stared out at the sunlit countryside flashing past. 'He's got no money, no resources. Maybe he'd feel happier there than moving back to civilisation. For that, he'd definitely need outside help.'

'And who's going to help him?' Lomax asked. 'He's got no friends outside immediate family. All his former Loyalist chums regarded him as a traitor for spying on them and he'll know the police will be expecting him to make contact with someone. No, I think he might be quite content to stay in the Chase – wait until the hue and cry dies down and we assume he's moved on.'

'At least until winter,' Johnson murmured.

'Until then,' Lomax agreed.

'It's imperative we locate his son and this Ferguson woman. Of course, we're watching Heather's house and we've officers at the hospital in case he tries to contact his mother.'

'How is she?'

'Latest wasn't good. It could be curtains any time.'

When they arrived back at the Visitor Centre, they discovered that the dog teams had met with failure. They'd rapidly picked up the scent from Keegan's hide at Anson's Bank and had followed it across the Country Park to the stream in Sherbrook Valley. Just as Ned had predicted. But there Keegan had obviously waded up or downstream for some distance before striking out again, and the animals failed to pick up the new trail.

Silly really, he knew, but Lomax couldn't help feeling just a little smug.

'A strong lead,' Johnson announced triumphantly at the Visitor Centre briefing the next morning. 'Someone broke into a caravan near Penkridge Bank. Stole fifty quid and enough food to last someone a week.'

Lomax smiled; it was just what he'd predicted. 'How far is that from the trenches at Anson's Bank?'

'Scarcely two miles.'

'Do you want me or the dogs?'

Johnson looked suitably abashed. 'I've learned my lesson, Chris. You do your stuff. Call in the dogs if you want them.'

On the journey by car to the caravan site, Johnson brought Lomax up to date with his investigation into Keegan's background. 'We traced Keegan's supposed mistress, Susie Ferguson, through Social Security. She's been living in Manchester. Local officers called to visit her bedsit last night – she disappeared the day after Keegan's abduction.'

'Sure she's not on holiday?'

'Place was cleared out. The day before, she'd taken a neighbour's kid to London. Came back and seemed perfectly normal. The next morning she walked out with a suitcase and hasn't been seen since. Maybe she'd informed on him to the IRA. Maybe she knew about the transfer.'

Lomax made a counter-suggestion. 'Perhaps she was afraid Keegan would come looking for her and didn't want to get involved? That must be a dilemma for a loved one. Do you harbour an escaped prisoner and risk jail yourself, or betray him?'

Johnson shrugged. 'Whatever her reasons, she's gone to ground. Mind you, she's on the dole, so hopefully we'll trace her soon enough next time she claims benefit.'

'What about Keegan's son, Tim?'

'No luck at all there. The French military are being very – er – French. Code of silence in the Legion and all that bullshit. They say they've no record of a Tim Keegan, but then they pointed out he would have been allowed to enlist under any name he chose.'

'You sound suspicious.'

'I would be, had Keegan not been abducted by the IRA and we know, roughly, where he is. If he'd been sprung under other circumstances, I'd be mightily suspicious if his nearest and dearest had vanished.' He shook his head slowly. 'Something about all this isn't adding up. I just can't put my finger on it. If

Keegan decided he'd do better to break out of the Chase, we wouldn't be able to stop him and I wouldn't have a clue where to start looking. We've got nothing on his background, his old friends or enemies in Ulster, ideas where he might go. I've never seen such a thin file.'

'Sanitised by MI5?'

'By someone. I've made an application for an interview with the Anti-Terrorist Branch to fill me in on some details.'

They arrived at the caravan park and drove towards the rear where the scene-of-crime officer and his group had taped off the area around a caravan.

Lomax climbed out and looked up at the clear September sky. This certainly beat working for a living.

'It's an old Provo trick,' Susie Ferguson said, 'but it works.'

They were sitting in a quiet corner of the sea-front cafe in Brighton, nursing mugs of tea and bacon and tomato sandwiches.

The sun streamed in from a porcelain sky. Outside, the air was full of salt and the screech of gulls; men were wearing baggy shorts and the girls skimpy dresses. It was all a far, far cry from G Block at Stafford. This was the first time since boarding the 125 at the Shugborough Tunnel that he had really believed he was free. Even his fumbled, hurried lovemaking with Susie, for the first time in six years, had been a misty dream, distorted by the effects of the celebratory champagne. Alcohol was something his body had forgotten how to handle after long years of abstinence.

Now was his fourth day of freedom. This morning, when he pinched himself, for the first time it hurt.

'Tim chose Brighton because there's a high proportion of pensioners,' Johan van Niekerk said in his distinctive South African drawl. 'Tomorrow is Thursday, payout day. The money arrives at the depot today by security van at five thirty, after the post office closes.'

Keegan's son Tim was quiet and thoughtful, having ridden through the night from Cannock Chase on his motorcycle. Wearily, he said: 'It's a bit cruel on our victim, but he'll soon get over a few hours of anxiety. His biggest problem afterwards will be his embarrassment.'

'You've done a good job, son, I'm proud of you.' Keegan placed his hand over Tim's in a gesture of affection. 'Have you any idea what this might net?'

Tim shook his head. 'I've had no time to go into all that. A few hundred thousand if we're lucky.'

'It's a start,' van Niekerk said and pushed the photograph of a woman, pram and young girl across the table. 'This is our man's wife and kids. I took it with a telephoto lens. Wednesday is her shopping day, which is doubly useful. She spends the afternoon at the shops and doesn't usually get home until six. By which time it'll all be over.'

'Her husband always goes to the same pub for lunch,' Tim added. 'Creature of habit. Always visits the gents just before he leaves. That's when we get him.'

Van Niekerk said: 'Remember, Tim, we must put the fear of God into him. If he doesn't *believe* we mean it, everything could all come horribly unstuck.'

Keegan was beginning to feel uncomfortable; they'd been at the cafe for almost an hour and it was too long. 'Time to split,' he decided. 'Susie and I will go first.'

They had two cars, both stolen in the Midlands by van Niekerk. Both were popular models, an Escort and an Astra; the plates had been changed. Without the financial reserves to hire lock-up garages, the cars had been legally street-parked in a neighbouring town until last night.

Keegan took the wheel of the Escort and drove it out of the multistorey. At eleven forty-five a parking bay across the street from the post office became free. He pulled in, fed the meter and settled in for a long wait.

At the same time, his son and Johan van Niekerk were watching the semidetached suburban home of Frederick Bates. Mild-mannered senior postal clerk, aged forty-six. Weeks earlier Susie had telephoned their home and spoken to his wife. A marketing survey, she'd said, answer a few simple questions about shopping habits – just ten minutes – and a wonderful free gift would be hers.

Within that ten minutes, Susie knew the family's ages and Christian names, their make of car, television and PC, their eating, drinking and smoking habits, that they had a fifty-thousand mortgage and couldn't afford holidays abroad.

From the Astra, the two men saw wife Jocelyn close the front door and start to push the pram containing baby Henry, while little Louise skipped happily behind. As soon as they'd turned the corner, van Niekerk opened the driver's door and stepped out. Moments later, the telephone line to the house was cut.

He returned to the car and the two of them set off back to the centre of Brighton.

Tim and van Niekerk were already waiting, sitting at different tables, when Frederick Bates entered the pub at five minutes past one. He ordered toad-in-the-hole and beans and his usual half of best, found a corner seat and opened his newspaper.

There was an anxious moment for the watchers at ten to two when another man walked across to the lavatory moments before Bates went in. It seemed like an age that both men were in there, yet it was only seconds. Tim began to sweat. Blow it now and they'd have to wait another week to try again some-where else.

Tim and van Niekerk looked at each other across the bar room. Tim nodded, they had to make their move. Both rising, moving in from different directions towards the door. It opened and the first man appeared.

Thank God. Tim brushed past. It was a matter of seconds, touch and go.

Van Niekerk was behind him, closing the door. Cramped in the short passage that separated the inner and outer doors to the urinal. Balaclavas on. Barely time to straighten them and the inner door opened. Bates coming out.

The South African pushed forward, grabbed the man by the throat and threw him back into the lavatory. Bates squealed as the hand tightened round his neck, forcing him back past a row of china stalls and slammed him against the wall of a cubicle with crashing force.

'Shut up!' van Niekerk ordered, left hand pinioning Bates's

149

throat as his right brought up the automatic under the man's nose. Bates's eyes crossed as he tried to focus on the muzzle.

Tim moved in behind and waved a photograph in front of the hapless post-office clerk. 'Jocelyn, young Louise and baby Henry!' he snapped. 'We've got them at your house. Co-operate or they die. Just one word from us.' The harsh Ulster accent was unmistakable.

Van Niekerk squeezed his clawed hand into Bates's larynx to emphasise the point. 'You listening, scum?'

The man's eyes were bulging out of his head and he gasped as the South African relaxed his grip. 'Please,' he breathed.

Tim said: 'The security van delivers at five thirty. When it goes at five forty, leave the gate and back doors unlocked. That's all you have to do. Our man stays with your family until you've done it and gets the all-clear from us.'

'If we get a smell of police,' van Niekerk added, 'or they come to your house, our man will take your kids out first. Got that? You fuckin' got that?'

Bates nodded, trembling uncontrollably.

Tim jerked at van Niekerk's sleeve; it was time to go. 'Wait here five minutes before you come out,' the South African added. 'We'll be watching you, Bates.'

Both men moved back through the inner door. Someone was trying to enter from the pub bar. Van Niekerk jammed his foot against the outer door to give them time to pull off the balaclavas. Then they pushed their way out, barging the male customer aside and walking out into the street.

Twice during the afternoon Tim and van Niekerk went in separately to buy stamps, the second time near to closing. On both occasions, Bates could be seen at his desk.

At five thirty the main doors were closed and a few moments later the Securicor van arrived, swung off the road and nosed up to the steel side gates. Bates appeared, looking nervous as he proceeded to unlock them. The van went inside and disappeared.

Keegan and Susie Ferguson sat in the parked Escort and watched. The minutes dragged by. Their hearts were racing and it felt unbearably hot. The digital clock on the dash flick-

150

ered with tantalising slowness. Five forty-one, forty-two, forty-three.

Running three minutes late. Was something going down? Had Bates snapped, poured out his soul to his superior? Had he been unable to resist the call home and got the dead line? And if he had, had he broken down with hysterical tears? Decided to call the police?

Keegan glanced in the side mirror. Looking for cops, uniformed or plainclothes. Anyone loitering, a stakeout, a pounce taking shape. He could see no one, nothing.

Susie nudged him. 'Here it is.'

Bates was back at the gate, the blunt nose of the security van behind him. Sunlight glinted on the keys. Keegan's hand tensed on the steering wheel, knuckle bones showing white through the skin, as the postal worker dragged back each barred gate in turn.

A glance in his mirror told him that Tim and van Niekerk were ready, exhaust trickling from the rear of the pulled-over Astra.

The van rolled away and Bates began closing the depot gates, going through the motions of turning the lock. At least Keegan hoped. The not-knowing was getting to him, the tension shrivelling his insides until it almost hurt. Sweat was seeping into his eyes. He caught the movement in his mirror, the Astra cruising past, van Niekerk and his son with collars up and cloth caps pulled low over their foreheads.

If the police were waiting, now would be the time. The Astra reversed up to the gates, inching back to push them open.

Keegan breathed again as the Astra backed up and out of sight inside the post-office yard. Then van Niekerk returned to shut the gates before disappearing again.

The next eight minutes were even worse. Waiting was unbearable, an almost physical pain. Susie saw it in his eyes, and reached across to grasp his hand. He was grateful for that; in fact, grateful to her for so much.

'Nearly over,' she whispered.

No, he thought, it hasn't even begun.

Van Niekerk reappeared at the gates and held them open

while Tim drove out. The suspension of the Astra was noticeably lower, a tarpaulin covering the load in the rear luggage space. Despite his own frayed nerves, Keegan couldn't help smiling as the South African sauntered back to close the gates and returned to his seat. So goddamn cool, the man was a gem.

The Astra signalled, waited patiently for a gap in the passing traffic, and joined the flow heading west; Keegan followed.

They swapped the load at a remote woodland car park outside town where Tim had left his motorcycle. He used it to follow the Escort after the Astra was abandoned.

Van Niekerk's old camper van was in a New Forest caravan park in a little woody alcove not overlooked by others. It was dark when they arrived and backed the Escort up to the rear door of the van. In the morning, the Escort would be driven away and abandoned before they left the area. Keegan, Susie and van Niekerk would seek to rent a house, which they could now afford, in an isolated location, while Tim returned to Cannock Chase.

'That's it,' van Niekerk said as the last neat bundle of used notes was transferred into the camper and stacked.

'Takes up more space than I thought,' Keegan said.

Tim had been staring in silence at the growing wall of money bricks. 'I'm not surprised.'

'What d'you mean?'

'I reckoned this haul might net a few hundred thousand if we were lucky.'

'Well?'

'A rough guess, Da, but I think this is closer to two million.'

Keegan stared. He always knew it would take a lot of money to launch a war.

Seven

The previous day Lomax had lost the trail at Stony Brook. He'd called the dogs in and run them east and west along the embankment of the stream. At last light they'd picked up a new scent.

Since just after dawn, Lomax had been following the trail. A half-mile loop and at noon he found himself back at the stream. Again the tracks and scent vanished. He could almost believe Keegan was giving him a deliberate run-around.

Idly he circled the area. The trail was too cold, nearly two days old now. There'd been nothing last night. No eyeball sightings and nothing from the helicopter's thermal imager. With a stocked larder of stolen food from the caravan, Keegan was sitting tight.

Lomax stopped and looked down at the boggy ground by his feet. A clear footprint in the mud, filled with brackish water. He took the length of tube and rubber bulb from one of his bellows pockets, then stooped, poking the end of the tube into the water. He squeezed and released the bulb to suck the print dry.

It was a similar size, but it wasn't Keegan's print. A flat sole and heel, slightly worn on the outer edge. Maybe a desert boot.

He glanced back over his shoulder. The stream was a mere ten yards away at the point where Keegan's trail had abruptly ended.

How old was this print? Impossible to tell. This ground probably never dried out from one year to the next. It was under firs and virtually never saw the sun. He used the pacing stick set at Keegan's stride, rotated it and found another print. Then another.

And then they vanished. Here the ground was hard and if the grass had been crushed, it had now recovered. He called in a dog team, but they could pick up nothing.

The nagging thought wouldn't leave him. Had Keegan

changed his shoes? How could he? He wasn't carrying a spare pair when he was abducted from the taxi. It was a nonsense. Something else too, but he couldn't put his finger on it. A small voice told him he'd overlooked a glaringly obvious clue.

He was just dismissing the thought when he saw the Ranger Service Land-Rover approaching along the firebreak. It stopped beside the dog team and Ned and Bill Johnson alighted.

This was the first Lomax had seen of the detective super-intendent today; he'd had an early morning appointment in London with the Anti-Terrorist Branch to try and glean some-thing of Keegan's history and previous contacts in Ulster.

'How'd it go, Bill?' Lomax asked.

Johnson didn't smile. He walked straight past him with a terse: 'Over here!'

The former SAS man was taken aback, shrugged and fol-lowed the policeman across the firebreak to where they couldn't be overheard.

'What's wrong, Bill?'

Johnson's face was grim and stony. 'Don't "Bill" me, Lomax! What the hell do you think you're playing at?'

'I don't understand.'

'I had a meeting with the ATB this morning.'

'I know.'

'They told me you're the brother-in-law of Rodney Little-child – this Loyalist on the Fitzpatrick murder charge.'

Lomax saw no point in denying it. 'So?'

'Why didn't you tell me?'

'You never asked, Bill. Anyway, it's irrelevant.'

Johnson's eyes narrowed fiercely. 'It can't be that irrelevant considering you'd been to see Keegan the day before his ab-duction, passing yourself off as his solicitor's clerk!'

'Oh, that!' That, he had to admit, was a little embarrassing.

'How the hell do I know you're not something to do with Keegan's abduction?'

Lomax couldn't prevent the smile. 'Don't be daft. Me with the IRA? The Regiment put you in touch, remember?'

154

'They wouldn't even know, would they? The ATB think you could be involved – at least they're not discounting it.'

'Do you mean the ATB, Bill?'

'What?'

'Was it just the ATB you saw?'

The policeman looked bemused. 'You know it wasn't. They're my link to MI5. It's MI5 and Army Intelligence who've got Keegan's file.'

'And they want you to kick me off this hunt, yes?'

'No, not like that.' He stared around the firebreak as though seeking inspiration for the words. 'They've advised that you be quietly dropped in case you're compromising the search.'

'That's rubbish, Bill, and you know it.'

'I hope so.'

A thought occurred to Lomax. 'How many people were at this meeting from MI5?'

'Just the one. Keegan's former case officer I imagine.'

'Was his name Prendergast by any chance?'

Johnson was taken off guard, and blinked. 'Er – Prendergast? Yes, I do believe it was. But how . . .?'

'Just a lucky guess. Keegan said someone by that name was taking an unusual interest in our legal visit before the abduction. Said he was sure the man was some kind of spook.'

The policeman looked uncertain. 'Well, he wasn't wrong about that.'

'So it seems. Look, Bill, if anything, I want to find Keegan even more than you do. He's the only person who can verify that my brother-in-law was an acting agent for MI5.'

'I don't know anything about the Littlechild case.'

Lomax held his gaze for a moment. 'Perhaps you should.' He glanced at his watch. 'I can't do anything more here. Why don't you join me for a pint and a bite to eat? I'll put you in the picture.'

Johnson agreed with some reluctance and Lomax drove them back over the M6 to a pub in Penkridge. Over a couple of pints of bitter and prawn salads, Lomax told the policeman everything he knew about Roddy Littlechild, his history and the alleged murder of the Provisional IRA's Donny Fitzpatrick.

After listening without interruption, Johnson pushed aside his plate, half the prawn salad untouched. Carefully he said: 'As far as I am concerned, Chris, I never heard what you just told me.'

'Why not? It's true.'

'How many times d'you think I've seen villains going down still swearing blind that they're innocent?' Johnson's eyes were hooded, his smile knowing. 'And every villain's wife and mother believes him, despite the evidence. Unless his defence team can *prove* what you've just told me, then forgive me if I file it away in the realms of fantasy. Call me a cynic, Chris, but I've been in this game a long, long time.'

Lomax was disappointed at the reaction, but was not surprised. 'Well, we *are* trying to *prove* his innocence. That's why I went to visit Keegan in prison, because he can at least verify Roddy worked for MI5.'

'It won't prove he didn't kill Fitzpatrick.'

'But it's a start. Make a jury think that perhaps other things aren't quite right about the whole business.'

'Like what?'

For a moment Lomax hesitated, not sure how much he should say. Yet instinctively he trusted the stolid career policeman with whom he'd just shared lunch. 'Fitzpatrick was murdered at an MI5 safe house and yet they or the police had it on outside surveillance. Why? And if so, how was Roddy allowed to get inside?' He paused again. 'I've been to the scene of crime, Bill. It's been redecorated, but I got inside before they'd finished. The ATB say Fitzpatrick was shot through the door, but I don't believe he was. I think he was shot by someone inside and then the shots put through the door to fit the story.'

Johnson's eyes said he didn't believe a word of it. 'Can you prove that?'

Lomax was reluctant. 'No, probably not.'

'Look, Chris, as a friend, let me give you a word of advice. Don't go running round making these wild allegations. Do you realise just how serious they are? That MI5, a government agency, first tried to get your friend Roddy to murder someone he knew in the Loyalist paramilitaries, then persecuted him

156

when he refused to co-operate. Then proceeded to arrange for Fitzpatrick's murder themselves and put Roddy in the frame for it. Think on, Chris, it's just not credible!'

Lomax finished his beer. 'You ever been to Northern Ireland, Bill? On secondment or something?'

'Never set foot in the place,' the man confirmed.

'I thought not,' Lomax replied quietly. 'If you had, you'd realise that anything is possible. There are a lot of secrets over there that a lot of people don't want to be known.'

'Yeah, I realise that,' Johnson conceded.

Lomax said suddenly: 'You didn't get far with your questions into Keegan's past, did you?'

'Bugger all.'

'Despite the fact yours is a genuine investigation that might help recapture Keegan. Despite that, Prendergast told you nothing.'

'Nothing of value, no contact names.' Johnson shrugged. 'National security, I suppose.'

'Or people watching their own backs, Bill. Tell me, what are you going to do now about Keegan's background?'

'Nothing I can do really, I suppose.' He sounded depressed.

'There is someone,' Lomax suggested. 'Someone who should know all about Keegan's background and contacts.'

'Your lawyer friend, this Browne woman?'

Lomax shook his head. 'No, Keegan would have told her only the barest essentials because he opted to plead guilty to conspiracy to murder. Therefore no details would have come out in court.'

'So who do you have in mind?'

Lomax didn't know why he hadn't thought of him before. 'The police chief from the mainland. He investigated the original allegations of the security forces giving confidential information to Loyalist terror groups. I think he was from the West Weald. I expect he's Commissioner of Police or something by now.'

Realisation dawned on Johnson's face. 'Ah, the Penny Inquiry. You mean Derek Penny. Yes, he was Assistant Chief

157

Constable of West Weald. But I'm sure I've read he's left the force.'

'Anyway,' Lomax said. 'He was the one who'd have known everything there was to know about Keegan's background.'

Johnson sounded suddenly more cheerful. 'That's a smart idea, Chris. I owe you one.'

'You owe me a pint.'

The detective picked up the empty glasses. 'I still don't believe a word of your brother-in-law's story, Chris, but I don't like being told how to do my job by an oily bureaucrat like Prendergast.'

'Meaning?'

'As far as I'm concerned, you're still on the case.'

'Is that an Australian accent, Mr Steyn?' the flying club secretary asked as they walked out of the hut and onto the airfield.

'South African.'

'Really? I'm no good with accents.'

There were two parking areas, one filled with a range of fixed-wing aircraft, from Pipers, Cessnas and Beechcraft to Piaggios and a restored Tiger Moth biplane. Some bore For Sale signs in the cockpit windows. The helicopter area was smaller, containing just three machines.

They approached the largest. 'The Agusta A109 is a good choice for an air courier service,' the secretary thought aloud. 'Flexible internal layout and a lot of cargo space available. Rugged, reliable. Bit expensive to run, of course, with the two engines.'

'I intend to make it pay for itself.'

'I'm sure. And where are you setting up?'

'The Irish Republic. I'll reregister the Agusta there.'

'Well, the owner will be pleased to sell. It's a slightly bigger beast than most people want. I expect you'll get it for a good price.'

The man called Steyn spent an hour going over it with an expert eye, prodding and poking around and then running up the twin Allisons in preparation for the test flight.

It landed again half an hour later and the secretary emerged quite white and visibly trembling. Never had he been flown so low and so fast before.

'I'll make the owner an offer,' the South African said. 'If he accepts, I'll get the paperwork done and arrange the money transfer by tomorrow, and I'll collect the day after. Okay?'

The secretary swallowed, rediscovered his voice and said: 'Fine.' And watched as the tall stranger turned and walked away with long and purposeful strides.

Not a man to cross, he decided. An ex-military flyer. Had to be. And he imagined him swooping hard and fast over the treetops during some faraway African bush war.

Bloody good, but bloody frightening. Wouldn't want another trip like that one. Not ever.

For the next four days, Lomax's work fell into a predictable routine.

Every night would end with a clue to the whereabouts of the elusive Peter Keegan. Usually the thermal imager on the helicopter would pick up something, always in a different part of the Chase. But come the dawn, when Lomax and the dog teams went in to pick up the trail, it soon became cold, usually when the footprints disappeared into a stream or pond. Yet tantalisingly he would find something to confirm that they were on the right track. Mostly tins and wrappers from food that had been stolen from the caravan.

One morning, the owner of a nearby smallholding reported that eggs and a chicken had been snatched from the wire-mesh run. The next day's tracking led Lomax to the charred aftermath of a fire, along with skeletal remains of legs, wings and wishbone.

When it was decided to do a night sweep, immediately following a thermal image sighting, their quarry vanished into thin air. Even while the helicopter remained hovering on station, the image of Keegan below just melted away before their eyes. On the ground the trail went cold after a hundred yards.

Midweek, Browne had phoned Lomax just as he returned to his hotel room.

She couldn't keep the excitement from her voice. 'Remember

you told me about your visit to Keegan's wife, about his son going off in a huff to join the Foreign Legion? The other night I spent hours on the office computer and found some of the Keegan trial papers. I'd misfiled them in our changeover to Windows 95.'

'You discovered something?'

'On the family history notes, about Tim. Peter was very proud of his son. Mentioned he'd no flair for languages, yet Tim had got Spanish A-level. I must have scribbled it in my note-book and it got typed up.'

'Is it relevant?'

'It wasn't then, but it may be now. I looked up Foreign Legion in the encyclopaedia and found that there are two. The French and the Spanish. *La Legion de Extranjeros.* I didn't know they had one.'

'Not many people do.'

'Anyway, I made the obvious conclusion and phoned the Spanish military attache's office in London. Laid on the charm with a shovel. They phoned back five minutes ago. A Timothy Keegan left the Legion almost a year ago!'

'Brilliant, Holmes,' he congratulated. 'But I'm not sure if it helps us.'

'It could mean that Peter Keegan has somewhere to go, someone to help him, couldn't it?'

He'd agreed that it could and had hung up in a thoughtful mood, churning various possibilities over in his head.

The next morning he had mentioned it to Bill Johnson, who was clearly impressed with the detective work. Nevertheless, as Keegan was still clearly at large on the Chase, he wasn't sure that the information was of any immediate use. But if their quarry left the area, then it might well be to find his son.

Nothing more was mentioned until the Friday night at a small impromptu celebration of Ned's birthday at the Visitor Centre. The head ranger produced a couple of bottles of Scotch and poured glasses for the police duty team and two rangers who'd volunteered for a night shift.

Detective Superintendent Johnson was in no hurry to return to Stafford HQ to face another pile of memos from his superiors demanding a result, and Lomax had no desire to return yet again to an empty hotel room.

It had been a long, tiring and frustrating week. Every day the weather had become progressively hotter and, with high pressure wedged firmly over the British Isles, it promised more of the same for the foreseeable future. And tempers were beginning to fray.

'Our main hope is,' Ned declared with a light belch, 'that the bleddy streams dry up, so our friend Keegan can't keep giving us the run-around.'

Johnson moved his glass to follow the waving bottle as Ned attempted to pour. 'His luck can't last for ever.'

'Dunno, Bill. If old superman tracker Chris 'ere can't trace him, perhaps no one can.'

Run-around. Lomax had only been half-listening, his mind wandering to the last time he'd spoken to Browne.

Run-around. Ned's word again, swimming about in his brain.

He turned to Johnson. 'Have you heard anything else about those IRA men who snatched Keegan in the first place?'

'No, Chris, they've vanished into the ether. Why?'

'Just suppose they weren't IRA.'

Johnson hid his irritation; this was a party. 'That old chestnut again. I know you've never completely swallowed that line, but all the indications are . . .'

'That they were from Northern Ireland. Period.'

The policeman sighed. 'You think it was Loyalists out for revenge on the man who betrayed them?'

Lomax shook his head. 'Not necessarily.'

'What are you driving at?'

'It's something Ned said. About Keegan giving us the run-around. He's right. That's almost how it feels. As if he's laying a trail and he knows where we are and what we're planning before we know ourselves.'

Johnson looked pained. 'How could he do that, Chris?'

Lomax had to admit he wasn't sure. 'With some sort of outside help? Maybe Keegan hasn't any friends left. But there's still Susie Ferguson and his son, Tim. One of them could be helping him.'

'C'mon, Chris. He's stolen food to survive; what else would he need?'

'One thing's been bothering me,' Lomax replied. 'Keegan himself told me he weighed around eleven stone, yet the depth of his footprints suggests a much heavier build. Unless, of course, he is carrying a load. That load's hardly likely to be a carrier bag, more likely some form of rucksack.'

'Where the hell would he have got that from?' Ned asked.

It was a question that had been nagging at Lomax for days. 'Say that, somehow, we've got it wrong. Whoever snatched Keegan came from Ulster – agreed – but say they weren't enemies but friends?'

'What about the spent bullets and fresh blood?' Johnson interjected.

Lomax waved that aside. 'Just bear with me. Assume they were friends. They could have fired the rounds and left blood samples – probably their own – to throw us. We now know Keegan's probably very familiar with the Chase, so what better place to go to ground? They snatch him from the taxi, remove his handcuffs and kit him out with whatever he needs to survive, including a rucksack and several pairs of boots or shoes.'

'Shoes?' Ned queried.

'An idea I got the other day,' Lomax admitted. 'If he had a change of clothes and shoes, that could help throw the dogs and me off the trail whenever he chose. And let's face it, that's what's been happening.'

It made sense to Ned, although in his current state of inebriation, almost anything would. 'A run-around,' he repeated.

'I still don't buy it,' Johnson said.

Lomax raised his hand. 'Okay, okay, Bill. We can argue this one until the cows come home. But let's change tack and get proactive rather than reactive.'

'How d'you mean?'

'Well, as far as I'm concerned Keegan's laying trails for us, then vanishing when it suits. It's as though he'd done far more than a routine two-day survival course at some time, yet we know from army records that he hasn't. So instead of chasing

162

after every sighting, let's look at what I would do if I were him and follow that up instead.'

The drink was getting to Johnson now and he was tired, mellowing. 'Okay, Chris, what would you do?'

Lomax lit a cigarette and savoured his first one in several days. 'Firstly, I'd like a main base. A hide I can make comfortable and relax in, knowing no one's likely to find me. Then, night by night, I'd strike out to a different area, lay a trail and leave some clue. Then scurry back to my main hide and keep my head down for the day.'

'Okay,' Johnson said, playing along, 'where?'

'For a start, nowhere the public goes.'

Ned walked over to the wall map. 'Then you can ignore Seven Springs and Marquis Drive.' His finger kept jabbing. 'Brindley Heath, Brocton, Milford Common, the White House or Penkridge Bank – all popular with dog walkers.'

Lomax regarded the ranger for a moment. 'So if Keegan knows the area, Ned, where might he make his main base?'

The man scratched at his ginger beard and then pointed to the north-east of the crescent. 'Wolseley Park is dense pine and remote, but maybe a little further to the west. Around Cherrytree Slade. More comfortable. Deciduous woodland but dense undergrowth. Fallow deer lie up there during the day.'

'Always trust animals to know best,' Lomax said, joining Ned at the wall map. 'And two running water supplies within a mile either way, Sherbrook and the stream from Seven Springs. Some three square miles of really dense cover.'

'So what do you want to do?' Johnson asked.

'Organise a sweep. On foot and with backup from mounted units and scrambler bikes. Regardless of where Keegan leaves clues tonight, we sweep Cherrytree Slade and move progressively east through the Old Buffs and Abraham's Valley and then Wolseley Park. Inch by inch.'

'It'll take a few days,' Johnson said, warming to the idea.

'That doesn't matter, Bill, as long as we hold the line at night and put out patrols so he can't escape the dragnet.' He added: 'Maybe tonight we should get the chopper to concentrate solely on this area.'

'Consider it done.' The policeman consulted his watch. 'I'm all in. Want a lift back to your hotel in my car, Chris? Wouldn't want you to get done for drink driving?'

They sat in the back while the police driver took the road back to Penkridge.

'I'll get everything set up for a dawn start,' Johnson said.

'I just hope it's a good idea.'

'It'll make a change to take the initiative. This operation is costing a bomb.'

Lomax stifled a yawn. 'It's all I can think of, Bill. If Keegan's behaving like he was Hereford-trained, let's try to out-think him.'

'But he wasn't, of course,' Johnson replied softly. 'That's the only puzzle, except I've just been thinking about that.'

'Yes?'

'Keegan never went on a Hereford course. But I had his son's army file sent up from the MOD in London after your solicitor friend found he'd left the Spanish Legion. Tim Keegan did a full course with the SAS. Escape and evasion. Perhaps he gave his old man some tips. I forgot to mention it earlier, and something else that'll make you smile.'

'What's that?'

'You were his instructor.'

Of course, Lomax couldn't remember Tim Keegan, even the next morning when Johnson brought the MOD file from his office. The plumpish, grim-faced headbanger in the maroon beret staring blankly out of the mug shot meant nothing to him. He'd seen a thousand faces like that over the years – not only failed and successful SAS recruits on Selection, but others from the Army, Marines and Air Force sent on specialist courses, often prior to deployment in a hot war zone.

At least this Saturday morning was different from all the preceding days. The previous night there had been a brief ten-minute sighting on the helicopter's thermal imager at Rainbow Valley, way to the south, followed by reports of a break-in at a golf club. Food and money were taken. But today the searchers were following their own agenda and the change of plan, from what had become a boring routine, lifted morale.

Something else had cheered him too. The previous night he'd spoken to Browne, told her that they'd discovered he'd once trained Tim Keegan and that the next day the searchers would be changing tactics.

'Will it work?' she'd asked.

'Impossible to say, but I think so.' He grinned at her down the phone line. 'It's a feeling we blokes on Planet Mars get. If Keegan's using tactics I taught his son, then I think Peter will be back behind bars before the weekend's out. Or soon after.'

'Really? I ought to be there for him. See what I can do.'

He'd seen his chance. 'Then come up and watch the fun. It's Saturday tomorrow.'

'I've a mountain of work.'

'You always have.'

There was a thoughtful pause. 'You're right, Chris. Keegan might need me and *I* need a break. Even twenty-four hours would be nice.'

It was a misty start to the day as the army of volunteers mustered with police officers who were more than happy for the overtime. Soldiers from the Staffordshire Regiment and the Military Police had been drafted in, swelling the strength of the sweep teams to over two hundred personnel.

The new arrivals left their transport in the three car parks off the A513 and congregated at the Punch Bowl rendezvous where a constant shuttle of police Range Rovers and Ranger Service Land-Rovers ferried them south to their various start points.

By nine, the mist was breaking up under a strengthening sun to herald another scorching day. Now the startline ran for nearly two miles north to south at the edge of the dense Cherry-tree Slade woodland. As the line began its slow movement east, it would sweep the entire top corner of the Chase's crescent shape. Observation posts and mobile stop-groups with armed backup were posted in the open fields on the far side of the forest to the east, so cutting off the town of Rugeley, should Keegan be successfully flushed out of hiding. Meanwhile, ahead of the sweep, horse-mounted policemen and officers on scrambler bikes would patrol the various trails and firebreaks that crisscrossed the woodlands, hoping for a chance sighting should Keegan break cover.

Overhead, the helicopter circled with its thermal imager. At nine fifteen, whistles began blowing down the long line of searchers and they started moving off like beaters at some vast pheasant shoot. The area was so big that it was hardly a fingertip search, each man having to cover a frontage of some fifteen yards, but it would still be a daunting prospect for anyone hoping to escape detection.

Lomax waited with the dog handlers next to Johnson's Range Rover which served as a mobile incident control centre.

'Best we can do,' the policeman said. 'The budget just won't run to any more.'

'It's an impressive turnout, Bill,' Lomax replied, and meant it.

'It's an expensive turnout, that's all I'm being told. The ACC's put his neck on the block by agreeing to this and keeps reminding the area commander.' He looked anxious. 'I don't know what we do if this doesn't turn up a result.'

'Try again in the next most likely area,' Lomax offered.

'I wouldn't like to have to sell that one. Still, cross that bridge when we come to it, eh?' He glanced across at the nearest sweepers now almost hidden in the undergrowth. 'Given any thought to what we discussed last night?'

'Only that we might not be hunting Keegan at all. That it could be his son.' Lomax gave a half-smile. 'Impossible to work it out, Bill. If it *is* Tim we're hunting, we've got to ask why?'

'I got to wondering the same thing. Couldn't sleep last night, tossed and turned, thinking it out. The wife's getting pretty brassed off with me.'

Seeing that Johnson was looking profoundly depressed, he changed the subject. 'Any luck in finding the chap who headed the inquiry in Ulster and caught Keegan?'

Johnson nodded. 'Funny you should mention that. There's a note on my desk this morning. Records have finally come up with a phone number for him; seems like someone had put a

166

block on his file, so I had to pull a few strings. Anyway, he's left the force, like I thought – and the whole human race by all accounts.' He raised his eyes heavenward in a gesture of despair. 'Still, if we get lucky today, I won't need to contact him.'

Momentarily, Lomax thought of Roddy Littlechild incarcerated in Belmarsh, desperate for news of Keegan's recapture and his own possible salvation. 'Let's hope.'

It was impressive, Tim Keegan had to admit, as he watched through binoculars from his vantage point in the Satnall Hills just north of the A513.

Below him he could see the car park full of police vehicles and even a couple of army lorries as a steady stream of people headed into the Chase on the south side of the road. High above he heard the distant whir of a helicopter.

A close-run thing, he decided, but the game was up. He had to concede that now as he listened to the squawking of the radio scanner and pieced together the scale of the operation.

Had his motorcycle not developed fuel-pump trouble, he might well have been trapped in the dragnet set to sweep through Cherrytree Slade, the Old Buffs and the Wolseley Park plantation. He had been returning after laying a trail from the break-in to the golf club, miles to the south in the lower quarter of the Chase, when the engine began misfiring.

By the time he'd solved the problem it was almost dawn; back on the A513, where he'd planned to park his bike before retreating to his hide, he became aware of the vastly increased police activity. Something was up, something big. He'd pulled off the road into the Satnall Hills to the south of the Shugborough estate and tuned into the police frequencies on his scanner. He realised then that it was all over. Not bad though, he thought with considerable satisfaction. The objective had been to keep the manhunt tied down in the Chase for fourteen days; time for his father to disappear without trace, mount the post-office raid and complete the first phase. While everyone was convinced they knew where Peter Keegan was, they wouldn't be looking for him elsewhere. And he'd virtually succeeded, just one day short.

Tim glanced at his watch. In just a few hours' time the last element in the first phase would be executed. A fine achievement. Especially when he'd been pitted against his old SAS instructor in a battle of wits. Funny that, seeing the article on Chris Lomax in the *Sun*. The man had been regarded as some sort of legend on the course, his powers of tracking verging on the paranormal. Invoking the spirits of the old Plains Indians, Lomax himself had once joked. Tim had been in absolute awe as he watched the soldier follow a spoor that looked nonexistent to the untrained eye; only Lomax, he was sure, had never really noticed him. Just another face, but one that had been destined to come back to haunt him.

Time to go. A pity he couldn't clear the hide as he had planned, remove the evidence and perpetuate the mystery. He'd have liked that.

Tim shoved the scanner back inside his leather jacket, stood up and returned to his motorcycle. After putting on his helmet, he sat astride the machine and gunned it into life before negotiating the earth track down to the road.

At eleven, Lomax returned to his hotel to pick up Sam Browne who'd just driven up from London. He took her back to the sweep area in his Cavalier and introduced her to Bill Johnson. The policeman seemed uncharacteristically cool towards her, congratulating her rather stiffly over her earlier detective work on Tim Keegan's whereabouts.

Was there just a hint of professional rivalry, of the man's nose put a little out of joint, Lomax wondered, or was it something else?

Yet he was to notice with amusement that, after only a few minutes in her company, Johnson's thinly disguised hostility began to thaw. Lomax decided the man was clearly distracted and not a little smitten by her.

Thirty minutes later, the detective superintendent was called to the radio. 'Chris, we've got something!' he shouted across.

'Where?'

'Between Cherrytree and Haywood Slades.' He replaced the receiver. 'Let's go.'

It took twenty minutes to cover the rough ground – dense bracken surrounded by oaks and beeches. At last they came across the cluster of police officers pleased at an excuse to find some shade and open cans of soft drinks. A roll of white tape was being strung out between the trees to seal off the area.

'Any sightings?' Johnson asked.

The sergeant in command of this sector shook his head. 'Quiet as the grave, sir. Wouldn't have found this if one of our blokes hadn't fallen into it.'

Lomax stepped forward. The hatchway to the hide was constructed of two-foot lengths of branch lashed to form a frame, then covered in chicken wire to support a layer of turf. It hadn't been strong enough to take the full direct weight of a policeman in boots and had partially collapsed.

Taking a torch from his fatigue trousers, Lomax ventured down into the four-foot shaft. The hide itself went off at right angles, a rough four-foot square cave dug out of the soft earth. A light green tarpaulin had been pegged to the roof struts that supported some two feet of sun-dried earth.

'What's that?' Johnson asked, dropping down behind him.

Lomax reached up and unpeeled the edge of the tarpaulin. 'To stop loose earth dropping on him.' He turned over the surprisingly lightweight material. The upper side was bright silver. A space blanket. 'Aha.'

'What?'

'It might also explain why the thermal imager never picked him out in hiding,' Lomax answered. 'Or how he disappeared from view whenever he chose. The foil blanket would hide his body heat. Very professional.'

'Bloody cunning.'

Lomax edged forward. It was all very neat. A green Pertex and fibrepile sleeping bag on a kip mat. Beside it was a pair of boots, each covered in a thick polythene bag to act as a galosh that would not leave a discernible footprint.

'No rucksack?' Johnson asked.

'Maybe he had it with him last night if it was him who raided the golf club.'

'Perhaps he got wind of what was happening? Saw all this activity and scarpered.'

'Perhaps.' Lomax scanned the water bladder hooked to a tree root and the provisions, including some of the grocery items reported stolen from the caravan, stacked tidily on a plastic sheet. A neat Trangia meths stove, fuel flask and boil-in-the-bag meals. There was enough for days; whoever lived in the hide hardly needed to go out stealing food; he was well-prepared. Other items had been stored in a carrier bag and Lomax tipped them out onto the sleeping bag. A mess tin, eating utensils, a torch, spare batteries – and an assortment of paper in a polythene envelope.

Lomax read the first item with interest and handed it to Johnson. 'That's how chummy knew our every move, Bill. An instruction leaflet for a radio scanner.'

The policeman looked at it in grim-faced disbelief. 'He's been making right idiots of us.'

'He certainly has.' Lomax had found a series of rough sketch maps of the Chase. Instantly he recognised the dotted lines marking the trails his quarry had deliberately laid. There was another folded sheet, a photocopy of an Ordnance Survey map of the Chase. A red marker with the word Cyclist written beneath it ran from Grenville's Wood, where the abandoned Safrane had been found, along the tracks of the woods and heathland to the Satnall Hills in the north. The marker came to an abrupt end at the Shugborough railway tunnel.

It made no sense for a moment until something clicked in Lomax's memory. 'Bill, did you say something about the sighting of a mountain biker on the day of the ambush?'

'Yeah. A family reported seeing him in the area about the time of the incident. They were trying to be helpful, but no cyclist came forward, despite radio appeals. Like the bloke with the rucksack seen crossing the A34 – our poacher. A negative there, too.'

Lomax shook his head and waved a small handwritten receipt from a film-processing shop in Stafford. The customer's name was T. Keegan – a bit careless that – but no address. 'What's the betting they were reconnaissance photos?'

170

Johnson took the receipt. 'I'll check it out, but I'm not sure we'll learn anything.'

'Well, we've learned something, Bill. This *was* Tim Keegan's hide, not his father's. I think Tim could well be your mysterious poacher. And the cyclist.' He handed over the map.

The other man stared, tilting the map to catch the shaft of daylight from above. 'Peter Keegan was the cyclist?'

'Could that have been a copy of the route he took?'

A frown creased Johnson's forehead. 'It stops by the railway line. Is that right? No, he was probably picked up by car.'

'I thought you'd had the roads sealed by then. Must have taken a while to cycle right across the Chase.'

'You're right, Chris, but maybe they got through the cordon?'

'I suppose . . .' Lomax pondered.

'What?'

'No, it's not possible.'

'What isn't?'

'To board a moving train.'

That evening the gathering at the Hatherton Country Hotel of police officers and Ned's rangers, reminded Lomax of an end-of-ops party.

With Keegan still at large, it was hardly a victory celebration, but at least the mystery had been solved and life within the Staffordshire police force could return to normality. No trace of the man's son had been found. But, as far as the police were concerned, ex-Para Tim Keegan could run around Cannock Chase living wild for as long as he liked. After the haemorrhage of police costs, no one was going to waste more time and effort playing his game. On the basis that he'd almost certainly left the area for good, it was no longer their concern alone. No doubt he'd get picked up eventually and be charged for his part in the freeing of a prisoner.

Meanwhile Bill Johnson would remain in a nominal co-ordinating role with a much reduced team and the job of liaising with other police forces. At least an ill wind had blown Lomax a little good with a useful proportion of the operational costs ending up in his wallet. Or at least it would when he sent his bill.

Manda had already badgered him over the phone to write out his invoice.

'She's right,' Sam Browne said. 'Bang it in as soon as you can. Getting money out of the police is worse than getting it out of solicitors.'

'Another drink?'

She shook her head. 'The car's exhaust box is about to drop off and I've just discovered my road tax ran out last month. Any more felonies and I'll find myself sitting alongside Roddy in Belmarsh.'

'It's late for driving back to London tonight. Why don't you stay over? It's Saturday night, so the hotel will have rooms spare.'

'I was planning to work tomorrow.'

He thought how tired she looked. 'You need more time off.'

Irritation flashed in her eyes. 'What are you, my nanny?'

This time he wasn't going to bow to her blistering anger. 'Well, maybe somebody needs to be. You'll work yourself into an early grave.'

'That's my problem.'

'Roddy's too. Where'd he be if you end up with a nervous breakdown?'

That brought the flicker of a smile to her lips. She regarded him with curiosity over the rim of her glass. 'I wasn't planning to have one.'

'I didn't think nervous breakdowns were planned,' he said, fixing her gaze. 'I thought it was like falling in love. It just happens. And you can't do a damned thing about it.'

He saw her jawline stiffen, and the sudden narrowing of her pupils. Immediately he regretted his choice of words. They hadn't been intended as they sounded. Or had they? Suddenly he wasn't sure. Their last meeting had ended when he'd felt a compulsion to make a clumsy pass. He'd been lucky then, her response had been kindly, almost flirtatious. But barely. Had he read the signals wrongly? What was it with him? Was this the start of the male menopause or something? He wasn't even sure he liked her. And she certainly didn't encourage familiarity with the opposite sex. In fact, she sometimes came across as the

172

original ice maiden. So what was it – the challenge? Or was there some perverse joy in risking that he'd get his face slapped?

As these confused thoughts rushed through his mind, it took him a moment to realise he'd broken through her defences. There was a sad expression in her eyes as she examined the remains of the gin and tonic in her glass, her voice so low it was barely audible. 'I'm being ratty, Chris, sorry. The truth is I was *so* sure you were going to find Peter Keegan out there. Or even his son – that might have given a lead. That man's evidence is so *important* to your brother-in-law's trial.'

'I know.'

She sighed wearily. 'Now he seems more out of reach than ever.'

'Cheer up!' a voice said suddenly from behind them.

Bill Johnson had elbowed his way through the clamour of off-duty policemen and rangers, protecting his pint of bitter from flailing arms.

'What kept you?' Lomax asked.

'Following up your crazy notion.' He sipped at his beer. 'God, I needed that! Been on the phone to Railtrack, bullying them to dig out details of all trains that ran to London on the day of Keegan's escape.'

'And?'

'Driver's report, Chris. There was an incident on the eleven thirty from Manchester. The train made an unscheduled stop at Shugborough tunnel. Apparently a child pulled an emergency lever before the adult with her could stop her. No charges were brought. The child's guardian was one Susie Ferguson.'

Browne stared. 'Keegan's girlfriend? I don't believe it.'

Lomax was stunned too; Keegan had actually pulled it off. 'So it was all a put-up job. Peter cycled across the Chase and somehow boarded the train. Then left his son to lay a false trail.'

'Bloody clever,' Johnson admitted reluctantly. 'There's a crew entry button on the outside of each door. That's how he must have boarded.'

'But what was the point?' Browne asked. 'Or am I just being dim?'

'The point, dear lady,' Johnson said, 'is that while we thought we *knew* where Keegan was – here in the Chase – there'd be no "all-cars" alert throughout the country, no roadblocks or "Wanted" leaflets or TV newsflashes with every copper in the land on the lookout for him. And no special watch on airports or ferry terminals.'

Browne looked aghast. 'You mean he might have left the country?'

'I'm afraid it's highly probable.'

'Back to Northern Ireland?'

'I doubt that, but anyway I've already contacted the RUC.'

'Maybe Spain,' Lomax suggested, 'or one of their former colonies. His son might have made some useful contacts in the Legion.'

'That's more likely,' Johnson agreed. 'But I might get a better idea if I could get some decent background material. At least I seem to have had a breakthrough with Derek Penny. Remember the man you suggested, the ex-ACC of West Weald who unearthed the Keegan case?'

'You've made contact?'

'He finally returned my call. I've had a helluva job reaching him. I'd left half a dozen messages on his answering machine. I hate those bloody things.'

'Has he agreed to see you?'

'Very reluctantly. I'd been warned he'd gone a bit reclusive and paranoid. They weren't kidding. It was his wife who phoned back first, playing the verbal bodyguard. Made it quite clear I was lucky to get any response at all. Penny refuses to have anything to do with the police. Even his old colleagues are *persona non grata*. He just doesn't want to know.'

'So how did you persuade him?'

'Told him the truth. That I desperately needed background to get a lead on Keegan and that I was getting no co-operation from those who were in a position to tell me. He actually laughed at that. Not the most cheerful of souls is Mr Penny. But I think telling him my inquiry was unofficial helped persuade him. He's suggested we meet tomorrow. That won't please the wife, but – ' He shrugged as though to say, but what can you do?

'Where does he live?'

'Retired to a little place outside Tunbridge Wells. Rose Cottage. Sounds idyllic, doesn't it? Wondered if you'd like to come with me?'

'Why?'

'Because you know Northern Ireland and you worked with Keegan. Anything Derek Penny knows will mean more to you than it does to me.'

'Ask him what the fee is?' Browne suggested mischievously.

Johnson gave her a disapproving glance. 'Once a lawyer always a lawyer.'

'Go on, ask him,' she pressed. It might have been Manda talking.

'It's unofficial,' Johnson said. 'If you come it'll be as a favour to me.'

Lomax relented. If it brought them closer to recapturing Keegan, then it was worth it for Roddy's sake.

Emboldened by drink, three cheery young police officers who'd clearly taken a shine to Browne, began distracting her with a distinctly ribald joke in a feeble attempt to chat her up.

Johnson took Lomax to one side and they quietly arranged to meet the next day at the Clacket Lane service area on the M25 in Kent at two in the afternoon. Then Johnson made his apologies for being a party-pooper and left. After all, as he'd explained, he did have his marriage to save.

Browne extricated herself from the unwanted attentions of the increasingly drunk young policemen and returned to Lomax's side. 'I'll check with reception about that room.'

'What's brought about this sudden change of heart?' he asked.

'Does there have to be a reason?' She smiled disarmingly. 'A woman's privilege. It's the way we do things on our planet, remember? Besides, I seem to recall you said you wanted to take me for a meal the last time we met. Now would seem a good time, before the drink goes to my head.'

'We could eat here,' he said. 'Or there's a Chinese restaurant in the village.'

'That sounds nice.'

She handed him her glass and walked away. He found himself

175

grinning rather stupidly, watching the elegant sway of her hips as she moved through the crowd, mesmerised momentarily by the languid shift of the beige shantung trouser suit that emphasised the contours of her long legs. And he noticed the lingering glances of the police officers who parted to let her through. There was something about her, her slightly above-average height and the way she carried herself, a natural poise that drew the eye.

Perhaps her mouth, the lips set in a naturally impudent pout, was a little too wide to be perfect, her smile showing too much pink gum against the startling whiteness of her teeth. Her eyes just too big and intelligent, unnerving in their eagerness to learn from what they saw. And the hint of slack skin at her jowl where the years had begun their cruelty, trying but failing to flaw the stunning beauty of her youth. For all that, Lomax knew that in a room full of pretty women half her age, Sam Browne would be the first one you noticed.

Clearly he wasn't alone in his assessment. Ned, drunk and swaying a little, sidled up to him. 'Your missus is a cracker all right, Chris boy, if you don't mind me saying.'

Lomax smiled. 'She's no one's wife, Ned, she's Keegan's solicitor.'

'Go on, the lucky beggar. Only women solicitors I've ever seen are frumps in black suits with woollen tights.'

Lomax laughed. 'I expect she's got them too.'

'Yeah, but she'd look a million dollars in 'em. And not married you say?'

'Don't think so.' He lifted his left hand. 'No ring.'

'And what about you?'

'Separating. Painful business.'

Ned nudged him and winked. 'Then go to it, old son, and see if you can't fill your boots.'

Eight

Later, Lomax smiled as he recalled Ned's words while he and Browne walked the short distance to the village. For an irrational second he was tempted to recount the ranger's words, thinking it might amuse her. But decided against it. Why was it he felt he was handling nitroglycerine here? Unpredictable and volatile.

Yet she seemed more relaxed than he had seen her before, sauntering by his side, inhaling the country air and watching the sweeping aerobatics of house martins overhead, their migration delayed by the prolonged good weather.

'There's a storm brewing,' he said.

'Are you sure? The TV forecast didn't say.'

'A local thunderstorm. See how low the birds are flying.'

Her eyes were wide. 'You can tell by that? I don't believe you.'

He grinned at her expression of incredulity. 'Air pressure forces the insects to fly lower, so the birds have to. There are other signs too. Have you noticed the smell?'

'What smell?'

He stopped beside a cottage garden. 'Earth, vegetation.'

She sniffed tentatively; her eyes said she wondered if this was a wind-up. 'Roses.'

Lomax laughed. 'Apart from roses. Background smells.'

Again she sniffed the air, closing her eyes. 'Maybe. Yes, you're right. Earthy, leafy.'

'Not what you usually get on a hot September night. It means rain's on the way. Like the clarity of distant noise.'

'Really?'

He glanced at the distant rolling banks of cumulonimbus in the westering sunset. 'Smell and sound. And in the fields there'll be a lot of rabbit activity.'

'Doing what?'

He laughed. 'Doing what rabbits do.'

And she laughed too, realising what she'd said. 'Oh, you mean eating!' she said with a mischievous glint in her eye. 'Why does the threat of rain make them do that?'

'I've really absolutely no idea.'

It suddenly seemed ridiculously funny and neither really knew why. Perhaps it was the end of the week's tension and drama, the sudden change of pace and scene, the tranquillity of the warm evening as it gathered in around them.

Somehow Lomax sensed that a barrier had broken, that some invisible river had been crossed.

'I miss the countryside,' she confided as they sat in the restaurant and scanned the menu. 'I'm a green wellie and jeans girl at heart. Labrador and checked cloth cap.'

'The shootin' and fishin' type.'

'I'm not so sure about that. Not hunting defenceless animals.'

Lomax said, 'I know what you mean. I'd rather shoot people.'

She peered at him over the menu for a moment. 'I suppose that was a joke. I mean, was it meant to impress me?'

'Not really. Hunting's more for officer types. It's the main preoccupation of a lot of them. Talk about nothing else.'

'Is that a chip I see on your shoulder?'

He glanced down at his jacket and flipped the top of his sleeve. 'I don't see anything.'

'It looks pretty large from where I'm sitting,' she goaded with a smile.

He remembered his assessment of her when they'd first met. She'd been surprised he wasn't an officer and he immediately sensed she herself was an officer's daughter. 'If I'd gone to university, Sam – and I could have done – I'd have been an officer. But I chose not to go. I've enjoyed some hunting and fishing in my time. But I like to do it for the pot, not for a hobby.'

'And shooting people?'

'You were right. It was a bad joke. Not really a fun experience.'

'But you've done it?' As soon as she asked she wished she hadn't.

Lomax tried to pretend he hadn't heard; the question was too intrusive, and the answer would take much too long. 'Have you tried Peking duck?'

'No. I'm not very *au fait* with Chinese cooking. I'm more used to Indian. I grew up on that.'

Bingo, Lomax thought. 'Don't tell me, your father was in the Indian Army?'

She smiled at his perception. 'Close. Royal Air Force. He was stationed there during the war and stayed on after independence on secondment to the Indian Air Force. My first nine years were spent there.'

'Good?'

'Magical. I used to run around all day in just my knickers like a female Gunga Din. A real tomboy, climbing trees, swimming, even riding elephants.' She looked suddenly sad, her voice trailing. 'But all good things come to an end.'

The waiter appeared and they vacillated over their choice under the man's infinite patience which clearly paid off as they ordered far too many dishes for two people.

Lomax poured the wine. 'I'm not normally a rosé man, but I always think it goes well with Chinese.'

'A connoisseur, are you?'

'Absolutely not. What the lads in the Regiment might call a plonker. Any old plonk will do, it's just that some are better than others.'

She was leaning closer across the table now, he realised with mild surprise, her grin wide as she began to forget herself and enjoy the repartee. His training instinctively noted her body language, moving into his domain; he didn't feel inclined to pull back. Her pupils were large and bright.

'My first husband was a wine bore,' she said with a slight giggle and shrug of her shoulders. 'But he'd rather hoard the stuff than drink it. I was twenty-five when I married – a silly move.'

'Why?'

'Because I'd just passed all my law exams and the world was at my feet.' There was candour in her eyes now, maybe the drink was helping her to talk, to open up. 'But I was afraid of being left on the shelf. It's different nowadays, of course. Girls have

179

their careers first and start families later. But then – he was handsome, dashing and played polo. A former Guards officer, I'm afraid, Mr NCO. Five years older than me. I let him whisk me off to his country estate.'

'Your green wellies and Labrador period?'

She gave a bitter little laugh. 'Yes, and I hated it. No, not so much life in the country as *him*. He was so boring, so precise. We rarely went out unless it was to meet his cronies in the hunt or the polo crowd. Roast beef every Sunday, the house always spick and span, a place for everything and everything in its place. He loved his home and never saw a good reason to leave it. Even for a weekend away, let alone a holiday.'

'So it didn't last?'

'Three years of purgatory. Our sex life was nonexistent and I felt incarcerated and marooned in deepest Somerset. What I wanted, what I *needed* was to be working, preferably in London. To smell the beeswax of the courtroom, the challenge and excitement.'

'So what happened?'

'He came back late one night from one of his Masonic meetings and found me drunk out of my skull. Surrounded by empty bottles from a crate of his prized Chateau de Tircgand! He slung me out.' She added impishly: 'The brute.'

They were interrupted by the arrival of corn and crabmeat soup.

'You said that was your first marriage,' Lomax coaxed.

She nodded. 'The second was seven years later. In the meantime I'd returned to London and thrown myself into work. Quite successfully, I suppose. I was actually featured in *Cosmopolitan* once. You know, professional women who've made it in a man's world. A bank manager, a company director, a chef – and me. Then in 1985 I met Ian, a lawyer from Belfast. It was one of those wild Christmas parties that barristers throw for solicitors.'

'Wild? I find that hard to believe.'

'Trust me, Chris. Wild is an understatement. Actually it was Tristram's chambers who threw it. Anyway, it was love at first sight with Ian and me. A sort of instant chemistry. It had never happened to me before. Or since.'

Lomax felt mildly discouraged by that, but said nothing; what had he expected?

'We married within a month,' she added. 'I went back to Belfast with him and we joined an established practice, him on the civil side and me on the criminal.'

'That's when you defended Keegan?'

'Yes, in '89. About the time the marriage started falling apart.'

'I'm sorry.'

Her eyes were clear and bright as she looked at him. 'Don't be, Chris. It was my own fault. I wanted kids before it was too late, but I just couldn't conceive. I blamed Ian, but it wasn't his fault – one of those things, I suppose. In my anger and frustration, I threw myself into work with a vengeance. The Keegan case came at just the right moment to distract me. I was working every evening, every weekend. Then I discovered it. He was having an affair.'

Outside there was a distant rumble of thunder. It had grown prematurely dark.

She looked up as the waiter cleared the plates and laid out the barbecue ribs. 'You were right about the storm.'

'Did you doubt me?'

'Mmm. Actually I did.'

After a few minutes of concentrating on the ribs, Lomax said: 'So no marriages since?'

'I think two is quite enough.'

'Plenty of boyfriends though.'

This time she looked mildly hostile. 'No. I've never had much luck with men.'

'I don't believe that.' He wished he'd kept his mouth shut, but it was too late now. 'A beautiful girl like you.'

She regarded him slowly, pushing her plate away and reaching for her wine glass. Would she go for a complete demolition job, he wondered, or let him off with a lacerating wound to his pride? 'I've never thought of myself as beautiful. My mouth's too big – my father said as a baby I looked like a hammerhead shark. As a teenager, I was gawky and sometimes

181

I think I still am. I've got no tits to speak of and when I smile I'm all gums. Without make-up I crack mirrors.'

His eyes fixed on hers and held them, daring her to break contact. 'Then you manage to keep such profound ugliness well hidden.'

'Max Factor is my best friend.'

'You're beautiful. Everyone says so.'

She raised one finely arched eyebrow as that curious mad eye regarded him coolly. 'I know. I don't think I am, but I've overheard enough people say it to know what they think.' Then the fierceness ebbed from her voice and a certain vulnerability softened her features. 'All I can tell you, Chris, is if this is being beautiful, then being beautiful can be a very lonely business.'

Her eyes seemed to draw him in, mesmerise him, he was lost for words.

'See what I mean?' she observed. 'Tongue-tied. Men are scared by beautiful women. Or at least women they regard as beautiful. They think beautiful women are unattainable, way beyond their reach. Only ugly men get the truly beautiful women – had you noticed that?'

'What?' He didn't follow.

'Ugly men know they don't stand a chance with beautiful women, so they don't care. Most normal men stand back, scared of rejection. But the ugly men just bowl in regardless with no expectations.'

'And get the girl?'

'Sometimes.'

'I've asked you out,' he said pointedly.

She fenced with him. 'True, you're not particularly ugly. But would you have asked me if business hadn't brought us together first? If we'd seen each other in a bar, would you have just walked up to me?'

'No,' he answered truthfully. 'Even a soldier's courage fails him sometimes.'

Her smile was gentle. 'See! Being beautiful can be lonely.'

'And your husbands?' he teased.

'The two ugliest bastards you've ever seen in your life!'

They both laughed at that and toasted ugly men and

beautiful women, and then ugly women and beautiful men. It was getting silly; the wine was going down. Outside fat droplets of rain were splatting on the pavement and the thunder rolled, suddenly very loud and close.

Lomax winced.

'What is it?' she asked, alarmed.

He smiled uncertainly. 'Sorry. I'd forgotten the storm. The noise made me jump for a second.'

She looked perplexed.

'For one split second I was back in Bosnia,' he explained. 'Artillery, incoming.'

'My God,' she breathed, 'are you all right?'

'Fine. It was just a reflex, the drink's addled my brain. We were guiding in an airstrike in Tuzla against the Chetniks when we nearly copped it. A howitzer round landed just yards away, buried us in our foxholes. I got shrapnel in my leg.'

'How awful.'

'Not so bad. One of my best mates lost an arm, so I can't complain.'

A bit of a conversation stopper that, he thought and cursed himself for flinching involuntarily at the sound. He was thankful when the waiter brought the duck and they both watched fascinated as the man shredded it with two forks before their eyes.

'What d'you do with these pancakes?' she asked. 'They're almost as thin as rice paper.'

'Spread them with the plum sauce, add the sliced cucumber and onion, then some duck and roll them.'

She tried and bit into the pancake, tasting it tentatively. 'God, that's delicious.' A trickle of plum sauce escaped the corner of her mouth.

'Allow me,' he said and reached his hand across to her face.

Her eyes were just inches from his. Greeny-blue, bluey-green, flecked with dancing light reflected from the candle flame on the table. Hypnotic. Angry and warm. At the same time? Deep limpid pools that he could not fathom, could not read.

His index finger touched the soft down of her chin. Her skin was cool and he felt her jaw stiffen as he caught the runaway trickle.

She said stiffly: 'You are in my space, Mr Lomax.'

He blinked and withdrew his hand, wiping his finger on the napkin. Damn her, he wasn't going to let her get away with this. No wonder she was bloody lonely. He ignored her put-down, made light of it. 'It's always a problem. Do you tell a guy his zip's undone or let him get on with it and watch the fun?'

It did the trick because a half-smile returned to lighten her face. Somehow he'd struck a chord. 'It's like leaving the loo with your skirt caught in the back of your knickers. Every girl's done it.'

'Not recently?'

Her eyes were deadpan. 'Not recently, no.'

She drew back into her chair. Things had gone far enough, he could read her now, re-establishing some formality into their relationship. She pushed aside her plate. 'I'm afraid I'm not hungry. Do you mind if I smoke?'

He shook his head and accepted one of her cigarettes and lit them both.

'And you, Chris, I don't get the feeling you're married?' Despite the personal nature of the question, he could tell she was deliberately making it sound like polite conversation. Neutral.

'Nisi verging on absolute.' His smile was tight.

She blew a neat little ring of blue smoke. 'You still love her.'

He frowned. 'Is that a question or a statement?'

'An observation. Am I right?'

'Very astute.'

'Not when it's written all over your face. We aliens can do that sort of thing. That's why we make good lawyers.' She tapped her cigarette on the edge of the ashtray, creating a pause, not wanting to rush him. 'How does she feel?'

'Relieved, I should think. Glad to be out of it. She's got someone new now, a new life. I'm happy for her. I'd given her a hard time.'

'I'm not sure I believe that.'

'I didn't believe it myself at the time; you don't always realise,

184

you know. I'd got pretty ratty, not much fun to live with. I couldn't take it out at work, not on ops or with my mates. You don't risk stupid upsets when your lives depend on each other. So I took it out on Fran.'

'Sounds like you've analysed it.'

'Not me. My daughter Manda. After my wife left she sat me down and told it to me straight. No messing.'

'She sounds very bright.'

'Just like her mother. As I've said, she was Business Student of the Year. I just wish she'd told me earlier.'

The waiter came with more dishes, but Lomax sent them back with apologies to the chef for their lack of appetite, then called for coffee and brandy.

'What got you into that state?' Browne asked. 'If that's not a personal question.'

'Well, it is, but I've learned to live with the answer. To be honest, I think it was one tour too many in Belfast. That's when it started, about the time I was minding Keegan.'

Her eyes were wide now, very intent. 'I don't really know what sort of thing you did.'

He shrugged and stirred a spoon around in his cup. 'Mostly sneaky-beaky, undercover stuff. Jeans and trainers, looking scruffy. Going right into the heart of the Republican ghettos – the Bogside or the Falls, or some other stronghold. Merging in. Keeping some Provo player under surveillance in his own backyard. Or else acting on some intelligence tip-off that some aggro or other was going down. On other occasions it was minding someone like Keegan. Not usually close protection work, more mingling close by just in case.'

Memories of her time in Ulster were flooding back; he knew that as her eyes misted. 'I can't imagine what that sort of work must be like. I mean, it's not like a soldier's war where you know the objectives, know the enemy.'

'You get used to it,' Lomax said, then realised that was a nonsense in view of what happened. 'Or you think you do. Maybe age has something to do with it. I was approaching forty then, and that's some sort of milestone because you realise that probably over half your life's gone. And it's going to be downhill all the way.' There was a flicker of recognition in her eyes, an understanding, but she said nothing, just sipped her brandy as she watched him.

'I became convinced I wouldn't survive the tour. Just couldn't get the idea out of my head. I thought, some bastard out there is determined I'm not going to make it for Manda's fourteenth birthday.'

'Why fourteenth? What was so special about that?'

He grinned at the painful stupidity of the memory. 'God knows, you tell me. It was just a fixation. Then my unit was pulled out and I transferred back to Escape and Evasion for a while – that was always my speciality. Things calmed down a bit at home then, but not for long.'

Her head tilted to one side, a comma of loose fair hair falling over her forehead. 'The Gulf War.'

'That was fun,' he said drily.

'I read *Bravo Two Zero*,' she said helpfully. 'It sounded like a nightmare.'

'Well it was, but we had no cockups like theirs. It was still bad enough. Mostly because I was still convinced some bullet had my name on it. Probably made worse because I knew there were only a few years left to retirement and just didn't think I was going to make it.'

'I can understand that.'

'You start to realise why armies rely on youngsters for their cannon fodder. They don't realise it can happen to them and probably will. Unlike others, I knew it *could* happen to me, because it already had at Goose Green. I should have got out then, after the Iraqi surrender. But then life fell back into a pattern, back to Escape and Evasion. I didn't want to admit I couldn't hack it any more.'

'So you took it out on your wife?'

'There's only one thing worse than living with a coward, and that's when the coward is yourself. And as they say, you always hurt the one you love.'

'I can't believe anyone else thought you were a coward. I mean you obviously went to Bosnia after that.'

'I knew it, Sam, and that's all that mattered. Besides, Bosnia

186

really did my head in. The carnage and the senseless brutality of it all. No one should witness sights like that.' He paused and sipped his brandy. 'Funny thing was, when I was hospitalised after that shelling, it sort of broke the spell. I thought – shit, that's the second time a round *has* had my name on it. And I've survived again.'

'When did it happen?'

He smiled then and glanced at his watch. The hour hand nudged past twelve. 'Funny, you're not going to believe this. A year ago today.'

It was still raining when they left, the dark sky trembling in awesome rage but the downpour restrained with lazy, heavy drops. She started to run, he did not.

'C'mon, we'll get drenched!' she called back, her hair already plastered wetly to her skull, her mascara melting down her cheeks.

Lightning crackled and fizzed, illuminating his face. He was laughing. 'We're drenched already.'

'Chris, for heaven's sake!'

He caught up with her. 'Enjoy it. You can't be wetter than you are now.'

Glancing down at the sodden trouser suit, feeling the warm water on the skin of her back, she couldn't say that he wasn't right.

'Stroll through one of nature's most spectacular shows. It's all free.'

Another tremulous roar, the rain drilling faster now. More lightning spat across the western sky, its brilliance reflected on the bruised thunderheads.

'You're crazy,' she challenged.

'Maybe.'

'I'm scared,' she said, glancing up. 'We might get struck.'

He continued his ambling walk. 'Not likely in the village.'

'Just because you survived that shell with your name on it,' she said, half-joking.

'I'm your lucky mascot.'

She felt calmer now, slowing down, walking by his side. It seemed ridiculous not to clutch his arm, but she felt mildly annoyed when she glanced sideways and saw his grin. So goddamn smug.

But he was right. Slowly her fear ebbed and, despite being soaked until her clothes clung like a second skin, she found herself enthralled by the natural *son et lumiere*, the crashing drums and dazzling swords of light tearing jagged scars across the sky.

They stood in a puddle of their own making in the hotel lobby. 'This is stupid,' she said, making a fist of her hair to squeeze the water out.

Their rooms were adjacent, they found. 'Come in for coffee,' he said, as they reached his door.

'That's not a good idea,' she replied quickly, then realised she'd been harsh. Her smile was brief and apologetic. 'I've got to get out of these things.'

'Yes.'

She looked at him, recognised the intensity in his eyes. Aware of each pore on his rain-flecked face, the darkening stubble on the angular chin. 'You don't mean it.'

'I do.'

'About the coffee. You don't mean coffee.'

'No.'

'Haven't you learned anything from tonight? I don't have good luck with men and I don't go to bed with clients.'

'I'm not a client.'

'Or with colleagues, with anyone.' Suddenly she looked embarrassed and smiled awkwardly. 'You'll have to get yourself touched with an ugly stick.'

'A what?'

'An American expression, I think. Forget it, Chris, it wouldn't work.'

His anger flared suddenly. Anger at her, at himself. Why did he let her get to him? He found himself saying: 'This beauty and the beast stuff, Sam. We've a saying in the Regiment. Your shit smells as bad as mine.'

She blinked, shocked, but quickly smiled, uncertain. 'That's the most endearing chat-up line I've ever heard!'

'And the truest you'll ever hear,' he snapped back. 'Just look in the mirror.' He hated himself. Why the hell had he said that? The drink? Maybe. Or the hurt pride?

She was still standing there, pale and stunned, dripping on the carpet.

'I'm sorry,' he said, 'that was out of order. A triumph of misplaced hope over experience. Forgive me?'

She nodded numbly.

'Good night, Sam.' He closed the door.

For a moment she stared after him. Bastard. Bastard, bastard, bastard. Then slowly she turned back towards her own door. Out of the corner of her eye she caught the movement, her own reflection in the hallway mirror above the half-moon table and cut flowers.

She gasped for a moment, her hand flying to her cheek for reassurance. She was a monster. A hideous apparition with wet spiked hair and wild eyes without make-up. It had run in the rain and smeared her face like the grey skin of a corpse. Her mouth was a red gash where the lipstick bled and smudged.

And then she remembered. Out there in the storm. Or were the drink and her memory playing tricks? Out there in the storm, in one mad and crazy moment, he had kissed her.

Lomax awoke late. He had no hangover and the storm had cleared the air. Sunlight streamed through the window as he made himself a strong sweet black coffee and drank it as he shaved.

He showered and dressed quickly, keen to make his peace with Sam Browne over breakfast, and wondered if she'd surfaced yet.

As he reached to turn off the radio he heard the local news-flash: *'Reports are coming in of a daring escape bid at Stafford Prison in the last half-hour.'* The announcer gave the impression that this was the most exciting thing that had happened in his sleepy town for years. *'An unmarked helicopter landed in the exercise yard then took off again, heading east. Early reports suggest that two prisoners are missing. We will bring more details as soon as we get them.'*

Wondering if life could ever be the same again in this rural

189

backwater after armed abductions, manhunts and now a spectacular aerial jailbreak, Lomax left the room. He knocked on Sam Browne's door but drew no response. Downstairs his disappointment mounted when he found she wasn't sitting at one of the breakfast tables. Finally he went to reception only to be told she'd checked out an hour earlier.

So he really had blown his chances. Hell, he thought, what had been his chances anyway? So she'd lifted off back to the planet Zeus. So what?

He put her from his mind and settled instead for the consolation of a high-cholesterol fry-up of which nearly two weeks of early starts had deprived him. Taking his time, he finally packed and hit the road at eleven thirty. A steady ninety on the motorway, he decided; the police rarely bothered unless you went above that. And good lane discipline, tucking into the nearside lane after overtaking so as not to draw attention. A relaxed cruise in the sun and Pavarotti singing his big heart out on the tape. He ate up the miles to London, relaxed and enjoying the drive even when momentary thoughts of a sodden Sam Browne flashed through his mind.

Afterwards he would find it hard to recall exactly when he first thought that he was being followed. Certainly it wasn't on the M40 to London; it was more probably at some point along the M25 ringroad around London where the traffic slowed for roadworks.

He wasn't immediately aware, it was a gradual thing. Glimpsing a car overtake two behind in his rear-view mirror, taking a bit of a chance; another a few minutes later. Even that was innocent enough. Had it not been for his anti-surveillance training and some sixth sense that came from sheer experience, he might not have realised at all.

As it was, his skills were rusty. Five years since his tour in Northern Ireland, with just a short refresher course before Bosnia. Two cars, he decided. Always two cars, one of them just in sight, though never close enough for him to be certain of the model. One dark blue saloon, probably Sierra or Granada. The other lower, sleeker, an orangey colour – a sporty number which in itself was unusual for a surveillance car.

Several times he slowed and speeded up, but one or the other of them seemed always to be there, rarely falling back and never catching up. He wasn't especially perturbed, logic telling him it was just coincidence and an overactive imagination. Anyway, there was nothing he could do about it on the motorway, short of making a time-consuming detour and he had no intention of doing that. The dash clock read one forty-five and he was in good time for his rendezvous with Bill Johnson.

The blue sign for Clacket Lane services flashed past. One last go, he decided, and pushed his foot down hard. His Cavalier leapt forward, the needle creeping round the dial to one hundred, one hundred and ten. In his mirror the following cars fell back until they were indistinguishable specks. Then, without signalling, he veered suddenly onto the slip road before braking hard and changing rapidly down through the gears.

He circled the car park once; using his mirrors, he saw only a red van and a Rolls-Royce come down the slip road after him. He smiled at his own irrational imaginings and found a space near the shops and restaurant. There was no sign of Johnson by the entrance, but then he was ten minutes early.

Switching off, he climbed out and lit a cigarette, leaning against his door and shutting his eyes to enjoy the warmth of the sun on his face.

It was then that he heard it. The throaty crackle of a tractor engine combined with a metallic clanking noise that sounded remarkably like a tank.

He opened his eyes to see the battered Celica sports spluttering into the car park. Heads turned at the racket just in time to see the exhaust pipe finally detach itself amid a belching cloud of fumes. It pulled into a space opposite and stopped. He'd been right after all.

Sam Browne's long legs appeared first as she climbed out, elegant in a pencil skirt and matching navy jacket with power-padded shoulders and white piping. And a wide-brimmed blue-straw hat. For a moment she removed her sunglasses to stare back at her car with disgust, then replaced them before crossing the traffic lane to where Lomax watched in total astonishment.

She did not smile. 'You did ninety all the way.' It sounded like an accusation.

'I didn't know we were travelling in convoy.' He indicated her hat. 'Are you going to a wedding?'

'No, I'm going with you and Detective Superintendent Johnson to see Derek Penny. I know him. Penny's a very proper sort of chap. Very formal.'

'Have you cleared this with Bill?'

She looked pointedly across at her Celica. 'I think she's had it, don't you? A new exhaust would cost more than the car's worth.'

'If you'd asked, I'd have given you a lift.'

'I was going to ask you last night,' her expression was deadpan, almost aloof, 'but the moment never seemed right.'

'So you followed me?'

'Obviously.'

'So you *haven't* cleared it with Bill.'

Before she could answer, they heard Johnson's familiar voice calling from the entrance steps. 'There you are!'

He trotted across, smiling. 'Am I late, Chris? Sorry.'

'No, I'm early.'

Johnson took a second to recognise Browne behind her disguise of dark glasses and floppy hat. 'Oh, hello, what are you doing here?'

She said quickly: 'Chris thought it would be a good idea if I came too. I know Derek Penny from the time of Keegan's trial. As I represent both Peter and Roddy Littlechild, there might be something useful to learn for the defence.'

Lomax opened his mouth to protest, then shut it again.

The detective was clearly unhappy. 'Look, Penny took a lot of persuading to see me. If I go in mob-handed he might change his mind. Besides, this is an investigation connected with Keegan's recapture. That's hardly a matter for you – and Rodney Littlechild's defence case certainly isn't a matter for me as a police officer.'

'While Keegan's missing,' Browne replied smoothly, 'Rodney Littlechild doesn't *have* a defence case. Yet he's totally innocent.'

'So Chris here tells me,' Johnson said tetchily.

'But Derek Penny *might* just know what Keegan knows – that my client was a reputable agent helping MI5. If he can confirm that, then my client still stands a chance.'

'I'm sorry.' Johnson was adamant. 'That's not my problem. This investigation is strictly police business and confidential. If you want to speak to Penny you must make your own arrangements.'

Suddenly Lomax felt sorry for Browne. Such was her zeal to snatch at any meagre straw to save his friend and brother-in-law that he felt compelled to overlook her devious method. 'Hang on, Bill. This meeting isn't official, you told me yourself. I don't think your senior officer even knows you're here. I'm doing you a favour, so do me one for the sake of a friend who once saved my life. Just let Sam sit in on it, eh?'

Her face lightened at the words of support from an unexpected quarter. 'I won't say a word, Bill, I promise.' She added: 'Trust me.'

Johnson heaved a sigh. 'Just a minute, Miss Browne.' He beckoned Lomax to follow him out of her hearing. His voice dropped to a whisper. 'Listen, Chris, your lawyer friend is a known troublemaker, bad news. They told me at that meeting with the Anti-Terrorist Branch. She's on the unofficial blacklist for causing problems.'

Lomax regarded the detective closely. 'You mean for being good at her job.'

'That's not how the police see it. She's caused upset and mayhem in dozens of cases.'

'Which she's won.'

Johnson was losing patience. 'What is it with you, Chris? Have you got the hots for her or something? She knows how to switch on the charm when she wants to, but that woman isn't doing you or your friend Littlechild any favours. She just gets up people's noses.'

He couldn't resist a smile at that. 'I know what you mean. But I still want her to come.'

The detective relented. 'Okay, under protest. But do your friend a favour, eh? Tell him to fire her and get a lawyer who's not on some evangelical crusade to take on the entire police force and legal system single-handed.' He glared back at Browne who stood decorously beside Lomax's car, smoking a cigarette. 'I just hope I won't regret this.'

They walked back to Browne, and Johnson said: 'No point in bringing your car, Chris, we may as well all go in mine. I'll drop you both here on my way back.'

Neither Lomax nor Browne mentioned her car; she was more than relieved to abandon it as, from the rear window of Johnson's Toyota saloon, she saw a police patrolman taking an interest in the rusted exhaust pipe lying on the tarmac. It would be a matter of seconds before he discovered her vehicle licence had expired.

'I'm very grateful, Bill,' she said brightly. 'You won't regret it.'

He glanced up into his mirror. 'I hope not. I've enough problems for one day.' He looked sideways at Lomax. ''Course, Chris, you probably won't have heard. There was a breakout at Stafford nick earlier today.'

'There was something on the news. A helicopter?'

Johnson nodded as they swung back onto the M25, heading east. 'Very audacious.'

'Will you be involved in the case?'

A shake of the head. 'Not really. Only to keep a watching brief. You see, the two cons they spirited away were known friends of Keegan's.'

'Surely not . . . ?'

Johnson laughed. 'I hardly think so. Those two had no connections with Northern Ireland or any terrorist movement. Just happened to have once served in the same regiment as Keegan. So best to keep an open mind.'

'Haven't air-traffic control been able to trace the helicopter?'

'Not yet. It must have been hedge-hopping. Vanished into thin air.'

They left the motorway at Junction 5 and took the A21 south towards Tunbridge Wells.

Rose Cottage was at the end of the little row of roadside dwellings that constituted the village. There was no shop or post office, just a pub and a small Methodist chapel, and fields all around. Derek Penny's place was pure chocolate box: thatch, crumbling red brick with cross-ties painted black and an ash picket fence squaring off the neat front garden. Not unexpectedly, rows of standard roses provided a guard of honour to the low timber door.

A woman in her late fifties stopped her pruning and watched as Johnson parked on the grass verge and the three strangers came through her gate. She wore an old-fashioned floral dress, no make-up and had permed grey hair.

Her smile was thin-lipped, her eyes flinty. 'Detective Superintendent Johnson, I presume.' The title tripped easily and familiarly off her tongue. 'My husband's expecting you. I hope you don't mind being inside. Poor dear's allergic to the sun, brings him out in a rash.'

At that moment, the door swung open and Penny's tall, lean frame filled the entrance, stooped to avoid the overhead beam. Lomax's first impression was how gaunt he looked, the skin of his skeletal face and balding crown having the waxy texture of a potato.

Policeman's eyes, seen-it-all-before-and-not-much-liked-it, darted down the row of visitors; he did not smile. 'A deputation?'

Johnson beamed, but it broke no ice. 'Sorry, sir. Didn't mean to overwhelm you.'

'Not sir,' Penny said sharply, 'I've retired. So who are these people? I thought it was just me and you.'

'Er – this is Chris Lomax. He was with the SAS in Keegan's time and knew him. Backup, minder stuff, I gather.'

'We don't need him here.'

'Er – sorry, sir – Mr Penny. I asked him because I know little about Northern Ireland and he can explain things I don't want to trouble you with. I hoped he could sit in.'

Penny's eyes moved down the line. 'And the lady?'

'Miss Browne is a solicitor. She's working on a related case. If you want I'll ask her to wait in the car.'

Penny shook his head, clearly deciding it wasn't worth the fuss. 'No, no. Just come in and let's get it over with.' He called to his wife. 'Meredith, bring us a pot of tea, will you?'

They followed him into the dim interior, Lomax noticing that the man's grey flannel trousers hung like windless sails around a ship's masts and that he wore a sleeveless pullover despite the warm weather. Beneath the low ceiling, the furniture was inexpensive and uninspiringly antique, a well-worn Persian carpet covering the cold stone floor. The neatness of everything was inescapable, from the shelves of books in descending order of size and the perfectly symmetrical stack of *Police Review* on the coffee table to the orderly row of family portrait snaps on the mantelpiece. One wall displayed pen-and-ink drawings of English cathedrals.

'Your garden's very nice,' Browne said, making conversation. 'Very pretty.'

'That's Meredith's doing, not mine.'

She removed her sunglasses. 'A lovely home.'

'All of you sit down,' he said. Derek Penny spoke as if he was still ACC of West Weald Constabulary. He sat in a leather club chair by the fireplace with its display of dried flowers. The chief's seat. 'I can't give you long,' he said as his wife brought in a tray of tea and digestive biscuits, 'because I'm taking choir practice at four.'

'Then I'll get straight to it,' Johnson said. 'Firstly, I'd like to emphasise this meeting is strictly off the record. As you know, Peter Keegan has escaped from prison – '

'I thought he was abducted?' Penny interjected immediately.

'We now know otherwise. He had accomplices and laid a false trail to throw us off the scent. My job is to investigate his background for any clues that may lead to his recapture.' Penny nodded his understanding. 'There's virtually nothing in his file and when I spoke with the Anti-Terrorist Branch and the Security Service, they made it clear I wouldn't learn anything worthwhile from them.'

For the first time an expression that could have been a mirthless smile appeared on Penny's face. 'That sounds familiar.'

'I'm not at all sure my senior officers would sanction this meeting,' Johnson continued, 'but I see no other way forward. Obviously it is imperative to recapture Keegan, if for no other reason than while he is out of our custody, his life could be at risk from former Loyalist colleagues or the IRA.'

Penny steepled his fingers across his chest. 'Highly commendable, Superintendent. It's good to see an officer who refuses to be deflected from his task nowadays. Too many bow to political expediency and financial pressures. Better to have faith in yourself knowing you are doing the Lord's work.'

Johnson gave a polite smile. 'Quite. Perhaps we should start at the beginning. What do you know of Peter Keegan's history?'

The former police chief stretched out his hands on his knees and contemplated the bony fingers. 'Let me see. Born in Portadown in 1945. Bright although not especially academic. Came to England when he was eighteen, trying to get a job as a cub reporter. But he failed – insufficient qualifications.' He looked up from his hands. 'On the rebound he walked into an army recruitment office and signed up for the Cheshires. God knows why. That would have been 1963. The life suited him and he got on well. Of course the Ulster Troubles broke out in '69 and he did at least one tour before he left the army in 1971. By then he'd attained the rank of corporal, acting sergeant.

'He went back home to Belfast and by the next year had joined the Ulster Defence Association. What happened over the next ten years is a bit of a mystery. He worked as an insurance agent, but his spare time was dedicated to the UDA paramilitaries. He claims to have been an RUC informer, but they deny that. God knows what the truth is.'

Sam Browne had been listening intently, her wide hat resting on her lap. 'I think you'll find Peter joined the UDA in order to fight the Provos. Then he found that elements of his own side were behaving as badly or worse, damaging the Loyalist cause. That's when he contacted the Royal Ulster Constabulary and became an informer in order to rein in the wilder elements.'

Penny's eyes focused on her, his eyes narrowing. 'Who told you that?'

'He did.'

'And your name again?'

'Sam Browne.'

The former police chief blinked slowly, reminding her of an

owl as recognition dawned. 'I knew you looked familiar. You were Keegan's defence solicitor.' He said it as though he'd just tasted something unpleasant. 'I recall prosecuting counsel described you as fighting like a tomcat behind the scenes.'

'Meow,' she replied demurely. Penny glared. 'Obviously I didn't fight hard enough or he wouldn't have gone down. If my client had listened, we'd have contested all charges all the way.'

Penny said stiffly: 'He'd have gone down anyway. The man was – is – a murderer.'

'But he'd have taken others down with him, Mr Penny. If he'd fought and not plea-bargained, he'd have exposed his controllers and the whole dirty tricks mob who'd thrown him to the wolves.'

'The wolves?' Penny repeated. 'Like Detective Superintendent Johnson here, I was just doing my job. In the public interest.'

Browne nodded. 'And Keegan would have argued the same. Just like you he was acting for and paid by the Crown.'

A film of ice seemed to glaze over Penny's eyes. 'The difference is, madam, that I never murdered anyone.'

'Now look, let's not get into all this,' Johnson interrupted, scowling at Browne. 'We're not here to discuss the morality of everything, just to get the facts.'

Browne said: 'The *fact* is, Bill, Peter Keegan sacrificed his entire life and eventually his freedom to helping the RUC, then MI5 through Army Intelligence.'

'So he told you,' Penny observed sceptically.

'He had no reason to lie to me. He was fighting a life sentence.'

'Then he had every reason to lie to you, to win you over.'

'I believed him,' Browne said flatly, 'and I still do. In 1983 he managed to penetrate the Ulster Defenders – an extreme hard-line faction – and that's when Army Intelligence took an interest and took over running him from the RUC.'

'On that I agree,' Penny said. 'What do you know about the Defenders?'

Browne shook her head. 'I was only ever told the bare facts.'

'It draws its membership from all the various groups. The

198

UDA, the UVF, and others. At its head is a nasty piece of work called Stevie Gavin. His *nom de guerre* is Rattlesnake, but he's always been known as Rattler. Very appropriate. He and Peter Keegan knew each other from childhood. That's why Keegan was so easily accepted. But by '85 Keegan had had enough of his undercover double life and the family emigrated to South Africa.'

'But not for long,' Browne recalled. 'According to Peter, MI5 was really missing his intelligence and begged him to go back and work for them again.'

'That's true,' Penny agreed. 'You see, strange as it may seem, Rattler – Stevie Gavin – had killed suspected IRA members on information supplied by MI5, but he was really crafty about it. In fact, he's survived to this day because of his natural cunning. For a start he never fully trusted MI5 – very wisely. So if he was given a target and a date for a kill, he'd use his own team to carry out an independent assessment and surveillance operation. Then he'd strike at a different location on a different date. That way the army or MI5 could never stitch him up, if it suited them.' He sighed deeply. 'I do believe he has murdered well over thirty people to date. But there has never, ever been evidence for a conviction.'

'Forgive me,' Johnson said, 'but if Rattler was obligingly killing IRA men for MI5 why also plant Keegan as an informer?'

Penny gave an impatient sigh. 'Because Rattler has always been a loose cannon. Always ran his own agenda, which didn't always square with what MI5 wanted. Keegan's presence was a check and counterbalance so they'd know what else he was up to.'

'And none of this ever came out in court at Keegan's trial?' Johnson asked.

'They made bloody sure it didn't,' Browne interrupted.

Johnson asked Penny: 'What happened when Keegan went back to Belfast after his spell in South Africa?'

'He rejoined the Ulster Defenders. That was in 1987. Rattler appointed him intelligence officer with the job of targeting victims. This really suited MI5 who wanted to distance themselves from Rattler – Stevie Gavin could easily prove an embarrassment. Now they could use Keegan as their conduit, feeding him the targets while getting information back on Rattler's other activities.'

'And that's when you became involved?' Johnson asked.

'Yes,' Penny said. 'Within a few months of Keegan rejoining, there was a spate of sectarian killings. A lot of Catholics were shot. One in particular Sinn Fein made a great fuss about, claiming the man was totally unconnected with the IRA. An innocent man shot at his front door, his blood and brains splattered over his wife and three-year-old son. It got a lot of sympathetic press coverage.

'This riled many of the Ulster Defenders' people. Rattler, of course, ordered the usual *omerta*. Complete silence and no comment. But one of their number felt he *had* to say something. He contacted a highly respected Belfast journalist and arranged a secret meeting. He showed the man a highly classified RUC dossier on the murdered Catholic, exposing him as a major player in the Provos. Within days it was splashed all over the papers with pictures of the dossier. 'RUC Feeds IRA Target Information to Loyalist Killers.' You can imagine the sort of headlines. There was a tremendous stink, media coverage and questions in the House.'

'I remember reading about it,' Johnson said.

'An internal police inquiry was set up and I was appointed to head it. As you might expect, my arrival in Belfast wasn't exactly welcomed. I was shunned in the RUC headquarters at Knock. The top brass were polite enough, but made it quite clear they thought the inquiry should never have been set up, but now that it had, I shouldn't dig deep and should just do a whitewash job. Papers and files mysteriously disappeared and people's memories became conveniently short. Army Intelligence, who were actually running Keegan, tried the same sorts of tricks.'

Lomax said: 'Maybe the whole idea *was* that you shouldn't have looked too hard.' There was an edge to his voice; he remembered the terrible mental torment Keegan had been through as an undercover agent.

'*If* that was the case,' Penny retorted, 'they chose the wrong man. I made it plain from the start I'd leave no stone unturned and I didn't. I found the link between the RUC and Army Intelligence and MI5 – and Keegan. The whole sordid business.'

'How did it work?' Johnson asked.

'It was Keegan's job in the Ulster Defenders to come up with target intelligence for Rattler or his hit squads. He was to pass details of planned assassinations to his army handlers who would take steps to ensure they failed. A convenient vehicle checkpoint to intercept the hit squad by apparent good fortune or cause them to abort. Or to flood the target area with troop activity, random house searches nearby – anything to disrupt the plan.'

'But MI5 wasn't just out to save lives, was it?' Browne asked pointedly.

Penny hesitated. 'No, I'm afraid it wasn't. As that very first newspaper scoop suggested, the killings that went ahead – many of them, anyway – were a result of information passing the other way. MI5 supplied RUC intelligence dossiers to Keegan via his army handlers. Those names were added to the list Keegan gave to Rattler for execution.'

'Good God,' Johnson said.

Penny gave the detective a reproachful glare at his mild blasphemy before adding: 'In the end none of this came out in full, but you can see why my investigating team was unpopular.'

'Is there anyone who Keegan might be able to rely on from that period?' Johnson asked. 'Anyone who might spring him from prison?'

'Certainly not Rattler. Stevie Gavin regarded Keegan as a traitor. Quite honestly, I think Keegan alienated himself from all his old friends when his work was discovered.'

Browne leaned forward. 'Did Rodney Littlechild's name crop up during your inquiry?'

Johnson's eyes widened as the blood coloured the veins in his cheeks. 'Miss Browne, we are not here to waste Mr Penny's time discussing your client's case.'

'Oh, come on, Bill,' she said with her little-girl smile, 'there may be a connection and I'm getting desperate.'

'Roddy Littlechild,' Penny interjected. 'The murder of that IRA thug Fitzpatrick? Is that the related case you referred to earlier?'

Johnson looked defensive. 'We're not *actually* sure it is related.'

'I certainly believe it could be relevant,' Browne insisted.

'Mr Penny, I really must apologise . . .' Johnson began.

But the former police chief appeared not to hear, his attention now solely on the solicitor. 'So now you are defending Rodney Littlechild as well?'

'Yes, and by coincidence, Mr Lomax here happens to be his brother-in-law.' After her earlier antagonism she decided that a sweet smile might be appropriate. 'I was wondering if Rodney Littlechild featured in your investigation?'

Penny nodded. 'Yes, his name cropped up. And I must admit I was very surprised – maybe shocked is a better word – to read about Littlechild's arrest for murder. It didn't seem to fit the profile I had of him. He was a very trusted MI5 agent.'

Lomax found his eyes meeting Browne's eyes across the room and saw the expression of relief in them.

'He was?' Johnson asked, clearly not persuaded.

'Oh, yes. I was shown a number of confidential personal assessments from the Security Service. Keegan was regarded as a bit of a wild card. That meant, as we now know, that he could prove to be a liability. Rodney Littlechild on the other hand was reliable and rock solid for some twenty years. I don't know exactly what service he provided before my team investigated, only that he made fairly frequent journeys back from Africa and knew all the top Loyalist players who all trusted him completely. They'd bring him up to date and he'd pass any information he gleaned back to MI5.'

'Did Keegan know that Littlechild was also an MI5 agent?' Johnson asked.

'No, not until the trial,' Penny answered. 'But the two of them did arrange an arms deal together in 1986. After the Anglo-Irish Agreement, Ian Paisley set up the Ulster Resistance

Movement, although he soon lost interest in it. A lot of factions got involved, including the Ulster Defenders. Stevie Gavin – Rattler – decided a massive arms shipment was going to be needed for the concept to work in reality. He sent Keegan to South Africa to organise it. Littlechild was serving in a special police intelligence unit there and showed Keegan a range of weapons that could be made available and introduced him to executives from Armscor.'

Browne said: 'Rodney's always denied he set up an arms deal.'

Lomax heard the disappointment in her voice and he shared her feeling of betrayal; if his brother-in-law had lied about this, what else had he lied about?

'He *would* deny it,' Penny said easily, 'because he made sure it never happened. Or tried to. Littlechild informed his controller at MI5 who decided to let the deal run.'

'Why?' Johnson asked.

'On the basis that while the Loyalists thought they were certain of a deal, they wouldn't try elsewhere – other transactions that MI5 *weren't* aware of. Not that there was much chance of that because Keegan, not knowing Littlechild had MI5 connections, was also informing his army handlers about the shipment.'

'What happened to the arms shipment in the end?' Browne asked.

'It was seized by the RUC in Belfast as planned,' Penny replied. 'Well, actually, not *quite* as planned. In truth some of the arms got through, unaccounted for. No one quite knows how or why; it's always a risk when you let something run. It's not certain where the arms ended up, although there's no sign that they've ever been used as far as I know.' He glanced pointedly at the Henri Jacot carriage clock on the mantelshelf. 'There was an arrest made at a Paris hotel – two members of the Ulster Defenders and a South African business man.'

Lomax felt a weight lift from his shoulders. 'At least we now know the foundation of all the media rumours. Roddy reckons they were started by MI5 when he stopped co-operating with them.'

'I am not in the least surprised,' Penny said. 'The secret state can be very vindictive as I have found out to my cost.'

'You have?' Johnson sounded surprised.

'Oh, indeed, Superintendent. Look at me here, in this cottage. Do I look like the sort of man who wants to spend his time kicking his heels at home, gardening and making jam with Meredith? I took early retirement, but I didn't jump. I was pushed. It's clear to me now, as you suggested, that I was expected to go along with a cover-up over the Keegan affair. I didn't and I've since paid the price. Afterwards, questions were asked about my integrity, my personal relationship with a businessman friend who was falsely accused and later cleared of fraud charges. Doors closed to me and it was made clear there was no prospect of promotion. People who knew me well turned their backs on me and there was talk of my suspension because of my links with my friend. I had no doubt what was expected of me. So I fell on my sword and left the force.'

A silence fell over the room, accentuated by the heavy ticking of the clock.

Browne said: 'Would you be prepared to repeat what you told us today at Roddy's trial? Confirm that he was an MI5 agent.'

'Miss Browne!' Johnson protested. 'Do I have to tell you again?'

But Derek Penny raised his hand. 'Please. Miss Browne, I can do more than that. During my investigation several sensitive documents passed across my desk, so to speak. Realising that there could be repercussions for myself later, I took the precaution of taking secret copies of the most sensitive material. Some of it acknowledges Rodney Littlechild's role in the affair, if that would help?'

'Oh, yes!' She was overjoyed.

At that moment the door edged open and his wife's head peered round it. 'Would anyone care for more tea?'

'No, thank you, Meredith,' Penny said, rising to his feet. 'Our friends are just leaving. But perhaps you'd get that package from the bottom of the freezer. And something for them to carry it in.'

'Freezer?' Browne asked as his wife disappeared. 'Did I hear right?'

Penny smiled properly for the first time. 'It always struck me as a good place to hide something. In with the frozen peas and sweetcorn.'

'I'm really grateful,' she said minutes later when Meredith returned with the icy package in a Safeway carrier bag.

Penny looked at Johnson. 'I only wish I could have been of more help to you. I fear Keegan has no friends left in the world. I don't know where to suggest you start looking. Except that the last place would be Northern Ireland. His old friends in the Loyalist paramilitaries have put a price on his head.'

Harry Grisewold watched from the driver's seat of the dark blue Ford Orion. The three of them and Meredith Penny seeing them to the gate. No sign of her husband.

Nothing different. He lifted the handy Tasco 8 × 21s to his eyes. Wrong, something different. He flipped the focusing wheel of the tiny binoculars. A Safeway bag. Carried by the solicitor Samantha Browne. She hadn't had that on the way in.

He murmured: 'He's given them something.'

Margie Lewis sat beside him, black jeans and jumper, black hair coiled into a bun. She was stuffing prawn-flavoured crisps into her scarlet mouth; another day without a decent meal, she thought, and swallowed. 'What?'

'Not groceries. But it's a Safeway bag. Browne's got it.'

'If Browne's got it, it's about Littlechild,' Margie decided.

'How d'you work that out?' Her powers of deduction and intuition never ceased to amaze Harry Grisewold and he'd been in the job for years. By comparison, she was a baby. A tough one though. Brains and fuck-crazy, too. Sometimes he couldn't believe his luck.

She said: 'Johnson's investigating Keegan, so if it was about Keegan, he'd have it.'

He didn't take the binoculars from his eyes. 'She looks happy. Nice smile, lots of ivory. Nice arse.'

Margie didn't comment, was well used to the man they all called 'Dirty Harry'.

'Lomax looks pleased too,' Grisewold added. 'Johnson looks like he's eaten something that doesn't agree with him.'

She put the last of the crisps in her mouth and scrunched up the packet in her fist. 'That's conclusive then. Penny's given them something on Littlechild. How d'you want to play this?'

They were running a four-car box. But on the long journey down from Stafford, Grisewold thought he might have compromised himself on the M25. He hadn't counted on the Browne woman following Lomax in her clapped-out car. He hadn't wanted to overtake her, but he didn't want to lose sight of the former SAS man either if she couldn't keep up.

Grisewold made up his mind. 'They've got to go back to the service station to pick up Lomax's car – I don't know what they'll do about hers. You follow them up, then get Eddie and Greg to take over. To his place or hers, I expect.' He lowered the binoculars. 'Sod it, I've had enough of this. I'm indenting for a tracer.'

'Pinfold won't like that.'

'Pinfold wants everything on the cheap. Just get it done. Lomax isn't your run-of-the-mill dummy. So do it, will you?'

'What about you?'

'I'm calling it a day.'

'Bastard. Filling your face again.'

'I'll pretend I didn't hear that. And if it makes you feel better, I'll be reporting in to the weasel himself. Wanna swap?'

'No thanks, Harry. I'll leave that honour to you.' She reached across and kissed his unshaven cheek. 'You deserve it.'

Then she was out. He watched her in his wing mirror as she walked back to the red Peugeot parked behind his on the farm track. Still looking good, he thought. Hard, compact body, fit. But putting on a few pounds. Too much hanging around in cars eating junk food. Needed more exercise. More shagging. They hadn't had one for days.

She swung the Peugeot past him and with a wave turned right to follow Johnson's car.

Nine

'This, dear heart, is absolutely bloody brilliant,' Tristram Meyrick said.

The QC was seated at his leather-topped desk in 10 Paper Buildings, a sheaf of documents spread out before him. Lomax and Sam Browne sat opposite, both hanging expectantly on the barrister's words. Ronnie Rock, the junior counsel from Jamaica, had perched himself on the desk edge and was plucking out and studying samples at random.

'Bloody brilliant,' Meyrick repeated, running his right hand over his bare crown. 'Seem like genuine Security Service documents. File referencing *and* sequential numbers. Very useful, makes it more difficult for anyone to deny their existence.'

'These are intelligence assessments of Loyalist paramilitaries,' Rock said, examining the paper in his hand. 'Stevie Gavin, Keegan – ah, and our client Rodney Littlechild. A complete character reference, confirming his length of service. Oh, yes, I love these words, man. Loyal! Trustworthy! Nonviolent nature! We couldn't ask for more.'

Meyrick chuckled. 'Didn't write these yourself, did you, Sam?'

She was feeling pleased with herself. 'I couldn't believe it either. Was worth the time Chris and I spent defrosting them and drying them out.'

'Defrosting?' The barrister was baffled.

'It's a long story, Tristram. The point is how important are they?'

He arched his eyebrows. 'Well, short of actually saying our client didn't murder Fitzpatrick, they're the very best you could hope for. It's a pity they're photocopies, but I suppose originals would be too much to hope for.'

'Of course, we'll call Derek Penny to verify they're genuine, that they came into his hands during the Keegan trial.'

'Man, that wouldn't be bad,' said a mirthful Ronnie Rock, 'a former ACC as a defence witness.'

'Well, it's about time we had some luck,' Browne replied. 'The RUC still haven't come up with anything on the whereabouts of Billy Baker who could yet be our key witness. And I'm still getting no co-operation from the police. Still no witness list or access to forensics.'

'That's nothin' new,' Rock observed unhelpfully.

'You said earlier that wasn't unusual,' Lomax said.

Browne nodded. 'The police like to do things their own sweet way. Can't see why we don't just sit on our arses and wait for the committal bundle. They've got stalling down to an art form.'

'Like solicitors who don't pay their bills,' chipped in the chief clerk Keith Billbury who had just breezed in, carrying a pile of pink-ribboned papers.

Browne ignored that. 'The longer they leave it, the shorter the time for us to prepare a proper defence, examine statements, etc.'

'It's just a game,' Billbury said lightly.

'But not a very funny one when your client's going down for murder.'

'I thought I'd remind you,' Billbury added, 'that Littlechild's got a remand hearing coming up next week at Woolwich. Maybe we can put some pressure on then.'

'I certainly will,' Ronnie Rock promised. As junior counsel, the task would fall to him.

'At remand hearings, solicitors can address the Bench,' Billbury explained to Lomax. 'And Cruella here is dynamite. Missed her vocation.'

'You'll be banging your head against a brick wall, young Ronald,' Meyrick observed lightly.

'It's worth trying,' Browne insisted. 'I'm afraid it makes me bloody angry. I'm not supposed to interview prosecution witnesses without notifying the CPS. But as the police still haven't told me who they are, how am I supposed to know who they are?'

Lomax said: 'I thought you said your staff were trying to find witnesses.'

'Yes, Totty and Wayne have been down to the pubs and done some spadework. They've got a few names. If I tell the CPS it'll alert the police to those we're interested in. Or else, if they decide someone may be a prosecution witness after all, that person is hardly likely to revise his story to me with DS Henwick standing over him.'

'You know I've offered to talk to them. I'm a third party. Technically it would be my decision to do it, not yours.'

'I'm not sure that would be strictly ethical.'

'Bugger that, Sam.'

'It could easily backfire. There's a risk of a charge of perverting the course of justice.'

'Just a risk?' He couldn't resist adding: 'Who dares wins.'

She smiled at his enthusiasm. 'The police will have told some of these people not to speak to anyone about the case. You'll have to be very persuasive.'

Lomax considered for a moment. 'I will be.' And as he said the words it flashed unbidden to his mind. Goose Green. The freezing night and his body sweating with adrenaline and fear. Screaming silent terror as the Argentinians' Italian-made 105s opened up, pouring in high-explosive and lung-searing white phosphorus. Finding their range and turning Camilla Creek into hell on earth. The distant thud from *HMS Arrow* as the frigate opened up in support, like lightning flashes out over the loch. The confusion, the pinned-down horror. And big Roddy by his side, teeth grinning amid the cam cream. Both scared, even petrified, but somehow loving it. Invincible together as they emptied their lungs and charged into the valley of death. A lifetime ago, yet only yesterday. Then he was back in the room with its rows of leather-bound law books and teetering stacks of legal briefs. He said: 'And I'll do whatever it takes.'

'Look, Chris, I'll give the police another couple of weeks to cough up a witness list. If nothing happens by then –' she took a deep breath, her decision made, 'then you're on.'

Lomax decided to attend the remand hearing, and afterwards wished he hadn't.

It was so depressing. More than bright autumn sunshine

would be needed to cheer the bleak estuary landscape; as it was, the sky was filled with murky low cloud and a bitter wind blew in off the water. Belmarsh Magistrates Court was part of the daunting concrete-and-steel complex that made up the new high-security Woolwich Crown Court. Lomax felt his spirits sinking by the minute.

As such hearings were most usually the domain of junior counsel, Browne and Rock were surprised to find the prosecution team being led by Henry Halifax QC. He was solidly built like a rugby prop forward with a broad florid face and iron-grey hair so crinkled it could have been permed. He greeted the opposition jovially; one of those loud laughs of the friendly bar-room bore that rings with insincerity.

'And how is the delicious Miss Browne today?' he ventured dangerously with a baritone chuckle.

'Pissed off, since you ask, Henry,' she responded flatly. 'And what on earth are *you* doing here? Has the CPS really got that much money to burn?'

He chortled loudly. 'Ah, they want the best on this one. You've a reputation as one slippery little fish, Sam, and this is a very high-profile case. They don't want any mistakes.'

Browne glowered. 'And who exactly is *they*, Henry?'

The barrister ducked that one and just said in a conspiratorial whisper: 'I also hoped I might have a quiet word.'

Reluctantly she allowed him to take her arm and lead her out of earshot. 'What are you up to, Henry?'

He indicated a tall man in an immaculate suit who stood talking to the CPS solicitor Ian Spinks. 'A gentleman from the Home Office legal department taking an interest.'

'The big guns, eh?' she observed sarcastically.

'This is off the record, Sam. But Mr Prendergast there has the ear of the Attorney-General's office. If your client pleads guilty, I'm given to understand there'll be a nod and a wink. He could be out on licence in ten. With a new identity if he wants.'

Browne blinked; she couldn't believe she was hearing this. 'You're being a bit previous, aren't you, Henry? I wasn't expecting this until after committal. If the police are to be believed, they haven't seen all the evidence themselves yet.'

Halifax gave a smugly sympathetic smile. 'They've seen enough, m'dear, I'm afraid. It's cast iron.'

She ignored that. 'But why now?'

He shrugged. 'Let's just say some people would like to know which way the wind's blowing. Unofficially, you know.'

'So they can sleep easy in their beds at night?'

'Quite possibly. But let your client know what's on offer. I'm sure he'll listen to you. A life sentence is indeterminate. Ten years is better than for ever. Think about it.'

Her jaw tightened, but she bit her tongue. This was high-stakes poker. 'Okay, I'll think. And while I'm thinking, you tell me when the hell am I going to get access to the forensic evidence?'

His big eyes widened with mock sympathy, taking in her face and dropping unguardedly to her breasts. 'My dearest little piranha, I'm doing my best but it really is out of my hands. I've badgered Spinks, your opposite number, but he says the police just can't speed things up. The Met lab at Lambeth is swamped by the current crime wave apparently.'

'We're talking murder here, Henry.'

'Ah, but you know these boffins, Sam. Everything in its turn and nothing will shake them.' He leaned forward so that his broad face was just inches from hers. 'What say you and I get together and discuss a joint deputation to ask them to speed things up? Over wine and a candlelit supper, perhaps?'

'In your dreams, Henry,' she replied tartly and turned away.

Not easily put off, Halifax moved across the lobby and spoke to Totty. 'And you're looking very – what shall I say? – *vol-uptuous* today, young lady.' He was almost drooling as he said it.

She fluttered her eyelids. 'That's very kind of you, Mr Halifax. Tell me, was you born to it or did you have to work at it – to become what you are today?'

'It always takes *hard* work to become a successful barrister.'

'No,' she said with a bright, chubby-cheeked smile, 'I meant to become such a creep.'

This time his jowls reddened and the ready smile collapsed. 'I can see the Ice Queen has created you in her own image. Pity she hasn't taught you a little civility.'

As he strode away, she turned to Lomax. 'Pompous prick.' She blushed, covering her mouth with her hand. 'Pardon me. But it's still true. 'E only does CPS work cos it's easy money. Doesn't give a stuff about anyone, he doesn't.'

'Not quite true,' Browne interjected. 'He appears to give quite a big stuff about a certain Mr Prendergast.'

Lomax immediately picked up on the name. 'He's here?'

Browne nodded. 'He's talking with Halifax now.'

'I suppose it's the same man who visited Keegan and briefed Bill Johnson?' He shifted position so he could see over Totty's shoulder without making it too obvious he was taking an interest.

Prendergast was laughing now with Halifax and the CPS solicitor. But the humour did not reach his eyes, Lomax noticed. Those eyes, so deep and blue. I know those eyes, I know that face. The cool bravado. I know this man. From when? From where?

'From the Home Office legal department,' Browne was saying. 'Wants us to know there's something on offer in return for a guilty plea. All unofficial, of course.'

The eyes were the same, Lomax decided. But not the face. The beard had been matted then, the hair long and greasy. There had been no Savile Row suit and shiny brogues, just a bomber jacket and dirty trainers.

Lomax said quietly: 'Prendergast isn't his name.'

Browne was taken aback. 'What?'

'And he's not Home Office, he's Box. MI5. Our paths crossed a couple of times in the province. He was a field operator then, undercover. His name's Pinfold, not Prendergast. Roger Pinfold. Looks like he's come a long way since then. Promoted. But I doubt to the Home Office legal department.'

The solicitor glanced at the man again. 'Do you think he's recognised you?'

'I doubt it. I was one of a group and not the leader. He'd have no reason to remember me.'

'We're being manipulated,' she said. 'And it's not a nice feeling.'

212

Lomax nodded. 'At least now it's confirmed. We know *exactly* what we're up against.'

Browne suddenly felt the need to loosen her collar. It was an inexplicable sensation, like suffocation.

Then the usher called the case and the opposing legal teams shuffled in.

The courtroom was spartan, harsh white paintwork and bland teak. Lomax sat beside Totty and Browne as though a member of the team, with Ronnie Rock in the next front row, resplendent in one of his elaborate fancy waistcoats.

Littlechild appeared in the dock, handcuffed to two prison officers, apparently having made the journey from prison to court via the 'rat run', the aptly named tunnel that connected the two buildings and stank of seeping marsh water. No proper daylight for his friend today, no view of the normal outside world that was rightfully his. Just mean glimpses of an equally mean patch of dull sky.

He looked awful, Lomax thought. Like a wild animal in captivity, his strong broad-shouldered body hunched in submission, his spirit clearly broken.

All rose as the magistrate entered and began by giving a sickeningly obsequious acknowledgement to the unexpected presence of such a renowned and revered silk as Henry Halifax. Then the proceedings fell into a predictable routine with Ronnie Rock making an impassioned but futile plea for bail. The prosecution promptly objected and requested that the prisoner continue to be held in custody. Which was granted, as they all knew it would be.

'Sir, I regret I must again raise the question of defence access to crucial forensic evidence being denied by the police.' Rock was on his feet again, addressing the Bench. 'And, although it is now nearly six weeks since my client was charged, neither have the police given an indication of the witness evidence against him.'

The magistrate nodded without concern. 'Counsel for the defence will be aware that these things take a little time.'

'Indeed, sir, but six weeks is more than sufficient for the police to question witnesses near the scene of crime and provide a list. Possibly more important is the question of forensic evidence. I understand that this is being examined by the Metropolitan Police laboratory at Lambeth. Whilst I understand there may be a backlog, there appears to be no valid reason why the defence should not at the very least be granted access to these forensic exhibits.' Rock was charm and reasonableness itself. 'I should add that some forensic evidence may degrade with time and we believe it may be crucial to the defence case.'

The magistrate peered over his spectacles in the direction of the prosecution team. 'Mr Halifax.'

'Sir, I should say firstly that I am informed that the police investigation in this matter is continuing and may do so for some time. I'm sure the officers concerned would say they themselves do not yet know which witnesses they will call. But, of course, a list of prosecution-witness statements will be provided at the appropriate time. That is, with the pre-committal bundle.'

'When it's too bloody late,' Browne rasped beneath her breath.

Halifax was continuing expansively: 'Moreover, I am at a loss to understand why my learned friend is concerned about the forensic evidence as the police themselves have not yet had the results. When they do receive written results, a copy will be forwarded to the defendant's solicitors in the usual manner.' He sat down.

'There you are,' the magistrate said. 'Does that answer your question?'

Ronnie Rock rose again. 'May I ask my learned friend how long Lambeth has had the forensic evidence?'

Now Halifax was up. 'I understand for the past few days.' Down.

Ronnie Rock up. 'Sir, I understand it to have been three weeks already.'

Another jack-in-the-box. 'Sir, I can only report what I am told.'

Ronnie Rock back on his feet. 'May I ask my learned friend

when he believes the results *will* be available and access granted to an independent expert for the defence?'

There was a discreetly smug smile on Halifax's face as he shot a glance at Rock. 'If the court pleases, this case cannot jump the backlog at Lambeth. However, it is hoped to be dealt with in the next two months.'

'Two months!' Browne repeated as she feverishly lit a cigarette in the corridor outside. 'The same old game. Dump it in our laps just before committal.'

'And what exactly is committal?'

'It's held in a magistrate's court to determine whether there's a case to answer,' Browne explained. 'So it's fundamental we know the forensic findings. I can't see how there *can* be anything that'll stand up. And if that's the case, we'll have very little time to wade through the witness statements to discover the holes and get the case dismissed. It'll be all *so* last minute.'

'It seems very unfair,' Lomax observed.

'It's the system, Chris.'

'It's also wishful thinking, Sam,' Rock said. 'It's too high profile. No magistrate is going to stick his neck out unless the police have made a complete balls. It'll go to trial.'

'We'll see.'

'Tilting at windmills again, Sam?' Rock chided.

'That's what I'm good at,' she replied testily. 'Anyway, it's too unbearable for Roddy not knowing just how strong their case is. If it's as flimsy as it must be, it'll be a comfort if I can assure him the prosecution case will fall apart at the seams. And dammit, I'm going to do something about it.' She turned to Totty. 'Which of the magistrates here has a soft spot for me?'

Her assistant averted her eyes. 'None that I've noticed. Sorry.'

'Then I need one who doesn't know me at all.'

Rock said: 'Old Caskin likes a well-turned ankle.'

'Right then, Totty. Speak to that usher who's always chatting you up. Find out when Caskin is next sitting.'

Rock looked suspicious. 'Just what are you up to, Sam?'

An impish smile hovered on her lips. 'I'm not going to tilt at this particular windmill, Ronnie, I intend to flatten it.'

In the week that followed, Lomax tried to keep up a cheerful pretence for Evie; he was just thankful he'd dissuaded her from attending the remand hearing.

He reassured her that it had gone as expected and that her husband had looked relaxed. It was doubtful he'd convinced her but, typical of Evie, she'd put on a brave face. She must have known the truth about Roddy's depressed mental state from her last visit, so perhaps they were both putting on an act for the other's benefit.

It came as a relief when Browne finally telephoned with her decision. As the police had still not provided a list of prosecution witnesses, she wanted to take up his offer to try and interview everyone who might be relevant, starting with the two pub landlords.

Deciding that it might be wise to have someone with him who could corroborate whatever he was told – not to mention give moral support – he called Joe Monk.

His friend didn't hesitate, agreeing with almost indecent eagerness. He arrived the next day and Lomax opened the door to find Monk with a wide tombstone grin on his face and a large kitbag grasped in each huge fist. 'Room for a little 'un?'

Lomax was taken aback. 'Travelling light, are we?'

'Nope, I'm here for the duration,' Monk replied, struggling to manoeuvre his luggage through the doorway. 'I've split with Marsha.'

'You're joking!'

'I was, she wasn't,' he answered and dumped his bags on the sofa. 'She gave me the ultimatum yesterday. Get a nice civvy job or she was off.'

'But you had a job.'

'Till this lavatory supervisor from the council came round to tell me I wasn't doing it right. Me!' He glowered with indignation. 'Me who's dug latrines from Borneo to Bosnia.'

'What happened?'

'I poured the slops bucket over his head and told him to stuff

216

it.' He meant it. 'So I had this row with Marsha, then you phoned. So I thought, right, that's it. Told her she could keep the house, I'm off.'

He flopped down on the sofa beside his luggage.

'I am sorry,' Lomax began.

'Don't be, mate.' He was grinning again. 'I haven't felt like this in years. Free! After you phoned, I called up Rob D'Arcy's outfit. He'll have a contract for me in Kazakhstan starting in three months.'

'That's great news. But you can't stay here until then. It's too small for two, let alone a big lump like you.'

Monk waved it aside. 'No problem. I'll rent a place and help you out in the meantime.'

'Listen, Joe, I've already told you the money will be lousy.'

'I know, I know. But I can scrape by on my army pension, it's bigger than yours. And Roddy's a mate of mine too.'

'You've only ever met him when you've been pissed. You two would pass each other in the street.'

Monk looked suddenly serious. 'The two of us spent a night together in the same bed.'

'I know. Both paralytic.'

'Exactly. You can't get closer than that.'

They left the flat half an hour later, picking up Totty from the offices of Eisner, Pollock and Browne before continuing on to the Duke's Head pub. It would be her job to point out customers she had already identified as potential witnesses to events on the night of the murder.

The manager of the Duke's Head was a big, surly man in his fifties. A professional London publican with mean eyes that said he'd seen it all and mostly hadn't liked what he saw. He was reluctant to talk, but when he did, he confirmed Littlechild's version of events. Fitzpatrick had been having a quiet drink alone when the manager received a call for him. He then left.

Other customers confirmed that no one followed him. Finally, the manager made it clear they were no longer welcome on his premises.

'Some people shouldn't be in the pub trade,' Monk said

darkly as they left. 'Nowadays it seems the main qualification to run a pub is to hate people.'

The atmosphere in the Mortar and Pestle was noticeably different from the first pub; it was fuller and there was lively chatter around the bar. Lomax went through the same routine, but had to wait half an hour before there was a lull in demands for service and the landlord slipped from behind the counter for a quick smoke.

His name was Sid Salmon. He was in his early thirties, unmarried, and this was his first pub. Full of nervous energy and nervous smiles, chatty and all too eager to please.

But as soon as Lomax explained why he was there, the shutters came down. Salmon was a changed man.

'I told the police,' he said sharply, almost angrily, his eyes darting towards the door as though expecting the boys in blue, or someone, to burst in at any moment. 'I didn't see no one answering those descriptions in here.'

'Not two men coming in about ten forty?'

'No. I'd have remembered.'

'And a couple, man and woman, almost on the bell.'

'No.'

'What about your customers?'

He shook his head, seeking a way to terminate the conversation. 'The police have interviewed them. They were mostly regulars. It was someone's work-leaving party that night and they were all fairly rat-arsed. They wouldn't have noticed if the ceiling had fallen in. That's it. Sorry.'

His relief was almost palpable when a customer banged his glass on the counter, giving Salmon his excuse to go.

Monk watched him as he went. 'I could smell the fear on him. One scared little bunny.'

Lomax lit a cigarette. 'Something certainly smells.'

'See no evil, hear no evil. Deny everything. Someone's got to him. The cops?'

'Somehow I doubt it. My guess is they're being strung along like everyone else.'

'I tell you what, Chris. If I wasn't convinced Roddy was telling the truth, I sure as hell am now.'

218

For the rest of the evening they sat with Totty who identified regulars as they drifted in. Their reaction to questions varied, but mostly they were happy to talk while Lomax and Monk were buying the rounds. But Salmon was right, no one had noticed Littlechild and Fitzpatrick on the night of the murder, or the couple who Roddy claimed had come in after them.

But of course, Lomax reasoned, they'd been having a party and all were half-drunk. The one person who *would* have cause to remember them, because he served them, was Salmon. And Salmon was keeping his mouth firmly shut.

As the hands of the clock edged towards closing time, Lomax was growing steadily more depressed and frustrated. He *had* to do something. When Totty went out to the ladies', he said to Monk: 'I'm thinking of having a private word with chummy.'

'Is that wise?'

'Probably not. Sam Browne would kill me.' He gave a short laugh. 'Sometimes I think she's just looking for the excuse.'

'Well, that would certainly give it to her.'

'We've got to break down this brick wall and we both know that bastard's lying through his teeth.'

Monk nodded his agreement. 'What? The bog dodge we used in the pub in Lurgan?'

'Why not?'

When Totty returned, Lomax gave her money for her cab fare home and sent the bemused girl on her way. Monk went to the gents' lavatory first, when Salmon was busy serving. Picking his moment, Lomax followed a few minutes later. They took a cubicle each and listened until the bell rang for time, then waited for the twenty minutes' drinking-up time to pass.

Finally the steady succession of drinkers tramping to the urinal ended and silence fell over the bar outside. A few minutes after eleven thirty they heard the outer lavatory door open; Salmon having a last look round. Monk left his cubicle and moved swiftly to position himself behind the door, his back jammed against a machine selling whisky-flavoured condoms, he noticed from the corner of his eye. God Almighty, whatever next?

The door swung open and Salmon stepped in, whistling as he

walked. Abruptly the sound stopped as his eyes registered Lomax leaning back against the cubicle doorpost, his arms folded across his chest. He'd adopted a particularly mean expression; under the circumstances it wasn't difficult.

Salmon's mouth dropped open. 'You!'

Monk slammed the door shut behind Salmon as the man jumped in shock and spun round, the colour draining from his face.

'W-What is this? A robbery?' he blubbered. 'I knew you two were . . .'

'Bad news?' Monk suggested helpfully. 'You're right there.'

'Calm down, Mr Salmon,' Lomax said. 'This isn't a hold-up and you won't get hurt if you simply tell us the truth.'

'*If* you know the meaning of the word,' Monk added menacingly. 'Otherwise you may find all your fingers getting broken. One by one.'

Salmon's head was turning to and fro between the two men like a demented tennis spectator. 'What's this all about?'

'We asked you questions earlier,' Lomax said. 'Now tell us the truth.'

Salmon shook his head wretchedly. 'I can't. I mustn't speak to anyone.'

'Who told you that?'

'People.'

'What people? The police?'

Tears were beginning to run down the man's face as he looked round the cramped tiled room, searching for inspiration, salvation – praying for escape. 'I don't know.'

'Did they threaten you?'

'No.' A gulp. 'Yes.'

'With violence?'

His head was shaking.

'*I'm* threatening you with violence,' Lomax said. 'When did these people speak to you?'

Salmon took a deep breath and attempted to compose himself. 'The morning after the murder. Two blokes. They came into the pub around midday.'

'And?'

'They said I could expect a visit from the police. Said when the coppers came, I should answer no to all their questions. Just say I didn't remember to everything they asked.'

'Did you ask them who they were?'

He nodded. 'They said to never mind. That they were acting on behalf of a friend of theirs. I don't know, I hadn't even heard about the murder then. Later I assumed they were villains working for the murderer.'

'And you did what they told you?'

'I told the police I saw nothing. Not the bloke who got murdered or the one they arrested, not the couple who followed them in.'

'Why?' Lomax demanded.

Salmon stared at him as though he were mad. 'Because I was fuckin' scared, damn it.'

Monk frowned. 'But you said they didn't threaten you with violence.'

'Not with violence, no. But they had this paper.'

'Newspaper?'

'No, no. Some police indictment document.'

'Explain.'

His shoulders sagged; it was almost a relief to tell someone, anyone. 'I've got a record. I did time, way back. Receiving stolen goods. The brewery doesn't know about it. If they did I'd be out on my ear. These people said they'd let the brewery know if I didn't do what they said. I'd never work in the trade again. They'd see to it.'

'And you believed them?'

'Oh, yes. And this is my first pub, my lucky break.'

'So you *did* see the two men, Littlechild and Fitzpatrick?'

He nodded. 'Two pints of Guinness.'

'And a couple?'

'Not long after. Half of lager and an orange juice with lemonade.'

'What did they look like?'

Salmon searched his memory. 'He was in his fifties. Sort of ordinary looking. Except for a small colourless mole on the

221

edge of his nose by his cheek. I remember that. And he was unshaven.'

'And her?'

'Good-looker with black hair. Maybe early thirties. Nice figure, but quite stocky, if you know what I mean.'

Monk said: 'Did they leave immediately after the two men?'

A shake of the head. 'They moved to the table the blokes had used. Probably to get out of the draught, the door doesn't always shut properly. Then they left, but not immediately. Maybe about five minutes.'

'Do you remember *anything* else?' Lomax pushed.

Salmon seemed more relaxed now, out of immediate danger. 'Just one thing was odd. One of the two blokes nicked a Guinness glass. You know, with the little gold harp emblem on it.'

'You noticed that?' Monk was surprised.

'I was running low on them, so I was a bit brassed off about it. People like Guinness in a proper glass.'

Lomax considered for a moment. 'I want a statement from you, verifying what you've just told us.'

'No way. I'm telling you in private and if it gets out I'm finished.'

Lomax's anger flared. 'You've just told me in front of a witness. If you say anything different in court, that'll be perjury. A very serious offence.'

But Salmon wasn't backing down now; he sensed he was no longer in physical danger. 'I'll take the risk. Those two thugs who visited me just threatened to put me out of business. But if they was friends of the killer, they could turn real nasty. According to the papers we're talking Irish terrorists here, for God's sake!'

'It'll still come out when the case gets to court,' Lomax warned.

'I'll cross that bridge when I come to it.'

Monk made a move forward but Lomax reached out a restraining hand. 'Leave it, Joe. I can see Mr Salmon's in a difficult position. Let him chew it over. His problem isn't going to go away.'

Monk added darkly: 'And we're not going to go away.' He

stepped aside and indicated for Salmon to go through into the pub. He and Lomax followed, heading for the door. Their last impression of the publican was of one very small and frightened man hurriedly bolting the door behind them.

'Curiouser and curiouser,' Lomax murmured as they began the drive back to Evie's flat.

'Those heavies,' Monk said. 'They've got to be connected with Box. The murder went down at midnight and by the following midday they've got confidential info on Salmon to ensure he sings to their tune. That's fast work. And the method reeks of MI5.'

Lomax thumped his fist on the wheel. 'It makes me bloody sick.'

But Monk's thoughts were elsewhere, trying to unwrap the puzzle. 'And what's this business about the Guinness glass? Was Salmon winding us up, or what?'

'God knows. I don't see Roddy or Fitzpatrick as the sort to go in for petty pilfering.'

Monk shrugged. 'Still, you never know.'

It was twelve thirty when they arrived back at Evie's flat and were surprised to find her waiting for them on the landing.

'What the hell have you been up to, Chris?' She was still dressed in her black barmaid's skirt and jumper and sounded very angry. 'You've left the place in such a mess I can't even get to the bedroom.'

Lomax jumped the last few stairs. 'What d'you mean, sis?'

She glared as he brushed past her. 'This fixation you've got about bugging. You could have put things back!'

On the threshold he halted abruptly. The flat was a shambles. Furniture had been moved and the carpet rolled back, blocking Evie's bedroom door.

Monk peered over his shoulder. 'You've been burgled, mate.'

'Burgled?' Evie echoed. 'You mean you haven't . . . ? But hang on, I don't think anything's been taken.'

Lomax quickly scanned the few items of value, all in their wrong places. 'The portable TV.'

'Isn't it there?'

'I can't see it.'

223

'Burglars,' Monk repeated. 'Must have come in while you were at the wine bar.'

Lomax took a step forward, noticing the prised-up floorboards for the first time. He knelt down beside the hole. 'Taking the television was just to make it look good. It was no ordinary burglary. They've taken my copy of Derek Penny's documents.'

The day began much the same as any other for Albie Nairn and a few dozen other chosen individuals in the province of Ulster.

Yet it was going to be a day that would change the rest of their lives, for good or ill. A day when they would hear the word they had waited to hear for almost a quarter-century. So long ago that most had almost forgotten, thinking perhaps now that it would never come.

Nairn always walked Toby, his collie cross, before breakfast. Out of his remote bungalow beside the narrow road in rural Keady, South Armagh, over the stile and into fields or the nearby copse. He enjoyed the early morning air, the freshness of it, and the birdsong. Before traffic began rattling along the main road, before this Indian summer sun became too warm. But he also enjoyed it in winter, when snow or ice crackled underfoot or, more usually, when the sky was cheerless and low, and the air dank and chill. It was still his time of day. His and Toby's, their own little carefree world.

His family had owned the adjoining land for generations, but to old man Nairn's disgust, Albie was no farmer and when his father died he'd begun renting out his fields to others. He'd cleared the ramshackle outbuildings around the bungalow, thrown out all the rusty farming paraphernalia, and set up in business doing what he loved best, restoring vintage cars. It didn't earn a mint, but as his wife worked as an optician's receptionist in town, it was enough.

A few years earlier, if he'd become bored walking his own land with Toby, he'd simply have crossed the road and entered the gate onto his neighbour's sprawling acres of grazing land. Not now, though. Eric Gibson had been shot dead by the Provos five years earlier. Then each of his two sons had been targeted, the first murdered as he walked in the morning darkness to the milking shed. A year later the youngest, a handsome strapping lad of twenty, after another shooting had been left with a steel plate in his skull and a mental age of three. His mother put the farm up for sale and moved out immediately. There were no willing Protestant buyers for a place with such a history and in such a notoriously dangerous area.

Albie Nairn had desperately tried to raise enough money, but no bank would touch the deal. Then the Doyle family had moved in from County Wicklow in the South. Local gossip had it the Doyles had bought the farm on a two per cent interest loan from the Catholic Church. It didn't surprise Nairn. Creeping ethnic cleansing, he called it, using the popular catch phrase from Bosnia. The process had been going on for twenty years, although it had accelerated noticeably in the past decade. First the Provos targeted Protestant farmers in the border counties that already had Catholic majorities, then the farms were sold, and were snapped up by immigrants from Eire. What were the figures he'd heard recently? Seventy-eight per cent of farms in the rural areas had been taken over by Catholics in the past twenty years. They were not statistics you'd ever hear the mainland politicians quoting; they kept it very quiet.

Short and stocky with a quiet voice and kindly face that was older than his fifty-five years, Albie was not a violent man. Indeed he had never even contemplated a personal act of violence. Or even helped plan it against others.

But for years he had known in his own mind what would eventually *have* to happen. Open civil war. It saddened him. The unpalatable and unspoken truth that in the end the only way to stop the violence would be to drive the Catholics out. Lock, stock and barrel. Because until that happened, there would never be peace. While the terrorists had a bedrock of tacit support in their aims from such a large minority of the population, then they would continue to thrive – like a virus for which there was no cure.

Albie Nairn threw a stick for Toby and while the dog rooted for it in a thick clump of dead undergrowth, he leaned against the gate and stared up the road to his bungalow.

His home, he thought, his land. His country. His family's

country. Once he'd traced his ancestors back in the parish records to the time of Elizabeth I. His family had lived here longer than the Virginia settlers had lived in America. And no little bastard with a balaclava and an Armalite was going to drive him out. Ever.

He glanced at his watch. Gone seven thirty. Time to get back for the Ulster fry his wife would be preparing for him before she left for work.

Calling Toby to heel, he started back and found himself humming that tune again. A sort of catchy rock-opera number. Just a few weeks back it seemed like it was always being played on the radio. Stirring lyrics that certainly stirred his blood. 'Red is the colour of anger. And black is the colour of hate. And yellow the colour of those who look on, doing nothing to alter their fate . . .' No doubting the meaning there. A call to arms, at least metaphorically speaking.

It was sung by a group of students called the Tain. That made Nairn smile. But the Tain and their song 'Colours' hadn't made everyone smile, far from it. Complaints flooded in from the Republican community. The BBC banned it overnight and projected concerts were cancelled in the interests of public order. Now tapes of the group's songs could only be bought privately by mail order and to hear them live you'd have to go to the packed bars and clubs in the Loyalist strongholds.

Nairn reached the gate, slipped on Toby's choke-chain and stepped onto the road. His son was coming out of their drive in his Mini, waving as he passed on his way south to Drogheda. After studying computer science at Queen's University in Belfast, young Brian had landed himself a plum job maintaining the Bank of Ireland's computer network.

Then Nairn stopped walking. A cold finger of fear ran down his vertebrae. Toby's hackles rose and he gave a low growl.

The nondescript saloon was pulled in on the verge opposite the drive to his bungalow. In the days before the Provo Army Council had announced its ceasefire, Nairn would always park an old wreck of a car to block the gateway. But now there was free access. He forced his legs to move; it took a strong physical effort, edging closer to the roadside opposite the car, ready to leap for the ditch. His eyes darting left and right, then glancing over his shoulder in case he'd missed someone behind him. His heart was thudding in his chest, his palms sweating.

He squinted, trying to see beyond the sheen of light on the car windscreen. Just a driver, he thought, but couldn't be certain. Toby's teeth clenched now, his growl deep, straining at the leash.

The side window suddenly rolled down. Inside a face was smiling. 'It's Albert Nairn, isn't it?'

God, the man was going to shoot him. Had a gun hidden on his lap. Nairn heard the words, but they weren't his. Some disembodied voice. Firm, confident. 'Who wants to know?'

'*Cuchulainn*,' the answer came.

Strange accent, Nairn thought abstractedly. Australian or American perhaps, not Irish.

The man's right arm was moving, his hand slipping beneath the lapel of his jacket.

In his mind Nairn was going over the word the stranger had said, picking out the phonetic breakdown. Koo-hull-in. *Cuchulainn*.

My God! His mouth dropped open. It had been so long since he'd heard that word. So long.

And yet only minutes ago he'd been humming that tune.

The driver's hand withdrew from his jacket. Not a gun in his hand, but a buff envelope. He reached out, offering it to Nairn.

Nairn just stared at it. *Cuchulainn, Cuchulainn, Cuchulainn.* The word spinning round and round inside his skull. *Cuchulainn*. The mythological Hound of Ulster. Dating back to the third century BC or even beyond. To times before there was the written word. *Cuchulainn*. The heroic Hound of Ulster who rose to resist the invaders from the southern kingdoms. Who fought alone while Ulster's warriors lay sick and helpless.

'Take it,' the man said. 'Quickly.'

Trembling fingers clutched the paper. Then suddenly his mind cleared, and he stuffed the envelope into his side pocket.

The car drew away, leaving Nairn standing and staring after it for a full minute before he walked slowly up his drive, his mind reeling.

'Albie, sure your breakfast is cremated,' his wife chided as he entered the kitchen to the smell of burnt bacon. She regarded him with concern. 'What is it? You look like you've seen a ghost.'

He smiled weakly. 'It's nothing. I just felt a little dizzy.'

Then he sat and tried to eat, thankful when his wife left a few minutes later to drive to work. He reached into his pocket, opened the envelope and spread the single sheet of orange-tinted paper on the table before him.

It read simply: TONIGHT. BE AT THE LAKE CAR PARK AT SUNDOWN. FOLLOW THE RAVEN VAN. HAVE A FACE MASK WITH YOU TO WEAR WHEN YOU LEAVE YOUR CAR.

YOU WILL BE BACK HOME BEFORE MIDNIGHT. TELL NO ONE OF THIS MESSAGE AND DESTROY IT IMMEDIATELY.

PS. YOUR NO IS 25.

He stared at it for a full five minutes before screwing it into a tight ball and dropping it into the furnace of the Aga boiler. Then he stepped into the front parlour and ran his eye over the three neat shelves of the bookcase. They were not a family of great readers. He found what he was looking for. A battered Oxford University Press paperback edition of *The Tain*, printed in 1970. A translation and interpretation of Ireland's most ancient fantasy legend, 'The Cattle Raid', a scholarly work by Thomas Kinsella. He flipped through the yellowing pages, the strangely powerful and mystic illustrations of the French artist Louis le Brocquy grabbing his attention as they always had. Semiabstract brush drawings that made him think of the cave drawings from the very dawn of time. Why did they make him shiver?

Page ninety-eight.

He read the verse:

> Dark one are you restless
> do you guess they gather
> to certain slaughter . . .
> the raven ravenous

>   among corpses of men . . .
>   death of sons
>   death of kinsmen
>   death death!

And there on the opposite page the inky blob. Like a psychologist's test. What does this remind you of? Nairn didn't really understand the words, but he understood a raven of death when he saw one. He'd had enough and replaced the book quickly amongst the other volumes. Why had it always made him feel like that?

He went to his writing desk and took the set of keys from the maker's secret compartment, then walked outside to a large outbuilding made of breezeblock and tin. Releasing the padlock he entered and switched on the fluorescent tube lighting. The large hut had been constructed in 1974 and had only ever been used for storage of the junk he habitually collected. Boxes and boxes of car parts and racks of panels prised from wrecked vehicles, all of which he thought might one day come in handy.

Carefully he picked his way through towards the back, remembering the day when the walls and roof had been completed, leaving an earthen floor. When the local builders had left, another team arrived with a small mechanical digger. Not usual workmen types, but quietly efficient, almost military in their manner. They did not speak much but when they did there was no mistaking the English accents. Hidden from prying eyes by the shell of walls and roof, they had finished their work in just a week. Then they left, never to be seen again. The concrete floor was a legacy of their handiwork. But only one.

At the rear half a dozen crates had been deliberately left empty and were therefore easy to shift. Beneath, the steel trap door glinted under the overhead light. Six heavy-duty padlocks: three combination types and three needing different keys. Once these were freed, he struggled to lift it open, the smell of musty air overwhelming him. He felt suddenly like the violator of a tomb, intent on plundering the treasure of the pharaohs.

To his surprise, the light switch worked, the flickering tubes below illuminating the steel ladder that descended vertically.

Gingerly he began his climb, down through two feet of reinforced concrete into the underground bunker.

He reached the bottom and looked around. Perhaps thirty feet by thirty. Wall-to-wall racking and more racks dividing the area into low corridors. It was amazing how much could be stored in such a confined space. Literally hundreds of weapons: assault rifles, sub-machine-guns, pistols and revolvers, all pristine and oiled direct from the manufacturers and all carefully wrapped in oilskin. None had ever been fired.

Other racks held metal ammunition cases, hundreds of them. Yet more held crates of grenades of every description. Another row was filled with radios and transmission equipment. A little dated now, but all still functioned perfectly well. Another wall of shelves was filled with anti-vehicle mines and another piled high with boxes of PE4 high explosive, detonators and coils of wire.

It had never really occurred to Albie Nairn before to ask whether or not all this stuff was still stable after nearly a quarter-century underground, whether he and his family were sitting virtually on top of one gigantic unexploded bomb.

Quickly he left the bunker and resecured the trap door before restacking the empty crates to hide its existence. When he'd finished, he felt a little shaky, a bit breathless. Like a mild anxiety attack. Going down there had been like passing through a time warp. Like becoming suddenly, brutally, back in touch with reality. The reality of over twenty years ago. He'd been a young man then, thirty-four and fit, admittedly a little overweight, but still fit. Now he had rheumatism in his fingers, a bad back and a spot of gut trouble.

He stepped out into the sunshine that was now breaking up the cloud and felt a sudden relaxing of tension as he locked the doors. But despite the fresh air, the smell of the mustiness and oiled gunmetal persisted in his nostrils.

Calmer now, he started walking back towards his bungalow. Then something made him stop and turn and look. Down the slope of the drive, across the road, over Doyle's pastures to the hills beyond.

On the other side of those hills was the enemy. The nearest

Catholic-dominated town, steeped in hard-line Republican tradition.

If – no, when – the enemy came over the hill, maybe now they would be ready for them.

Ten

While Albie Nairn was wondering exactly what was afoot, an increasing number of people were similarly approached as the day progressed.

Most were respectable and respected members of their communities: shopkeepers, farmers, teachers, businessmen, bank managers, solicitors – even police officers and clergymen. None had ever been connected with the Loyalist paramilitary gangs.

All, however, had at one time belonged to the Frontline Ulster Movement, an embryonic resistance organisation whose members had shared Albie Nairn's fears of an ultimate doomsday confrontation since the dark early years of the latest conflict. Everyone in the Northern Ireland community knew of its existence from its occasional strident proclamations, but also that it had withered on the vine over the years. Its long slow decline had been speeded by the conviction of its founder Wallace McIlroy on paedophilia charges; he later hanged himself. Since then the FUM was rarely found to be worth quoting by the media, and at most, its continued spluttering survival was seen as an irrelevant joke.

But that morning, before Nairn had taken Toby for his walk, all that had begun to change.

Stevie Gavin, known to everyone as Rattler, lived in the staunchly Loyalist area of the Shankill. Years before, he had selected the two-up two-down terraced house at the end of a cul-de-sac street that was marked by two gigantic gable-end murals, one depicting William of Orange astride his white charger and the other the red hand of Ulster in clenched-fist salute. The kerb stones were painted red, white and blue. No one, let alone an innocent Catholic, was ever going to wander into that dead end without knowing he was walking right inside the lion's mouth.

So there was only one way in to find Stevie Gavin, but there was another way out for him – at the back, through a specially concealed gate in the fence and into the adjoining rear garden, then through the neighbours' house and out into the street. He had a set of keys and he used them often, at any hour of the day, or more usually night. And, inexplicably, the streetlamp opposite that house had been the frequent target of vandalism. It had been permanently out of action for as long as anyone could remember.

Neither was Rattler on the telephone; there was no point as all calls were routinely monitored by intelligence agencies. So if someone wanted to reach the Ulster Defenders' chief, they had to be 'connected', to know who were the runners who had access to him. And even they did not know his whereabouts from day to day; he was always on the move and rarely at the place he called home. Sometimes with his girlfriend, sometimes not; like so many of the paramilitary leaders of all persuasions, he had sacrificed his wife and child and normality in general to the cause he believed in.

There were plastic venetian blinds at all the windows and they were always shut. Stevie Gavin lived perpetually in a world of artificial light, in constant fear of surveillance and the assassin's bullet, both here and wherever else he stayed. The front door was never answered and those who knew the routine would go down the side of the house to the back door, so triggering the infra-red light switch and the audio alarm inside. That would give Gavin time to arm himself and identify the caller on closed-circuit TV before his bodyguard opened the steel-plated door.

Peter Keegan remembered the system of old and Johan van Niekerk, who knew Rattler from the past, had recently dropped in to check it out. It had been a friendly reunion and over tea both men had speculated on the mysterious escape from a mainland prison of Rattler's erstwhile friend who had betrayed his organisation. Before he left, van Niekerk had arranged to see Gavin again in a few days' time.

That was how Keegan could be certain Rattler would be home this night.

And Rattler's escape route, his way out, would be the way

in for them. All four approaching singly and from different directions on opposite sides of the street. Keegan and van Niekerk from the east, Gaza and Hutch from the west. Converging to meet in the patch of shadow beneath the shattered streetlamp.

Gaza jemmying the window, slipping inside and letting them in through the front door. All on tiptoe so as not to wake the family sleeping above their heads. Out through the back into the garden adjoining that of Stevie Gavin.

Van Niekerk's steady aim on the infra-red security light, taking it out with the second silenced round. Then go. In through the concealed door in the fence. Sledgehammers coming out from under long raincoats.

A sudden rain of blows shattering the urban quiet, rending timber, locks and hinges torn from their mountings. Bolts and chains ripped free under the frenzied pounding. Seeming like minutes because their lives depended on the speed of entry, but in reality only thirty seconds.

Then in. Team splitting: van Niekerk and Hutch into the living room, catching the bodyguard groggily awake, still tangled up in his sleeping bag on the sofa.

Gaza already heading up the stairs, Keegan trailing. The younger man going through the bedroom door like it wasn't there. Which was as well because it was bolted and the sheer force of his shouldered entry had ripped it clear.

Light from the landing fell across the carpet and the bed. A woman sitting upright, her face as white as the sheet she had clutched to her chest. Caught midway between the bed and the window was Rattler, dressed in boxer shorts and carrying a Magnum. He froze, startled, unsure whether or not to shoot it out.

'HALT OR I FIRE!' Gaza yelled, already on one knee and his gun unwavering in a double-handed grip.

'Fuckin' army,' Rattler muttered in disgust as he realised he was a second too late.

Keegan entered behind his friend. 'Not the army, Stevie, we're friends.'

Rattler's jaw dropped and a fringe of lank black hair fell

across his forehead to half-obscure his dark and glittering eyes. 'You?'

'The gun, drop it!' Gaza snapped. After tours on the streets of Londonderry and Belfast he knew better than to take any chances with a terrorist gunman. Especially one with the reputation of Rattler.

Gavin let it clatter to the linoleum floor. 'I don't believe this.'

Keegan thought how vulnerable the other man looked now, vulnerable and harmless. His face gaunt and his body thin to the point of emaciation, stripped of its flesh by years of nervous tension, of never knowing. The skin was so pale it was obvious he hadn't seen proper daylight for months. Not for Rattler casual weekend strolls with the family in the park or sunning on a beach. His was a dark secret world of rooms with the shutters down and cars with tinted windows. Scurrying furtively from bolt hole to bolt hole, seeking safety. Knowing that to stay in any one place for too long was to die. And his face now said he'd been in this house one fateful night too many.

'I've not come here to kill you, Stevie.'

The eyes did not blink. After a moment, Gavin said hoarsely: 'So what the fuck?'

'We're going to take a trip.'

On the bed, the woman whimpered, still clutching the sheet.

'Shut up!' Rattler ordered, not taking his eyes from Keegan.

'You'll be back here tomorrow night, Stevie. That's a promise.'

Then van Niekerk appeared at the door, pushing the hapless minder before him. 'So you can tell your goon here and your lady friend not to send the boys out looking.'

'Johan?' Rattler squinted at the light. 'You bastard, you were in on this. You bloody set me up.'

'It had to be done,' Keegan said. 'We need your help.'

'My *what*?' The man stared, incredulous. 'You fuckin' Brit informer, you want my help! Like shit!'

There was a slight smile on Keegan's face. 'That's why we had to do it like this. Sorry. Things are about to change.'

'What things?'

'We're activating the Frontline.'

Rattler started as though the other man was mad. 'This has to be a joke.'

'No, Stevie. It's time to activate the FUM,' he repeated.

'Any time until last year was time to activate the Frontline,' Rattler jeered. 'Not now in the middle of this laughable bloody peace process. I know it won't last, but I'm buggered if I'm goin' to be the one to restart it.'

'That's why I want you to come with me now,' Keegan said softly. 'To listen to what I have to say.'

Rattler shook his head. 'And why should I listen to you? Correct me if I'm wrong, but didn't you spy on me for over twenty years on and off, reporting everything back to the army and MI5?' He almost spat the words in his contempt.

Keegan considered that for a moment. 'At the time I thought I was right to do it, and mostly I still do. I didn't want it degenerating into a full civil war. You and the Ulster Defenders have always been at the centre, Stevie, the hard core. Not afraid to commit any atrocity . . .'

The eyes facing him hooded fractionally; Rattler didn't like terms like that.

'It played into the hands of the enemy,' Keegan concluded. 'A bad press. Got Whitehall and the general public thinking we're as bad as the Provos, so wash their hands of the lot of us! That's why I did what I did.'

Rattler snapped back: 'Kill six Taigs for every one of ours – random terror of the innocent – it worked well enough to drive the Provos finally to a ceasefire!'

'I won't deny that,' Keegan replied. 'And it also worked well enough for the Gestapo.'

The man ignored the jibe. 'And if I refuse to come with you?'

'We do need you, Stevie. I'm sure we can put our differences behind us. We need you and your experienced players to form –' he hunted for the right word ' – our tungsten tip.'

That brought a thin and humourless smile to Rattler's lips. 'Very poetic. But, I repeat, what if I want no part in this?'

Keegan placed a hand on the man's shoulder, but Gavin drew back. 'Okay, Stevie, the bottom line is I can't afford not to have you with us. You and your people are too dangerous to have as enemies.'

Behind them van Niekerk raised his silenced pistol. He said nothing, didn't have to.

A pink tongue flicked along Rattler's lips and his eyes shone darkly as he glanced momentarily at the woman on the bed and then down at his boxer shorts. 'You would seem to have me at a disadvantage.'

At twenty minutes to seven, Albie Nairn drove into the lakeside car park.

His heart was thudding. What the hell was he getting himself into? Ceasefire or no ceasefire, this could be a setup. He could just have accepted an invitation to his own funeral. Anyone could be behind it, an old enemy or a new one. Provo or Loyalist, who knew? Anyone who thought he was connected might have a grudge.

And here he was, driving slowly into the car park glowing in the golden light of a blood-red October sunset over the lake, a mist floating above the still green waters. Perhaps the last sight he would ever see.

There were four cars already there, each facing towards the view. He made a wide circling sweep, getting as close to each vehicle in turn without making it too obvious he was checking the occupants. But there was no one he thought he knew or even recognised.

One car was empty – no doubt its passengers out walking by the lake – a courting couple huddled lovingly together in another. Single men sat in the other two and Nairn wondered why? Snatching a few moments away from nagging wives, pondering their fate – or was it something more sinister? Both had glanced at him as his car rolled by. Furtive eyes, he thought, wary. Much like his own.

Don't park too close, he told himself, just in case. If they make a run at your car, give yourself enough distance to get clear. He slowed and stopped. Facing the lake because that could be the only reason for being here. But leaving the bumper six feet from the fence and putting the wheels on full left-hand lock so he'd have space to clear in one sweeping movement if he needed to drive out fast.

He switched off the engine and waited.

Five minutes. Twilight dimming quickly; now cars on the road had their lights on. The courting couple drove away. Then another car swung in.

Nairn's mouth went dry, watching in his mirror as the car crossed behind him, kept going and parked at the far end. No one got out. He breathed again.

More lights on the road, something else entering the car park. A white van, Transit type. It cruised slowly in a wide circle, past each vehicle in turn but without stopping.

What the hell was the driver playing at?

As it drove back past him, he saw the emblem on the side. A black blob design, the unmistakable drawing by Louis le Brocquy. Above it the words: Raven Laundry.

Already the vehicle was disappearing, working its way back to the main road, flasher going, indicating right. Nairn fumbled for his key, rushing to start the engine. Stalled it in his haste. Tried again. Sod, have I flooded the carb? he asked himself. He closed his eyes in relief as it fired at last and he engaged gear.

By now, the van was on the road, another car already following it out. He recognised it as belonging to one of the solitary men. Damn, he might block his view of the Raven Laundry van. Light shone in his rear mirror. Someone falling in behind him.

Too late now. He joined the main road, the car behind still following. Following him? His heart began to thud again.

It took ten minutes and several distinct changes of route before he slowly began to realise. All three cars were following the Raven van. He was in a convoy.

'It's been organised like a rave party,' Keegan explained. 'The people we've called up have no idea of the final destination.'

Rattler was in the back of the car, squeezed between Keegan and van Niekerk. They'd been travelling in darkness down country roads for almost an hour and he'd lost all sense of direction. Somewhere in Armagh or Tyrone, on the borders. 'It

238

won't work, Peter. You'll be riddled with informers.' He smiled then at the irony of his words. 'You should know – you were one. Perhaps you still are, getting in on the ground floor of this new outfit.'

'You'll have to trust me, Stevie. This is clean. Pure driven snow.'

'Forgive me if I laugh.'

'Laugh all you like. Just listen to what is said.'

But with quiet satisfaction, Keegan noted that Gavin wasn't laughing. As each hour had passed since they'd snatched him that morning, Gavin had become steadily more thoughtful.

'We're here,' Gaza announced suddenly and pulled off the road onto a narrow tarmac track. Ahead was a cluster of car lights.

'And where is here?' Gavin asked.

Keegan tapped his nose. 'Need to know, Stevie, need to know. Things are going to be very different from now on.'

Gavin could see now that they'd stopped in a private car park. There were scores of vehicles: family saloons, estates, muddy four-wheel drives belonging to farmers, a couple of motorcycles, two small lorries – and vans. He noticed three white vans, each with a strange symbol and the words Raven Laundry.

People were everywhere, milling around and waiting, but not talking. It was a mild shock to see that everyone was wearing some kind of mask, whether a balaclava or handkerchief.

Van Niekerk nudged him and handed him a woollen ski mask. 'Put this on,' he ordered.

Rattler obeyed, still bemused by the entire business.

Then they were out, fully masked and standing around with the others. A little farther ahead, he saw the lights of what was undoubtedly an Orange Lodge hall. The sign outside had been thoughtfully draped in black cloth to emphasise that this was unofficial business.

One hooded figure wearing a red armband detached itself from a group nearby and walked up to Keegan. 'It's gone well. I reckon we've had an eighty per cent takeup.'

'Well done, Tim. Right, let's get everyone inside.'

His son walked away and, with two other masked men, began

acting as usher to shepherd the bewildered gathering into the hall.

Stevie Gavin walked alongside Keegan. Despite himself, he found his excitement and expectation mounting. He was beginning, just beginning to be impressed. A month ago Keegan was in a mainland prison with six years left to serve. Now this.

They shuffled through the double doors and into the hall. Limp flags of the local Orange Order stood racked along one wall like the forlorn pennants of a defeated army. A trestle table had been set out on the stage and above it hung a stencilled banner in Gaelic script. *Cuchulainn*.

'You've not forgotten,' Gavin remarked.

'No,' Keegan said. 'And it's never been more appropriate.'

The other man indicated the rows of plastic-backed stacking chairs put out for the audience. 'Where do I sit?'

'On the stage with me. It's all right, no one else here knows who you are. I want you to see them, see how they react. I want you to feel part of this, Stevie. It's important.'

Rattler shrugged and followed up into the wings and to the seat that was indicated to him. He felt uncomfortable. A sea of masked faces, eyes staring at him expectantly. He didn't like it at all. His was the world of shadows, of not being seen.

Then the double doors were shut, Hutch and Gaza standing guard. Keegan rose to his feet.

He paused, savouring the atmosphere of nervous anticipation. Total silence, not a shuffle, not a cough. 'Gentlemen, I will keep you for only a short time. And afterwards we shall not meet again like this until it is all over.

'What is over, you will ask? I shall explain. The Frontline Ulster Movement is at last, after twenty years, being called to arms in defence of the province. It is a long time since you pledged your allegiance to fight for your homeland and I understand that some of you may have modified your views. That is your individual choice and it will be respected. If at any time during the next half-hour you decide you want no part of this, you may just walk out. You have been specially chosen. Also each of you was issued with a number when you were summoned. Just give it to the usher on your way out and wait outside. We will all leave *together*, not before. And I assure you, no harm will befall any of you who decide to go.' He hesitated. 'However, your silence about this meeting *will* be absolute, whether you leave or stay with us. There will be no bar gossip and no pillow talk. For *anyone* found to have talked, retribution will be swift and deadly. Remember that. This meeting has never taken place and to talk of it will be considered as treason by Frontline's war council and dealt with accordingly.

'My identity is known to just a few people here and I intend to keep it that way. Your identities are known *only* to me *en masse* and individually you will only ever be referred to by the number you've been given. My number is One. Further, your names do not appear on any government intelligence data as being members of Frontline. I cannot tell you how this has been achieved, but rest assured that it has.

'It is our intention to organise you into four-man cells of complementary talents. This will support cells for our active service units, providing logistical and technical support, from storage and false documentation to transport, communications, and safe houses. No one will be asked to carry out active service missions which will be conducted only by volunteers with professional military training. Units will be drawn from cells and tasked to individual assignments.'

'Wait a minute!' interrupted a large man rising to his feet in the front row; judging by his clothes, he was a farmer. His borrowed pink ski mask looked incongruous in this setting. 'What the hell is all this about and why now, in the middle of a ceasefire? It doesn't make sense. We've got peace for the first time in a generation and I for one intend my grandchildren should enjoy it!'

Keegan nodded his understanding. 'Believe me, I know exactly how you feel. And I also know how you'd feel about your grandchildren growing up in the Republic of Ireland, knowing that you did nothing to stop it.'

That produced a rippling murmur of agreement through the audience.

'We will do nothing to shatter that peace although we know it is just a callous tactical manoeuvre,' Keegan assured. 'All of us

241

in this hall tonight know that it will not, cannot, last without a massive breach of faith by the British Government. None of us on the platform have any doubt that they will not dare openly betray the Protestant majority of Northern Ireland and be seen to submit to PIRA terrorists, however much they would like to. That means that they cannot give the terrorists what they demand. And therefore they cannot square the circle. This ceasefire is the cruellest deception yet to be presented to the decent, law-abiding folk of Ulster. And because the Provos cannot have what they demand, they will return to violence, sooner or later. Even if Sinn Fein got as far as all-party talks, within a month they would realise that ten per cent of the electorate cannot dictate its will to the rest.

'And when the war returns to the streets of London, Belfast and Londonderry, then we must be ready. That is why we are calling you to arms NOW!'

This time the murmur from the crowd was more than a ripple. Keegan had hit a chord, echoing what most had been thinking privately.

He continued quickly: 'For a quarter-century this organisation has stayed its hand. Has trusted the British Government to do its duty by us, its loyal citizens. But clearly we can now see that our trust has been misplaced. Tempted by the ceasefire, London is contemplating the unthinkable, the reunification of Ulster and Eire by stealth and sleight of hand. Note that there is only *one* topic on the agenda. Not whether Eire left the Commonwealth illegally to set up the Republic or that it should rejoin the United Kingdom. Oh no, not that. So in truth there is only one subject to be discussed – how our homeland can be pushed closer and irreversibly into the arms of Dublin. That and nothing else. And I can tell you exactly what the plan is. To set up so many cross-border institutions and to involve the Irish Government in every aspect of the province's political decision making, that Ireland becomes united in all but actual name. It will ruthlessly use the bribe of funding from the evil European Union and its creeping federalism and the ERM in order to achieve its aims. The result of any so-called referendum in Ulster won't mean a thing. It won't change the *reality* of the situation.' He paused to allow his words to sink in, and knew he had his audience rapt. Was speaking aloud the thoughts of every one of them. 'And when the ceasefire ends – as it will – are we again going to sit confined in our homes for the next twenty-five years and watch this country being raped again, its people and its policemen killed and maimed, the fabric of our society ripped to shreds? Watch while the British Government again does nothing and ties the hands of all those who can with its legal niceties and yellow cards? We know who and where the Provos are, so does Whitehall. They always have done, but they've never done anything about it. Nor will they in the *next* twenty-five years!'

More nods and murmurs of approval. But not everyone was convinced; the farmer was on his feet again. 'If you're right and the ceasefire ends, then surely we Protestants and Loyalists will have no fears of being pushed into a United Ireland in the way you've said.'

'I wish you were right,' Keegan answered quickly. 'But have you really thought it through? I have. Already we have enjoyed a year of peace. And we'll continue to do so. Until next month, next year. Just when the British Government thinks it has lasting peace in its grasp, it will be snatched away! What do you think their reaction will be to that? Think about it. They will fall over backwards to make even more concessions. If PIRA resumes its bombings and shootings, then, for a while at least, Sinn Fein will be excluded. But the SDLP, Dublin, Whitehall and Washington will beaver away to get some solution that will still persuade the terrorists to stop. They will still try, *even harder*, to give the Provos what they want. Nothing will have changed.

'Already the British have opened all doors to Sinn Fein, including PIRA Army Council members; they've given way on the argument of the permanence of the ceasefire and accepted weasel words instead. They've allowed Adams and his ilk to go to the mainland and lifted the media ban and they're releasing terrorist prisoners early. Now they're talking of a twin-talk approach to get round the cornerstone condition of disarmament-before-talks. They've taken the troops off the streets, torn

243

down the border checks and have started a phased military withdrawal. All for nothing, absolutely nothing in return. How many more concessions will they make in their desperation to get a settlement? To get rid of us at any price? They will find some format, some formula. All this encouraged by a duped Washington regime in the thrall of the papist Irish lobby and desperate to claim credit for peace before the presidential election!

'And do you really think a British Government – of any colour – will resist? You've seen how far down the road of appeasement they've already gone. Peace at any price, no matter how unjust!'

'Bloody true!' someone called, and his words were answered by cries of agreement.

Keegan knew he had them then, was talking their language. 'We have been and are being betrayed by the leaders of our own nation. And I ask you this:

"Treason doth never prosper, what's the reason?
For if it prosper, none dare call it treason." '

He stared defiantly at the packed rows of people. 'Well, we dare!' Then his voice rose to fill the rafters. 'NO SURRENDER! GOD SAVE THE QUEEN!'

Abruptly he resumed his seat as the audience erupted, leaping to their feet with fists and voices raised in a chant of approval, chorusing his last words, turning to each other, hearts burning and eyes on fire beneath masks and balaclavas. At last a voice had been heard in the wilderness, a voice that echoed every personal belief and fear they had each had for so, so long. Just when their spirits were finally crushed, their will to fight eroded by a smothering sense of helplessness, with their politicians mouthing the same old no surrender rhetoric as they again gave away a little more of their cultural identity, their heritage and their birthright to Southern neighbours who had chosen to become a foreign nation state. Now, suddenly, it was as though a banner had been unfurled, a battle ensign fluttering before them. In their imaginations they could already hear the flutes and the heavy beat of the Lambeg drum. And above the triumphal marching band, the voice of a leader calling them to arms.

The ovation continued, the cheering and the clapping rolling on, even when Keegan once again rose to his feet. Van Niekerk glanced pointedly at his watch; the longer this rally ran, the greater the danger of being compromised.

Keegan raised his right hand and to his surprise the noise died away immediately. Total obedience. 'Gentlemen, if any of you wish to leave, now is the time to do so. To remain, you should be *totally* committed – otherwise go. We respect your view. But you must wait outside with our usher until we all leave together.'

Again he was surprised when only two people, decidedly embarrassed, rose and edged awkwardly to the side. There were a few low hisses and boos, but mostly the eyes inside the masks watched them go with disdain.

As the exit door closed, Keegan said: 'Our intelligence tells us that Dublin anticipates the withdrawal of British troops from our province soon, to be replaced by some other international force. Perhaps London does not foresee it, but the Irish Government expects a badly organised Loyalist uprising, an apocalyptic pogrom as bad as anything we've witnessed in the former Yugoslavia. And it has contingency plans, as it always has, for its army to rescue the Catholic population. After which, you may be assured, it will not again retreat.

'We have evidence that Dublin has spent millions of punts of EU grant aid in the past few years to totally re-equip its armed forces beyond any self-defence or UN peace-keeping role. So you can see that time is short. But rest assured our plans are well in hand. We have communications, sophisticated arms and explosives and we have a campaign. Not a campaign of slaughtering the innocents like the butchers of the Provisional IRA, but a campaign to bring the Republic to its knees economically and spiritually. And our demands will be simple and clear.

'To withdraw from the Anglo-Irish Agreement of 1986, giving Dublin a say in the running of a foreign nation state, and to intern all members of the IRA south of the border.

'And, most important of all, to remove from that country's written constitution – and from its very psyche – its claim on Ulster. Because, my friends, despite all the talk and hollow promises of the past ten years, it remains. The *one* thing that Dublin could have done during twenty-five years to allay our fears and to discredit and disinherit the IRA, and still it has not done so.

'So we will do it for them and hit them so hard they will no longer *want* our homeland for their own! They will realise we are not worth the Holy Roman candle!

'*Cuchulainn* has arisen. Collectively we are now the Hound of Ulster, so appropriate to come again to the rescue of our people from the southern invaders while our warriors lie sick and defenceless. We are at war with Dublin.' He raised his right hand in a clenched salute – all but Rattler, who stared in incredulity, suddenly noticing that every other man on the platform wore a red glove. '*CUCHULAINN! CUCHULAINN! CUCHULAINN!*'

The voices of the audience rose as one, seeming to shake the roof and walls like an earthquake. Everyone was on their feet, shouting their support, carried along by the excitement of it all.

It was then that one figure of slender build stood to one side of the platform. Only as the mouth within the balaclava opened and the first pure notes floated above the audience, was it realised that the singer was a girl. The effect was shocking, her voice like crystal and needing no accompaniment as the words now familiar to everyone present rose to a soul-rending crescendo. 'Red is the colour of anger, And black is the colour of hate, And yellow the colour of those who look on – doing nothing to alter their fate!'

More rapturous applause. Keegan turned quietly to Rattler. 'Okay, Stevie, we leave now. Quick, on your feet.'

Still bemused the man joined the departing group from the platform, down the steps and past the waving forest of arms reaching to touch them and slap their backs like fans of a winning football team.

Suddenly they were outside in the clear night air, all relieved to be away from the heat and clamour of the packed hall.

246

'Back to the car?' Rattler asked.

Tim tugged his arm. 'No, the other way. To the helicopter.'

Rattler did a double-take and changed direction. 'A chopper? Are you takin' the piss?'

'No,' Keegan replied, lengthening his stride. 'We'll be out of the province and over the border in five minutes. Low level all the way.'

'Am I supposed to be impressed?' he sneered.

Keegan pulled off his balaclava and ruffled his hair to let the breeze cool the perspiration from his scalp. 'Were you?'

'It was like a fuckin' Nuremberg rally.'

'That good?' van Niekerk joked.

'That good,' returned Rattler, 'if you're a fan of Adolf Hitler.' He continued walking, clearly turning something over in his mind. 'So what's this campaign you were talking about?'

Keegan didn't even have to pause to think. 'We're going to hit them where it hurts. Destroy their tourist industry and agriculture, their banking system. Then their infrastructure – transport, electricity, water, gas. We'll make it impossible for them to sell their produce abroad. I've had years to work this out.'

For once Stevie Gavin let his mask slip a fraction. 'Well, if that rally was an example of your planning, I suppose you could just succeed.'

His former friend stopped walking. 'With you and your people with us, Stevie, we can't fail.'

Rattler's eyes narrowed. 'Why the hell should I help you?'

Keegan looked up into a clear sky full of stars, something he had rarely seen for over five long years. 'Because in the end, Stevie, you were right and I was wrong. Those bastards in Whitehall betrayed me then, just like they're betraying the entire province now.'

Rattler didn't answer as they continued walking, but he began to feel something, a sensation filling his chest. A sensation he had not experienced for many a dark year. Pride.

Back at the hall car park, Albie Nairn was one of the last to leave. He sat in his car, humming that tune as his mind reeled and he watched the vehicles queuing to go through the gate.

247

Then he remembered he was still wearing his balaclava and swiftly pulled it off. He realised that his eyes were full of tears.

The monthly progress meet was on neutral ground. Old habits died hard and anyway Roger Pinfold knew that Harry Grisewold would insist if he himself had not.

Everything boxed and separate. That was how to keep secrets secret.

Too many prying eyes and ears in London, so Pinfold took the suburban line rattletrap out of Waterloo to Surbiton. He knew Grisewold lived in the area somewhere, sharing his flat with Margie Lewis. Both reliable, both former staffers and now running one of several private investigation agencies that the Security Service frequently used.

However, he made sure that Grisewold's outfit only ever worked for him; that way no documentation would exist at Thames House. Pinfold was in a position of such authority to allow him to syphon off whatever funding was needed from other deniable and highly classified black operations as was necessary. No one above him would ever call him to account.

Everything boxed and separate.

His mind was preoccupied on the journey by two things. Both, as far as he knew, unrelated. The first was the continuing disappearance of the prisoner Peter Keegan. No hint, not even a whisper of where he might be. Nothing from immigration, the Prison Service, Special Branch or the Anti-Terrorist Branch. Zilch. He had disappeared off the face of the earth. Fine, Pinfold thought, as long as he stayed that way.

Of course, Curtis Manning of the CIA would be clucking around like some paranoid chicken looking for its head. Always running scared when he'd lost control of someone who knew too much, especially if he thought this might upset his beloved President's peace process. Pinfold had been fielding phone calls for a week, allowing his secretary to do the stonewalling.

The other subject that niggled at the back of his mind was an intelligence signal that had come through from Northern Ireland. An uncorroborated report that there'd been stirrings in the Frontline Ulster Movement, a quasi-paramilitary group that Pinfold's department had long regarded as toothless and moribund. Probably it was another of their occasional outbursts of predictable vitriol which even the Belfast newspapers ignored. Rumour of a meeting or rally in some remote rural backwater near the border. A bunch of anal-retentive, teetotal churchgoers, thought Pinfold dismissively, that's all the Frontline had ever been. All bullshit and no action in twenty-five years.

But once again it might just be enough to get Curtis Manning twitchy, so Pinfold for one was not about to tell him. He just hoped Manning hadn't learnt that once, as impressionable youths, both Peter Keegan and Rodney Littlechild had been members. That would really get him going.

The train pulled in and Pinfold alighted, making his way across the high street to the dingy little cafe that served breakfasts all day long. It was nearly empty and Grisewold sat at his usual table, munching on a fried egg wedge. Pinfold collected a chipped cup of stewed tea from the counter and joined him.

Grisewold nodded without speaking because his mouth was full and shoved the plastic folder across the table.

'What's this?'

'It's what that ex-cop Derek Penny gave Lomax,' the other man replied, and a tiny gobbet of chewed egg landed on the folder. Pinfold flicked it away distastefully as Grisewold swallowed and cleared his mouth. 'They're keeping several copies at different locations – I thought it was less obvious to snatch the one from Lomax's pad – especially as we've already been inside the place.'

'How long have you had these?'

'Couple of weeks.'

'They aren't photographs.'

Grisewold sniffed. 'We didn't have time before the sister came back. Devil of a job to find it as it was. We just snatched it and ran. Made it look like a burglary.'

But Pinfold wasn't listening. 'God, Harry, have you seen this stuff? It's all highly classified department material. Where the hell did Penny get it from?'

'From when he was running his inquiry in Belfast, I should think. When he discovered what Keegan was up to.'

Pinfold nodded. 'Through the RUC, or maybe the army,' he agreed. 'I certainly had no idea he'd got hold of this stuff.'

'It'll interest the jury,' Griswold said absently, pausing to call to the waitress for a jam doughnut. 'Reads like Roddy Little-child was the best agent the Brits ever had.'

No panic, Pinfold thought. His mind raced ahead, a mind endlessly practised in the art of damage limitation, seeking for the weakness that he knew must be there somewhere. Then he saw it. 'Of course, Harry, these are only photocopies. Who's got the originals?'

Griswold smiled, not an especially edifying sight. Pinfold, the smug bastard, wasn't always as smart as he thought he was. 'Your department, I should think, boss. Tucked away in the vaults. No one would have handed over original classified stuff to Derek Penny. They'd have swung for it. You're looking at copies of copies.'

'Ah,' Pinfold said, suddenly seeing the light. 'Forgeries.'

'Don't look like the real thing to me, boss,' he said with a dry chuckle. 'Given the sequential numbering, I'm sure you could trace the actual originals.' He lit a cigarette.

Pinfold considered for a moment. 'That still leaves us with the problem of Derek Penny himself. He can give evidence as to his source and the authenticity of these documents.'

'Perhaps he can be persuaded otherwise.'

Pinfold shook his head. 'Not Derek Penny. That's why Keegan is,' he corrected himself, 'was doing a stretch. His army handlers and the RUC put real pressure on for Penny to drop it. He refused point blank.'

'And your department?' Griswold asked casually; but he was never a good actor when performing in front of Pinfold.

'I think you know the answer to that,' he replied reproach-fully. 'My department were remitted to run a different agenda by then, looking to the future.'

Griswold chuckled. 'A rogue element, eh?'

A patina of ice crystals seemed to glaze Pinfold's eyes. 'Quite the contrary, Harry, my department's instructions have always come from the very top. And at that time we were beginning to realise that Keegan and his ilk would become an embarrassment and a liability.'

'So you let him go swing?'

The MI5 man's expression didn't alter. 'You'd do well to remember that, Harry.'

Oh, I will, you bastard, Grisewold's eyes said. But his voice spoke different words: 'Problem with people like Penny is that they don't bend.'

'What do you mean?'

'Any engineer will tell you. Things that don't bend under pressure – well, they snap.'

Pinfold regarded the other man carefully. 'I don't see Penny snapping. Not the sort.'

'He's exactly the sort. He's bitter and twisted, full of disillusion with his former police colleagues, the Home Office, the government. He's not exactly hard up, but he's got to be careful. And he's not well.'

'How d'you know that?' Pinfold began and stopped himself; his department did it all the time. Banks and NHS regional authorities with their central computer records were an open book to the Security Service.

'He suffers with nerves. Regular prescriptions for Valium and sleeping pills. He's got a small overdraught and negative equity. I don't think it would take much to push him over the edge.'

'What do you have in mind?'

'Something Margie suggested.'

Momentarily Pinfold imagined the two of them in some squalid little flat. The insatiable slag up to all her old tricks that were legendary in the service; then after, lying in their stale sweat, having a cigarette while they picked over the intimate personal details of Derek Penny's life. 'Tell me.'

'He prides himself on his integrity, always has. But if some question was to arise of some impropriety . . .'

At that moment Pinfold's mobile began bleeping. 'Okay, Harry, leave it with me.' Irritably he tugged the telephone from his jacket. 'Hello,' he snapped.

'Mr Prendergast?' It was a woman's voice. 'Jane Wednesday

251

here, Attorney-General's Office.' Her tone was very self-assured but, he detected, slightly ruffled. 'I thought you'd want to know of a most extraordinary occurrence in the case of Police v. Littlechild.'

'That's most kind of you, Miss Wednesday.' His oily response disguised the fluttering he felt in his heart. 'What's happened?'

'Sir Joshua Stokes has had a witness summons issued against him. I think it's quite unprecedented.'

'I'm sorry, who?'

'The director general of the Metropolitan Police Forensic Science Laboratory at Lambeth. A witness summons has been issued obliging him to appear before an examining magistrate at Woolwich to explain why forensic samples have not been provided to the defence – or at least access granted to the defence's own experts. Sir Joshua is absolutely outraged.'

'Who's responsible for this?' Pinfold wasn't even aware that it could be done.

'The defence solicitors, Eisner, Pollock and Browne.'

Pinfold closed his eyes. 'Her!'

'Yes, Samantha Browne. She might just as well have subpoenaed Her Majesty or the Prime Minister. Sir Joshua is just not treated in this manner.'

'Is it legal?'

She hesitated. 'Unheard of, yes. Actually illegal, no. Browne has clearly browbeaten and misled the magistrate into issuing the summons. I am fully aware that she's a canny operator – after all, she is on our unofficial blacklist.'

'So what can be done about it?' Pinfold cut in.

'Well, I can certainly have the CPS refer the matter to the Law Society. Such an action is clearly a breach of the agreed code of conduct.'

But Pinfold's life had been dedicated to circumventing codes of conduct in all respects. 'No, I mean what can be done about the summons itself?'

'Well, I'm sure the Met and your department have no intention of having Sir Joshua dragged before some magistrate like a common criminal any more than I do. Lambeth will just have to give the Littlechild case top priority – and give way to Browne's demands.'

Pinfold didn't mention that the case results had been given priority on his personal instruction, but also with the heavy hint that there should be no great rush to release them to the defence. He said: 'Well, thank you for advising me, Miss Wednesday. Please continue to keep me informed of any further developments.'

As he folded away his mobile, Grisewold asked him what had happened. When Pinfold explained, the investigator scratched thoughtfully at the day's growth of stubble on his chin. 'Well, if the CPS is going to refer the matter of the Browne woman's conduct to the Law Society, they can add something else.'

'What's that?'

'The defence has been sniffing around prosecution witnesses without agreement with the police or CPS.'

'How d'you know that?'

'We've got Lomax under twenty-four-hour surveillance.' He gave a smug little smile. 'That tracer I indented for – the one you complained about – well, it's paid off. If my team had to be right up his arse, he'd have spotted them by now.'

'Lomax?' Pinfold repeated. 'You can't report *him* to the Law Society.'

'He's acting for Browne, boss. Her junior clerk did the legwork in her free time, then Lomax and a mate of his followed up with the actual questioning. Browne's hired Lomax to act as a private dick. He's spoken to Salmon, the landlord of the Mortar and Pestle.'

'Interviewed him?' Pinfold paled. Salmon's evidence could be crucial.

'More like threatened to break his legs.'

'Did he say anything?'

'I don't think so. My boys paid a little follow-up call. He's more scared of losing his pub. But just to be sure we roughed him up a little bit, broke a few optics. He's more scared of us than Lomax.'

'Be careful, Harry. I don't want this blowing up in our faces.' He glanced at his watch. 'Look, I've got to catch the next train back into town. Meanwhile, I want Browne and Lomax watched like hawks.'

'I'm doing my best, boss. They're both fully wired to sound, so to speak. But my team's pretty stretched. They're exhausted – there's only so much four people can do.'

Pinfold didn't like that, even if it was stating the obvious.

'I've got to keep the lid on, Harry, so I can't draft in staffers. Haven't you any more people you can hire?'

Grisewold smiled. 'You can't get the quality nowadays, and when you do it comes expensive.'

'I've got to keep the budget under control or else it'll start to show.'

God, Grisewold thought, he'd find the funding soon enough if things went wrong and his own neck was on the line. He said: 'Then there's not a lot *more* I can do.'

Pinfold rose to his feet, leaving his tea untouched. 'Leave it with me, Harry, I'll see what I can do.'

But on the train journey back to Waterloo, he did not give it too much thought, preoccupied as he was with the meeting he was due to have with Lord Moffat and the American Curtis Manning. When he called in at his office in Thames House before going to the electronically swept conference room, he glimpsed the letter on the top of his IN-tray. Recognising the crest of the Staffordshire Police Force, he snatched it up.

'Jesus,' he breathed as he scanned its contents. 'That's all I need.' He stuffed it into his pocket and set off for the basement.

Curtis Manning clearly considered himself to be a mover of mountains, and preferably before breakfast. Big and raw-boned, he had the bearing of a military commander who had never contemplated defeat in his life, even when it stared him in the face. It showed in his glittering gimlet eyes and the defiant jut of his chin.

In his mid-fifties, he'd cut his teeth on the Bay of Pigs operation in Cuba and had been immersed in the sewerage of US clandestine ops ever since. Nam, Cambodia, Laos, El Salvador, Nicaragua, Afghanistan and South Africa. More recently he'd been involved in rearming the Croats in the former Yugoslavia.

And, of course, Northern Ireland where he'd had an interest for many years, even before this latest involvement in the ceasefire and peace process on behalf of the White House. Curtis Manning was a man who liked to be trusted as the one who got things done.

He was in typically bullish mood when Pinfold arrived to find him drinking coffee with Moffat. Typically the American was already in rolled shirtsleeves, on his feet and pacing the room impatiently. The comparison with the relaxed Moffat, over-weight and pin-striped, lounging in his chair, couldn't have been more marked.

'Hi, Roger,' Manning greeted, turning sharply. 'Thought we might have to start without you.'

Pinfold hid his irritation. 'I've just come up on the train.' He didn't say where from.

'Your trains still running late, eh? So much for privatisation.'

It was meant to be a joke, a typical Manning Brit-bashing joke, but Pinfold wasn't in the mood. 'In fact the railways aren't *actually* private yet, Curtis. I just thank God we've *still* got a railway system worthy of the name. I really do wonder how you Americans manage.'

Manning saw the barb and ducked. 'We fly, Roger, we fly!' And he chuckled heartily at his own quick wit.

Moffat moved quickly to defuse any further antagonism. 'Let's get ourselves up-to-date, gentlemen. I have to report to the Cabinet Intelligence Unit at six, so I really have little time. If you'd like to kick off, Roger?'

Pinfold settled in his chair, having decided how not to give the impression that their plans were falling apart at the seams. 'Just to remind ourselves, the purpose of Operation Gadfly is two-fold. To ensure that the PIRA ceasefire holds and the peace process maintains its momentum, given the government's balancing act. That is, between how many concessions it can make and still keep the Protestant majority on board.'

'And without admitting the inevitability of reunification,' Manning chipped in. It was part of his bravado to call a spade a shovel – no point in fudging the bottom line in private, had always been his maxim.

'Quite,' Pinfold murmured. 'The most immediate danger to this *had* been Donny Fitzpatrick, a highly influential member of the PIRA Army Council who was dead set against the ceasefire. On the Loyalist side, we have most of the paramilitaries under control, the little shits see themselves as budding politicians. The biggest danger is the man they call the Rattlesnake or Rattler, Stevie Gavin.'

'And he's the guy you tried to get Littlechild to top?' Manning asked.

'Yes, that was just before the ceasefire was announced. We thought it best to get Rattler out of the way at the start. As you know, Littlechild refused. As an ally, Littlechild was invaluable, but as a potential enemy, he is very dangerous. He has considerable military experience and exceptionally good contacts with South Africa and other arms-supplying countries who will trade with anyone for hard currency. We couldn't risk him possibly switching loyalty back to Gavin.'

'I am aware of his CV,' Manning said acidly. 'That's why I wanted him blocked out.'

Pinfold continued: 'The second purpose of Operation Gadfly has been to silence anyone who can reveal any previous activities of the British,' he glanced pointedly at Manning, 'or other allied governments that could cause great embarrassment or misunderstanding. Revealed at this critical time, the first casualty would be the peace process. The second would be the credibility of the British Government and especially the integrity of MI5 and certain operations mounted by the CIA. That would hardly allow the United States to present itself as an honest broker.'

'I know all that crap,' Manning intervened. 'Hell, we've all got skeletons in our cupboards. The question is will they rattle? That's why we're all here.'

Pinfold held up three fingers. 'Only three people can do any real damage. Rumours are one thing, we've always lived with that. But Stevie Gavin, Peter Keegan and Rodney Littlechild are the ones with credibility.'

Manning hissed gently through his teeth; he didn't like the sound of that. 'Who rattles loudest, Roger?'

'Reverse order,' Pinfold replied. 'Stevie Gavin knows the least and he's so deeply implicated in over thirty murders, it's hardly in his interest to talk.

'Keegan and Littlechild are different. The media already know that Keegan was an army agent and have speculated that Littlechild was too. Now, until a month ago we thought we had the two of them safely out of harm's way for several more years . . .'

'Don't remind me,' Manning interrupted. 'So is there any news on Keegan?'

Pinfold shook his head. 'I'm afraid not. But, as he's on the run, he's not likely to want to attract media attention either.'

'I wish I had your faith,' Manning muttered. 'So anyway, Roger, you're telling me the real danger is still Rodney Littlechild.'

Moffat said: 'We must be sure we have that situation under control, Roger, so you'd better update us.'

Pinfold told them about the evidence that Littlechild's defence team had unearthed from the former DCC of West Weald, Derek Penny, Lomax's questioning of witnesses and Browne's provocative ploy to get her hands on forensic evidence. He then indicated without detail the countermeasures he'd taken to neutralise any potential damage to the prosecution case.

'There has been one other new development you should know about,' Pinfold added, addressing his words to Lord Moffat. 'A request has come through from the Assistant Chief Constable of Stafford for us to arrange an interview with Colonel X.'

'Who's he?' Manning asked.

'A former colonel in Army Intelligence who was running Keegan for us. The request was made on behalf of a Detective Superintendent Bill Johnson who's in charge of the operation to recapture Keegan.'

'Why should he want to speak to this Colonel X?' Moffat asked.

'He's dissatisfied with the co-operation from the Anti-

Terrorist Branch and my department – we've instructed only the bare minimum on Keegan's background to be released.'

'Why, for Godsakes?' Manning asked. '*We* want that bastard back inside.'

'It's a delicate balance, Curtis. Tell Johnson too much and heaven knows what he might accidentally unearth.'

Moffat agreed. 'Let me have a discreet word about Johnson with the Chief Constable, Roger.'

Pinfold looked down at the letter on his lap. 'I've a sneaking suspicion Johnson is doing more than hunting down Keegan. It could be that his unauthorised interview with Derek Penny has aroused his curiosity.'

Manning could see that. 'The fact he took Lomax and the Browne woman in tow suggests he sees a link between Keegan and Littlechild. That's a very dangerous turn of events.'

'I agree,' Moffat said. 'Do we have any knowledge yet how Littlechild's going to plead? Has he taken the bait?'

The MI5 man shook his head. 'Not yet. It's still fighting talk. Mind you, they haven't seen the forensic evidence yet.'

'I don't like it,' Moffat said. 'It's that damn Browne woman. She just won't accept defeat – thinks she's on some bloody moral crusade.'

Pinfold almost smiled. 'Perhaps she is.'

'We need more insurance,' Manning decided. 'There's no way they must be allowed to fight this case. We must make them see there's no way out. Any ideas, Roger?'

The other man had an idea all right; he'd been mulling it over for a couple of weeks. 'There is a possibility. Something that would make the defence realise that Littlechild was going to face a prison sentence whatever the outcome. There's a connection that would put Littlechild neatly in the frame, but there's a risk involved.'

'Why?' Manning asked.

'Because we can't control the defence reaction, only surmise the most logical outcome. And then you can never rely on any jury. Nevertheless, on balance it's virtually foolproof.'

'You'd better give us your idea in full, Roger,' Moffat decided.

It took Pinfold ten minutes to outline what he had in mind.

He concluded: 'It'll box him in so tight, he'll be forced to take the line of least resistance.'

'The Browne woman won't like that,' Manning observed.

'But it won't be her neck on the block,' Pinfold replied. 'In the end it'll be Littlechild's decision. So the risk is minimal.'

Manning could see that. 'I'm more worried about this Lomax guy. He's too much of a loose cannon. His background makes him dangerous and he knows where to poke around. I'd be happier with him on a tighter rein.'

'We have limited resources, Curtis, you know that.'

The British excuse for everything, Manning thought, and let his contempt show in his voice. 'Look, just over a month and the President goes to Belfast. I can't afford any shit hitting the fan. You need resources, I've got 'em. Zack Ryan and his boys are running all over Ireland lookin' for work to do. He'd be more than happy to lend you some manpower. I insist.'

Moffat smiled. 'It's nice to see the old special relationship isn't dead.'

'Just sleepeth,' Manning quipped. 'I'd consider it a discourtesy if you turned my offer down.'

'We wouldn't dream of it, old man,' Moffat said. 'Would we, Roger?'

Pinfold didn't answer. Harry Grisewold was going to love this.

Moffat added: 'That's settled then. And I think we'll have Mr Littlechild so tightly chained up, the Browne woman's going to need Houdini to get her client untied.'

Eleven

Lomax arrived at the offices of Eisner, Pollock and Browne at just before one. He was in high spirits as he parked and sauntered in out of the late October sunshine and up the paper-cluttered staircase.

Following the witness summons issued against Sir Joshua Stokes, things had started to move, although not quite as fast as Sam Browne would have liked. Lambeth had telephoned direct to say that a copy report of the forensic findings would be available within a fortnight and access granted to a defence expert. Bullseye!

That morning Browne had phoned him with the news that a package was on its way by courier from the CPS. She was delighted with her coup, not least because the day before Evie had visited her husband in Belmarsh and reported he was deeply depressed at the lack of any progress.

'I'm going to see him this afternoon to give him the good news,' she'd said over the phone. 'Come with me, Chris, and help boost his morale.'

'If you let me take you to lunch first,' he'd replied, half-joking.

She relented. 'Well, just half an hour for a pie and a pint.'

'Not exactly seductive.'

Her voice hardened. 'Don't even think about it, Chris. We've done the candlelit supper bit and it didn't work out, remember?'

Was he still really getting the cold shoulder or was she just playing a game? He wasn't sure, any more than he was sure he wanted to pursue her.

Those thoughts were still tumbling through his mind as he entered the solicitor's chaotic outer office. Browne was leaning against Totty's desk, long trouser-suited legs outstretched and her hair the soft, pinned-back muddle he'd got used to. The two of them were raising glasses of champagne with old man Eisner and the pimply-faced clerk called Wayne.

'Can anyone join the party?' Lomax asked.

Browne peered over her reading specs. 'Chris! Come and have some bubbly – celebrate my victory over the system. Only Sainsbury's own, I'm afraid.'

'We Eisners have our reputations to keep up,' the senior partner said, shaking Lomax by the hand. 'I hope you're as proud of her as we are.'

'Well, let's say I'm very pleased for Roddy's sake.'

She noted that, he saw; her eyebrow arching in a quizzical sort of way. 'The messenger should be here any minute. Then we can *really* get to town on Roddy's defence.'

'Don't forget Bill Johnson,' Totty chimed in with a champagne giggle.

'Oh, yes, it slipped my mind. Bill phoned earlier, trying to track you down.'

'What does he want?'

'A word apparently. He's down at Scotland Yard today on some briefing and would like to see you. I said he could join us at the pub across the road.' She noticed the flicker of disappointment in his eyes. Teasingly she added: 'I thought it would be a good idea for us to have a chaperone.'

Before Lomax could respond, a leather-clad spaceman in visored bonedome staggered to the top of the stairs clutching a large padded envelope.

'Package for Mr Browne,' he announced.

Browne sprang to her feet. 'Gimme, gimme,' she laughed, snatching it from him. 'Sign for it, Totty, will you?'

Feverishly she plucked at the staples, breaking a nail in the process, and pulled out the file. 'This is what I want. I'll read it over lunch.' She grabbed her shoulder bag and turned to Lomax. 'C'mon, let's go.'

They crossed the street to the crowded pub and weaved their way through the lunchtime drinkers. By the time Lomax had fought his way to the bar to get the drinks and sandwiches, Browne had charmed two burly workmen into giving up their table.

'How'd you manage . . .?' he began. But she wasn't listening. Her specs were on and she had the lab report open on the table. She was staring in disbelief, her face ashen.

He put down the glasses and plates. 'What is it?'

Her head was shaking slowly. 'Oh, Chris, I don't believe this, I really don't. They must have it wrong.'

'What, for God's sake?'

'According to this, Roddy's fingerprints have been found on the gun, the murder weapon.'

'That's impossible.'

'I know. Of all the things I was expecting, that wasn't one. It *must* be a mistake, although I don't see how.' She shut the folder with a snap. 'For many things there might be a rational explanation. But fingerprints, that's a killer.'

'Somebody must have faked it. I mean, we know it's a setup.'

She gave a sad, sympathetic smile. 'I'm not sure it's possible to fake that, Chris.'

'These people have got limitless resources, technology.'

'Even so, fingerprints are like DNA. Virtually non negotiable.' She glanced at the plate of sandwiches, her appetite gone. 'I can only imagine they got him to handle the weapon at some time, then kept it for when it was needed. But I'm snatching at straws. Only Roddy can answer that.'

Suddenly a cheerful voice intruded. 'You two look like you won the pools but forgot to post your coupon.'

Lomax turned. 'Bill! Good to see you.'

'But a bad moment?' Johnson asked.

'Worst possible,' Browne said. 'We've just had the forensics through. Roddy's fingerprints are on the murder weapon.'

If Lomax thought the policeman's reaction was going to be one of I-told-you-so, he was mistaken; he accepted the news quite calmly. 'Some things aren't easily explained, but to be honest I'd be a bit suspicious about it anyway.'

'You've changed your tune, Bill.' Lomax nodded towards the bar. 'A pint?'

'No thanks, I need to keep a clear head for this afternoon. I just wanted to speak with you for a minute.'

'You could have phoned.'

'Too many ears twitching. I'll be honest with you, I was rather disturbed by our meeting with Derek Penny. Admittedly, I didn't like the man, but I was very unhappy that his inquiry had ever been allowed to get off the ground in the first place. Keegan was obviously someone's sacrificial goat, whatever the misdemeanours to protect his cover. However, that's just a personal opinion. What deeply concerned me was that our Assistant Chief Constable knew about the meeting within twenty-four hours. Penny wouldn't have told him, so I can only surmise that someone was following me or one of us. I can't think why anyone should take that close an interest in my investigation into Keegan's whereabouts, unless *someone* is concerned that I might discover something they don't want me to.'

'What happened?' Lomax asked.

'I was rapped over the knuckles for making an unofficial visit. Fine, a small blot on my record; I can live with that. Then I got to thinking about Keegan's controller in Army Intelligence, the Colonel X who gave evidence at his trial. So I asked the ACC if I could make a request for an *official* meeting with him. Struck me Colonel X might know even more about Keegan than Penny. The ACC saw no problem with that.'

'But?' Lomax guessed.

'The next thing we know is the Chief Constable himself gets involved. Word has come down from on high that certain powerful people are unhappy with my inquiries. It's not in the so-called national interest. In short, I'm treading on someone's toes. And Colonel X is strictly off-limits.'

'Why are you telling us this?' Browne asked.

Johnson shrugged and smiled uncomfortably. 'Maybe Penny's zealous seeking after truth got to me. Maybe pricked my conscience. But your client's history seems inextricably entangled with Keegan and hearing what Penny had to say about those MI5 reports, it seems to me that Littlechild could be just another victim of some unofficial cover-up.'

'What are you going to do about it?' Lomax asked.

'I'm afraid there isn't much I can do about it, Chris. I've been officially warned off and that's it. I shall ask to see the Chief

Constable personally and register my dissatisfaction in writing. He'll listen and might even be sympathetic. But I'm not kidding myself; it won't change anything. There's no more I can do.' He glanced down at Browne. 'But you can. If they're putting this Colonel X out of bounds, it's because he knows too much about Keegan. And if he knows about Keegan, he knows about Littlechild. Don't either of you know his identity?'

Lomax shook his head. 'I realise from Keegan's trial that I must have operated under his overall command, but always through intermediaries. I was at the bottom of the pyramid and he was at the top. No name was ever used.'

'What about you, Sam? He was one of your defence witnesses.'

Browne smiled tightly. 'But it was a Diplock Court and there were strict conditions if I wanted to use him as a character witness. No pre-trial interview and a screen in court. We were only allowed to converse in open court during the trial.'

Johnson grunted. 'Then you know as much about him as I do. Bugger all. But if anyone can shed light on your client's case he must be the best bet yet. The only crumb I've had is that he's retired.'

'Where would *you* start looking for him, Bill?' Browne asked.

'I'm sorry, Sam. I haven't a clue.'

The prison officer looked up from his desk. 'Ah, Miss Browne. I did telephone your office, but you'd just left. I wanted to save Mr Lomax a wasted trip.'

'What's the problem?' she asked.

'Littlechild's a Cat A, ma'am, and this is a legal visit. Brief only, I'm afraid. Not even a legal assistant. He'll have to apply for a social visit. There's two a week.'

She smiled demurely. 'Couldn't you make an exception?'

'Not for a Cat A, sorry.'

Lomax shrugged. 'I'll wait outside in the car. Give Roddy my best.' He turned and walked back to the gatehouse.

'Usual procedure,' the officer said. 'No tape recorders and no files. You can take in a pen and paper, that's all. If you'd leave your bag with us, a female officer will give you the usual search.'

Browne walked through the metal detector then gritted her teeth as expert hands ran over her body. Even having had the foresight to wear trousers did little to make it more bearable. No concession was made to her professional legal standing. She supposed that the lawyers of terrorists and major criminals might sometimes be as committed or as bent as their clients, but it didn't help the feeling of utter degradation.

She was taken through numerous locked gates and feature-less corridors. Two plain wooden upright chairs and a table were the only items of furniture in the small, empty glass cubicle. A tin-foil ashtray was overflowing and cigarette ends had spilled onto the bare tiled floor at her feet.

God, she thought, it was impossible to feel optimistic in a place like this. If it depressed her, what on earth was it doing to Roddy Littlechild?

Then the door on the far side of the cubicle opened and the prisoner was shown in. Immediately, she could tell he'd lost weight, even since her last visit three weeks earlier. His shoulders sagged and his eyes were sunken and void of expression. He nodded to her as he dropped into his chair, took a tin of rolling tobacco and some liquorice Rizla papers from the pocket of his prison fatigues, placing them on the table.

'How are you, Roddy?' She knew it was a fatuous question even as she asked.

'Do you really want to know?'

'If it'll help.'

He glanced back at the stone-faced warder who'd taken up position outside. 'This place is doing my skull. Twenty-three hours a day locked in a cell with a psycho who thinks he's the second coming of Christ. It's like living in a lavatory. I was used to army life, but not this. I'm starting to get claustrophobia, panic attacks.' He was fiddling with his tobacco, trying to roll it into a paper, but his trembling fingers were making a mess of it. 'One shower a week and one change of underpants. Sorry, Sam, but you asked. There are no recreational facilities, no work to do.'

'I know it must be awful.'

'And I haven't even been tried yet,' Littlechild added. 'I'm

265

beginning to think I'm guilty myself. I can even see the doubt in Evie's eyes.'

'That's not true, Roddy. She's with you all the way.'

He didn't argue, didn't have the energy. Finally he'd managed to get the roll-up into shape and light it. 'No point in asking if there's any news?' he said, inhaling deeply.

'We've had the forensics through at last.' There was no point in overegging the optimism. 'At a glance there's nothing much that can't be explained. Except, the report states that your fingerprints were found on the murder weapon.'

Cool green eyes stared at her through the drifting veil of smoke. 'That's not possible.'

'Obviously I'll have to verify it, Roddy, but it's unlikely to be a mistake.'

'It's not possible,' he repeated, half to himself.

'Perhaps there's something you've forgotten to mention? Did Fitzpatrick show you a gun when you were together in the pub?'

'No.'

'Are you absolutely sure?'

'I think I'd remember that.' Sardonic.

'Because if he did and you touched it?'

His eyes narrowed. 'Are you putting words into my mouth, Sam?'

'Of course not.'

'It just didn't happen.'

She made light of it. 'Well, you just keep trying to remember, until our next meeting. It weighs the scales dramatically against you. So think *very* carefully.'

His eyes held hers steadily, telling her he saw where she was coming from, knew she couldn't put it into words. 'I'll see if I can't jog my memory.' He dragged hard on the roll-up and exhaled. 'Has Peter Keegan been recaptured yet?'

'No, I'm sorry. But I've been to see someone. Someone who can vouch for your credentials with the Security Service.'

'Who?'

'It's better I don't say. But he's got written evidence and he's more than willing to testify on your behalf.'

'Will that help?'

He found himself staring into her frank blue eyes. 'At best it'll make a jury question the prosecution case and possible motives for our argument that this is a frame-up. It's the best development so far.'

'Forgive me if I don't give three cheers.'

She overlooked his scepticism. 'This witness says you assisted MI5 in stopping an illegal arms shipment from South Africa to Loyalist paramilitaries. Is that correct?'

That stopped him in his tracks, his facial muscles momentarily frozen as he stared at her, a cloud of anxiety casting a shadow behind his eyes. 'Ah.'

'Well?' Her eyes bore into his like a hypnotist's.

The roll-up burned down to his fingertips, but it took a moment for him to feel the pain. He stubbed it out in his ashtray. 'I've always denied involvement in arms dealing. It's easier than getting into convoluted explanations. And once people start throwing mud, some always sticks.'

'So what happened?'

'Stevie Gavin – Rattler – got mixed up with Paisley's Ulster Resistance movement in the mid-eighties. The politicians soon lost interest, but Gavin wanted to make it work. He got funding from some source or other and approached the South Africans. As he and I knew each other from way back, my chief in police intelligence in Jo'burg ordered me to play host when Gavin came to visit. I showed him what was available and gave him the price list. After that I was only involved on the edge of the deal.'

'And you informed MI5?'

He nodded.

'Why, if Gavin was a friend? And anyway, I thought Stevie Gavin himself had worked for the Security Service.'

'He wasn't a close friend, more a casual drinking pal. We'd just known each other a long time. And he only worked for MI5 when it suited them and it suited him. If something fitted with his agenda, then he'd co-operate, but not otherwise. And this arms shipment thing was dangerous. If Gavin had access to a massive arsenal he was quite capable of starting a civil war all by himself. Besides –' he hesitated as he concentrated on another roll-up.

'Besides what?' she urged.

Again he hesitated. 'There are other measures in place in case the Ulster situation ever degenerates into civil war. It's in safe hands and will stay that way.'

'Do you want to tell me about it?'

'It wouldn't help. It has no bearing. Anyway, there are some things it is better for you not to know.'

It was not a meeting that left Browne feeling at all optimistic. There were so many secrets in Rodney Littlechild's life and he clearly found it difficult to part with some of them. And it was impossible for her to know if any could yet prove to be his downfall.

But as she walked out from under the shadow of Belmarsh that day to rejoin Lomax in his car, she was unaware that those exact fears were to be realised three days later.

It was to have been a routine remand hearing at Woolwich and she was therefore mildly surprised to see that Henry Halifax QC was present again. This time with DCI Millman and the CPS solicitor Ian Spinks. Halifax was unusually subdued, acknowledging her only with the polite smile and nod of a courtier, and keeping well away. There was an unmistakable air of superiority in his manner, a look of self-satisfaction in his eyes. A signal to Browne that he had a surprise in store and she wasn't going to like it. Something was afoot, but she wasn't sure what.

After the defence's junior counsel Ronnie Rock made an eloquent, impassioned and ultimately vain plea for the early release of witness statements from the police, she found out.

Halifax rose to address the Bench: 'Sir, if it pleases the court, in view of certain new evidence that has come to light, the prosecution requests that the prisoner be remanded into police custody for seventy-two hours pending consideration of further charges.'

Browne's mouth dropped open. Of all the things she had been anticipating, it certainly wasn't this.

'Which police officer is making this application?' the magistrate asked, taken aback.

'Detective Chief Inspector Millman of the Anti-Terrorist Squad, sir,' Halifax replied with a triumphant glance in Browne's direction, 'who is now present in court.'

Ronnie Rock took a moment to recover, turning to Browne. 'What the hell's going on?' he asked in a hoarse whisper.

'You tell me,' she replied testily. 'Just get in there and stop it!'

The defence lawyer sprang to his feet; there was no need to act out his genuine sense of indignation. 'SIR! I really must protest! This is absolutely outrageous! I beg the court to turn down this request outright. It is clearly a flagrant abuse of police privilege, an attempt to intimidate and undermine my client who is *already* accused of the most serious of all possible crimes.'

'Yes, yes, Mr Rock,' the magistrate said patiently. 'I understand your consternation. And indeed I shall ask Mr Halifax for the fullest explanation.'

The prosecution silk rose obligingly. 'Yes, sir, of course. I am informed by Detective Chief Inspector Millman that he wishes to arrest and question the prisoner further with regard to a charge of conspiracy to murder.'

Browne was shaken. Littlechild, unmoved, stared back at his accuser.

'I would ask you to elaborate further, Mr Halifax,' the magistrate said.

Halifax nodded. 'Of course, sir. The police have reason to believe that on August 5th 1987, the prisoner may have conspired with person or persons unknown to murder one Dominic Smals in Belfast and assisted by supplying the firearms in full foreknowledge of their intended use.'

Ten more minutes of ferocious argument followed, but in the end, the magistrate acceded to the police request before nodding obsequiously in Halifax's direction.

'The court will rise,' the usher announced.

As soon as the magistrate left, Browne rushed towards the door but found her path blocked by a gathering of Halifax and his prosecution team.

'Dear me, Cruella,' the barrister said in feigned surprise, 'you

269

are in a hurry. I do believe someone's gone and upset your applecart.'

'You have already told us in previous interviews, Roddy, that you were in a branch of the South African Security Police,' Detective Chief Inspector Millman said in the custody suite back at Paddington Green, following Browne's privileged consultation with her client. 'And you were in this unit in 1987?'

'Yes.'

'And you went to Belfast on home leave in July of that year through to August 10?'

Littlechild felt his heart skip a beat and the blood rush to his face. He was aware that Sam Browne was watching him closely, scribbling in her notebook in a spidery scrawl. 'Yes', he said.

'At the same time that a man called Dominic Smals was shot dead on the streets of Belfast?'

Littlechild's voice had lowered to a murmur. 'I know nothing about that.'

'Speak up for the tape, please, Roddy. Do you know who Smals was?'

Another nod. 'According to the newspapers he was a white South African journalist. A freelance.'

'Did you know he was an active campaigner against apartheid?'

'I think that's what the papers said.'

Millman raised his heavy eyebrows like two halves of a bridge. 'I think you knew that *before* you came home to Belfast for your leave.'

Henwick added: 'His killers have never been caught.'

Littlechild looked at him directly. 'Are you saying I killed him too?' he challenged.

It was Millman's turn. 'Did you?'

'No.' Flat denial.

'But you know who did, don't you?'

Littlechild's mouth clamped firmly closed and he averted his head.

'Well, do you?'

There was no response.

270

'I'm asking you for the third time.'

Browne said: 'My client is not able to answer that question.'

Millman glanced sideways as though some aggravating little dog was pulling at his trouser cuff and he wanted to shake it off. 'Can't or won't answer, Roddy? Well, what is it?'

'I have just told you, Chief Inspector,' Browne repeated. 'My client is *unable* to answer the question! Please respect that.'

'You realise his refusal to reply could harm his defence?'

Her mad eye widened a fraction. '*I'm* his lawyer, Chief Inspector, and I am advising my client here and now, not to answer your question. Do *you* understand?'

Littlechild added: 'I won't be answering it, ever.'

'Thankfully,' Millman said, 'you weren't so reticent when you were boasting to your previous cell mate.'

That really shook Littlechild. 'Do you mean Reg? Reg Turtle? You must be joking, I wouldn't tell that paedophile the time of day!'

'Ah, but you told him more than the time of day, didn't you?' Henwick interrupted. 'Why was that? To frighten him, or to shut that irritating, gabby mouth of his? Or was it just to boast how big you were and what a little nerd he was?'

Browne said: 'What does this man *claim* my client told him?'

Millman swelled his chest, wanting to get it all just right. 'That the murder of Dominic Smals was carried out by a South African hit team. Government professionals. Smals was an effective anti-apartheid campaigner and agitator who caused considerable embarrassment to Pretoria. And you, Roddy, by your own admission, used your contacts in the Loyalist paramilitaries to supply them with handguns to do the job.'

'That,' Henwick added emphatically, 'is conspiracy to murder.'

'Where is this,' Browne glanced at her notes, unable to read her hasty hieroglyphics, 'this Reg Turtle now?'

'He's been transferred to Risley,' Henwick said, 'for his own safety. But we're not relying on his word alone. We've checked with the RUC in Belfast and with the Security Service. It all fits.'

She shut her eyes. Not again. The Security Service. She

271

should have seen it coming. Taking a deep breath to steady her nerves, she said: 'And what deal has this Reg Turtle been offered?'

Millman lowered his voice. 'I'll pretend I didn't hear that. Now I think you and your client might need some time to consider your position. We'll continue tomorrow when we have more data from the RUC and other sources.' He leaned towards the tape recorder. 'Interview suspended at 16.30 hours.' And switched off the machine.

'This is another stitch-up,' Littlechild said angrily. 'The Security Service knows it's a lie.'

Something snapped inside Browne's brain, a short-circuit, a connection. 'Who put you onto this, Chief Inspector? It wasn't this Reg Turtle person, was it?'

Millman hesitated. 'No, it came through the Home Office.'

'Let me guess. Mr Prendergast.'

His silence gave her the answer.

Her eyes blazed. 'Doesn't that strike you as a coincidence, Chief Inspector? We're not talking Home Office here, are we? We're talking MI5.'

'Look, Miss Browne, my patience is wearing thin. The Security Service is responsible to the Home Office as I'm sure you're aware. Mr Prendergast's legal department liaises between the two. After so many previous convictions against terrorists have been subsequently overturned, its remit is to ensure that every legal procedure is properly followed and *safe* convictions secured. That is in your interests as well as ours and it is why Mr Prendergast's department interviewed all prisoners who have had direct known contact with your client. And in view of what's been discovered, I for one am very pleased they did. Because then one of my own officers was able to follow it up and take a statement from Turtle.'

'After he was primed by MI5.'

'You mean interviewed.'

She searched his eyes for some sign of self-doubt, however small. 'You just don't see, do you?'

'Meaning?'

Turning, she shook her head. 'It doesn't matter.' Then she

struggled to get some authority back into her voice. 'Look, Chief Inspector, I need to talk with my client.'

'Of course,' he replied.

'But not here. Another interview room.'

Millman looked perplexed. 'Why?'

'Because this room could be wired, bugged.'

A pained look of incredulity showed on the inspector's face. 'Miss Browne, you are being ridiculous. You can see for yourself the tape machine is off. And I give you my personal guarantee this room is not bugged, as you put it.'

'With respect, the deepest respect, your guarantee is worthless. We're dealing with the Security Service here. If they decided to put a microphone in here, it's doubtful anyone would even know.'

Millman and Henwick glanced at each other; there was no doubt what they both thought. The woman should be certified.

'No offence meant,' she added with a tight smile.

'Interview room next door?' Henwick suggested with an inane and patronising grin.

Her relief was genuine. 'Thank you.'

After they had changed rooms, Browne lowered her voice to a conspiratorial whisper as Littlechild leaned towards her across the table. 'They're getting desperate.'

'How the hell do you work that out? They've got me twice over now.'

'Exactly, Roddy, they only need to get you the once. I've been here before – with Peter Keegan. They're working up to a plea bargain, I can feel it in my water.'

'I don't understand.'

'As you didn't opt for a confession, they're getting twitchy that the murder charge won't stick.'

'Not even with the fingerprint evidence?'

She shook her head. 'I don't know *why* they're getting twitchy, Roddy, just I sense they are. By going for a second lesser charge, the temptation for us is to go for a guilty to conspiracy in return for them dropping the big one.'

'And I still go to prison for something I haven't done.'

'It happens all the time, believe me.'

'So I'm finished.' There was utter despair in his voice. Enemies he could see, he could fight. But this?

'Only if you play their game,' she said with more optimism than she felt. 'Prendergast and his lot are betting on a guilty plea and the presentation of minimal prosecution evidence in court. They won't have to *prove* their case. I remember MI5 sweating over the Keegan trial in Belfast until he pleaded guilty. If he'd fought, then God knows what would have been made public.'

'And that's what you wanted him to do, right?'

She smiled gently. 'You can't win them all.' Looking at her notes, she said: 'How strong a conspiracy case can they bring against you, Roddy? Be honest.'

'Well, I never said a word to Reg Turtle, I promise you that. But I imagine they could make a convincing case for conspiracy if they've got MI5's connivance. All circumstantial though.'

'Okay,' she said decisively, 'this is what we'll do. I'll come back tomorrow and stay with you until they've finished questioning you. Wait until we've got the full picture. Then I'll set up another meeting with your barrister, Mr Meyrick, and consider all the options.'

'He seemed like a good bloke. Didn't say a lot.'

'He *listened*, Roddy, that's what matters. He's the very best and he's very keen on defending you. We're lucky to have him on board.'

A wry smile broke on his lips, but the humour failed to reach his eyes. 'Luck. That's a commodity that's been in short supply just lately. If you see some, buy it for me, will you?'

The next day Rodney Littlechild was formally charged with conspiracy to murder Dominic Smals in 1987 and was duly remanded back to custody in Belmarsh.

It was a crushing blow to Lomax and especially to Evie. Despite Sam Browne's best efforts to reassure them that nothing was as bleak as it at first looked, it was of little consolation. Late into the night Lomax sat with his sister, trying to allay her worst fears yet at the same time feeling a fraud for even trying. They demolished a bottle of whisky between them, but it didn't help. Despite the alcohol, neither of them slept.

A week later, Browne paid a legal visit to see her client in Belmarsh with Tristram Meyrick QC. They both saw it as imperative to boost Littlechild's morale which had clearly taken a battering. The barrister tackled the murder charge first. 'Don't be too downhearted by the initial forensic report, Mr Littlechild. These things can often be explained by independent experts and we've got the very best. They've been granted access to all the evidence.'

'It's been an uphill struggle,' Browne admitted, 'but we're starting to get some co-operation at last.'

Meyrick said: 'Let's leave the murder charge to one side for a moment, Roddy. We've already got all the angles covered on that. So let's look at this conspiracy business. Sam's kindly dug up newspaper reports from the Belfast papers at the time – the mainland nationals barely mentioned it. According to the police you were at home on leave in Belfast when Dominic Smals, a white South African journalist, was murdered by a South African hit team. Did you know this man Smals?'

'Only by reputation because there was a security police file on him.'

'Tell me.'

'Smals was actually an Afrikaner. Wrote about politics and social history. Pretoria knew he had strong links with the African National Congress and marked him down as a propagandist and activist. Life got pretty uncomfortable for him and he left the country in the early eighties to settle in Belfast. Then he got in with Sinn Fein and started writing pro-Republican stuff for the foreign press.'

'How did you regard him?' Meyrick asked.

'At the time he was just a name on a file. He was irrelevant to me. We were pretty used to woolly-minded liberals all around the world declaring what ogres we all were in South Africa. One more didn't make any difference.'

Browne frowned. 'You approved of apartheid?'

He shook his head and sighed wearily. 'No. To my mind it was a stupid concept that was crumbling away, dying of natural causes. The signs were everywhere. It was unjust and vindictive.'

'So Smals was right?'

Littlechild shook his head. 'I had no time for apartheid, but then I didn't want black majority rule, especially under a Communist government. That's where Smals and I would have disagreed.'

'Communism has collapsed since Smals was murdered, Roddy. And South Africa now *has* black majority rule. Isn't that only just? Is that so bad?'

He gave a mirthless chuckle. 'Do you have time to read newspapers, Sam? The place has slipped into total anarchy. Murder, robbery, rape and mayhem – you'd make a fortune out there. The poison from Smals and the others did its job all right. Created a nation of disaffected and disillusioned people getting angrier and angrier as the ANC's promises come to nothing. And it'll get worse. Watch this space.'

Browne said: 'But you only knew about Smals after his murder, is that right?'

'Obviously I took more of an interest after his killing and looked up his file when I returned to South Africa.'

Meyrick's mind went into overdrive. 'But *had* you taken part in this conspiracy, the prosecution could claim you had a double motivation. Smals was in league with your two most hated enemies, the Provisional IRA and the ANC.'

Littlechild shrugged. 'I suppose so.'

Browne said: 'According to news reports, Smals was assassinated by unknown gunmen and the murder has remained unsolved. At the time it was assumed to be some Loyalist hit team.'

'So where have the police got this information that it was a South African death squad?' Meyrick asked.

'There can only be one source. MI5 have known it was a South African team all along. That's how they've been able to suggest there's a link with me.'

Browne lit a fresh cigarette from the stub of the first and inhaled deeply to help her concentration. This was not looking good. 'Roddy, you were on leave from the South African Security Police – a covert unit at that – in Belfast at that time.

Are you seriously telling me there is no connection with you and Smals?'

'I knew *nothing* about it until after it happened.'

'And you did not use your Loyalist contacts to supply the murder weapon?'

He could see the doubt in her eyes, could understand it. 'No, Sam, I did not.'

Meyrick interrupted. 'Do you know who did?'

Littlechild lay back in his chair, an ironic smile on his face. 'I found out later.'

'Who?' Browne pressed.

'You're going to love this.'

'Tell me.'

'Peter Keegan.'

Her mouth dropped. 'But Peter was an army agent.'

'Exactly. He supplied the weapons because MI5 told the army that he should.'

Meyrick said: 'That's just not credible.'

'Oh, it's credible all right,' Littlechild answered. 'Smals had just returned from the US lecture circuit on Sinn Fein's behalf, raising money for Noraid. He was also trying to set up a deal to buy Stinger anti-aircraft missiles for the IRA. So when Keegan reported that a South African team wanted rid of him as well, they thought why not? All MI5 had to say was one word on the phone, and all their dirty work was done for them.'

'My God,' Browne breathed, shutting her eyes momentarily. When she opened them again, Littlechild was watching her closely. 'And, Roddy, do you know who actually killed Dominic Smals?'

He held her gaze. 'Yes, Sam, I do. But I'm not saying, because it would put lives at risk back home.'

'Ulster?'

'I meant South Africa. The ANC is purging the old white security apparatus and digging up all the old skeletons. Whether what they did was right or wrong, the South Africans believed it was necessary. At that time the frontline of the Cold War wasn't Europe, it was southern Africa. The men who did it were good friends, honest, courageous and patriotic, whatever you may think of them. And I know they would never betray me if the situation was reversed. I'm not in the betrayal game. I'll leave that to this country's politicians.'

Meyrick plucked a hair from his sleeve. 'Apart from Reg Turtle's testimony, the police claim a certain Billy Baker saw you hand over the weapon to the killers.'

'That's rubbish. King Billy's an MI5 puppet. He's just saying what he's told.'

'He's becoming a rather important puppet,' Browne pointed out. 'A key figure in both cases. He's the one who told you Fitzpatrick was going to be in touch, and therefore the only person who can give evidence it was Fitzpatrick who'd asked to see you. Now he appears to be the prime prosecution witness in the conspiracy case.'

'And still can't be found?' Littlechild asked, appearing already to know the answer.

'The RUC claim to have no knowledge of his whereabouts. I've got my old practice in Belfast putting out feelers, but they're not hopeful.'

Meyrick said solemnly: 'From what I understand of the situation so far, the only way we may be able to raise doubts about your guilt is if you can name the men who actually did the killing. I don't think a denial of involvement will be enough.'

'I can't do that.' It was as though the logical conclusion of it all was just sinking in. 'I'll just have to plead guilty to the conspiracy.'

Browne looked aghast. 'That's *just* what they want. They're banking on this King Billy never being cross-examined.'

'I know.' His voice was very flat.

'Do you still believe he wasn't involved?' Meyrick asked as they drove back to London.

'Yes,' Browne replied firmly. 'Everything he's ever told me has been backed up by events.'

'Doesn't mean he's not telling porkies on this one, dear heart.'

'Except I've heard through the grapevine that the CPS has

dropped the charge against Reg Turtle. That dirty little paedophile has been released for lack of evidence.'

Meyrick shook his head. 'That's not conclusive, Sam, although I suspect you're right. It'll be the deal he's got for promising to give evidence against our client. Never mind, I'll tear him to pieces in the witness box.'

'If you get the chance, Tristram. They're banking on us offering a plea. And I've a nasty feeling in my water that's what Roddy's going to go for.'

'Mmm,' Meyrick said. 'This is getting to be like a game of poker, Sam.'

'And they've got the best hand.'

He nodded. 'And upped the stakes. But it's a high-risk strategy to them. If all MI5's dirty linen gets washed in public, heads are going to roll. Bringing up Dominic Smals' murder at this stage of the game would be a helluva gamble for them if they've got it wrong and Roddy stands on a not guilty. There'll be an absolute stench of rotten fish if he gives evidence – even if only half of it's to be believed.' He squinted his eyes in concentration. 'So what does that tell us? That the murder charge isn't watertight.'

'I agree, but they hold all the aces.'

'No, they don't. We're playing with a card sharp. All these aces are pulled from up his sleeve. They're all fake and he knows it. Therefore, he's relying on huff and bluff to persuade Roddy to throw in his hand without looking at his cards.'

'Very eloquent.'

'A good analogy. We must hold on to it, make Roddy see it that way too.'

'Well, Tristram, we'll soon know how fake their aces are. I've got a pathologist from the independent labs coming over this evening with her report.'

Twelve

When Meyrick dropped Sam Browne back at her office, she was pleased to find Lomax there, laughing and chatting with Totty.

'Glad you could make it, Chris.'

'Wouldn't miss it for the world,' he replied. 'Evie was furious she had to go to the wine bar. I've strict orders to phone her as soon as I've heard the forensic results.'

Browne smiled tightly. 'Let's hope there's nothing to alarm her unduly. We'll know soon enough. Miss Sixsmith should be here at any minute.'

Totty interrupted: 'A couple of things, boss. Mr Eisner's received a letter from the Crown Prosecution Service. It claimed you was in breach of the code of practice between them and the Law Society.'

'Bloody cheek.' Browne took the offered letter and one-handedly manoeuvred her reading specs into place. 'Mmm. Interviewing prosecution witnesses without agreement from the CPS or Millman and without a police presence. Tough, as the police wouldn't tell us who they were. And likewise visiting the scene of crime under false pretences without waiting for a court order. Phooey!'

'What'll happen?' Lomax asked.

'They suggest I should be removed from the case in the interests of the accused receiving a fair trial – very funny – and are sending a report to the Law Society. Oh dear, I do seem to have been a naughty girl.'

'Mr Eisner was furious,' Totty said.

'With me?'

'No, the CPS.'

Lomax said: 'They're a bit slow off the mark, aren't they? That all happened weeks ago.'

'That's the legal system for you, Chris. Never do anything in a week when you can take a year.'

Totty said: 'I picked this up from your flat this afternoon. From the Kent Police, giving notice that you're being summonsed for driving without a valid vehicle licence.'

Browne slapped her forehead. 'That's all I need.'

'Does this mean I'm working for a criminal lawyer?' Totty asked chirpily.

'Not funny. Another crack like that and you won't be working for anyone. I'm lost without wheels and I just haven't got time to go looking.'

'I'll ask me brother. He's in the trade. Anyway, that car was a heap.'

'I loved that car.'

'You need something with a bit more class. Something that fits your image.'

'You mean a middle-aged spinster who's got more wrinkles than a walnut. What've you got in mind?'

Totty grinned. 'A Sherman tank.' She looked past her boss and indicated the door. 'I think this is Miss Sixsmith.'

Wendy Sixsmith was in her late thirties and stood five foot four in her sensible grey pumps which matched her sensible grey suit. The frilly ruff at the neck of her blouse was the only concession to femininity. She wore little make-up and had her silver-rinsed hair pulled tightly back into a no-nonsense ponytail.

'Sam Browne?' They shook hands. 'Lovely to meet you after we've spoken so often on the phone.' She held up a weighty Gladstone leather case. 'Shall we get straight down to it?'

'Yes, but not here.' Browne obviously felt rather stupid saying it. 'The walls could have ears, as they say.'

Sixsmith smiled. 'Very cloak and dagger. You really have upset some people, haven't you?'

Totty had hired them one of the small upstairs meeting rooms in their local pub.

As they walked, Wendy Sixsmith explained that her partnership was one of only five fully qualified independent forensic science practices in the country whom defence lawyers could call on.

As the only source of training was the Home Office, most of

the seven hundred scientists were retained by the government. That left an assortment of partially or ill-qualified so-called 'expert witnesses' with some kind of scientific qualification available for defendants to challenge forensic findings in court. Many of these offered their services as a sideline and in some cases were little more than well-meaning amateurs.

'So you can see that all forensic evidence weighs overwhelmingly on the prosecution side,' she said. 'And, of course, everyone tends to accept the Crown's forensic evidence without question – or at least without the *right* questions. Defence "expert witnesses", if they're any good, don't specialise sufficiently to know what to ask. And it's simply above the heads of lawyers, judges and juries.'

While Lomax was buying drinks from the bar, Wendy Sixsmith spread out her file of reports and findings on the billiard table in the upstairs room.

When all three were together, Sixsmith began: 'The thing that really disturbs me is that the first people on the scene were from the MI5 surveillance team outside. They claim to have discovered the body at eleven forty-five, immediately after the killing. Yet it was not until one fifteen that the police were called in with a fully trained scene-of-crime officer. That was one and a half hours with people clomping about the murder scene, contaminating the evidence. Why the delay, I wonder? Perhaps they were awaiting instructions from a higher authority?'

'Or rearranging the evidence,' Browne suggested and lit a cigarette.

'I can't speculate on that. What I *can* tell you is that the scene-of-crime officer was not as thorough as he might have been.'

'Do you know why?' Lomax asked.

'No,' Sixsmith answered with a tight smile, 'but I can guess. When the police arrived, the version of events would have already been established by the Security Service people present. It was self-evident that your client had shot the victim through a locked door. Therefore not much point in trying to find forensic evidence to put your client *inside* the flat. And I can imagine the police officers being a little overawed and intimidated by the presence of MI5 – perhaps being hurried along or else not questioning MI5's analysis of events too closely. Why should they?

'The SOCO took fibre samples from the dead man's clothing as a matter of routine, blood samples from the hall and lounge carpet, then concentrated on the door and corridor. Mostly footprints – these are virtually invisible dust imprints that are in fact very clear when lifted onto an electromagnetic foil sheet – and, sadly for your client, fingerprints. Then there were the bullets embedded in the hall wall.'

'So did you discover anything to support my client's case?'

'The short answer is yes and no.' She smiled sympathetically. 'Sorry. On the up side, Lambeth didn't bother analysing the fibres and hairs from the dead man's clothing. No point for them to, as I've explained. But I did and isolated over thirty-three of them. A mixture of animal, vegetable and man-made. Most were associated with clothing – wool, cotton, goat, vicuna – and others with furnishings. In particular, I noticed an unusual accumulation of a reddish velour fibre taken from the trousers. That suggests the victim may have sat recently on newly upholstered material, which could possibly confirm his whereabouts just before the killing. Within a few hours I would have expected such a density of fibres to have been reduced to lower levels by natural fall-out, brushing, rubbing and sitting down on other surfaces. But I'll discuss that with you later.' She was talking faster now, excited about something else. 'But the best discovery was the human hair analysis. Four types of human hair, excluding the victim's own.' She paused and smiled, savouring her moment. 'And one is a perfect DNA match to your client.'

Browne and Lomax both stared in disbelief.

Sixsmith laughed. 'Don't look so surprised. Your client said he'd met the victim before the killing and this proves he did.'

'That's wonderful!' Browne said.

'There's more. Fibres taken from the dead man's jacket cuff matched those taken from your client's jacket – probably transferred when they shook hands.'

Lomax found himself grinning like a child; this was just too good to believe.

'Another point,' Sixsmith continued, 'is that of all the three dozen footprints successfully lifted from the corridor outside, not one matched your client's shoes. That could be construed as strange, but not conclusive either way.'

Browne sensed that was the last of the good news. 'And the fingerprints?'

The scientist shook her head. 'I'm afraid I just can't explain it. Your client's thumbprint on the doorbell. Clear as anything, no doubt. And the murder weapon was found in a dustbin just outside the back door of the apartment block. A perfect set, see for yourself.' She fanned out the numbered police exhibit prints.

'But my client was never there,' Browne protested.

Sixsmith shrugged. 'Then it was his doppelganger.'

'A .45 automatic,' Lomax observed, leaning forward.

'Yes, it fired six metal-jacketed rounds, four of which passed through the body and all embedded in the wall.'

He frowned: 'Were they the only prints on the gun?'

'Yes, you can see. It's been dusted all over.'

'No palm prints?'

'Doesn't look like it.' Sixsmith was curious. 'What are you driving at?'

Lomax held out his hand, closing his fingers slowly as though grasping a gun butt. 'I would have expected the fingertip prints to have been in a line on the leading left-hand edge of the butt, and maybe an index print on the right-hand side while he kept it away from the trigger.'

Browne raised an eyebrow. 'I see what you mean; that is how you hold a gun after all.'

'It's almost as though someone had wiped the thing clean,' Lomax added, 'then picked it up once. Not by the butt, but gripped it along the barrel.'

'I'm sorry,' Sixsmith said, 'but the bottom line is, they're still your client's prints. But, anyway, let me give it some thought. I'll see if I can't make sense of it. And, if you'll allow me, I'd like to consult a ballistics expert because that's not my speciality. With my limited knowledge I can see nothing amiss, but if this *is*

284

some sort of elaborate plan to implicate an innocent party then it could well be worth further investigation.'

'I'm not sure the Legal Aid Board will agree to that,' Browne replied. 'Can you put a price on it?'

'Between one and two thousand as a ball-park figure.'

Lomax didn't hesitate. 'Do it,' he said. 'Whether they agree or not.'

'Can you afford it?' Browne asked later, after Wendy Sixsmith had left and she had returned to her flat with Lomax. She'd found a bottle of Glenmorangie in the kitchen cupboard and poured some into two tumblers.

He savoured the smooth liquid. 'Like a good malt, some things are beyond price.'

'Like friendship?'

Momentarily he was back. The room darkened and muzzle flashes briefly illuminated the unforgiving Falklands landscape of Goose Green all around him. His companions behind him and on both sides, faces pressed into the damp peat as the shrapnel sliced over their heads. The Argentinian lines ahead and the smell of fear and death and cordite all around him.

He had physically to shake his head to clear it of the memory. 'Friendship,' he repeated. The word seemed so inadequate. 'Something like that, something more than that.'

She was on the sofa beside him now, her legs curled beneath her and her shoes discarded on the carpet. He was aware of her watching him closely as she nursed her tumbler in both hands. It was then that he realised that her hair was down, hanging lankly to her shoulders. In need of a thorough shampoo and conditioning rather than the hurried attention it received when she was working all the hours God gave. Somehow it made her look unusually vulnerable and very ordinary. This was the price she paid for trying to help a man who'd saved his life but whom she scarcely knew. His heart went out to her and he realised then just how grateful he was to have her fighting by his side.

'Blood brothers?' she asked gently, as though not wanting to intrude into this exclusively male domain.

He smiled at that. 'Oppos, mates. Nothing more fancy than that.'

Her cheeks coloured. 'I'm sorry. That was impertinent.'

'No, it's just something that's hard to explain. When you train together, then fight together. It was all so new. We may have been Paras, but none of us had ever experienced anything like the Falklands, not a real fighting war. You just can't share that with anyone who wasn't there.'

She nodded. 'Yes, but I'd like to understand, to know what happened.'

He was dismissive. 'It's not important, not now.'

'It is to me.'

'To you?' Surprised. 'Why?'

Browne looked sheepish. 'Because I want to know what makes you tick. And to have had your life saved by Roddy that time must have been the single most important event that ever happened to you.' With a smile she added: 'After all, if it hadn't been for what happened then we could never have met.'

He frowned. Where was she coming from? 'And is that important to you?'

'I don't know. I think it might be. What happened that night?'

He didn't answer immediately. First he poured more malt whisky into his glass. Then said in a quiet voice: 'It was Goose Green, we were advancing on the Argentinian positions. Our company was pinned down. Roddy and I were together as the Argies got our range with their mortars. The air was thick with shrapnel. But we both knew we couldn't stay there all night. We just looked at each other, sort of unspoken words. Then Colonel H began his charge.'

'The man who died?'

'Colonel H. Jones.' Lomax smiled in grim admiration at the memory. 'Daft bugger. He led from the front, charging towards the Argie positions. It broke the spell, then Roddy and I were hard on his heels.' He heaved a deep sigh. 'It was a pretty messy business. Fixed bayonets. First time I'd ever, you know, killed someone. About five went down. Then it was my turn. A high-velocity round caught me in the left arm, shattered the humerus. I went out like a light. Our line swept on apparently

286

and in the heat of the moment no one knew what had happened to me. As soon as Roddy realised I was missing he came back alone to find me.'

Browne's room seemed suddenly very hushed, except for the exaggerated ticking of the mantelpiece clock, as he continued. 'I came to and found this Argie soldier creeping past, trying to slip away. He must have seen me move. I don't know if it was anger or fear, but he swung his assault rifle in my direction. I can see the smile on his face even now. So maybe it was vengeance. It must have been obvious I couldn't move and I'd lost my weapon. But still he pointed his rifle and I could see his finger tightening on the trigger.'

'God, how awful,' she whispered.

'I remember thinking, well, this is it. I tried to conjure up a picture of Fran, my wife, and Manda in my mind. Manda was just five then. But the images wouldn't come. That's when I realised there were tears in my eyes. When I couldn't even say goodbye. Then there was a shot from close by and the bastard was blown off his feet.'

'That was Roddy's doing?'

He nodded. 'He'd found me. But the muzzle flash alerted an Argie machine-gun nest that had been missed in the advance. Rounds were landing all around us. Roddy didn't hesitate. Just threw me over his shoulder like I was some rag doll and ran like hell after the rest of our company. He should have got a medal.'

'He didn't?'

'Nothing's fair in love or war. Life isn't fair.'

'It certainly hasn't been fair to Roddy. But what's unfair, Chris? Being born crippled or blind is an unfair we can't do anything about, like accidents and diseases. We can only do our best.' He saw the fire of deep anger in her eyes. 'But there are some unfairs we *can* do something about, *should* do something about.'

He guessed then; it wasn't difficult. 'That's why you chose law?'

'Yes.' She hesitated. 'But in my naivety I was wiser than I realised. Only later I came to understand how many innocent victims there are in our so-called civilised society. There are victims of bureaucracy and state power as well as criminal injustice. Little people, Chris, who don't have the knowledge or the money to fight the big guns. The single mother fighting a local council to get herself rehoused. Parents whose children are wrongly taken into care. An asylum-seeker resisting a Home Office extradition order back to some murderous regime. All that sort of thing is pretty intimidating to little people. It crushes them, ruins their lives. And there are thousands of people in jail who shouldn't be there, convicted on the flimsiest of evidence. Because magistrates always believe the police rather than the accused. Because a duty solicitor couldn't be bothered to do his job properly. And that's before you get to the big stories of people like Peter Keegan and Roddy. I mean, you expect that sort of thing in dozens of corrupt countries around the world, but not here.'

'You sound bitter.'

She placed her glass on the coffee table and reached for her pack of cigarettes. 'Do you remember when you were a kid? I spent most of my childhood in India and then moved with my family to Aden when Dad was in the RAF. Grown-ups seem to have everything under control, don't they? They seem to know everything, what to do and when. Tell us how to behave and have their own code of conduct, of fairness, right and wrong.'

He smiled at that. 'And it's only later you realise they make mistakes and get things wrong just like you.'

Browne laughed. 'Too bloody true!' she said with feeling. 'And as you grow up you expect governments and officials in authority to behave just like your parents did. To be all-knowing and incorruptible, tireless and benevolent to their people. Then you learn the truth and when you do it comes as a terrible shock.'

'You sound like a little girl lost.'

Her smile was mischievous. 'Sometimes I think that's exactly what I feel I am.'

It was then that he had an overwhelming urge to kiss her. To risk it yet again. But she was too far away because her legs were curled up beneath her with her knees brushing his thighs. If he reached across, she'd have too much time to resist, to turn her head away.

To hell with it, he thought, and instead took her hand, gently prising the burning cigarette from her fingers. 'What are you doing?' she demanded.

He stood and stubbed out the filter in the ashtray. 'What I should have done a long time ago.' He leaned over her, taking her wrists and easing her to her feet.

'Chris? I don't think . . .' she began, but did not struggle.

'That's right,' he said harshly, 'don't think. Just shut your eyes and don't think.'

To his surprise, she obeyed, her lashes fluttering closed like a child trying not to peep. His hands were on her arms now and he felt her body tense. Knew that at any moment she would pull away. Then his lips feathered against hers and her mouth opened a fraction in a small gasp that might have been surprise. The faint mix of whisky and tobacco was perversely exciting in his nostrils. Exciting because he didn't care. At that moment he wanted only to kiss this woman, this aloof ice maiden. She had melted him and now the only stupid thought in his head was to melt her.

He brought his mouth fiercely down on hers, bruising her lips against her teeth. Lust, anger and maybe something else. He was aware of her back arching, her arms struggling to be free as he pinned them to her sides. She was surprisingly strong; he could feel the flexing of her biceps beneath his fingertips. Then suddenly the power seemed to drain from her and her mouth yielded. Her tongue tasted sweet against his, unmoving at first, then responding tentatively.

Gradually he released her right arm. She allowed it to hang by her side as his palm glided from her sleeve to lift and gently cup her breast. Against his skin, the material of her blouse was fetchingly limp from the perspiration of a long day. There was something raw and animal about her now, not freshly bathed and scented. He felt the blood rushing to his loins, involuntarily pressing against her. A soft gurgling sound, almost like the purr of a cat, escaped her throat. Then, to his surprise, her right hand was on his shoulder, her cool fingers curling the hair at the nape of his neck. The sensation sparking down his spine like a mild electric current.

Then the telephone rang, and the spell was broken.

She pulled away sharply and glared at him. 'Don't try that again, Chris! Ever! Or you'll find yourself on a charge for indecent assault – or worse.'

He stared at her, stunned, not believing. But before he could reply she turned away to answer the phone, snatching up the handset. 'Browne speaking. Who?' Her tone softened instantly. 'Oh, Evie, yes. We've only been back a few minutes. Chris was about to call you.' She glanced up, then. 'Evie, hang on a minute and I'll update you . . .'

Lomax was walking towards the door.

'Chris!' she called. 'Where are you going?'

He hesitated and turned. 'Back to my planet, Sam. And out of your life.'

She opened her mouth to speak but couldn't find the words. Then she was staring blankly at the closed door, aware of a strange and empty sensation as though something deep inside her had just died.

It was mid-December but there were no decorations up and definitely no festive spirit at the remote farmhouse in County Longford in the Republic of Ireland.

As daylight faded over the washed-out rural landscape and an icy north-easterly picked up, a group of men gathered around the television in the kitchen. They stood and watched with a detached and cynical air, drinking from their mugs of hot soup.

The President of the United States was in Ulster. Standing outside Belfast City Hall, talking into the microphones, his voice croaked with emotion. Eyes glittering with unshed tears for the benefit of the crowd, and CNN.

'Turn that fuckin' shit off,' someone said, 'before I throw up.'

'Poking his nose in,' Albie Nairn said, reaching for the set. 'Trying to take the credit to get the Irish American vote. Doesn't he know how it's all going to end?'

As the picture cut out, the door opened and Gaza stepped in from the yard. 'Car coming, boss. Flashed his lights.'

Lights flashed three times on the approach track. So one of ours, Peter Keegan knew. As expected and on schedule. So no nasty surprises. No Irish Special Branch raid or random Garda patrol. So everything ready for the council of war.

It had been a busy couple of months since the rebirth of *Cuchulainn*. A suitable headquarters had taken time to find, because many criteria had to be met. This farm had been available for immediate vacant possession, was a good mile from its nearest neighbour in all directions and a clearing in the adjacent copse provided a suitable site for a helicopter to land and take off unseen. And there was an airfield ten miles away where Johan van Niekerk was able to set up the office of his courier cover firm.

This had been used to ferry down quantities of explosive and handguns for self-defence from the secret cache in Albie Nairn's garden.

A number of cheap second-hand vehicles had been pur-chased and used for various reconnaissance missions ranging the length and breadth of the country. Yet that had not long begun; there was much more still to do. But Keegan was delighted with the progress.

He turned as he heard the car pull up outside. Moments later, Rattler entered, rubbing the circulation back into his bony hands, the collar of his black raincoat turned up against the cold.

'God, Pete, you could have got a car with a friggin' heater that works,' he said, as van Niekerk stepped in behind him and closed the door. 'First this mad South African scares me shitless with his flying, then tries to freeze me to death.'

Keegan grinned. 'A good trip then?'

A lank comma of black hair fell over the forehead of Stevie Gavin's pale, gaunt face as he laughed. 'Yeah, a good crack, I suppose. How're things going?'

'Much advanced since we last met, Stevie. We'll bring you up to date – once you've got some hot soup inside you.'

Gavin dumped his raincoat on a chairback and lit himself a cigarette. 'Just coffee, Pete. Black.' He glanced around at the faces he didn't know. 'You lot heard the latest?'

'We were watching on the box,' Nairn said innocently.

'No, not that smarmy nerd. The word on the street?'

'We've been a bit cut off here,' Keegan admitted.

'So I see. I'll get that put right, plug you into the Defenders' intelligence wing in the North.'

'That would be useful, Stevie, thanks. So what have they got?'

Gavin stared down at the cigarette burning between his nicotine-stained fingers. 'The IRA is reforming its leadership under a new so-called Continuity Army Council. The hard men are back in control.'

Keegan felt the flutter in his heart and the knot of tension tighten in his belly. 'Is this official?'

'Not yet, but it'll be rubber-stamped in January. Word is they'll resume bombing on the mainland by February.'

'Christ,' Keegan breathed.

For a moment no one spoke. They didn't have to. Now they all knew. When their final preparations were ready, it wouldn't be a moment too soon.

'So,' Gavin said, 'are you going to introduce me to my new comrades-in-arms?'

Keegan went clockwise around the kitchen table, giving first names only: Tim, Albie, Gaza, Hutch. 'And you've met Johan again, of course.'

Van Niekerk smiled and introduced the remaining five new faces. 'All old friends of mine from South Africa. You probably won't remember, but you've met at least one of them before. When you set up that arms deal with us in '87.'

Gavin glanced at Keegan. 'The one you and Roddy Littlechild tried to scupper between you,' he accused, still not completely forgiving.

'Tried?' Keegan asked with a grin.

'Yeah,' Gavin replied with laconic self-satisfaction. 'Over half of it got through.'

Van Niekerk laughed as he read Keegan's expression. 'It's a little secret I've yet to share with you, Peter. In South Africa we had a lot of experience in avoiding arms embargoes and foreign intelligence services. Therefore we used a method we often employed when there was a danger of infiltrators discovering a deal. We went ahead with part of the shipment as planned. Then we went to Stevie here – the personal end-user himself – and set up a completely different routing with no intermediaries.'

At that, Keegan couldn't resist a smile. 'As it's turned out, I'm glad you did.'

'Never did trust me, did you?' Gavin challenged. 'Too much of a wild man to be trusted with enough weapons to start a war?'

'It's true, Stevie, your reputation goes before you.'

Gavin waved his index finger. 'Let me tell you, Peter, those weapons have been kept under lock and key from that day to this. I've never let the UVF, the UDA or anyone else get hold of them. And now *you* want them.'

Keegan shook his head. 'They might be needed in the fullness of time, but I hope not. If they are, our plans and our strategy will have failed. I admit I misjudged you, Stevie, and I'm sorry. But the truth is Frontline – *Cuchulainn* – has ample weaponry and always has done.'

Gavin shook his head in disgust. 'Don't give me that bollocks, Peter! Frontline has always been piss and wind since the start. For all the rumours of hidden arms over the years, I've never seen so much as a water-pistol! MI5 set up Frontline and MI5 closed it down.'

'Wait a minute,' van Niekerk interrupted. 'Let's just get this straight, because if I'm getting deeper into this, I'd like to know exactly what's going on. I thought Frontline was set up as a middle-class resistance movement by this Wallace McIlroy character. And you needed the arms my South African department supplied to Stevie to get it up and running.'

'We want Stevie's expertise and his experienced colleagues,' Keegan said firmly, '*not* his arms. At least not yet. I didn't want to mislead you, but . . .' He glanced around the room at the expectant faces. 'I've kept all this a secret for so long that it's difficult to let go. I guess one day the wilderness of mirrors will shatter and we'll all see who's been behind them pulling the strings.'

'So it *was* started by Wallace McIlroy?' van Niekerk persisted.

'Yes. Wallace McIlroy was a very charismatic but rather

strange character, full of contradictions. He was fiercely against the Roman Catholic Church, saw the Pope as a symbol of the Antichrist. He was a student of Irish prehistory and used to argue that the Protestants were the original people of Ireland, driven out to seek sanctuary in Scotland by the later Celtic invaders.'

'A weird guy,' van Niekerk murmured.

Keegan shook his head. 'Not weird, just an original thinker and a bit zealous on the religious front. He served with the Special Operations Executive during the war, then afterwards ran an operation smuggling Bibles into the Soviet Bloc. So you can see the roots of his intelligence connections. He foresaw the current Ulster conflict and set up Frontline in the late sixties. Later MI5 found him a useful and willing ally. They financed him and arranged for a number of Frontline members to go to Rhodesia for proper military training. Roddy Littlechild was one of them. Of course, we were all young and naive then; no one knew MI5 was behind Frontline, supplying the arms. That only emerged gradually over the years.'

Gavin gave a snort of derision. 'Don't overegg the pudding, Peter. What bloody arms? There *are* no bloody arms. That was all McIlroy bullshit.'

'That's what I always thought,' Keegan agreed. 'Until recently. But they came in all right, two large shipments organised by MI5 contacts in Belgium. Heckler and Koch G3 rifles, M16 Armalites, Walther sub-machine-guns.'

'Nah.' Gavin shook his head in disbelief.

Keegan grinned. 'Here's a memory test for you, Stevie. You remember the Ulster Workers' Council strike in 1974? When Loyalists brought the province to a standstill to bring down the power-sharing executive in Stormont after the Sunningdale Agreement?'

'Sure, how could I forget?'

'And do you recall that Frontline took a full-page ad in the Ulster edition of the *Daily Mail* and the *Newsletter* beseeching the unions to call it off?'

Gavin scratched his head. 'Yeah, I do vaguely. I thought it

very odd. I'd always believed Frontline was opposed to the executive.'

Keegan said: 'Well, the reason was, the dockers were going on strike at the very moment hundreds of tons of weapons for *Cuchulainn* were sitting in containers at Larne docks.'

The other man's mouth dropped open for a second. Suddenly his scepticism evaporated. 'You mean it, don't you?'

'Every word.'

'And now you want to combine your armoury with that of the Ulster Defenders and,' he gave an evil little grin, 'go to war.'

Keegan's eyes hardened perceptibly. 'No, Stevie, not yet. We'll not motivate the general population until the situation really goes down the tubes. From the hard core of recruits at our rally, I want to train a cadre of instructors to teach new recruits tactics and weapons' handling as things worsen. In the next year or two. The timing rather depends on the politicians and what decisions they make.'

'So where do my people fit in?' Rattler asked, beginning to see yet another excuse for Frontline's ongoing history of inaction.

'As I said at the meeting, it's time to bring the battle to the South,' Keegan replied, 'and just as soon as possible.'

'Now you're talking.'

'But I'll not resort to barbarism,' Keegan warned. 'There'll be no bombing of civilians on the streets of Dublin. No assassinations of Irish politicians.'

Disappointment showed in Gavin's eyes. 'It has to be all or nothing, Peter, or it will fail. That's one thing we can learn from the Provos.'

'Just listen!' Keegan snapped back. 'I agree with you, but it must be done with a strategy that does not alienate us from our friends and natural allies. Not the governments in London or Dublin who'll hate us for destroying their plans. We must know that whatever words the politicians use to condemn us, the *people* are with us in their hearts. I want their sneaking admiration that someone's fighting against all the IRA stands for, to foster a sense of shared pride.'

Van Niekerk saw what he meant. 'You want them thinking

good for you, doing what no British Government has ever had the balls to do.'

Keegan's eyes were suddenly alive with a fire that none of those present had ever witnessed before. 'Exactly. *Cuchulainn* must be regarded in the public perception as a modern-day Robin Hood. We have to be audacious and daring. And that way recruits for the ultimate resistance will be beating their way to our door.'

Stevie Gavin thought for a moment. 'What about the enemy, Peter? And I don't mean Dublin, I mean the Provos. When do we start taking those bastards out?'

'We are guerrillas, freedom fighters, Stevie, not terrorists. I don't intend to stoop to their level. Bring Dublin to its knees and they'll get rid of the Provos for us. They've interned them twice before in their history. We'll make sure they damn well do it again!'

'You're wrong. Take out the Provo leadership if you really want to hear the cheers in the Shankill.'

There was a natural authority in Keegan's voice. 'You're with the Frontline now, Stevie. You made your choice and now you take orders like everyone else.'

Rattler shrugged and grinned stiffly. 'Sure, boss, anything you say.'

The days were shortening and the shops were filled with Christmas glitter.

Evie was over eight months gone and the impending birth brought the only glimmer of happiness into her life. Lomax spent many hours traipsing round the shops with her, sharing the experience that was rightly Roddy's, buying all the paraphernalia that would be needed for the new arrival.

When she came home with a plastic bag of second-hand baby clothes from the Oxfam shop it almost broke his heart. After that he insisted he went with her and purchased everything she needed new. Well, not quite everything. He picked up an old rocking cradle from the Portobello Road and spent hours stripping it down and repainting it in bright colours with stencils of fairytale characters. Never having thought of himself as artistic, he was rather pleased with the professional-looking result. The baby might not have a nursery of its own in the poky flat, but at least the cradle would be something special.

The work helped take his mind off his and Evie's other problems: Roddy's committal hearing date was now set for mid-January but his prospects looked no better and Lomax's cash reserves were dwindling fast. Every time his thoughts wandered to Sam Browne, as they frequently did, he tried his best to stop them, although without much success.

Manda was in regular contact by phone from the family home in Hereford where she'd taken it upon herself to organise his job-application campaign in her spare time.

She would scour all the appointment pages of the national newspapers in the college library and post details to him with carefully crafted letters for him to sign. As a result he'd actually been asked to attend six interviews, although as yet no job had materialised.

It was looking more and more likely that he would eventually have to follow his friend Joe Monk's example and work abroad for Rob D'Arcy's security company. But there was no way he could entertain that idea until after his brother-in-law's trial.

Evie now went to the occasional progress meeting at Eisner, Pollock and Browne and only once asked him why he no longer spent so much time with the solicitor.

'No point, sis. Nothing much will happen now until the trial,' he'd answered glibly.

Then in late December she'd returned from a visit to Browne's office looking deeply despondent.

'What's up? Want to talk?'

She looked around the small room, its walls seeming to close in on her. 'I need some fresh air, Chris.'

So they went to the park as the clear day began to die, the bare chestnut trees casting their elongated shadows across the dewy grass. There was no one about.

'So what happened, sis?'

She shrugged, taking his arm and huddling close to him for protection against the chill damp air. 'Nothing really. I was just told the truth. Sam was her usual bright and cheerful self. I couldn't bear it. I challenged her to level with me, no sweet talk. What was the bottom line?'

They'd slowed to a standstill. Twilight was falling, the landscape mellow and diffuse in the gathering mist. Not a breeze stirred. 'What did she say?'

'I could see she didn't want to tell me, but in the end she did. All they've got is Derek Penny's evidence and that by itself just won't be enough. Not to be certain of an acquittal, not with the fingerprint evidence against him. And she's *still* waiting for the witnesses' statements from the prosecution.'

'I can hardly believe that.'

'She's sure they'll come anytime. They'll have to now the committal date's been set.' She stared unseeing along the avenue of trees. 'But she really needs to talk to the man they call King Billy – Billy Baker who phoned Roddy to say Fitzpatrick wanted to get in touch. He's also involved in the conspiracy case. He's somewhere in Ulster but she can't trace him.'

Lomax wasn't surprised at that. 'What about Colonel X? Has she had any luck with him?'

'No, the MOD clammed up tight when she made inquiries.'

He nodded thoughtfully. 'It needs a backdoor approach.'

By the time they left the park, it was dark.

Two days later Lomax arrived at Belfast's Aldergrove airport. He had talked only to Joe Monk about going and swore his friend to secrecy. Nothing of the purpose of his visit was mentioned to Manda or Evie. Or even Roddy Littlechild.

Lomax was fully aware of the dangers. He was out of the secretive brotherhood of the SAS now. He couldn't just pick up the phone to the 'Kremlin', the Regiment's intelligence section, and call in a favour. At least not this sort of favour. Further he had no doubt his telephone was bugged, probably at some remote exchange, and anyone else closely associated with Littlechild was likely to be under surveillance. If the opposition got wind of what he was up to, then he could be in deep trouble. If they could stitch up Roddy for murder, then they were quite capable of anything.

So he had discussed his options with the only person he could trust and who knew the problems. And Monk hadn't been optimistic. Then Jerry Tucker's name had cropped up.

Lomax had last seen Tucker at his retirement party. He was a lieutenant in Army Intelligence in Northern Ireland who had worked with both men during their secondment to the ultra-secret unit generally referred to as 14 Int, although its name was changed frequently to keep its enemies in the Ulster paramilitaries guessing. On the last count it was DARG, the Defence and Research Group. Tucker was a chubby, cheerful man with ginger hair and a faceful of freckles; thanks to his easy-going nature, Lomax and Monk had quickly become firm friends with him.

As the aircraft had descended out of the wintry sky, Lomax had looked down at the dull sheen of Belfast Lough and felt the old dark fears closing in on him. A knot of anxiety tightened in the pit of his stomach. It would be all right now, he'd told himself. All different, not like before the ceasefire. But he'd been lying to himself, and he'd known it all along.

There were spits of light rain in the air and a raw wind was blowing down from the north-east. He went straight out to the airport concourse with his overnight grip. The terminal had been extensively refurbished since he'd last been there and there was no obvious sign of heavy security, not even the inevitable plain-clothes officer from Special Branch with an eye out for the regular players.

He told the taxi driver to take him to the Malone Lodge Hotel and settled down to enjoy the journey and relive some of the more pleasant memories of the province. There were quite a few, a fact that the bad ones tended to overshadow.

The permanent checkpoint on the airport road had gone, the brick blockhouse now boarded up and derelict at the roadside.

'You'll see a big difference, so you will,' the driver had told him. 'Belfast's fair bustling nowadays. People are coming in to shop who haven't dared to for years. Sure, I've doubled my income since those bastards stopped. It's been good for business.' He glanced up into his mirror. 'You're not a squaddie, are you?'

That wasn't a question anyone would have dared ask before the ceasefire. 'Not now.'

'You've got the look. But then I thought you were probably too old.'

'Thanks a bunch. You've made my day.'

They both laughed.

On arriving at his hotel, Lomax put a call through to Tucker's office, but it was a full twenty-four hours before his friend came back to him with effusive apologies, explaining he'd been out 'walking the parish boundaries' as he put it. Lomax told him he was over from the mainland to look up some old mates, including him; perhaps they could meet for a drink? Tucker was pleased. A drink for old times' sake seemed like 'a good crack'.

'Where d'you want to meet? Spoiled for choice now,' the man said. 'Restaurants opening up all over the place. The peace seems to have given everyone an appetite. What d'you fancy?'

'I really don't mind.'

'The Garage is an in-place for the smart set. Do a nice cajun chicken. And some of the prettiest waitresses in town. It's on the east side of City Hall. See you there at around eight.'

Lomax found no difficulty in locating the converted warehouse with its brick walls, black-painted steel joists and wrought-iron minstrel's gallery; the place was heaving with Friday-night revellers and he was lucky to find a spare table.

This was not the Belfast he remembered, not the place where you existed in a perpetual dank twilight and an atmosphere of brooding menace. The ceasefire had transformed the city. Army and RUC patrols were off the streets, the shopping-centre barriers were open and the bag searches at every store and restaurant had stopped. It was all bright lights, chatter and ringing cash registers. It had even stopped raining. He felt his apprehension begin to ebb away.

Tucker was twenty minutes late. He arrived flushed from the exertion of running to make up lost time but seemed as jovial as usual, if a little preoccupied.

'Something cropped up just before I left,' he apologised. 'Anyway, great to see you again, Chris. Let's order – I'm famished – then we can catch up on gossip.'

They talked pleasantries and reminiscences while they ate, yet Lomax sensed that Tucker was distracted, his humour a little strained.

'So how's life with the slime?' he asked, a reference to the 'green slime', army slang for intelligence units. 'Pretty dull, I should imagine.'

Tucker wiped his mouth on a napkin. 'Dull but busy. With all the VCPs off the streets and army patrols restricted to the border bandit country, we've lost our information infrastructure. Not so easy to keep track of the major players if you've got to eyeball everyone. Before the ceasefire, we could plot their movements from all the sightings reported in.'

'Are the leprechauns still active?'

'Little buggers never stop. They're still recruiting, training and doing dummy runs to keep their hand in, although South Command is more active than up here.'

'So will the ceasefire last?'

The other man grinned. 'That's the million-dollar question. Even with my lot, opinion is divided and we're supposed to know. Personally I'm sceptical, but then the politicians reckon they know best. A triumph of optimism over reality.'

'And the reality?'

'It'll break down.' Tucker was emphatic as he waved to the waitress to bring more beers. He stopped talking as the waitress arrived and kept quiet until she'd gone before he said, lowering his voice: 'What's the real reason you're here, Chris?'

Lomax felt that old sensation return, the shuddering dread that caused his heart to flutter in his chest. 'That's very perceptive of you.'

The laughter had gone from Tucker's eyes. 'Not really. The reason I was delayed was because something crossed my desk that I had to check out.'

'Something?'

'Something about you. I'm routinely copied relevant reports from Box. This one had your name on it. You're under covert surveillance.'

Lomax's face was a mask, his flesh stiffening like cooled wax.

Tucker said: 'Somehow I don't think that surprises you.' His grin was fading. 'Well, it surprised me. So I called up Group to query it. After a few minutes' pow-wow amongst themselves, the duty officer came back on and said it was all a mistake. Told me to shred the copy.'

'And did you?'

He nodded. 'Old habits. So, Chris, what gives?'

Lomax explained at length, including both Rodney Littlechild's predicament and his hope that Keegan would be recaptured and persuaded to give evidence for the defence.

'We've been put on alert for Keegan,' Tucker confirmed, 'although this is the last place anyone expects him to turn up. It sounds as though your friend Littlechild is between a rock and a hard place.'

'Believe it.'

'Oh, I do, Chris. I've been associated with Box for long enough in this business to know what some of their operators get up to. And I've known you and Joe long enough to know there's something in it if you're convinced.'

'That's good, Jerry, because I'm desperate for some help. I need to find the Colonel X who gave evidence at Keegan's trial. All I know is that he's retired.'

'Just as well, because no serving officer would give you the time of day.'

'I need a name and an address. Or at least a phone number.'

Tucker looked uncertain. 'Well, I can tell you his name was Colin Roebuck; he used to be my CO. But we wouldn't have details any more, Chris. The only hope is Army Records or that someone at the office is still in contact with him. I could ask around . . . But everyone's cagey about addresses and phone numbers.'

'I'd be grateful. And there's something else.'

'Isn't that enough?'

'I need to contact King Billy. Billy Baker.'

His friend glanced nervously around to be certain no one could hear, before turning back to Lomax, his voice a fierce whisper. 'For God's sake, Chris, are you crazy?'

Lomax held his gaze. 'I wouldn't ask if it wasn't absolutely essential. Just an address, a phone number, just a contact name. Anything.'

'Not that easy. Billy seems to be in Box's domain nowadays. I've had nothing on him in months. He's not in his usual haunts. In fact, the rumour is he's gone to ground. Not receiving visitors.'

'Couldn't you make discreet inquiries?'

Tucker looked uncomfortable. 'Not without raising eyebrows. You're entering dangerous territory. If half what you've told me is true, certain people are going to get very upset if you go prodding in dark corners.'

'I don't have any choice. It's that or see the man who once saved my life banged up for a crime he didn't commit.'

'But I do have a choice. I've no doubt the report on you I saw was genuine. The mistake was sending the copy to my department. If anyone realises I'm helping you, the brown stuff could fall on me from a great height.'

Lomax's heart sank. 'So you won't help?'

'I didn't say that. Just that we need to be careful. As it is, I've been told that report was an error, so I'm ignoring the implications and seeing you – why not? But if it's true, then someone probably already knows I'm with you here.' He avoided the temptation to look around for likely watchers. 'Perhaps we could find out?'

'What d'you mean?'

'Do a little fieldcraft, find out if you've got a tail.' All humour had drained from his eyes now. 'It's you they're watching, not me. Let me leave now as if I'm going home. You have a beer, then walk out and back towards your hotel. Do a lot of stopping and starting and I'll see if I can pick anyone out.'

'It might be someone you know.'

Tucker shrugged. 'At least then we'll both know the score.'

There seemed to be nothing to lose by trying, so they made a show of their farewell and Tucker wandered out while Lomax went to the bar for another pint of Guinness. He made a point of glancing at the girls in their weekend 'curry-and-a-disco' microskirted finery – a typical male alone and at a loose end. But all the time his eyes focused beyond the obvious subject of

303

his attention, scanning the rows of smiling, perspiring faces. Nothing, and no one looked out of place.

Just after ten, he finished his drink and stepped out into the street, heading towards City Hall without a backward glance. Minutes later he passed the refurbished Europa Hotel, remembering the days when there would have been few venturing out at night into this mile or so of restaurants, bars and discos. But now it was filled with a colourful lively throng with long queues forming on the pavement as people waited for tables. Clearly capacity was reaching saturation point. He stopped frequently to look in shop windows or to study menu cards in bistro doorways. It felt strange using the old techniques, studying reflections in mirrors and glass. But there were too many people. If you want to lose a tail you travel to suburbia where you could be sure you've shaken it off in the near empty roads. Tucker would be in a better position to judge, standing back and seeing who responded to his movements. Who walked when he walked, who stopped when he stopped.

Twice he diverted down isolated side streets, then hailed a taxi back to his hotel.

He'd barely closed the bedroom door when the telephone rang.

It was Tucker, phoning from a call box and not giving his name. 'I've flushed two of them out, Chris. I thought I'd picked one up earlier and I was right. When you flagged the taxi, a car pulled in almost immediately after. Two males came from different sides of the street and jumped in, then followed you. They're probably sitting outside your hotel now.'

'Nice to know someone cares,' Lomax murmured, feeling resentful of this invasion of his privacy.

'I'll check out the car reg tomorrow, see if that tells us anything. At least now we know. I'll be in touch.'

The absolute certainty of what was happening was in a strange way a relief. 'Thanks, pal. I owe you.'

Thirteen

Christmas didn't prove as restful and uneventful as Lomax had hoped.

At Manda's suggestion, he and Evie would spend the holiday back at his home in Hereford where they would be joined by Joe Monk. Lomax was quite looking forward to it until his sister had dropped her mini bombshell a few days earlier.

'I've invited Sam Browne to join us, Chris. When we were chatting, it cropped up that she'd be at home alone. That seemed terrible at Christmas.' She saw the look on his face. 'Oh, it's all right, I checked with Manda first. She said fine, the turkey's plenty big enough.'

'Browne's not family,' he replied coldly.

'That's the trouble, she's not anybody's family. She was delighted when I mentioned it. I think she leads a very lonely life.'

'Perhaps she deserves to.'

'That's not very charitable.'

'No, I suppose it isn't.'

It came as no surprise when Browne arrived in her rented car with a holdall and a briefcase stuffed with papers.

'Can't you ever leave work alone?' Evie asked.

'It's our Christmas prezzie from the CPS. The prosecution bundle. Arrived on Friday, at last. Thought I'd continue going through it when I've got a minute.'

Her meeting with Lomax had been stiffly polite and he'd obligingly kissed her on the cheek. They regarded each other cautiously, neither knowing quite what to say. The atmosphere improved during the evening at a local pub and then on Christmas Day itself, but both of them kept their distance.

Over the prolonged lunch, Lomax noticed Browne become more animated as the wine flowed. She'd been seated next to Monk who flirted outrageously with her, but she didn't seem to mind. In fact, she rather gave the impression she was enjoying it. Even when he caught her under the mistletoe in a passionate embrace.

Lomax turned away, but not before his eyes met hers for a moment. One frozen, questioning moment. What was she doing? Was she deliberately trying to punish him? Then she'd turned her face back to Monk's and they'd both laughed at some joke or other. To Lomax it was salt in the wound.

That night he might well have hit the bottle hard if only Evie hadn't started her contractions and he'd had to race with her to the hospital.

Evie and Roddy Littlechild's son was born one month prematurely on Boxing Day afternoon.

'It would have been nice to have called him Noel,' Evie said the day after, as they all stood around the tiny shrivelled baby in the incubator.

'You still can,' Lomax said. 'I think Boxing Day is close enough.'

'He's gorgeous,' Browne observed. 'Now Roddy has *another* special person to fight for.'

The visit had left them all feeling more cheerful as they returned home for lunch. But while Manda was preparing sandwiches in the kitchen, Browne brought Lomax and Monk rudely back down to earth.

'I've had time to go through all the statements in both cases now,' she announced. 'It's pretty much as I expected. No more nasty surprises in the murder case, thank God.'

'What about the conspiracy charge?' Lomax asked.

She extracted some papers from the file on the dining table. 'The most damaging statement is the one from William Baker, this King Billy. Yet, perversely, he'd be the best defence witness in the murder trial – if we could find him.'

'Still no luck?' Lomax asked, but didn't mention he was following his own line of inquiry.

'No, he's a pretty shadowy character. In fact, I hardly know anything about him.'

'Last I heard of him was about six years ago,' Lomax said. 'A local Loyalist warlord, he ran a drinking club off the Shankill.'

'Oh, he's still around,' Monk confirmed. 'Or at least he was just nine months ago when I was running a covert OP on him. Fat bastard. Still into protection, extortion and pirating porno videos, but mostly it seems to be hard drugs now.'

'Liked to think of himself as the leader of a major Loyalist paramilitary group,' Lomax recalled, 'but his gang was just a bunch of thugs.'

Monk added: 'He's been mixed up with the UDA, the UVF and others at different times, but he never had any real political commitment. Case of what was in it for him. I think he fell out with all the Loyalist factions at one time or another.' He paused for a moment's thought. 'There were rumours in the early eighties that he'd done a job or two for the Brits.'

Alarm bells were ringing louder in Browne's head. 'You mean MI5?'

'Quite possibly, but I've never had proper confirmation. Anyway, I think any sort of co-operation with him died out a few years later.' He tugged absently at his moustache. 'Mind you, there were strong rumours that King Billy played a part in tracking down the PIRA bomber they called AIDAN just before the Downing Street Declaration.'

Browne's eyebrow arched. 'So Billy Baker could be back on board with MI5?'

Monk grimaced. 'That's a difficult one.'

'C'mon, Joe,' she flared, 'you said you ran an observation post on him and he was into narcotics.'

'That's what Int reports said.'

'So why wasn't he arrested?'

A shrug. 'No evidence, I guess, just hearsay.'

'Were you looking for evidence?'

'No.' Monk shook his head. 'It was routine surveillance because he's a major player and isn't trusted. If we'd discovered anything on drugs it would have been passed on to the RUC for action.'

'But via MI5,' Lomax pointed out.

Browne gave a soft grunt. 'So if you or some other surveillance team learned anything, ultimately it would be MI5 who would decide what, if anything, was passed to the RUC?'

307

'I guess so.' Monk's eyes hardened. 'All I know is, Sam, that in Northern Ireland nothing is ever quite what it seems.'

She gave a brittle laugh. 'I think I've learned that, Joe. And now we have an *unconvicted* narcotics dealer and gangland leader giving testimony that he saw Roddy hand over weapons to the killers of Dominic Smals in 1987. It's a shame he's vanished just when we want him to help prove Roddy *didn't* murder Fitzpatrick. If it went to a second trial for conspiracy, what's the betting King Billy would magically reappear?'

'Heads they win, tails we lose,' Lomax murmured.

Browne sighed. 'To look on the bright side – if there is one – at least I'm in a position to request interviews formally with those prosecution witnesses we haven't already spoken to.'

'You haven't got long.'

She smiled tightly. 'Don't I know it. Committal's just two weeks into the New Year.'

The conversation was broken by the telephone ringing in the hall. They heard Manda leave the kitchen to answer it. 'Dad, it's for you! Won't give a name!'

Lomax levered himself from his chair and quickly left the room. Manda handed him the receiver. 'Hello?'

'Ah, Chris, tracked you down at last!' It was Jerry Tucker's voice. 'Listen, mention no names. I'm on home leave, but before I left the province I ran a check on the car that followed you over there. It was one of our pool cars, but lent out to some American operators.'

'American?'

'Yeah, I know that sounds odd. But we've had a lot of sneaky-beaky teams from the US out here since just before the cease-fire. Mostly opening up secret lines of communication with the State Department, Dublin and Sinn Fein from what I gather. We've got the infrastructure and kit on the ground, so we help out. None of us like it much, but you know – '

'Orders is orders?'

'Just be careful, right? There're a few rumours flying around about these boys and they're not good, even if it's only half-true.'

'What sort of rumours?'

'You don't want to know. But they can be quite heavy if they put their minds to it, so watch your back.'

'Any news on the two names?'

'Not yet. I'll let you know if I get anything. And don't forget, watch your step. You're walking blind in a minefield.'

Lomax hung up in deep thought.

'Sandwiches everyone!' Manda called.

But suddenly he'd lost his appetite.

On their first morning back at work in the New Year, Sam Browne and Totty began bombarding the Crown Prosecution Service and DCI Millman of the Anti-Terrorist Branch with formal requests to interview confirmed prosecution witnesses in both the Littlechild cases.

Crown prosecutor Liz Shilling of the CPS hid behind her stonewalling secretary for four days until an inadvertent slipup by a receptionist put Browne's call through.

The prosecutor's tone was terse. 'This is an unusual case in that it directly affects national security. The Director of Public Prosecutions might not be pleased for me to sanction your request.'

'We do not yet live in a total police state, Miss Shilling, and I'd respectfully remind you of the long-established principle that there is no property in a witness. Sound familiar? I'm informing the CPS of my intention, not asking permission.'

Shilling wasn't backing down. 'And I'll remind you, Miss Browne, that you've already been reported to the Law Society for approaching prosecution witnesses without notifying me first.'

'When the police wouldn't tell us who their witnesses were,' Browne replied tartly. 'Which is anyway why I *am* informing the CPS now.'

'You say you've already written. Then, if you're determined to go ahead, that should suffice.'

'If you've read my letter, you'll see I've requested CPS assistance in asking the police to co-operate, given their stubborn reluctance since the very beginning of this case.'

'I haven't seen your letter personally. It's in the system.'

'That's why I've been driven to phoning as I haven't had a reply in nearly a week.'

'I'll see if I can find your letter.'

'I'll fax you a copy.'

'I can't act on faxes. It has to be a proper letter.'

'Then I'll messenger one round immediately.'

'If you wish, but you'll be wasting your time.'

Browne growled down at the receiver in her clenched fist. 'This conversation is being taped.'

'Oh, yes?' Slightly taken aback. 'For what purpose?'

The solicitor ignored that. 'Why will it be a waste of my time? Because you do *not* intend to act with the *impartiality* incumbent on the CPS?'

'I don't mean that. Your request will be considered in due course and go through the proper channels.'

'Meanwhile, DCI Millman is steadfastly refusing to communicate with me. He's permanently out of the office, on vacation, in court or in the sodding bog!'

Browne sensed Liz Shilling blanch before she replied: 'I'm sure DCI Millman is very busy, Miss Browne. But you might find him a little more communicative if you could only learn to be civil. Good day.'

The line went dead, leaving Browne to fume at the dialling tone. Totty came in with a pot of black coffee as her boss slammed down the phone and angrily lit her twentieth cigarette of the morning.

'You'll smoke yourself to death,' the girl observed.

'They're my kippers,' Browne snarled. 'And have you had any joy with Millman – or need I ask? What's the excuse this morning?'

'Off with a cold.'

'What about the organ-grinder's monkey, DS Henwick?'

'One fax every thirty minutes like you said. A phone call every hour, plus telex, and letter every night. They must be drownin' in bleedin' paperwork.'

'Double it,' Browne said, then changed her mind. 'No, hang on.' She reached out for the phone. 'I just do not believe

Millman has a cold – men like him don't even admit they get them. What's the number?'

Totty told her. She dialled and composed herself while the telephone rang. 'Oh, good morning. It's Hammersmith Hospital here. I'm sorry to trouble you, but I need to speak to Detective Chief Inspector Millman.' She put her hand over the mouthpiece. 'Is he married?'

The girl shrugged. ''Ow should I know?' Eyes heavenward.

'No, no,' Browne said into the phone. 'I'm afraid it's his wife.'

Totty's mouth dropped open.

'Chief Inspector!' Browne said as though he were a long-lost friend. 'I'm so glad I caught you. You must be so busy.'

'Switchboard said you were the Hammersmith. My wife . . .'

'Oh, gosh no, that was a misunderstanding. I was having a conversation with my partner when I rang. His wife's having a baby. Sorry, it must have confused your receptionist.'

'Hmm,' Millman said. 'Anyway, Miss Browne, what is it?'

'Have you received my request to interview witnesses?'

'I can hardly have failed.' Cold.

'I was expecting you to call.'

'Yes, well, as you know, I've been busy.'

A girlish laugh. 'Not to worry, we're talking now.'

Millman decided to grab this particular cow by the horns. 'Well, look, you've already had your people contact the two publicans in the murder case without my agreement so that really leaves the MI5 operator who identified your client outside Fitzpatrick's apartment. And I'm afraid the Security Service has refused point blank to talk to you. Not much I can do about that, I'm afraid.'

'What about the taxi driver who picked up my client and drove him to the King's Head? His is a key statement.'

'He's abroad, I'm sorry to say. Won't be back until just before the trial.'

'Where abroad?'

'Er, Trinidad, I think. Holidays.'

'Is he Jamaican?'

An involuntary laugh. 'No, an IC One male.'

Then a sudden thought occurred to her. 'This taxi of his, is it a minicab?'

'No, it's a licensed black cab.'

Browne moved on to the conspiracy case. 'There's another MI5 man's evidence in this.'

'And the same answer. Sorry, out of my hands.'

She read down her list. 'Reg Turtle and the Loyalist paramilitary, William Baker – King Billy.'

'I might be able to arrange something with Turtle.'

'No, thank you. He's an out-and-out liar – I'm not worried about him. My QC will tear him to shreds in court and I don't want him to see it coming.'

'I see.' Millman sounded just a little surprised at that.

'But I am still interested in King Billy.'

'Ah, yes, as a defence witness in the murder case. As you know, I have put your request to the Royal Ulster Constabulary, but frankly I'm not holding my breath. You probably appreciate he's a slightly dodgy character – I never said that, mind – and not easy to pinpoint. Always "on the gallop" I think the expression is. I am sorry, Miss Browne, it's the best I can offer.'

After a couple of pleasantries, they hung up. 'Damn and sod it!'

'Nothing doing?' Totty asked.

'More brick walls than Parkhurst.'

There was a knock at the door. It was Lomax. 'Who's died?'

'You, if you make another crack like that!'

'Drawn a blank on interviewing any prosecution witnesses what matter,' Totty explained.

Browne said: 'How many taxi drivers d'you know who can afford six weeks in the Caribbean? We seem to have picked the only one who can.' She sighed and forced herself to relax. 'Anyway, it's a long time since we've seen you in the office, Chris. Just passing?'

'Taking Evie to Belmarsh,' he said. 'Thought I'd drop in with the glad tidings.'

'What about?'

'I had a call from my friend Jerry Tucker in Belfast this morning. I'd asked him for any info on Colonel X, Colin

Roebuck. Well, Jerry has been clearing up his chief's office, taking down cards and decorations before he gets back from leave. Anyway, there were some cards that came in late, just before Christmas. His chief had just opened them before he rushed off to catch the shuttle. One was from Colin Roebuck.'

'Was there an address?'

'No, but the envelope was franked in Banbury, Oxford.'

Browne's face lit up. 'That's wonderful, Chris! Brilliant! I'll get a local solicitor to check the electoral register . . . God, I needed some good news.'

He hesitated, not really wanting to drag himself away. 'Right, well, I'd better be on my way. Evie's waiting in the car. Sends her love.'

'And how's little Noel?'

'Loud and smelly.' Lomax grinned. 'Not a born traveller.'

'It'll make Roddy's day to see his son.'

Lomax was still reluctant to go, trying to find something sensible to say. 'Our holidaying taxi driver, the one who drove Roddy to the pub the night of the murder, right? I suppose he *is* kosher?'

'Why shouldn't he be?'

A shrug. 'It's just that nothing else seems to have been that night. Only a thought. See you.'

Browne said suddenly: 'Hey, Chris!' He turned at the door. 'It's good to see you around here again.'

He smiled uncertainly. 'Sure.'

'Pax, eh?'

'Sure, Sam, pax.' And then he was gone.

Totty studied Browne for a moment. 'What's all this pax stuff, boss? You two fallen out? How d'you always manage to do that? He really fancies you, you know.'

Browne regarded her assistant over the top of her specs. 'Don't talk nonsense. Now go away, you horrid child.'

With a knowing grin on her face, Totty sauntered back to the chaos of the outer office. One of Wayne's elaborate paper darts landed with stealth-bomber accuracy in her ample cleavage.

'Oh, do grow up,' she barked without her usual tolerance.

'And make yourself useful. *Who* would have a list of London taxi drivers?'

'The Public Carriage Office, of course.'

Totty looked it up and dialled the number. Ten minutes later, she called Browne on the intercom. 'Your taxi driver witness, Mark Wortle.'

'What about him?'

'He's not listed.'

It was just one week before the scheduled committal hearing of Police *v.* Littlechild, and Derek Penny, the former Deputy Chief Constable of West Weald, was unaware that his world was about to be cruelly shattered.

He had spent a pleasant couple of hours at the church directing the junior choir in rehearsals while his wife Meredith pottered around with the flower arrangements.

The boys were doing well really, considering that they had come straight from school and would have almost certainly preferred to have been doing something else before knuckling down to an evening's homework. Lovable rogues, the lot of them, but Penny would sort them out. A little carrot and a little stick. He had a way with kids. The shame was he and Meredith hadn't been able to have any of their own.

Still, give the choir another month and maybe they'd be good enough to enter in the southern counties' competition. Another silver cup to go in the display cabinet with the others.

They finished just before six when he and Meredith left for home, dropping in at the pub for a quick drink before returning to catch the Channel 4 News.

It was a surprise to find the unmarked police car by the gate and a local detective sergeant with a DC waiting at the door.

'Hello, Reg,' Penny greeted. 'What's this in aid of, not one of my angelic choirboys been drawing on walls?'

The sergeant did not smile. 'Bit more serious than that, Mr Penny,' he said tersely.

Penny frowned. That was unusually formal. Reg was Reg and he was Derek; the sergeant's son was the solo soprano of the choir.

'Perhaps we could talk inside,' the sergeant said. Glancing sideways at the worried look on Meredith's face, he added pointedly: 'Best if it's just you and my DC, I think.'

Penny put his key in the lock and let them in. His wife said: 'I'll put the kettle on.'

Once they were seated in the front room, the sergeant chose his words with care. 'This choir-singing thing of yours, how long have you been doing it?'

That took Penny by surprise. 'My involvement with choirs? I was brought up with it from the age of five. My parents were greatly involved with the local church. It's been a hobby ever since.'

'And you've often been involved with choirs through your local community work as a policeman?'

Penny nodded. 'On certain postings, yes.'

'Including at the time of your secondment to Salford in Manchester in 1975 and '76?'

'Yes, I was assistant choirmaster at St Bartholomew's.'

The sergeant smiled thinly; it was all tying up. 'And do you remember a boy there called Tommy Aitken?'

Despite his growing unease, Penny's dry laugh was involuntary. 'We're talking twenty years ago, Reg, I can't remember the names of all the boys.'

'You can try,' the other man pressed.

A shake of the head. 'I'm afraid not.'

'Well, Mr Penny, I'm afraid he claims to remember you.'

'What do you mean?'

'He says he was in the St Bartholomew's choir and alleges that you subjected him and other boys to acts of gross indecency.'

'It's a lie. I've never laid a finger on a child. Never! Ask anyone, ask your own son, dammit, Reg!'

'He's pressing the charge, Mr Penny.' For the first time there was a softening of the sergeant's expression. 'Sounds like he's been talking to a shrink, if you ask me.'

The truth was sinking in and Penny asked, his voice quavering: 'What happens now?'

'I'm going to ask you to come down to the station and make a statement.'

'Am I going to be arrested?'

'Obviously that depends.'

'My God.' Penny felt that he was suffocating.

'If it's any consolation, Mr Penny, in my experience there's every chance he'll change his mind before the case gets to court. And even if he doesn't, he may have difficulty in convincing a judge and jury after such a long time's delay. But then there is one other former choirboy who is backing his allegations.'

'That's impossible!'

'I'm afraid not, Mr Penny. So let's get down to the station and get this over with.'

Meredith opened the door. 'Nice cup of tea, anyone?'

Tension and anxiety were mounting relentlessly as the date of the committal hearing approached. It was a blessing for Evie that the demands of baby Noel absorbed her completely, leaving her so exhausted that sleep came easily.

Sick of lying awake each night and walking around like a zombie all day as he tried to distract himself, Lomax took to visiting the offices of Eisner, Pollock and Browne more regularly again. Unsure of the reception he'd get, he was pleased when Browne and Totty welcomed the extra help.

At least he felt he was doing something useful as he was given the task of finding a firm of local solicitors in Banbury to look up Colonel Colin Roebuck's name on the electoral register. He spoke to five before he found one who was willing and sounded reasonably efficient.

When he sauntered into Browne's office, she glanced up. 'What were you saying the other day, Chris, about black cabs?'

Lomax nodded. 'It just struck me as convenient for the police to have found the taxi driver whose evidence condemned Roddy, but not the one on the return trip who could confirm his alibi.'

'That's the way it goes sometimes.'

'Sure, but it made me think. We're certain Roddy's phone was tapped and the flat bugged. MI5 would have known when he was leaving to see Fitzpatrick. It would have been easy for them to have a cab cruising past just as he left.'

Browne looked thoughtful. 'Roddy said it was a bit of luck, because you don't get many black cabs in Southall, and it was raining.'

'And MI5 use black cabs.'

'What?'

'They've got their own fleet. BT vans for static ops and black cabs for mobiles. No one ever looks twice and they don't get parking tickets.'

'Do you really think so?'

Lomax said: 'Why don't we check this taxi driver out? I know he's away but his wife or girlfriend might know something.'

'Well, I – I suppose so.'

They both knew they were clutching at straws again.

'I'll call Joe. The three of us could go round this evening.'

The home of taxi driver Mark Wortle was in a block of council flats in Romford, Essex, on the north side of the Thames.

Lomax and Monk stood well back so as not to present an intimidating presence when Sam Browne rang the bell. From inside they heard a child screeching above the noise of some junk television game show. A young female voice shouted at the youngster to shut up as she opened the door.

'Yes?' Her face was pinched and white, the skin beneath her eyes grey with fatigue. The baby in her arms gurgled and its tiny little fingers toyed with the mother's lank hair.

'Mrs Wortle?' Browne asked politely. 'I'm sorry, this obviously isn't a convenient time to call. Oh, what a pretty little baby. What's her name?'

'Johnny. I was just putting him down.'

'Of course, silly of me. He'll be a handsome chap when he grows up.'

'What d'you want?'

Little Johnny regurgitated his supper over Browne's gently prodding fingers and she withdrew her hand with an embarrassed smile. 'I'm Sam Browne, a solicitor. I really wanted to see your husband. He's the witness in a case – someone he picked up in his cab – ' Warm, sweet-smelling vomit dripped off her hand and splashed down her skirt.

'Mark's away and he doesn't talk to me about his business.' She stared at the mess on the solicitor's clothes. 'That looks like an expensive suit. You'd better rinse it off or you'll never get the stain out. Come in for a minute.'

'Would you mind?' Browne's foot was already in the door. 'That's most kind.' Mrs Wortle stepped aside as Lomax and Monk followed her in. 'These are two colleagues from work, Chris and Joe.'

The woman regarded them suspiciously, evidently wondering why, as solicitors, they weren't wearing suits and ties. 'Best come in the kitchen.'

The two men drew back towards the living room. 'We'll wait here, okay?' Lomax said.

A little girl in pink pyjamas was sitting on the floor playing with the remote control in front of the television. About six, Lomax guessed, with an open face and big brown eyes.

'What's your name?' Monk asked.

'April. What's yours?'

'Big Joe.'

'That's a funny name. Why *Big* Joe?'

'Why d'you think?'

And while Monk engaged in banal conversation with the youngster, Lomax idly cast his eye round the room while listening to what Browne and Wortle's wife were saying in the kitchen.

'So where is Mark?'

'In Jamaica, jammy beggar.'

'Not many taxi drivers can afford that sort of holiday.'

Mrs Wortle gave a cynical little laugh. She'd put the baby in its highchair and was on her knees in front of Browne, sponging the material. 'Mark's not on holiday, he's working. And he's not a taxi driver.'

'No?'

'Not as such. He's a driver, does all sorts.'

'I thought he had a black cab.'

318

'He has. It's in his lockup. But he does private work for companies, not the general public.'

'Isn't that unusual?'

'No, according to Mark a lot of business people prefer black cabs to cars. More space, more comfort.'

'I agree, I much prefer them. So what's he doing in Jamaica?'

'Relief chauffeur while another bloke's on holiday.'

'Sounds very grand.'

'The British High Commission might sound grand, but Mark says he's just a glorified lackey.' Mrs Wortle stopped scrubbing and climbed wearily to her feet. 'There, that should do it. Anyway, Mark'll be home in a few weeks. Leave a card and I'll tell him you called.'

'That's kind, but no matter,' Browne said. 'It's not important. Thanks for the clean-up.' She turned towards the living room. 'Come on, you two. And stop chatting up the girls, Joe.'

Lomax replaced the faded framed photograph on the mantelpiece. A good-looking if dour-faced man with a moustache wearing a Number One dress uniform and cypress-green beret.

Once outside, they sauntered along the balcony towards the steps. 'I think you were right, Chris. He's working for the High Commission in Jamaica.'

'I know I'm right,' Lomax replied. 'There's a photograph of him in the living room, taken some years ago. Army uniform.'

'Is that significant?'

'The cap badge. He was in the Intelligence Corps. So at some point in his past, Wortle would have been known to the Security Service.'

'I reckon it's a stronger connection than that,' Monk said. 'My best guess is that Wortle's on their payroll as an A Branch surveillance driver. All that tosh about private clients, that's just what he tells his missus. Now they've shipped him out to Jamaica to keep him away from the likes of us.'

Realisation dawned on Browne's face. 'Until the trial.'

Lord Moffat loathed mobile phones. He hated people having loud and animated conversations on them in restaurants. Or showing off their business prowess when negotiating on trains for the benefit of fellow passengers. And he hated the thought that there was nowhere he could go to escape if someone wanted to reach him; no sanctuary fishing on a river bank or even in a lavatory. Of course, you could switch it off, but then what was the point of having one in the first place?

Anyway, he'd borrowed the confounded thing now from his assistant. Because, just this once, he was anxious for the call, even if it meant using the mobile. Because today was the committal hearing in the case of Police *v.* Littlechild. He just hoped it didn't bleep in the middle of lunch with the minister.

Of course it did.

It made Moffat jump and he splashed soup over his tie before fumbling to find which pocket he'd put it in. Heads turned as the sound continued, most embarrassing; mobiles were frowned upon in this establishment.

'Hello, yes?' Moffat demanded, listened intently for a second, then shook it irritably.

'Press the receive button,' the minister suggested helpfully.

'Ah.' Moffat remembered the instruction then, thumbed it roughly and tried again. Static whistled in his ear.

'Allow me,' the minister said and reached over the table to pull up the little aerial. 'Better reception.'

Moffat smiled, thinking what a fool he must seem. 'Hello?'

It was Roger Pinfold.

'What happened at the committal?'

Pinfold sounded irritatingly calm. 'He was committed, of course. Rodney Littlechild will appear at the Old Bailey in nine weeks.'

That was a relief. Somehow he half-expected the Browne woman would have magically pulled some sort of rabbit out of the hat. At least that was the bottom line; but not quite all he wanted. 'The Bailey? I wanted this to be low profile, Roger.'

'I know, sir, but the fact is any judge will want the prestige of the Central Criminal Court.'

Bloody bewigged fools, Moffat thought, considered themselves just one down from royalty and one up from God. 'I can't believe that Browne woman didn't rock the boat. They didn't go for no-case-to-answer?'

A light laugh at the other end; Pinfold was clearly relieved and feeling pleased with himself. 'No, she and Tristram Meyrick are not fools. It would have taken an absolute miracle and a barking mad magistrate to have had the case thrown out. And defence wouldn't want to reveal their hand to us at this stage. They'll plan to keep their powder dry for the trial . . . *Our* next concern will be the judge.'

Moffat grunted. 'I'll put that in hand, talk to the Lord Chancellor's department. They know who's who and which ones have conventional values.' Followed the Establishment line and had their eyes on the New Year Honours List, he meant, and Pinfold knew it. 'But tell me, Roger, are they going to fight?'

'That's a difficult one, sir. Looks like it on the face of it. But Browne took Henry Halifax aside after. Said she thought her client wouldn't go through with it. Would probably offer a plea at the eleventh hour.'

'Did she mean it?'

'Or getting us to drop our guard? That we just can't know, sir. But I'm optimistic he'll cave in eventually.'

'Good.'

The minister regarded Moffat carefully as he packed away his mobile and stuffed it in his pocket. 'You look pleased, Anthony.'

'Just a little problem sorted.'

A few days after the committal, they located Colonel X at his Tudor farmhouse in the rolling Oxfordshire countryside on the outskirts of Banbury.

Colin Roebuck stood on the low roof of the derelict annexe surrounded by piles of local stone which he was using to restore the building. He watched as Lomax's car turned off the road and approached along a muddy track.

A frown creased his forehead as he saw the woman emerge and he took in her dark business suit, the raked-back fair hair and power shoulder pads. He had no doubt where she was from.

'Colonel Roebuck?' she called up, friendly enough.

He looked down and felt a little easier when he saw she'd been joined by a man. Men in positions of power were usually more reasonable, more pragmatic. He curbed the urge to hurl a solid Tudor brick through the windscreen of the car below and send them both packing.

Instead he thrust his thumbs into the front pockets of his old cords. 'If you're from the planning department, I don't see anyone without an appointment.'

'We're not,' Lomax called back.

Roebuck looked again at the woman, and thought of the other major problem dominating his life. 'The Inland Revenue?'

Lomax grinned at that and shook his head. 'No, sir. I'm a former soldier who served on attachment to your unit and Miss Browne is a solicitor who represents Peter Keegan and Roddy Littlechild.'

The colonel stared, taken aback, the colour draining from his thin weathered face as the names sank in. After a moment he recovered and said: 'Let me get down. We can't shout about that sort of thing.'

He was clearly fit, moving swiftly for a man in his mid-fifties, descending the ladder with boyish agility. Despite the chill, a green army-surplus body warmer and a flat cap were his only concessions to the weather.

'Planning department's been giving me hell over this restoration,' he explained with a wary smile. 'I think they'd prefer the place to remain a ruin. Trouble is they don't live here.' He stared hard at Browne. 'I know you from the Keegan trial. Defence lawyer, weren't you?'

She smiled, flattered at being remembered. 'Unfortunately, we never got to talk. Only the barristers and judge spoke to you. But we were all grateful you put in a good word.'

Roebuck grunted. 'Not sure it did Keegan much good. It certainly did nothing for *my* career.'

'No?'

But the man refused to be drawn. 'You'd better come inside.'

Apart from the absence of the bitter northerly wind, it was

little warmer in the dark flagstoned interior than it had been outside. The big fireplace was empty. Colin Roebuck clearly wasn't one to feel the cold. 'The wife's out at SCATS picking up some fencing,' he said unnecessarily. 'We'll go through to the kitchen and I'll put some coffee on. It's only instant, I'm afraid.'

As the water splashed noisily into an old-fashioned whistling kettle, he glanced up at the former SAS man and repeated the name. 'Lomax, Lomax. Rings a vague bell, but I don't recognise you.'

'I was on attachment from 22. We never met as far as I recall. I did some minding and close protection work with some of your agents in the field. Pretty menial stuff.'

Roebuck placed the kettle on the Aga and smiled. 'Also pretty essential stuff. Dangerous too. I'm afraid we got so engrossed in our Machiavellian schemes that we sometimes forgot about you chaps who did the legwork. You're out now, I presume?'

'A few months.'

The colonel grinned. 'And missing it like hell, I bet?'

Lomax laughed. 'And then some.'

'So what do the two of you want with me, something to do with Roddy Littlechild's trial, I imagine?'

'Yes,' Lomax replied. 'I'm his brother-in-law and Miss Browne and I are trying to prove that he didn't murder that IRA man Fitzpatrick.'

Roebuck's face was deadpan. 'Naturally you are.'

Lomax said: 'The problem is we're convinced that Roddy was set up by the Security Service, which means by implication that they were somehow involved with the murder.'

'Ouch,' Roebuck replied. 'That's dangerous territory and I'm not sure you should be telling me about it.'

Browne intervened. 'We have to tell someone, Colonel, to trust someone, and I notice you didn't even blink at the possibility it could be true.'

Absently he took three mugs from the stripped-pine dresser. 'I could believe anything in connection with Northern Ireland, especially at a time like this. And, please, do me the honour of dropping the colonel title. I've left that all behind me now. I no longer feel much pride in my work over in the province.'

'Really?' Browne asked innocently. 'I remember you speaking at the trial. Emphasising the importance of your work and Peter Keegan's contribution.'

Roebuck gave a wry smile. 'That was then. Looking back now, I sometimes wonder if we weren't all just pawns in someone else's game. Anyway, despite being flattered that you feel you can trust me, I don't really see that I can be of much help. You see, I ran Peter Keegan for Army Intelligence, whereas Roddy Littlechild was purely an agent for MI5.'

'There's a good chance the prosecution will deny he was an agent.'

'I'm sure they'll at least play it down,' Roebuck agreed, 'but I *can* confirm he was a key player in MI5's intelligence network. He was on good terms with all the major Loyalist figures, like Keegan, of course, and Rattler, Mad Dog, King Billy and the others. They'd confide in him and it would all get fed back to MI5. I know it was through him that they managed to intercept a major arms shipment from South Africa.'

'Would you be prepared to confirm all that in court?' Browne asked.

A bleak look came into Roebuck's eyes. 'Giving testimony in Peter Keegan's trial was the worst career move I ever made. After that I was sidelined and given dead-end postings.'

Lomax said: 'That's what Derek Penny reckoned happened to him over his investigation into Keegan.'

Roebuck was surprised. 'You've spoken with Derek Penny, have you? I wouldn't have thought he'd have given you the time of day.'

Browne noticed his tone. 'Do I gather you didn't get on?'

The kettle began to whistle and Roebuck removed it from the hob, filling up the line of mugs. 'You could say I wasn't too happy when he started stomping all over the province in his big copper's boots. Of course, you could argue that the inquiry should never have been set up. But after revelations in the press that Loyalists had been given information from RUC files about likely PIRA targets there was quite a furore. Someone somewhere had a vested interest in letting it go ahead. I can't believe Derek Penny was chosen by accident.'

'What do you mean?' Lomax asked.

'Derek Penny was known as an evangelical zealot, a sanctimonious and self-righteous little prick – excuse me.' He stirred the mugs, taking his time as he remembered. 'Penny's main claim to fame was terrorising motorists in West Weald. The biggest catch of drink-drivers every Christmas, that sort of thing. Always rabbiting on about Christian ethics in policing and that sort of thing. Very naive in his way about people and certainly about the facts of life in Northern Ireland. There were plenty other senior officers who would have had the wit and wisdom to walk on eggshells over there, who would have understood the delicate and difficult nature of intelligence work. But not Derek Penny. Everything to him was stark black and white. Whoever chose him must have known that.

'He'd already upset the RUC before he came to my department and started ferreting. I tried to tip him the wink, hinting that it would be unproductive to dig too deep. But he already had wind that Peter Keegan had allowed murders to go ahead to protect his cover, and then Penny was like a pit bull. Wouldn't let go however hard you hit him.'

Browne looked puzzled. 'Why should anyone in Whitehall have wanted Keegan to be exposed? I don't understand that.'

Roebuck handed out the mugs of coffee. 'I think someone saw it as an opportunity to expose British intelligence activity. I asked myself why a million times all through Keegan's trial. I'm sure you did yourself. It's only since that I've come to realise that sometime in the late eighties the agenda began to change. Some civil servants and politicians began to see Ulster as a no-win situation and began preparing the ground for a British withdrawal.'

'Roddy has said something similar,' Lomax recalled. 'That the Brighton bombing was the real watershed, followed quickly by the Anglo-Irish Agreement. His belief is that there was one faction of new wave thinking battling with the old Northern Ireland hands.'

Roebuck nodded. 'He could very well be right. But it was all quite subtle. As you know, I was in the thick of the intelligence war, but you were never aware of the gradual shift in the political landscape. In the early days, some of the Loyalist para-military groups were regarded almost as allies, doing favours for us. Gradually that stopped. Then, bit by bit, our orders were to turn on them and regard them in the same light as the Pro-visionals. Whitehall wanted the security forces to be seen as even-handed, no matter that the Loyalist groups only existed to counter PIRA.

'I only began to learn of the real turf battle going on after the trial. While I was running Keegan I had to keep MI5 briefed. I never did like their liaison officer – man called Pinfold. When everything went pear-shaped, Pinfold was more than happy to abandon Keegan. I insisted on giving evidence and Pinfold objected strongly. It was only when I went over his head to his boss, a man who was only referred to as Mr Grey – rather appropriate that – that I finally got my way. The three of us had an unholy row. It was then that I got an insight into the real divisions. Grey was old school, willing to fight on against PIRA, while Pinfold wanted to negotiate a settlement with Dublin behind the scenes. I gathered the split in opinion ran right through Whitehall and government to Cabinet level.'

'And who won?' Browne asked, anticipating Roebuck's reply.

'I think events have shown that. The British Government has made a series of concessions from before the Downing Street Declaration and since. That's when the Americans started getting heavily involved, politically active in Belfast and Dublin. So far, it's very nearly worked, but in the end it won't be enough for the Provisionals. For me the last straw was Foxtrot Four Zero.'

Lomax recognised the reference. 'The downed Chinook?'

'Mmm,' Roebuck confirmed, and leaned back against the pine refectory table, cradling his mug of coffee. 'That crash wiped out virtually the entire intelligence old guard in Northern Ireland. RUC, army and MI5. It was lunacy putting them all on one flight to an anti-terrorism conference in Fort William, Scotland. Even top commercial companies don't allow their key executives to fly all together. I would have been on that flight if my son hadn't had a car crash and been taken to hospital. I received the news and got off at the last minute. I remember several people weren't happy about me leaving. Funnily enough, I recall Pinfold was one of them. Lectured me about duty before family. I told him to stuff it.'

'Are you saying the crash wasn't an accident?' Lomax asked.

There was a sad, weary look in Roebuck's eyes. 'I can't say that. I can't know for sure, no one can.'

Browne said: 'Could it have been the IRA?'

'Very unlikely. If it was deliberate it would have required highly sophisticated knowledge and equipment to interfere with the navigation and radar equipment.'

Lomax frowned. 'You're saying one of our own government agencies was responsible?'

Roebuck shrugged. 'Responsible, involved? In collusion? It's guesswork, except that it's common knowledge that the crash site was sealed off for several days and the CIA had a unit in there searching the scene. You have to ask yourself why? Removing evidence? I don't know. All I know is that the crash cleared the decks in Northern Ireland of all the old intelligence dinosaurs like me. Within a few months the Provisionals announced their ceasefire. And for many, the reason for the crash has never been satisfactorily explained.' He gave a rueful smile. 'Anyway, it was enough for me. I left the army as soon as I could after that. I've been happy enough since. This place keeps me busy and I have time to devote to my hobby.'

'What's that?' Browne asked.

'Sky-diving.'

She winced at the thought.

'You should try it sometime, both of you. Be my guests at the club.'

The idea appealed to Lomax. 'It's a while since I've done it. Thanks, might take you up on that.'

'Meanwhile I have to ask you,' Browne said, 'if you'd give evidence for the defence. Confirm that Roddy was a loyal MI5 agent and helped the Crown. If you can corroborate what Derek Penny says, it'll strengthen our case no end.'

Roebuck grunted. 'Well, in your position I wouldn't want to

rely on Penny's testimony alone. He's a strange character. His obsession with truth can be counterproductive. He may confirm your client's good points but he'll also have no compunction about saying anything derogatory either. He could well prove to be a liability.'

'Thanks for the warning,' Browne said. 'But is that a yes?'

Roebuck half-smiled. 'I thought life was getting too boring to last. Hell, why not? Someone's got to make a stand against these people, so it may as well be me.'

'It's much appreciated,' Lomax said.

'I'm just not sure it'll be much help. But I have kept copies of many documents that crossed my desk in Northern Ireland. Some may well refer to Roddy Littlechild.' He saw the expression on Lomax's face. 'Yes, I know everything should have been shredded, but I looked at things differently after the Keegan trial. I was covering my back. I suppose I wanted an insurance policy in case anyone turned against me.'

Browne said: 'Derek Penny did much the same thing.'

The colonel nodded. 'He upset different people for different reasons, but he'd have found himself feeling just as vulnerable as I did.' He drained his coffee. 'Anyway, I don't keep that sort of stuff here. It's all safely under lock and key. Let me have your card, Miss Browne. Perhaps I can give you a call if I find anything.'

Fourteen

Two weeks later Sam Browne received a call from Colonel X.

'Got some stuff that might be of interest to you,' Colin Roebuck said in a distinctly enigmatic way. 'Can't go into detail over the blower, and I don't want to risk the post.'

'Then let's meet,' she said. The calendar on her desk read Friday 9 February. 'Maybe over the weekend?'

'Fine. I'm at the parachute club every Saturday. Why don't you come up and see the fun?'

It was agreed. She felt a thrill of anticipation but made a deliberate attempt to subdue it; there was no point in building her own or Roddy's family's hopes up, only to see them badly dashed. Roebuck's find *could* be everything, or nothing.

She put a call through to Evie's flat which Lomax answered. 'I've heard from a mutual friend of ours, Chris, that builder who specialises in Tudor restoration. Thought I'd go and see him tomorrow and wondered if you'd like to come along?'

Lomax picked up on it immediately, deliberately playing it down for the benefit of any eavesdropper. 'Well, if you'd *really* like my company, I suppose a breath of country air would do me good.'

'I'll pick you up at ten. Show off my new motor.'

'Can't I drive? It'd be nice to get there in one piece.'

'Chauvinist pig!' she laughed.

'I'm going on the razz tonight with Joe, so I could be in a fragile state. Promise you'll take it slow?'

'Promise.'

But, of course, she didn't.

They went like a rocket along the M40 towards Oxford in the second-hand silver sports coupe that Totty's brother had procured for her. And their speed seemed only to drop marginally when they turned off for the airfield.

He glanced sideways at her and was reassured to see that at

least she was concentrating fully for once. And looked more happy and relaxed than he'd seen her for a long time, her hair casually up and wearing a lumberjack shirt, jeans and trainers. Almost a different woman.

It was just twelve when Lomax said: 'Can I put the radio on? I missed the news last night.'

'So did I, but it sounds to me as if you and Joe missed last night, period.'

He turned the dial. 'Looks complicated.'

'It is. Radio, CD and cassette. The instruction book's bigger than the one for the car.'

Suddenly the announcer's voice filled the cockpit. Neither of them registered exactly what he said, just key words leaping out to stun the brain. '*Last night's IRA bomb in Docklands . . . Two dead and dozens injured. Some horrific . . . Lacerations from flying glass . . . Timed for maximum casualties . . . Condemned by London, Dublin and Washington . . . Ceasefire at an end . . .*'

'BASTARDS!' Browne shouted at the road. 'God, Chris, can you believe it? Starting all over again.'

He shook his head. 'You know, even I was thinking it might last.' Momentarily he remembered his trip to Belfast just before Christmas, the happy faces of the shoppers and late-night revellers. He murmured: 'So it was all just a cruel deception.'

'And now everything's back to normal then,' she said, accelerating with the turbo kicking in at four thousand revs as they overtook a lumbering juggernaut. Air horns blasted from the opposite direction as she cleared the oncoming tanker by a few feet.

Lomax blanched. 'Either you're the best woman driver in Britain, Sam, or the luckiest.'

'What?' She hadn't even realised how close she'd come.

'Sure, be angry with the terrorists, but don't take it out on the roads. Not while I'm with you. When you said you'd bought a Nissan, I didn't know you meant a bloody 200SX.'

She laughed then, her black mood broken, and grinned at him. 'Yeah, they've come a long way since they built those tin huts in the Second World War, haven't they?'

Lomax smiled. 'Very funny, but different spelling, I think.

330

Anyway this isn't another Celica, this is a monster. One of the fastest of its class.'

'But a beautiful monster,' she replied lightly. 'A poor girl's Porsche.'

'It needs to be treated with respect and caution – like all monsters.'

She flicked a look in his direction. 'If that's a very unsubtle allusion to me, Mr Lomax, then you'd better believe it.'

The distant speck of a high-flying light aircraft in the porcelain sky indicated that they were nearing the airfield. Even as Lomax pointed out the machine, half a dozen tiny black figures spiralled away from it in free-fall. After a few seconds they edged together, holding hands to form a circle, then breaking again, going their separate ways. Then the canopies mushroomed and disappeared beyond the treeline.

'You haven't changed your mind then?' Lomax asked.

'Are you joking? They must be mad. You'll be suggesting I go bungee-jumping next.'

'Can't be any more dangerous than driving with you.'

Deliberately she put her foot on the gas.

As they entered the wire-mesh gates, the Cessna 208 Caravan touched down while its former passengers, carrying their parachute bundles, were still trudging back across the field towards the clubhouse. Browne parked beside the concrete apron on which a number of tables and chairs were set out for onlookers.

Roebuck, wearing a red jumpsuit and his face grinning beneath the bald sunburnt crown, recognised them and rose to his feet. He waved and beckoned them to join him. His bone-dome helmet and goggles were on the table, surrounded by coffee cups and the remains of a sandwich lunch.

A handsome woman in her forties with straight silver-grey hair sat next to him. Looking very much an army officer's wife, she wore an old Barbour and a tweed plaid skirt against the nagging wind that blew uninterrupted across the field. 'Nice to see you, Miss Browne, and you Lomax. This is my wife Arabella.'

'You're not jumping?' Browne asked as they shook hands.

'Good grief, no! I'm just here for moral support while the little boys play their games.'

Roebuck turned to Lomax. 'What about you? One of our members has to leave early, so there'll be a spare place on the flight after next.'

Lomax was delighted. 'Great idea. I've brought my log. A jump today will keep it up to date.'

'Then I'm happy to oblige,' Roebuck replied, pleased to have found a like-minded soul. 'I've got a spare chute in the back of the car,' he glanced at Browne, 'along with some copies of documents I've found for you.'

'What have you got?'

With a grin and a conspiratorial flourish, he tapped the side of his nose. 'Reports that I originally unearthed for the Keegan trial. There are two references in official secret documents confirming that your client Roddy Littlechild was an acting agent for MI5 and that, with Keegan, he was directly responsible for the seizing of Loyalist arms smuggled in from South Africa in 1988. And I can vouch for the authenticity of those documents. One was an analysis by Army Intelligence and the other was from the Security Service.'

'That's brilliant,' Browne said.

'There was something else I'd completely forgotten about. An old RUC investigation report from 1987 into the murder of a South African, Dominic Smals. Highly classified and before my time in the province. Only reason I kept it was because it referred to Keegan who I was then running. And it begged more questions than it answered. Part of it refers to an interview with an RUC informer who claimed he saw Keegan, who was then in the Ulster Defenders, hand over small arms to two unidentified visitors from South Africa in return for money. This was just twenty-four hours before Smals was shot.'

'Keegan must have just returned with his family from South Africa,' Lomax added, 'after he'd decided he'd had enough of the undercover life.'

Roebuck said: 'I remember checking my predecessor's files, but there was no reference to the incident. If it was an Army Intelligence job, then it was highly irregular and suggested to

332

me an MI5 involvement. Naturally I never asked Keegan about it because, officially, it never happened.'

'This is dynamite,' Browne said, scarcely able to keep the excitement from her voice.

'I don't know about that,' Roebuck cautioned. 'It's far from conclusive. My predecessor died aboard Foxtrot Four Zero and the informer isn't specifically named in the report. To identify him you'll need the co-operation of the RUC and I doubt you'll get it. At least it suggests that at the time the police's prime suspect was Peter Keegan and not Rodney Littlechild.'

'And Keegan wasn't arrested because Army Intelligence and MI5 were protecting him,' Lomax guessed.

'You can see how times have changed,' Roebuck said grimly. 'Anyway, it's a pleasure to be a bringer of good tidings.'

'It'll fully back up Derek Penny's evidence,' Browne told him, 'which is *just* what Roddy needs.'

The former Army Intelligence officer frowned. 'Then it's a double pleasure, because I've a feeling Derek Penny's evidence is no longer worth what it was.'

'What do you mean?'

Arabella said: 'Then you haven't seen today's paper.' She lifted the folded tabloid from beneath Roebuck's helmet. 'We don't usually get this rag, but when Colin saw the front page . . .'

Browne almost snatched it from her and stared open-mouthed at the lurid headline.

EX-POLICE CHIEF IN CHOIRBOY SEX SCANDAL

Lomax peered over her shoulder with a sinking feeling in the pit of his stomach. 'Has he been arrested?'

She was fumbling in her bag for her reading specs. 'I don't think so. Wait a second. No, it says held for questioning.'

'Then surely they can't name him,' Lomax said.

'They haven't,' Roebuck confirmed, 'but it's Derek Penny all right. It'll be clear enough to anyone who's ever known him. What does it say? Former high-profile senior police officer of West Weald. No newcomer to controversy after investigating allegations of RUC collusion with Loyalist terrorists in Ulster. And a well-known choirmaster in amateur circles.'

Browne shook her head. 'This is a disgusting piece of journalism. And an interview with two alleged victims. You're right, they might just as well have yelled his name from the rooftops.'

'Do you think there's any truth in it?' Arabella asked.

'I've always thought I could smell closet gays at fifty paces, but I've been wrong before,' Browne said furiously. She slapped her hand against the paper. 'But look at this *crap*, pointing out he and his wife had no children. Bloody innuendo! The poor man – I must call him later; he needs legal help.'

Lomax said: 'I think you've got enough on your hands right now.'

She glared at him. 'Do you now? I don't seem to remember asking your opinion.'

Roebuck and his wife exchanged bewildered glances. The colonel said quickly: 'Look, I'm due to go up now. You two have a coffee with Arabella. I'll be back in half an hour and then we can run through those files.' He looked at Lomax. 'You still on for later, Chris?'

'You bet.'

This time it was the two women who looked at each other, shaking their heads in unison. Boys will be boys. They'll never grow up. Incorrigible.

Roebuck disappeared into the clubhouse with his helmet and re-emerged some five minutes later with a group of skydiving friends. Laughing and joking, they sauntered across the turf to where the Cessna pilot was winding up the revs and checking the flaps.

'They're mostly ex-army,' Arabella explained. 'There's a lot of military people in this area. Just as well, otherwise it would have driven Colin mad. He's not very used to talking with civilian types. He really misses army life.'

'But not you?' Browne asked.

'I'm just glad he got out in one piece. I wasn't happy with what he was up to in Northern Ireland, all that dangerous covert work.' She glanced at Lomax. 'And you, Chris, I gather you worked with my husband's unit?'

334

'Yes, but we never met.' He didn't shatter her illusions by telling her it was men like him who faced death every day on the urban frontline, not the desk-bound spymasters like her husband.

Browne said: 'I think Chris misses the army life too.'

'I miss the life,' Lomax replied, 'but not some of the work. I'd had enough.'

Arabella laughed brightly. 'I'm not at all sure I believe you, you know.'

But Browne saw the dark shadow fall across his eyes and instinctively knew he wasn't seeing the sunlit green of the airstrip as the Cessna taxied ready for takeoff. Remembered secrets he'd shared with her that night of the storm. Knew he was in the black hell of Goose Green. Or was he on the rainsodden Bosnian hillside when an enemy round again had his name on it? Or was it behind Iraqi lines, with the young goatherd's warm blood on his hands, on the day that Lomax lost his soul?

Beneath the table, she moved her fingers across his knee and he looked towards her as she took his large hand in hers and squeezed.

But she'd been wrong. For that transient moment he'd been back in the run-down Bogside ghetto. Lounging against a wall, scruffy in jeans and trainers, eating from a greasy bag of chips. Watching, and suddenly knowing he was being watched. Microphone clipped to the neck of his T-shirt, but the enemy too close for him to talk. The Browning High-Power bulky and comforting in his waistband, but too far away to reach it if things went wrong . . .

A premonition. In just those few seconds, as the Cessna gathered speed and its nose lifted, he knew. Knew he'd be going back. Back to face the demons on the dark, dank streets. Demons he thought he'd left behind for ever.

'That was a smooth takeoff,' Arabella observed. 'The pilot's really very good.'

The Cessna swept skyward, skimming over the trees at the field edge as it rapidly gained height, the engine noise receding to become a lazy distant drone. Sunlight glinted on the canting wings as it swept over the distant spires of Oxford.

'They usually jump from around twelve thousand feet,' Roebuck's wife said. 'We can expect them back over the field in about ten minutes. Let me get you both a coffee.'

She returned a little later with a tray carrying sturdy china cups and saucers bearing the paraclub's crest. As she sat and passed the sugar lumps and plastic packs of milk, she said suddenly: 'I do hope you realise the risk Colin is taking for you. At any trial it's going to come out that he kept copies of classified documents and made them available to you.'

'I realise that,' Browne said, 'and we're very grateful.'

Arabella smiled stiffly. 'I hope you are. It's a serious contravention of the Official Secrets Act. People at the Ministry of Defence can take great exception to that sort of thing. And to them it won't make the slightest difference that it was being used to save an innocent man. I've seen how vindictive they can be, especially if it casts government departments in a bad light. He could end up in court himself.'

Browne shook her head. 'Not if we win our case. They'll not want to stir it all up again.'

'That's a very big "if" I'm afraid.'

'If your husband was ever charged, Mrs Roebuck, I can promise you he'll have the best lawyer money can buy.'

Arabella held the other woman's gaze. 'If that's a joke, Miss Browne, I'm afraid it's a very bad one.'

'I wasn't joking.'

A voice called out from one of the adjoining tables as the young son of one of the skydivers was first to spot the returning Cessna. All eyes turned in the direction of the pointing finger. Family members brought out binoculars and telescopes; children jumped up and down with excitement while wives looked on with slightly anxious expressions.

'I'm not sure I want you to do this,' Browne murmured to Lomax.

'I didn't know you cared.' But behind his throwaway response he felt a small glow of satisfaction that she evidently did. It was a start.

336

They could all see the Cessna now, hear the faint buzz of its engine high above and downwind of the airfield. One of the wives nearby gave a little gasp as the first dark speck detached itself from the aircraft's minuscule silhouette. It was followed by another, then another. Within split seconds, six parachutists were free-falling towards the earth, edging in towards each other in readiness for linking hands.

A small cheer went up from the onlookers and some clapped spontaneously. It had been perfect aerial choreography.

'Bravo,' Arabella breathed. 'That's the best one this year. Colin's training them, you know. He'd like to form a competition team. If he could do that, he might even stop missing the army.'

The circle broke, the individual skydivers bursting away to give themselves space to deploy, bodies now rapidly becoming identifiable as they plunged groundward. One canopy snapped open, jolting the body in its harness and they could see the man looking up to check the rigging lines. Another opened, and the others deployed in quick succession, drifting gracefully over the Oxfordshire countryside. All moving towards the X-marker of fluorescent orange plastic. It was looking good.

'Christ,' Lomax gasped, 'someone's in the shit.'

'What?' Arabella said.

But she didn't need an answer. Now she and Browne could see it too. The last skydiver had failed to deploy. He was hurtling to earth, overtaking the staggered row of floating canopies.

'Your reserve,' Lomax urged beneath his breath, 'pull your reserve.'

'My God!' Browne exclaimed, hand to her mouth.

Instinctively Arabella knew. 'Oh, Colin!'

At last the reserve began to unravel, but it was all too late.

They sensed rather than felt or heard the bone-shattering force of the impact at the far corner of the field. One of the wives screamed. Then, for a moment, there was a shocked silence.

'Call an ambulance!' someone shouted. People began running forward.

Suddenly Arabella shook herself from her paralysed stupor.

337

'I'll get the car,' she said and broke into a run, leaving Lomax and Browne to follow.

She had the engine started even as they scrambled in, driving off before the doors were properly closed. 'We don't *know* it's Colin,' Browne said hopefully.

Arabella didn't reply.

Giving the X-marker a wide berth to avoid the other sky-divers who were now landing, they overtook the running helpers and raced towards the field edge. As they neared, Lomax recognised the red jumpsuit. Arabella pulled up sharply and leapt out, leaving the engine running.

Roebuck was on his back, his face hidden behind the helmet and goggles. His body appeared normal at first glance, with no grotesquely distorted limbs, but it also looked strangely slack as though the jumpsuit contained crumpled newspapers rather than solid flesh and bone. Lomax guessed the man's skeleton was shattered to smithereens.

He knelt down and checked the pulse. It was there, but feeble.

'Is he alive?' Arabella asked, stooping on the other side.

'Yes.'

Carefully, Lomax eased the goggles up onto the helmet. Roebuck's eyes were closed and the trickle of blood from his mouth exaggerated the waxy whiteness of his skin. He looked strangely calm, almost peaceful.

'Colin?' Arabella touched his cheek with her fingertips. 'Colin, can you hear me?'

The eyes fluttered open, unfocused. Parched lips mouthed his wife's name silently.

'You're okay, Colin. You'll be okay.'

Browne looked across the body and caught Lomax's glance; his face was impassive. She guessed he'd seen this many times before, probably even worse.

Arabella leaned over her husband, her ear close to his mouth to catch his last words. Slowly she regained her feet, trembling slightly as she looked down at the eyes staring sightlessly at the sky he'd loved so much.

'He said something about the ripcord,' she murmured, too numbed to know what she was doing or thinking.

Browne put her arm round the woman's shoulder, gathering her in like a hurt child. But Arabella's tears wouldn't come, not yet.

The remaining skydivers had now joined the others who had run from the clubhouse; all stood in a semicircle, looking on in dread horror, not wanting to intrude on the moment of private grief.

'Let's take you back,' Browne said tentatively. 'Some hot tea, something stronger.'

Arabella stared at her, scarcely comprehending. 'Tea? That's what Colin always says. Tea in a crisis. Things never seem as bad . . .'

'Would you rather stay here?'

The woman stared down at her husband's shattered body. 'He looks so restful, at peace.' She sniffed heavily, straightened her back. 'I can do nothing here, not now. Tea, yes. I need some tea.'

Lomax watched as they turned back towards the car, then knelt again and gently closed Roebuck's eyelids. Then he noticed the colonel's fist. Clutched in his fingers was the ripcord, the strap sheared neatly. Almost as though it had been cut.

Not cut, of course, he told himself, because if it had been, Roebuck would have spotted it when he checked his rig before the jump. He slid the strap from the fingers and examined it carefully, noticing the staining and slightly acrid smell. The material wasn't cut, he realised, but rotted.

Then the answer came to him. Acid.

He stuffed the cord into his pocket as the crowd edged forward, and left to join Browne and Roebuck's wife. They sat in the back of the car and he took the wheel, driving slowly back to the clubhouse, passing the deflated canopies that had been abandoned where they landed.

Parking beside Browne's 200SX, they returned to the tables. The club steward saw them and rushed off to fetch teacups and a bottle of brandy from the bar. The Roebucks' friends came up, shocked and offering hesitant commiserations.

It was another five minutes before the police arrived, followed closely by an ambulance. People drifted back as police taped off the scene of the accident and photographs were taken for the record before the paramedics stretchered Roebuck's corpse into their vehicle.

A police sergeant approached and spoke with Arabella for a few moments, offering his sympathies and a lift to her home or to the hospital, whichever she preferred.

'I'll be another five minutes,' he told her. 'Then I'll pick you up.'

As he walked away Arabella turned to Browne. 'You'd best have those papers my husband promised. He wanted that.' There was a lump in her throat. 'It can't do him any harm now. Would you mind?' She held out the car keys.

'It's okay,' Lomax said, 'I'll get them.'

He took the keys, stood and turned. Three paces took him to the first row of parked cars. Several people were milling around, still in a state of shock, still talking it through with friends, somehow not wanting to leave in case it seemed they didn't really care.

For a moment he thought Roebuck's car wasn't where he'd left it. Next to the glistening sleek body of Browne's 200SX was a different vehicle. He knew it was a different vehicle because someone else had the boot lid open and was shouldering his parachute pack. The man closed and relocked it and began walking away towards the airfield gates where a nondescript grey car waited, its engine idling.

Lomax did a double take. The car *was* Roebuck's. What in hell? Instead of running after the man, instinctively he called out. That was stupid, he realised almost immediately. But it was already too late as he heard his own words, 'HEY! YOU!' screaming in his ears.

The man turned for a second, then began to run. Lomax could see then that, apart from the parapack over his shoulder, he carried a briefcase in his left hand. Briefcase. The realisation struck Lomax like a thunderbolt. Roebuck's briefcase. Containing the classified documents for Roddy Littlechild's defence.

'What is it?' Browne called.

But he wasn't hearing. Instead he broke into a sprint, trying in desperation to make up the distance before the man reached the waiting car. It was hopeless, of course, because he already had the rear door open and was hurling in the parapack before scrambling in after it.

Lomax redoubled his effort, legs pounding and his heart thudding as he willed himself on. He was within reach of the rear, when he was caught in the sudden burbling cloud of exhaust. It clawed at his throat, the car tantalisingly close, the rear bumper edging away from his outstretched hand. In a final effort he flung himself at the smooth metallic surface. One hand snatched at the radio aerial and his other sought a grip, any grip. But there was nothing, just polished steel that was slippery beneath his palm. He felt the surge of power trying to pull him off, was aware of the rear door flapping, not even closed before the driver took off.

The aerial snapped. Immediately the force of his effort to hold on propelled him backwards, his fingernails tearing as he vainly tried to dig them in. He felt himself going, and the next second was dumped unceremoniously on the gravel by the gate. Dust from the spinning wheels enshrouded him as the car accelerated away.

'For God's sake, Chris, what are you playing at?' He turned to see Browne running up to him.

Lomax gulped for breath. 'Those bastards have just taken the papers from Roebuck's car.'

Her mouth fell open.

'Don't stand gawping, woman. Get your bloody car!'

She went to retort, changed her mind, then turned and started running back towards her 200SX. Lomax crawled painfully to his feet. His trousers were in shreds, two gaping holes at the knees, and his skin red with grazing.

There were a dozen or so people around the car park who glimpsed some or all of what had happened. Now they looked at him with the bemused and silent stares more usually reserved for drunks and lunatics.

'Did anyone get the number of that car?' he called out.

No one had. And neither had he, damn it. He was angry with himself for not having stopped and noted the registration rather than gone running after it like some macho hero in a Hollywood movie.

It seemed an embarrassingly long wait before Browne's 200SX pulled up alongside and he leapt in.

'Go right!' he snapped, and yanked the seatbelt harness across his body. 'And step on it!'

'Yes, boss,' she murmured, swinging the long nose out through the gates and accelerating so hard that the rear wheels spun and fishtailed on the dusty tarmac.

Nought to sixty in seven seconds, Browne had told him earlier. Well, it would need to be for them to stand a chance of catching up with the thieves.

'What sort of car was it?' Browne asked, trying to think logically as they flashed through a sun-dappled tunnel of trees.

'A Ford, I think.' He tried hard to recall. 'Yes, a Mondeo. Just a 1.8. But if this is MI5, there'll be something different under the bonnet.'

'MI5?' She glanced at him.

'Watch the road!' he ordered angrily. 'God, Sam, you don't think it was a bloody coincidence, do you? Roebuck dies and a passing thief just happens to steal the stuff from the back of his car. It was planned. The bastard didn't even have to jemmy the boot, he had a skeleton key.'

'Jesus.' She stared blindly at the road ahead, understeering as they took the bend wide, drifting onto the offside.

'Concentrate, Sam,' Lomax said. 'Use the right gears – always max power. Brake hard before the bend, change down and accelerate out, foot right down!'

'You can fucking drive!' she retorted.

'No time. Just do it.'

'Shit!'

Another bend. She braked too late, fumbling the gears, losing

342

power and ground. Then she found second, and floored the gas peddle.

'That's better,' he said charitably, but she knew he didn't mean it.

'Are you saying Roebuck was murdered?'

'Virtually. His chute was tampered with. It looked like the reverse of the ripcord strap had been scored with a razor blade, then some form of acid applied. Maybe brake fluid.'

'You didn't say anything to his wife.'

'I think she had enough on her plate. Anyway, I couldn't be certain then. I am now. Why else would they take his spare parachute?'

'The one you were going to use?'

'Whoever sabotaged them wouldn't have known which one Roebuck was going to jump with.'

'God, Chris, that means it could have been you back there.'

It was a chastening thought on which he didn't want to dwell. 'I imagine that's why they've taken the spare. Any inquiry might ask how his parachute was damaged, maybe snagged or stored next to corrosive liquid. But with two of them identically tampered with, the police would be virtually certain it was deliberate sabotage. The thieves probably planned to lift it while we were all out at the accident. Taking the car with us messed up their plans.' He glanced forward. 'Careful!'

But he needn't have worried. This time Browne's timing was perfect as the bend loomed. She braked hard at the last moment, deftly switched gears, and gunned up the power almost immediately she began turning the wheel. The 200SX went round tight and hard, nearside wheels virtually touching the embankment, clinging tight as the rear started to break away, so she was already lined up for the next straight. Up ahead brake lights blinked momentarily in the gloom of overhanging trees as the Mondeo vanished around another twist in the road. Maybe two hundred yards ahead. Not bad. Not exactly good either, but at least they were gaining.

The sight of their quarry spurred Browne on, and Lomax found his knuckles whitening as the car's speed increased perceptibly. She was good, he conceded; at least when she put her mind to it. Then she went into the next turn a shade too fast, the tyres shrieking in protest and the rear beginning to slide before she throttled up. Momentarily, he glimpsed the Fiat Panda heading towards them, the startled white faces of the elderly couple. Heard the warning bark of the horn as the little car crunched into the offside hedge.

'Sod,' Browne chided herself, her gaze fixed ahead on the Mondeo. 'Are they all right?'

Lomax glanced over his shoulder. 'I should think so. Just a dented wing.'

They'd entered a straight avenue of towering limes and now they were really shifting, the 16-valve turbo kicking in to launch them forward like a jet fighter with afterburners full on. It ate up the gap of worn tarmac behind the leading car, clearly taking its driver by surprise.

'Keep your nerve,' Lomax said, 'and don't go mad. If only you can get close enough to get the registration number.'

'Sod that, Chris. I'm going to drive the bastard off the road and make a citizen's arrest.'

Despite himself, Lomax had to smile; she clearly meant every word. But now that the Mondeo's driver had picked them up, he was doing something about it. Whatever he had in the engine compartment, it was more than 1.8 litres. Almost immediately he began to surge ahead again, stretching out the distance between them before he disappeared round another hairpin.

Browne followed, managing her best racing change and holding the bend like a limpet. They'd regained their loss and begun closing the gap again. Then the Mondeo flashed past a red Roadworks Ahead sign on the verge, moments before it leapt a humpback bridge, the chassis lifting high on its springs until the wheels all but lost contact with the road. The car plunged out of sight. Browne followed. It felt like taking off from a ski jump, the suspension shuddering under the impact of their landing.

Suddenly everything came into view. Their side of the road coned off and the Mondeo reaching the line of cars that waited for the red traffic light to change.

But the Mondeo driver wasn't about to join the queue.

Although a Rover saloon was heading towards him, past the steamroller and generator abandoned for the weekend, the Mondeo driver swung out to pass the waiting line. His hooter shrieked out a heart-stopping warning. A blaze of headlights reflected in the Rover's windscreen as the other car headed straight for it.

Browne didn't hesitate. She changed down and followed the Mondeo, bypassing the queue as more hooters joined the cacophony of protest. Meanwhile the driver of the Rover lost his nerve and spun the wheel as the racing Mondeo bore down on him. With a nauseating crunch of steel and shattering of glass, the Rover burst through the red tape and into the heavy front wheel of the steamroller. Traffic cones were scattered everywhere. Browne ploughed through them, now right on the Mondeo's tail as it gathered speed. Lomax could clearly see the tense white face of the thief glaring back at him. In the excitement of the moment he almost forgot about the registration number; he took a pen from his jacket and hastily scribbled it down in his pocket book.

'Okay, Sam, I've got his number. You can ease off now before we kill someone or ourselves.'

'You're joking,' she snapped back. 'If they've got Roebuck's evidence, we'll never see it again. And you don't think they're genuine plates, do you?'

Of course she was right. Did he really think he could trot down to the local police station, report the theft and the car number and seriously expect anything to happen as a result?

She clung tenaciously to within inches of the rear of the Mondeo, matching his acceleration and braking when he was forced to slow for a bend. He couldn't shake her off. Then twice he tried braking without warning, forcing her to swerve, her bumper just missing his offside light cluster.

'Try that just once more,' she willed.

He did. And this time she was ready. Instead of braking, she threw the wheel hard over to the right and pushed her foot to the floor. As the 200SX swerved out, she double-checked the short, straight ahead was clear and let the turbo kick in. The coupe surged forward alongside the Mondeo.

'Don't do it!' Lomax warned.

The Mondeo's driver glanced sideways as they passed, a look of consternation on his face. He was young, still in his twenties. Lomax shut his eyes. The two cars were neck and neck, the 200SX squeezing ahead, the speedo needle sweeping past the hundred mark. Then she swung the wheel left, hard without warning, cutting right across the Mondeo's path.

The driver reacted wrongly. Perhaps he was too new to the game, or rusty, or tired or just badly trained. Or perhaps he simply wasn't expecting such a dangerous and deadly manoeuvre by a good-looking middle-aged female solicitor.

In any event, he was caught off guard. Instead of accelerating, driving the 200SX into a spin or cutting Browne up before she cut him, his reaction was that of any layman. Instinctively, he swung his wheel left to avoid her.

It was all over in a second. Once he'd made his error, he was travelling too fast to do anything about it. The Mondeo bounced over the rough turf of the verge and down the other side, out of view. Browne stood on the brakes and the 200SX went into a shrieking, slewing skid until the ABS cut in and they straightened up. Jamming the gearshift into reverse, she backed up at speed to where the Mondeo had disappeared. Before it had stopped, Lomax was already out and running up the low embankment where he paused.

The Mondeo had careered off the verge and taken flight across a drainage ditch before smashing through a wire fence into a wheatfield. It had landed nose first, buckling the bonnet and causing the doors to burst open. The driver was hanging half out, restrained by his seat belt.

Lomax edged down the grassy slope and jumped the ditch.

'Wait for me, Christ,' Browne called, her trainers skidding on the long grass.

He offered his hand to help her across the ditch then they proceeded to pick their way through the tangle of wire and uprooted fence posts. By the time they'd cleared it, the driver had recovered his senses and was struggling to release his seat belt.

'Stay where you are!' Browne yelled.

346

'Sam!' Lomax warned.

But the young man was already out. In jeans and nondescript bomber jacket, he looked mean and fit with close-cropped hair and an earring. Despite a cut above his eye and his slightly groggy stance, he'd made a quick recovery and was now moving towards Browne in a low crouch.

'Fuck off, cow!' he demanded.

She stared at him, suddenly filled with abject horror. He raised his arm, bent at the elbow to give her a back-handed slap and clear his escape route. Instinctively Browne ducked and parried with her left forearm, knocking his aside. As his guard opened, she swung her right fist hard and low, hunching so that the full weight of her shoulder went in behind it. The blow struck him squarely in the abdomen and he collapsed onto his knees, winded.

Browne looked in surprise and amazement at what she'd just done, then a smug little smile broke on her lips.

'You bastard,' she said flatly. Then she brought up her knee, catching him hard under the chin. He toppled over, unconscious.

Lomax turned to locate the passenger who'd taken Roebuck's documents and parapack. He was staggering out of the rear door and beginning to run across the field, still clutching the briefcase. Lomax sprinted after him, pounding across the grass, then launched himself in a rugby tackle. As his arms encircled the thrashing legs, the passenger toppled forward with his hands outstretched to break the fall.

The man began kicking, trying to break the grip, but Lomax held fast, clawing his way slowly up the body under a rain of blows. A fist caught him on the cheek, then full on his nose. It was an excruciating pain, but he forced himself to ignore it until he could grab the flailing limb with both hands. Executing a stabbing knuckle-punch to the man's bicep, Lomax momentarily disabled him. That gave Lomax the opportunity to sit up and pinion the man to the ground with his knee while dragging the numbed arm securely up into the small of his prisoner's back.

'One squeak,' Lomax warned breathlessly, 'and it snaps. Okay?'

There was a muffled surrender mouthed from the face pressed into the grass. Then the body relaxed, the fight gone. Lomax dragged the man to his feet and picked up the briefcase before frog-marching him back to the car.

Browne had found a wheel brace in the boot of the battered Mondeo and stood with it at the ready as the driver stirred on the ground.

'I thought you'd killed him,' Lomax said. 'That was some road rage.'

'I should have kicked him in the balls,' she replied tersely.

'I think you've done him enough damage.' He pushed the second man roughly onto the ground beside the driver. 'Right, now you two have got some explaining to do.'

'Who's this?' Browne said suddenly. She stood facing the road and could see a couple scrambling down the bank from a car that had pulled up behind her 200SX.

The man was middle-aged and wearing a flat cap, but the woman looked several years younger.

'What's happened?' the man called out. 'Is anyone hurt?'

'Damn,' Lomax cursed. 'That's all we need. I wanted a few moments alone with these two.'

The man was slightly out of breath as he arrived. 'Goodness me, what a smash! Are these two injured?'

Browne forced a sweet smile and reached out for the man's shoulder, starting to turn him away. 'It's just minor cuts and bumps, but would you mind going to the nearest phone and calling for an ambulance. They ought to have a proper checkup.'

'No need, I've got a mobile phone.'

Lomax's heart sank as the man reached into the pocket of his short driving coat and pulled out a Browning 9mm.

'What the hell?' Lomax began, then stopped. He didn't have to ask what was going on. It was all too clear and he kicked himself for his own ineptitude. Of course, MI5 wouldn't have sent in one team for a tricky operation like the one at the airfield. Anything could have gone wrong, as indeed it had. And he and Browne had been so busy chasing the Mondeo it had never occurred to them that they in turn were being chased.

'Open the boot of the car and get inside,' the man ordered.

'You bloody murderer!' Browne snarled.

It was the woman now who stepped forward. She was in her late thirties, solidly built although not unattractive. Without hesitation, she slapped Browne hard across the cheek. The solicitor fell back against the side of the car; when her hand came away from her mouth there was blood on her fingers. 'Do as you're told,' the woman ordered. 'Or we'll bloody well torch it with you inside!'

The man glanced down at the two men. 'Eddie, Greg, on your pins. And you've got nothing to laugh about. Get that briefcase and the parachute and get over to our car. I'll talk to you later.'

Browne was now reluctantly climbing into the boot, still glowering. Lomax held his tongue and watched, looking for an opportunity to take them on. But the odds weren't good and the woman might also be armed. He studied the gunman's face carefully until the woman saw Lomax staring at him. 'Now you. Get in with her.'

'We hardly know each other.'

'Well, now's your chance to get acquainted. Shift!'

Browne squeezed up as tightly as she could to allow room for Lomax. 'I'll see you in court one day,' she told the gunman who said nothing, but slammed the lid.

They were immediately entombed in absolute blackness, sounds from outside cut off and a faint smell of petrol in the air.

'I hope that was an idle threat about torching the car,' Lomax said.

Browne's face was only inches from his, but he could see nothing. 'God, Chris, they wouldn't, would they?'

Now he wished he hadn't mentioned it. 'I shouldn't think so.'

Alarm remained in her voice. 'We'll suffocate, I'm feeling claustrophobic already.' She hammered her fist on the metal pressing down on her head; not a sound came from outside.

'Someone will be along soon.'

'We're in the middle of the countryside, Chris.'

'There's always *someone* around. We'll be seen from the road,' he assured. 'Now, is there some sort of fastener or catch behind you? We might be able to let the back seat down and get out that way.'

'I can't move.'

'Let me try.'

'Get your hands off my tits!'

'Sorry.'

'Liar!'

He chuckled. 'True.' He couldn't find any form of catch as he ran his fingers along the top edge of the seat. 'It's no good.'

'Oh, God,' she wailed.

He changed the subject, trying to imagine her in the darkness. 'Where did you learn to pack a punch like that?'

'Barney's Gym. I box there.'

'No kidding. No shortage of sparring partners, I bet?'

He could tell somehow she was smiling when she said: 'No, why? Fancy your chances in a couple of rounds?'

'Not after I saw the way you floored that bastard.'

'Better than he deserved.'

'Still, that woman had a point.'

'What?'

'Said this was an opportunity for us to get acquainted.'

'He was gross!'

'I thought I recognised him.'

'That pig?'

'Something familiar.'

'I'm scared. I can't breathe. The air's running out.'

'No, it's not.'

'Chris, what are you doing?'

'Kissing you.'

And that was the bizarre scene that greeted the bemused police officer who released the boot. They had been incarcerated for barely ten minutes when he'd seen the crashed car while passing on Panda patrol.

'You're not going to believe this,' Lomax began, shielding his eyes from the sudden influx of light.

And clearly the young constable didn't. Neither did the desk sergeant at the local police station. Browne let Lomax do the talking and took her cue from him. He missed out all speculation about tampered parachutes and just reported that after Roebuck's death he'd seen a stranger stealing belongings from the widow's car. They'd given chase and the thieves had gone too fast and driven themselves off the road. He didn't mention that Browne had forced them off. The sergeant was obviously sceptical about the arrival of two strangers – Lomax omitted mention of guns – although he didn't challenge the statement. However extraordinary it sounded, he couldn't fathom how else they could have ended up in the boot of a crashed car that wasn't theirs.

'I'm glad you didn't mention I hit that creep,' Browne said as they were driving back to London afterwards. 'With the state of British law, I'd have probably been arrested for criminal assault.'

'There was no point trying to get the police involved. Even if they believed half of it, MI5 would arrange to have it hushed up. Look what Bill Johnson was told when he started taking an interest. And your joke about an assault charge isn't that funny. If we kicked up a fuss you might just get charged with dangerous driving for real. As it is, I expect the local plod will just file the incident away and forget about it.'

'Well, I certainly won't. If someone really did murder Roebuck, I want him to swing for it.'

'They *did* murder him, Sam. It's getting nasty.'

'But they didn't kill us. Why?'

'Not a time of their choosing. Or else we're too close to a high-profile trial.'

'Chris, I'm frightened.'

'You'll be okay. They only bump off lawyers in Italy.'

'That's not funny.'

'Anyway,' Lomax said, 'let's forget about it. Let me take you out for a meal tonight.'

She shook her head. 'I'm not in the mood. Not after what happened to Colin.'

'We can commiserate together. Like we did in the car.'

'That was a moment of madness, Chris. I was scared.'

'At least you didn't threaten to have me charged with attempted rape this time.'

'You were lucky.'

He shook his head sadly. 'Why do you always pull back, Sam? What is it with you?'

'Look, Chris, I don't want to get involved, that's all. Not with you, not with anyone. And I'm not pulling back. I told you I'm not in the mood. Besides, I've got work to do. I want to phone Derek Penny when I get home.'

'It's Saturday.'

'The world doesn't stop just because it's the weekend, Chris. We've just lost one of our two star witnesses. With all this stuff in the papers about child abuse, I don't want Derek Penny going wobbly on us too.'

Reluctantly he had to admit she was right. He'd seen the mountain of files she had to work through. Since the late arrival of the prosecution's huge evidence bundle prior to committal she'd been wading through the reams of papers. On the murder charge it seemed the police had interviewed every other inhabitant of south London and had obligingly sent her the lot. It had all but swamped her as she was duty-bound to read and sift out anything that might be relevant to the defence and follow it up.

Now he felt bad. 'If there's anything I can do to help?'

'Sure, I'll let you know.'

Almost as soon as she'd dropped him outside Evie's flat in Southall, Browne regretted it. She glimpsed his receding figure in her rear-view mirror and felt a small tight knot of fear forming in her chest. Why did she do it? Why did she seem deliberately to set out to destroy any relationship she'd ever had? She was losing Lomax again, she could sense it, feel it. Now that he was seeing her more regularly again she felt almost depressed when he wasn't around. She used to enjoy her own company, her freedom and space to do what the hell she liked when she liked. But now when he wasn't there, her flat felt empty. Desolate. The residence of a dried-up old spinster who had never known love. No, not never known. A spinster who had turned her back on it, because she couldn't bear the thought of love in case she lost it once again.

Thinking of Lomax made her decide to stop off and buy a Chinese takeaway before returning home. The building was cold and airless and she opened a window before checking the answerphone and settling down to eat. With a bottle of red wine on the table, she began working through the prosecution files. She hardly tasted the chicken chow mein and barely registered a word she read.

A vision kept creeping into her mind's eye. The cloudless blue sky. A ragged little bundle, a distant speck, the red jumpsuit tugged by the wind. Her ears heard what Roebuck heard. Nothing but the awesome silence of the sky. The whistle of gravity's pull and the slipstream snapping at the material of his clothes. And she saw what he saw. Earth spinning up to meet him. And she felt his dread, his horror as the parachute ripcord came away in his hand. The lingering horror – seconds seeming like minutes as he waited to die – that he took with him to the grave.

She heard and felt the thud of impact and closed her eyes. No one should ever have to face death like that.

Again she tried to read. The blue Mondeo. That car chase. Already it was a bizarre dream that had never happened. Had she really forced it off the road? And the passers-by. That middle-aged man with his flat cap. The awful woman, the bitch. Had she had a hand in Roebuck's death? Suddenly these weren't half-imagined phantoms that had set up Roddy Littlechild for murder and hindered her progress in his defence. Now the phantoms had faces; now she *knew* they were for real. She had seen them. Dammit, she had touched one. Hit him. God, had she really done that?

Unconsciously she glanced down at the knuckles of her right hand, saw the bluish tint of her bruised skin. She smiled at the memory. Barney should have seen that, he'd have been proud of her. Like Lomax had. He hadn't exactly said, but he didn't have to. She could see it in his eyes.

Lomax. Locked in the bloody boot with Lomax. Suddenly she felt an overwhelming urge to phone him. Tell him to come over because she was frightened and she was lonely. And she wanted him.

No. She pushed away the half-eaten takeaway and lifted the telephone onto the table. Consulting her notebook, she dialled Derek Penny's number.

It rang for a long time. She checked her watch. Nine thirty. Not in bed yet and the Pennys wouldn't be out socialising if they'd read that morning's newspapers. Perhaps they'd gone to ground?

She was about to replace the receiver when the ringing stopped and a woman's voice came on the line. 'For God's sake, can't you leave us alone!'

'Meredith? It's Sam Browne here.'

'Who?' The voice quavered.

'Sam Browne. I'm a solicitor, we met the other week.'

'Oh, my dear, I'm so sorry. I thought it was the press again. The phone hasn't stopped all day. It's been perfectly beastly.'

'I can imagine. Look, I read the story today and I thought your husband might need help.'

'He didn't do all those awful things, you know,' Meredith said with breathless indignation.

'I imagine not, that's why I'd like to help.'

'He might not want to talk to you,' she said defensively. 'He's not in a very communicative mood. I'll ask him.'

Browne waited for several long minutes before Derek Penny came on the line. 'This is none of your business, Miss Browne.'

'I think perhaps it is. If these stories are unfounded, then someone may be trying to hurt you because you're a trial witness.'

There was a hesitation. 'I suppose that's possible. I certainly can't think of any rational explanation.' Finally he agreed to meet her at her office on Monday morning.

She had just hung up when the telephone rang.

It was Lomax. 'Sorry to interrupt you.'

Browne was pleased to hear his voice. 'I've just been talking to Derek Penny. He's coming to see me Monday morning. Will you be doing anything?'

'Only writing for job interviews.'

'I may need a gumshoe. Penny's due at nine.'

'I'll be there.'

'So why are you disturbing me, Mr Lomax?'

'That man in the flat cap – '

'Yes?'

'Remember I said he looked vaguely familiar. Well, he's changed a lot since I last knew him. Name of Harry. I've just been cracking a couple of cans with Joe. He knew the man even better. Was a field operator for MI5 in Northern Ireland way back. Joe knows his full name.'

'So what have you got?'

'Harry. Harry Grisewold.'

'No kid.'

'Known behind his back as Dirty Harry.'

Fifteen

'So you haven't even been charged?' Browne asked.

Penny was sitting stiffly upright in the solicitor's office while his wife regarded him with silent concern. 'No,' he said. 'I was just interviewed by the local police and asked to make a statement. Obviously I denied the allegations and said that I did not recall the names of the people who were accusing me. Well, I wouldn't after twenty years.'

'Did the police indicate that they intended to prosecute?'

'Not specifically. Just said the usual, that their investigation was continuing. Then last week our local paper ran the story without naming me. Of course it was obvious to everyone. The entire village turned its back on me.'

'You wouldn't think people we've known for years would believe Derek capable, would you?' Meredith asked plaintively.

'I'm afraid people believe what they want to believe,' Browne said. 'And some like to see the mighty fallen.' She turned back to Penny. 'You think the local police tipped off the paper?'

Penny shrugged. 'They say not, but it doesn't matter now the tabloids have picked it up. One claims to have investigated and named all the names, mine included.'

'They won't do that again,' Browne promised. 'I'll get an injunction slapped on them and we'll start suing for libel damages.'

'Oh dear,' Meredith said, 'I couldn't bear all that sort of thing.'

In a rare show of emotion, Penny reached out and took his wife's hand. 'She's right. The mud's been thrown now and it'll stick whatever I do. Going to court will just drag it all up again.'

Lomax had been leaning against the wall. 'These two men who made the allegations, do you know where they live?'

Penny shook his head. 'No, the police won't give that sort of information. At first I thought they might be ex-cons I've put away trying to get revenge. But if they are, they aren't names that ring any bells with me.'

Browne said: 'There's not a lot I can do if I don't take out an injunction.'

'I don't want to get embroiled, Miss Browne. I'd rather let it blow over if I can.'

Lomax said: 'What is it you're afraid of?'

Penny glanced up at him. 'Very perceptive of you. To be honest, I wasn't the most popular man amongst my police colleagues. If I fight a newspaper in court, God knows what sort of lies it might dig up. It could even affect your client's case.'

'Are you still prepared to testify on his behalf?' Browne asked.

'Of course.' He sounded almost indignant. 'Provided you still consider my testimony of value after this scandal.'

Later that day Lomax used a call box to telephone Detective Superintendent Bill Johnson in Stafford.

'Hello, Chris, nice surprise.'

'How's life?'

'Bit quieter now that manhunt for Keegan's on the back burner. Vanished into thin air. Incidentally, read all that stuff about Derek Penny over the weekend. Quite incredible.'

'That's why I'm phoning. I think it's part of a deliberate smear campaign because he's a witness.'

'Isn't that a bit unlikely?'

Lomax said: 'Did you also read about that skydiving accident in Oxford? A man called Colonel Roebuck.'

Johnson was hesitant, perhaps starting to guess. 'Yes.'

'He was Colonel X at Keegan's trial. Do you get my drift?'

There was a brief considered silence on the other end of the phone. 'Before I got involved in all this, I'd have laughed in your face. How can I help?'

'Some info from Penny's local coppers.'

'I can try,' Johnson said guardedly. 'Someone on the Kent force owes me a favour.'

Three days later, Johnson called back with the addresses of Penny's two former choirboy accusers. Both lived in cheap short-let bedsits in different parts of north London. And the following evening Lomax and Monk planned to approach the two men simultaneously so that neither could warn the other.

They went in at seven and in both cases got the same reply from their respective landladies. Earlier that day the occupant had upped and flown leaving no forwarding address.

Half an hour later Lomax and Monk kept their pub rendezvous to compare notes.

'Mine had barely been there a month,' Monk said.

'Any clues?'

'Told a neighbour he'd been a seaman in the Merchant Navy.'

'Could be a connection,' Lomax thought aloud. 'I said I'd consider renting the place and had a look round. He'd left behind a copy of *Globe and Laurel*, the Royal Marines' magazine. Said he'd just got a job on the oil rigs.'

'Could be ex-cabbage hats,' Monk decided.

'Oil rigs, divers,' Lomax followed his train of thought. 'Divers could be Commachio Troop or Special Boat Service.'

'Navy is Navy. Mean Royal, but say Merchant. Always keep your cover story close to the truth.'

'If they're ex-SBS, it could mean they'd cross paths with the intelligence community.'

Monk wiped the froth from his moustache with the back of his hand. He grinned. 'That's what I call making two and two equal five.'

Lomax laughed. 'If we're right, I call it bloody good detective work.'

'I'm beginning to like this business. Philip Marlowe, eat yer heart out.'

'Trouble is, we're not getting paid.'

'There's always a snag.'

But on this occasion there was an even bigger snag as they discovered when they called at Sam Browne's flat to give her their news. Her footsteps were heard racing down the stairs inside before she flung open the door. 'Chris – er, hello, Joe. Where on earth have you been all this time?' she demanded.

Lomax was taken aback. 'I told you earlier, looking up Penny's accusers.'

'Did you find them?'

'No, they'd both upped sticks and flown.'

'Then they've served their purpose.'

'What?'

'Of course, you don't know. I had a distressed call from Meredith, Penny's wife, not long after you left. He's hanged himself.'

Lord Moffat was returned to his Victorian apartment in Cadogan Gardens by ministry car.

He had spent an hour and a half in the Cabinet Intelligence Unit meeting doing his best to persuade the Prime Minister and others that all was not lost just because the Provisional IRA's ceasefire had collapsed.

He had told his despondent colleagues that it was only to be expected. 'We allowed the Unionist politicians to dictate too much of the agenda. Difficult, I know, with them demanding a referendum on the final outcome of any talks – a virtual veto on anything they don't like. And then insisting on a start to paramilitary disarmament even before talks begin. A resumption of violence was therefore inevitable, as I predicted in my memorandum six weeks ago.'

'I see no realistic way forward now,' the Prime Minister had responded gloomily.

'Not at all, sir,' Moffat replied. 'You're still pushing ahead with elections of those participating in the talks. That's good.'

'But little hope of all key parties participating,' the Northern Ireland Secretary had interrupted wearily. A large man with gravitas projected with a cultured public-school accent and a diplomat's evasive turn of phrase, Sir Ralph Maynard had been in the job too long. It had simply worn him down and now his plans to retire from his thankless task were public knowledge. 'Or, indeed, all parties being able to qualify to participate.'

That was a reference to the suspicion that the Provisional IRA would decide to renew its ceasefire. Moffat had waved the problem aside. 'It may be no bad thing if Sinn Fein doesn't attend. If the Republican diehards are not there, then the Unionists may be persuaded to relax their stance.'

There was a steely glint of interest in the Prime Minister's eyes that belied his benign appearance. 'I think I understand what you're getting at, Lord Moffat.'

'We have no doubts about what both PIRA and Dublin want, Prime Minister, and the stepping stones to get us to an agreement that sits comfortably with everyone. Namely, so many joint cross-border collaborations in health, tax, police and currency that eventually the infrastructure of North and South becomes as one.'

'So continue,' Maynard suggested. 'Softly, softly? But nothing too extreme, too sudden?'

'Exactly that,' Moffat had exclaimed. 'Without feeling Sinn Fein is pushing them into a corner, the Unionists will agree to far more co-operation with Dublin than they would otherwise. The key, as I've said before, is to keep the legal actuality of all these decisions and changes deep in all the small print. Leave it to the Brussels lawyers to pronounce one day exactly how tightly bound Ireland has become as one state. No need for any British Government to take the rap for what'll seem as Europe's meddling. All of us in this room recognise the inevitability of the future of the island of Ireland, and we should not reproach ourselves if we adopt less than straightforward means.'

All in all, it had been a satisfactory meeting, Moffat concluded, as he took the ancient elevator cage to the top floor of the mansions.

Entering the stillness of his high-ceilinged apartment, he made his way first to the walnut credenza and poured himself a stiff gin and tonic before settling down in his favourite leather club chair to catch ITV's Early Evening News.

He wasn't fully concentrating, the sound too low and Moffat feeling too weary to reach for the confounded remote control. Reporter outside Leinster House. Looking serious. *'A quarter of Dublin without electricity . . .'* Moffat frowned. Had he heard right?

Cut to a talking head. An inspector in the Irish Garda.

Moffat found the control, thumbing up the volume. *'A main powerline was brought down by an explosive device in a remote region of County Wicklow. Police have sealed off the area.'*

'*Have there been any arrests?*' the reporter asked.

'*Not so far. It is possible the explosive device was time-delayed but that's yet to be confirmed.*'

'*Do you think this is the work of Loyalist terrorists from the North of Ireland?*'

'*I really cannot speculate at this time.*'

Cut back to reporter. '*A spokesman for the government told me earlier that it could be at least two days before full power supplies are restored to affected areas of the city.*'

Back to studio, the announcer saying: '*While official sources in Dublin refuse to confirm or deny that the explosion is the work of Loyalist extremists from Northern Ireland, in the province itself a group calling itself* Cuchulainn *or the Hound of Ulster has claimed that it carried out the attack in response to the ending of the IRA ceasefire. We go direct now to our reporter outside Belfast City Hall.*'

Without realising, Moffat had already finished his gin, getting a mouthful of lemon peel; he put his glass aside without taking his eyes from the screen.

'*Hello, John,*' the studio anchor said. '*What can you tell us about this new terrorist organisation?*'

'*Not a lot, Michael,*' replied the Belfast reporter in front of a crowd cheering and waving Union flags. '*No one appears to have heard of them until today when they claimed to be responsible for the explosion which denied electricity to up to a third of Dublin. It is a Loyalist grouping that says it is the military wing of the Frontline Ulster Movement.*'

'*And what is Frontline Ulster? That name isn't familiar to me.*'

'*No, Michael, it wouldn't be. But it's known to most Ulster people from the early 1970s when it pronounced itself to be some sort of resistance movement to meet a doomsday scenario of total civil war. Until now it has been regarded as moribund.*'

Back to studio. '*So why have they chosen this moment to take military action, do you think?*'

The reporter waved a thin sheaf of orange-tinted paper for the benefit of the camera. '*Well, Michael, I have here their official communique which says it now considers itself to be at*

361

war with Dublin. It claims Ulster has been betrayed by the Westminster Government, which is continuing a policy of eroding the civil liberties and rights of their Unionist majority and which continues a policy of pushing – I quote – "the province's loyal subjects of the Crown into the arms of a foreign nation state". An awkward smile at the camera. '*Meaning Eire, of course. The communique says it is not prepared to wait until this happens or for another twenty-five years of urban warfare while Westminster continually fails to take necessary effective action to destroy the Provisional IRA.*'

'*What does it expect a British Government to do?*'

'*I don't think this organisation expects it to do anything; that is rather the point.*'

'*So what's the purpose of bombing power supplies to Dublin?*'

The reporter tapped the communique with his forefinger. '*It's clearly stated here that the intention is to force Dublin to take the action these Loyalists think is necessary.* Cuchulainn makes two demands. Firstly that the Dublin Government cracks down on the IRA in the South by interning all suspected members – which they say has been done twice before, in 1939 and 1957, with great effect. Then they demand that Dublin revoke Clauses Two and Three from its constitution, which lay claim to the Six Counties. And finally that the Anglo-Irish Agreement be scrapped.*'

'*Has there been a response from Sinn Fein or from any of the other Loyalist paramilitary groups?*'

'*None so far, it took everyone a bit by surprise when the announcement was made a couple of hours ago.*'

'*And yet I see quite a few people behind you, apparently expressing approval of the action that's been taken. Is this orchestrated support?*'

'*Michael, yes, this is rather a strange phenomenon. A local pop folk band broke on the Loyalist pub and club scene a couple of months ago. They called themselves the Tain after the book of Irish mythology which features the Hound of Ulster. This band makes no secret of its affiliations with Frontline Ulster, which is a perfectly legal movement, and has had great success with an own-label record called "Colours". It is plainly a recruiting song aimed at the Loyalist community. The people behind me claim to be fans of the band. Perhaps it would be helpful if I read out the chorus from that song.'*

A wry smile from the anchor man. *'As long as you don't attempt to sing it, John.'*

'Certainly not.' Joke shared. The reporter referred to his notes and cleared his throat:

> *'Red is the colour of anger,*
> *And black is the colour of hate,*
> *And yellow the colour of those who look on,*
> *And do nothing to alter their fate.'*

'Thank you, John. And now next tonight . . .'

Moffat switched off the set and stared at the blank screen for several seconds in deep concentration.

What the hell was going on? The Frontline Ulster Movement. Impossible! What the hell was Roger Pinfold playing at?

As his fingers reached towards the telephone, it rang and made him jump. He snatched at the receiver. 'Moffat.'

'Pinfold here, Lord Moffat.'

'I was just about to call you, Roger. What in damnation is going on, all this nonsense about Frontline . . .?'

'Not over the phone, sir,' Pinfold hissed. 'I'm calling from my car. If it's convenient, I'll be with you in ten minutes.'

'I'll be waiting, dammit, and expecting answers too.' He slammed the receiver into its cradle and walked unsteadily to the cabinet to pour another drink.

He had barely regained some composure when Pinfold arrived.

'I came as soon as I could,' the MI5 man said breathlessly.

Moffat glared at him. 'Really, I *cannot* believe what I've just seen on the news.'

'It's worse than that. The media reported one pylon blown up. But in fact there were three. Three main electricity feeder lines into Dublin are down. And there's been major disruption to the railways with tracks blown up.' He took a deep breath, hardly believing his own words. 'Dublin's in the process of slapping on a news blackout and is setting up a crisis news management team. I've just come from an emergency meeting with the director-general. Not a pleasant experience. Anyway, we're putting a D-notice on the media regarding any future developments. A couple of minutes ago the Taoiseach was on the telephone to the Prime Minister. They'll both want to play down the seriousness of this development.'

'Seriousness?' Moffat countered. 'How *can* it be serious, Roger, with Frontline under your personal control?'

The man smiled defensively. 'Not exactly *control*, sir.'

'Let's not bandy words.' Lord Moffat felt his blood pressure rising. 'It's your personal area of responsibility. Your job to maintain accurate files on the membership list, to know what individuals are up to.'

Attack was always the best form of defence, Pinfold thought. 'My department has done that. For a start, all weapons caches were closed down by my predecessor. These explosives have come from some other source and that suggests this is some kind of splinter group.'

'So what do you intend to do?' Moffat demanded.

'Nip it in the bud. This development is serious in terms of its timing and the apparent professionalism. But, as you say, we have an up-to-date membership list for Frontline. The RUC and army are now making plans for a massive dawn swoop in the province tomorrow morning. They won't know what's hit them.'

Moffat took a deep breath, swelled out his chest. 'I hope so, Roger, otherwise neither will you.'

It was one of those uncannily still Sunday afternoons and bitterly cold.

Lomax stood by the dormer window and sipped at a mug of soup. From one of the long row of gardens below, woodsmoke spiralled into the wintry sky and flecks of snow eddied about but didn't settle. Rows of snowdrops stood bravely in the window box.

364

'I've toasted some crumpets,' Evie said, coming in from the kitchen.

'I can smell them,' Lomax replied, turning back into the room.

'One of Roddy's favourites. With butter and strawberry jam. The other day he said that's one thing he missed. Silly, isn't it? All that business with Derek Penny and we talked about crumpets. I don't believe he could bear to think about it, about just how bad things are now.'

'We've still got the documentary evidence.' Lomax tried to introduce an optimistic note into his voice.

She shook her head. 'Roddy doesn't think it'll be worth much without Penny himself to back it up. We've talked it over and we've accepted that he's going down. If he fights it'll be a life sentence and if he doesn't he's looking at fifteen years.'

Lomax felt a rush of anger. 'Don't talk like that. Have some faith.'

'In Sam Browne?' Evie gave a pained little expression. 'I don't have to because I'm not the one who's besotted with her, Chris. However good she is – and I know she and that barrister Meyrick will do their best – neither of them can work miracles.'

He sat down beside his sister. 'I know it'll be tough.'

'It'll be tough on you if you bankrupt yourself.'

'I won't. Besides, Roddy can sue for thousands when we win.'

'We can't win if we go for a plea bargain.'

'For God's sake, Evie, Roddy can't do that.'

Her eyes flashed. 'We're not on a holy crusade, Chris. It's mine and my husband's life we're talking about. And our baby. I want us back together as soon as possible. If we listen to Sam Browne, Roddy'll end up doing at least five years more than he needs to. Noel will be grown up by the time he gets out.' She sniffed heavily to stop her tears and pushed away her plate, the crumpet untouched.

Lomax sat in thoughtful silence. He understood the reasoning, and could only wish that he didn't.

Evie said: 'So *please* will you start looking for a job. Properly, I mean, not half-heartedly.'

It was then that he realised. 'Has Manda been talking to you about this?'

Evie bit her lip. 'Oh dear, I promised her I wouldn't let on.'

'And she promised me she wouldn't breathe a word to you.'

'Chris, she's not a fool. Manda knows the perilous state of your finances. Nearly all your savings have gone on living and travel expenses since this business began. That's before your divorce settlement. Fran will expect half the value of the house and half the savings you've already spent!'

Lomax seethed. 'Manda had no right.'

'She had every right, Chris. She's your daughter and she's worried about you. How many old soldiers are there sleeping rough under Waterloo Bridge? Or on park benches throughout the country?'

Lomax didn't reply immediately. He sat back and drained his soup. What could he say? Evie was right, Manda was right. He was trying to juggle what remained of his finances with one hand tied behind his back. He was already a month behind on the mortgage.

At last he said: 'Don't worry about me, sis, I'm a survivor. I'm prepared to face anything provided Roddy doesn't throw in the towel. If he does, then it will all have been a waste.'

Evie frowned. 'Don't lay that on me, Chris. It's not fair.'

'I think it is,' he answered, more harshly than he intended. 'Your influence over Roddy is crucial. He knows my view, but *you're* his wife. You're the one who matters. You and Noel. And what sort of world do you want to bring the child up in?'

She gave a bitter little laugh. 'Not the deceitful and corrupt one he's been born into, that's for sure.'

'Exactly. So do something to change it. Roddy *can* win. He didn't commit murder so there *has* to be a way to win. And we'll find it. Even if Roddy goes down, we'll appeal and I personally will go on digging until I find the truth. Don't let Noel grow up being ashamed of his father.'

'For God's sake!' Angry.

'No, sis, it's got to be said. Give the kid something to believe in. When he's old enough to understand, he'll know his father served his time defiantly declaring his innocence. In a way,

366

better that than spend a shorter time having confessed to a crime he didn't commit!'

Then the tears began to well in Evie's eyes. 'Oh, Chris, I don't know what to think.' And she began to sob as he took her in his arms.

'Mr Justice Todd!' Browne fumed for the umpteenth time. She strode across the pavement towards Belmarsh Crown Court with the rest of them striving to keep up. It was the day of the pre-trial review and a plea and directions hearing.

'Repeating his name won't make him go away, dear heart,' Tristram Meyrick admonished as they reached the court steps. 'It's sounding like an incantation.'

'A prayer even,' offered the Jamaican Ronnie Rock.

She stopped and turned. 'Not a prayer, Ronnie, a curse. You'd know all about that. Voodoo. Don't you know a friendly village witch doctor who can make a doll for me to stick pins in?'

Rock laughed. 'All the witch doctors I knew have got practices in Harley Street now.'

'Just how terrible is this Todd?' Lomax asked.

'Last of the hanging judges,' Browne said contemptuously. 'Establishment all the way. A bloody arse-kisser.'

'Sweeney Todd,' Totty added helpfully as she struggled with the enormous bundle of papers. 'That's what Wayne calls him.'

'For once, Wayne's said something sensible,' Browne snapped. 'Amazing how Todd's name pops up – supposedly an unbiased choice by the Lord Chancellor's Department – whenever the government is determined to win a case. It's either him or one of about four others in the same mould.'

'And, of course, the Lord Chancellor is a Cabinet Minister,' Rock pointed out.

Meyrick said: 'I don't believe anyone's yet managed to overturn a Lord Chancellor's judicial selection since he was given the powers of discretion in 1925. Anyway, Todd's not so bad,' he reassured. 'I've conducted a defence under him before. Strict but fair. You just need to know how to handle him.'

'And how's that?' she asked.

Meyrick grinned. 'With kid gloves.'

Browne had calmed a little. 'I shall smile sweetly at him across the court room all the way through the trial.'

'Please don't do that,' Rock replied. 'We want to *win* this.'

With a half-smile, she pushed open the doors and stepped into the courthouse lobby. Barristers and solicitors stood around the bare and soulless room in animated groups with their clients or with court officials.

She picked out the rival prosecution team immediately. It wasn't difficult, Henry Halifax's baritone laugh was like a ship's horn in a fog as he recounted some story to the phlegmatic CPS solicitor. Ian Spinks was the antithesis of his barrister, painfully lean in a dark suit and bland tie with the sort of schoolboy face that Browne associated with anoraks and trainspotters. The impression wasn't helped by the lank wing of oiled hair across his brow and spectacle frames that were too dark and heavy for such a pale and youthful face.

It took a second for her to place the other man, but Lomax got there first. 'Roger Pinfold,' she heard him breathe beside her.

Pinfold was on his mettle, had obviously seen them and mentioned it because Henry Halifax turned. No second thoughts, no hesitation from the barrister; immediately his arms outstretched in exaggerated welcome, his florid face beaming beneath the horsehair wig. 'And how is the loveliest woman that God created?'

'I don't know, Henry,' she said, attempting to retreat as Halifax embraced her and kissed her cheek, 'you'll have to go and ask her.'

'Put her down,' Meyrick said. 'You don't know where she's been.'

'And is this a red knickers day, I wonder?' Halifax whispered quickly in her ear as she pulled away. 'Ready for mortal combat?'

'Wouldn't you like to know?' she replied acidly and straightened her crumpled jacket before turning to Pinfold. 'Here to see justice done, are we? And is it Pinfold or Prendergast today?'

Spinks looked bewildered. 'What do you mean, Sam?'

Browne gave a wan smile. 'Just that your Mr Prendergast is a bit of a chameleon. Mr Lomax knew him by a different name.'

The prosecution solicitor looked none the wiser, but Pinfold stepped quickly in with a suave smile. 'I'm afraid your boyfriend's mistaken. They say we all have a doppelganger – an exact double – somewhere, don't they?'

'Saddam Hussein and Adolf Hitler used them, I do believe,' she replied with an innocent smile. 'Oh, and for the record, Mr Lomax is not my boyfriend.'

'Then I'm still in with a chance,' Halifax rejoined swiftly.

'You and the nearest leper colony. Or is that unfair to lepers?'

'Ouch,' said Halifax. To his credit he looked genuinely abashed. 'I see you've mellowed since our last encounter. Talking of which, does your client still intend to run in the face of all the evidence?'

'He's pleading not guilty, Henry, if that's what you mean.' As she said it, it gave her a small sense of satisfaction to see the concern in Pinfold's eyes.

Halifax said: 'Pity he doesn't just save the taxpayer a lot of wasted money.'

'Some of it yours, of course. That must rankle.'

'It does, if I dwell upon it.'

'Don't let it. This time it'll be money well spent. There's always a price to pay for justice.'

It was then that the case of Regina v. Littlechild was called and both teams of lawyers began making their way to the courtroom.

'What was that about a red knickers day, Sam?' Lomax asked innocently.

Irritation flashed in her eyes for a moment before she relented.

'It's all about the psychology of colour. It can help influence a jury about how they perceive people. That's the theory – at least in the States. Of course, all barristers have to dress the same here, but we can use it for witnesses and, of course, the defendant. Roddy will wear a nice new suit, a light blue-grey suggesting openness.' She lowered her voice. 'Most of the prosecution witnesses, the police, will almost certainly wear very sombre dark colours.'

'And you believe in such nonsense?'

The mad eye. 'Yes.'

'And the red knickers?'

'The French philosophy,' she explained wearily. 'You are what you wear and you dress from the inside out. Put on green knickers in the morning and you feel cool and relaxed. Yellow, cheerful. Black, sexy or white, submissive. Red for anger, for a fight.'

'And today?' Bemused.

'Bright scarlet. If I'm run over by a bus they'll think I'm a hooker.'

'And Henry Halifax knows this?'

'My fault,' Totty said, as they shuffled into the teak pews before the Bench. 'The boss explained it to me once and I made the mistake of confiding in Wayne. Now the entire Inns of Court know about it.'

Browne smiled, grimly. 'It did my reputation no end of good.'

'THE COURT WILL RISE!' the clerk announced and the red-robed figure of Mr Justice Todd swept in from the door beyond the Bench. As he sat, Lomax squinted to get a better view of the man's features. Tall and large-boned, he carried himself with the air of a man who had no self-doubt, who knew exactly what he was doing. In another life he could have been one of the few senior military officers whom Lomax had come across and instantly disliked. It wasn't difficult to imagine the impassive broad face with its stern bluish jaw and humourless dark eyes, ordering thousands of troops over the top without a moment's prudent second thought. A man who believed in making decisions, even if they were the wrong ones.

After the clerk's preamble, listing the charges, Halifax rose to his feet. 'I represent the prosecution in this case, Your Lordship, and my learned friend, Mr Meyrick, appears for the defence.'

'If it pleases Your Lordship,' Meyrick said, standing swiftly, 'I should like to request most strongly that the two cases before you be heard concurrently. The defence believes this is the only way for the jury to understand the full and somewhat confusing background story that links both charges.'

Mr Justice Todd peered down. 'That is a most extraordinary request.'

'But not unprecedented, Your Lordship. And this *is* a most extraordinary case.'

'Mr Halifax?'

'The prosecution would object equally strongly to any linkage being attached to these two cases. One relates to the murder last year of a British subject in London and the other to the conspiracy to murder a South African national in Belfast some eight years ago. To suggest any linkage other than that the same man carried out the crime is preposterous.'

Meyrick was adamant. 'The defence believes that it can draw a very clear link between the two cases, that link being the work my client loyally conducted on behalf of the Security Service and the repercussions of such service. If this is not fully understood and appreciated by the jury, then they will not be able to reach a decision in either case with the benefit of all available evidence before them.'

'Mmm,' said Mr Justice Todd. 'Well, Mr Meyrick, it may come as a surprise to you to know that I take my duty of studying each case before me most seriously. Having scrupulously read those details, I am of the opinion that any linkage is purely coincidental and in no way affects the basic decision facing the jury in each case. Was the defendant guilty as charged on two separate occasions distanced by the best part of a decade, each under totally different circumstances?'

'With respect, Your Lordship,' Meyrick began.

'That is my decision, Mr Meyrick,' Todd came back swiftly. 'Moreover, I do not believe it to be in the defendant's *own* best interest to run the trials concurrently. These are two very serious charges and to be found guilty on either count will have serious consequences for him and his family. He will be ill served if the jury is overwhelmed by an unnecessary and bewildering torrent of evidence.'

Meyrick knew he was beaten; it was no surprise, he'd been expecting it. 'As Your Lordship pleases.'

371

Halifax was on his feet. 'Your Lordship will be aware that the Home Secretary's Office seeks to preserve the anonymity of those members of the Security Service – more commonly referred to as MI5 – who will be appearing for the prosecution. I would beg assurance on behalf of the Crown that the applications be granted?'

Mr Justice Todd looked towards Meyrick.

'We would oppose any such restrictions, my lord, for reasons that will become clear during the trial.'

'Really, Mr Meyrick?' He might just as well have said, 'Must you?' 'Very well. The clerk will set a date for a meeting with me and the two parties in chambers at the Old Bailey. I think probably tomorrow, if that would suit all concerned?'

There was no dissension.

The clerk of court then read out each charge and asked how the defendant intended to plead.

'Not guilty,' Meyrick replied firmly to each.

The detail then seemed endless, the prosecution listing the number of witnesses it intended to call, the broad nature of the evidence and other legal technicalities, and how long the respective sides anticipated the first of the trials would last.

Unusually, the murder case would commence in just six weeks' time. Littlechild's legal team guessed the government was anxious and would be putting pressure on to get the entire thing wrapped up and allow any dust to settle before the Forum elections in Northern Ireland scheduled for early June. Two weeks was set aside, assuming an end by the Easter Bank Holiday. Only after the verdict would a decision be made on the second conspiracy-to-murder case. If the defendant was found guilty, then the CPS would most likely just leave the second charge on file.

However, if there was a not guilty verdict, the conspiracy trial would surely follow.

'A double-barbed fish-hook,' Browne described it rather graphically to Lomax as they waited in the rain for a taxi to return to 10 Paper Buildings. 'A damn cheek saying it wasn't in *my* client's best interests not to run the trials concurrently. It reduces it to a seemingly black-and-white case of a Loyalist with

372

paramilitary connections seizing an opportunity to kill an IRA leader. Open and shut. I know what I'd believe if I was on the jury.'

'C'mon, Sam,' Meyrick chided. 'Once we knew Mr Justice Todd was running the trial it was a foregone conclusion. It makes our job harder, but not impossible.'

'How can you get round it?' Lomax asked.

'By working in cross-references to the other case,' Rock explained. 'Teasing out the truth, so the relationship with the second charge is exposed.'

'Easier said than done with Mr Justice Todd in the hot seat. He'll see what we're trying to do and so will Halifax. We'll be fighting them both all the way.'

'Desperate times call for desperate measures,' Monk said that night as Lomax explained what had happened during the day. They were having a couple of pints at a pub near Evie's flat.

'That's the drink talking,' Lomax replied irritably. 'Who Dares Wins – until you wake up with a hangover the next morning.'

Monk looked hurt. 'I'm serious.'

'Okay, what *can* we do?'

'First, what exactly is the nature of our problem?'

'You got all night?'

'All right, what's the most *immediate* problem?'

Lomax lit a fresh cigarette. 'Fundamentally, according to Sam and Meyrick, we've got a judge who's virtually in the prosecution's pocket. If they say it's raining, he gets an umbrella. If they say it's sunny . . .'

'Yeah, yeah.' Impatient. 'Can't our lot complain about his appointment?'

'No, it's just not done. Even Sam says that's not worth trying.'

'Is there another way?'

'No.'

'C'mon, Chris, you're not helping. Remember the old Chinese Parliaments in the mob? Tossing ideas around till we come up with something.'

Lomax relented. 'Okay.'

'So, what would happen if Todd was taken sick? He couldn't conduct a trial from his hospital bed.'

'I'm not taking to beating up judges, Joe.'

'Or running them over? Hit-and-run would do nicely.'

'I wish. But I don't think that or food poisoning's on the agenda.'

'Abduction,' Monk said brightly. 'Just for a few days until another judge is appointed.'

'Joe, us ending up in jail isn't going to help Roddy.'

Monk saw the funny side of that. 'I don't know. With the right judge he might win – and be free to visit us when we're inside.'

'You're right in one respect,' Lomax said thoughtfully. 'If only Todd could be indisposed long enough for another judge to be appointed . . .'

'Any ideas?'

'None.'

'I suppose we ought to know more about him. Where he lives, his family, his recreations? Something might give us an idea. Perhaps we ought to follow him.'

Lomax shrugged; he really wasn't sure this was a good idea. 'We know there's a meeting in his chambers with Meyrick and Halifax tomorrow . . . I could find out the time from Totty.'

'At least we'll be doing something,' Monk said with his usual enthusiasm.

His friend nodded uncertainly. 'Just one thing, Joe. Don't breathe a word of this to Evie or Sam. Especially Sam.'

It was big boy's stuff behind closed doors in judge's chambers at the back of the Old Bailey. Mr Justice Todd and heavyweight barristers in genteel, yet bloody-minded combat. Solicitors excluded, Sam Browne and the prosecution's Ian Spinks feeling like rejected ringside seconds in the draughty corridor outside.

She didn't know her opposite number well, she realised. Perhaps that was a mistake. He seemed an unemotional sort, but it could be shyness. 'D'you smoke, Ian?' she asked, offering the pack.

'No, filthy habit.'

Her smile wavered. 'Yes – er – it is, isn't it? I try to give up, but times like this – Doesn't it get to you?'

Dark eyes blinked behind the old man's hornrims on the young boy's face. Boy? A man in his mid-thirties was hardly that. Yet she couldn't get the image of anoraks and trainspotting from her mind.

'It doesn't worry me, Miss Browne. We win the majority of cases for the CPS. Bound to really as they're virtually all guilty as sin.'

'Oh, yes?'

'Otherwise they wouldn't have been charged in the first place. When some do get off, it's usually thanks to some clever lawyer conning the jury or some technical point of law, isn't it? No offence meant.'

'Not related to Mr Justice Todd, are you?'

'Pardon me?'

'Nothing, just an idle thought.' Dammit, she thought and lit her cigarette despite him. Or perhaps to spite him. 'And my client?'

'I've seen the evidence.'

'So have I. And?'

'A personal view?'

She nodded.

'He's a vicious killer with terrorist connections who should be put away for a long time. The Security Service has told us exactly what he is and they should know.'

'No doubts?'

'No. I am a man who likes dealing in certainties.' He had the good grace to blush. 'Well, near certainties. That's why I work for the CPS. Frankly I wouldn't like to be in your position. Trying to defend the indefensible.' He indicated her cigarette. 'I expect that's why you find it such a strain.'

Suddenly she had an overwhelming urge to smack him in the mouth. Instead she said: 'Ian, I expect you're probably right. In fact, between you and me, I wouldn't be surprised if my client changes his mind at the eleventh hour.'

'Meaning?' The eyes behind the lenses were suddenly alive with interest for the first time.

'A change of plea, perhaps. He's wavering, I can tell.'

'He'd plead guilty to murder?' Overhopeful there.

'Of course not. He's caught on a double barb. If he was going to put his hand up to conspiracy, he'd have to see there was something in it for him.'

'Like?'

'Oh, don't play dumb, Ian. My client isn't suicidal. He might do it, though, if you dropped the murder.'

'I'd have to talk to my superiors.'

'Of course. When you speak to her, please remember me to Miss Shilling. Mind you, I expect she's forgotten all about me.'

Ian Spinks gave an inscrutable little half-smile. 'Somehow, Miss Browne, I don't think she has.'

At that moment the doors to the judge's chambers swung open and Henry Halifax's voice burst forth into the corridor like the howl of a monsoon. Meyrick trailed in his wake.

'Never mind, Tristram, old chum, it was a foregone conclusion.' Halifax waved in Browne's direction. 'You didn't stand a chance. Got me red Y-fronts on today!'

His chortling receded along the corridor as Spinks scurried after him. News that Littlechild was wavering would soon reach Pinfold and hopefully the prosecution would lower its guard.

'That bad?' Browne asked Meyrick.

'Worse,' he answered. 'Any MI5 witnesses to remain strictly anonymous and I get the impression we'll find Public Interest Immunity certificates have been allowed, denying us access to any government papers that back defence claims.'

'Oh, God.'

'Todd was in the foulest of moods. That man really is monstrous.'

Browne's shoulders slumped. 'Okay, let's go back to your chambers and go through what it means.'

'A beer on the way,' Meyrick said. 'I *need* one.'

When Mr Justice Todd later emerged from his chambers, he was wearing a jacket and pinstripes. Without the wig he looked far less forbidding and several pounds lighter. That was Lomax's impression as he stepped out of the archway and ambled casually behind the judge in the direction of his parked car.

Monk had stopped Lomax's Cavalier on a double yellow in view of the exit; he had the bonnet up and the emergency lights flashing. His friend approached, closed the lid and climbed into the driver's seat as Todd pulled out in his Bentley two-litre.

The two cars travelled south and over Blackfriars Bridge before picking up the South Circular and finally taking the A23 towards Reigate. The destination wasn't Todd's home as it turned out but a country hotel nearby.

Leaving Monk behind, Lomax followed Todd inside. Minutes later Lomax returned to his car.

'Well?' Monk asked.

'He's having a drink with a familiar face.'

'What? Who?'

'Roger Pinfold,' Lomax said, a rising sense of anger replacing his initial shock.

'What is it? Bribes?'

'I doubt it, Joe. No bags of gold anyway. I expect Pinfold's just playing his role as legal watchdog for the Home Office.'

'This whole thing stinks, Chris. I'm getting fucking pissed off with it, to be honest.'

Lomax couldn't have agreed more. He wasn't sure what was worse, the anger he felt or the sense of helplessness. That Sam and her legal team were dancing to a predetermined tune. The end would never really be in any doubt.

An hour and a few gin and tonics later, Pinfold and Todd went their different ways. It turned out that the judge's home was a vast detached Georgian house within its own high rhodo-dendron borders. Monk backed into a leafy track and they settled down to wait and watch.

In fact, Lomax was to do a lot of waiting and watching over the following six weeks as the trial date approached. Whenever he had a day free – and he had too many of them – he would watch the house and take notes, borrowing different cars from friends and making superficial changes to his appearance. As his notebook filled, so the pattern of activity became estab-lished.

377

Mr Justice Todd lived with his wife of similar age. They had a maid who came to clean each morning and a gardener arrived to mow the lawn once a week. There were no children still living at home and Mrs Todd went out most mornings. Lomax followed her to various minor social events in the village. Coffee mornings, WI meetings and flower-arranging classes. Her husband usually left for work early each morning and invariably visited the country hotel or played a round of golf before returning home in the evening. The greetings and goodbye kisses were perfunctory.

'Bet he's got a floozy somewhere,' Joe said, who'd just returned from four weeks in Kazakhstan in his new job. 'Or a rent boy. Find one of them and tip off the papers. Like they did to poor old Penny.'

'We should be so lucky, and there's no sign yet.'

On the fifth Friday, Mr Justice Todd's wife went to the local supermarket to do her regular weekend shopping. That was when they broke in. Access was easy: after scrambling through the hedge they were able to scale a drainpipe to a first-floor bedroom window that had been left open, so the antiquated burglar alarm didn't trigger.

They located the judge's study and Monk picked the lock. Then they went through all the papers on the desk and worked their way through each drawer. There was nothing concerning the trial.

'Look at this. Dirty sod,' Monk said, holding up a tatty ancient copy of *Rustler*. 'A pile of them.'

Lomax picked up a gold-edged invitation card by the green-shaded lamp. 'Interesting. A supper invitation for the night before the trial opens. RSVP Lord Moffat.'

'Who's he?'

'No idea,' Lomax replied, 'but it means they'll be out.'

Monk had hardly heard. 'Hello, what's this?' He was opening an envelope and tipping out the contents. Two glossy photographs of some luxury villa and a yacht. Palm trees and happy Jamaican faces in the background. And an attached note. He held it up. *Thought you'd like to see the place. Villa and boat all yours for a month, December 15 to Jan 15, as promised. With my compliments in anticipation of a job well done. Roger P.*

'Our friend?'

Monk turned the envelope over. HMSO envelope. SW1 postmark. 'Could well be.'

'The bag of gold. A jolly in the sun.'

'Bastard. Both of them. Bastards,' Monk seethed.

'Todd and his wife will be out on Sunday night,' Lomax repeated.

'You just said that, Chris. What you thinking?'

Lomax glanced up at the ceiling, so angry that now he was actually thinking the unthinkable. 'I was just wondering how long since this house last had its electric wiring checked.'

Sixteen

The new Director General of the Security Service was not his usual equable self when Roger Pinfold entered his office in Thames House with its panoramic view of the river.

'I've a meeting in an hour with the Cabinet Intelligence Unit,' John Nash said testily. 'I'm going to be asked questions, and I don't have any answers. Has RUC Special Branch completed its report yet? Those raids were weeks ago.'

Pinfold smiled uneasily. 'Just about, sir. It's taken time to find and interview everyone on the Frontline Ulster membership list. Nearly all the stragglers are in now.'

'Nearly?'

'Some were abroad and others are – er – well, dead and buried. It wasn't the most up-to-date list in the world. None claimed to know anything about *Cuchulainn*. They pay their subs and read the FUM's newsletters and that's about it. Mostly middle-class and living in rural locations. Not a major player amongst them and not a weapon found except those held by RUC cops or gun-club members.'

Nash grunted. This was not what he wanted to hear. 'What about the leadership?'

'A lawyer, a bank manager and a couple of academics. Oh, and a printer who runs off their pamphlets. Well, their interrogators are fairly sure they don't know what's going on. Of course, they're rather pleased someone's claiming to be their military wing and one or two are being a bit coy, as if they know but aren't saying.'

'But there's no hint of evidence that they're at all involved?'

Pinfold shook his head. 'Doesn't look like it, I'm afraid, sir.'

'What about this student pop group, the Tain?'

'They were taken in for questioning. Apparently they were approached about a year ago by a mysterious Englishman called Tim or Tom Smith. Befriended them when they were playing in

380

a pub, said how good he thought they were and suggested they write resistance songs for the Loyalists. He gave them some guidance to get them going, suggested they change their name from Reservoir Dogs and that they should join the FUM.'

'They went along with it?'

'And haven't looked back.'

'But otherwise they're unconnected?'

'Appears so.'

'And this Tim or Tom Smith, what happened to him?'

'Disappeared. They say they haven't seen him since mid-summer last year.'

Nash shook his head in despair. 'What's the word from our informer network?'

'Well, it's not what it was,' Pinfold pointed out.

The director general sighed wearily. 'My predecessor warned the Cabinet this would happen if we continued the new policy of isolating the Loyalist groups. They used to consider us as allies, now most regard us as much the enemy as the IRA. Frankly, I think we've lost control of them.'

'We've still got friends.'

'If you mean King Billy's lot – ?' Nash didn't even bother to hide his contempt. 'What does he know?'

'There's a rumour that Rattler's involved.'

'That I can believe. Where's Rattler now?'

Pinfold shrugged. 'On the gallop.'

'On the gallop in the Irish Republic!' Nash said in exasperation. 'Have you read these reports from Dublin? More power lines down, more railway bridges. It's creating major chaos. The media blackout won't last.' Another weary sigh. 'Still our political masters call the tune. And they, of course, know best. Even if we haven't a friend left in the Loyalist camp.' That reminded him. 'Talking of old friends, Roger, what's going on in the case of Rodney Littlechild? I thought he was going to plead guilty to killing Fitzpatrick.'

'The defence has dropped hints he will – at the last minute.'

'But you said he was virtually caught red-handed. Tabitha actually identified him at the scene.'

'That's right, sir. But he's got a top legal team. One can't count one's chickens.'

'And that's why you introduced conspiracy to the Smals murder?' There was a hint of disapproval in his voice. 'Was that wise? Weren't some of our people involved in some unorthodox ops at that time, running the old agenda?' He meant when it was still thought the war against the IRA could be won.

'Don't worry, sir. I had Lord Moffat's approval. It was introduced to pressure Littlechild into a plea bargain so details won't come out in court.'

'But it hasn't worked, has it?'

'Er – not yet.' Sheepish. 'But the defence know we'll drop the murder for a plea to conspiracy.'

'But if he doesn't co-operate and he's found not guilty on the murder charge, the Smals case could still go to trial, couldn't it? That could be a bit uncomfortable for us.'

Thank God, Pinfold thought, for the time-honoured Service ethos of keeping everything secret. Boxed and separate, never letting the right hand know what the left is doing. So the DG only has half the picture, if that. Just like his predecessor and the one before her.

'Littlechild is the prime suspect in that too, sir. Well in the frame. And I don't believe any of our people were involved. There's a witness to what went on.'

'Yes?'

'King Billy; he's still on board.'

'Oh dear.' Nash drummed his gold Sheaffer pen on the leather blotter pad. 'Still, you know what you're doing, Roger; I've every faith. Meanwhile, though, we've *got* to dig deeper into this *Cuchulainn* business. Who shut the operation down? Before your time, wasn't it?'

Pinfold smiled. 'My old boss, Walter.'

'You should have a word.'

'Difficult that, sir. He's in a hospice. Big C, I'm afraid. Refusing to see anyone.'

'Oh dear. Poor Walter.'

Pinfold agreed. 'He's dying, only given days to live.'

John Nash turned in his swivel chair and took in the spring

sunshine reflecting brightly on the grey river water. 'Anyway, I don't suppose he'd be of any help. The answer won't lie there.'

'No, sir.'

'But I tell you, Roger, it lies somewhere. And we've *got* to find it before the whole Irish situation blows up in our faces like an atomic bomb.'

As both Lomax and his sister were to be called as witnesses, neither would be able to sit in on the hearing in the public gallery. Nevertheless, both felt a burning need to be at the Old Bailey on the opening day. To be there for Roddy and for themselves, to experience the atmosphere and to get an impression of how the trial was going to progress.

Manda had come down from the family home in Hereford to babysit while her father drove Evie and Monk to the Central Criminal Court in the City of London.

The trial was scheduled to start at ten thirty and, when they arrived with twenty minutes to spare, Browne was waiting for them. She gave an uncertain smile of greeting. 'Evie – ' A kiss on the cheek – 'Chris, Joe. Look, I'm afraid there's been a delay. They've just announced that Mr Justice Todd won't be conducting the trial after all.'

'What's happened?' Evie asked.

'Apparently he had a house fire last night. A faulty fuse box or something. The house was gutted. Thank God there was no one inside at the time.'

'How awful,' Monk said, straight-faced.

Browne nodded. 'Apparently they lost everything. So Todd and his wife have got to find temporary accommodation, buy clothes and essentials, sort out the insurance.'

'A nightmare,' Lomax agreed a little sheepishly. He wasn't proud of what he'd done and felt particularly sorry for Todd's wife.

Evie was more concerned at how her husband would take the news of further delay. 'How long will the trial be postponed? Days, a week?'

'Hours, thank goodness,' Browne answered. 'At the Old Bailey you can't just bring forward other big cases without warning. They're hopeful they can start at two thirty, provided they can find a senior judge willing and able to hear the case.'

'At least,' Monk said, 'I suppose any judge would be better than Todd.'

She looked at him curiously; there was something slightly smug about his expression. 'Not necessarily, Joe. It's just we *know* how bad he was for us. Another *could* be even worse.'

Monk caught Lomax's eye and both men shrugged. They'd done their best.

And they learned the results of their best at lunch as they sat at the pavement tables in the mild sunshine outside the Chambers Wine Bar across the street. They'd just ordered spritzers, beers and a range of salads when Ronnie Rock appeared, having rushed straight from the court building.

'Well, who've we got?' Meyrick demanded.

Rock gulped for breath. 'You won't believe it.'

'Do come on,' Browne urged. 'Is it that bad?'

'Mr Justice Quigley.'

'Oh, my God!' Meyrick blinked. 'You've got to be winding me up, young Ronald.'

Browne was momentarily bewildered. 'Is that the one with the chauffeur-driven Morris Traveller?'

'That's the one,' Rock confirmed. 'Mad as a hatter.'

'A bit strong,' Meyrick chided. 'Mischievous, eccentric, cantankerous even, and certainly cunning. But mad? I'll reserve judgment.'

'I don't know whether to laugh or cry,' Browne confessed.

Lomax was horrified. Just what had he and Monk achieved? 'Surely he'll be better than Justice Todd?'

For Evie's benefit, she said: 'I'm sure he will. But he'll also be unpredictable if he's true to form. He's due to retire – in fact I thought he had. That's probably why he was free.'

'Did you say he gets chauffeured in a Morris Traveller?' Monk asked, sharing Lomax's sense of doom.

'His pride and joy,' Meyrick confirmed. 'I've seen it. A real collector's item, the shooting-brake type with timber window frames. He gave up driving years ago and hired a driver.

Refused to go for a more suitable limo. I remember the *Mail* ran a story on it.'

'There's one consolation,' Browne pointed out. 'If we're apprehensive about Quigley's appointment, Henry Halifax will be having apoplexy.'

And so will Roger Pinfold, Lomax thought. The prospect of that cheered him up no end and he lifted his newly arrived beer. 'A toast. To Roddy and Evie. Good luck to them both.'

Browne saw the tears in his sister's eyes and reached across to her, taking the small pale hand in her own. 'Tristram and Ronnie and I are going to fight like the devil for Roddy, I promise you that.'

'Thanks, Sam,' Evie sniffed.

Lomax felt immensely proud of Browne at that moment. This was most definitely a red knickers day.

'I am minded,' said Mr Justice Ernest Quigley, 'to follow the decision of my erstwhile colleague, Mr Justice Todd, and run these trials for murder and conspiracy to murder completely separately as the *prima facie* evidence suggests that they are indeed unrelated events.'

Sam Browne slumped back in her seat having heard the pronouncement by the rasping squeak of a voice from the Bench. It had followed Meyrick's robust and impassioned plea to have the court's earlier decision reversed.

Quigley's style was markedly different from that of Todd. As he came, bent-shouldered, into court, Browne was reminded of a bewhiskered dormouse, swamped by the massive wig and voluminous red gown. Far from generating authority, his voice and manner suggested a mischievous sense of humour, happy to share jokes with counsel and to lighten the solemnity of the proceedings. He was clearly a man who enjoyed his work and wanted others to do likewise. Once or twice, she noticed, the judge's comments even brought a half-smile to Roddy's lips and she was thankful for that.

'Of course,' Quigley was saying, 'Mr Justice Todd had more time to study the papers that are before me now, so I feel I should respect his judgment. However, my brief reading does lead me to believe that there *may* just be a thread linking the two cases. And I will bear that in mind during this hearing. I may, therefore, allow a certain amount of relevant – I repeat relevant – evidence from the defence counsel to be raised until I have made up my mind whether the second charge in some way pertains to the first. I make this decision because of the gravity of the two charges and because of certain restrictions that will necessarily face the defence since the case involves the intelligence services and could affect the national interest.

'Nevertheless, I do not intend to make judgment on the second charge, nor prejudice any future trial on that indictment which, I repeat, remains separate.' He peered over his gold pince-nez. 'I would warn counsel for the defence not to be tempted to take advantage of an old man's generosity.'

Meyrick couldn't keep the grin from his face; the suppressed fury of the prosecution bench was almost palpable. He bowed from the waist. 'As Your Lordship pleases.'

Browne glanced up at Littlechild who stood with his hands white-knuckled on the rail of the dock, looking quite taken aback at the first small glimmer of good fortune in months.

'Let's proceed,' Quigley said briskly and the trial began to unfold.

Roddy Littlechild stood tall in the dock. Somewhat to Browne's surprise, there seemed to be more colour in his cheeks, as his slumped posture of recent months straightened and his soldierly bearing returned. It was the old Roddy that Lomax had described to her, had fought alongside all those years ago. It was the relief, she felt sure, that battle, however unequal, had at last been joined.

Halifax caught Browne's eye for a moment and she knew he was wondering. Would there be the last-minute change of plea she had hinted at?

She shook her head with a knowing smile.

Minx! Halifax mouthed. Then he turned away and was on his feet to deliver his opening address. With thumbs hooked aggressively into the armholes of his waistcoat and his chin jutting, he said: 'My lord, ladies and gentlemen of the jury, on first impression this trial may appear to be somewhat out of the

386

ordinary, indeed extraordinary. Talk of the Security Service, which as the country's counter-espionage force is known to most people as MI5, talk of safe houses and terrorists – But that first impression could not be further from the truth. For this is a squalid tale of nothing more or less than vindictive sectarian murder. Moreover, the murder of a man who was a crucial player in the achieving of the ceasefire in Northern Ireland. A ceasefire that has, lamentably, collapsed in recent weeks. And who knows – a ceasefire that may have still been in place had it not been for the untimely demise of this murder victim.'

'Makes him sound like a bloody saint,' Browne murmured to Totty.

'Yes, the dead man was a former member of the Provisional IRA,' Halifax was saying, 'but as such he was a man of passionate – you may think misguided – belief, an Irishman's belief in the rightfulness of eventual unity in his country. He considered himself to be a freedom fighter in a long Irish tradition. To him all actions taken were on behalf of his fellow countrymen. But in the end he saw the folly of violence and was instrumental in no small way in persuading the men of violence to lay down their arms and end over twenty years of bloody conflict.

'And so it was that the victim, Mr Donal Fitzpatrick, came to be in an MI5 safe house in south London last August while conducting delicate peace negotiations with members of Her Majesty's Government.

'The prosecution intends to prove – beyond any doubt – that the defendant, Mr Rodney Littlechild, a former Loyalist paramilitary and secret policeman in the reviled South Africa of apartheid, received a tip-off from terrorist colleagues by telephone of the presence and location in London of his old enemy, Donny Fitzpatrick. That he watched the public house where Fitzpatrick was drinking and stalked him back to the safe house where he was staying and then brutally shot him dead.

'You will have presented to you conclusive forensic evidence of the defendant's guilt as well as reliable eye-witness testimony to confirm it.

'This then is a wicked crime, compounded by the fact it has

no doubt gone some way to wrecking the Northern Ireland peace package that it was hoped would end nearly a quarter-century of violence!'

He resumed his seat in the hushed court before the first witness was called.

Halifax began by registering a complaint to Mr Justice Quigley about the improper conduct of the defence-team solicitor concerning the first prosecution witness to take the stand, one Mark Wortle, a taxi driver.

'Miss Browne improperly attempted to make contact with this police witness by visiting his home,' he accused. 'This without notifying the police or the Crown Prosecution Service. By good fortune the man was on holiday abroad and in fact has only just returned to learn of this intimidating visit during which his wife was interrogated in his absence.'

Quigley nodded his acknowledgement. 'I understand the prosecution's displeasure at this visit and I myself find it disquieting that a member of the legal profession should behave so unconventionally.'

Halifax's face creased into a satisfied grin as he listened.

'I am even more disquieted,' Quigley continued, 'that the defence solicitors appear to have been so frustrated by lack of co-operation from the police and CPS in this case as to take such drastic steps in the interests of their client – in what is the most serious crime it is possible to commit. There is no property in a witness, yet the prosecution seems to have been hellbent on holding on to witnesses with a ball and chain.'

Suddenly Halifax's face resembled a deflated balloon.

Quigley smiled kindly in Browne's direction. 'The defence solicitor's actions may not have been conventional but, strictly speaking, they were not improper as earlier witnesses interviewed had *not* at that time been identified by the police. And as for Mr Wortle, *he* is the prosecution witness, *not* his wife. Now, Mr Halifax, you may continue.'

'As Your Lordship pleases,' Halifax grumbled and called Wortle to the box.

The witness was slight and wiry and in his mid-thirties. His cropped hair sun-bleached and his somewhat gaunt face tanned after his absence in the Caribbean.

Halifax led him quickly through his evidence. He had been passing down Littlechild's road in Southall on the night of the murder and had been waved down by a pedestrian. He described Rodney Littlechild in perfect detail. His passenger had asked to be taken to the Duke's Head public house in south London, but on arrival had asked the driver to drop him a hundred yards farther on. In his mirror, the taxi driver had seen the passenger enter a telephone call box; he had picked up the receiver but made no attempt to make a call.

'Why was this, do you think?' Halifax asked.

'I got the impression he was just making it look like he was making a call. All the time he was watching the pub across the street.'

'Thank you, Mr Wortle.'

This time Ronnie Rock was doing the cross-examination.

'Make a point of watching passengers you've just dropped, do you, Mr Wortle?'

'No, I just happened to notice.'

'Then you must have been noticing for some time to convince yourself he wasn't actually making a call?'

'No, maybe thirty seconds.'

Rock held up his flashy gold wristwatch. 'If the court will bear with me. Thirty seconds from now . . .'

The silence seemed to stretch into long minutes. The prosecution team began to fidget; one of the jurymen coughed.

'There we are,' Rock said, 'thirty seconds. A long time for a busy taxi driver to sit doing nothing, idly watching a complete stranger.'

'Maybe it wasn't that long.'

'Then how long?'

'Ten seconds.'

'And then what did you do?'

'Made a U-turn. That's how I could still see he hadn't dialled.'

'You managed to do a U-turn, looking both ways for traffic

and were still able to be sure he hadn't dialled? You must be very observant?'

'I suppose I am.'

'Is that due to your army training in the Intelligence Corps?'

Wortle's mouth sagged for a moment, his eyes darting towards Halifax for help. The barrister slowly shook his head, unable to intervene.

'Is that relevant?' Wortle asked. 'Surely my past career has absolutely no bearing on this case.'

Quigley frowned. 'I'd have thought if you have past service in the Intelligence Corps, it might *strengthen* your evidence, add more weight, Mr Wortle. A man trained to observe.' He looked towards the defence counsel. 'Carry on.'

Rock continued. 'Do you own the taxi that you used to pick up Mr Littlechild?'

'Yes.'

'You're an owner-driver?'

The witness nodded.

'But you are not a licensed taxi driver, are you? You are not among the twenty thousand black cab drivers registered with the Public Carriage Office?'

Wortle paled. Again, there would be no help from Halifax on this one.

'Come on, Mr Wortle,' Rock pressed. 'Yes or no?'

'No.'

'So you picked up the defendant illegally that night?'

Hesitant. 'I suppose so.'

'Do that often, do you? Taxi-drive illegally?'

'No, it was a one-off. An indiscretion. Mostly I do private work for regular clients.'

'What sort of clients? Name some. Individuals, companies?'

'I don't recall off hand. I'd have to check.'

Rock smiled with full white-toothed Jamaican charm. 'I'm not going to push you on that, Mr Wortle, because I don't believe you are in a position to tell the court who you really work for.' He paused. 'Now, during your time in the Intelligence Corps you served in Northern Ireland, right? And as such you'd have had regular contact with members of MI5, isn't that so?'

390

'I can't comment on that.'

Rock brushed his answer aside. 'And both the police and MI5 regularly use black cabs to mount surveillance operations, don't they?'

A light gasp went up from the public gallery as Wortle retorted: 'I wouldn't know about that.'

'Mr Wortle, you have a nice tan; where did you get it?'

'I've been in Jamaica.'

'My home country. How nice. Since when? Since about a week after the events you have just described?'

'About then.'

'Lying doggo? Keeping a low profile? But some nine months must have made it an expensive holiday?'

'It was.'

'Or were you working?'

Wortle now had the look of a trapped animal. 'Yes, I did some to pay my way.'

'Driving?'

'Yes.' Uncertain.

'A bit of casual driving?'

'Sure.' Escape in sight.

'For the British High Commission, no less?'

'Er – yes.'

'I know something of Jamaica, Mr Wortle. Isn't it true that the Commission simply doesn't take on casual drivers? Their drivers have to be fully trained in defensive driving and various other security techniques, don't they? Full-time professionals with an impeccable pedigree. Now, please tell the court who you really work for?'

Wortle's eyes flickered shut for a moment. 'I've told you, I'm self-employed.'

'The truth is, isn't it, Mr Wortle, that you are on the staff of the Security Service, most probably as a surveillance driver with your taxi? On the night in question you were instructed to park near the defendant's house?'

'No, sir.'

'You then received a message by radio to say the subject had left his house and was looking urgently for a cab, didn't you?

And no doubt he was very pleased and relieved to find one in such a remote street at such a time.'

Wortle raised his voice. 'That's just not true.'

'Thank you, Mr Wortle,' Rock ended with a note of contempt.

The next prosecution witness to be called was the manager of the Duke's Head public house. He confirmed that Fitzpatrick had been drinking alone in the pub and had received a telephone call.

Rock got confirmation that Fitzpatrick had not appeared nervous or unduly wary and that the caller had an accent which was definitely Ulster rather than Southern Irish. The caller had said quite distinctly that he 'couldn't make the meeting' with Fitzpatrick before the bar manager had handed over the receiver.

Earlier, Halifax had established that there was no way of knowing who had called the pub. The barrister left the inference hanging that the caller was probably an accomplice of Rodney Littlechild, who knew and was trusted by Fitzpatrick, and who set him up so that the assassin knew where to find him.

Although a relatively small part of the prosecution case, it was a convincing and damning point on which to end the first day.

At the start of the second day, the stand was taken by 'Officer A' of MI5, giving evidence from behind a special security screen and visible to no one except the judge, opposing counsels and the jury.

Meyrick lifted his eyebrows. Somehow he hadn't been expecting a woman. Severely attractive, she appeared to be in her mid-forties although the sparsity of her make-up and unflatteringly bunned grey hair could have been making her look older.

Halifax began prompting her gently through her evidence. Firmly and fluently she explained how she had been the officer responsible for Fitzpatrick's safety, how she had been in the car outside the apartment block and had recognised, albeit belatedly, the face of Rodney Littlechild as he entered. Then what she had found on reaching the apartment.

Only minutes into her testimony, Littlechild appeared to freeze like a statue. Totty sensed the reaction first and turned to see their client speak to the prison officer with him in the dock.

She nudged Browne. 'Something's wrong with Mr Littlechild.'

As the solicitor glanced across, the prison officer beckoned. Swiftly she made her way back to the dock where Littlechild leaned down to whisper: 'That voice, Sam, I'd know it anywhere. It's Tabitha White.'

Browne's eyes widened. 'You're sure?'

'I'll never forget it.'

'Okay, I'll tell Tristram.'

A ripple of whispers ran along the defence bench, the assured words of Agent A hardly registering as the news was rapidly digested and notes scribbled.

The witness's evidence was brief almost to the point of indecency.

Meyrick took the floor. 'Now, Officer A, I understand you are a highly experienced and senior MI5 case officer of many years' service?'

'Er – I'm afraid I can't answer that.' She knew the defence had been given no such details.

'And you've had many dealings with the defendant?'

An awkward half-laugh. 'Er – no.'

'A few dealings perhaps?'

'None.'

Meyrick held her gaze and said very, very slowly: 'Are you *quite* sure – on your oath – that you've *never* met the defendant?' He noted the concern in her eyes. How cold they looked. Maybe not concern, but most definitely hatred. And it was directed straight at him.

'Quite sure,' she said firmly.

Meyrick gave a dramatic sigh. 'Because I suggest that you were in fact the defendant's controller?'

'I was not.'

'But you are a controller, handler of agents?'

'On occasions.'

'Isn't it true that you once told the defendant the government's agenda on Northern Ireland had changed? That they recognised the IRA could not be defeated militarily and that in the end there would have to be a political settlement?'

'I never said any such thing.'

'Not to the defendant?'

'Not to anyone.'

'Did you not once ask the defendant to co-operate in the murder of a fellow Loyalist known as Stevie Gavin?'

'Certainly not. That sort of thing *isn't* done.'

Meyrick ignored that. 'And when the defendant turned you down, wasn't he then considered to be a dangerous liability? Untrustworthy? Is that when you threatened him if he didn't leave the country, and subsequently began a smear campaign against him?'

'No, never.'

'And isn't it true you were afraid the defendant was going to reveal this and other dubious MI5 tactics in Northern Ireland in a television documentary?'

'Hardly, as I don't know the man!'

'But someone in your office knew about the documentary, didn't they? Because the production company was warned off, wasn't it?'

'I wouldn't know. Not my department.'

Meyrick paused. 'Tell me, Officer A, did you give the defendant's telephone number to the late Mr Fitzpatrick and suggest that they meet?'

The witness stared impatiently at the ceiling of the courtroom. 'No.'

'Did you or someone you work with conspire to have Fitzpatrick killed and set up the defendant to be in the wrong place at the wrong time?'

Her answer was hardly unexpected. 'Most definitely not.'

Meyrick continued: 'We've heard you were in a car outside the victim's apartment block. How many of you?'

'Three in total.'

'Wouldn't your presence have been more effective if you had

been in the flat *with* your charge, Mr Fitzpatrick? That, I believe, is usual procedure?'

'In hindsight, yes. That had been the arrangement for many weeks and it was getting on Fitzpatrick's nerves. Some people find it very irritating and claustrophobic – the lack of privacy.'

'But you could have insisted?'

'He was in dialogue with the government *voluntarily* and we couldn't force protection on him, merely advise most strongly. But he threatened to leave our safe custody altogether and make his own arrangements. He was adamant, so that night we compromised with the car outside.'

'So Mr Fitzpatrick was aware of your presence?'

'He was, and he was able to call us by mobile telephone if we were required.'

'Which I believe he did on the night in question?'

'Yes. At ten thirty that evening he phoned in to say he was going down the road for a quick drink alone. At the Duke's Head public house.'

'Anything else?'

'He didn't want any minder or protection officer to accompany or follow him. As I say, he wanted some private space to relax.'

'And you respected his wish?'

'Not entirely. I was responsible for his safety. I followed at a discreet distance, observed him drinking alone and then followed him back to the safe house.'

'And you saw no one following him?'

'Not that I was aware – ' she hesitated, 'although clearly I was wrong.'

'Or right,' Meyrick countered. 'And what time did he return?'

'He was logged in at just before eleven twenty-five. The safe house is a ten-minute walk from the pub.'

'Then, approximately five minutes later, a stranger walked up to the block and entered. You said his back was to you, hiding what he did at the door? That he hardly hesitated, suggesting that he was able to punch in the correct code or else found the door ajar?'

'Correct. At first I thought it was another resident who'd been out for the evening. They were of similar build and both had beige raincoats which were almost identical.'

'No beige raincoat was ever found in the defendant's possession, was it?'

'I wouldn't know. All I know is that, according to the police, it has never been found.'

'So how did you see his face if he had his back to you? He had to walk down a thirty-foot path to reach the door and his back would have been towards you all the way, surely?'

'We were parked outside and he walked towards us and past us before turning in.'

'And the street lighting?'

'It was fair, good.'

'Which? It can't have been both."

'Good.'

'And so you were able to see his face clearly?'

'Yes. Reasonably so.'

'Yet you still thought he was this innocent neighbour?'

'Yes. I was tired, it'd been a long day. My reflexes were slow. I assumed it was the neighbour, then thought – wait a minute, that *wasn't* him. Do I know that face?'

'And did you?'

'Yes, but not well. Only from security files. He was known to have associated with Loyalist terrorists in Ulster.'

'That is all? Just known to associate with them?'

'Yes.'

'So hardly a priority for MI5 concern?'

'No.'

'Then you must have a remarkable photographic memory, Officer A, to recall such an insignificant character whom you'd never met.'

'Yes, actually. Part of the training. I had a brief discussion with my colleagues in the car, deciding what to do.'

'Hardly the time for a conference at such a crucial moment, surely?'

'A few seconds, maybe a minute.' She sounded angry now.

'By which time, this person had disappeared inside, right?

You have said you rushed inside and when you reached the apartment door, you found the corridor deserted and six bullet holes in the door.'

'Yes.'

'Don't you *do* things to a safe house *to make* it safe?'

'How d'you mean?'

'Come now, Officer A, you are an experienced operator. Isn't it commonplace to reinforce the external doors and replace windows with bullet-proof glass, that sort of thing?'

'Sometimes, it depends.'

'You mean Fitzpatrick wasn't important enough for that?'

'There were bullet-proof windows.'

'But not the door? Why was that?'

'I don't know.'

She was flustered now, he could tell. 'Don't know? You were responsible for the man's safety. The officer in charge; you've already admitted that. That apartment was even purchased in your name.'

Halifax rose swiftly to his feet. 'Forgive me, my lord, but this is entering into an area of national security. Moreover, my learned friend cannot possibly know the name of the witness. And if he does, she may not be able to continue giving evidence as her personal safety could be placed in jeopardy.'

Quigley said coldly: 'I'm not aware that anyone has given the lady's name in open court, nor is about to.'

'Certainly not, Your Lordship,' Meyrick confirmed. 'But I would ask Officer A to tell us why the door was not protected against firearm rounds?'

'It just wasn't,' the woman replied. 'A separate department advises on that sort of thing. I'm not qualified.'

'Isn't it a fact that there had been a bullet-proofing panel in position, but it had been removed?'

'Not that I'm aware of.'

Meyrick pressed on. 'And is that not the real reason that access to the scene of crime was denied to the defence?'

'That was not my decision.'

'Don't tell me – another department?'

'As it happens, yes.' There was a smirk of triumph on her face.

Meyrick turned towards the Bench. 'My lord, I would ask that the court instruct the Security Service to provide a witness or affidavit explaining whether and when and why a bullet-proof panel for this door was removed.'

Quigley frowned. 'I'm not sure that it's truly relevant, Mr Meyrick. It is *accepted* that such a panel was not in place at the time. This is not a civil court to apportion blame for the purpose of a claim for damages by the deceased's family, although perhaps it should be, given the apparent level of incompetence.'

An undercurrent of amusement flowed through the court, but stopped short of the prosecution bench.

'Incompetence yes, my lord,' Meyrick cut back in, 'unless there was another motive, as the defence believes there was. The circumstantial evidence facing my client is such that we must strive to persuade the jury that others might have far stronger motives for wanting Fitzpatrick dead and my client indicted for the crime.'

'I am afraid, Mr Meyrick, that I am not convinced.'

'Then will Your Lordship allow me to convince this court that there is something very strange about this case, something that is not right. Some minutes ago you heard Officer A claim that she previously had no dealings with Rodney Littlechild and indeed had never met him. Yet a message was passed to me from my client identifying Officer A by her voice alone. I crave Your Lordship's leave to cross-examine this witness further to establish whether she is indeed known to the defendant. And, as important, vice versa.'

Halifax piped up on cue. 'This really is most improper. We're talking here about the interests of national security.'

'No, Mr Halifax, we are talking about the interests of a fair trial,' Quigley corrected. 'This is an important point to establish one way or the other. Therefore I propose to allow Mr Meyrick to cross-examine the witness in camera tomorrow morning. Meanwhile, Mr Meyrick, do you have any further questions for this witness?'

'Just a couple more. Officer A, presumably you had spent some time with Fitzpatrick in his flat?'

'Yes.'

'And did you gain some insight into his political views?'

'Some.'

'Is it not true that, far from being in favour of the IRA ceasefire, he was dead set against it? And as such was an obstacle to the peace process?'

'He never expressed such an opinion to me.'

Meyrick waited for the jury to digest that before continuing. 'You discovered the body of Mr Fitzpatrick at fifteen minutes to midnight. Yet it was one fifteen before the police were notified. One hour and thirty minutes. Why was there this unpardonable delay?'

'I don't think it is your place to tell me what is unpardonable or otherwise. We are not the police force – our prime consideration is national security and we answer to the Home Office. In a case like this there are many implications to be taken into account – the peace process in Northern Ireland and the private talks the victim was attending. Superiors had to be consulted and they in turn had civil servants, and no doubt, politicians to consult. This takes time after midnight, people have to be roused from their beds.'

'Or was it,' Meyrick said, 'that you needed the time to move the body, remove the bullet-proof panel and have shots fired through the door?'

The public and press gallery joined in a united gasp of astonishment. Halifax was up immediately. 'My lord, the defence is attempting to put words into the witness's mouth.'

'Indeed,' Quigley agreed. 'If you ask a question, Mr Meyrick, it is best not to answer it on the witness's behalf.'

'Very well. So Officer A, did you need the time to interfere with the scene of crime?'

'No, that's ridiculous. You've been reading too many cheap spy novels.'

'I have read *Spycatcher*.' A titter came from the press gallery and died out quickly. 'So are you telling this court that no one –

with or without your knowledge, from or connected with MI5 – could have killed Fitzpatrick?'

'Categorically!' the woman snapped. 'This court will realise what a preposterous suggestion that is. We are answerable to the Home Office and have to act within the law at all times!'

'Methinks,' Meyrick murmured, 'thou dost protest too much.' His voice rose: 'Thank you, Officer A, that is all.'

Fergal had chosen the Fakhreldine, the exclusive Lebanese restaurant offering a splendid view of Piccadilly and Green Park from its first floor windows. It was Fergal's favourite and he always dined there whenever he was in London. And Lord Moffat had grudgingly come to admit he enjoyed its calm and understated opulence and the warmth of welcome from its staff. He was not one for foreign food, more instinctively inclined towards the plainer fare and schoolboy puds of London's clubs, but even he had to admit the Arabs had a pleasingly different and imaginative range of dishes.

However, he drew the line at wines from the Middle East and ordered a bottle of heavyweight Nuits St George before Fergal arrived. They had barely finished exchanging pleasantries and were just beginning their starters of *muhamara*, a Syrian dish of chopped mixed nuts in a hot pepper sauce, when the bleeper started.

He was more used to the mobile now, even beginning rather to like it. Kept him on top of the situation at the Old Bailey and enabled him to give instant advice when Pinfold phoned in with his regular progress reports. Not good news this time, but not too bad.

'Nothing we can't get sorted,' he told Fergal as he put the thing away.

'I'm pleased.' As always his friend was engaging and polite. 'I only wish some of our larger problems could get sorted.'

'Meaning the campaign against Dublin? I thought that's why you wanted to see me.'

Fergal stared forlornly at his plate and shook his head. 'The situation's bad, really bad.'

'I know.'

The Irishman looked up. 'No, Anthony, you don't know the half of it. Most of Dublin is without electricity again this morning. More power lines were blown up. Yesterday it was Cork's turn.'

'I hadn't heard.'

Fergal's smile was without warmth. 'We Irish are known for gabbing and blabbing, but some of us know how to keep a secret when it's necessary. The US has put a special counter-terrorist unit at our disposal. We've imposed a media blackout and we're feeding out a story about major technical problems with electricity distribution. Saying the stories being put about by Loyalist terrorists are just opportunist propaganda, cashing in on what is a serious, but transient problem. A failure in the computer-controlled grid system – we've had the electricity board's boffins come up with some convincing nonsense. Bullshit baffles brains and all that. Everyone thinks the power failures are highly localised – if they realised how widespread they are, there'd be a public outcry. The Taoiseach hasn't even informed your Prime Minister how bad it is, because he hasn't been fully informed himself.'

'That's absurd, Fergal.'

'No, Anthony. Once the politicians learn the extent of the attacks on the South, it'll soon be in the public domain. There are many with axes to grind who won't be afraid to wield them. Old animosities and old scores to settle. Demands for retali-ation, marches in the streets. Our fragile coalition government might well collapse and more extreme nationalist elements seize power amid demands for action. Even military action of some sort.'

Moffat sat back, feeling slightly shocked. 'Against whom?'

'You Brits in the North, of course.'

'Don't be ridiculous, Fergal.'

'I'm deadly serious, Anthony. If your government can't root out the Loyalists who are causing this mayhem quickly, then someone could behave rashly, however much they may come to regret it.'

Moffat had suddenly lost his appetite. He dabbed his mouth

401

with his napkin. 'I think you're exaggerating the position somewhat.'

'Last night a bomb went off at Blarney Castle.'

'What?'

'No one was hurt, it was the dead of night. Simultaneously another small device was detonated near the Cork ferry terminal. Do I have to spell it out, Anthony? They've already hit our infrastructure, blown up rail and road bridges. Nothing too bad yet, but they're playing merry hell with electricity. All police and army leave's been cancelled, but there's no way we can protect everything short of general mobilisation. Now Blarney Castle and the Cork ferry. They've started on our tourist industry.'

'I see,' Moffat said softly, chastened, as he felt a small sinister shiver radiating out from the back of his neck.

'Last night there was another development. Our agriculture ministry received a letter claiming to be from this Loyalist outfit, *Cuchulainn*. With it was a phial which they said contained deadly prion protein which causes BSE, or Mad Cow Disease as the popular press calls it. They threatened to infect our dairy herds. Said that contaminated Brucella vaccine was already in widespread use on our farms. Just before I left our embassy to come here, I had the laboratory results phoned to me.'

'And?'

'The phial indeed contained prion protein.'

'God, these people,' Moffat growled in suppressed rage. Only days before Britain's health minister had informed Parliament that scientists could not rule out the possibility that BSE could jump the species gap to humans. A media outcry was already beginning. 'At least you are not alone in that.'

Fergal's eyes hardened. 'No, and we'll make damn sure we aren't. We're taking steps within the EC to ensure this British scare is blown into a major catastrophe of global proportions – just a little media and committee management amongst allies in Europe. The world's attention will be so focused on Britain's beef crisis that any news of this *Cuchulainn* threat will be drowned out in the uproar.'

Moffat leaned forward. 'We're doing all we can, I assure you. All members of the Frontline Ulster Movement in the province have been questioned.'

'I know, the Americans have told us.'

That took Moffat somewhat by surprise; the entire operation had the highest security classification. Bloody Curtis Manning! 'Ah, well.'

'And I also know that you haven't caught the ringleaders. Don't take us for fools, Anthony. The Americans have already informed us that nothing incriminating was found during any of the raids. I doubt there's even one who would raise his voice in anger, let alone a gun. Whatever lists you've been using, it appears they are hopelessly out of date.'

The colour had left Moffat's cheeks. 'I know investigations are ongoing,' he blustered.

'Take it from me, Anthony, the Loyalists have already slipped loose their dogs of war and whatever your government is doing is too little and too damn late. Unless they are stopped and quickly, I can see this turning into a major international catastrophe. Lighting the touchpaper for a civil war – or worse – that could set the whole of Ireland ablaze. Trust me, Anthony. At this moment we are staring into the abyss.'

Seventeen

After the early in-camera session the next morning, Mr Justice Quigley addressed the jury when they were readmitted. 'Yesterday you will remember counsel for the defence asked leave to cross-examine the witness known to you as Officer A in order to compare her name to the name given by the defendant, Mr Littlechild, who claims to have had extensive dealings with this person from MI5. A claim Officer A denied in court.

'I have to tell you that the surname is different. However, the Christian name is the same. A name that is very unusual in this day and age. So much so that I cannot recall in all my long years ever having met someone with such a name. Until yesterday.

'Whether or not this is the same woman as is claimed by the defendant, it is up to you, the jury, to decide the balance of probability. Only I feel it my duty to remind you that in intelligence circles real names, or real full names, are rarely used, especially when members are what is termed "in the field". That is all I have to say on the matter.'

Browne was delighted, exchanging congratulatory smiles with Meyrick and Rock and giving Littlechild an encouraging thumbs-up sign. Without putting it in so many words, Mr Justice Quigley was saying that the likelihood was that Officer A and the unnamed Tabitha White were one and the same person.

The next session began with the showing of various police exhibits, including the murder weapon and spent rounds, and photographs of the scene of crime. Meyrick drew attention to small screw holes just visible around the edge of the bullet-torn door.

In answer to this, Halifax begged leave to introduce a new witness from MI5's administration directorate responsible for property. The anonymous officer declared under oath that the panel had been removed sometime previously during redecoration. Due to an administrative oversight, it had not been replaced.

Then the next witness was called, an experienced police examiner called Laboratory Sergeant Ted Manning, who had attended following a call from the first police officers at the scene. A rather dour but plain-spoken man, he related his attendance at the apartment. It was straightforward, he said. Bullet holes in the door and rounds embedded in the wall on the far side of the hall. Blood on the carpet and a trail leading to another pool in the living room where Fitzpatrick finally expired, all cross-matching with the victim. A range of hair and fibre samples were taken from the dead man's clothing, then fingerprints and footprints from the corridor outside.

'Were you alone at the scene of crime, Sergeant?' Meyrick asked.

'No. There were other local officers with me, a police photographer and members of the Anti-Terrorist Branch.'

'What about MI5?'

'I wouldn't know.'

'Were there any civilians there who clearly were not police?'

'Yes. A man and two women as I recall, they didn't give their names.'

'Did they give you any instructions?'

'No, I know my job.'

'Did they tell you what had happened?'

'Briefly, yes.'

'Did they appear anxious or agitated?'

'Not that I recall. Maybe a little impatient.'

'Did that make you feel pressurised?'

'Not really, I still did the job.'

'But you felt rushed – they were in control, yes?'

'Only in that they seemed to know what had happened.'

'Did you look round the walls and behind the furniture in the living room?'

He looked baffled. 'No, there was no point. I knew what had happened. The victim was shot in the hall through the door.'

'Would it be truer to say,' Meyrick asked carefully, 'that you *thought* you knew what had happened?'

'Well, yes, I suppose. It seemed clear to me.'

'Was there a bullet-proof panel fixed to the door?'

'Of course not, otherwise the victim wouldn't have been shot.'

'Quite. And did you see the screw holes where such a panel could have been fitted?'

'I don't recall.'

Browne passed a hastily scrawled note over the bench to Meyrick who glanced at it quickly before asking: 'And did you check the deceased's possessions?'

'Yes.'

'It is claimed he called his MI5 minders in the car outside by mobile telephone. Do you know if there was one in the flat?'

'There was. It was in the deceased's jacket pocket. The one he was wearing.'

'So, having been badly shot, the victim would have had no need to drag himself into the living room to phone for help, would he?'

Manning shrugged. 'No, but then I expect he was disorientated . . .'

'You expect that because there *is* no other *rational* explanation, is there?'

'No.'

'Thank you.'

After lunch Meyrick resumed his questioning. 'Let us return to the question of the murder weapon. A Heckler & Koch .45 automatic pistol, I understand?'

'Yes, fitted with a special silencer. It was found in a dustbin at the rear of the building. There was a clear set of fingerprints on the weapon.'

'And on the doorbell outside the flat you also found a fingerprint, isn't that so?'

Manning nodded. 'Matching the defendant's prints.'

'Please show me, Sergeant, how you would press a doorbell.'

'I beg your pardon?'

'Just pretend. Imagine a bell in front of you and that you are about to push it. Demonstrate, please.'

The Lab Sergeant pointed his right hand. 'Like this?'

'Your index finger, right? The print you found was from my client's thumb. Correct?'

'Yes, but then I myself on occasions may have used a thumb. There is no rule.'

'But you'd agree it's more normal, natural, to use the index finger.'

'Yes.'

'And how would you explain three fingerprints – including neither thumb nor index prints, on the barrel of the gun, but no palm print on the butt?'

Manning was unfazed. 'If the killer was professional he or she probably wore gloves. Possibly surgeon's gloves as there were no traces of material. Then in panic he removed the gloves and threw the gun away using a bare hand.'

'So not so professional after all. Let me ask you, Sergeant, is it possible to transfer a fingerprint successfully from one item to another?'

Manning shook his head. 'I do not believe so.'

'Thank you, Sergeant. No more questions.'

Next to give evidence was the senior hospital pathologist who performed the postmortem, reporting on the state of Fitzpatrick's body while alive and the cause of death. Namely a .45 round passing through the heart, two more through the lungs and another through the stomach. Entry and exits points and the horrific amount of internal damage was given in nauseating detail.

Meyrick cross-examined. 'The deceased was supposedly shot through a timber door, wasn't he? Were any wood fragments found in the wounds, any microscopic particles?'

'No.'

'Wouldn't you expect that?'

'I would anticipate, rather than expect. Bullets and materials do not react together in any truly consistent way. There are all too many variables from one situation to another.'

Meyrick glanced down at his notes. 'Who apart from staff was present during the postmortem?'

'Detective Chief Inspector Millman.'

'Anyone else?'

'A Home Office representative.'

'Did he have a name?'

'It wasn't given to me.'

'Were you given a version of events leading to the death?'

'Verbally, yes.'

'And you put the place of shooting in the flat hallway and position of death in the living room,' Meyrick summarised. 'Isn't it highly improbable that a man with such terrible wounds to the vital organs could crawl all that distance, some fifteen feet – as has been suggested – to telephone for help?'

'Improbable yes, impossible no. He was a big, fit man with strong heart and lungs. It is amazing what feats the human body can achieve in a life-threatening situation.'

'Isn't it more likely that a thumping great lead slug through the heart killed him outright, doctor?'

The man nodded. 'That would have been my expectation. But the positioning of the corpse proves otherwise.'

'Unless the body was moved?'

The pathologist frowned; clearly that had never even occurred to him. 'Why should anyone want to do that?'

'Why indeed, doctor?'

A forensic scientist specialising in gunshot wounds, Dr Asmail Singh, was then called to the stand. He confirmed the murder weapon as a .45 Heckler & Koch of German manufacture which had been fitted with a silencer. The rimmed, round-nosed Teflon-coated lead slugs that had killed Fitzpatrick had been fired by that gun, characterised by the five rifling twists to the left and test-firing comparisons.

'A powerful weapon this,' Meyrick observed. 'Capable of passing through ten inches of timber, I believe? A veritable cannon.'

'Very much so,' Singh agreed. 'Six rounds passed through a two-inch oak door, four then struck the victim and all then embedded in the far wall, three to four inches deep.'

'Were any human tissue particles found on any of the rounds?'

Singh looked uncomfortable. 'I didn't examine for that.'

'Why?'

408

'There was no point, it wasn't in question.'

'Because you accepted the police version of events? Yes, Dr Singh, I fully understand that.' He glanced towards the pathologist's diagram of the corpse with all the wounds marked. 'With the exit wounds substantially lower than the entry wounds, doesn't this suggest to you that the victim was shot from above, perhaps while seated, and not while standing to open a door?'

'It could suggest that,' Singh conceded. 'But we don't know if the victim was stooping to release the lock or even ducking when he was hit – a reaction to the muffled sound of the first round. A silencer on a weapon of this power cannot fully subdue the noise.'

'And where in the wall were the rounds located?'

'In a cluster averaging fifty-five inches from floor level.'

Detective Chief Inspector Kenneth Millman of the Anti-Terrorist Branch was the final prosecution witness to be called. With a little prompting from Halifax, the large officer with his dark brooding features went through events of the night of Donny Fitzpatrick's murder.

He confirmed that the victim was attending delicate talks in London with senior civil servants from the Northern Ireland, Home and Foreign Offices. Therefore it was considered prudent to accommodate him in a safe house supplied by MI5, who were also maintaining a discreet and protective watch from a car outside.

'Did you have knowledge of this arrangement at the time?' Halifax asked.

'We were informed, but not involved. Although we co-operate regularly with the Security Service our organisations have very different functions.'

'So when did you first know of the events of the night in question?'

'I received a call at my home in the early hours of the morning. A duty officer at the Anti-Terrorist Branch had been alerted at one fifteen by an MI5 officer at the scene of crime.'

'And you went straight there?'

'Yes.'

'And what did you find at the scene?'

'That the victim had been shot through the apartment door. Six rounds had been fired. A trail of blood ran to the living room where the man finally died.'

'Did the MI5 officer say anything to you?'

'That the killer had been recognised and identified as the defendant, Mr Rodney Littlechild. I was given an address which meant that we could make an early arrest the next morning.'

'And the defendant denied the charge when he was arrested?'

'Yes, sir. He claimed he had not stalked the victim, but had met him at a public house earlier for a meeting and then gone straight home. However, the victim's address was found written on the telephone notepad in the defendant's flat.'

'Thank you, Detective Chief Inspector.'

After lunch on the third day, Tristram Meyrick rose to cross-examine Millman.

'Detective Chief Inspector, are you aware that Rodney Little-child has been an agent of sympathy – that is acting unpaid – of MI5 for over twenty years?'

'No, sir.'

'That was never mentioned to you by your associates at MI5?'

'No, sir.'

'At the time, or since?'

'No, sir.'

'But that is what Mr Littlechild told you in his initial interview with you, isn't that so?'

'He did.'

'Did you attempt to verify his claim?'

'I considered it irrelevant. No one is above the law, no matter who they are or what they've done previously. National heroes fall foul of the law regularly.'

'Please just answer the question.'

'I'm afraid I can't. I have received instructions not to discuss Security Service matters.'

Mr Justice Quigley looked up. 'This has in fact been covered by a Public Interest Immunity certificate, Mr Meyrick. But I think here the interests of justice must override the general public interest in protecting MI5. The witness will answer the question.'

'I did check with MI5. They denied he was ever an agent, just that they had knowledge of him.'

'Didn't that strike you as a somewhat evasive answer?' Meyrick asked. 'What does "have knowledge" mean?'

Halifax intervened. 'My lord, the witness has answered the question and the subject is irrelevant.'

Quigley gave a high-pitched grunt that was more like a squeak. 'I am minded to agree, Mr Halifax. I do not really see the relevance Mr Littlechild's previous job description has to his guilt or otherwise of murder on this particular night.'

Meyrick stood his ground. 'With respect, my lord, my client's relationship with the secret security apparatus of the state is absolutely central to this case.'

'Very well,' Quigley said, 'but Chief Inspector Millman has answered your question.'

Meyrick nodded acknowledgement, then turned back to the witness. 'This was a very odd place, this safe house, wasn't it? Indeed rather inappropriately named. As I understand it, "safe house" in the terms to which we're referring means a haven offered to those whom the state believes to be in danger and whom it wishes to protect. Isn't that so?'

'Yes, sir.'

'And it is normal for minders to live in the safe house with the person they are protecting? Not sit outside in a car. Did you not think this situation odd?'

'I queried the arrangement,' Millman said grudgingly. 'I was told it was a compromise arrangement.'

'So this was a recent development? How long had it been in place?'

'That was the first night.'

'Chief Inspector, it is this court's job to find my client either guilty or not guilty of this crime. Nothing more. But should he be acquitted, it will raise the question of who else could have killed the victim? So let me simply ask you this. Is it not possible that a friend or associate of Fitzpatrick, whom he trusted and who was in the flat with him, could have killed him – for whatever motive?'

Halifax was on his feet. 'My lord, this question is an impertinent and speculative fantasy.'

'What exactly are you suggesting, Mr Meyrick?' Quigley demanded.

'That it is not impossible that Fitzpatrick was killed by someone he trusted – even someone who was protecting him. As you will hear, far from wanting to prolong the Provisionals' ceasefire, Fitzpatrick wanted to destroy it.'

'My lord!' Halifax protested.

Quigley said: 'These are indeed realms of fantasy, Mr Meyrick. Perhaps you'd care to reword your question without attaching it to a statement of opinion which you are in no position to substantiate.'

'Of course, my lord. I submit that it is possible – I say *possible*, however unlikely it may strike the jury at this time – that a person or persons unknown within the safe house murdered Fitzpatrick. And then colluded with the Security Service to implicate my client in the full knowledge that Fitzpatrick had just had a meeting with him.'

'I really don't think I can answer that,' Millman said, not bothering to conceal his indignation.

'Indulge me.'

'In *theory* it could be possible. Except, of course, for witness and forensic evidence to the contrary.'

'In theory it could be possible,' Meyrick repeated, turning towards the jury with the unspoken implication that those words should be remembered. He looked back at Millman again. 'Let me ask you, Chief Inspector, how did the assassin enter the block? I believe you needed to know the code to punch into the keypad or be allowed in by the resident you'd first speak to on the intercom?'

'We've been unable to establish exactly how. Either the killer knew the code or someone hadn't shut the door properly.'

'Was it faulty?'

'Not to my knowledge.'

'Then the assassin was very fortunate that night, wasn't he?' Meyrick glanced down at his notes. 'When you first arrested Mr Littlechild at his flat, did he say something about his telephone answering machine?'

'Actually it was his wife. She said there was a message on it from Fitzpatrick. It was claimed he'd called the previous night asking for a meeting. We checked, but the message tape was clear.'

'Could someone have broken into that flat overnight and replaced that tape with a blank? Or pressed the message erase button?'

Millman shrugged. 'Are we talking theories again?'

'Your answer?'

'I don't believe so, because we also checked the telephone company records of both Littlechild and the safe house. No such call was made.'

'So, if my client is to be believed, someone would have made a very good job of a cover-up. Someone adept at breaking in and also with powers to alter public records if it were deemed to be in the so-called national interest?'

'Mr Meyrick,' Quigley warned quietly.

'Chief Inspector, why was the defence initially denied access to the scene of crime until a court order was sought?'

'Their request was put to MI5 and turned down.'

'Didn't that surprise you?'

'Yes and no. It was a safe house after all. A security matter.'

'An ex-safe house, don't you mean? It was put up for sale shortly after the crime, wasn't it?'

'I know nothing about that. We took advice from MI5 at the time. I saw no problem with this because all forensic evidence would be made available to the defence in due course.'

'A very *long* due course, as this court has already learned.'

'That matter wasn't in my hands.'

Meyrick paused for a moment. 'Are you a naive man, Chief Inspector?'

The policeman's cheeks coloured. 'I don't believe so.'

'Neither do I. Isn't it true that a certain gentleman by the name of Prendergast has been taking a special interest in this case?'

'Yes. He is a representative from the Home Office legal department. His presence is due to the political sensitivity of this case at this particular time. To ensure no trivial errors result in an unsafe conviction.'

'Are you aware that MI5 is answerable to the Home Office?'

'Of course.'

'And that both organisations have legal departments?'

'Yes.'

'Are you sure you know which Mr Prendergast represents?'

'The Home Office.'

'So it would surprise you to know that Prendergast is not his real name, which is why I have no compunction in using it in open court? And that we have witnesses who will testify that he is, or was, a serving officer in MI5.'

Millman shook his head. 'It wouldn't surprise me. He is an MI5 officer, but serving in a liaison capacity with the Home Office legal department.'

At that point Halifax sprang to his feet. 'If I may be permitted to interrupt, Your Lordship. My learned friend will find verification from the Home Office that Mr Prendergast is authorised in his capacity as consultant and liaison officer to its legal department, if he troubles to look in the unused material bundle supplied to him.'

Meyrick turned back to Millman. 'And can you tell me who from the Home Office was present with you at the postmortem?'

The detective shuffled his feet. 'Mr Prendergast. Officer A told me she'd called him to attend the scene of crime immediately after the shooting.'

'Before she called you?'

'Yes.'

He could see no further point in pursuing this; he'd established a seed of doubt and with it the start of a linking thread. 'No further questions, my lord.'

Before Rodney Littlechild was sworn into the witness box, Tristram Meyrick addressed the court. 'You are about to hear the

414

most incredible and extraordinary but true story. It is not an exotic tale of espionage or the world of James Bond so glamourised on celluloid. This is a story of sleaze and betrayal. Of corruption at the very heart of our society. Of a section of a state organ of security behaving in a way that might more befit some fascist state. A rogue element, perhaps, but certainly out of control and answerable to no one.

'Time and again you will hear protestations from the prosecution that it is a confection of lies and fantasy. I intend to prove to you that this is not so. That far from being the perpetrator of any crime, you will hear evidence to suggest that the defendant is in fact the victim. That the defendant – happily married and then expecting their first child – did not just one day last year receive a phone call tip-off telling him where he could find, stalk and murder a leader of the opposing IRA movement.

'It was a remarkably simple setup by, let us say, this rogue element of the Crown's security apparatus to rid itself of two embarrassments. One was Donny Fitzpatrick, a Republican utterly opposed to his own organisation's ceasefire, to be killed by I know not whom. And two, the defendant who had been a loyal and long-term agent for MI5 who refused to co-operate in the murder of a fellow Loyalist and was then regarded as a liability because he knew too much of the Security Service's dirty-war tactics in Ulster. And indeed had been driven to the point of revealing them in a television documentary.'

Henry Halifax rose to his feet in protest and asked the judge for leave to object in the absence of the jury. Mr Justice Quigley readily agreed.

'I really must object, my lord, at this outrageous slander against unnamed officers of the Crown,' Halifax said, after the jury had filed out. 'My learned friend is suggesting duplicity and, in his own words, *murder* by a government agency! This is in the realms of dangerous fantasy, of the penny dreadful spy story. I ask that Your Lordship tell the defence to contain its vivid imagination and keep strictly to events of the night in question.'

Quigley paused for several long moments, weighing his

thoughts carefully before speaking. 'I have heard enough evidence in this case so far to be satisfied that the defendant did have some form of association with MI5, possibly over many years. I can see more clearly now why the defence was keen to run both cases of murder and conspiracy-to-murder concurrently, because that background may yet prove relevant to its theory of the events leading to Mr Fitzpatrick's murder. Without that background knowledge, the jury will find it impossible to judge the weight of probability as to whether the defence's alternative theory of what happened that night is correct or not.'

'With respect, my lord,' Halifax countered. 'It is this court's job simply to answer the question, Did the defendant kill Mr Fitzpatrick or not, on the evidence before it? Yes or no? It is not to examine theories about alternative suspects – that is for the police.'

'Thank you for telling me how to conduct this trial, Mr Halifax.' Quigley's voice had risen an octave. 'The defence has merely suggested what it considers to be a plausible alternative scenario to explain what happened. Neither has counsel accused the government nor any specific person. I notice he was careful to use the words "rogue element". Therefore I am overruling your objection.'

The jury was recalled as a disgruntled Halifax resumed his seat, muttering beneath his breath.

Meyrick then picked up his theme. 'With Fitzpatrick dead and my client in prison for his alleged murder, the cover-up is complete and the decks cleared for continuing Ulster peace talks with no fear of embarrassing revelations. Events that fateful night last August were rooted in developments that had taken place over more than twenty years.'

A sudden ripple of muted excitement broke from the press gallery. The newshounds suddenly had the scent of a front-page scandal in the making.

Meyrick then went back over Littlechild's childhood years in Belfast where he went to school. Some of the pupils at the school were later to be major players in rival paramilitary organisations. One was Donny Fitzpatrick who was destined to

416

become Chief of Staff of the Provisional IRA. Another was Stevie Gavin, known as 'Rattler,' who headed a small Loyalist extremist group called the Ulster Defenders. One more was Peter Keegan, older than the others, who later became an informer for Army Intelligence until he was convicted for conspiracy-to-murder, and another Loyalist terror-gang leader known as King Billy.

With the scene now set, Littlechild was sworn in. 'In 1969 when the current troubles started,' Meyrick began, 'how old were you?'

'Eleven.'

'Did you get caught up in any of the violence?'

'Not for the first four years. I had a very strict father who kept me off the streets.'

'But by 1974, aged sixteen, you were becoming a more rebellious adolescent, is that right?'

'Not so much rebellious, more politically aware. I began making up my own mind about things. I joined the UDA.'

'Which is?'

'The Ulster Defence Association. It had been set up to protect Protestant communities from IRA attacks.'

'Did you ever carry a firearm?'

'No. I was a runner, a messenger boy.'

'But you drifted away from the UDA. Why was that?'

'What they were doing seemed senseless to me, just making matters worse. On a trip to England I heard people saying the Protestant Loyalists were as bad as the Provos. I knew it wasn't true, but unless you've lived in Ulster it's hard to understand that.'

'Then you read a pamphlet by an organisation called the Frontline Ulster Movement.'

'Yes. It made a lot of sense to me.'

'For the benefit of the court, what was the philosophy of Frontline Ulster?'

'That the Protestant population should leave it to the police and the army to counter terrorism. Instead, the country should prepare for a doomsday scenario which foresaw open civil war.'

'So you joined Frontline and met its leader Wallace McIlroy?'

'Yes, we became firm friends in a sort of father–son relationship. He became my mentor.'

'Did he ever tell you about his background?'

'He told me he'd been a member of the Special Operations Executive during World War Two and after retained links with the British intelligence.'

Halifax intervened. 'This is hearsay unless evidence is to be brought to substantiate it.'

Meyrick riposted: 'Certainly, McIlroy's SOE career is well documented in the public domain. I wish to establish the man's links with the intelligence community.'

'Then leave it at that,' Quigley ordered.

'In 1975 did McIlroy make a suggestion to you and other young Protestant men of similar age?' Meyrick asked.

'He said the resistance movement would need people of sound military experience and encouraged some of us to go to Rhodesia – now Zimbabwe – and join the army. See active service and get experience.'

'You were introduced to someone?'

'Yes. A man called Walter Grey.'

'An Englishman?'

'Yes, apparently an old friend of McIlroy. He came across from London, talked to us, encouraged us. Said he had contacts in Rhodesia and could arrange everything including paid flights, pocket money etc.'

'Did you go?'

'I couldn't wait. It was very exciting. I joined the Territorials there and did my basic training before joining the Armoured Car Regiment, 2 Brigade, fighting the Communist ZANLA and ZIPRA terrorists. Later I transferred to the brigade's intelligence cell.'

'And during this period, until 1990 you returned regularly on leave to Ulster to see McIlroy and your other former friends in the Loyalist paramilitaries. On one of these trips did you learn something that came as quite a shock?'

'Yes, when I was in my early twenties McIlroy thought I was old enough and mature enough to understand. We met Walter Grey who told me he was a very senior MI5 officer and that he

418

and McIlroy had conceived Frontline and its ultimate military off-shoot *Cuchulainn*. Vast arms caches and explosives were in place, secretly supplied from Belgium using MI5 black funds.'

'And did Grey ask a favour of you?'

Littlechild nodded. 'To keep in touch with my former friends and report back to him.'

'Then in 1980, you returned to Ulster, but you could see no future for you there as the Troubles continued. So you decided to try South Africa for a while. What happened?'

'I met an old friend from Rhodesia who was then in a branch of the South African Security Police. He was setting up a special covert operations group. He invited me to join them and I did. My job was to collect, collate and disseminate information on any terrorist threat.'

'That was in late 1982,' Meyrick confirmed. 'And I believe that continued until 1984 when your unit's remit suddenly changed. Why was this?'

'The ANC planted a car bomb outside the Air Force HQ in Pretoria. Just after this I went on leave to Belfast where Walter Grey contacted me. He handed over details of information concerning Provisional IRA links with the African National Congress guerrillas. The Provos were given training facilities in remote areas of Mozambique where they could plan and perfect mortar bombs in particular. In return the Provos passed on their bomb-making and setup planning knowledge. My unit discovered that this had been used in the Pretoria bombing.'

Now in the public and press galleries there was a ripple of speculative whispers and hushed conversations.

After Quigley demanded order, Littlechild continued: 'As a result of receiving this information, the South African National Intelligence Service set up a small group to explore the links between the Provos and the ANC.'

'What happened as a result of this?'

'The bond between MI5 and South Africa was cemented in fighting a common cause and mutual enemies.'

'But this being the murky world of intelligence, double-cross was soon to upset this rosy relationship, was it not?'

'A year or so later, when my unit had got to know many of the

Loyalist people well, especially Stevie Gavin – known as Rattler – my police boss realised that they wanted arms, particularly for a new military movement called Ulster Resistance. It was formed in protest over the Anglo-Irish Agreement in 1986. The South Africans saw it as an opportunity to get their hands on British missile technology from Shorts in Belfast. They offered arms in return for secrets.

'Rattler and Peter Keegan came over and I was asked to play host. They were shown a wide range of weapons and ordered what they wanted. Their offer of money was turned down if they could supply the secrets.'

'Did this deal go through?'

'Yes. Armscor weapons were provided via the Lebanon.'

'Did you do anything to stop it?'

'Yes. Rattler was a wild card, and I realised it would be dangerous for vast supplies of arms to be in his possession. I didn't know it at the time, but Keegan was an Army Intelligence agent and was also trying to stop the deal. Anyway, I informed my contact Walter Grey.'

'Those arms were eventually intercepted in Belfast?'

'Yes, in 1988. Not all, though, I believe some got through to Rattler.'

'And the missile secrets?'

'I've heard reliable rumours that details of Javelin and Firestreak were stolen in 1988.'

'But you had done your bit for God and country.'

Littlechild managed a faltering ghost of a smile at that. 'I thought so at the time.'

'You clearly had a good, if periodic, relationship with MI5 at that time. So what went wrong?'

'I think it began in '89, the year that Peter Keegan was arrested and jailed for conspiracy to murder. My contact Walter Grey retired shortly after and that's when things cooled. MI5 virtually ceased all relationships with the Loyalists and Grey was replaced by someone else. And I had a new handler assigned to me. A person called Tabitha White.'

'And did your new handler tell you something that surprised you?'

Littlechild nodded. 'She told me that the political agenda was changing, that Ulster was no longer of strategic national importance. In the end there would have to be a political settlement.'

'When did she say this?'

'About three years ago. I'd just returned to the UK to settle down and get married.'

'What did she ask you to do?'

'To set up a meeting with Stevie Gavin.'

'That is Rattler – the leader of the outlawed Ulster Defenders?'

'Yes. He's exceptionally difficult to track down. Never stays two nights at the same address. It's why he's survived so long.'

'Why did she want you to have this meeting?'

'There was only one purpose. To set up Gavin for assassination.'

'Were there any witnesses to this astonishing request?'

'Yes, a man known as King Billy. He was another Loyalist gang leader, more than willing to do MI5's bidding for the right price.'

'He couldn't set up Gavin?'

'No, Gavin loathed him. My handler hoped King Billy could persuade me.'

'But he couldn't?'

'I detest King Billy as much as Gavin does.'

That extracted a general chuckle from the courtroom.

'Why did your handler want Gavin dead? Hadn't he himself worked for MI5 in the past?'

'*With* them rather than *for* them. Wet jobs, when it suited him.'

'Wet jobs?'

'Assassinations.'

'On behalf of MI5?'

'Yes.'

Halifax was up. 'I really must protest, my lord, at these outrageous accusations.'

'Carry on, Mr Meyrick,' Quigley retorted irritably.

'Please continue, Mr Littlechild,' Meyrick said.

'Gavin was volatile and unpredictable,' Littlechild said. 'And now he had access to quantities of South African arms he was considered to be a big liability. Besides MI5 wanted to clean up their act in advance of a political settlement. It was also under pressure to become more accountable to Parliament.'

'You mean they didn't want journalists and such revealing past misdemeanours by a government agency?'

'Exactly that. I was told that was one reason no one rushed to Peter Keegan's defence during the Penny Inquiry.'

'And what did you do to help MI5 with this meeting with Stevie Gavin?'

'Nothing. I refused.'

'Did your handler respect that?'

'Hardly. Made various threats. It got worse over the next few months.'

'Why was that?'

'Because I refused to set up Gavin and then refused to have anything more to do with MI5, she and others began to suspect I'd arranged for some of those earlier South African arms to escape the net and reach Gavin.'

'What did she tell you?'

'She wanted me out of the country. To set up a life elsewhere so I couldn't embarrass the government with my revelations. I never intended to do that, of course. But I refused to go.'

'Why?'

For a moment, Littlechild stared at Meyrick as though he'd asked the most stupid question imaginable. 'Because this is my country, my home. I'd hoped to resettle in Ulster with my wife and start a family.'

'And after you refused to emigrate, the smear campaign started?'

'Yes. Newspaper reports and a TV documentary suggesting I'd smuggled arms to Loyalist terrorists.'

'When, in fact, all you'd done was try to stop them?'

'Yes.'

Meyrick turned to Mr Justice Quigley. 'Thank you, my lord.'

The next morning, Henry Halifax dispensed with any preamble

and launched into his vicious counterattack, cross-examining Littlechild in a manner that suggested he was beneath contempt.

'When, at the age of sixteen, you joined the Frontline movement in Ulster you were quite the little innocent, weren't you?'

'I wouldn't say that.'

'No, neither would I. Frontline preached a policy of ethnic cleansing, of driving all Catholics back to the Republic?'

'No, they predicted that *could* be the final outcome if things came to civil war.'

'And that idea appealed to you?'

'It didn't appeal, it just seemed like a realistic prediction.'

'And you spoke with the leader, Wallace McIlroy, about his views?'

'Sometimes, he was very busy.'

'McIlroy was later found guilty of having under-age sex with boys in a youth club he ran linked to Frontline, wasn't he? Not to put too fine a point on it, he buggered them.' His eyes blazed at Littlechild. 'Did McIlroy ever bugger you?'

Instantly Littlechild's cheeks were inflamed with fury. 'No. And I never saw him behave incorrectly in the presence of youngsters.'

'Just answer the question please,' Halifax reprimanded.

'No, I was never buggered.'

'Because the truth is, isn't it, that you were brought up by a strict Presbyterian family which believed that the Pope was the Antichrist? Therefore, you virtually never mixed with Catholics as a child, isn't that so?'

'I wouldn't deny that.'

'The truth is you hate Catholics. You were drip-fed hatred of Catholics with your mother's milk, weren't you? All this cosy stuff about being playground chums is all make-believe to fool the jury.'

'I never said chums . . .'

Halifax cut in. 'The truth is you loathe all Catholics and you'd certainly not give the likes of Donny Fitzpatrick the time of day, would you? Certainly not as a leader of the Provisional IRA whom you detest and see as the destroyers of your homeland. You saw your family's view fully vindicated by the Troubles. It was a view shared by the Frontline Movement which so appealed to you. The only time you'd ever agree to meet the likes of Fitzpatrick would be to kill him.'

'That is not how it was.'

Again Halifax ignored the reply and steam-rollered on. 'And this man Wallace McIlroy. A convicted child abuser who later hanged himself – are you really asking the jury to believe this is the sort of man MI5, a government agency with a reputation to uphold, would employ?'

'Some people believe the charges were trumped up when he fell out of favour.'

'Full of stories of trumped-up charges, aren't we, Mr Littlechild?'

'McIlroy was married with three kids,' retorted Littlechild.

'The truth is, I believe, that you recognised yourself in McIlroy. A former SOE man, a soldier. A man who sang the same anthem as yourself. A fellow Spartan, a born soldier, and maybe recognised and even admired McIlroy's latent homosexuality.'

'The man's dead, for God's sake!' Littlechild snapped back. 'He can't defend himself.'

'He doesn't need to, but you do. Because, Mr Littlechild, you are a born soldier. A natural-born killer. I've no doubt McIlroy suggested you went to fight in Rhodesia and I've no doubt that appealed to you. We've already learned you are a xenophobic, racist bigot. What better than to go and fight for the reviled regime of Ian Smith, kill black people you regarded as scum? No better, I imagine, than the Catholics in your homeland?'

'That's not true!' Littlechild protested.

Rock glanced at Meyrick, wondering why he didn't intervene. But the senior counsel was happy for Halifax to show himself being exactly the sort of man he was claiming Littlechild to be.

'Isn't it?' the prosecution barrister asked. 'Let's examine the facts. As soon as Rhodesia's white regime collapsed, you came back to Britain. After a short spell in the British Army here, you joined the armed forces of an even more vilified regime, apartheid South Africa. And when black majority rule came there under President Mandela, you left that place too. Your actions speak all too clearly.' Halifax smiled smugly, convinced he'd made his point. 'Would you like to tell the court why you left?'

'It was the end of an era.'

'The end of apartheid.'

'Not that, the end of white rule.' He remembered Meyrick's warning not to try to convince the court that he believed South Africa would degenerate under an inevitable black one-party state. 'I saw no future for me.'

'Because you were a secret policeman?'

'No, but that didn't help.'

'I don't expect it did. As you told police in your interviews, your job was to make intelligence assessments of ANC activity, then assassinate them.'

Meyrick stood. 'My lord, I have read the transcripts. My client said that his unit would sometimes assassinate or ambush. He would have added that more often than not the result was to put suspects under surveillance.'

'And then assassinate them?' Halifax asked mischievously.

'Be careful when quoting transcripts, Mr Halifax,' Quigley warned.

'Of course, my lord. Now, Mr Littlechild, the police asked you how many men you killed personally. You answered three. And two other men, Argentinians in the Falklands War, one of whom you bayoneted.' He paused for effect. 'Asked how many men you'd *commanded* to be killed in South Africa, you answered – and this is verbatim, my lord – "I don't recall." Mr Littlechild, you are certainly no stranger to weapons and killing, are you?'

'I must object, my lord!' Meyrick called. 'My learned friend is putting an inappropriate slant on what has been a courageous and quite proper military career.'

'I agree, Mr Meyrick,' Quigley decided.

Halifax gave a little bow of acknowledgement before continuing: 'But it wasn't always a courageous and proper military career, was it? Sometimes it was sleazy and decidedly illegal – and not always in your own country?'

Meyrick glanced back at Sam Browne who looked up from the bundle of papers she was reading. She'd only half-registered the change of tack.

'In 1987,' Halifax continued, 'you were in Belfast at the same time as a two-man hit team from your unit was sent to kill a South African ex-patriot, weren't you?'

Littlechild paled; he used his tongue to wet his suddenly parched lips. 'Yes.'

Meyrick saw what Halifax was doing; he was referring to the conspiracy-to-murder case, having previously insisted that it be tried separately. What the hell was he playing at? 'My lord, this can hardly relate to the murder of Mr Fitzpatrick last year.'

Quigley peered over his pince-nez. 'The defence really cannot have it both ways. At your request, I am allowing you to paint a broader background to the circumstances relating to that charge. You cannot now object if the prosecution adds its own colour to that background picture.'

'Very well, Your Lordship,' Meyrick said reluctantly as he resumed his seat.

Halifax looked well satisfied. 'The target of this hit team was one Dominic Smals, a journalist from Johannesburg, isn't that so? Also a vehemently outspoken critic of South Africa and apartheid on the international stage?'

'He was also involved in Sinn Fein and the . . .'

'Please!' Halifax interrupted. 'Confine yourself to yes or no.'

Littlechild slumped back. 'Yes.'

'And you supplied the murder weapon from your Loyalist friends, didn't you?'

'No, I didn't. I only knew about the assassination *after* it had happened.'

Halifax hammered on. 'And you know the identity of those killers, don't you? They are friends of yours, aren't they?'

'They were from my unit.'

'So who were they?'

'I can't answer that.'

'You're under oath. Please reply.'

426

'I'm sorry.'

Meyrick could only listen helplessly. He knew nothing of this as it was an area that Littlechild had always been reluctant to discuss.

'I can understand your shyness in this matter,' Halifax continued. 'Planning an assassination on sovereign foreign soil is not something one likes to talk about.'

Meyrick had to do something. 'If Your Lordship will pardon my interruption, I wonder if my learned friend would tell the court from where he obtained details of such a fanciful tale?'

Halifax bowed from the waist. 'From police files containing information supplied by the Security Service.'

Meyrick resumed his seat. He now knew what had happened. Halifax had filleted the information from the conspiracy-to-murder case to show Littlechild in potentially damning light.

'And you would have this jury believe,' Halifax resumed, 'that you are the sort of man who was a loyal and trusted employee of MI5 for over twenty years, is that right? Likewise have them believe you received a call from a sworn enemy, Fitzpatrick, then calmly agree to go and have a quiet beer with him in a London pub, is that right?'

'That's what happened. I telephoned him and arranged to meet in another pub.'

'Yet, you'll be aware that the landlord of that other pub says in his statement to the police that he never saw you.'

'It doesn't mean we weren't there.'

Halifax gave the court one of his smug smiles. 'The truth is, isn't it, that this meeting *never* took place. Fitzpatrick drank alone at the first pub and you, following a tip-off, stalked him to his flat and shot him. It was just unlucky for you that an MI5 officer recognised you because of your known connections with Loyalist terrorists and illegal arms shipments.'

Meyrick intervened. 'My client is not, has not and will not be charged on anything connected with illegal arms smuggling, my lord.'

'I concur,' Quigley said. 'That last phrase, which I instruct the jury to ignore, shall be struck from the record.'

'My apologies,' Halifax replied graciously. But still he'd made his point. 'I have no further questions.'

It was a sour note on which to begin the weekend.

Lisa Hardcastle was called the following Monday morning. She was a good witness, with a firm and confident manner, and her recollections of her early dealings with Rodney Littlechild appeared to back up everything the defence had claimed, especially his desire to quash the rumours about his involvement in arms dealing. The fact that Double Vision Productions had been 'leant on' to drop the programme added a nice sinister spin to her testimony.

But Halifax tore into her. Within minutes he was making it sound as though Littlechild was only on the make: inventing uncheckable fairy tales of conspiracy against MI5 and happy to betray old comrades in return for cash.

Meyrick had seen it coming, of course, and had emphasised points of evidence to the jury knowing full well which weaknesses his legal rival would go for. It was still galling to watch it happen, and left the defence team with jaded spirits.

A fierce legal wrangle then began in the absence of the jury when Meyrick presented a short deposition statement by the former Deputy Chief Constable of West Weald, Derek Penny. It had been made just days before his untimely suicide.

'If Your Lordship pleases,' Halifax protested. 'I would argue that the deposition by a dead man should not be allowed to be entered. It boldly, and in my view mistakenly, states Mr Penny's belief that Rodney Littlechild was a long-term and valued MI5 agent. This belief gleaned from classified papers improperly photocopied in contravention of the Official Secrets Act and hoarded by Mr Penny at the time of the 1989 Regina *v*. Keegan trial in Belfast. Unfortunately, my lord, I respectfully submit that the deposition be ruled inadmissible as the prosecution cannot cross-examine a piece of paper.'

That amused the court and Quigley evidently had no objection to lightening the tone of proceedings. 'Just so, Mr Halifax, but I believe that were he able to be here today, Mr Penny would repeat his deposition statement of how these papers came into his possession during that trial, supplied by persons from within the Security Service. Those documents speak for themselves – Mr Penny merely gives deposition evidence as to their source.'

'With respect, my lord, those documents are not going to be permitted to speak for themselves. As Your Lordship will be aware, as classified material they are the subject of a Public Interest Immunity certificate which your predecessor Mr Justice Todd upheld at the pre-trial review.'

'I am indeed aware,' Quigley replied evenly. 'But we have here a man on trial for murder. The defence claim that he was a loyal and long-serving MI5 agent has a great bearing on the veracity of his evidence regarding the state of his relationship with this somewhat – how can I put this? – shadowy organ of the state at the time of this murder. I am therefore minded to overturn my predecessor's decision and disclose the contents to the jury. Also, as these documents are referenced and sequentially numbered, they would suggest untampered evidence. Do you wish to consult with me in chambers as to any names or other sensitive material you would wish to have blacked out before distribution to the jury?'

Halifax glanced back at Ian Spinks, the CPS solicitor, who was seated in the row behind; the man shook his head. 'In that case, no, my lord.'

Quigley raised his eyebrows. 'No? Very well. Mr Penny's documents may be read to the jury after lunch.'

'The court will rise.'

Meyrick turned to Littlechild and winked. But Browne was less happy. 'Henry's up to something, Tristram, I can feel it coming.'

And, as usual, she was right as they discovered when the court reconvened in the afternoon and Halifax addressed Mr Justice Quigley.

'If it please my lord, we did not wish to make deletions to the defence documents for the simple reason that they are forgeries. And I beg leave to call evidence in rebuttal.'

Quigley looked distinctly irritated and it showed in his voice. 'What is the nature of this evidence?'

'My lord, it has only just been released from Security Service archives. It is the *original* documentation, with all sequential numbering and references, of the copied papers provided by the late Derek Penny. You will see, my lord, that the contents, however, are markedly different from those already before the court. Far from recognising the defendant Littlechild as a trusted MI5 agent, it clearly shows that he was a long-term Loyalist terrorist suspect and contact was made on occasions to lull him into thinking that they trusted him. This, of course, done in the interests of national security.'

'So what are you saying about Mr Penny's documents?' Quigley demanded.

'That they are crude photocopies of the originals which were clearly tampered with by parties unknown for the Regina *v.* Keegan trial. In short, forgeries.'

'But the defendant here was not part of that trial,' Quigley quickly pointed out. 'So why would anyone want to alter what was said about him?'

Halifax shrugged, 'Alas, my lord, I cannot answer that. Nor can the court question Mr Penny about the source of his documents.'

Browne glared across at Halifax who stared into the middle distance wearing the expression of an angelic choirboy. 'Nice one,' she snarled beneath her breath, then turned to Meyrick. 'That's what they did after stealing those copies from Evie's flat. They simply replaced and altered the originals in MI5's archives.'

'Bastards.'

The uproar and confusion led to the court going into early recess for half an hour until Quigley returned to the Bench to instruct the jurors to disregard all evidence relating to the Derek Penny documents.

Halifax's proposition, that Littlechild's claim to be an MI5 agent was pure fantasy, was surely and steadily gaining ground.

As Ronnie Rock succinctly pointed out: 'We're going to be left to fight this one on purely technical grounds.'

Eighteen

Next into the witness box was Mike Salmon, the former manager of the Mortar and Pestle public house.

'You, Mr Salmon, could be described as an unwilling witness, could you not?' Meyrick began.

Salmon gave a nervous smile. 'You could say that.'

'Because you were visited by two men the morning after the murder. Who were they?'

'They didn't say. I assumed they were – er – friends of the killer, although I didn't know about the murder until they told me. I sort of assumed later they were connected with Loyalist terrorists.'

'You now know differently?'

'I know they weren't connected with the man in the dock.'

'What did these men tell you?'

'Not to say I'd seen the people I now know as Fitzpatrick and Littlechild had come into my pub the night before when the police came around asking questions.'

'Did these men threaten you?'

'Not with violence, but they said if I spoke up they'd inform the brewery I had a criminal record.'

'How could they know that barely twelve hours after the murder?'

Salmon shrugged. 'I can only think they had access to police records, but I didn't stop to think about it for some time. I was in a state of panic.'

'So you told the police no one came into your pub who answered that description?'

'Yes.'

'So what persuaded you to change your mind?'

'Well, the brewery got to know about my record anyway. I'm now without a job. So I thought, to hell with it.'

Ronnie Rock leaned back towards Browne. 'I wonder who told them?'

Browne gave a tight-lipped, embarrassed smile. 'I'm afraid I did. He wanted to keep his pub too badly. Sorry, it had to be either Roddy or Mr Salmon.'

'You're an animal, Sam.'

'I know.'

The witness was saying: 'Fitzpatrick and Littlechild came into my pub at about ten to eleven, ordered a couple of pints of Guinness and then left at about ten past.'

'Had someone else entered the pub at that time?'

'Yes, a couple. A middle-aged man and a woman. They stayed until just after the other two went, virtually on the bell.'

'Did something odd occur?'

'Well, they changed seats, sat where Littlechild and Fitzpatrick had been sitting. I thought vaguely it was hardly worth moving for the odd five minutes.'

'Was there something else?'

'After that, I discovered one of the Guinness glasses was missing. I assumed one of the two men must have snitched it.'

'But it could as easily have been the couple?'

'Yes.'

Meyrick nodded. 'One more question, Mr Salmon. Had the seating in your pub been recently reupholstered?'

'Yes, it was finished just a week before the murder.'

The mild-mannered Salmon was to have his confidence rudely shattered by Halifax's opening volley. 'So you are a self-confessed liar, are you, Mr Salmon?' The man coloured and opened his mouth searching in vain for a reply. 'Well, answer, yes or no?'

'Er – I suppose so.'

'Is that yes?'

'Yes.'

'You admit you're a liar. You lied to the police following this alleged verbal threat. Putting your own selfish interest before the search for truth in a murder investigation?'

'I suppose so. I wasn't proud of it. I was afraid . . .'

432

'I don't need a speech, Mr Salmon. Just for you to admit to the court you are a liar who can be easily persuaded to change your testimony whenever it suits you.'

'That's not true.'

'Really? Were you not visited some weeks later by the defendant's brother-in-law and his friend?'

'Yes. They said they were acting as private investigators.'

'Did they intimidate you?'

'No.'

'Where did they interview you?'

'In the gents' lavatory.'

There were some titters from the public gallery. 'At what time?'

'Just after I'd closed.'

'They were waiting for you?'

'Yes.'

'That sounds pretty intimidating.'

'Well, I thought so at the time, but later I realised they just wanted me to tell the truth.'

'Mr Salmon, you wouldn't recognise the truth if it leapt out and stared you in the face, would you? You just change your story whenever it suits, don't you?'

'No.'

'What did you tell the defendant's brother-in-law?'

'That I wasn't changing my story.'

'But you have now. Why?'

'I've already said. I lost my job and my pub anyway. So I had nothing more to lose.'

'Thank you, Mr Salmon.'

Lomax took the stand the following morning.

'You are the defendant's brother-in-law and an old friend, is that right?'

'Yes.'

'The court has already heard that you and another friend of yours have been acting as private investigators in this case. Why is this?'

'Because I'm convinced of his innocence, and because the

433

smear campaign has left him and his wife destitute. So I lent a hand.'

'You're a former SAS soldier who reached the rank of Staff Sergeant by the time you retired last year after twelve years' service?'

'Yes.'

'What was your speciality in the SAS, Mr Lomax?'

'Tracking and fieldcraft.'

'In fact, you were the Regiment's top expert in a craft that means reading footprints, blood trails, spoor, etc, is that right?'

'Yes.'

'A highly respected and reliable professional soldier, you are also well versed in, shall we say, the *modus operandi* of intelligence agencies such as MI5?'

'I've had a fair bit of experience.'

'When you spoke to the witness, Mr Salmon, did you form any opinion as to whom his previous visitors might have been?'

'My immediate reaction was that they were MI5 officers, or had been sent by . . .'

Halifax interjected. 'This is pure supposition, Your Lordship.'

'I agree,' Quigley said.

'As Your Lordship pleases,' Meyrick relented. 'Mr Lomax, can you confirm that you did not intimidate Mr Salmon into changing his story?'

Lomax swallowed hard. 'Well, we did come on a little strong to persuade him to tell the truth. But he was more scared of his previous visitors than of us. He told us he wouldn't repeat his story to us in court.'

'Although he since has?'

'So I believe.'

'Then, some time after the defendant was charged, you and a colleague gained access to the scene of crime, didn't you? This despite the fact that the defence solicitors had initially been denied such a request by the police and the Security Service on the grounds that it was an MI5 safe house? Why did you do this?'

'Because it was an *ex*-safe house. Once a safe house is

compromised it is never used again. It was clearly to cover up something.'

'And did you discover what that something was?'

'I discovered two things and my friend took date-timed photographs.'

'Exhibit G,' Meyrick advised the judge and jury. 'So what did you find, Mr Lomax?'

'Decorators were repainting the flat, replacing the front door and removing the bullet-proof glass from the windows. Our photographs showed in particular a close-up of screw holes in the old door that once would have held a bullet-proof plate in place and deep plaster repairs in the living-room wall.'

'How high were these plaster repairs from the floor?'

'Six of them were in a cluster about eighteen inches from the floor.'

Quigley interrupted. 'What is the significance of this?'

'I shall explain in detail with later expert witness evidence, my lord. But will meanwhile ask Mr Lomax what *he* considered these repairs to signify?'

'It's my belief there were six bullet holes.'

'Anything else?'

'There was a much larger bloodstain in the hallway than in the living room.'

'Is this significant?'

'I believe so. If a man crawls after being wounded, then lies undisturbed for a period, as in this situation, I would expect the largest deposit of blood to be in his final resting place.'

'Suggesting to you?'

'That Fitzpatrick was shot in the living room, then crawled – or was carried – to the hall and left.'

'Thank you, Mr Lomax.'

Lomax had lost his appetite for lunch, just toying with a sandwich over a beer in the Magpie and Stump across the road from the Old Bailey.

His growing sense of apprehension was well founded when they returned to court for Halifax's cross-examination.

'How long have you known the defendant, Mr Lomax?'

'About fifteen years.'

'Did he ever mention his claim to be an agent of MI5?'

'No, not until about a month before the murder.'

'What, not once in fifteen years? Not even a hint?'

'Never. It's not the sort of thing he'd talk about.'

'Doesn't that strike you as odd?'

'No.'

'Come now, Mr Lomax, you were a soldier in the SAS; you have experience in the cloak-and-dagger world. Surely it would have been the most natural thing in the world to share a confidence or two? Or even a joke about his work?'

'Roddy's not like that. He's quiet and introspective.'

Halifax nodded and changed tack. 'Maybe he didn't mention it because he hadn't thought of it? At that time he didn't need some cock-and-bull story because he didn't have a murder charge hanging over his head.'

Lomax glanced across and met his friend's steady gaze. 'To be honest, I don't think his imagination would run to that.'

A hint of a smile fluttered on Littlechild's lips and a few people in the public gallery chuckled.

'You and he are firm friends, aren't you?'

'Yes.'

'In fact, more than good friends. You consider that he saved your life during the Falklands War?'

'I don't *consider* it – I know he did.'

'Yes, I appreciate that was your perception in the heat of battle. A perception that may have coloured your view of this man, don't you think?'

'I think that question is beneath contempt.'

'You're not here to express opinions about my questioning, Mr Lomax. Isn't it the case that your perceived sense of gratitude to Littlechild disturbed your sense of judgment and has led you to breaking and entering and intimidating prosecution witnesses?'

'So shoot me.'

Quigley frowned. 'The witness will be deemed in contempt of this court if he replies in a like manner again. Meanwhile, Mr Halifax, the gentleman you refer to, Mr Salmon, has already told us he didn't consider himself to be intimidated by Mr Lomax. And as regards breaking and entering, I consider the judgment of those who denied access by the defence to the scene of crime to be flawed in the extreme. It was an over-zealous use of secrecy.'

'As Your Lordship pleases.' Halifax turned back to Lomax. 'The simple fact is, Mr Lomax, that you have no way of *knowing* what caused those holes in the living-room wall that you had so studiously photographed, do you?'

'I can't be certain.'

'It's purely convenient supposition? Yes or no?'

'Yes.' Reluctant.

'Similarly, the size and positioning of the two bloodstains are not *absolutely* conclusive as to the place of death, are they?'

'Not absolutely, no.'

'So all this is wishful thinking on behalf of a man to whom you feel you owe the debt of life itself, isn't it?'

Lomax didn't answer; it was heads I win, tails you lose.

'No more questions,' Halifax said.

Stepping down from the stand, Lomax felt gutted. Surely he could have done better, not allowed himself to be caught in the prosecution's verbal traps? Even kind words from Browne did nothing to stop his sense of guilt that he'd let his friend down when he was most needed.

'How was last night?' Danny asked, looking up from his desk and the early reports from the money markets around the world.

'Grand,' came Liam's slightly smug reply, slipping off the jacket of his sharply tailored suit. 'Better than yours, and that's a promise.'

Rivals in romantic conquests and rivals at work, the two young men were always first in on the international floor of the Bank of Ireland in College Street opposite Trinity. No time for backsliding when you were aiming for the top and playing the game of trying to pull every girl in Dublin's nightclub mile. Danny couldn't resist rising to the bait. 'Who was it?'

'Would you believe me if I said Shelagh O'Flynn?'

Danny's mouth dropped. 'You never did.'

'Promise you,' Liam said with a lascivious grin. 'So if you want to know about the birthmark on her bum – ?'

'Sure you never did.' The most sought-after girl in Investments, next floor down. Most sought-after girl in Dublin come to that. Or so it seemed to Danny.

Liam played it cool; he sat down at his terminal and threw the switch. 'What's wrong? Your screen's not on.'

'No, they've been down again. Another bloody power cut. You'd think, when they landed a man on the moon a quarter century ago—'

'Ah, well,' Liam said, 'it's okay now. Here it comes.'

Danny busied himself with his market reports. Questions about the voluptuous Shelagh would have to wait. It took a moment before he realised that something odd was occurring. When he looked up he saw that Liam was staring at his monitor, mouth agape.

'What is it?'

Liam was frowning. 'I'm not sure. Somehow I've got into the wrong programme.'

Danny propelled his rollerball swivel chair to his friend's side. 'No, it's not, look – IT-FinFast.'

'I know what it says, but look at the text. It's some foreign language version.'

It was Danny's turn to smile. 'Not foreign, Liam, it's Irish. Gaelic, your mother tongue.'

'Is it? Oh, yeah, of course it is. Oh, holy shite, they don't expect us to work in Gaelic, do they?'

'I bloody hope not.' Danny booted up his own machine. 'Expect it's a test programme of some sort. Let's see what I've got?'

Both men stood up now, concentrating on the second monitor.

The page pinged onto the screen. 'Oh, Mary and Joseph, this can't be right.'

At that moment the department manager's door opened and their boss strode into the open-plan office. He looked harassed and was sweating as he walked past the empty work stations. 'You've seen it then, lads?'

438

'What happened?' Liam asked.

'You tell me,' the manager replied tersely. 'Overnight our entire system's converted to the Gaelic language. Must be some kind of virus. I've just called in our expert. Brian Nairn should be here in half an hour. From what I've told him, he reckons it could take weeks to replace all the programmes – every branch appears to be affected. And if all the hard-drives are infected, the cost of this could run to millions.'

Danny was hardly listening. He was back at his keyboard, delving into each menu along the toolbar, trying to make some sense of it. That wasn't easy, as now even the command titles were in Gaelic and he had to trust to memory.

'Look, Liam,' the manager was saying, 'I'm going to an emergency meeting right now. When everyone's in, find out who speaks the bloody language in all departments – we'll form an emergency team to try and keep the bank ticking over until the technical wizards sort something out.'

'It's that bad?'

'It's a bloody catastrophe!'

When he was gone, Liam turned back to Danny. 'What you trying to do?'

A shrug. 'I don't know – find some sort of explanation. It must be some sort of logic bomb.'

'What?'

'A logic bomb. I read about it somewhere. A sort of virus bomb. It gets imported innocently through internal E-mail – say, placed by a disgruntled employee – and just sits there on a timer or using a command signal to release it.'

'You think that's what this is? Where are you now?'

'File Manager – thought I'd . . .'

'What's that there, that icon?'

'Never seen that before.'

'Maximise it,' Liam suggested.

Danny clicked on. Suddenly the entire screen was filled with the image: An orange hand and the legend: *Cuchulainn. The Hound strikes back! Hands off Ulster!*

'Christ.'

*

439

So far the trial had been running on a knife-edge, Lomax realised. Meyrick believed they were ahead on points, but Browne was not so sure. It was still far from conclusively proven that Littlechild had ever been an MI5 agent.

The evidence of the expert witness, Wendy Sixsmith, could push it either way.

'You have studied fibre samples routinely taken by the police from both the deceased's clothing and that worn by the defendant on the night of the murder?' Meyrick asked. 'Would you tell the court what you found.'

She ran swiftly through the list, then returned to the important points. 'In particular, I found cross-matching fibres of each man's clothing. Taken, according to police notes, from the right arm of both men's jackets.'

'What does this tell you?'

'That the two men most certainly met that night. There had been definite physical contact. Most likely the fibres were exchanged when they shook hands or sat side by side in a public house. I also found cross-matching hairs from both men, two from Fitzpatrick and one from the defendant, each on the other's clothes.'

Halifax raised an objection. 'While Miss Sixsmith may feel these two men had met, it is not for her to say *where* they may have done so.'

'On the contrary,' Meyrick replied, barely concealing his sense of triumph. 'Perhaps, Miss Sixsmith, you would tell us of your other finding?'

'I also examined a collection of reddish velour fibres taken from the back of the legs and seat of both men's trousers.'

'What did this tell you?'

'That they'd both been sitting on the same seat. The unexpected volume of fibres suggested to me that the seat had been recently reupholstered.'

'Did you discover where this seat was?'

'Taking advice from the defence solicitors, I visited the Mortar and Pestle public house. The bench seat, including a window alcove, had been refurbished last summer. The fibre match was identical. This evidence was subsequently served on the Crown.'

'Why do you think the Home Office forensic science laboratory missed this?'

'Oh, it's nothing sinister. Given that the manner of death was known – well, was thought to be known, there was no need to cross-match these samples which were routinely taken. As the men were not believed to have met before the killing, there was no point. In their position I'd probably have committed the same oversight. No one is looking for unnecessary extra work.'

'Now we come to an extremely important item of forensic evidence,' Meyrick continued. 'Fingerprints of the defendant on the murder weapon and a thumb print on the doorbell to the murdered man's flat. The court heard earlier from the laboratory sergeant at the scene of crime that he did not believe it possible to transfer fingerprints successfully. Would you agree, Miss Sixsmith?'

'No, I would not. It is a contentious issue, and I believe the police and judicial system,' she inclined her head towards Mr Justice Quigley, 'if Your Lordship will forgive my frank speaking – ' the man's eyes twinkled as he acknowledged her, ' – have perpetuated the myth that this can only be done under strict laboratory conditions. Not true. I have conducted experiments myself in a domestic kitchen. If His Lordship would permit me to demonstrate?'

Halifax rose. 'I really must object. The defence has not approached us and the prosecution would certainly not agree to this. The courtroom is not the place for conjuring tricks. We shall be bending spoons by telepathy next!'

'Come, come,' Quigley scolded. 'You say it's not possible and the defence says it is. The jury and I do not know who to believe. A demonstration may help clarify the matter.'

'Very well,' Halifax muttered.

'If Your Lordship will permit us,' Meyrick said and turned to Wendy Sixsmith as she pulled on a pair of yellow rubber gloves, then carefully removed two straight pint beer glasses bearing the Guinness harp emblem from a plastic carrier bag. 'These were thoroughly cleaned, dried and polished and bear no fingerprints.' He glanced at Halifax. 'Perhaps I may invite my learned friend to take one glass.'

'I want no part in this,' Halifax protested.

'Do go on, Mr Halifax,' Quigley urged. 'We might all learn something.'

Reluctantly the barrister took the offered glass from Sixsmith. She then took it back with her gloved hand, placed it on the bench in front of her and accepted a strip of clear Sellotape that Ronnie Rock had prepared. Carefully she placed it over the imprints of Halifax's fingers, pressed down, then carefully peeled it off. She took the strip to the jury to see more closely before pressing the adhesive side down onto the second clean glass.

Sixsmith peeled the strip away again with a dramatic flourish and returned to the jury. There for all to see was a near-perfect set of Halifax's prints.

'I am not an expert,' Sixsmith admitted modestly, 'but I'm told it is more effective with practice. You will note also that I will need another strip of Sellotape to move the thumb print.'

Quigley said: 'If this method is feasible – and it has been well demonstrated here – how are you suggesting, Mr Meyrick, that prints of the defendant's hand were obtained in the first place?'

'Your Lordship will recall the evidence of Mr Mike Salmon, the manager of the Mortar and Pestle. He is adamant that an empty beer glass was stolen, he thought by Littlechild or Fitzpatrick. It is my submission that it was taken by neither of these men, but by the couple who stayed after them and swapped tables.'

'Are you suggesting these were police officers?' Quigley asked.

'No, my lord, that they were acting for this rogue element of MI5 we've heard so much about. There was an hour and a half after Fitzpatrick's death for them to arrange things before the police arrived.'

After lunch, a chastened Halifax concentrated on one point only in his cross-examination. 'Miss Sixsmith, while I and the rest of the court were impressed with the demonstration this morning, would you not agree that this is no more than a fanciful notion? You have no proof that this is what *was* done, have you?'

'No, sir.'

'And the red fibre velour is a material popularly used in public houses, is it not?'

'That's true.'

'In fact, thousands of metres are used in the pub trade every year throughout the country, aren't they?'

'I don't know, but I expect so.'

'Probably many pubs in the area of the crime?'

A shrug. 'It's possible.'

'So, forensically, the prosecution version of events remains sound?'

'On my evidence alone, yes, I suppose it does.'

The six-day Easter recess was just a day away and the trial was clearly going to overrun due to unexpected complications and frequent adjournments to sort out technicalities.

On the last day before the holiday, Adam Snaith, an independent ballistics expert, was called by the defence. It marked the start of a complex debate over details of the shooting which required Dr Singh to be recalled and re-examined and recross-examined by both sets of counsel.

Snaith's arguments were based on the angle at which the bullets had passed through the victim's body. He claimed they were in keeping with Fitzpatrick having been shot whilst *sitting*, when the bullets would have embedded low in the wall. This fitted with Lomax's evidence and suggested that the murder took place in the living room after all. Dr Singh disputed that this was necessarily the case.

What had seemed beforehand a solid defence argument became confusing and muddled as the two experts constantly disagreed and became deeply engrossed in complex statistics regarding geometry, velocity and deflection. When Browne saw one of the jurors dozing, she knew the case was slipping out of their hands. Having earlier captured some of the high ground of probability, it was beginning to look now as if the defence was just throwing everything at the prosecution, however bizarre.

443

For all their considerable success in establishing an alternative explanation to the police's version of events, they had not managed to *disprove* that Littlechild killed the victim.

A weary Justice Quigley drew a halt to proceedings at four in the afternoon. The court would reconvene the following Wednesday for the closing addresses and the judge's summing up.

Both teams of lawyers met at the Magpie and Stump for a much needed round of long, cool beers before going their separate ways for the holiday weekend.

'How'd it go?' Lomax asked; he'd been pacing the public area antechamber for most of the afternoon.

'I'm not happy,' Browne confided. 'Tristram and Ronnie have done a brilliant job in casting doubt on much of the prosecution case and establishing our version. But doubts may not be enough; we haven't been able to *disprove* anything.'

'But the ballistics expert?'

She shook her head. 'Dr Singh wouldn't give an inch. Didn't want to lose face, I expect. In the end it just confused the jury.'

'Two thousand down the drain.'

'Sorry, Chris.' She touched his arm. 'But without evidence from Penny and Colonel Roebuck, it would have made little difference. Those two would have given Roddy real credibility. The only other possibility . . .'

He got there first. 'Billy Baker? I'm not sure he's star witness material.'

'But King Billy knew what was going on, Chris. He contacted Roddy to say Fitzpatrick wanted to get in touch and Roddy says he's in MI5's pocket. If we can get him to the stand, Tristram will prise him open.'

Lomax looked sceptical. 'He's just a thug. Even his own side has disowned him.'

'That doesn't matter. He knows MI5 *wanted* Roddy and Fitzpatrick to meet. In essence that's all he's got to say. And he'll bring a real feel and smell of Belfast treachery to the courtroom.'

'Anyway, it's irrelevant. If the RUC and our Belfast solicitors have failed to find him . . .'

Totty had been listening intently. 'If it's that important why don't you 'ave a go? There's six days before the trial restarts.'

'Don't be a silly girl,' Browne chided. 'If MI5 wants him to hide, he'll stay hidden.'

'I don't believe you, boss.' Totty looked genuinely annoyed. 'You've always taught me not to give up.'

'This is different.'

'Chris managed to find Penny and Colonel Roebuck. And them two blokes who said Penny'd abused them.'

Lomax shifted his feet. 'That was luck, I had inside help.'

'Yes,' Totty replied defiantly. 'One was your mate in Army Intelligence.'

'Yes, and he's also keeping a lookout for news of King Billy, and so far he's come up with nothing. He can't keep asking questions about MI5 matters that don't concern him. He'll lose his job.'

'But *you* can,' Totty persisted, 'if he told you where to start looking. You could go places no solicitor would dare to go.'

Lomax half-laughed. 'You want to get me killed?'

The girl looked sheepish. 'Course not.'

And then he saw Browne staring at him, her eyes questioning. He knew what she was thinking. 'No, Sam, definitely not a good idea.'

Of course it was dark. Of course it was raining. It always was in Belfast, or so it seemed. A cold persistent drizzle that worked its way down your neck and into the cuffs of your jacket. After a while, the damp and chill gnawed into your bones.

And it was one of those typical streets; Lomax had walked down hundreds of them in his time. Thousands even. Endless streets of featureless brick. Small sideroads and alleyways everywhere. Providing shadows in which someone could hide and wait unseen. Blinds drawn at every window, blacked out to give no shadow target for a passing gunman. But those same windows offering sanctuary to anyone watching him. And he knew they were.

Should he loiter? Lean against a wall with a newspaper and

merge in. Another unkempt, unemployed layabout. Or should he walk?

Of course he had to walk. He was looking for someone and King Billy wasn't going to come to him. So he forced one step along the glistening black pavement. Legs like lead, his soles sticking to the concrete. God, he hoped he wouldn't have to run. Heart thudding against his ribcage and the nausea of fear draining in his gut like water down a plughole.

They were there, at each alley. Sheltering in doorways. Monk in the first, cammed up but those tombstone teeth giving him away. A grin. Got you covered, mate.

A gap in the rickety fence. Monk there too and another thumbs-up sign. And he was at the next street corner beyond the pool of lamplight.

Another alley. Lomax jumped forward, the old familiar Browning in his hand. No Monk this time. Just the enemy, crouched and charging. The gun shook in Lomax's hand, its muzzle flashes blinding him.

And when the smoke cleared the enemy was nothing more than a holed plywood cutout in black and brown. Standard MOD target Figure 11/59, the grotesque charging trooper.

Then Browne stepped out from behind it, taunting him with that enigmatic smile of hers. Eyes laughing at his fear, mocking his cowardice.

'Are you all right, Chris?'

He spun round. Evie standing in the middle of the street, coat and hair sodden, eyes dark and lost. Looking so sad and lonely, head bent as she gazed at the open coffin at her feet, Roddy lying within its white satin walls, his dead arms clutching the baby that wriggled and screamed. 'You were too late for him,' she said, and lifted her eyes accusingly.

And the baby still screamed as, one by one, the lights came on all along the street.

'Are you all right, Chris?'

'Aaaagh!'

He awoke with a jolt, his body drenched in sweat.

'Chris?'

Breathless, he turned his head towards the bedroom door.

Instantly he recognised Evie's silhouette against the hall light. 'What? Evie?'

'I heard you calling out.'

He rubbed his eyes. 'Sorry, a bad dream. Did I wake you?'

She shook her head. 'No, I couldn't sleep.'

'The baby?'

'No, Noel's good as gold. Just my usual insomnia.'

'You should take some of my tablets.'

'No. I mustn't fill myself with chemicals. I'll make some tea. Want some?'

'Sure.' He wouldn't get back now, he knew that. The bedside clock flicked on to five o'clock. And before the day was out he'd be back across the water.

He pulled on his dressing gown and wandered out to the kitchenette where Evie was filling the kettle.

'It was Northern Ireland, wasn't it?' she said.

'Yeah,' he replied lightly. 'A bit different this time.'

She turned to look at him, her eyes very wide and candid. 'I know how difficult it must be for you to go back.'

He shrugged dismissively. 'I went back earlier.'

'That was different, Chris, we both know that. The ceasefire was on. Now it's all back to how it was.'

'It's still quiet.'

'But it's dangerous again. For people like you.'

'I'll have Sam and Joe to protect me.'

'Sam? Fat lot of good she'd be.'

'You should see her straight-arm jab.'

'She'll be the one to get you into trouble.'

'Quite a girl.'

'Hardly a girl, but yes, she is. You just be careful. She's very good at her job but she's impetuous. And you're . . .' Her voice trailed.

'I'm what?'

'Besotted enough to follow her anywhere.'

'Me? Besotted?' But his laugh of indignation had a distinctly hollow ring.

Evie poured the water into the pot. 'Yes, you're like a dog

with two tails whenever she's around. If she beckons, you follow.'

'I'm going because I'm the only one who can. I know the turf.'

Evie reached across the table and took his hand. 'Roddy and I are grateful for what you're doing, Chris, really we are. But not if it ends up getting you killed.'

He met her eyes. 'I owe Roddy.'

'I understand. Just be careful.'

'Sure,' he said. 'Now take your tea back to bed and rest even if you can't sleep.'

And when she'd gone, he washed and shaved and began to pack his rucksack. By then it was six fifteen and dawn was breaking. As the sun rose, so the memory of his nightmare faded with the shadows.

Monk arrived at lunchtime and the two of them drove in Lomax's car to Sam Browne's south London flat. She was already waiting outside on the pavement with her case when they arrived. Dressed stylishly in a beige two-piece and chocolate blouse, and with her hair flowing freely, Lomax thought she looked more relaxed than he'd ever seen her.

'I can't wait to get away from the courtroom,' she admitted. 'It almost feels like going on holiday.'

'Damn,' Monk said with a grin. 'Forgot to pack me bucket and spade.'

They drove off in good humour and once they'd cleared the suburban traffic made good time down the M4 towards Wales.

It had all been planned with indecent haste the evening before. Browne had phoned from the Magpie and Stump on her mobile to book the car onto the next evening's Swansea to Cork ferry sailing. At that time of year there were still several places available and she was offered an upgrade from a two- to four-berth cabin for the crossing.

That news had filled Lomax with anticipation and not a little trepidation at the prospect of a romantic voyage. But those hopes were dashed while he and Browne were back at her flat. Joe Monk phoned in, back on leave from his new job in Kazakhstan and anxious for news of the trial. When they all met at a pub later that evening, Monk immediately volunteered his services. It had seemed churlish and unwise to turn him down and so the romantic voyage sank without trace at the very prospect of the tomb-toothed chaperone sharing the cabin with them.

As nothing sinister had happened during the weeks of the trial, Lomax felt fairly relaxed about visiting Ulster.

It was Monk who had introduced a note of caution. 'Maybe people have stopped watching and listening, Chris, but maybe not. You and Sam suddenly charging off to Ulster will certainly renew their interest.'

'I realise that,' Lomax replied. 'It's why we're going via Eire. We'll slip quietly over the border.'

'Using your car?'

'C'mon, Joe, we'll just be tourists not terrorists. One of thousands of cars crossing every day.'

'Do me a favour, swap cars in Cork. Hire one to cross the border.'

'It all costs, Joe, and times is hard.'

'I'll pay,' his friend insisted. 'There's been bugger all to spend it on in Kazakhstan. Just cos we're paranoid doesn't mean they're not out to get us.'

Twice on the journey to Swansea they pulled off into a service area and went inside for a coffee. Monk loitered to study any cars pulling in soon after them. At the second stop, he reckoned he'd identified a suspect vehicle.

Lomax was sceptical.

'It arrived three minutes after us,' Monk insisted as he joined them in the cafeteria, 'so it can't have had visual contact. A red Volvo. Male and female couple. She stays on board and he saunters in and wanders round the shop. Pretending to browse, but not buying anything. He's positioned so he can see us when we leave.'

His friend was so certain that Lomax was now starting to take it seriously. 'If the Volvo hasn't had visual contact then they must have placed a homing device on my car.'

'Surely not,' Browne said.

'You're getting a bit lax in your old age, Chris,' Monk scolded. 'Should have thought of that.'

'And have you checked *your* car?' Lomax asked.

'Sure,' Monk answered a little too glibly; he wasn't the best of liars. 'Anyway, *my* car isn't the problem, is it? I'll go out and have a look for it. Probably a magnetic job stuck on the chassis.'

As Monk quickly drained his coffee and rose to leave, Lomax said: 'If you find anything, Joe, don't chuck it. No point in letting them know we know.'

He and Browne followed ten minutes later. Monk had the engine hood up and was making a show of wiping oil from the dipstick.

'Any joy?' Lomax asked.

'Finally. Not on the chassis at all. They'd opened it up and put it in the engine compartment. I thought it was part of your alarm system. Very professional.'

'Where is it now?'

'In my pocket. And their car's on the other side of the park. Don't look now, but the bloke's pretending to make a phone call.'

Browne, however, couldn't resist sneaking a glance. An edge of fear had crept into her voice as she whispered: 'God, I'm not sure, but I think it's the man who forced us into the boot of my car after Colonel Roebuck's accident.'

'Harry Grisewold?' Lomax said. 'I didn't get a clear view.'

'Time we taught that bastard,' Monk growled. 'Got something in mind?'

Lomax had.

He turned off at the next junction and headed north towards Stroud, taking it steady while he looked out for a busy petrol station. A short while later he found one, pulled in and parked behind an empty estate car whose driver was walking towards the shop to pay for his fuel. Lomax opened his door, sauntered to the gap between their two vehicles, dropped to one knee and shoved his hand under the other car's rear. The homing device was snatched from his hand, the magnet clamping hard to the underside of the fuel tank. After testing that it was secure, he stood up and glanced at the price board with a look of disapproval. He then casually returned to the driver's seat, started the engine and swung out onto the road.

Realising that his quarry had stopped, Grisewold, or whoever it was in the Volvo, would have pulled over back down the road to avoid visual contact. When the homer started moving again, Grisewold would find himself unwittingly following a boiled sweets-and-candy salesman around the Gloucestershire countryside.

Lomax then took the next left turn and drove west down a series of narrow lanes until he was able to pick up the M5 running south before picking up the M4 again to resume their journey across the Severn Bridge to Swansea beyond.

By late afternoon, Harry Grisewold realised something was wrong. The car he was following had travelled from one town and village to another across the county, stopping at each for twenty minutes before moving on.

'Get an eyeball,' Margie urged.

So at the next village he did, slowing in the main street as the bleep from the homing beacon became progressively louder.

'No sign of Lomax's car,' he thought aloud. He pulled up, double-parking beside a pale blue estate car. Its owner was carrying a large cardboard box across the pavement to a tobacconist and confectioner's shop.

'They've made a switch, Harry.'

'Shit.'

'You were right first time. M4 to Wales and not for a weekend pony trekking. Swansea or Fishguard.'

'There was nothing on the tapes.'

'C'mon, Harry, they got wise to that months ago.'

He made his decision. 'Get that thing off the car or we'll have to pay for it. I'll just have to make Pinfold's day.'

While Margie opened her door and climbed out, Grisewold called up Pinfold on his mobile. The reception was terrible and his master irritated at the breach of security.

Grisewold was brief and practical. 'Sorry to interrupt you, but the birds have flown and we'll need backup.'

'Official?' Horrified.

'Don't know. I think they're taking a ferry. Fishguard or Swansea. They were using his car.'

'What are they up to?'

'How the hell – but no good, you can be sure of that.'

'Okay, leave it with me.' Pinfold knew now he'd have to alert the American and swore beneath his breath. 'I'll talk to Curtis Manning. He's got a team in Dublin and they're thick with Garda Special Branch. We'll have to pull in some favours. They'll find them.' He hung up without saying goodbye.

Margie returned with the homing device secreted in her palm. 'How was he?'

'On a scale of one-to-ten, about fifteen. Just short of ballistic.'

She made a face. 'Oops, there goes your New Year Honour. Still, now we can take some time out. Get a hotel room for the night, eh?'

'Yeah,' he said wearily. 'I'm shagged.'

'Not yet,' she said with a grin, 'but you soon will be.'

Nineteen

The Emergency Contingencies Committee met in closed session at Leinster House, Dublin. Minutes before, the room had been electronically swept by security experts and the plain-clothes detectives guarding the door were armed.

A senior Cabinet Minister chaired the meeting; also in attendance were senior civil servants from the departments of foreign affairs, finance, industry and commerce, justice and communications. In an advisory capacity were members of the Council of Defence, comprising defence and state ministers, the Chief of Staff, the Adjutant General and the Quartermaster General.

It was to this sombre and tense gathering that the 'chair' invited Fergal to present his review of the latest developments concerning the terrorist group known as *Cuchulainn*.

'It is my unpleasant duty to confirm what most of you will have already heard,' he said, 'that two days ago an implanted crypto-virus attacked the Bank of Ireland's entire computer system. It will take weeks to correct and the cost will run to millions of punts. Our friends in the US Treasury are flying out a team of anti-virus experts from the States to assist us and I understand we may receive some emergency grants from the EU to pay for essential work. Of course, our concern is that information technology in other essential service sectors may also be vulnerable.'

'Are we prepared for this?' the chairman asked.

'Not immediately. Unfortunately there are so many insti-tutional systems for the enemy to target that we cannot possibly cover them all. However, those regarded as essential will from now on be subjected to twice-daily security sweeps. All of this, of course, is a new worry to add to the continuing attacks on our telecommunications, electricity and transport systems.'

453

'Has there been any improvement here?' the chairman asked, directing his question at the Chief of Staff.

The Lieutenant General cleared his throat, obviously not as confident as he was trying to appear. 'It is my view that we have stabilised the situation as far as possible, given our current resources. Only two explosions last night, both minor. One cut power supplies to parts of Limerick and the other shut off all telephone links with the town of Ennis.'

'*Only* two?' the chairman reprimanded. 'Important enough if you happen to live in Limerick or Ennis.'

'I'm sorry, badly phrased,' the COS conceded. 'Trouble is, we are faced with an ongoing dilemma. Do I swamp Clare and Limerick with soldiers to back up police in guarding every pylon and telegraph pole to prevent a repeat attack? If I do, the Loyalists will strike somewhere else, maybe in the east. One thing we've learned is that they are exceedingly mobile.'

The Adjutant General broke in. 'Of our eleven thousand troops, we currently have only some seven thousand available for this work. If we were to consider calling up all-service reserves, we could bolster this by some fifteen thousand. That would make a difference.'

There was a shake of the head from the chairman: 'The Taoiseach has considered this and he's not keen. We'd hardly be able to maintain the current level of secrecy and media coverage would panic the community and cost the country dear in lost resources.'

'And I doubt,' Fergal added, 'it would make a real difference. Like all terrorists, they will always have the advantage of choice – when and where to attack. And they appear to have unlimited access to plastic explosive.'

'Do we know where it's coming from?' someone asked.

All eyes turned to Fergal. He smiled his winning easy smile, but his stomach was churning and his mind spinning. How long should he keep it from them? How would they react? Probably calmly, but you could never tell. The Taoiseach had taken it responsibly enough, and he was the one who held the ultimate power.

He said softly: 'It's our understanding that *Cuchulainn* has a near inexhaustible supply, mostly due to an unfortunate accident of history. The origins of the *Cuchulainn* group can be traced to a political movement in the late sixties called Frontline Ulster. What was not known at the time was that it was a cover operation by MI5 for a full-scale British "stay behind" policy against any contingency, including full British withdrawal.'

A ripple of quiet gasps and murmurs eddied round the table.

The Chief of Staff had trouble containing his sense of outrage. 'Are you telling us that *Cuchulainn* is that same organisation, Fergal?'

'The same or not, we can't be certain. It seems that it has been taken over – hijacked may be a better word – by other Loyalist organisations.'

The chairman grunted, his knuckles white and clenched before him on the table. 'Then it's down to the British Government to sort out the *Cuchulainn* group.'

'With respect,' Fergal responded, 'it always has been. As the Chief of Staff has pointed out, there is little we can do to protect ourselves effectively. The group can only be attacked and destroyed in its own spawning ground – the North. And, to be fair, the British have done all they can. They understood all the arms caches were withdrawn years ago, but obviously some were missed. They've organised a massive security round-up of Frontline members and increased border protection to match our own.'

'Tell us, Fergal,' the chairman asked, 'how do you and your intelligence people see this *Cuchulainn* campaign developing and what would be its outcome?'

The man sighed; how in the Dear Lord's name did you predict the unpredictable? 'I fear it is almost certain they will be able to sustain their attacks for the foreseeable future. And once the news finally leaks out we fear an upsurge of Loyalist support could lead to a massive campaign of ethnic cleansing in Ulster to drive out the entire Catholic population.'

'And there would be grass-roots support for this?' the chairman asked.

'In the present climate of bitterness over the end of the IRA ceasefire, it is likely to grow. There are daily signs of a change in public opinion. I fear the touchpaper has already been lit.'

'Touchpaper?' queried the Chief of Staff.

'For civil war in Ulster, maybe even the border counties of our Republic. And no one can guess the outcome.'

'That serious?'

'I'm afraid so. We're staring into the abyss.'

The senior civil servant from foreign affairs said in a small voice: 'There's only one thing to do when you stare into an abyss.' He paused, aware that all eyes were on him. 'You step back.'

'Meaning?' Fergal asked.

'Give them what they want. Drop our constitutional claim on the North and take immediate steps to set up the necessary referendum. And pull out of all political dealings with the North. Intern all known IRA members. It would be simple enough to give them what they ask.'

'And throw away our trump card?' Fergal came back barely hiding his disgust.

The foreign affairs man withdrew like a tortoise into the protection of his shell. He was heard to say quietly: 'Then we step over the edge with our eyes open.'

'It's out of the question to give in to terrorists – of whatever persuasion,' the chairman said decisively. 'The Taoiseach has already ruled that out. There would be a most humiliating loss of face with the Forum elections looming and talks to follow. It would be a terrible climb down and would inevitably lead to the breakup of this fragile coalition government. And if hardliners come to power, God knows where it all might end.'

For several long moments a disturbed and thoughtful silence settled over the room.

It was the chairman who finally spoke. 'If we allow this situation to spark a civil war, then our country will never be reunited. Only the British can prevent this and clearly – despite their best intentions – they have failed. We must signal our displeasure in the strongest terms. Signal in a way that will give them a message they cannot ignore.'

The Chief of Staff straightened his back. 'There is only one thing that has ever made the British sit up and take notice.'

'A bomb in the City,' someone said, and the mirth was as spontaneous as it was self-conscious; you weren't supposed to laugh at jokes like that.

'A repeat of Autumn Gold,' the COS said icily. 'Deploy all armed forces units to the border in full battle order. Move our armoured reconnaissance units and artillery. Let them see just *how* seriously we take the *Cuchulainn* threat. They haven't liked that in the past and they won't like it now.'

Fergal added: 'Especially if they don't know whether or not we mean it.'

The chairman was warming to the concept. 'I propose we put this forward as a recommendation to the Taoiseach. Those in favour?'

There were only two dissenters round the table.

'Carried.'

'Just one thing,' Fergal said, addressing himself to the Chief of Staff. 'May I suggest no one in the armed forces is told this is only an exercise until the very last moment. If the troops believe this is for real, so will everyone else.'

The chairman gave a tight nervous smile. Maybe then the British would actually *do* something about the *Cuchulainn* menace.

'That's pushing the old pals' act too far, Chris,' Jerry Tucker warned.

Lomax had telephoned that morning and arranged for them to meet his old friend from Army Intelligence at a quiet country pub not far from its Northern Ireland headquarters in Lisburn.

Monk said: 'It's not that much to ask, Jerry. We're not asking you to take us to King Billy personally, just point us in the right direction.'

'His testimony could be decisive,' Sam Browne said earnestly.

Tucker shook his head. 'You don't understand. If the RUC's not telling you where King Billy is, it's because MI5 don't want them to. They ultimately call the tune and Billy Baker's become one of their biggest assets in recent years.'

'He's a thug and a crook,' Monk said with disgust. 'He hasn't been a serious player in the Loyalist paramilitaries for years.'

'Maybe not, but he's singing MI5's tune now.' Tucker glanced nervously about him, taking care that there was no one within earshot. 'I shouldn't be telling you this, not least because it's mostly rumour. Box plays its own game over here and only tells us what we need to know. But it's common knowledge on the grapevine that King Billy's up to his fat armpits in drugs. He's pushing everything, but mostly ecstasy and cannabis to the kids. There's a theory that it's some bizarre conspiracy to knock the fight out of the young Loyalist hotheads.'

'I don't follow,' Lomax said.

'Look, during the IRA's ceasefire, the province was transformed. New clubs and nightspots opened almost every day. The kids – the teens and twenties – have been enjoying the time of their lives without fear for the first time ever. In the lull, a lot of the Loyalist yobs have lost their cutting edge. More interested in scoring dope and getting a legover. If you listen to their parents in Protestant ghettos, they swear it's a deliberate policy to keep them subdued. So they're no longer inclined to mix with the Provos. They're already being called the lost generation.'

'Surely that couldn't be government policy?' Browne asked, incredulous.

Tucker grimaced. 'Not government's, but it *could* be *someone's* policy. Who the hell can tell, who would know? All I can see is King Billy, the main supplier responsible, walking around with impunity.' He shook his head sadly as if not wanting to believe his own words. 'Thing is, Box has managed to alienate most Loyalist factions who no longer see it as an ally. There's been too much betrayal, like Keegan and your friend Roddy. Box just isn't trusted any more.'

Lomax said slowly: 'So MI5 has only got King Billy left?'

'Spot on,' Tucker said. 'They found he would dance to their tune for the right incentive. Now I don't know what he's done or does for MI5. All I know is we've been told in no uncertain terms to leave him and his gang alone. If any of my bosses in Army Intelligence have taken an interest in King Billy or got too close to one of his operations they've received a swift rap on the knuckles from on high. No doubt the RUC would say the same.'

Browne was chain-smoking in her anger and frustration; as she lit her third cigarette of the meeting, she said testily: 'Well, we know MI5 used him to get to Roddy. And, if things go the course, they'll use him to bear false witness in the conspiracy case. Surely you can't go along with that, Jerry?'

Irritation rarely showed on Tucker's cherubic face, but this time it did. 'Of course not, Miss Browne, but my job is closely defined. Put simply, what MI5 gets up to is none of my business unless they decide it is. A fact of life, I'm afraid.'

She watched him coolly for a moment. 'I understand that.' Her smile was a little oversincere. 'But if you were us, how would *you* go about finding Billy Baker?'

Tucker glanced at Lomax with the expression of a drowning man pleading to be rescued. But his friend's face remained unsmiling and inscrutable. Crunch point, Lomax thought. Sam Browne was playing the loyalty-to-comrades-in-arms card because it was all she had left. It was make or break. Tucker would either cast them a joker or throw in his hand, stand up and walk out.

The tension in the smoky little corner of the pub was palpable. Tucker thought for a moment as he lifted his glass and swallowed the last of his ale. Then he said: 'It would be a long shot.'

It was the joker. Yet Browne was desperate enough to pick it up. 'Yes?' Her eyes glistened with steely intensity.

'A man called Spike. Spike Scott.'

Monk said: 'I know that name.'

Tucker nodded. 'You would do. He used to be King Billy's head honcho, a young tough in his late twenties. To be honest, whatever respect Billy ever had as a paramilitary was down to Spike. But the two of them fell out a couple of years ago over Billy's dabbling in drugs. Now Spike does his own thing, got aspirations to be a politician. He's given up his T-shirt and jeans for a sharp suit.'

'But if he's fallen out with King Billy –' Lomax protested.

'They parted company, Chris, but they're still on speaking

terms. King Billy respects him, maybe even fears him a bit. After all, he's all too aware of Spike's capabilities. If you can get to Spike, it's just possible you'll get to Billy Baker.'

'Got an address for Spike?' Monk asked.

'I know it all too well. My people have got a permanent OP opposite his place.'

'Oh,' Lomax said.

Tucker's smile was grim. 'That's the rub, I'm afraid. OP and phone taps. If any of you make contact you'll get clocked and there's no way I can put my head on the block by interfering. Not during this current crisis.'

'End of the IRA ceasefire, you mean?'

Tucker looked momentarily flummoxed, then appeared to realise the misunderstanding. 'Sorry, Chris, I was forgetting you wouldn't know about it.'

'About what?'

'The Loyalist attacks in the Republic.'

Lomax frowned. 'I caught something on the radio some weeks back.'

'You wouldn't have known because of the news blackout imposed by London and Dublin. Only the first incidents were reported before the shutters came down. It appears to be the work of a new Loyalist grouping called *Cuchulainn*. The Hound of Ulster.'

'Who are they?'

'Some sort of splinter group of the Frontline Ulster Movement.'

'Frontline?' Lomax queried. 'Weren't they that defunct resistance lot Roddy was involved with years ago?'

'That's who they claim to be. Whoever they are, they're wreaking chaos south of the border. We organised a swoop a few weeks back and pulled in all known members for questioning. When we did, we found these people knew nothing about *Cuchulainn*. Zilch.'

'How embarrassing,' Monk said with a smile.

'Very. Not least for MI5, because it was they who actually set it up over twenty years ago.'

'That's how Roddy and Keegan got involved with MI5 in the first place,' Browne murmured.

'I don't think any of those young lads realised they were dealing with MI5 at the time,' Tucker said. 'Only later they realised they were in fact working with MI5. They thought that gave them a kind of legitimacy.' The Army Intelligence officer turned to Browne. 'But as your old client Keegan found out, that wasn't quite the case.'

'They allowed him to be thrown to the wolves,' Browne confirmed bitterly.

Tucker nodded. 'At the time, Colonel Roebuck was my boss, and he was personally running Keegan through one of the field operators when Derek Penny started investigating. Keegan was sure MI5 would somehow get it stopped.'

'I know,' Browne said, remembering her client's utter sense of betrayal at the time.

'The colonel agreed, wanted to pull strings and call in favours. But even then MI5 wanted to wash their hands of Keegan because his use to them was over. The man who had the say-so was a right bastard, a young Turk called Roger Pinfold.'

'We've met,' Lomax murmured.

Tucker looked mildly surprised. 'Small world. He was adamant that Roebuck should dump Keegan. The colonel decided to go over Pinfold's head and speak to an MI5 supremo known as Mr Grey.'

'Very appropriate,' Browne mused, then added: 'Wait a minute, Colonel Roebuck mentioned this Mr Grey at our first meeting with him.'

'Grey had known McIlroy since they'd served together in the Special Operations Executive during the war. They'd been close friends at one time. Anyway, Grey wasn't long off retirement at the time of Keegan's trial, but he still had authority over Pinfold. Keegan was right that Grey would be on his side, but Pinfold put up a helluva fight. Pulled every stunt in the book to get his way. As he was due to be Grey's successor in a few months, his opinion had to be taken into account. The result was an unhappy compromise. No one attempted to halt the inquiry, but Colonel Roebuck was permitted to appear as a witness for Keegan's defence, as you know.'

'But it wasn't enough,' Browne observed.

'Grey wanted to do more. After all, Frontline had been his concept, his baby. Roebuck once told me that Grey felt as terrible as he did about not being able to get Derek Penny's inquiry stopped.'

A thought occurred to Browne. 'Is this Mr Grey still alive?'

'I've no idea. The last I heard he was in bad health and that was four years ago. Roebuck reckoned the Keegan trial broke him. Why are you interested?'

'Because we're in desperate need of a credible defence witness now that Penny and Roebuck are dead,' she said.

Jerry Tucker nodded his understanding. 'The news of those two came as a bit of a shock, I can tell you. I still can't come to terms with Colin's death. He was a great bloke – best officer I ever served under. He lived for free-fall parachuting; he'd done over a thousand jumps when I worked with him. Who'd have thought he'd get killed in a freak accident. I thought he was indestructible.'

Lomax said: 'It wasn't an accident.'

His friend stared. 'Say again?'

'It wasn't an accident.'

Tucker pulled back in an expression of disbelief. 'How d'you know?'

'Sam and I were there. His parachute had been tampered with.' Lomax explained the sequence of events and Tucker listened intently, his jawline hardening as the story unfolded.

At last he said: 'Dirty Harry! Are you sure?'

'It's a long time since I'd last seen him, Jerry, but I'm as sure as I can be.'

'Harry's no longer with the Service.'

'Ah.' Lomax's exclamation was edged with disappointment. 'We're talking about the same man? Harry Grisewold?'

'Grisewold is it? I only ever knew his first name, but there is only one Dirty Harry. It must be six years since he left them.'

Lomax was puzzled. 'So maybe Box isn't mixed up in this.'

There was an edge to Tucker's voice now. 'Oh, I think it is,

Chris. Harry set up a private investigation agency, I believe. With some other former Service field officers. Box uses freelancers like them a lot, especially when they want to cover their tracks.'

'I see.'

'No, you don't, Chris, not fully. You remember you were followed when you were last over here and I traced the car being used back to Group's motor pool? It was being used by a group of Americans, maybe CIA or some other outfit. Well, I got intrigued and made a few discreet inquiries. It took a while, but eventually I got the name of Zack Ryan. Probably a cover name, but it's something. So I went on the booze with an old mate from Box. When he was well pissed I started running down the Yanks and, of course, he joined in. The long and short of it is that this Zack Ryan is running some sort of op with your old mate, Dirty Harry.'

'What sort of operation?' Monk asked.

Tucker gave him a pained look. 'No idea, Joe. My mate didn't say, though I doubt if he knew. Russian dolls, one inside another, inside another and all that – and I certainly didn't ask. But we know that at one time at least they had Chris in their sights.'

'Do they know we're here now?' Lomax asked.

'Not that I've heard, but that means nothing.'

'It was Joe's idea to pick up a hire car in Cork.'

'Wise move,' Tucker agreed. 'Did you have any trouble crossing the border?'

'None, just the usual. Glanced at my driving licence and asked what we were doing, where we were going. I said touring and they waved us through.'

Tucker nodded, satisfied. 'You'll be okay then.' He reached across for Lomax's cigarette packet and scribbled an address inside the lid. 'That's where you might find Spike Scott. But as soon as you go there, 14 Int will take an interest in you, and I may not be able to help.'

'You've helped enough,' Lomax said. 'Thanks.'

'It's what mates are for.' Tucker glanced at his watch and climbed to his feet. 'Time I was going. I'll see if I can find out

463

where that Mr Grey's living now. Or where he's buried. Happy hunting.'

After Jerry Tucker left they drove on to a country hotel and booked two rooms, the men sharing. They wrote false names and addresses in the register, Monk signing as his friend Len Pope whose credit card he had borrowed. Following supper they retired to one of the bedrooms, raided the minibar, and discussed how they could approach Spike Scott.

'We can't just phone this Spike character up,' Lomax said. '*Even* if he believed our explanation, we know 14 Int will be listening in. So we can hardly arrange a meet either.'

'What about posing as a market researcher?' Browne suggested. 'Going down the entire street, then Jerry's people wouldn't know we're only interested in Spike.'

'You can't go knocking on doors in Belfast,' Monk said. 'People don't answer to strangers.'

'Especially someone like Spike Scott,' Lomax added. 'Even to a pretty woman.'

She faked a flattered look. 'Meaning me? Oh, Chris, how *sweet*.'

'Maybe we can follow him,' Monk suggested, 'then try an approach when the coast is clear.'

Lomax shook his head. 'That won't be any easier if he's under constant surveillance.' He consulted his large-scale street atlas. 'We don't even know if he's living there or what he looks like. We're going to have to start at the beginning. A covert recce.'

'Middle of Loyalist heartland?' Monk observed. 'I wouldn't fancy hanging around there for too long.'

'Could I get away with it?' Browne asked brightly.

Lomax considered for a moment. 'What about the break-down wheeze?' he asked Monk.

'Yeah, why not.'

'It'll get you close enough to see what's going on,' Lomax told Browne, 'but without alerting suspicion. If any neighbours do get nosy, you can even ask them to help. Just hope they're not mechanically minded. If it works, it'll give you an hour or so to observe what's going on. Get an idea if Spike's in the house, if he's leaving for work, if he has a car – anything at all that might show us how to approach.'

Browne frowned suddenly. 'Is it dangerous?'

Lomax looked at her candidly. 'For Joe or me it could be lethal. But a daffy gal who knows nothing about cars – you could pull it off.'

Browne's mad eye widened a fraction.

They parked just short of the luridly painted gable end which marked the entrance to the estate. It was eight fifteen and already a queue of cars was forming to turn out onto the main road as residents made their way to work.

Browne took over the driving seat as the two men climbed out. She released the catch so that Lomax could lift the bonnet and loosen two of the spark plug caps.

'Okay, try it now,' he called.

The engine struggled into life, coughing and spluttering until it was ticking over unsteadily. It sounded pretty sick, but should allow the car to keep moving for another few miles. It was not, however, a precise science.

Lomax slammed the lid down and returned to the driver's door. 'Okay, Sam, off you go. Joe and I will be nearby, but we'll have to keep out of Spike's actual street. One of us will try to pass the end of it every ten minutes or so to check you're still there, okay? When you decide to pull out, we'll RV – sorry, rendezvous – at the car park I pointed out. All clear?'

'I must be mad,' she said, drumming her fingers on the wheel.

'You'll be okay. Good luck.'

She shoved the car into gear and let out the clutch. Reluctantly the stammering engine took up the load as she signalled and edged out into the traffic.

God, the engine sounded awful, she thought, expecting it to cut out at any minute. But she pushed the thought from her mind; there was too much to occupy her as she turned into the estate where Spike Scott lived.

The wall murals were huge, badly proportioned paintings

465

of men in balaclavas carrying rifles, William of Orange on a demented white charger and motifs of the red hand of Ulster. Daubed slogans screamed at her: 'The UVF lives – Provos die!', 'Stop the Priest Process!', 'Peace – but not at any price', and 'United Ireland not wanted here!' She could feel the vitriol in the hands of those who had written the words and a sense of uneasiness crept over her as the car shuddered its way into the first street.

Cuchulainn – the Hound of Ulster is with us now.

She'd just glimpsed it as she passed, registering the freshness of the crimson paint on the old brick wall. That name again. What was happening here?

Her heart fluttered in her chest. Leaning forward, she squinted for a better view along the straight narrow street of terraced houses. It all looked innocent enough: rows of Victorian two-up two-downs opening onto grey slabbed pavements and lines of parked cars. But every window, it seemed, had blinds or curtains drawn. A neighbourhood of unease, where privacy was paramount and every innocent passer-by could be a harbinger of death. Strangers were not welcome here. She could feel it, smell it.

For a moment, she was so overwhelmed by her desire to swing the car round and retreat, she almost missed the first left-hand turn.

She braked, allowing a dour-faced woman with a child and pushchair to cross the mouth of the street; there was no wave of thanks, just a glare from the hard, pinched, pale face beneath the headscarf. Young men leaned against the red-brick walls and talked in small groups, all in trainers, faded jeans and bomber jackets with the ubiquitous hood. Always hoods in Ulster, it was almost the national costume. Funny how you forgot these small things. Hoods against the fickle weather, against the frequent drizzle, against the bitter north-easterlies. Hoods against the prying eyes of strangers who might not be your friends.

Her eyes flicked right to more youths gathered around a lamppost. The crushed drink can clattered in the gutter where it was thrown, the noise through her open window making her tense suddenly. In the rear-view mirror she saw dark eyes turn to watch her pass. Shaven heads, cigarettes smoked to the butt between fingers with bitten nails.

Not a good idea after all, she thought. How could Lomax have said it was? How could he have gone along with it?

There it was. High on the right, the street name above the corner shop. She took a deep breath and turned the wheel. Panicking now, she tried to take it all in. Spike Scott's street. A little wider than the last, these houses with handkerchief front gardens, low walls and trim little privet hedges. She glanced left and right, trying to pick out the numbers. Even left, odd right. So she wanted right. Number Twenty-nine. Quick mental arithmetic. Fifteen doorways. Or was it fourteen? How many had she already driven past? Shit, she'd already lost count.

The car shuddered on. People on their way to work turned and looked as they walked. Someone laughed with his companion.

Not Twenty-nine, not Twenty-nine. Had she passed it already? Should she stop now? Was it safe? She thought how calmly Lomax and Monk would have handled this – made her feel stupid. Well, sod them both. Twenty-seven.

God, she'd almost got too close! She slammed on the brakes, and fell back breathless against the seat and shut her eyes. Well, this was it.

Taking a deep lungful of air, she braced herself and threw open the door. She scarcely had to act out her anger, stomping to the front of the car and throwing up the bonnet in disgust. Give it a minute or so, she told herself, let them see you peering at the engine and listening to the dreadful racket. Let the neighbours see you've got a problem, let Jerry Tucker's OP boys share a chuckle.

After a few minutes, she leaned against the offside wing, facing towards Number Twenty-nine, and took the mobile telephone from her shoulder bag. She went through the motions of making a call. 'Hello, yes, is that the RAC? Yes, a roadside breakdown. My membership number? Yes, it's . . .'

All of this was for the benefit of any pedestrians on the pavement a few feet behind her. Lomax had told her not to call the breakdown service straightaway in case they arrived *too* promptly. Was that a joke? She'd make a genuine call after forty-five minutes. In the meantime she had a perfect view of Spike Scott's house.

She returned to the driver's seat and made as though to read the morning paper. All the time her eyes moved back and forth over its top edge, trying to make mental notes as Lomax had instructed. Almost immediately she'd been aware of twitching blinds and curtains. A car outside. Someone placing a mobile bomb? A gunman waiting for a kill? Or someone watching. In Belfast there was always *someone* watching. An IRA 'dicker' or a Special Branch or army covert car? You could never be sure.

She concentrated on Number Twenty-nine. There was no sign of life: curtains closed on the upper floor, venetian blinds firmly in place on the little bay window downstairs. The owner could already have left for work. Could even be on holiday. Except there were full milk bottles in the small porch, not yet taken in. And there was a rusty blue Escort on the patch of tarmac where a garden had once been. She jotted down its number on the corner of her newspaper. Lomax would be pleased with that.

'Gotta wee problem, have we, love?'

The sudden intrusion of the harsh Ulster accent made her jump.

She jerked her neck round to see the hard, blunt-featured face of the shaven-headed young man pressed against the window. He was smiling but his eyes were cold. Recovering from the shock, she wound down the window to increase the gap by a few inches. 'Car's broken down, I'm waiting for the RAC.'

'RUC?'

It took a moment to realise he was joking. 'Oh, I see. They said they won't be long.'

'Not from these parts, are you? From the mainland.'

She gave a tight smile. 'I'm a solicitor,' she said as though that explained everything.

'What you doin' here?'

'On business.'

'No, I mean *here*. In this street? Seeing a punter, are we?'

'What?' She had trouble with the rapid words wrapped in such a thick accent. As she deciphered them she struggled to recall the line Lomax had told her. 'No, I was taking a short cut.'

'This is a dead-end estate, so it is.' He grinned unpleasantly at his own words. 'In more than one sense.'

She laughed it off. 'I realise that now. I used to live over here and thought I knew where I was. My memory was playing tricks, so many of these streets look the same.'

'Sure it's very confusing to strangers.' As he spoke, his eyes were darting around the interior of the car, looking for something. A weapon stuffed beneath a front seat, perhaps, or the tell-tale wires of a radio, or a telephoto-lensed camera on the back seat. At last he seemed satisfied and pulled back. 'I'll keep an eye on you till the RAC comes, make sure you get no hassle. Hear all these stories about women alone breaking down in their cars.'

'That's most kind.' And she watched, trembling slightly as he moved away along the pavement and disappeared into the doorway of one of the houses. It occurred to her then that the man could have been anyone, even a member of Tucker's OP team. A shiver of apprehension trickled down her spine.

Again she lifted the newspaper and adjusted her reading specs so she could watch Number Twenty-nine over the top of the sheet. Minutes ticked by, her own watch audible in the silence of the car. In the mirror she noticed the wafts of cigarette smoke from the doorway where the young man remained half-hidden.

Forty-five minutes passed and Browne began to feel flat with disappointment. Nothing and no one had stirred in Scott's house, and now it was time to phone the RAC for real. With a sigh of resignation she climbed out of the car and made a show of appearing irritated at the long wait for anyone who might be watching. Putting the mobile to her ear she paced up and down on the pavement as she made her call.

She had just finished and snapped shut the mouthpiece when the door to Number Twenty-nine opened. Her eyes widened in surprise and she quickly averted her gaze as a woman emerged. Although she was only in her twenties, the faded print dress, unkempt hair and flat shoes made her look frumpish and middle-aged. She crossed the street towards Browne with arms folded across her chest.

'D'you mind telling me what you're doing here?' she demanded coldly. 'This is a private street.'

It occurred to Browne that it was a stupid thing to say. The street was as public as any other; the woman meant they didn't tolerate unknown cars parked in it.

'Look, I've broken down, that's all . . .' And she stopped herself, almost losing this opportunity before she realised. 'You must be Spike's wife.'

Suddenly the woman's eyes glazed with fear; she instantly took a backward step.

Browne moved forward, her arms open in a gesture of reassurance. 'No, don't be alarmed. I need to talk to your husband.'

But the woman backed away again, her mouth contorting silently around the word: 'Peelers!'

'No, no, I'm not from the police. I'm a solicitor defending someone your husband might know.'

The woman glared defiance. 'Then why not telephone or knock at the friggin' door?'

Browne held her gaze. 'Because your husband's under surveillance by the army.'

'What?' Now her eyes were wide and wild. 'How d'you know? What is all this?'

'Your husband sent you to check on me, right?'

The bewildered look told Browne she was correct. Well, almost. 'Spike's my boyfriend.'

'Okay, fine. I need to see him urgently. Tell him I'll be at the Clandeboye public house at one o'clock. My name's Browne, Sam Browne.'

But Spike's common-law wife was still backing away like a frightened rabbit.

'*Please* tell him,' Browne pleaded as the woman turned and ran back to the house. The door slammed shut and silence settled again over the street. A puff of cigarette smoke from the doorway told her that the other watcher was still watching. A few minutes later an upstairs curtain twitched at Twenty-nine. Spike Scott was clocking her, making up his mind.

Thankfully it was only a few more minutes before the RAC van arrived and a patronising patrol man gave her a lecture on the rudiments of car-engine maintenance. He secured the loose spark plug caps, tested the engine and waved her on her way.

Browne swallowed the double brandy in three hard gulps. Lomax sat watching her from the opposite side of the small table in the Clandeboye saloon bar. It was gloomy, with lack-lustre mahogany panels, a threadbare carpet and a pervasive smell of yeast. Monk sat alone by the door, backup if needed.

An old grandfather clock gave a belated and melancholy chime at ten past the hour.

'I've never been so terrified, Chris. Look, I'm still shaking. I don't know how you did it for all those years.'

'You get used to it. Sort of.'

Browne looked around the bar at the small gathering of lunchtime regulars. 'He's not going to come, is he?'

'He's coming.'

'How can you be certain?'

He indicated a stout middle-aged man in a tweed jacket who was leaning against the bar. 'Because someone's casing the joint. Watching us through the mirror behind the bar. He's been watching us ever since we came in. Spike's not going to want to walk into an ambush.'

'Who'd want to do that?'

'No idea. More to the point, neither does he. Life can be quite interesting in the province.'

'A nightmare.'

At that point the man in the tweed jacket saw Lomax watching him and approached slowly across the room. He looked amiable enough, but his eyes were suspicious. 'Someone wants to meet Spike Scott, is that right?'

'I do,' Browne said.

'A solicitor? From England?'

'I want your friend's help.'

The man indicated Lomax. 'And who's your boyfriend?'

'He's my client's brother-in-law.'

Gimlet eyes regarded Lomax for a moment. 'Never a soldier, were you?'

A cautious smile showed on Lomax's face. 'Is it that obvious?'

'Aye, well you've got that look. Is that how you know our mutual friend is under surveillance?'

Lomax cast a glance at Browne; she shrugged in response. 'It just slipped out.'

'Spike's grateful for that,' the man said evenly. 'You can never be sure.' He looked pointedly in Monk's direction. 'And your pal by the door, another soldier?'

Lomax knew defeat when he stared it in the face. 'Another ex. An old comrade – he's just keeping an eye on us.'

Browne was becoming impatient. 'Is Mr Scott going to see me?'

'That's down to me. Depends what I think.'

She met his gaze and held it. 'And what *do* you think?'

The man hesitated. 'I think you were the solicitor who handled Peter Keegan's defence back in '89. Now you're looking after Roddy Littlechild.'

The solicitor tried not to let her rising sense of panic show. 'You're very well informed.'

'It's my job.' He straightened his back and looked at Lomax. 'Roddy's brother-in-law, eh? I know a bit about you too. Okay, Spike'll see you, but not your friend over there. He stays put till we've had our wee conversation. Go tell him, then follow me outside.'

The rusted blue Escort that had been outside Number Twenty-nine was waiting in the pub car park. Its driver was in his early thirties, short dark hair razored at the sides and back, an aggressive cut that hardly went with the flash silvered suit and loud tie. Bright blue button eyes scrutinised their approach, fingers beating a rapid tattoo on the sill of the wound-down window.

'The woman in the front with me, Albie,' Spike Scott said. 'You go in the back.'

He made no attempt to address them before he swung the vehicle out into the stream of traffic with scant regard for any highway courtesy.

'Were you followed to the Clandeboye?' Lomax ventured.

'Probably,' the man answered, looking into his rear-view mirror, 'if you say I'm under observation. But then why should I give a shit? I've got nothing to hide.'

Damn, Lomax thought. Spike Scott might be brazenly indifferent to an Army Intelligence tail, but it meant Tucker's team would start asking questions and taking an interest.

'Where're we going?' Browne asked nervously.

'Just a wee drive,' Albie Nairn replied amicably. 'Take in the view.'

Spike Scott said: 'So you want my help, is that it?'

'I'm defending Roddy Littlechild in London. D'you know him?'

Spike was noncommittal, but Nairn replied: 'There's not many in the Loyalist community who don't know Roddy. I think Spike's met him once or twice.'

Browne pushed on. 'We're looking for an important witness for his defence.'

'Billy Baker,' Lomax added.

The silence in the car was abrupt, the tension almost palpable. At last Spike said: 'That's a good crack. The big fella giving evidence in court. Sure who'd believe a word from the likes of King Billy?'

Nairn chuckled. 'No one this side of the water, that's for sure.'

'Someone told us you used to know him,' Browne said anxiously. 'I wondered if you could put us in touch. Act as go-between.'

Spike studied the road ahead. 'I'm not sure I want to be associated with the likes of King Billy nowadays. If someone told you I know him, then that someone would know I'm standing for election in June. For the all-party talks. I don't want to be tainted by the likes of that fat maggot.'

473

Nairn said helpfully: 'William Baker is no longer regarded very highly in the Loyalist ranks.'

'He's a fuckin' pusher!' Spike added angrily. 'And we all know why. He sits at the right hand of Her Majesty, so he does. Or at least those slimeballs who do the Queen's business.'

'Can't you just give us a lead?' Browne pleaded.

'Oh, we can do better than that,' Nairn said expansively, 'for our friends on the mainland. Sure young Spike has been wanting a wee word with King Billy for a while now, only your man has been avoiding him.'

'Money in it, is there?' Spike asked. 'A wee backhander, a palm-greaser for old Billy boy.'

Browne glanced at Lomax in alarm. 'I'm not here to bribe a witness.'

'Oh, sure, you are,' said Nairn. 'Because King Billy isn't having visitors at the present. We've been trying to see him for weeks ourselves. But an offer of cash might just open the door, let me tell you.'

Lomax said: 'How much would do the trick?'

'Maybe five big ones.' Nairn smiled. 'As your opening bid.'

'Do it.'

Browne was aghast. 'Chris, you can't, you haven't got that sort of money,' she blustered. 'Besides, it's – it's – '

'Unethical?' he asked cynically.

'Downright illegal,' she replied.

'So is framing an innocent man for murder.' He turned back to Nairn. 'It's my money and my decision. Please go ahead.'

The Yank was on to it, and Harry Grisewold was well displeased.

Displeased to learn that Lomax and the bitch solicitor had indeed turned up in Northern Ireland. Even more displeased that Zack Ryan had been the one to tell him.

Ryan's boys were in Dublin and Belfast, doing their bit to get the peace process back on course for their President. Their little American liaison unit was plugging itself into every British intelligence and police agency over there, co-operation given on orders from Whitehall. No one liked that much, of course, they were all well used to guarding their own little piles of excretia from each other, let alone some know-it-all big shots from Langley. But Zack Ryan understood British reticence and stonewalling and had set about building up his own network. Plying contacts with lunches and gifts of bourbon or tickets to take their kids to Disneyland. Christ, Grisewold thought, it was just like the wartime GIs with their nylon stockings and chewing gum. It made him sick, but it worked.

'So maybe you'd best get your butt over here pronto, Harry,' had been his parting shot on the telephone.

It had felt to Grisewold like an order; the more so because, of course, that's exactly what he had to do. And he certainly didn't need the Yank to tell him.

He took Margie Lewis with him on an early shuttle to Aldergrove. They grabbed a quick fry-up breakfast at Heathrow, then she watched with bemusement as he ate another on the plane.

'Jesus, where d'you put it all, Harry?'

'I eat when I'm worried,' he replied testily.

'C'mon, you're always eating lately.'

'That's because I'm always worried lately.' He grinned lasciviously. 'I need the oral satisfaction. It's my sex substitute.'

'Don't complain, Harry. It was you who fell asleep again last night.'

'This sodding case is knackering me. Seven days a week, twenty hours a day.'

'Then tell Pinfold to piss off.'

'We need the money.'

'Then stop moaning.'

He wiped his lips with a tissue and gave her a none-too-gentle nudge. 'Fancy joining the mile-high club?'

When they landed, Zack Ryan was waiting with an unmarked pool car. The American was mean and lean, and young. And to make matters worse he kept giving Margie the eye. And Margie being Margie didn't discourage him. Making matters worse, she wound Grisewold up in private about toyboys and clean-cut all-Americans, going on about Zack's pecs and his cute army-academy haircut.

'I had the Garda check all the car rental companies in Cork.

They crossed over from Eire the day before yesterday,' Zack said, driving lazily with one hand on the wheel. 'Thanks to your pals' anti-American zenophobia, I didn't get a routine print-out of the list until yesterday afternoon. Then another pal of mine from Army Int tipped me off.'

Another flight to Disneyland, Grisewold thought, forcing himself to listen. Zack Ryan – everybody's friend.

'Lomax's car stopped outside a house under surveillance. But his boss pulled the information before passing it up to his superiors. A guy called Tucker.'

'Tucker?' Margie asked. 'Jerry Tucker's a friend of Lomax.'

Grisewold was irked, again. He knew Tucker and Lomax went back a long way, had served together in the province. Tucker was *his* secret, dammit. When Lomax was in Ulster, Tucker was his first port of call. Watch Tucker and you'd find Lomax. Now, here was Zack telling him like he didn't know.

'You oughta pull this Tucker creep,' Zack said. 'He's a security risk.'

'I'm letting Tucker run,' Grisewold answered dismissively and moved on: 'Whose house?'

'Guy called Spike Scott. Some Loyalist hardman. Hung up his balaclava and bought himself a politician's suit.'

'Why should Lomax want to contact him?' Margie asked.

Grisewold knew instantly, but wasn't going to say anything in front of the American. He just shrugged and asked: 'So where's Lomax now?'

'Last seen yesterday evening,' Zack replied. 'Passed through an RUC checkpoint at Katesbridge in County Down. Nothing since.'

'I suppose the solicitor Browne was travelling with him.'

'And his pal Monk.'

Grisewold reached a decision. 'I know we want to keep this low-profile, but we'll have to have the RUC put out an "all-cars". We've got to locate Lomax. It'll be discreet – they're used to it over here. Once he's clocked, we'll put one of our own tails on the job.'

'Sure, let's get some action,' Zack said, eager to go as always.

476

'Now, Zack, much as we enjoy your company, Margie and I've got work to do. I'll catch up with you later.'

When the American had dropped them at Grisewold's private Belfast office, Margie said: 'What's going on, Harry? You've got that look.'

'Who has Browne been desperate to get as a defence witness?'

'Billy Baker.'

'And who used to be Billy Baker's right-hand man?'

Margie's eyes widened. 'Christ. Spike Scott.'

The grin on Grisewold's face was smug and wide as he dug in his raincoat pocket for a roll of Rolos. 'Bloody Zack doesn't know *everything* yet.' He popped one of the chocolate toffees in his mouth.

She frowned. 'Where is Baker?'

Grisewold shrugged. 'No idea, that's the rub. He's gone to ground. Under strict orders to keep hidden till after Little-child's trial.'

'So it's follow Lomax and find them both?'

'If King Billy is breaking cover, then the Browne woman must be offering money. And if she *is* meeting with him, then this is getting seriously out of control.'

'Not much we can do about it.'

'Oh, yes, there is, sweetness, and I know Pinfold's desperate enough to agree.'

'To what?'

'To handing it over to Zack's boys. Give them a free hand.'

'You're joking.' Her face was momentarily white. Dirty tricks were getting dirtier by the day. 'They'll negotiate them, you know they will.'

'It'll be nothing to do with us and a problem solved.'

'You can't, Harry,' she protested.

'Not like you to be squeamish.'

'I'm not. Fitzpatrick was a shit.'

'And Roebuck?'

She frowned. 'An unfortunate accident.' There was something about the expression on his face. 'Wasn't it?'

'Sure.' Some things were best for only the boys to know.

'But Browne and Lomax . . .'

477

Grisewold swallowed the remains of his Rolo. 'Browne's broken the rules and she knows it.'

'God, Harry, that's hardly a hanging offence.'

'It is when the stakes are this high.'

'If we're implicated –'

'Still a babe in some respects, aren't you, Margie? Zack's people are pros. It'll look like some paramilitary feud that Browne and Lomax have got caught up in.'

She shook her head, but had to smile. There really was no one quite like Harry. 'You really are a bastard.'

'And you love me all the more for that.'

'Maybe.' She forced the unpleasantness to the back of her mind. 'So what now?'

'To our hotel for an hour or two, I think.'

'Lunch,' she said with disgust. 'Not another meal.'

'I had in mind a quick shag. All that talk of the mile-high club, I've lost my appetite.'

'I love you when you're masterful, Harry Grisewold. And you know me, I'll do anything for a Rolo.'

Twenty

'I must be off my bloody rocker,' Tucker said.

Moments before he'd scared the life out of them when Lomax, Monk and Browne had stepped out into the hotel car park on the Sunday morning. None of them had seen the Army Intelligence officer lurking beside a parked van.

'How'd you find us?' Lomax asked.

'Someone in Box has put out an "all-cars" for your hire car. It was routinely copied to my desk. When I saw it, I got a chum in the RUC to give me first news of any sighting. A passing cop car recognised it about two hours ago.'

'It was bound to happen,' Monk reflected gloomily.

'I've had an hour's head start, so someone from Box could be down here at any moment. That's why I've brought the car. You can have it for a couple of days.'

Lomax was astounded. '*Your* car?'

'A pool car. It's supposed to be in the workshop for a service, but it goes okay. I've juggled the paperwork so no one'll miss it for a day or two. But you'll have to give me a lift back to my place.'

'No problem. I can't tell you how much I appreciate this.' Lomax was under no illusion as to the risk Tucker was running if he were found out. His career would be over and he'd face court martial.

Tucker smiled. 'Just do me a favour and don't get noticed, eh?'

His easy manner belied the stress he was under and he was clearly relieved when Lomax was driving away from the hotel in the anonymous grey Rover.

Whatever the risk to Tucker's career, the move couldn't have been better for them. It was proved at the first RUC police road check when the Rover was waved through as a 'listed security vehicle'. The grin on Monk's face was huge.

They dropped Tucker in a quiet suburban street in Lisburn, close to army headquarters. There was little they could do then until noon when they'd agreed with Albie Nairn to telephone his home number for any news.

They parked in a Belfast multistorey and passed the time having a coffee and doing some window-shopping before Lomax made his call from a box in the near deserted centre.

'The fish has taken the bait,' Nairn's quiet voice told him. 'We'll rendezvous at five this evening.'

It was a location that had already been agreed so there was no need to confirm it on an open line.

Harry Grisewold watched in his rear-view mirror as Lomax and the others returned to the Rover in the parking stack.

This time they wouldn't find the homing beacon, not unless they stripped out the entire car. He'd fitted it in a rear-door panel – a quick job with a skeleton key and simple screwdriver. But not so quick to find unless you knew exactly where to look.

Doors slammed and the Rover came alive, Lomax reversing out and heading for the exit. Moments later Margie Lewis appeared at the exit stairway, dressed in headscarf and an old gaberdine raincoat.

'He made a call,' she said simply. 'Just one. That was all.'

'If it was to Spike Scott, we'll have a trace,' Grisewold replied and started the engine, swinging out and heading for the exit ramp.

'I'll check.' Margie was already on the mobile. Minutes later, when they were out on the Belfast streets following the steady bleep from Lomax's Rover, she had an answer. 'No one's called Spike today and the OP thinks he's had a tip-off and given them the slip. Maybe he got out over the garden wall during the night.'

'Ah,' Grisewold said. 'So chummy's on the gallop. So it all fits. They've set up a meet. The Browne woman and Lomax with Spike to introduce them to King Billy.'

'You're enjoying this, aren't you?'

'I'm going to enjoy telling Zack where to find Lomax.'

'So you were right about Tucker. You said if we watched Tucker, we'd find Lomax.'

Grisewold's smile became a little smugger. 'Even I didn't reckon the bugger would be daft enough to get a pool car for his old mate! Smart move, but a bloody stupid one. Tucker's finished.'

Five o'clock. Church car park, the tarmac lacquered black after an unexpected downpour. Half the spaces vacant and the crowd of worshippers dispersing.

Lomax and Browne in the Rover, waiting. Monk leaning against a wall, reading a newspaper. But not reading, watching. An overview, looking for anything out of place, anything or anyone unusual.

A small blue van pulled up alongside the Rover, Albie Nairn at the wheel in a Marks & Spencer cardigan with a polyester tie. He wound down his window and Browne did the same.

'We'll go in my car, if you don't mind,' he said. 'You can come back and collect yours later.'

When he'd locked the car, Lomax stooped and pushed the ignition keys into the exhaust pipe. Without a backward glance at Monk, they joined Nairn, Browne beside him and Lomax in the rear where he found Spike Scott waiting.

Monk continued his lonely vigil.

A few minutes later he knew he had them. A couple who had driven into the car park not long after the Rover ... So not needing to be in visual contact with it – Surely that didn't mean there was a radio tracer beacon on the Rover? Surely not? How? Then he remembered it had been unguarded in the Belfast stack.

The couple hadn't gone inside the church, but had remained in their seats. He didn't recognise the woman, but the man's face was familiar. Although not in direct view of Lomax's Rover, they would have witnessed the vehicle switch.

That's why the man looked tetchy, chain-smoking as he spoke into his mobile. Was calling for backup because now he couldn't follow Nairn's van on eyeball for fear of being spotted.

Dirty Harry, Monk decided, was not a happy man.

It was a quiet lay-by on the Newtownards–Greyabbey road beside the unruffled aluminium surface of Strangford Lough. That was where the compact grey Fiat Panda waited.

When Albie Nairn pulled in and stopped facing it, the driver climbed out and approached cautiously. He was young and hard-faced with straggly long hair that was in need of a wash, as were the muddy jeans and faded anorak.

'King Billy's scraping the bottom of the barrel,' Spike murmured, seeing his replacement as Baker's henchman.

The man didn't introduce himself, didn't need to. 'I trust no one's tooled up?' he asked warily.

'Don't be silly, son,' Nairn replied.

'I'll have to check.'

He did the job quickly and inexpertly, then peered inside the van before saying: 'Okay. Get back in and follow me. It's not far.'

The Panda led the way to Greyabbey where it took the B5 to the coastal village of Ballywalter before turning north alongside the wind-swept sand flats of the Irish Sea. After a mile or two it signalled and swung into the entrance to a caravan park where a line of European national flags snapped raggedly in the stiff offshore breeze. Most of the caravans were locked and curtained, only a few hardy holiday-makers brave enough to endure the fickle spring weather.

King Billy's mobile court was set in a far corner of the park where the perimeter fence adjoined open pastureland. It was a bright chrome-and-cream affair that was as old as it was luxurious and looked too large to have ever done much travelling on the road.

So this was the man's little bolt hole, Lomax thought, where he could disappear into anonymity when he needed to.

The Panda pulled up and Baker's henchman climbed out. He glanced around the deserted, wind-scoured field for a moment, like an animal sniffing the air for scent of danger. Deciding nothing was amiss, he rapped briskly on the door.

When it was opened, King Billy filled the entire aperture with his bulk. He looked pleased to see them, the incongruous cupid's bow grinning in his chalky, flaccid face. The fingers on the huge extended hand were of the dimensions of pork saveloys.

'Come on in, will you,' he said, greeting Spike first. 'Good to see you again.'

'And you, Billy,' Scott replied. 'This is Albie who I believe you've met before. And these are our friends from the mainland. Chris Lomax and Sam Browne.'

King Billy's interest in Lomax was perfunctory; it was Browne whom he fixed with his powder-blue eyes, the palest eyes she had ever seen. 'Charmed, so I am. Heard so much about you lately.'

Browne laughed awkwardly. 'None of it true, I hope.'

The man saw his opening. 'Well, sure it was true about the legs.' He guffawed at his own sally. 'What an exquisite creature.'

Inwardly Lomax winced, but Browne appeared unaffronted by the gross flirtation, playing his game.

Baker shuffled breathlessly into the lounge area, sofa seats ranged along three sides of the caravan. Despite its size, the presence of the big man made it appear small. He seemed aware of the fact. 'Sorry if it's a bit cramped. That's the trouble bein' a big fella – you take up all the space.'

Lomax sensed he was in a relaxed mood, vividly expressed by the voluminous short-sleeved floral shirt and casual slacks that must have taken yards of material to make. After ordering his henchman to wait outside, Baker waddled over to the built-in cocktail cabinet. 'Anyone for a wee drop of Blackbush?' he asked.

Only Browne declined, settling for a mineral water. She came straight to the point: 'Mr Baker, I'm here concerning the trial of my client Rodney Littlechild.'

He gave a demure little smile, his lips taking the shape of a pink rosebud, and sipped at his drink before replying. 'And how is my good friend Roddy?'

'Not very happy that you've disappeared when he most needs you.'

'Needs me for what?' He was smiling, enjoying this.

'I think you've a good idea, Mr Baker. You contacted him to say Fitzpatrick would be in touch. You persuaded him it was safe to have the meeting.'

'Really?' The pale eyes widened in feigned surprise. 'I can't say I recall.'

'Did you know why MI5 wanted Roddy to meet Fitzpatrick?'

'MI5?' Any humour drained from his eyes. 'Don't be fanciful, m'dear. Sure it doesn't suit you.'

'No one knew his number, Mr Baker, not even his own brother-in-law. Certainly not you. You were given it by MI5, probably by a woman called Tabitha White.'

That seemed to surprise him. 'Been doing some homework, haven't you?'

'Did you know why she wanted Roddy and Fitzpatrick to meet?' she repeated, realising by the look in his eyes that he'd never tell her the truth. 'It was to have Fitzpatrick got out of the way and to have Roddy take the blame.'

King Billy's face was a picture of childlike innocence. Of course he knew, she decided, and didn't even care. With a cold thrill of fear she realised she was staring into the hypnotic eyes of a multiple killer. A man who'd committed or ordered countless summary executions, created widows and orphans and cripples on the merest whim.

She was thankful when Lomax said curtly: 'Six thousand pounds, Billy. My life savings. Half before and half after you've given evidence.'

'You just walk into court,' Browne added quickly, 'and tell the truth. It's that easy. Say who told you to phone Roddy, who wanted him to meet Fitzpatrick. That it was all MI5's idea. Say that and Roddy's a free man.'

An enigmatic smile played on King Billy's lips. 'Is that all? Just the truth. And what will my friends in MI5 think about that?'

'It doesn't matter what they think,' Browne insisted. 'They are not above the law. If I call you to the highest criminal court in the land you are expected to attend. And tell the truth. Your MI5 chums might not like it, but they'll have to respect it. You've nothing to fear, you just did what they told you. Now you're obliged to tell a judge and jury what that was.'

'Even if it puts me in personal danger?' He was still playing games, and they all knew it.

'They're not going to bump you off,' Lomax countered. 'From what I hear, you're the only friend they've got left. They need you more than you need them. And they've more reason to be scared of you and what you know than you have of them. But I think you've worked that out already, otherwise you wouldn't have agreed to see us.'

Baker blinked. There was something about the tone in Lomax's voice that warned him he'd gone far enough. 'Okay, I'm persuaded. I am a great believer in justice . . .'

'In that case, there's something else,' Browne cut in quickly. 'You've told the police that in 1987 you saw Roddy hand over weapons to a South African hit team. The day before Dominic Smals was killed. That's a lie.'

'Ah, well. It was a long time ago.'

'Just the truth, Mr Baker,' Browne persisted. 'It really is that simple.'

'Not for six thousand it isn't,' King Billy replied. 'Twelve.'

'Eight,' Lomax bartered.

'Ten.'

'I'll settle for nine.'

Baker looked triumphant. 'Done.'

Browne was angry. 'For God's sake, Chris, you haven't got that sort of money.'

'I'll find it, borrow it.'

Further discussion was halted by a sharp knock on the caravan door.

'What does the imbecile want now?' Baker said irritably, struggling to his feet; he glanced at Scott. 'Can't get the staff nowadays, Spike. You really shouldn't have left, y'know.'

Spike nodded with a smile. 'Yeah, miss you too, you old bastard.'

Baker's chuckle was like a bubbling volcano as he reached the door, and began to open it. 'What is it this time?'

Without warning, the man's huge bulk was thrown back inside the caravan. An unseen wave of air pressure seemingly flung him against the wardrobe, the plywood splintering loudly. Browne gasped as the acrid stench of gunsmoke drifted in from the doorway and they heard the sound of feet on the metal step.

Peter Keegan lowered the silenced pistol.

The Eagle patrol had picked them up, the Puma hovering at ten thousand feet. At maximum altitude, it presented no more than a tiny blur to anyone on the ground, the clatter of its rotor blades reduced by distance to the faint drone of a flying insect.

To the occupants of the little Fiat Panda and the blue van that followed, it went unnoticed.

To the pilot of the helicopter, the vehicles resembled plastic N-gauge models moving across a miniature railway layout. He was well pleased, having followed instructions from Griswold at the church, updated by an RUC sighting on the road. His message was relayed via ACC headquarters Aldergrove and Security Service headquarters to Margie Lewis as Harry Griswold was driving them past the flat, still waters of Strangford Lough.

'A caravan park near Ballywalter,' she reported.

'Where are Zack's boys now?'

'On the Newtownards Road. Maybe twenty miles.'

'So they could make it in twenty minutes?'

'Sure, the way some of Zack's boys drive.'

'Then give them the co-ordinates.'

Margie looked uncomfortable. 'You *really* sure, Harry?'

'Just do it.'

Moments later, the Eagle patrol peeled off, its task complete, and headed towards County Armagh for its next job in yet another routine day's work.

Peter Keegan hardly needed to examine the body. Its size seemed somewhat diminished as a crumpled heap of rags on the floor oozing blood from the four puncture marks around the chest and abdomen. Already King Billy's brightly coloured shirt was sodden as the vermilion pool began creeping across the caravan floor. That almost pretty mouth half-formed around a cry of surprise, or was it pain? Eyes staring sightlessly at the ceiling.

'Peter?' Browne said hoarsely, not believing the evidence of her own eyes.

Keegan straightened his back and shoved the gun into the waistband of his jeans. 'Hi, Sam.' He grinned. 'Sorry to bust up the party.' He inclined his head towards Lomax. 'Chris.'

'What is this?' Browne asked, her voice quavering as the shock set in.

They could see that there was another man behind Keegan; a gaunt figure with unkempt black hair and eyes that smouldered with an unnerving intensity. Lomax looked across at Spike Scott and Albie Nairn; one smiling gently and the other impassive.

'We've been set up,' Lomax told her.

Keegan shrugged. 'Yes, I'm afraid you were. King Billy had to go.'

Spike said: 'We've been trying to get to him for weeks.'

'Your offer was just too much for him to resist,' Keegan added.

'Murder,' Browne mumbled, staring at the corpse. 'Cold-blooded.'

Keegan shrugged. 'I suppose I can't expect you to defend me on this one, Sam?'

'That isn't funny, Peter,' she snapped back. 'Not remotely funny. Chris was going to pay him to tell the truth.'

'And d'you think he would?' It was the thin dark stranger who spoke for the first time. 'He'd have taken your money, or half of it, and just gone his own sweet way. Said what his master'd told him to. He knew where his bread was buttered.'

Keegan stepped to one side to introduce the man. 'This is Stevie Gavin. You've probably heard of him. More usually referred to as Rattler.'

Browne caught the look on Lomax's face. Rattler, the most

deadly Loyalist hit man in the province. The string of killings attributed to him went back over twenty years.

'King Billy was the last Loyalist in MI5's pocket,' Keegan said. 'They've given him *carte blanche* to run his narcotics, to poison the Protestant youth, to keep them cowed.'

'Getting in the way,' Spike said. 'That's why I left him. I'm with *Cuchulainn* now; we all are. A united front against the Provos and against Dublin.'

'*Cuchulainn*?' Immediately Lomax picked up on the name. 'You're with *Cuchulainn*?'

The four Ulstermen looked at each other and grinned; there was no mistaking their pride. Keegan said: 'We are *Cuchulainn*.'

At that moment, the caravan door flew open. 'TROUBLE!' someone yelled from outside.

Rattler turned and sprang down the steps, followed by Keegan. Spike was on his feet, moving to the window, Lomax close behind him.

From their vantage point on the slight rise, there was a view across the undulating grass of the park to the main road. A second car was screeching in after the first, leaving the concrete ringway to bounce over rough ground in the direction of Baker's caravan. A family playing ball stood and gawped, then ran for cover as the cars drove straight at them, intent on only one thing – reaching their target before anyone had time to react.

Nairn paled. 'Provos?'

'Could be anyone,' Spike hissed. 'Maybe peelers. Let's get out of here.' He turned to Lomax. 'You'd better come too. Don't stick around to get shot.'

There was no time to discuss the wisdom or otherwise of Spike's advice, because outside, Stevie Gavin and Peter Keegan had opened up on the two cars that were bearing down on them, lined abreast.

Phut! Phut! Silent rounds spat from the muzzles in angry whispers, sparks flying as the lead embedded in the bodywork of the cars. One driver spun his wheel. The car slewed and at once the windscreen disintegrated. Doors flew open and the four occupants threw themselves out.

Lomax grabbed Browne's wrist and dragged her out of the

caravan, jumping the step and forcing her to the ground. 'DOWN, DOWN!' he yelled.

The second car gave up an attempt to get closer and the doors opened, the passengers using them for cover as they opened fire.

Lomax could scarcely believe what he was seeing. There must be seven or eight of them out there, pumping out the rounds. No uniforms, just casual urban garb, except for the balaclavas. This was turning into a major firefight and for a second he was back in the Falklands as the bullets zipped above his head to riddle the side of the caravan.

Keegan and Stevie Gavin were holding their own with Spike, who looked incongruously like a Capone mobster in his spivvy business suit, joining in the shooting with a gun thrown to him by one of the others.

Lomax tried to shield Browne's body with his own and looked around for some way of escape. To his surprise, he found a body lying beside him. It took a moment to recognise the contorted face. King Billy's henchman, who had been on guard outside, had died whilst trying to loosen the garrotte wire from around his throat.

With a clear field of fire into the adjoining meadow, their attackers had no compunction about pressing home their advantage, free to fire indiscriminately. The caravan bodywork was studded like a colander and windows were exploding all around them as stray rounds hit.

On Browne's other side he saw Albie Nairn, face down in the grass and covering his head with his hands as shards of glass showered on top of him.

They had only seconds, Lomax realised, before their attackers found the range, or Keegan, Gavin and Spike Scott had to stop to change magazines.

'BACK!' he yelled in Browne's ear. 'UNDER THE CARAVAN!'

She glanced over her shoulder, saw what he meant and began to wriggle backwards. He slapped her backside hard. 'KEEP IT DOWN! MOVE YOURSELF!'

Forcing her belly into the grass, she stretched her thighs to get some momentum going. Now that she was underway, Lomax nudged Albie Nairn and indicated for him to follow.

By the time all three were sheltering in the shadows, probably only sixty seconds had passed since the firefight had begun. But, as always in combat, split seconds of action seem to stretch on for ever.

Browne was sheet-white and trembling, her eyes wide like a startled animal, begging to be told what to do.

'Over the fence,' Lomax decided, 'into that meadow and run like hell.'

Out in the open the firefight was petering out. Keegan, Spike and Rattler had retreated to the sides of the caravan, using it to provide a small measure of protection. Their attackers were losing impetus as several of them paused to reload.

Lomax shoved Browne unceremoniously out into the open behind the caravan, then half-dragged her along behind him as he raced towards the perimeter fence. Albie Nairn stumbled breathlessly after them.

At the fence, Lomax dropped to one knee and cupped his hands to give Browne's foot a lift up, propelling her over the top wire. Nairn was next, putting up a manful but clumsy effort, tripping over the top wire and falling into a cowpat on the far side. Lomax himself was about to follow, when Keegan, Spike and Rattler pulled him back.

'Stay put, Chris,' Keegan gasped. 'Then we'll give you covering fire.'

Keegan's foot landed in Lomax's cupped hands and he, too, was over. The Ulsterman turned, aimed his automatic and let off a short burst at the attackers while Gavin, then Spike and finally Lomax vaulted over the fence.

'To the right!' Gavin shouted. 'Into that copse!'

Keegan remained to hold off the pursuers as the rest of them ran raggedly across the tufty rough ground to the sanctuary of the treeline.

'Where to now?' Lomax asked breathlessly.

'This way,' Gavin said, as Keegan finally rejoined them, and led the way into dense undergrowth. In a final glance back, Lomax saw their pursuers gathered by the fence of the caravan park; they were making no attempt to give chase. There was much head-shaking and he guessed they would be thinking about their own survival if police or army patrols had been alerted by the shooting.

Lomax followed for several minutes before they reached the woodland dell. Sunlight lit the bright paintwork of the Agusta helicopter.

Lomax's mouth dropped in amazement.

'God is airborne,' Keegan said with a grin as he saw the look of astonishment. 'And looks like today He's on our side.'

Harry Grisewold leaned his crossed forearms on the roof of his car and idly watched the civilian helicopter droning its way south out over the Irish Sea.

God, that's what he'd like to be doing now. Flying away from this mess, preferably down to one of his favourite haunts in Tuscany. With Margie.

His eyes wandered back to the entrance to the caravan park, now full of RUC and army Land-Rovers as the area around King Billy's caravan was being sealed off with tape.

What a disaster! Roger Pinfold was going to love this. He turned as another car pulled up onto the verge behind his own. Zack Ryan emerged, long-limbed and moving with a lazy grace, doing his usual James Dean impression in black jeans and jacket and wraparound shades.

'You've heard?' the American asked, jaw jutting as he chewed on a wad of gum.

Grisewold nodded, trying to hold back his anger. 'What the hell went wrong?'

Ryan shrugged. 'One of those things. Someone saw us comin' and opened up. It was like a Nam war movie. Pretty hairy shit. I'm afraid Lomax and the woman got away.'

'Your boys okay?'

'Yeah. A lotta rounds but piss-poor marksmanship all round.'

'Not that poor. Several rounds hit King Billy, I'm told. Taking him out wasn't in the plan – he was one of our best assets.'

'What? Baker wasn't there?'

'He was inside, didn't you realise that?'

'Holy cow – of course, we didn't see him outside.'

'Don't worry, it wasn't down to you. Looks like your boys put a few more rounds in his corpse. Nothing's certain yet, but from what the police said, I think he'd been killed minutes before you arrived. He'd been shot at point-blank range and his minder had been garrotted.'

'Who the hell would do that?'

'Anyone. Baker had a lot of enemies. Provos or Loyalists. Course, at the moment, the police think your boys did everything, it's just a question of whether they think you were Taigs or Prods.' He looked back across the road. 'Did you see Lomax or Browne there, or Albie Nairn and Spike?'

'Sure, but they legged it over the fence before we could get a bead. I don't know Nairn to look at, but that's his van still parked outside. They were making for that wood over there on the hill.'

Grisewold nodded. 'I think some witness has already told the police that. I've seen a search party heading that way.'

Ryan said suddenly: 'But I'll tell you who I *did* see? Man, I had to do a double-take because I've only seen some old mug shots.'

'Who?'

'That Rattler guy, Stevie Gavin. And, wait for it – '

Grisewold smouldered. 'Don't piss me about with silly games, Zack. Who?'

'I *could* be wrong, but somehow I don't think so. It was Peter Keegan.'

It was an exhilarating flight, skimming low over the wave tops, the downdraught creating a wild screen of spume all around, hiding the helicopter's outline in the wash of grey tones between sea and sky.

'Who's your pilot?' Lomax asked, shouting at Keegan above the roar and clatter of the engine.

'Superb, isn't he? Johan van Niekerk. Used to be a bush pilot before he joined the South African Army. An old friend, met him through Roddy Littlechild.'

'What the hell's he doing here with you?'

'Not just with me, Chris – with *Cuchulainn*! We've a few South Africans on the team! Didn't wanna stay there no more, so starting a new life in the province!'

'Helluva way to start a new life, isn't it? Joining up with you lot, with *Cuchulainn*! I'd have gone for the quiet life, Canada or New Zealand!'

Keegan grinned and Lomax couldn't help noticing how different he appeared from the last time they'd met in Stafford Prison. Now he looked alive and full of zest, as though he now had some purpose in life. 'The South Africans identify with us, Chris, that's the difference! A beleaguered country, but with everything to fight for! Old Protestant standards and values! We're the same breed!'

The pilot had swung landward now that they were well clear of the Anglo-Irish border. Dunany Point passed below. Empty fields and hedgerows were flashing by, so breathtakingly close that Lomax was sure if he reached out he could grab a handful of leaves from the treetops.

'No one's yet twigged how we get about,' Keegan explained. 'Johnny's set up a little flying courier service as cover and we can basically go where we please! We log official flight plans, of course, but no one ever checks! Why should they? Besides, when necessary we travel under radar level and avoid built-up areas!'

'Where the hell did you get the money?'

'Don't ask!'

After a while Keegan produced some strips of rag from the storage compartment. 'I think it best for all concerned if you put on blindfolds for the rest of the trip. Sorry, just a security precaution!'

It was never a pleasant experience to be blindfolded while in the company of men quite capable of cold-blooded killing, but Keegan continued to put them at ease, until the pitch of the engine changed and they became aware of the descent.

'Somewhere in the Irish Republic,' Keegan said in a deliberately dramatic voice, before leading them out of the helicopter and across rough ground.

No traffic noise, Lomax noted, and just the smells and sounds of the countryside. Once indoors the blindfolds were removed.

They were in a spacious farmhouse kitchen filled with the heavy aroma of fresh coffee which emanated from a pot on the wood-burning stove. Three men, younger than Keegan and Gavin, were already there, lounging in chairs and smoking.

'What's this, boss? Takin' prisoners now, are we?' one asked.

'That's Gaza,' Keegan introduced. 'Ex-Para, ex-con and a nut case. And his pal, Hutch. They were both doing stir in Stafford with me.'

Lomax remembered the news story about the helicopter jail break. 'God Almighty, Peter, that was you? I'd never have dreamt it in a million years.'

That amused Keegan as he indicated the third man; despite the cropped red hair, the resemblance was quite striking. 'And this is the man you were hunting all over Cannock Chase. My son, Tim.'

Young Keegan was unsmiling as he leaned forward to shake hands with some reluctance. 'No hard feelings?' he asked gruffly.

'I've no cause to complain,' Lomax said. 'The longer that search went on, the more money I made. You did well, both of you.'

Keegan said: 'Coming from Chris Lomax, that's a real compliment, son, believe me. He's the best.'

Lomax said: 'But obviously not as good as I thought I was. We realised what had happened eventually, but you were well away by then.'

'I needed a breathing space,' Keegan explained, 'and time to move freely and get things set up.'

But Tim was looking decidedly unhappy. 'So why are they here, Da? Did something go wrong?'

Keegan took the coffee pot from the stove and began pouring the contents into a row of mugs lined up on the table. 'Well, something went different. Mission accomplished – King Billy's reign is over for good. But we'd just topped him when two

494

carloads of gunmen turned up. We saw them coming and just started zapping.'

'What d'you mean, gunmen?' Tim asked. 'Billy's boys?'

A shrug. 'We didn't stop to ask. Seemed a bit efficient to be any of Billy's hoods. Maybe Provos. Frankly, I just don't know. Anyway, we had to change plans in a hurry. Basically we all just ran. And obviously we couldn't leave Chris and Sam there with Billy's corpse – not after that shoot-out. They'd get caught up in a murder inquiry and God knows what as witnesses. Best to spirit them away, I decided. If they were never there, they won't be put on to give evidence against me and Stevie.'

The man called Gaza said darkly: 'There's only one way to make sure of that.'

Lomax didn't like that at all. He was aware just how easily a comment like that could turn attitudes of ruthless men concerned about their own survival. 'Like Peter said, we were never there. We saw nothing and no one.'

He was acutely aware of Browne's presence beside him, the questioning gaze of her eyes and the smell of fear on her.

'You say,' Gaza sneered.

Lomax turned to face him. 'Exactly that, big mouth. What d'you want me to do to prove it? Join your merry gang?'

'You could do worse,' Keegan interjected. 'Still looking for a job?'

That hurt, but it gave him an idea. 'Why, are you offering?'

Keegan didn't blink. 'Why not? We need the best and we can afford to pay for the best.'

'Chris, you can't join them!' Browne protested. She knew it was stupid, but it was out before she could check herself.

He turned on her sharply. 'Do shut it, Sam. This is none of your business. I think even you realise by now I'm not exactly cut out to be a solicitor's clerk. And I'm on my uppers.'

'And you'd be fighting for a worthwhile cause,' Keegan added, clearly taking to the idea. 'Fighting alongside fellow pros.'

But Gaza was still regarding Browne with hostility. 'Don't think we've need of no prissy lawyer though, boss.'

Lomax noticed the slight widening of her mad eye as she said slowly: 'On the contrary, the way you're all going that's exactly what you're going to need.'

'Okay, okay,' Keegan said quickly to defuse the situation. 'We can't expect Sam here to understand or respect exactly what we're fighting for. But I can tell you, she's a fine lawyer and a fighter.' He looked at Rattler. 'There'll be time enough for you to explain things to her. Win her round.'

'Time?' she asked, feeling suddenly more threatened than ever. 'We need to be getting back.'

'Back?' Keegan smiled. 'Back to where?'

'Ulster.'

'Not a good idea,' Lomax said.

'He's right,' Keegan added. 'Army Int was on to Spike here and Box was on to you.'

'How would you know?' Browne asked.

Stevie Gavin answered for him. '*Cuchulainn*'s got friends in very high places, including the RUC. It was known you wanted a meet with King Billy, that you were in the province.'

'And now King Billy's dead,' Keegan said, 'you and Chris could end up being squared away for murder, just like your client, Roddy. Or worse,' he added ominously. 'And don't think it couldn't happen.'

She gave a snort of derision. 'They wouldn't dare.'

Lomax said: 'Don't bet on it.' He turned to Keegan. 'Did you notice anything unusual about our attackers this morning?'

'Er – not especially.'

'The way they carried themselves, covered each other when a mag went dry . . . They'd had military training, specialist close-quarters stuff.'

'American.' All eyes turned on little Albie Nairn. Still in a state of shock, he was clutching his mug of coffee as if it was giving him physical comfort. 'I thought I heard American accents.'

'You thought fuck,' Gavin retorted. 'You with your head under your arms and your arse in the air.'

'Leave him be,' Keegan warned. 'Albie's never claimed to be a fighter; he's a planner. He was entitled to be scared shitless, he didn't even have a gun.'

Lomax said thoughtfully: 'It's not as preposterous as it sounds. A friend in 14 Int told me I was followed by a group of Americans when I was last over here. Maybe CIA, who knows? Somehow they're linked in with elements of MI5, although God knows how.'

Keegan nodded. 'I've heard similar reports – various US teams trying to push the peace process along.'

'Last year, some Yanks approached the Ulster Defenders, my group,' Gavin added. 'We told them to get stuffed.'

Browne regarded Lomax with increasing concern. 'Are you saying what I think you are, Chris?'

He took a cigarette pack from his pocket before answering. There was an uncharacteristic tremor in his fingers as he lit one of them. 'It's possible those people at the caravan park weren't out to get King Billy. Rather – somehow – they knew we were going to meet him and used him as bait to get to us.'

'What d'you mean, *get* to us?' she asked, hoping she was wrong.

He blew a ring that hovered magically over the table before dispersing. 'I mean get rid of us. Negotiate, that's the jargon.'

'God, Chris.' Now she sounded really scared.

'It could fit,' Keegan agreed. 'They wouldn't have been expecting Stevie and me to turn up at a critical moment and blow away their plans.'

'So,' Lomax concluded, 'returning to Belfast wouldn't be the smartest move.'

'But, Joe,' Browne remembered. 'He'll be worried, won't he?'

'Joe'll handle the situation, worried or not,' Lomax assured. 'He knows we'll make contact as soon as we can.'

'We can fly you back to the Welsh coast tomorrow,' Keegan promised. 'In good time for when Roddy's trial resumes. When is that?'

'Wednesday,' she replied.

'And how's it going?' He asked it casually, like an afterthought.

'How d'you think, Peter? No evidence from King Billy, none from you.'

Keegan's eyes hardened. 'Roddy and I are both fighting the

497

same enemy, Sam. A cowardly British Establishment with no stomach for standing up for itself. Christ, no wonder we lost an empire. Well, we're fighting back now. Dublin and the South's been crippled for weeks. Power lines down, rail tracks blown, gas pipelines and telecommunications . . .'

Lomax frowned. 'It's all been kept pretty quiet.'

For the first time Keegan looked less sure of himself. 'Well, you're not wrong there, Chris. I hadn't anticipated how efficient their news management would be.'

'That's why we've been forced to change tactics,' Gavin interrupted. 'Like I always said we should.'

'In what way?' Lomax asked.

'That's enough, Stevie,' Keegan intervened. 'The least said the better.' He straightened his back and forced a smile. 'Right, we'd best get our unexpected guests billeted. That includes you, Albie.'

Nairn looked bewildered. 'My wife will be expecting me for my tea.'

'Your car was left outside King Billy's caravan,' Keegan explained patiently. 'You'll be a wanted man. We'll let her know you're all right. But meanwhile you're in for the duration. The war has started.'

For a moment, the older man stared into his empty coffee mug, his hunched figure on the stool looking very lost and alone. He wondered if he was really the only one who understood what was coming. The predictions of Wallace McIlroy were echoing down the years from those early Frontline rallies. Predictions when the days would be as dark as night, the darkness caused by smoke from the burning and ransacking, the explosions and gun fire of the civil war that was about to tear the very soul out of his homeland. And now he would have to play his part, there was no escape.

Keegan said: 'We're a bit short on accommodation, but if some of us double up, it'll give us a spare room for Sam. And, Chris, I'm afraid I can only offer you the barn – if you don't mind sharing with a couple of horses.'

Browne noticed Stevie Gavin's stare; it made her flesh creep. There was no doubt he agreed with Gaza that she and Lomax were a liability that should be dispensed with. But after what, she wondered? Gaza's lascivious leer gave her a good idea. She said: 'If you don't mind, I'd like to stay with Chris.'

The smirk disappeared instantly from Gaza's face.

Keegan grinned. 'Fine, I'm sure Chris won't object. As long as you don't mind roughing it.'

She regarded them all coldly. 'I can rough it with the best of them.'

'I'm sure,' Keegan said. 'I've got some army-issue kit you can wear so you don't ruin that pretty outfit.'

Gaza's smirk returned.

Later Lomax and Browne were shown to the timber barn with its dirt floor and horse stalls built along one side. 'There's plenty of fresh straw and I'll have some bedding brought out; you'll be comfortable enough,' Keegan said. 'And you can light a fire, Chris, as long as you promise not to burn the place down.'

It was a relief to be left alone in the tranquillity of the old barn as a blood-red sun dipped behind the treeline.

Browne looked suddenly relaxed and dropped her shoulders. 'For a moment back there I thought they might decide to kill us.'

Lomax nodded. 'If it was down to Rattler or that guy Gaza, I think they would have. That's why I've said I'm interested in joining them.'

She stared at him, hardly believing. 'Oh, God, I'm sorry. My big size eights again. I didn't think.'

'That's okay. Your disapproval would be expected and at least it sounded genuine.'

'I didn't want to be left alone in there in case one of them did something. They probably trust you more than me.'

'And I thought it was because you couldn't bear to be parted,' he teased.

'Don't get any ideas, Chris.'

He didn't even bother to answer that, turning away to leave her staring at his back as he set about building a small fire. He made it in the earth floor using a ring of stones. A small pile of straw, bark scrapings and some cotton wool was all he used to get it going. She watched in silent fascination as he worked, patiently feeding the growing flames with larger scraps of collected wood. It was a mild night but it would have still been chilly without the extra flickering heat; once the embers began to glow it was almost cosy, the air rich with the smell of hay and hazy with woodsmoke. Tim brought in a couple of spare DPM camo smocks with the blankets, one of which Lomax hung up to create a snug corner behind the door. Mess tins of lamb stew followed and Lomax set a borrowed tin coffee pot amongst the embers.

They ate in silence, and he watched Browne, not too obviously, as she sat cross-legged opposite him, wolfing down the food. With her fair hair a soft muddle and tumbling in marked contrast against the greens, browns and sand colours of her camouflage jacket, he thought how much like a child she looked. A bit of a tomboy. Was that how she'd once been? He remembered her description of her childhood in India. Scampering about with the boys in just her knickers in the tender years before innocence was lost. Imagined her swinging on the branches of the tropical riverbank trees, dropping into the water with squeals of self-induced fright and helpless laughter.

For a moment he felt an inexplicable regret, almost an ache, that he hadn't known her then, hadn't shared those carefree days that moulded her, that made her what she was today. Had never known her before she'd become obsessed and driven, before she'd collected the baggage of life and lost hope around her.

'You're staring.'

He blinked. 'What? Sorry, I was miles away. Just wondering what you were like as a little girl.'

A half-smile. 'Sugar and spice.'

'I'm not sure I believe that.'

'Daddy loved his little girl.'

'Daddies always do.'

'Even when I was horrid.'

'Were you horrid?'

'You won't believe this, Chris, but I had my moments. My practice for being grown up. I never wanted to grow up.'

'I couldn't wait,' Lomax said.

'Little boy soldier, I bet.'

He laughed. 'Not far off. From tin soldiers to army cadets. It was in the family blood.'

'I'd like to have seen you in shorts.'

'No, you wouldn't. I didn't like girls.'

'I bet you were a cute little chap. Very happy.'

He grinned. 'Never happier than with an air rifle or catapult.'

She laughed aloud at that, it struck a chord. 'Somehow I *do* believe that. What about your parents?'

'Dead, some years. And yours?'

'Mum died last year. But Dad . . .' For a moment her voice faltered and he realised she was on the verge of tears. 'Sorry. No, Dad died a long time ago. He really was still quite young.'

There was a noise outside the barn door, someone's footsteps. Lomax glanced up to see van Niekerk standing with another coffee pot in his hand. 'Replen,' he said. 'Hope I'm not interrupting anything.'

'No,' Browne said quickly. 'We were just about to start our camp-fire singsong. Want to join in?'

He dropped onto his haunches and placed the second pot beside the first. 'Camp-fire singsongs. God, that takes me back to the bush.' He laughed at the memory. 'With the army in Rhodesia. Great times. I thought you might do with this.' He fished in the bellows pocket of his combat trousers and produced a plastic bottle of Scotch.

Browne's eyes lit up. 'Oh, God, could I do with a shot of that.'

'Sam's an alcoholic,' Lomax explained helpfully, and shifted sideways to avoid the glancing blow.

'We haven't had a chance to speak,' van Niekerk said. 'I wondered how Roddy's trial was going?'

'Keegan said you used to know Roddy,' Lomax recalled.

'Know him?' van Niekerk replied. 'We were close mates. He was best man at my wedding. Don't get much closer than Roddy and me. In fact, we first met when he'd just come out to Rhodesia. God, when was that? Hard to believe it's over twenty-five years.'

'You served together in the Rhodesian Army?' Browne asked.

'Yeah, we had our moments with the "terrs", the Communist guerrillas. Later, when Roddy returned home to Ulster, I went south to join the South African security police. I was asked to set up a special unit and invited Roddy to come and join me.'

Lomax said: 'Yes, Roddy's told me about you. I just couldn't place the name.'

'Do I gather the trial's not going well?' van Niekerk asked.

Brown explained the situation while the South African listened in careful silence, passing round the whisky bottle.

When Browne finished talking, he said: 'I'm sorry, Sam, truly I am. Give him my best when you see him. And wish him all the luck in the world.'

'I'm afraid he's going to need it,' Lomax said.

Van Niekerk's expression was solemn. 'He's not the only one.'

'What, you?' Browne asked.

The man grimaced. 'Yeah, well, my own stupid fault. Getting mixed up with this lot.'

'Why did you?' Lomax asked.

'Seemed like a good idea. There was nothing left for ex-military like me in South Africa and the witch hunts had begun. And, well, me and others have always had a fascination with Ulster. There were quite a few Ulstermen like Roddy in Africa. It seemed to many of us they faced similar problems. Isolated in their way from a world that didn't understand, much less care. So when the crunch came, and Tim Keegan got in touch, asking for my help to spring his father who I'd known when he lived in Jo'burg for some time, well, it seemed like the right thing to do. The *Cuchulainn* idea sounded a bold and courageous move that might actually force a lasting peace. Their plans were subtle, clever. No one was going to get hurt.'

'But?' Lomax asked.

'It's not working out,' van Niekerk said. 'Not going the way we planned. There's this news blackout, no one knows the extent of the damage we're causing, and our demands – essential to the plan – have not been fully revealed by the media.' There was exasperation in his voice. 'Keegan's losing control. It's moving into Rattler's hands and soon the gloves will be

502

coming off. It'll be bombs and bullets, political assassinations, the works. Then the ethnic cleansing will begin.' Browne looked horrified.

'You've seen mild-mannered little Albie. He explained it to me. They've had twenty-five years of this and it's got to change. Says the only answer is to drive the Catholics out and torch their houses so they can't come back. Albie's convinced now it's the only solution.'

'Sounds more like Hitler's final solution,' Browne said. 'It's horrible, like Bosnia.'

Van Niekerk shrugged. 'Does it help that Albie was crying when he told me this? Said some of his best friends were Catholics, but it was no good, they'd still have to go. There was no other way now to achieve lasting peace.'

'There'd be civil war,' Lomax said darkly.

'Albie knows that. They all do. I think they've finally accepted it as inevitable. And when it comes, it'll spread across the border to engulf the whole of Ireland. They've come to believe that if Loyalists want their freedom, they'll eventually have to fight for it. And the sad thing is, they're probably right.'

Van Niekerk sighed deeply. 'Anyway, it's not exactly what I was anticipating. It's all gone a bit sour as far as I'm concerned.'

'You could get out,' Browne suggested.

'And go where? Not back to Rhodesia or South Africa, that's for sure. Besides a promise is a promise.' His grin was a little forced. 'Hell, they've got no one else knows how to fly choppers.'

He glanced then at his watch, deciding it was time to turn in for the night. At the doorway, he paused: 'Incidentally, Chris, that was a good move of yours to show an interest in joining us. Rattler was all for having you both topped.' Browne blanched. 'I think that swung it. If I was you I'd stay on until the lady's safely away from here. You can always change your mind later.'

Then he was gone.

'Christ, did he really mean that?' she breathed.

'Sounded like it. So I wasn't mistaken.'

'I don't want to leave you behind tomorrow.'

He was touched by the concern in her eyes and the dancing

light of reflected flames. His arm slipped around her shoulder and he urged her closer, brushing his lips against her cheek. 'I'll be okay.'

She turned to face him, her gaze mesmeric as though trying to understand something. His feelings, or her own? They both knew it at that moment, moving imperceptibly towards each other without a word being spoken. So close. Her lips parting a fraction and her eyelids fluttering momentarily like butterflies settling on a leaf. The smell of her filled his nostrils; not the usual smell of soap-scrubbed skin and a trace of perfume. After the traumas of the day, there was a raw earthiness, the smell of sweat and fear mingled with the natural fragrance of her hair.

He felt her lips on his even before they touched, remembered their taste, anticipating the sweetness of her tongue, the hint of whisky and tobacco. His loins stirred as his mouth came down on hers and he thought he heard her sigh.

'NO!' She pulled away suddenly. 'God, Chris, what is it with you? Whenever we're alone you try it on. I wanted you here for protection, not for a bloody screw.' She was trembling in her anger, her eyes accusing, her chest heaving in indignation.

Twenty-one

He stared back at her, still recoiling from her outburst. Christ, could he never interpret her signals right?

Her breathing slowed. 'This is hardly the time, the place . . .'

Something snapped in his head, pent-up emotion of being taunted and tantalised for so long exploding in anger. 'When are you going to stop playing these stupid games, Sam? It's never the right time or place with you, is it? What are you trying to do to me? Whoever named you Cruella got it right. Do you really loathe me that much?'

She seemed genuinely taken aback at that. 'No, Chris, you know I don't.'

He tilted his head to one side. 'Do I? Well, I thought I did. So what is it? Why are you so scared frigid to let yourself go?'

'I don't know what you mean,' she protested.

'I think you do. I think the prospect of love, of a relationship scares you silly. I think you're afraid of another failure. What is it? Two marriages down the tubes? God, well, I'm hardly surprised at that. I can see now what the poor bastards had to endure.'

'How dare you!'

'You're terrified of love and terrified of your own emotions. So you bury yourself in your work, in good causes, instead of getting yourself a life. You're working yourself into an early grave. For God's sake, stop hating yourself, because if you don't it'll kill you.'

She was reeling; it showed in her face. The mad eye up and a snarl on her lips like an animal at bay; barking crazy and fighting back in the only way she knew. 'You just see me as another conquest, another notch on the bedpost. To you I'm just another sodding challenge, another mountain to climb. C'mon, Chris, why the hell should you want to screw me? A bloody dried-up old spinster!' Her voice was quavering when she

505

stopped abruptly, realising what she had just said. She was visibly shaken and the sudden silence was stunning.

Lomax swallowed. 'Sam, you can't believe that. You are the most beautiful creature I've ever known.'

She blinked, tears clinging like jewels to her lashes, her mouth open. Speechless.

He grinned. 'Sure, not the *youngest* most beautiful creature I've ever known. And sometimes it saddens me that I never knew you in your first flush of youth, in your adolescence.'

At that she gave a dry half-chuckle and sniffed, trying to recapture some composure. 'I had terrible pimples.'

His eyes narrowed. 'Maybe that's it. You must know just how beautiful you are. You've got eyes and a mirror. You must see how heads turn when you walk into a room. A room full of beautiful women, yet it's always you they look at.'

Her voice was hushed, her gaze downward. 'You make it sound like it's something to be proud of. It's horrible. People expect . . .'

'Expect too much from a beautiful woman? Is that it? Men expect too much?'

'More than I can give, Chris. To you I might seem beautiful – whatever that is – but that's not what it feels like from this side. From this side I've always been gawky, teeth like a rabbit and no boobs. Men scare me, life scares me. I'm always getting things wrong, making a fool of myself or making enemies. Sometimes I feel . . .' For a moment she mouthed around words that wouldn't come. 'I feel so inadequate. At my job, at life itself.'

A fragile silence settled between them as they both watched the flickering small flames of the fire. He wanted to hold her, to comfort her. But he'd been down that road once too often already.

At length, he said: 'Once before I made a promise to get out of your life, but I came back. That was a mistake.'

Her lower lip crumpled like that of a crestfallen child. 'What d'you mean, Chris?'

'After Roddy's trial, whatever the result, there'll be no need for us to meet again. And this time I won't come back.'

She felt as though she had been pummelled, the stuffing

506

knocked out of her. She found herself staring dumbly at his back as he shook out his bedding, pulled off his shirt and snuggled into the blanket.

It seemed as though he was asleep in an instant. Maybe he was, maybe not. But how peaceful and content he looked, she thought. Like a little boy. Serene. Was it the relief at having finally made his decision to walk out of her world?

His eyes opened. Something had disturbed him. Had he been asleep for a minute or an hour? He shook his head to clear his mind, propping himself on one elbow. What was it?

The fire still spat and crackled a few feet away. It can't have been long then, unless Browne had added another log.

'I couldn't sleep,' she said.

He squinted in the direction of her voice, into the dancing shadows. It took a moment until the firelight lit the arched line of her neck and picked out the glistening whites of her eyes. Her shape was hidden by the DPM camouflage jacket draped over her shoulders, only the contrasting splash of fair hair visible as she knelt just a few feet in front of him.

She saw his look of momentary consternation as he focused in the dark. Knew now that he would see that she was almost naked beneath the jacket, would see the sheen of perspiration on the skin between her breasts. Felt his eyes penetrating the gloom, the confusion in his expression as he registered the ivory-silk boxers she wore.

'What is this, Sam?' His voice was a low growl.

'I'm frightened.'

'Of what?'

'Of everything. This mess we're in, the danger. Roddy going down.' Her hair floated around her as she shook her head in despair. 'I'm frightened of what Grisewold might do to us.' Her voice trembled. 'But mostly, I'm frightened of myself. Of losing you.'

'Don't wind me up, Sam,' he warned.

She shut her eyes at his words, convincing herself that she hadn't heard them. Not now, not at this moment. Not now that she'd decided. Without opening her eyelids again she reached out and took his right hand, lifting it from the blanket. She carried it very slowly, but very deliberately towards her. The small white fist of her hand brushed away the edge of the jacket and pressed his palm hard against her breast. She held it there until she felt her nipple harden in response, and knew that he knew.

'No more games, Chris,' she whispered and left his hand where it was as she reached across for him. And as he took her in his arms and rolled her over to lie on top of him, her jacket fell away.

'Sam,' he said, that was all.

She peered down at his face just inches below her chin. 'Yes, Chris.'

'I want you.'

An impish half-grin. 'I know, I can feel it.'

'Some things can't lie.'

'Don't expect too much, I'm not very good. Be patient with me. I don't know what to do, you know, not really. Teach me. I don't want to die dried up and unloved.'

At that moment his heart ached. This was Sam Browne, the real woman behind the façade. This woman, so frightened and too long alone, with tears in her eyes and trails of mascara down her cheeks. Why hadn't it been him and not two other men who had found and abandoned her first?

'Teach me,' she said again. Plaintive.

What could he say? 'I knew a man once, in the Regiment for a short while. Name of Kurt Mallory. Had a way with women – made even whores fall in love with him.'

'Let me be your whore.'

Lomax said: 'He believed the secret was just to concentrate on giving the other person pleasure. Simple as that.'

'Let me give you pleasure.' Her hand moved down across his chest. 'Tell me what you like.'

'No, you tell me what you like first.'

Her eyes were unblinking white and the irises dancing flecks of green amid the blue. So, so close. 'Take me from behind. Like a dog.'

A light frown creased his brow. 'I don't think so.'

'I want you to treat me like dirt.'

'Sam . . .'

'I deserve it, the way I've behaved to you. Besides . . .'

'What?'

'You asked me what I wanted.'

'When I make love to you for the first time, I want to see your face.'

'Then, afterwards?'

He didn't answer, but rolled her gently off his chest and over until he had her embraced beneath him.

The next half-hour passed in a haze. It was like a sweet hallucination under morphine, all shadows and golden light from the dying flames. Aware only of the tentative exploration of her fingers, the whispering touch of her hair on his skin, her moans. But when he finally drew aside the silk boxers and penetrated her, she froze. Her eyes were cloudy with concern, almost frightened, staring at him, knowing that this was the moment and that her muscles had involuntarily contracted, barring him at the very gate.

'YES!' she said.

And he pushed through until she yielded with a small cry, muffled by the small fist that she clenched at her mouth. Then slowly the waves began to mount, wave upon wave, taking their time until her head was tossing from side to side. As the momentum gathered, with increasing abandon it became a frenzied and almost violent coupling. When she came, several minutes after him, the power of release was tumultuous, her teeth sinking into his shoulder and tearing his flesh in her fevered climax.

Then everything went still, the dream dying away as all dreams do, but this time the vision and the memories lingered.

'Stay inside,' she whispered breathlessly. 'I'm afraid if you go, you'll never return.'

'I'll return.' He smiled. 'Trust me.'

'I do.' She relented then, and allowed him to withdraw. 'God, what have I done to your shoulder? You need stitches.' He rummaged for his cigarettes while she dabbed at the blood with her handkerchief. 'God, you don't think I'm a vampire do you?'

'Ah, that's it. I knew there was something.' He handed her one of the cigarettes and lit them.

They lay together for some time. Not talking, just getting used to the new experience of being this close to each other for the first time. Eventually, he asked her what he'd wanted to know since their very first meeting. 'What is it that's made you what you really are, Sam?' The admiration was plain in his eyes as well as obvious and total bemusement. 'Such a fighter for the underdog.'

'Oh, that.' She drew deeply on the cigarette and exhaled, closing her eyes. 'You really want to know?'

'Really.'

'It's not something I'm used to telling people, especially in law circles. They'd think I was the blindly biased daughter of a father who betrayed his country.'

'Your father? You said he was in the RAF.'

She reached for the whisky bottle and examined the last remaining inch. 'That's right. Then he spent years on second-ment to the Indian Air Force, helping it to develop and modernise – that's where I was born. Afterwards he was posted to RAF Khormaksar in Aden as Wing Commander, Admin, or "Wingco, drains" as he called it. That was in 1965, the year that Ian Smith's Rhodesian government declared UDI – its Unilateral Declaration of Independence.'

Lomax nodded as she swigged from the bottle and handed it to him. 'I remember. Harold Wilson was Prime Minister.'

'Wilson planned to send in troops to seize it back, which would have meant flying them to Africa via Aden. It caused an absolute furore at the base, apparently, a near mutiny at the prospect of the British fighting their own kith and kin so soon after the last war when Rhodesian pilots fought on our side.

'The C-in-C Middle East and Air Officer Commanding told London what they thought in no uncertain terms. Dad was furious too. He was putting up a visiting MI6 man at the time and they were lunching at the Rock hotel. They'd had a bit to drink and the argument got heated, especially when the MI6 man denied what was planned. Dad shouted in the crowded restaurant that he'd seen the effing Top Secret order, and produced a copy, waving it for all to see. Made it plain no flights to Rhodesia would be refuelled or serviced while he was at the base.'

'Like father, like daughter,' Lomax murmured.

'The government backed down, but they wanted a scapegoat, to set an example. My father was court-martialled for conduct prejudicial. Cashiered out of the RAF after years of exemplary service. No pension, no nothing. And no one lifted a finger to help. We returned to England penniless. Dad never really got over it. He died four years later. He was only forty-nine. When he really, desperately needed help, there was no one.'

'And you've fought for the underdog ever since.'

'When people are that far down, Chris, I'm often the only friend they have in the world.'

He was beginning to understand.

'At least Roddy's got Evie and Noel and you.'

'And now you've got me, Sam. If you want me.'

'I want.'

It had taken Jerry Tucker hours to get to sleep, tossing and turning in the narrow bed of his rented bedsit in Lisburn. Oblivion had finally closed in on him, only to be rudely shattered by the insistent trilling of the bedside telephone.

He snatched up the handset. 'Yes.'

'It's Joe.'

'Thank Christ for that! Where the hell are you?'

'A church car park.' He gave the location.

'We need to talk, urgent.'

'Agreed, but I've got no wheels. Correction, I've got the wheels you lent us, but the car's been clocked.'

'Who by?'

'Dirty Harry.'

'Shit, that explains it. Never mind. I'll be with you in twenty to thirty minutes.'

'*Ciao.*'

Tucker tumbled out of bed in a hurry and began pulling on jeans and a sweater over his pyjamas. If he'd slowed up physically over the years, he'd never moved faster than this night. He was out of his bedsit in five minutes flat and had his car out of the garage in record time. He crashed the gears and hit the gas pedal.

In just twenty-one minutes, he pulled up on the main road alongside the deserted car park. Only one car in the entire site, the pool car he'd lent Lomax.

His spirits collapsed. Normally a car like that left after hours would have drawn the attention of the RUC. And when it was known to be a pool car, someone would have collected it. The fact that it was still there meant someone knew it was there and was watching it.

Tucker's heart suddenly jumped as the big face with the walrus moustache appeared at the passenger window.

'God, you gave me a fright,' he said as Monk scrambled in.

'Let's get out of here, Jerry. I've been sitting under that fucking bush since dark. Feel like I've put down roots.'

Tucker swung out, checked his mirror for signs of a following vehicle, and headed off with no clear idea where to go.

Monk said: 'Something's gone wrong. Chris and Sam went to see King Billy and never came back to the car.'

'I know.'

'What?' He took a moment to absorb Tucker's answer. 'Are they all right? What's happened?'

'King Billy's dead. Assassinated.'

'Fuck me.' He shook his head in bewilderment. 'You don't think Chris . . .?'

Tucker shook his head. 'Two carloads of gunmen descended on Baker's caravan hideaway. There was some shoot-out and at the end of it the big fella was dead. The gunmen drove off and some people – who must have been with Baker before they arrived – were seen legging it across fields. One was a woman.'

'You mean Sam?'

'The description fits. Another of them could well have been Chris. Right age, build and hair colour.'

'What happened to them?'

'Vanished. Anyway, no sign as yet.'

'And they weren't injured?'

'Not as far as I know.'

512

'What about the gunmen? Who were they, any idea?'

There was a tormented look in Tucker's eyes. 'My boys just started to take an interest when the Security Service stepped in and took over. Complete clamp down. They're handling it all with an RUC Special Branch team. Frankly, Joe, it stinks of rotten fish.'

'Meaning?'

Tucker found he could no longer concentrate on his driving. He pulled into the roadside and stopped abruptly. He turned to face Monk straight. 'Look, Joe, I could be wrong about all this. I mean 14 Int – my lads – are being kept well out of all this. But some of them overheard some joke about Top Guns at the OK Corral.'

'Meaning?'

'The sort of disparaging stuff our people say when Americans foul up.'

'The gunmen?'

'I think so. And if that's true, it might not have been King Billy they were after. This special CIA unit is operating with Dirty Harry and King Billy was his man. *If* it was them, they might have been out to get Chris and maybe even Browne.'

'Why, for God's sake?'

'It would bugger Roddy's trial for a start. Everything's going chaotic over here, Joe, you wouldn't believe it! This *Cuchulainn* mob are really making their presence felt.' He hesitated.

'Yes?'

Intensity burned in Tucker's eyes. 'This really is classified. Top Sodding Secret. In the past week three top Provos have been assassinated.'

Monk blinked. 'I've heard . . .'

'Nothing. I know. Sinn Fein's keeping buttoned and so's the Northern Ireland Office with the Forum elections looming. But it's happened. Not well-known names, but the real power brokers.' He sighed and leaned back against his seat. 'Something's out of control, Joe, and I don't know what it is. But it's shitting well dangerous and you and Chris and Roddy are somehow caught up in the middle of it.'

Monk stared ahead through the windscreen at the line of

streetlights marching away to infinity. Suddenly it was hot and airless in the confines of the car. He wound down the window. 'You too, Jerry,' he said quietly. 'If we're caught up, so are you now.'

Tucker nodded. 'Yes, I suppose I am. It won't take long to work out who gave you the pool car. I'm finished.'

'I'm sorry.'

His friend sucked in his cheeks, deep in concentration. 'Don't be, Joe. 'Cause I don't give a shit any more. I didn't sign up for all this sort of crap. I'll be well out of it. You just can't trust anyone any more.' His jaw tightened as he came to a decision. 'If I'm not arrested the moment I put my foot inside HQ tomorrow, then I'll ask for a posting back to the mainland and get out of the army as soon as I can. But you,' he added, glancing at Monk, 'you're the one with the problem. You need to get out of the province fast, before Box or the Yanks – whoever – realise you're not going back to that pool car.'

Monk nodded. 'I was thinking of making it over the border on foot, get a bus to the ferry port.'

'No,' Tucker said suddenly, 'that'll take too long if Box are looking for you. You've got to move fast. Take my car.'

Monk was startled. 'Well, Christ, thanks, Jerry, but that won't help.'

'And my ID.'

'You can't do that.'

'I've just done it. Just shave that tash off and you'll get by. Drive over the border. Tonight. Get the first ferry from Cork. You can post my ID back when you get home. I'm in such deep shit anyway, losing my ID won't make it any worse. No one's going to be looking for my private car or me while I'm still around.' Then he remembered. 'Sam was asking about that retired MI5 chief, Walter Grey. His real name is de Witt. Apparently he's in a hospice. Somewhere in south Hampshire. It's all I could get.'

'Great! You're a pal.'

'If we haven't got each other, Joe, old comrades, who the fuck have we got?'

The return journey to Lisburn took a more leisurely thirty-five minutes. Two streets away from Tucker's digs they pulled in and Monk took the driver's seat. Tucker leaned in at the window. 'Take care, Joe, and watch your back.'

'Sure. And if you get word from Chris or Sam – '

'You'll be the first to hear. Don't worry, Chris can look after himself.'

'That's what I'm afraid of.'

The big man let out the clutch and the exhaust burbled softly away into the mild moist night.

Tucker stood and watched the receding taillights until they were swallowed up in the darkness. Now he felt totally alone. He glanced around the familiar suburban street. No one and nothing stirred. So deceptive, he knew. Such an ordinary place, Northern Ireland, which made events here over the years all the more extraordinary.

He'd seen it all, and suddenly the prospect of leaving for good seemed to lift some great burden from his shoulders. As he began the short walk to his home, his feet felt light as though they were floating. A new life ahead, beckoning. No more danger and deceit, no more not trusting any human, on your side or the other. Indeed, sometimes he hardly knew which side was which any more. Away from covert ops, the dirty tricks, the killing. Away from the fucking rain.

He must have been watching the car for several seconds before he realised it was moving.

It had been parked facing him, just beyond the house where he had his bedsit. A dark nondescript model with tinted windows. And no lights, because if it had had its lights on he'd have realised it was starting to roll silently forward, its soundproofed engine generating no more than a murmur.

He froze. For a second he considered running back the way he'd come. Or should he race forward, get to the house, hit the panic button? Twenty yards, no contest.

The indecision cost him vital seconds.

With a life and will of their own, his legs crashed into action, propelling him forward with the fear-induced power of an Olympian sprinter. The headlights of the oncoming car burst over him, showering him with blinding light. Lungs heaved to bursting as he stretched every sinew for that extra inch, that extra millisecond that would get him to safety. Past the neighbour's garden wall, past the gate pillar, those twin orbs like the light tunnels of an out-of-body experience. Bearing down on him, devouring him.

Sharp, hard right-hand turn. Into the garden, across the crazy paving of the drive. Now the car behind him, engine screaming as it mounted the pavement ramp, illuminating the entire front of the house.

Heaving for breath, he stopped before the garage doors and turned. He couldn't believe it. It was still coming, on top of him.

He scarcely felt the pain as the bumper crashed into his thighs and ground his bones and flesh into the unrelenting steel of the up-and-over doors. The screaming, mind-numbing agony only came after the driver crunched into reverse gear and the car backed off a fraction. It blew his mind like a tiny bomb planted in his skull.

His head filled with noise as the car slammed forward again. Again and again.

Thomas Harding, a signals lieutenant at headquarters of Western Command at Custume Barracks, Athlone, stared at the secret signal in front of him.

He felt a sick, sinking feeling in his stomach as he read it over again and the list of attachments to it. His eyes were dizzy and unfocused as he scanned the papers again and again for one word. In vain.

That word was Exercise, and it wasn't there.

Of course, it was not his job to reason why, as the poem went. Just to do and die. Wasn't that it?

Numbly he read over the units to be put on immediate standby. Not forty-eight hours, not twenty-four. Immediate. Christ, what was going on? He could imagine the panic, the confusion. Depleted battalions desperately trying to contact members on leave, or fly back subunits from training exercises or United Nations duties in some far-flung place. Workshops sweating to get every vehicle repaired and serviced to operational standards, getting the ugly wheeled French Panhard carriers, like something out of Gothic science fiction, up and running, the twin 7.62mm machine guns oiled and ready. The whole of 4 Brigade, including 1st and 28th at Galway and Donegal, Western Command – the entire goddamn shooting match – on a war footing and on the march north to join the regular border patrols. Reserves called up.

Harding flipped the page. Again he couldn't believe it. Similar orders for 2 Brigade in Dublin, the other border command, scrambling troops from the Collins and Cathal Brugha barracks. Even 6 Brigade from Curragh and Kilkenny and – he blinked again – Southern Command's 1 Brigade from County Cork. All the way up to the border. Talk about the big push, this was reading like all-out war.

And if he needed confirmation, there it was. The long list of field artillery barracks – McGee, Murphy, Columb, McCann and Dun Di Mhaoiliosa in Galway. Nine field artillery regiments. Heavy mortars and 105mm light guns. Plus the Air Defence Regiment.

He glanced back at the opening preamble of the message. '*To aid the civil power . . .*' The usual phrase. Balls, Harding thought, you don't deploy artillery and the Air Defence Regiment for that. This was armed forces *primary* role, this stuff. '*To defend the state against external aggression.*'

Was all this some administrative oversight? Or was it a reality training exercise when they would only be told to stand down when they reached their designated holding-up areas on the start line at the border? Just what the hell was it all about? He imagined the telephones at Dublin headquarters would be jammed with senior officers requesting clarification.

There was always one squadron of the Cavalry Corps' Panhards – No. 4 out of Longford – designated to support border security operations, he knew. But according to the signal, two other squadrons had been mobilised, one from Fermoy and the heavy mob, the 1st Tank Squadron of Scorpion light tanks from Curragh with supporting Timoney armoured personnel carriers.

No mention here of the army's Ranger Wing. In previous

exercises, the country's special forces had been earmarked to seize strategic buildings and facilities in the North. They included the ports of Warrenpoint, Belfast and Larne, Aldergrove airport, and all broadcasting studios and military barracks.

That in itself was strange, Harding thought, until he considered that if this was for real, the Ranger Wing's orders would be passed directly and secretly to their headquarters.

It was a relief when Major O'Hare, a bluff and stocky career officer, entered the ops room. His usually cheerful expression was clouded by genuine concern.

'Is this for real, sir?' Harding ventured.

The middle-aged officer shook his head slowly, clearly not believing himself what was going on. 'I don't know, Tom, honest I don't. Sure, no one seems to know and that's a fact. Everyone's in the dark.'

'Surely we wouldn't take on the English – not now? Not when they've got the elections and Peace Forum coming up.'

'Wouldn't make sense,' O'Hare agreed. 'Unless, of course, this is all about sealing off the border against the *Cuchulainn* group. You know, make a big public show. Because that's all it'd be. You don't stop saboteurs with armour and artillery.'

'That's what concerns me. It's more like a rerun of Autumn Gold, but on a much bigger scale, and we all know what the ultimate purpose of that was to be.'

The major nodded. 'Save the Catholic enclaves. Seize the facilities with special forces, grab the artillery base in Coleraine.' He paused, trying to recall the detail. 'The armour in north Belfast, then flying columns straight up the M1 to Belfast. Cutting off British reinforcements to the second pincer in the west which would have seized Derry, Strabane and Enniskillen.'

'Could that ever have worked?'

'I doubt it, we couldn't have held out for long. But the embarrassment to Whitehall and the international furore would have brought some kind of result. Diplomatic intervention, a UN presence, who knows?'

'So why now?'

The major smiled uneasily. 'My guess is it's to frighten the

English. A bit of good old sabre-rattling, Put pressure on them over the peace process and this bloody *Cuchulainn* threat.'

Now Harding felt a little reassured. 'Well, it certainly frightened me for a moment or two.'

It was then that Harding's shift finished and the replacement duty officer arrived. After updating the newcomer, Harding made his way towards the canteen. By the row of public wall phones he hesitated.

His was a Protestant family that had lived in Eire for generations; they lived happily amongst their Catholic neighbours, but also had many Protestant friends and acquaintances in the North.

It was to one of these that Harding felt compelled to make a brief call. A rendezvous was agreed. Then the signals officer hung up, turned away from the canteen and began walking towards the car park. The photocopied battle orders felt as though they were burning in his breast pocket.

He looked up from the mess tin of coffee bubbling on the embers. 'Breakfast.'

She was in the shadows, her hair up and stripped to the baggy camouflaged trousers that were several sizes too large. They emphasised the narrowness of her waist and the elegant arch of her back which she'd kept carefully to him as she sluiced with water from a galvanised bucket. Before turning, she replaced and buttoned the jacket.

'That's better. I haven't washed like that since I was a Girl Guide.'

'No cracked mirror then?'

'What?' Instinctively her hand went to her cheek as she realised what he meant. 'Oh, no make-up. Yes, ghastly, isn't it?'

'Not from where I'm sitting. Just makes you look – more ordinary. Vulnerable.'

'Ugly,' she helped out.

'Stop fishing for compliments and get your coffee. At least you didn't put your teeth in a jar.'

She took the tin mug he'd filled. 'Not while you were looking,' she replied lightly and sipped at it, scalding her lip.

He decided to brave the question he had to ask. 'No regrets, Sam? About last night.'

'*Je ne regrette rien.*' She took the cigarette he offered. 'Except for the straw up my arse and other uncomfortable places.'

'Sorry about that.'

'You're an animal.'

'I didn't mean to be.'

'That's a compliment,' she replied mockingly. 'I prefer animals to humans.'

'Not all?'

A hint of a smile. 'No, not any more. And maybe I'm getting too old for regrets.'

'Good.' He reached forward and kissed her gently on the lips. She didn't resist and, when he pulled back, she held his hands to her cheeks.

'I don't want you to stay here, Chris. Now I've found you – God, I really don't want to lose you.'

He couldn't explain what those words meant to him. After losing Fran, he'd wondered if he'd ever hear them again. 'You won't, Sam. But if I stay on for now it'll persuade them that we're not a threat. Half of Keegan's men were in favour of topping us as a security risk. They're all so far in now that another couple of killings would make no difference.'

She stared down at her coffee. 'I suppose so.'

'I'll wait my chance. In a few days, when the situation's right, I'll slip away and rejoin you in London.'

He'd barely said the words when Keegan and Rattler appeared at the barn door with Spike.

'Still staying with us, Chris?' Keegan asked. 'Or changed your mind?'

'I gave my word,' Lomax replied, adding with more humour than he felt, 'as long as we can agree a price.'

'I'm sure we can.' Keegan turned to Browne. 'Johan's gone to get the helicopter from the airfield. He'll touch down here to pick you up in about fifteen minutes. I want you packed, in civvies, and ready to jump aboard. Then he'll drop you on a secluded part of the Welsh coast. You'll have to make your own way from there.' He turned to Lomax. 'Come and let's talk while she gets sorted.'

As the men sauntered towards the nearby copse where van Niekerk would be landing, Keegan said: 'Square with me, Chris. Can she be trusted?'

'To keep her mouth shut about you and *Cuchulainn*? She's no reason to do otherwise. She *is* in the middle of a murder trial.'

'Never trust a woman,' Stevie Gavin said darkly. 'Can't help themselves. I never tell my women anything.'

Not out of the wood just yet, Lomax thought. 'Sam's different. Besides, if she talks she puts herself at the scene of King Billy's murder. She knows damn well MI5 would love to tie her in with that. Just think what her arrest now would do for Roddy's trial.'

Keegan appeared to accept the logic of that.

Lomax said quickly: 'So what about the contract?' He sounded eager.

'Not in writing.' A joke. 'We're paying mercenaries like Johan a grand a week. And a two-grand bonus if you finish a three-month tour.'

'You make it sound like a regular army.'

Suddenly Keegan's eyes were very serious. 'That's what it'll become if all this ends in civil war. And I think it will.'

'Cold feet already?' Gavin goaded Lomax, then turned as he heard the approach of van Niekerk's helicopter. 'Here he comes.'

The Agusta came in low over the treetops, then swaggered to a stationary hover before descending into the clearing.

'Where is she?' Keegan asked, turning.

Browne was running across from the barn, her shoulder bag flapping.

'Hurry up!' Gavin shouted. 'Every second he's down, there's a risk of being compromised.'

'Sorry,' she said breathlessly, 'I got taken short.'

Gavin's eyes rose heavenward.

'Good luck with the trial,' Keegan said. 'Do your best for him.'

'I will.' She turned to Lomax and kissed him briefly on the lips. 'I'll miss you.'

Then she was gone, bent low, and scampering beneath the thrashing rotors. No sooner was she aboard than the helicopter lifted skyward then, canting over, set course for the Irish Sea.

As it shrank from view, Lomax felt an ache in his chest, a pain that was almost physical. He stared blindly until he was left watching an empty sky.

'Let's get back,' Keegan said.

The rest of the morning was spent going over future plans for the next wave of operations against the Republic.

Lomax soon detected a difference in approach between Keegan and Stevie Gavin. While Keegan had masterminded the sabotage plan, it was Rattler who'd begun targeting members of the Provisional IRA and INLA leadership. The two men were co-operating but there was an underlying antagonism and the strain was beginning to show. Rattler made no secret of the fact he thought they should begin assassinating police and military in Eire and plan to take out some major political figures.

The argument was in full swing when van Niekerk arrived back from the airfield where he had parked the helicopter. It was a relief to see him.

'One fightin' lawyer back on the mainland,' the pilot announced. 'She's quite a girl, that one.'

'Impressed?'

'Could say.' He hesitated. 'Are you two an item?'

Lomax smiled. 'That's pretty hard to determine.'

Van Niekerk winked. 'Work at it. If you ask me, she's smitten. Thinks the sun shines out your backside.'

'It does.' And they both laughed, Lomax feeling particularly pleased to hear the South African's opinion.

The pilot helped himself to coffee and turned his attention to Gavin who was arguing for *Cuchulainn* to take a more aggressive stance.

'Problem is, Peter, no one *knows* what we're doing. But blow up a politician or two, or some gardai and that'll soon change.

Can't deny bodies on the street. That's what makes terrorism work. Terrorising.'

At that moment a car drew up outside and all eyes turned towards the door.

Lomax had not seen the man who entered before. He was tall and in his mid-thirties with neat dark hair and wary eyes; it did not surprise Lomax to learn later that he was a sergeant in the Royal Ulster Constabulary.

'So what's this news you're so excited about?' Keegan asked the new arrival.

The policeman extracted an envelope from the pocket of his jacket and slapped it on the table. 'I think we've finally stirred up the hornet's nest. Dublin's starting to do a little sabre-rattling. It's put the majority of army units on immediate alert for border manoeuvres. Our intelligence assessments indicate it's out of frustration over *Cuchulainn*'s activities. They think the Brits aren't doing enough to stop us.'

Keegan's grin was very wide. 'Shame they don't realise our HQ is behind their lines.' He picked up the envelope and shook out the photocopies of the Irish Army signals. Concern clouded his face as he read. 'Are you sure this isn't for real, Brian?'

'No way, even the Irish aren't that daft.'

Gavin jabbed a finger at the signal Keegan was holding. 'This is our golden opportunity!'

'What d'you mean?'

'That signal, does it give details of convoy routes, that sort of thing?'

His colleague glanced back at the papers. 'Seems to. Yes, the routes various columns will take. Copied to the Garda to keep the roads clear of traffic. Then timings and the location of marshalling points along the border.'

'Magic,' Gavin declared. 'So we pick on one of the columns and set up an ambush. Take 'em out and get the whole thing on video.' He grinned in triumph. 'I'd like to see Dublin or London keep the lid on *that*!'

Keegan looked up, uncertain, glancing at the faces gathered around the table. Gavin, Albie Nairn, Tim, Spike, Gaza, Hutch and the South Africans. And saw the smiles.

Their time had come.

Stevie Gavin turned to Lomax. 'And you?'

Despite the draining sense of dread in his gut, Lomax forced a grin. 'Count me in.'

That night, Albie Nairn and Keegan left with van Niekerk for the airfield. The helicopter would take them to some secret location over the border where apparently heavy weapons and anti-vehicle mines were stored. Meanwhile Gavin and the others pored over maps and the signal details to select their target.

Finally, the decision was made. The attack would go in the following night. They would take on the Irish Army's 1st Tank Squadron, or at least part of it. The elite, the *creme de la creme* of light reconnaissance tanks. It would be a day that Dublin would never forget and a day that the Loyalist paramilitaries would savour for ever.

At ten, the helicopter had still not returned and Lomax left the others to turn in. The barn suited him; there he could be alone with his thoughts.

He lit the fire and placed the coffee pot on the flames before sitting down and lighting a cigarette. His only concern was how best to get away and alert someone to what was going down. Armed pickets guarded the farm day and night. Given his training, that would be no great problem. But that would be if he left alone and he now had in mind to take one person with him. He'd have to be cautious though, not reveal his hand until his suspicions were confirmed.

The burden of responsibility was getting to him and he was feeling unaccountably weary. When he finally turned in that night, his last waking thoughts were of Sam Browne.

On the Tuesday morning he awoke to the bustle of activity outside and excited voices. During the night the helicopter had dropped Keegan, Spike and Nairn with supplies of heavy weapons. Now the mixed team of Ulstermen and South Africans were admiring and inspecting the formidable arsenal. Everything from handguns and assault rifles to anti-tank rockets, mines and heavy machine guns. Not the very latest designs but more than adequate for the purpose.

'How long have we got before the ambush?' he asked Keegan.

'Tonight, Chris. We cross our Rubicon at around midnight.'

God, Lomax thought, that gave him so little time.

The rest of the day was to pass in operational planning, creating a sand-pit model of the ambush area and weapons familiarisation. With the bantering and camaraderie, it was almost like old times. But not quite.

Time was running out and Lomax was starting to regret his decision not to leave the previous night. He had become the centre of attention, everyone wanting to draw on his experience and it was impossible even to attempt sneaking away.

That gave him only one hope, a telephone. There was one in the farmhouse but the use of that was severely restricted for security reasons. And only Tim and Rattler had their own mobiles.

So Lomax had no choice but to bide his time, even if that commodity was disappearing fast.

They stopped in mid-afternoon for a belated lunch break of sandwiches and coffee. Lomax wandered off to be alone, leaning against the fence and admiring the pastoral setting while he sipped from his coffee mug.

'Penny for them?'

He turned. Johan van Niekerk was standing behind him, a can of lager in one hand and a half-eaten sandwich in the other.

Lomax forced a smile. 'Just trying to get my head around this stuff. Going to war against Ireland tonight.'

Van Niekerk laughed. 'Hardly that. They won't be expecting it. It'll be a turkey shoot.'

'If it goes to plan.'

The South African raised an eyebrow. 'And it never does, right?'

'Your experience too, I expect?'

'You know how to make God laugh? Tell him your plans.' There was a bitter humour in the South African's chuckle. 'We'll have the Irish and British security forces down on us like a ton of bricks. I don't think we'll be able to continue like before. Events will take on their own momentum.'

'Sounds like you don't approve?'

Van Niekerk shrugged, cautious. He wasn't about to hand himself a death sentence by confessing his reservations to someone he hardly knew. 'I don't approve or disapprove. It's what's been decided. Fine. I'm not a general, just a foot soldier.' That engaging smile. 'If you can have a flying foot soldier.'

'But?' Lomax persisted. He had to know.

The man finished the last of his sandwich and accepted the cigarette Lomax offered. 'To be honest, it wasn't what I was expecting. I've followed the Loyalist cause for years, ever since Roddy Littlechild explained the situation to me back in Rhodesia all those years ago. Since then I've put my life on the line many times to protect a way of life. First Rhodesia – I still find it hard to call it Zimbabwe – and then South Africa. And both times I've lost.'

'And you're hoping Ulster will be third time lucky?'

Van Niekerk took a deep draught of tobacco smoke. 'I was feeling pretty down before Tim Keegan looked me up last year and put his proposition to me. That really cheered me up. I knew my life there was finished under black rule. Tim's visit seemed like – I don't know, providence. A message. A new life and new homeland. A future in my old age.'

'He told you his father's plans for *Cuchulainn*?'

'Sure.'

'It didn't put you off?'

Van Niekerk glanced sideways at him. 'Why should it? The sabotage plan sounded good. Give the Republic a thorough shaking up, make them do what they should have done years ago. And a clear set of political aims. And best of all, no one would get hurt. Probably like you, I've seen a lot of senseless killing in my time.'

'But now?'

He looked back out across the meadow. 'No one mentioned taking on the Irish Army. Brewing up innocent soldiers in their tanks. Like some boil-in-the-bag dish.' He almost spat the words with contempt. 'I've known many Irishmen in my time from North and South. It's killing your own.'

Lomax decided to take a gamble, more sure than ever now that he'd been right. Van Niekerk was wavering. 'It'll be worse if it all ends in civil war.'

'Yeah, and no one mentioned that. Didn't explain the way things would probably go.'

Push a little more, Lomax thought, one more little gamble. 'I get the feeling it's changed since Rattler came on the scene.'

Van Niekerk raised an eyebrow, unsure where Lomax was coming from. Was he being tested for loyalty? Cautiously he said: 'Gavin has different views. Believes in fighting fire with fire, pushing things to the edge.'

Lomax decided to go for it. 'I think Stevie Gavin's gaining the upper hand, starting to run things. Mind you, I'm the new boy. I could have it all wrong.'

The South African shook his head. 'No, you're right. And now I'm not sure I still fit in. I'm not even sure I want to be here.'

'Then walk away.'

A mirthless chuckle. 'You don't walk far with a bullet in your head.'

'Try flying. You're the pilot.'

Suddenly van Niekerk's eyes narrowed. 'What is this, Chris? You winding me up, playing games? This isn't a fuckin' joke, you know.'

Lomax knew he'd struck home. 'Listen, Johan, yesterday I thought a contract with these people for a few months could be good. God knows, I need the brass. But I was sold the same story as you. Sabotage work for a sound political goal is one thing. But I'm not about to become a terrorist – I've spent my whole life fighting them.' He added pointedly: 'Just like you.'

'Fine line that,' van Niekerk observed, 'between fighting for freedom and being a terrorist.'

'A line I'm not about to cross.'

A shadow passed behind the other man's eyes. 'I don't think you should be telling me this.'

'You want out, Johan, it's written all over your face. So do I.

527

We both got it wrong. Somehow we've got to put a stop to what's going down tomorrow – mass murder of innocent Irish troops on peacetime deployment.'

'So what do we do? You want to try walking out of here? Just see how far you get?'

'The helicopter?'

Van Niekerk smiled at that. 'You don't realise, do you?'

'What?'

'That chopper is their prized investment. I'm only allowed to fly with an armed guard.' He raised a hand. 'No, no one's ever *said* I'm not trusted, ever hinted. But I've noticed there's always a hard man with me since we started operations here. Whenever I've offered to fly alone, Peter or Stevie Gavin always insist on an escort, even if it's awkward to arrange. It's no coincidence.'

Lomax hadn't expected that. 'There's one other way. If I can use a phone I can get something sorted. I can't use the one in the farm, but if I could get hold of one of their mobiles?'

'Their?'

'Keegan's or Gavin's.'

'No need.' He smiled. 'I've got one. Need it in my role.'

Now this was totally dangerous territory. He had to know van Niekerk was on board. If he wasn't, if he hesitated, Lomax would have to kill him. Right here by the fence, using just his bare hands. And then run like hell, take his chances with the armed pickets.

He said: 'Let me use it. Alert someone to what's going down tonight.'

'You know who to call?'

'I've an idea.'

An easy smile crossed the South African's face. 'If I knew who to call, I might have done it myself.'

'Not here,' Lomax said. 'Too exposed.' He saw the farm track to his right, shielded by wild blackberry hedges on both sides. 'Let's take a stroll.'

They lit two more cigarettes and ambled like old friends, chatting and laughing for the benefit of anyone observing.

Once out of view between the hedges, van Niekerk said: 'I'll keep lookout,' and handed over his mobile.

Lomax took it and punched in Jerry Tucker's number. 'Hello, Jerry?'

'Jerry isn't here.' An unfamiliar voice. 'Who is that?'

'Never mind. Can I reach him? This is urgent.'

'Then tell *me*.'

'This is personal. It's got to be Jerry or no one.'

'Sorry, chum, Jerry's dead. Now, do you want to tell me?'

Lomax was stunned. 'Jerry dead?'

'A hit and run last night. Sorry. So, want to talk?'

He rang off, his mind in a spin. Still not fully registering the appalling news, yet feeling somehow responsible without even knowing why. Who else to call? Whose number? Which ones could he remember? Joe Monk. He ran his finger deftly over the key pad. The ringing tone began at the other end. On and on and on. No answer. Reason began to return. No, of course, yesterday Monk was with them in Belfast. No point of contact if he was still there. And no time yet to get home unless he flew. And if he flew, he wouldn't do so from Ulster. There probably had not yet been enough time for him to get home.

Who else? Sam Browne? Would she be back yet? He keyed in the office number. 'Eisner, Pollock and Browne,' Totty announced brightly. 'How may I 'elp you?'

'It's Chris here – '

'Oh, my God, where've you got to? We're all worried sick.'

'Isn't Sam back yet?'

'Back? No – oh, hang on a mo'.' A pause. 'I think that's her now. Expect you can 'ear the swearin' and cussin'.'

A second later a breathless Browne was on the line.

'Chris! Are you okay?'

'Fine. And you?'

'Apart from hitching a lift with a Welsh sex maniac lorry driver.'

'What?'

'It's all right. I gave him a black eye at the Severn Bridge service station, then persuaded a police patrol car to get me back . . .'

'Shut up, Sam,' Lomax interrupted, 'and listen. Things are about to get out of hand here. Keegan's lot intend to hit an Irish

Army convoy tonight. If we don't stop it, a lot of people will get killed and any peace process will be well and truly over.'

She blinked, trying to absorb what he was saying. 'What d'you want me to do?'

'I've tried to get Jerry Tucker,' he explained, 'but Jerry died last night. Car accident.'

'No!' Incredulous.

'This is going to go against the grain, but get hold of Prendergast – Roger Pinfold. He'll take it seriously and know the right buttons to push. Tell him *Cuchulainn* is going to hit a flying column of the 1st Irish Tank Squadron around midnight. Somewhere on the N15 along the Barnesmore Gap in Donegal. Got that?'

She was scribbling frantically. 'Er – yes.'

'Tell Pinfold to contact the SAS at Hereford and persuade Dublin to use them rather than their own. The Hereford lads know me and I'll have van Niekerk by my side. We're the good guys – make sure he knows that.'

Browne was horrified. 'You're going to be there?'

'I've no option.'

At that moment, van Niekerk said in a hoarse whisper: 'Wind it up, Chris, Stevie Gavin's wandering this way.'

Lomax acknowledged. 'Gotta go, Sam. Make it happen.'

'I love you,' she blurted, but the line was dead.

Her receiver had barely touched the cradle when the phone rang again. She snatched it up. 'Browne here.'

'Sam, it's Joe.'

'Oh, thank God it's you. Where are you?'

'Cork, about to board the ferry. What the hell are you doing in London? How . . .?'

'Long story, Joe, but listen. Chris has just called. Something bloody awful's about to happen.' Rapidly she brought him up to date.

He listened intently. Then he said: 'No, not Pinfold, Sam. I'll contact Jerry Tucker.'

'You can't, Joe. He died last night in a road accident. I'm afraid, given the time, Roger Pinfold is our only option.'

Monk didn't like it, but it wasn't up to him. Then he remembered Tucker's last message about the identity and whereabouts of the enigmatic Mr Grey of MI5. But Browne sounded too dazed to be taking it in. Moments later he hung up and stepped out of the call box. Yes, he could see why Pinfold was their only option. He knew exactly what was going down, would have the necessary clout and know exactly who to contact to get things done.

Yes, he understood, but he still didn't like it.

Sod you, Chris, he swore beneath his breath and returned to Tucker's car. He started the engine and threw the wheel hard round, taking the car in a circle and bumping up over the opposite kerb. Then he accelerated hard, back the way he had just come, this time heading for Donegal.

Twenty-two

'Remember this, Mr Prendergast,' Browne concluded. 'You owe us now. I expect it to be reflected in your actions at Roddy Littlechild's trial. Some honesty for a change.'

'I can't make any sort of promise, you understand,' he replied smoothly. 'But this information is truly appreciated. I shall see that your co-operation is brought to the notice of those who matter.'

'You *will*, won't you, Mr Prendergast?'

'Believe me.'

He hung up and lay back in his chair, assimilating the rapid speed of events and the ramifications. He swivelled round in his chair to face the window. The peaceful, timeless view of the Thames, glittering in the spring sunlight.

Fortuitous timing, he thought. Lord Moffat and Curtis Manning due for a routine progress meeting. He'd been expecting a difficult session over the way the trial was going. But now that would be replaced with a different agenda.

In fact, they arrived a few minutes later in a better mood than he'd anticipated, courtesy of an extended lunch at Moffat's club.

They listened in blank amazement to what Pinfold had to tell them.

'So we have the *Cuchulainn* group in the bag,' Manning said, his face lighting up. Already he was imagining his audience in the Oval Office.

'Many a slip 'twixt cup and lip,' Moffat cautioned. 'I must alert Fergal right away.'

'One moment,' Pinfold said. 'The Irish have brought much of this on themselves with these stupidly provocative manoeuvres. And we all know why – to force our hand to stop *Cuchulainn*. Huh, if only we *could* – until now. If the Irish are alerted, they'll just halt the column. The *Cuchulainn* group will slip away. After all, we don't have their exact location and it's rugged terrain around there, I believe.'

'And just how *good* are our Irish pals?' Manning asked.

Pinfold's silence answered that.

'Send over an SAS team as Lomax suggested?' Moffat said.

'Too sensitive on this one without Dublin's permission,' Pinfold replied. 'And we can't ask them without alerting them to what's going on.'

'Your boys in the Security Service?' Moffat asked hopefully.

Pinfold wasn't about to stick his head into that particular noose. If it went wrong, there'd be dead Irish soldiers splattered all over the countryside.

'I'm afraid we're not geared for that sort of operation,' he replied with a slightly plaintive air. And waited. Curtis Manning, stone cold sober over an orange juice and waffle breakfast, was predictable enough. After a long lunch and seeing success in his grasp, his response was a dead cert.

'Your guys ain't geared, Roger,' he beamed. 'But mine sure are. Tooled up and ready to go.'

Pinfold feigned surprise. 'What an awfully good idea, Curtis. Don't mind if I send Harry along for the ride, do you?'

Just so we can claim the credit if it works, he didn't actually say.

They deployed in two cars and pulled into a lay-by on the Donegal road, just south of Ballybofey, as the sun set behind the Blue Stack mountains. The sky was blood red and streaked with gold, throwing the basalt humps into bold relief until they resembled the outline shapes of fantastical prehistoric creatures.

Inspiration perhaps, thought Grisewold, for those ancient folklore tales of *Cuchulainn*? If he squinted he could almost see a hound's head up there.

'I like to be proactive, not reactive.' Next to him in the driver's seat, Zack Ryan was complaining again.

Grisewold dug the cigarettes from his pocket and poked one between his thin lips. 'Can't have it all ways. At least we've got

our lead at last. And your anti-terror squad gets all the glory.'
He spun the wheel of his trusty Zippo.

'Don't smoke in here,' Ryan replied, as he was engulfed in the cloud. 'What is it with you, Harry? Working with you, I'll die of passive smoking or passive drinking. You should see a psychiatrist. You're too dependent.'

A wintry smile crossed Grisewold's face as he threw open his door and stepped out into the twilight. The last thing he needed right now was a lecture.

Ryan joined him, sensing he'd been tactless. 'Sorry, it's just that I'm pissed.'

'You mean pissed off,' Harry corrected.

'What?'

'This side of the pond, pissed is drunk. So not much chance you're pissed. You're pissed off.'

'Hacked off, okay,' Ryan retorted. He hated playing these stupid word games with the Brits.

'No need,' Grisewold answered evenly. 'Like I say, you get the glory.'

'Not if we foul up.'

'You won't.'

'I'd like to be certain. There's twenty miles of road along the Barnesmore Gap, and *Cuchulainn* can be deployed anywhere along it. We won't know where till they hit the Irish column. Dublin should be in on this, get surveillance aircraft up so we can locate them, then move in.'

Grisewold gave a mirthless chuckle. 'I think some people will be more than pleased if the cavalry arrives a little late. Dublin's sabre-rattling hasn't been appreciated, so if they pay a small price . . .'

'As long as my guys aren't the ones who pay it.'

'It's unlikely, Zack. We're at one end of the road as the column's coming up from the other. You'll have a clear run to the ambush spot when it starts.'

Ryan grunted; he didn't like being used like this. Not a nice feeling when you didn't know who was pulling your strings.

'What about your informer?'

'What about him?'

'Any special instructions?'

'Like what?'

'Like don't shoot him.'

'I don't even know who he is,' Grisewold lied.

'Okay, then fire as necessary and only take prisoners when it's safe to do so. My men's safety first.'

'Sure, Zack. You're the boss.'

Ryan looked back to the cars. The rest of his men were out now, stretching their legs, making nervous jokes. The calm before the storm, all their weapons checked and primed.

'We've got several hours to wait,' Grisewold said, 'and I'm famished.'

'You're always eating.'

'Can't smoke, can't drink, can't eat . . .'

Zack Ryan shook his head slowly. 'Okay, I've got some C-rations in the car.'

Grisewold grimaced. 'Thanks, Zack, but I'm not that desperate.'

The helicopter had gone fast and low over the Ox Mountains in County Sligo, skimming the valley floors before heading north across the outer reaches of Donegal Bay.

Off their port wing the sun was dipping into the ocean, a vermilion wash that painted the waves the colour of diluted blood. Lomax shivered.

This was the second run for van Niekerk and his helicopter. The first had dropped the advance recce party of four and half the weapons. While the pilot returned for the second group, the first split into two, one couple guarding the remote landing zone and the other making the one-hour overland trek to the N15 road which ran along the Barnesmore Gap. Meanwhile, Albie Nairn and Spike remained at the farmhouse base in the South.

Nerves were chewing at Lomax's guts, his heart tripping unevenly. This wasn't like any pre-combat stress he'd ever known. It was totally different. *Cuchulainn* may have had its battle plan, but he did not. His survival, his life, was in the hands of others now. He and van Niekerk were expected to do their bit, yet both men were only looking for a way out. If it came, they'd seize it. But if it didn't –?

That was it, time for thinking over. The helicopter slowed abruptly as it cleared a high pass between two rugged peaks, then dipped and hovered, awaiting the flashlight signal, the all-clear from the recce party on the LZ.

The helicopter swayed, inching cautiously down until the wheels touched. 'Right, out!' Gavin ordered.

Each man grabbed his weapon and scrambled for the hatch. Lomax had not yet been entrusted with a personal firearm and was the last to emerge. As he did so he turned back to van Niekerk who sat with Gaza at his side, the Englishman's job to ensure that both pilot and transport remained there for the return trip.

'Keep your head down, Chris,' the South African said, his face impassive. It wasn't good luck to say good luck. Soldiers could be as superstitious as actors on a stage. Likewise the show had to go on, regardless.

Lomax gave a brisk nod of acknowledgement then shouldered the anti-tank rocket launcher and was gone.

He fell in second from last, the short column of figures bent under the weight of weapons and ammunition, disappearing into the shadows of the boulder-strewn mountainside. The dim glow from the Agusta's cockpit lights melted into the gathering darkness. A few stars were beginning to show; later it would be a clear sky and the full moon would shed a useful amount of ambient light.

A hushed, oppressive silence closed in around them, the only sound that of rubber soles on loose shale and the occasional whispered curse of missed footing. Lomax began to sweat with exertion and a mounting sense of anticipation.

If Browne had got his message through, he could expect an attack to come at any time without warning. But an attack from whom? The Regiment, he hoped, who knew what they were doing, who knew him. But would Dublin allow it? Whoever it was, whenever they struck, he'd hit the deck, find the biggest rock he could to shield behind. After that his plan was less sure.

Fifteen minutes. Half an hour. Still nothing had happened.

He trudged on, his calf and thigh muscles beginning to scream in protest. His months of retirement and relative inactivity were beginning to tell. Already the straps of the rocket launcher were biting into his shoulder.

Surely an attack must come soon. Any moment. But all around the utter silence remained, just the stolid clump of boots and laboured breathing. More minutes passed, the march seeming endless. Then he heard it. The faint sound of a vehicle. Heavy, a lorry, trundling along the Barnesmore Gap. Up ahead the sky lightened perceptibly above the humped horizon as the headlamps passed.

Nearly there. He glimpsed his watch. Spot on. For exactly an hour they'd been marching, their timing and navigation perfect.

More cars and lorries now, their engines clearly audible every few minutes, shattering the quiet at irregular intervals, their lights momentarily illuminating the roadside terrain.

A shadow detached itself from the rock. The man was expertly camouflaged with a scrim face veil, the same material used to break up every regular line of clothing and the assault rifle he carried.

It was only when he spoke that Lomax realised it was Tim. 'Hi, Da. Any problems?'

Keegan shook his head. 'And you?'

'No, all set. Six Claymores along the far-side embankment, the disused railway, and Hal's posted lookout one mile down the road.'

'Any news from Donegal?'

Lomax knew one of van Niekerk's South African friends had been sent by car to the nearby town for a visual sighting of the 1st Tank Squadron as it passed through.

'He radioed in five minutes ago. He's had an eyeball. Apparently they're reassembling before the final run up here. Reorganising and letting stragglers catch up.'

'Convoy pattern?' Lomax asked. He might as well sound as though he was interested, part of the team as he claimed.

'Appear to be moving in groups of ten to twelve vehicles,' Tim replied, 'each with two police motorcyclists, fore and aft.

Cavalry units first, then the Tank Squadron. That's five groups. Then the supply trucks and signals units.'

'So we want the fifth group?' Keegan asked.

Tim nodded, his eyes white and glistening between the dark smears of cam cream. 'Yes, hit the Scorpion light tanks. That places the armoured personnel carriers farther up the road, which is good, because infantry are our biggest worry. If the balloon goes up behind them, their instinct will be to take flight, even if they soon stop and come back.'

'But the rear units?' Keegan asked.

'Logistics, tail-end Charlies,' Tim said dismissively. 'They'll have no stomach for a fight when the lead starts flying.'

His father nodded. 'So we get in position now, right?'

'Yep. You and Stevie form the forward stop-group with Chris. The South African three will form the rear stop-group, and Hutch and me will take the centre with the heavy machine guns and grenade launchers.'

'Fine,' Keegan said, turning to Lomax and Gavin. 'Let's get going.'

The groups divided according to task, Lomax scrambling behind Stevie Gavin towards a boulder outcrop that offered a perfect view of the road some thirty yards away.

As they began sorting out the weapons, Lomax said: 'When am I going to get a firearm, Peter? I'm starting to feel a little undressed without one.'

It was Gavin who answered: 'Sorry, Lomax, I should have explained. You've carried that anti-tank launcher all this way, so you can have the privilege of firing it.'

Lomax winced inwardly. 'I'm a lousy aim.'

'Said you'd used the kit back at the farm.'

'I didn't say I was any good. I'm better with a rifle.'

Gavin's grin was more like a sneer. 'You wanna contract with us, Lomax, you got to earn it. Peter here might trust you, but in my book trust has to be earned. An ex-SAS man can do a lot of damage with an assault rifle.'

He realised then he was in a fix. Rattler was as canny as an urban fox. Shoot up an Irish tank and he was irrevocably committed. And murder was as committed as you could get.

'Stevie's right,' Keegan said, sounding almost apologetic. He slapped the green plastic sleeve of the launcher with his palm. 'So you'd better get it right.'

Lomax shrugged. 'I'll do my best.'

He removed the safety pins and end covers, then extended the telescopic inner tube of the one-shot launcher. His actions were reflex, his mind reeling with the problem he faced. There was no way he was going to fire the thing at innocent people. He'd just have to go through the motions and shoot wide, yet make it look convincing. If he failed, Gavin might decide then and there to dispose of him. And he would understand the reasoning: the seasoned Ulster veteran must have regarded Lomax's sudden involvement with their cause as suspicious to say the least. Only Keegan's trust and personal acquaintance gave him any kind of legitimacy. And now he had to convince Gavin to give him a firearm in order to stand any chance of escape.

A few minutes later a radio message came in from Donegal town: the Irish flying column was on the move at last.

Christ! On the move? Had Keegan's watcher got it wrong? He must have, but surely not. If he was right, then his message hadn't got through or hadn't been believed. Otherwise the column would have stayed put in Donegal. With a dread sinking sensation of nausea in his gut, he readied himself for the worst. Lomax checked over the M72 for the last time and aligned the backsight aperture with the luminous spot on the clear plastic foresight against each passing car on the road. He then sought the point at which an oncoming vehicle showed no lateral movement, but merely enlarged within the sights. At last he found his marker, a black-and-white metal pole that carried a Bend Ahead warning sign. When a vehicle reached that it would be heading straight for him for between five and seven seconds. Not long, and there would be no second chance.

Twenty minutes dragged by with excruciating slowness. *Surely* some sort of Irish dragnet must be closing in on them following his message to Pinfold? But somehow it didn't feel like it. A similar sensation to being stood up on a date: you knew

539

in the first few minutes that she wasn't going to show, yet still stood there, hoping in vain she was just running late.

A faint buzz and crackle came from Keegan's earpiece. 'It's Hal, on lookout,' Keegan said. 'He can see the lead vehicle.' Must be passing the Biddy's-O-Barnes pub now.

A few minutes later they saw it for themselves, the flashing blue strobes of the police escort appearing first round the farthest bend. Then the first angular loaf-tin shape of a Panhard armoured personnel carrier, an amber convoy lamp blinking out its warning. Another followed and then another, like a line of flickering fireflies emerging from the darkness.

By the time the first motorcycle and Panhard rolled past Lomax's position, Hal had reaffirmed the composition of the convoy. The Scorpion light tanks were in group five: eight of them and two Timoney APCs with a Land-Rover at their head.

'You ready?' Gavin demanded, lifting his assault rifle.

Lomax nodded, his mouth suddenly parched.

'Make sure you are.'

Gavin's rifle was pointed at his head.

'For Christ's sake!' Keegan protested.

'Just want to concentrate his mind,' Gavin answered tersely.

Lomax ignored him and hunched his shoulder under the firing tube of the launcher. He'd have to make this look good, which wouldn't be easy because the damn thing was notoriously inaccurate. And, as he'd warned, it was a long time since he'd used one and hadn't been very good even then. Sod you, Rattler.

Below them the first groups were rumbling past, totally unexpecting. Just helmeted heads of the drivers and commanders showing in the top-heavy-looking Panhards, concentrating on keeping to formation. Their ten-man squads locked inside for the claustrophobic duration of the ride. No one gave a sign of suspecting trouble, everyone looking straight ahead.

The first group cleared Lomax's position to join the necklace of lights moving like an illuminated worm towards Ballybofey and the border with Ulster beyond. Then followed the second, third and fourth groups.

Sweat formed in the small of Lomax's back, his hands warm

against the cool metal of the launcher. He forced the thought of Rattler's pointing gun from his mind, used his right hand to pull forward the safety catch to the 'arm' position and squinted down the launcher's sights.

There it was. The first Scorpion. Low, light and fast, it was not an easy target. Primarily a reconnaissance and light support vehicle, it relied on agility, speed and its low profile for survival. The aluminium armour was minimal and if Lomax's 66mm HEAT warhead struck, the effect would be devastating.

With its tracks spinning it was making a steady thirty miles an hour, its sleek lines and angled turret with the 76mm gun offering an oblique angle. Lomax rested the fingers of his right hand on the rubberised trigger cover on the top edge of the launcher, his thumb hooked beneath in readiness to squeeze. He held his breath, waiting as the Scorpion trundled round the curving road. His eyes darted sideways to the Bend Ahead sign, mentally lining them up, estimating the arrival time as the tank's nose passed alongside. Because every second would count. Fire early and more lives might be saved. Stop them before they reached his group and Keegan and Gavin would be shooting at longer range.

The plan had been simple. Take out the first and last tanks with rockets, then rake the vehicles between with armour-piercing and tracer rounds from heavy machine guns and grenade launchers. Anyone running for cover on the far side of the road would run straight into a tearing sheet of steel ball bearings from the line of Claymore anti-personnel mines.

At last the lead Scorpion came into the straight. Head-on profile. The sights wavered slightly as Lomax's heart tried to burst its way free of his chest. His fingers began to press down the trigger.

Twin sights lined on the sloping front glacis plate. NOW! He dipped the sights a fraction. A blurred image of dark tarmac. No time for second thoughts. He squeezed. The trigger went down, and down, and –

The meteor tongue of dazzling flame exploded from the tube. Momentarily he was disorientated, blinded and deafened by the hissing roar of the backblast in his ears, the vicious kickback jarring his shoulder. The vision of the arcing fireball in the darkness seemed etched in his retina, at once a lightning stab of power, yet at the same time tantalisingly slow and graceful as it homed unerringly on its target.

His eyes widened and jaw fixed in concentration. God, he'd got it wrong, misjudged. He'd fired at the tarmac in front of the tank, but the vehicle had been moving faster than he'd thought.

The sun's core burst white hot before his eyes as the rocket struck. Blinded again by the instant flux of light, he barely registered the tank lifting off the road. One foot, two. Then crashing back to earth, one caterpillar track unwinding like a steel serpent with a mind of its own.

'Fuckin' brilliant!' Gavin screamed. Hunched over his assault rifle, he emptied an entire magazine into the smoke and flames.

Lomax blinked again, his eyes adjusting. Then he realised: Gavin was wrong. The rocket had struck the tarmac a second before the tank rolled over it. Closer than he'd intended, but what the hell? The detonation of the warhead had lifted the tank's front end but the explosive power had dissipated in all directions. A track had been blown off and the tank was stopped, and no doubt the driver and gunner inside would have shattered eardrums and be badly shaken. But his shot *had* missed. With his lack of military training, Gavin had failed to realise exactly what had happened and, now the moment was past, he didn't care. He was on his own wave of excitement and adrenaline now, switching magazines and hosing the contents along the line of tanks as they stopped or crashed into the ones in front.

A second explosion rent the air, this time at the rear of the convoy. It was their rear-stop group, the South African trying to prevent a retreat and landing a rocket dead on target. There would be no escape for the second crew. The flash lit the surrounding landscape like a false dawn, shards of metal and bits of human body tossed high in the sudden pulse of igniting energy.

From the mid-section came the dull thud and crump of grenades as Tim pump-actioned the hand-held launcher at the chaos below him. It was joined by the hesitant stammer of Hutch's heavy machine gun stitching a line of fire up and down the column of stalled tanks. For several long moments the clamour of combat was ear-shattering, the constant crackle of small-arms fire interspersed by awesome, heart-trembling explosions that shook the earth they stood on.

Momentarily Lomax was back at Goose Green. Frozen in terror and mesmerised by brightly zipping lines of tracer and bursting flashes of orange flame. Then the scene of carnage was obliterated by a fast-gathering fog of smoke and burning oil. The stench reached his nostrils. That familiar acrid concoction that made him want to retch. Oil, rubber and burning flesh. Your turn next, your turn next! The voice of death seemed to be screaming in his ears. As it had that first time in Belfast. Then again, louder, in the Gulf War. And later on that wet lonely hillside in Bosnia.

Then, as though some mental switch had been thrown, he was suddenly back in the present. For the first time in the past hour his mind was crystal sharp, his brain functioning again, kicked into action by the sheer need to survive and to stop the horror.

While Keegan was standing next to him, unsure, and taking half-hearted shots at targets below, Stevie Gavin was still firing magazine after magazine into the turmoil on the road. Irish troops were now running back and forth between the vehicles which were stopped in a crazy zig-zag pile-up. Some were ablaze, others reduced to smouldering hulks. Other soldiers had orientated themselves, had taken whatever cover they could find and were returning fire with their Steyr bullpups. One or two unfortunates had sought refuge on the far embankment and had triggered Claymores which detonated without warning, spitting out their deadly steel seed at waist height.

Lomax looked towards the head of the convoy on the road to Ballybofey and the border. A trail of brake lights glowed in the darkness and torches were flashing as the earlier groups began to realise that something terrible had happened to the convoy behind them. Not knowing who or what they were up against, Lomax imagined it would take some time before they decided what to do, before some officer made the brave decision to engage a totally unknown and unseen enemy. And by then it would be too late, much too late.

His decision made, Lomax stepped towards Keegan and without warning swung his elbow hard back into the man's face. Bone met teeth and Lomax felt them give as Keegan yelped and let the assault rifle fall from his hands. Lomax snatched it up and jabbed the butt down onto the back of Keegan's head with all the force he could muster. His scream was stifled by the choking flow of blood from his damaged mouth and he collapsed to the ground, clutching his battered head. But even above the noise of battle, Stevie Gavin had heard something. He spun round, eyes glistening and his face shiny with all the maniacal excitement of the predator in at a kill.

It took a second to register what he was seeing. 'Lomax, you fuckin' bastard!'

Lomax turned Keegan's rifle in his hands and fired from the waist. He had no time to aim, couldn't give the man the chance to lift his own weapon. The rounds whipped viciously past Gavin, some ripping through the material of his trousers.

A mistake, Lomax knew, as he tried to correct his aim. But Gavin responded faster with a short return burst that sent Lomax diving for cover, rolling over and over to escape the fountains of earth that followed him. The shooting ceased abruptly and he rolled over one final time, ending on his stomach with legs splayed and his rifle pointing.

Gavin stood, now some thirty feet away, half-hidden between the shadows and the flickering light of flames. He'd momentarily lost sight of Lomax. Now he found him, and fired. Nothing. Dead man's click.

Lomax fired a three-round tap. And missed.

Shit! A perfect line-up, the bloody thing hadn't been correctly zeroed. Keegan had been out of the front line too long. As Lomax shifted his aim to compensate, Gavin melted into the shadows, leaving behind just the sound of urgent footsteps crunching on shale as he fled. Only escape was in his mind now, Lomax guessed.

He quickly checked on Keegan's condition. The man was

semiconscious, moaning softly, blood over his face and in his eyes. He'd be no threat to anyone tonight.

Lomax had other priorities. He took aim at the other *Cuchulainn* positions above the road, first at Tim Keegan and Hutch's mid-section group, then the South Africans' stop-group. The only targets offered were muzzle flashes, so he had little chance of hitting anyone. But, because he was firing at right-angles and from above the height of their positions, the rounds would land unnervingly close. He repeated the process twice and as he did, the muzzle flashes stopped. They had decided to call it a day. They wouldn't have known it was him, of course, would be assuming some Irish troops were turning their flank. Time to bug out. Up sticks and retreat to the landing zone. In the smoky half-light of burning carnage, he could just determine the retreating shapes.

He smiled to himself then, lowering the assault rifle. Well, they'd be in for an unpleasant surprise and a long walk. If all had gone according to plan, van Niekerk would have overpowered his minder Gaza when an opportunity presented itself, and relocated to a new agreed site.

But Lomax's small sense of achievement was short-lived as gunfire broke from the direction of the first convoy group on the Ballybofey Road. Rounds pinged and whined off the surrounding rocks, too close for comfort. He dropped to his haunches, shielding behind a rock slab. He was surprised that the Irish Army commanders were counter-attacking quite so swiftly.

Then he realised. They weren't soldiers. Two cars had slewed across the road just in front of the destroyed convoy. Men in civilian clothes were firing from the open doors, covering others who were scrambling up towards his position.

Instinctively he knew this was the belated help he'd been waiting for. These people had no hesitation, knew what they were doing and were manoeuvring like professionals. SAS, he wondered, or Irish Special Branch?

Whoever they were, they would shoot first and ask questions after. He was well aware of the rules in their game. They used to be his. Hastily he searched for the white handkerchief in his pocket and tied it to the barrel of his rifle. Keeping his head well down, he held the weapon clear of the boulder and began to wave. Not much else he could do now except pray.

It took a moment for him to realise that the shooting had finally ceased. Then he heard the crunch of nearby footsteps and the harsh breathing of exertion. In the dying light of the fires he was aware of shapes moving around him, encircling. Jackets flapping, men stood with handguns pointed in double-handed grips and their legs astride. Their movements nervous, hyped.

'Easy, buddy! Throw away that rifle! Nice and steady now!'

Was he hearing right? Americans?

He placed the weapon on the rock and raised his hands. 'Took your time getting here.'

'What?'

'I'm Chris Lomax.'

That cut no ice. 'Then get down on your face, Chris Lomax, and spread your legs.'

As he crawled onto all fours, a foot roughly kicked his legs apart and unseen hands quickly but thoroughly frisked him.

'He's clean,' someone pronounced.

Then the plasticuffs were snapped over his wrists, binding them together, and he was hauled to his feet.

'Who's this?' Someone had found Keegan, still curled in a whimpering ball.

'Peter Keegan,' Lomax said, 'the *Cuchulainn* leader. The rest are making for a helicopter landing zone – about two miles north-west.'

'Helicopter?'

'Yes, but the pilot isn't one of them. He was forced to co-operate at gunpoint. He's helping me, just waiting his chance to get away from them.' Not exactly the truth but it would do for the moment. 'Look, I don't know who you are but are you in touch with the British Security Service? They'll tell you who I am. I want to get untied.'

'It's okay, Zack.' Another voice, distinctly British, joined them from the darkness. 'I'll take care of Mr Lomax. You and your boys get after the others. We'll wait for your return.'

The American was pleased to be on his way, and led his men off in hot pursuit of the ambushers.

Then, as the man in the crumpled mackintosh stepped forward out of the shadow, Lomax's blood turned to icewater in his veins. It took a second or two for him to find his voice. 'Hello, Harry. We meet again.'

Grisewold regarded him dispassionately for a moment without replying. There was a movement behind him and an Irish Army officer appeared, scrambling over the rocks. 'Is it safe to send in the medics now?' he asked breathlessly.

'Well?' Grisewold asked Lomax.

'They've all left. But be careful, mines are placed on the far side of the road.'

'Holy Mother,' the officer said, seeing the extent of the destruction from this vantage point for the first time.

'There's an injured man here too,' Lomax said, pointing at Keegan.

'No,' Grisewold said quickly, 'I'll take care of him.' The officer nodded; he had enough on his plate. 'What about the Americans? Will they need our help?'

'I shouldn't go running after them. You'll end up shooting each other in the dark. Better to use your troops to seal off the area. Don't want any of those bastards escaping the net.'

Grisewold watched as the officer made his way back down to the road, then calmly extracted a packet of cigarettes from his pocket and lit one, cupping the match flame with his hands.

'Are you going to untie me?' Lomax demanded impatiently. 'Or am I under arrest?'

The man smiled at that, a sly cold smile. 'No, you're not under arrest. Box has no powers of arrest – not that I'm Box, of course. Officially, at least. Besides, this is foreign soil.'

'Then bloody well cut these ties.'

'Don't understand, do you? You're not giving orders to anyone any more, Lomax. You're not a soldier any more. You're a fucking unemployed civilian. A nobody. Worse than that

547

you've been upsetting some very influential people within HMG.'

Lomax restrained the anger he felt. Roebuck, Penny, Tucker. Not to mention Littlechild. How many others had Grisewold helped to destroy to keep the door closed on his dirty little secret world? 'Who are those Americans?'

'Them?' Grisewold shrugged dismissively. 'A special anti-terrorist unit. Something to do with the Defence Intelligence Agency, I think.'

'What the hell are they doing here?'

'On the President's orders. Assisting Dublin to keep the wheels of the peace process oiled.' He chuckled. 'A sanitisation squad, they like to call themselves.'

'Sanitisation?' Lomax thought he saw it then, a glimpse of what lay behind it all. 'Is that what all this has been about?'

'There's a lot to clean up.'

'You mean cover up, don't you?'

Grisewold didn't answer.

'So what happens next?'

He exhaled a stream of smoke and watched as it was whisked away into the night sky. 'That's just what I've been considering. There's one good thing about a firefight. Confusion, people get killed.' He removed the revolver from one pocket and sniffed heavily before hunting for the screw-on silencer in the other. Casually, with the cigarette hanging from his lips, he began to attach it.

'For God's sake, Harry. We've worked together. We were on the same side,' Lomax began.

Grisewold smiled bleakly at that. 'Yeah, then someone went and moved the goal posts.' He lifted the gun and fired twice at point-blank range into Keegan's head, shattering the skull beyond recognition. For a brief second the limbs twitched with a momentum of their own.

'Christ!'

'An old adage, but true. Dead men don't talk.' He switched his aim. 'Sorry, old soldier. Nothing personal.'

Lomax stared death in the face. And worst of all was the

totally impassive expression of the man who held the gun. Only the eyes were animated, glittering like mica chips in granite.

The finger curled around the trigger and instinctively Lomax shut his eyes, his body jerking at the crack of the pistol shot.

Nothing. Nothing happened. He'd felt no pain. He was dead. This was death. Silenced guns make no noise.

His eyes opened and he was staring down at Grisewold's sprawled body at his feet. There was an expression on the face now. One of surprise, the eyes looking up curiously as though trying in vain to see the neat hole drilled into his forehead.

Joe Monk stepped out of the darkness. 'Sod me, Chris, that was close.'

Lomax's mouth fell open in astonishment. 'Joe? How the hell . . .?'

'I spoke to Sam when I got to Cork. I turned round and came straight back. Got stuck behind that convoy. God knows why they let it run. Someone should have stopped it.' He peered over Grisewold's corpse. 'I thought it was Harry. Couldn't be sure in the dark. Then I saw him shoot the body.'

'Keegan,' Lomax told him. Then held up his wrists tied in the plasticuffs. 'Have you got a knife?'

Monk grinned. 'Good Boy Scout, me.' He took the Swiss Army knife from his pocket and began hacking through the bonds.

'Where d'you get the gun?'

'Off some poor stiff. I'm afraid there're a few about. Now do you mind if we stop chin-wagging and get the fuck out of here? I think I've just committed first-degree murder. My car's back there.'

Lomax shook his head. 'No, the area will be swarming with troops and police. There's another way.'

'What?'

'By helicopter.' He rubbed the circulation back into his wrists.

Van Niekerk's helicopter was a dark shape without lights, parked on a flattish area beside a stream bed.

'Who's that!' he demanded nervously.

'Johan, it's me, Chris. It's okay, I'm with a friend.'

The South African was white-faced and clearly on edge as he lowered his pistol. Lomax recognised it: the one Gaza carried. The man himself sat lolling in the co-pilot's seat, the sisal necklace still around his neck.

'You managed it then?' Lomax observed.

'Just. It's a long time since I've killed a man with my bare hands. He fought like a lion. Nearly ripped my bloody ear off.'

Lomax examined the blood-sodden flap of flesh. It wasn't an exaggeration. 'I'll put a dressing on it. Can you still fly?'

Van Niekerk gave a weary grin. 'Watch me.'

'You got enough fuel to cross the Irish Sea?'

'I reckon. If not we'll have to swim.'

For the first time in days Lomax felt the tension ebb. 'An old friend of ours is going to be mighty pleased to see you.'

Although still shattered from her experiences in Ireland, Browne hadn't been able to sleep and had drifted through the following morning in a daze. Worried sick about Lomax, she had barely registered the proceedings in court as the wrangle over ballistics evidence recommenced. There had been nothing on the radio news about an attack on the Irish Army and Roger Pinfold's number was coming up on answerphone.

At lunchtime she and the defence team were crossing the road from the Old Bailey to the pub when she stopped dead in her tracks. A taxi tooted and swerved.

'You got a death wish, boss?' Totty asked, pulling her onto the pavement.

'Eh, what?' She shook her head, trying to clear her brain. 'How in God's name could I have forgotten?'

'Forgotten what?'

'The name Jerry Tucker gave Joe in Belfast before he died. What have I done with it? It must be in my bag somewhere.' She stood on the pavement, a cigarette in her mouth, and began rummaging, becoming more agitated by the second. In exasperation she knelt and poured out the contents on the ground. Passers-by turned and stared as Meyrick, Rock and Totty gathered round her.

'What is going on, dear heart?' Meyrick asked. 'Can't you hunt for your lipstick in the pub?'

'Piss off, Tristram,' she answered snappily. 'Ah, here it is.' She scooped the spilled contents back into her bag. 'The real name of Mr Grey.'

'Walter Grey?'

'Yes, Grey,' she replied irritably. 'The man who set up Frontline with Wallace McIlroy. The MI5 man who originally recruited Roddy.'

'Ah, yes, I see. Roger Pinfold's predecessor.'

She smoothed out the crumpled piece of notepaper. 'Walter de Witt,' she read. 'Unfortunately no address. Tucker thought he was in a nursing home in south Hampshire. Tristram, you can manage without me in court this afternoon. I've got to get back to the office. We really must find this man.'

Meyrick agreed. 'It could be crucial, but you're in no fit state; you're like a zombie as it is.'

'I'll give you a hand,' Totty said resignedly.

Browne grinned at her. 'That's my girl.'

They arrived back at the office at two o'clock, walking in to find Wayne waving at them to be quiet as he tuned in to the radio news. 'It's about the attack in Ireland!' he shouted.

Within seconds the entire firm was huddled round the little transistor set as the BBC announcer told how news was just coming in of escaped convict Peter Keegan being shot dead while leading a Loyalist terrorist attack on an Irish Army border patrol the previous night. Browne's heart was in her mouth as the report went on to say that the man's son, Tim, was also killed together with several people believed to be white South African nationals. A notorious paramilitary leader known as Rattler was understood to be on the run from the scene.

Five Irish military personnel were dead and ten wounded, two seriously. One British civilian holidaymaker, thought to be backpacking, was killed when he was caught up in the fighting.

'God, not Chris!' Browne gasped. 'Oh, please God, no!'

Totty tried to console her and neither really heard as the announcer said that the gang calling itself *Cuchulainn* had been attacking utilities in the Republic for some weeks although editors on both sides of the Irish Sea had co-operated in a news blackout. The gang was finally destroyed by a garda force, assisted by US anti-terrorist experts in Dublin and information supplied by MI5.

The office switchboard began flashing and Wayne dragged himself away from the broadcast to take the call. His mouth fell open as he listened. Then he grinned. 'It's Mrs Littlechild, Sam. She's just had a call from Chris. He's safe and says he'll be in London tonight.'

'Oh, thank God,' she blurted, barely able to talk through her sobs of relief. 'Where is he?'

Wayne looked nonplussed. 'Er – she says Scotland.'

In a much lighter mood after Ernie Eisner opened a celebratory bottle of champagne, everyone joined in the frantic hunt to find the man who could just possibly still save Littlechild from a life sentence. Wayne called a friend who lived in Southampton and had him fax a copy of the nursing home list from his local Yellow Pages directory. They split the list between them and each manned a separate phone. For half an hour it became a madhouse, like a newspaper office amid some global catastrophe, everyone talking at once, then phones trilling madly as returned calls came in.

At three twenty, Wayne covered the mouthpiece of his receiver and called: 'I think I've got him! The receptionist's just going to double check with the matron.'

'Where is he?'

'St Luke's Hospice.'

'Oh shit.' Browne ended her own call and fairly flew across to Wayne's desk, snatching the phone from him. 'Hello, hello, hello. Oh, yes? Matron? Yes, a Mr Walter de Witt. Thank God for that. This really is a matter of life or death. Oh, no. That's awful. Could I speak with him? Well, can you ask him, *please*! Tell him it's Sam Browne. Oh, oh thank you so much. Yes, I'll hold.'

'What's happening?' Totty asked.

Browne was trembling with agitation, trying to light a fresh cigarette from the stub of her last. 'He's sick. Terminally ill with lung cancer.' She didn't seem to see the irony of that as she finally drew smoke. 'Now it's spread. He hasn't got long. The matron really didn't want to bother him.'

'So it doesn't look hopeful?' Eisner said.

'I don't think we'll get him to court.'

Then the matron came back on the line. 'I've spoken to Mr de Witt. He was very interested in your call.' She sounded surprised. 'He'd be pleased to see you.'

'I can leave right away.'

'What? Oh, I don't know about that. He's very weak, sleeps most of the time. He was already dozing off just now. Maybe another day.'

'Matron, believe me, I don't have another day. Let me come. If he's asleep, fine, I'll just wait till he wakes up.'

Reluctantly the matron agreed. 'Will you come with me, Totty? And bring the tape recorder.'

'You're not going in that death-trap rocket of yours? Not likely.'

'The 200SX? I'll go, boss,' Wayne piped up with enthusiasm.

Browne gave a pleading look at Totty, who shrugged reluctantly. 'Okay, I wouldn't wish *that* on anyone. Even my heartless slave-driver boss.'

They arrived at St Luke's Hospice, an old converted manor house surrounded by a crumbling red-brick wall in the New Forest. With a duckpond and spreading chestnut tree by the gravel drive through ornamental gates, it seemed to Browne to be a tranquil place to spend the last of one's days.

For most of the drive her mind had been on Lomax and whatever had happened in Ireland. Thankfully, her apprehension at having to rely on Roger Pinfold had proved to be unfounded and Lomax was safe. The question now was, would they see a change in the prosecution case? Strings pulled to persuade the CPS to stop the trial on some pretext? It was almost too much to hope for, so she must battle on.

As they were met in reception by the matron, she forced her mind back to the present.

'Walter is waiting for you.' A large, formidable woman in a dark blue tunic, her severe face was softened by kindly grey eyes. 'I'm surprised. He seems much brighter than usual.

Seems to be keeping awake without any special effort. I'll take you through.'

Old folk, frail and mostly in dressing gowns, tottered about with sticks or sat around playing cards in the communal rooms; another small group was gathered round a television set in one corner. No one seemed to notice Browne and Totty as they followed the matron through the French windows and into an elegant white-painted conservatory in Victorian style.

For one dreadful moment, Browne thought he was dead. He sat so still in his wheelchair, wings of unruly white hair splayed like a halo against the cushion and backlit by the low-angled sun that came in over the walled garden outside to cast long shadows across the lawn. His skin was porcelain white, yet not in texture. There was no firmness to the flesh where it sagged in the hollows beneath his cheeks and the livid veins ran like threads in marble.

'Walter. Your visitors have arrived.'

The watery staring eyes flickered with recognition, suddenly bright and focused as though someone had thrown a switch. Even as she watched, the irises seemed to clear as though a mist had lifted and the pupils sharpened with the glitter of anthracite. The transformation was almost unnerving as Browne noticed the beauty in those cobalt-blue eyes and realised that once he must have been a stunningly attractive man.

'Miss Browne.' His voice was a croak, parched as desert soil. He lifted a slender bony hand with effort. She took it and was surprised how strong the grasp was. But his skin was cold and for a moment he didn't seem to want to let go, as though drawing strength from the warmth of her flesh. Perhaps even holding onto life itself. 'Forgive me if I don't get up.'

'No, no, of course.'

'Just bring yourselves up some chairs.' He waved the frail hand. 'It's all right, Matron, you can leave us now.' And as Browne settled in a garden chair, he said: 'And is this charming girl your daughter?'

'What me?' Totty said, taken aback. 'I should 'ope not.'

Browne smiled awkwardly. 'No, Totty's my assistant. I don't have any children.'

His eyes crinkled. 'That's a shame. As the great Bard said, "Lady you be the cruellest she alive if you lead these graces to the grave and leave the world no copy." '

'She's cruel all right,' Totty blurted without thinking.

'Somehow I don't believe that. Then at least I'm honoured to enjoy your original graces, my sweet rosebud. Do you mind if I call you rosebud?'

Browne's cheeks flushed with colour. 'Me, rosebud?'

De Witt coughed and there was a distant gurgling noise from his chest. 'I named you that back at the Keegan trial in '89. Thought then you were my perfect English rose.'

'Quite an old rose now.'

'And old roses have the sweetest fragrance of all. I know about roses.'

'So you were there, Mr de Witt, for Keegan's trial?'

'Oh yes, I thought he should see at least one friendly face in court. And please call me Walter. I don't have time left to me for formalities.' Again he was racked with a dry cough. 'Please excuse me. Would you mind passing that glass behind you.'

Totty turned to find the glass of white liquid on the wicker table. 'The milkshake?'

De Witt accepted it with a chuckle. 'Liquid morphine. But you're right, perhaps I should flavour the milk with chocolate. This is the stuff that keeps me going, a balance to keep the pain in check without completely addling my brain. I can't let go yet. Not until it's finished.'

'What's finished?'

'The work I began with Wallace McIlroy in the early seventies, the Frontline Ulster movement. You know about that, of course. You're here because of Roddy Littlechild, I imagine?'

'Yes.'

'A smashing lad, had a lot of time for him. I had a son. Turned out to be a rotten bastard. Too many of my own genes, I suppose. I'd have liked a son like young Roddy. Hear he's got himself a wife, lucky woman. A good catch.'

'And a son now.'

'That is good. And how is the trial going? I've been following it in the papers, but you can't tell from that.'

Browne gave a brittle laugh. 'You can't tell from the defence bench either. To be frank, it's not looking good. He really *was* set up.'

'I know Roddy well enough to realise that. Pinfold is behind it, you'll find. Do you know Roger Pinfold?'

'Our paths have crossed.'

'Pinfold, the evil little bastard, and his other cronies. Lord Moffat and the rest of them – the other lily-livered grandees of the Establishment. No honour, no sense of history!' He broke off into a spluttering cough and gulped a soothing mouthful of his liquid morphine.

As she waited for him to recover, Browne thought over what the man had just said. 'Walter, you mentioned unfinished business with the Frontline Ulster Movement. What did you mean?'

'It doesn't matter, rosebud. Time will tell, only I don't have much of it left. I expect Tim will be in contact soon, bring me up to date.'

'Tim?'

A look of youthful anger flashed in his eyes. Not anger at her, but at himself, she could see that. Angry that the morphine had slowed his brain and loosened his tongue. 'Getting muddled,' he said dismissively.

But suddenly Browne saw it. 'Do you mean Tim Keegan? Peter's son?'

Then, in an instant the years rushed back and the brilliance of his younger days was once again trapped within the ravaged body of a dying man. 'I'm tired.'

'You *do* mean Tim Keegan. You know him . . . And so you do know about the *Cuchulainn* campaign?'

He sat up abruptly and for a moment she thought he'd had a seizure. 'How do you know about that?' Suddenly the switch had been thrown again. 'I've seen nothing in the news.'

'Oh my God, Walter, you're not aware of what's happened, are you?'

'Happened, rosebud?' Confusion returning.

'First tell me. About you and Tim and *Cuchulainn*.'

He sighed wearily. 'Nearly two years ago, when I knew I was on the final downhill run, I wrote a note to Peter Keegan in prison. For old times' sake, I suppose. He wrote back by return. It was like finding a long-lost chum. For both of us in a way. In one letter he said in passing how Ulster needed its defending hound now more than ever before. He meant *Cuchulainn*. That triggered the idea. Of course, he didn't know then what I'd done, what I'd set in place while I was still at MI5.'

'What had you set in place, Walter?'

'An insurance that *Cuchulainn* would survive. So I wrote and told him to send his son to visit me. Here. We talked in the rose garden. I call it my secret garden.' He smiled a twisted smile. 'I tell you, rosebud, one day the Hound of Ulster will arise!'

Browne took a deep breath. 'Obviously you don't know. Few people do. *Cuchulainn* has been mounting a campaign against the Irish Republic for the past two months.'

His mouth dropped in shock. 'That isn't true!'

'It is, Walter, I promise you. There's obviously been some kind of media blackout.'

'I might have known!' Saliva gathered as he spat his words of contempt. 'The bastards!'

She reached forward and clasped his bony wrist. 'Walter, I'm sorry to have to tell you this. Peter Keegan and his son are dead. It all ended last night. A gunfight with the Irish Army. It's all over.'

He twisted his wrist so he could take her hand. His grip was remarkably strong for one so frail and she could see the emotion in his rheumy eyes, the hurt and disappointment.

Then she saw her opportunity. 'You can hit back at them, Walter. Strike a blow against the likes of Roger Pinfold.'

It took a few minutes for him to absorb all that had just been said. For a while he appeared withdrawn, physically shrunken by the disappointment. Then slowly, very slowly, a fresh new spirit seemed to lighten his emaciated features. 'So Tim and Peter *did* do it! It all worked after all. And perhaps it still can, d'you think? Just a pity . . .' But he wasn't really listening; she could tell his mind was wandering.

'Walter, please, I need to know,' she said anxiously. 'Would you agree to give evidence at Roddy's trial? Tell them how you recruited Roddy and ran him for all those years? Confirm what people like Pinfold are capable of?' She was beginning to gabble now in her excitement. 'You wouldn't be expected to go, of course. In exceptional circumstances the court could convene here. Or maybe a video link . . .'

'At the trial, me?' A triumphant grin lit his face, and in a twinkling the years had momentarily vanished. 'An appearance at the trial of the decade, rosebud. Now there's a thought.'

Twenty-three

They had talked for another hour before the old man's strength started to wane and his eyelids closed. Then it was back to London as fast as she could to be reunited with Lomax. On the journey Totty used the mobile to pass on news of developments to Tristram Meyrick who was yet again working late in chambers. By the time Browne had dropped her assistant home and driven across London to Southall, it was nine thirty.

Having rung the bell she could scarcely wait for someone to descend the stairs to let her in, and still could hardly believe it when she saw Lomax standing there. Calm as you like, as though nothing much had really happened. That goddamn grin on his face, like some naughty schoolboy. She threw herself into his arms and just couldn't stop the flow of tears.

Eventually she regained control, gasping and sniffing, mascara streaked all over her cheeks. 'God, I'm blubbing like a schoolgirl.'

'It's nice to know you care.' He sounded pleased, as though he hadn't really been expecting it.

'Oh, I do, Chris. If ever I'd had any doubt, these past two days – I've missed you.'

He thrust a handkerchief into her hands. 'Don't start all over again, Sam. I can't stand to see a grown-up lawyer cry. Let's get upstairs, we've a lot to talk about. I've brought you back a present from Ireland.'

'What?' Perplexed.

'Not what, who? Come on up.'

She dutifully trotted up the stairs, trying to catch him, then followed into Evie's flat. Lomax's sister was there, cradling little Noel, Manda and Joe Monk.

And another man. She did a double-take. It was Johan van Niekerk.

*

The next day was to see the start of the summing-up for the prosecution, yet by the time the defence team arrived at the Old Bailey the urban message drums had already been at work and by some mental telepathy everyone in court knew that something was up. Halifax and Ian Spinks were subdued and watchful as Browne strode into the lobby ahead of Tristram Meyrick and Ronnie Rock.

'Definitely a red knickers day,' Halifax was heard to observe with a chuckle that lacked its usual heartiness.

And his smile vanished totally when Meyrick addressed Mr Justice Quigley in the absence of the jury: 'If it pleases Your Lordship, I have some unfortunate news to impart to the court. You, my lord, will be aware that we have been striving for months to locate a key defence witness from Northern Ireland, Mr William Baker. We believe he could vouch for the fact that the deceased Mr Fitzpatrick wanted to contact the defendant and not vice versa, and that the contact was the idea of MI5.

'I have to inform you that the defence solicitors established his whereabouts over the Easter weekend but, regrettably, before a meeting could take place the witness was tragically murdered by unknown gunmen.'

A low murmur of surprise eddied along the prosecution bench before Mr Justice Quigley replied: 'Mr Meyrick, that is indeed sad news and I am sure all in this court will join with me in extending our deepest sympathies to the deceased's man's family. Er – was there something you wished to add?'

'My lord, you will be aware that this murder of a key witness follows the suicide of Mr Derek Penny and the fatal accident of Colonel Colin Roebuck, after which certain irreplaceable documents were stolen from his car. In these circumstances the court may consider the defence in this case to be somewhat jinxed, or that it indicates something a little more sinister at work . . .'

'My lord,' Halifax interrupted, 'the implications of this remark . . .'

'Quite,' the judge agreed. 'By now this court is well aware of the defence's conspiracy theory, Mr Meyrick.'

'Thank you, my lord. And I would now beg the court's

permission to allow me to introduce two new witnesses for the defence. I further apologise for the belated nature of this request, but it is the result of new information that has only just come to light.'

Quigley didn't bother to hide his sigh. 'And who are these new witnesses?'

'If Your Lordship pleases, they are Mr Johan van Niekerk, a former South African officer in the security police and long-term associate of the defendant, and a former senior MI5 officer, Mr Walter Grey or de Witt, who originally recruited the defendant.'

Meyrick might as well have ignited an atomic bomb. Halifax leapt to his feet to protest and demanded an adjournment to consult with the CPS and government ministries concerning the nature and implications of allowing testimony from the surprise witnesses.

By the time the court reconvened after lunch, Pinfold had made an appearance and was seen talking in the lobby with the prosecution team. He had studiously avoided eye contact with Browne and she saw no advantage in appealing to his better nature. The man clearly didn't have one; if he had, the CPS would have withdrawn by now. The wrangling went on for the rest of the afternoon, both in court and in the judge's chambers.

Halifax argued, with justification, that van Niekerk could throw no possible light on the murder charge, and neither could de Witt who was still bound to silence by the Official Secrets Act. Meyrick countered that at last he could prove his client's long service with MI5 and show why that organisation might have wanted him silenced – by whatever means available.

Unusually, Mr Justice Quigley called the court back in the late afternoon to announce his decision.

'I am finding various aspects of this case increasingly disturbing. Whilst Mr Meyrick's earlier suggestion that the defence was jinxed can be put down to misfortune and coincidence, there appears to me to be a thread throughout every aspect of this trial. Three people who could testify to the defendant's good name and loyal service to the Crown are all dead by their own hand, fate or the hands of others. Two more, at the eleventh hour, have been found. Their evidence may not relate directly to the murder but may cast light on Mr Meyrick's oft-repeated theory of conspiracy. This can only be discounted if this court can penetrate the fog of secrecy surrounding this murder and the background to the main parties. I for one would welcome such light in the interests of justice. Therefore I shall permit these witnesses to give evidence to this court. Should such evidence relate to any other charge facing the defendant, so be it. For there is no more important crime in the land for a man to face than wilfully to have taken the life of another human being. And neither, Mr Halifax, do I intend a witness in my court to be gagged from free speech by the provisions of the Official Secrets Act.

'I also accede to the defence request that police protection be extended to both these witnesses until they appear. This court will reconvene tomorrow at ten.'

'The court will rise,' ordered the clerk.

Browne literally jumped to her feet in triumph, grinning stupidly at a very smug-looking Meyrick and a joyous Ronnie Rock.

For the next seventeen hours, Sam Browne was running on black coffee, a tot or two of whisky and pure adrenaline. With Evie's flat becoming overcrowded, Lomax and van Niekerk, together with his uniformed police minder, went to Browne's home to talk over his testimony with Meyrick and Rock. Meanwhile, Totty had been set another task. Walter de Witt could not make the journey to court and therefore a video link would be established once the old man could charm the matron of St Luke's into agreeing – which he did. As the Old Bailey's ageing video monitors were on the blink, Mr Justice Quigley had agreed to a single large multiscreen being installed by the Friday. As always, Totty's brother knew someone who could provide it.

At three in the morning, van Niekerk was asleep on the settee and his minder in an armchair by the door. 'Time for bed,' Lomax said.

Browne peered over her reading specs. 'Five more minutes, Chris.'

'Now.'

She put down her pen. 'Yes, master.'

'I'll kip in the spare room.'

'No, you won't.'

'You must be all in.'

'Almost, not quite. A little secret, I've got them on.'

'You are Johan van Niekerk?' Meyrick asked in court the next morning. 'Until recently a captain in the South African security police? Before that you served with the Rhodesian Army, I understand, where you first met Mr Rodney Littlechild?'

'Yes, back in 1976. We served in the same armoured-car regiment, in the field intelligence unit.'

'Did the defendant ever confide in you why he'd gone to Rhodesia to join up?'

'To get experience of a real fighting war – especially in intelligence and counter-insurgency warfare. He told me that it had been arranged by a Walter Grey – aka de Witt – who was connected with the FUM, a Loyalist resistance force set up by Wallace McIlroy.'

'Did Mr Littlechild tell you who these men were?'

'Not then, but later when he found out himself. Walter Grey was a senior MI5 controller and McIlroy was an old friend and an acting MI5 agent.'

'Did you meet either of these men yourself?'

'Not McIlroy, but I met Walter Grey on several occasions.'

'In what circumstances?'

'As representative of our countries' respective intelligence agencies.'

'So obviously you can vouch that he was not a fantasist, a Walter Mitty rather than de Witt?' That produced a titter of amusement as van Niekerk confirmed the man's official standing. 'Before we move on, may I ask if you heard or saw in yesterday's media news a story regarding an incident in the Republic of Ireland concerning a Loyalist paramilitary group called *Cuchulainn*?'

'I did.'

'Had you heard of them before?'

'Yes, about a year after I met Roddy Littlechild he told me it was the armed wing of the FUM, to be used as a last resort resistance movement to protect the Protestant population.'

'In case of what?'

A shrug. 'Civil war, or in case of outright hostilities with the Republic.'

'Did Mr Grey confirm this to you?'

'Much, much later when we knew each other better. He and Roddy and I got on really well. A lot of us had empathy with the Protestants in Northern Ireland.'

'In what way?'

'Unfriendly neighbours and terrorists in our midst, fighting the Soviet Communists by proxy. And a similar culture, hard-working and God-fearing.'

'And did the defendant tell you something else about his links with Mr Grey and his former Ulster homeland?'

Van Niekerk nodded. 'Grey was afraid of wild Loyalist elements running out of control. He used Littlechild as a conduit to keep him informed about what they were up to. Roddy knew all the major players over there.'

'This relationship between the defendant, Grey of MI5 and yourself was to grow over the years. Why was this?'

'It was discovered that the Communist government in Mozambique was allowing the IRA to train there with the African insurgents attacking Rhodesia. Our two countries had a mutual interest.'

'And the closeness between you developed even further after 1980 when you, Mr van Niekerk, then left Rhodesia – or Zimbabwe as it was becoming – for South Africa to work in the security police – of course, now with a new enemy, the ANC?'

Van Niekerk shook his head. 'Not the ANC, their armed terrorist wing the *Umkhonto we Sizwe*. An important difference. I was asked to set up a small covert ops unit under command of the Deputy Commissioner of Police. When Roddy Littlechild came back to Africa after two years in the British Army, I invited him to join me.'

'What was your unit's function?'

'To collate and disseminate intelligence about terrorist threats, then direct action against them. But a couple of years later, in 1984, our remit was changed.'

'What happened?'

'Well, I set up a sub-unit and put Roddy in charge. It was after the ANC's car-bombing of the Air Force headquarters in Pretoria. The National Intelligence Service discovered that it had involved IRA technology and planning. I wanted the sub-unit to liaise with MI5 and discover fully the links between the IRA and the ANC's armed wing. We found the two were swapping expertise for safe training areas and doing other favours for each other.'

Meyrick glanced around the court, pleased to see that he had his audience rapt. 'And did that give you an idea?'

'Yes, to do something similar with the Loyalist paramilitaries. MI5, through Walter Grey, liked the idea. Loyalist gunmen needed a safe training area which we were able to provide. We had a succession of visitors, some of them major players who then were alongside MI5. Big names like Rattler and King Billy.'

'Did it extend beyond that?'

Van Niekerk nodded. 'They would go on operations for us in Africa – strangers, unconnected foreigners. They could take out our ANC targets. As they were unconnected, they left no clues for our regular police.'

'And was there some reciprocation?'

Van Niekerk shuffled his feet. 'A few times. With MI5's connivance, our agents sometimes killed for them in Eire and Ulster.'

The court gave a chorus of gasped surprise, muffling Halifax's protest. 'My lord, as I warned, this is entirely unrelated to this murder trial.'

'Far from it,' Meyrick cut in. 'It is why elements of MI5 were having apoplexy at the prospect of the defendant revealing any of this to the media, having mistakenly decided he'd turned against them!'

'Beautiful,' Browne murmured and shared a grin with Totty. This was really taking shape now.

'Carry on, Mr Meyrick,' Mr Justice Quigley allowed.

The barrister turned back to the witness box. 'But in this murky world of spying and dirty tricks, even allies are betrayed when it suits, aren't they?'

Van Niekerk agreed. 'Yes, at about this time my superiors decided to supply the Ulster Defenders group, run by a Stevie Gavin, with advanced weaponry.'

'Who did you ask to set up the deal?'

'Rodney Littlechild. But I knew of his relationship with MI5, so I couldn't fully trust him not to report it back to them – and I was proved right. I made a second secret deal direct with Stevie Gavin and that consignment got through.' Van Niekerk glanced apologetically in Littlechild's direction and saw the ghost of a smile on his friend's face.

'Why did South Africa supply this Loyalist group? Not for money or belief in their cause, surely?'

'No. Instead of payment we suggested missile technology secrets from Shorts of Belfast.'

'And did you get them?'

'Eventually, yes.'

Meyrick said: 'One last question. Did South Africa receive defence material routed through Northern Ireland – despite sanctions?'

'Yes. Sophisticated communications equipment and Soviet weapons made in the West under licence. In part, it was used to arm the right-wing terror gangs of Renamo to destabilise Mozambique. I got Roddy to set it up for us through MI5.'

'Which country was the originator of this deal?'

'The United States of America.'

By lunchtime the stunning revelations were hitting the early editions of the *Evening Standard* and the court was besieged by reporters, radio and television news crews. Browne tried to run the gauntlet of questions, then abandoned her plans for a lunchtime rendezvous with Lomax.

In the afternoon, Halifax launched into his cross-examination. 'Mr van Niekerk, you mentioned earlier that your security police unit in South Africa hunted down ANC activists then took, in your words, direct action. By this, you mean ambush and murder without trial. Correct?'

'We were fighting a guerrilla war.'

'Nelson Mandela may disagree with you there. But, yes or no?'

'Sometimes.'

'And the defendant was part of your team, privy to these murders without trial and no doubt witnessed what you would call interrogation of prisoners? What other more civilised people may have regarded as torture?'

Van Niekerk glanced at the dock. 'As I said, we were fighting a war, following orders. Roddy's role was intelligence not executive action; that was a job for others. In fact, he was always mindful of events back in his homeland and would sometimes criticise the unit's more extreme activities. Like violent interrogation. On more than one occasion he caused me to examine my own conscience.'

Halifax looked pleased. 'But this did not prevent you sending him as part of a hit team to Belfast in 1987, did it? To kill an alleged ANC and Sinn Fein activist called Dominic Smals?'

Van Niekerk shook his head. 'The department head sent the team, not me. And Rodney Littlechild was not part of it. He just happened to be on leave in Belfast at the time, visiting his father.'

Halifax adopted an expression of sneering distaste. 'Isn't the truth that the defendant supplied the weapons from his Loyalist friends for this murder?'

'No. They were supplied by Peter Keegan, an army agent in the Ulster Defenders and he first obtained sanction from MI5.' Van Niekerk looked towards Tristram Meyrick, knowing what he wanted him to add. 'From Walter Grey himself.'

It was rare for Roger Pinfold to get home before eight in the evening. And tonight it was gone ten before his Daimler Sovereign swept into elegant Carlyle Square in Chelsea and reversed into the residents' parking space outside his house.

As he killed the wipers, lights and power and climbed out, he became aware of the woman standing by the railings, her black hair and gaberdine raincoat sodden.

'Margie?'

'What's going on, Roger? You haven't answered my calls.'

'Bad time, Margie.' There was an edge of irritation in his voice. 'And bad form. I contact you, not the other way round. You shouldn't be here.'

'I had no choice. I needed to talk.'

'Look, don't you think I've got enough on my plate with all this shit at the Old Bailey? Moffat's going stark raving mad over this and it's my head on the block. The repercussions are shaking Whitehall right up through MI5 to the Cabinet Office. Not to mention Washington.'

'Not my problem, Roger. We did our bit. The Yanks fouled up over Browne and Lomax, not us. And now *Cuchulainn*'s destroyed.'

'Yesterday's problem.'

'So, where's Harry?'

Pinfold paled. In the hurry to clean everything up, the trial going wrong – 'No one's told you?'

'Told me what?' There was something in his tone.

'Harry's dead. Caught in the crossfire when Zack's boys took out Keegan's lot. I'm sorry.'

She felt her heart turn to stone, sitting heavily in her chest, too shocked even to comprehend, let alone grieve. 'You bastard. You're not sorry. You couldn't even be bothered to let me know.'

'No, you're wrong, Margie, I am sorry. But look at it this way. It might be a blessing in disguise. After this trial, questions will be asked and Harry would have proved a liability. He was too involved in everything. I could never have used him again.'

'What?' She really wasn't hearing this.

'So maybe it's better it turned out this way.'

'You mean it saved you getting rid of him.'

He didn't answer that. She stared at him, trying to see something in those cold dark eyes. But all she could see was her own reflection. Turning on her heel, she walked away without another word.

I loved you, Harry. I shagging well loved you, you randy old sod. And now you've gone and died on me. And already Pinfold is happily pissing on your grave. God, she needed a drink. A drink and a packet of salted. She'd share it with him, like they always had. But this time her down here and him up there, shagging the celestials.

The pavements outside the Central Criminal Court were overflowing with onlookers the next morning, the police having had crush barriers put up overnight. Flashlights popped from the press pen as Browne and Lomax alighted from the taxi. They found Monk amid the gathering outside the doors.

'It's a closed session this morning,' he announced. 'No public.'

'It's as well you can't go in,' she said to Lomax. 'In case you get called back to the box; you never know.'

'CHRIS!'

Lomax turned at the sound of the familiar voice. 'Bill! What you doing here?'

Bill Johnson shook hands. 'Came down specially to see the trial, felt I had to after yesterday.' He glanced at Browne. 'You seem to be doing a good job, Sam.'

She looked abashed. 'Thanks. But I'm afraid they won't let you in this morning.'

Johnson nodded. 'Still, maybe I'll see the finish next week. I'd never have believed you could have put up such a convincing fight.'

'So you're on holiday?' Lomax asked.

'No, I've left the job, taken early retirement. After helping you two I kind of lost faith in my work.'

'I've got to fly,' Browne interrupted. 'See you at lunch.'

As she disappeared inside, Monk said: 'If we can't get in, let's go have a fry-up and a natter.' Neither of the other two were going to argue with that.

Inside the courtroom, the large multisectioned screen was flickering into life on one wall, the gnarled and shrunken Walter de Witt with his wispy halo of white hair appearing like the face of a wrathful alien god in some science-fiction movie. It totally dominated the proceedings and added to the electric tension in the air.

Proceedings were delayed as the matron came into shot, plumping the old man's pillows and refilling his glass of morphine milkshake. 'Please don't exhaust him.' Her whispered words were relayed and resounded around the courtroom.

At last the old man was settled, the jury and lawyers hushed in anticipation. The oath was taken, de Witt's voice croaky but strong, despite his obvious breathing difficulty.

'You are Walter de Witt?' Meyrick asked. 'Also known as Walter Grey during your time as a high-ranking officer in the Security Service, MI5?'

'I am.'

'When did you retire, Mr de Witt?'

The faded blue eyes flashed like sun on ice. '1989.'

'I understand that in the early 1970s you had responsibility for important aspects of security in Northern Ireland. With an old friend of yours, Wallace McIlroy?'

The old man cleared his throat. 'Yes. McIlroy had set up a political group called Frontline Ulster and I used this as a front to form a Loyalist resistance movement. It had a secret armed wing called *Cuchulainn* and it was provided with arms caches by the British Government.'

'Can you tell the court why this was done?'

'Cold War,' de Witt rasped, the words echoing loudly. 'Northern Ireland was of supreme strategic importance. The Soviets had large investments in the Republic, a big diplomatic mission in Dublin and a massive fuel facility in Shannon. Do I have to spell it out?'

Meyrick smiled gently. 'Sir, for the court's benefit it would help.'

De Witt took a shallow breath of resignation. 'The Soviets were cosying up to Dublin and the Provisional IRA was wreaking havoc n Ulster. In addition, elements of the rich Irish–American lobby had supplied secret arms caches in the South in case of all-out civil war spreading to both sides of the border. Thankfully, these were not in IRA hands.'

'So politically it was a powder keg?' Meyrick suggested.

De Witt gave a dry cough of a laugh. 'Not as stable as gun-powder. Nitroglycerin would be a more apt description. In view of these uncertainties, *Cuchulainn* was established for the ultimate defence of the Ulster people when London may politically have been unable to help them.'

'Do you feel any sense of shame or regret about having established this?'

There was a fierce light burning in those watery blue eyes on the screen. 'None.'

'Was Rodney Littlechild one of your recruits?'

The light in the huge projected eyes softened, moisture gathering in the corners. 'Yes, I had a lot of time for Roddy. A quiet, reflective lad. I almost regarded him as the son I never had. He became my best agent and a good friend.'

Meyrick waited for de Witt to nod and lift his morphine drink to his parched lips. 'Why did you and other MI5 colleagues seek to gain control of various Loyalist paramilitary groups?'

'We couldn't stop them existing to counter the IRA. But left to their own devices, they'd have slaughtered thousands of innocent Catholics. So we tried to control them, send them in the right direction.'

'You supplied them with the names of known enemies of the state. IRA, INLA, those sorts of people?'

The old man nodded, his eyes unfocused as he remembered. 'I'm afraid it didn't stop all the killing of the innocents. Never could, of course, but it contained it.'

'Surely this was not only unethical, but illegal? Particularly in a democracy.'

That fire was back in the eyes. 'A totally free democracy can never exist. To do so it would have to deny itself the very means that assured its survival. So technically illegal, yes. Unethical, no. Terrorism would have destroyed Northern Ireland twenty years ago had purely legal means been used. The RUC and army were generally the democratic face of the realm's defence. The operations of MI5 and others made it work.'

'Mr de Witt,' Meyrick said with great gravity, 'did you in 1987 sanction arms to be given to a South African hit team to assassinate Dominic Smals?'

'Yes. He was a fund-raiser for the ANC and IRA and was negotiating the smuggling of American Stinger missiles for the Provos. It was expedient to let the assassination go ahead.'

'Who was ordered to supply the weapons used? The defendant?'

'No, Peter Keegan. He was our man in the Ulster Defenders.'

At the bench behind Meyrick, Browne felt the tension ebb from her shoulders. Littlechild's conspiracy-to-murder charge had evaporated in a sentence.

The defence barrister then persuaded de Witt to confirm that Littlechild had proved to be his and MI5's most reliable agent throughout the entire period, culminating in the seizure of South African arms destined for a dangerous Loyalist leader called Rattler.

De Witt also confirmed the defendant's role in liaising with MI5 in the supply of military equipment from America to South Africa via Northern Ireland.

'Wasn't MI5's role breaking an embargo agreed by both Washington and London?' Meyrick asked.

De Witt had begun to look really tired now, his eyelids beginning to droop. He sipped more morphine and steeled himself. His task was nearly done. 'Remember what I said about democracy. Under President Carter the CIA was emasculated. It looked to its friends in London for help. Northern Ireland was virtually a secret state, all the intelligence agencies involved. The ideal conduit to move military material around the world. Apparently destined for a NATO ally, only to be rerouted. South Africa was one such destination.'

'But the embargo?'

'South Africa was of vital strategic interest to NATO. Moreover, it held rare and vital mineral resources only available elsewhere in the Soviet Union. However much apartheid was despised, the overriding priority for Washington and London was the survival of a friendly pro-West government. Besides, the war in southern Africa was seen as the cockpit of the war between East and West. It was why Britain never endorsed sanctions, which many didn't understand.'

'But all that has changed?'

There was a bitter smile on Walter de Witt's wizened face. 'Oh yes. The Soviet threat has gone and its mineral resources are available on the open market. Neither South Africa nor Ulster any longer plays a strategic role. So Washington sees more benefit in wooing the ANC and the pan-Irish nationalist movement in Ireland. By 1989 I could see the writing on the wall as clear as day.'

'Is that the year your MI5 chief ordered you to close down *Cuchulainn*?'

'That began two years earlier after the Anglo-Irish Agreement. It was completed by '89.'

'But in fact you hadn't closed it down, had you?'

His chuckle was dry and the physical pain of the effort showed in his face. 'I was not prepared to betray the Ulster people. I closed down most of the caches, but only after I'd moved many of the arms. Then I sanitised the membership lists, removing the names of my old and trusted friends.'

'How betrayed?' Meyrick asked.

'Appeasing terrorists step by step. Giving something here, something there. Taking the line of least resistance.' Spittle gathered in frothy bubbles at the corners of his mouth. 'Don't they realise the terrorists will just take what's given, then come back – for more!' He broke off into a spluttering cough which doubled him up with pain, then the matron's blue tunic blotted out the screen as she rushed in to assist.

Mr Justice Quigley peered over his pince-nez at the prosecution bench. 'You will wish to cross-examine?'

An ashen-faced Halifax looked towards Ian Spinks and the troubled CPS solicitor slowly shook his head.

'Then the court shall adjourn until after lunch,' the judge said, 'when the prosecution may begin its final address.'

As soon as Mr Justice Quigley had disappeared through his door, pandemonium broke out in the courtroom. The defence team burst into enthusiastic chatter and the prosecution benches and jury became alive with heated debate as everyone began filing out.

Browne lingered, looking up at the huge screen and the close-up of the face. His eyes were closed and he appeared

573

remarkably serene. At peace with himself, she thought, his life's work done. She leaned towards the microphone Meyrick had used. 'Thank you, Walter,' she whispered.

His eyes didn't open, but his lips moved almost imperceptibly and she only just caught the croaked murmur of reply: 'My pleasure, rosebud, my pleasure.'

The screen flickered into blankness as the video link went down.

It was twenty minutes before she escaped the waiting crowd of reporters outside and found Lomax and the others in the Magpie and Stump. They'd already heard news of what de Witt had said and it had clearly added an unneeded sense of euphoria to their shared state of inebriation.

'Dad's pissed,' Manda complained, offering Browne a bottle of mineral water.

'Don't be too hard on him, he deserves something to celebrate.' She took a sip. 'He knows it can still go either way.'

But Manda was distracted, thinking deeply. 'Dad and Joe have come up with this really stupid idea with Bill Johnson. And they sound serious, Sam.'

'Oh, what's that?'

'To start a private investigation agency. It's so ridiculous. Can you believe that?'

A smile slowly curled Browne's lips and an amused light danced in her eyes. 'Do you know, Manda, I really think I can.'

It was a female voice. 'Miss Browne?'

Sam Browne turned, feeling unaccountably unnerved. The woman was dressed in a gaberdine raincoat, her black hair in need of a brush. Tiredness detracted from the attractiveness of her looks. 'Don't I know you from somewhere?'

'I once made you get in the boot of a car.' As Browne's jaw dropped, the woman said quickly: 'Can we talk?'

Browne was surprised that Henry Halifax put up no objection to the appearance of yet another unexpected witness. In fact, he looked towards her and gave a sheepish smile and a gentle nod of approval. Even Henry was realising now that he'd been duped; Ian Spinks averted his eyes, looking suitably embarrassed.

'You are Marjorie Helen Lewis,' Ronnie Rock said. 'A private investigator and former employee of the Security Service, MI5. On the night of Donny Fitzpatrick's murder last August, where were you?'

She took a deep breath, her eyes half closed, as though she were deciding to step over the edge of a cliff. 'I was in the safe house at Bascombe Court with my boss Harry Grisewold.'

'Another former MI5 operator?'

'Yes. We're often hired for irregular work by the Service. Roger Pinfold – also known as Prendergast – asked us to be on standby. At about ten thirty we were radioed to follow Fitzpatrick to the King's Head public house and wait outside for the arrival of Rodney Littlechild. If he'd turned up we'd have entered the pub and arranged to pick up a glass he'd used in order to get a set of fingerprints.'

'But Littlechild changed the venue?'

She nodded. 'That wasn't unexpected – good fieldcraft. So we followed them to the Mortar and Pestle and did the job there.'

'What happened next?'

'Fitzpatrick returned to his flat and then we went in with Roger Pinfold. He introduced us to Fitzpatrick as a relief minder team then left. A few minutes later there was a ring at the door . . .'

Ronnie Rock interrupted. 'Was it bullet-proofed?'

'At that time, yes, they always are. Anyway, Harry opened it and brought this man into the living room. Fitzpatrick was completely unsuspecting. The man pulled out a silenced gun and shot Fitzpatrick on the sofa at point-blank range. Then he left.'

'Did you know this was going to happen?'

'No. I was a bit shaken, but then I'm used to dirty ops.'

'Did you know the killer?'

'Not then. Later Harry told me he was an East End hit man called Pixie Dean. Harry had paid him cash, half up front. Pixie took the Eurostar to France and went into hiding at some remote country house rented by Harry.'

'And a couple of weeks later, Harry Grisewold went to pay Pixie the second half?'

'Not exactly. Harry shot him and fed him to pigs kept at the house. Eat anything, pigs. The skull was smashed, burnt and the remains scattered.'

Someone in the jury threw up noisily. Ronnie Rock waited for silence before asking: 'Do you know who ordered Harry Grisewold to arrange this assassination?'

Before Halifax or the judge could intervene to stop the hearsay answer, Margie Lewis said quickly: 'Oh yes.' Hatred glittered in her dark eyes. 'Roger Pinfold.'

At that moment the case against Rodney Littlechild collapsed.

Albie Nairn heard the newsflash on the transistor radio as he worked on the restoration of an aged Wolsey saloon in the wooden shed beside his bungalow. Rodney Littlechild freed! Such wonderful news, worthy of a celebration, which was good because there hadn't been much to celebrate in the past few days.

There was a sound bite from the husky-voiced lawyer Sam Browne and hearing her words took him back to her unexpected arrival at the farm in Eire with Lomax. So much had happened since then. He and Spike Scott had known something was wrong when the *Cuchulainn* helicopter had not returned. The disastrous outcome had been confirmed on the early morning news and the two of them had left the farm immediately, travelling by car across the border.

His wife had known better than to ask him where he'd been and the next day an RUC detective called to ask him why his car had been found abandoned outside the late King Billy's caravan. He made a statement saying he'd been visiting when unknown gunmen had attacked. Terrified, he had run away and gone into hiding with friends. The detective was clearly sceptical, but then it was known from witnesses that Nairn wasn't responsible for the killing. His statement would just gather dust in some filing cabinet; no one in the RUC was going to shed a tear for the end of King Billy's reign.

Nairn turned off the radio, took the lead from behind the door and whistled for his dog. Toby bounded in and the two of them set out into the fields, passing the outhouse where the vast arms cache lay. All bolted and sealed again. The genie back in its bottle – for now.

Rattler back to his old life, always on the gallop, scuttling from one hideaway to another in the province. Spike electioneering and Susie Ferguson grieving for her few weeks of happiness after so many years of waiting.

He looked out over his neighbour's pastureland and wondered if he'd ever get the call again. He doubted it. Wondered if they'd ever find another leader like Keegan, another Hound of Ulster to take his place when they faced their darkest hour.

Littlechild swooped Browne into his arms and lifted her off her feet, whirling her around three times as the crowded court dispersed. Totty, Meyrick and Rock looked on with wide grins at the sudden and welcome transformation in the quiet Ulsterman.

'I never thought you'd pull it off, Sam, really I didn't.'

'Put me down this instant, you'll ruin my reputation,' she laughed as she landed and quickly smoothed down her rucked skirt. 'Anyway, you ought to thank Chris as much as me.'

'Where is he?'

'Gone to phone Evie with the news. Now come on and let's get this over with. Don't talk to the press; I'll read them a short statement. If you want it, I've an exclusive deal ready with the *Mail* and a TV documentary with Lisa Hardcastle.'

Lomax rejoined them in the corridor, hugged his old friend and gave Browne a congratulatory kiss. 'I told Evie to jump in a cab with the baby and get straight down here. She says Noel can't wait to crack a pint of warm milk with his old da. She's over the moon.'

A melee of media reporters was gathered outside the entrance, with flashlights blinking and microphones thrust towards them as Browne put on her reading specs and made the short announcement.

When she finished speaking and the reporters began dispersing to file their stories, she heard a voice behind her. 'Make the most of your moment of glory, Miss Browne.' She turned, startled. It was Roger Pinfold. 'I assure you it won't last. I'll make certain of that.'

Her eyes narrowed, but when she started to speak, he turned away. As he did so, she saw the tall, dark-haired detective step briskly in front of him. Chief Inspector Millman said: 'Mr Prendergast, I wonder if you would mind accompanying DS Henwick and me to Paddington Green. There're a few questions I'd like to ask.'

Pinfold shrugged and smiled coldly. 'Sure. Only to be expected.'

Millman left him standing with his sergeant and walked back to Browne. 'I'm afraid I owe you an apology, ma'am. You asked me once if I had doubts. I should have done. I've been used and it's not a nice feeling.'

She smiled. 'Thanks for the good grace to admit it.' She indicated Pinfold. 'It's good to see that justice is going to be done. He's responsible for at least three deaths.'

Millman sniffed. 'Don't fool yourself, Miss Browne. I intend giving him a hard time, but nothing will stick. Within a few hours I'll get a call from the Commissioner telling me to drop it. Word from on high. Sorry, but that's the way it is. Pinfold will walk.'

Browne looked aghast and glanced at Lomax. He shrugged. 'Some people are untouchable, Sam.'

She looked around and saw the press photographer fiddling with his camera. 'Have you got film in that?' she demanded.

He looked bewildered. 'Er – yes.'

'Well, here's your front-page picture for tomorrow.' She turned back to Millman. 'MI5 people need anonymity to do the job, right?'

She didn't wait for a reply, but spun on her heel and strode across to where Pinfold stood waiting beside DS Henwick.

Lomax frowned. What the hell was she playing at? It came so

fast he almost missed it as she threw back her right shoulder and elbow, then lunged. Her balled fist sped foward, a blur as her elbow snapped in to straighten her arm. The impact caught Pinfold square in the centre of his face. Lomax winced. Browne yelped at the pain in her knuckles. And Pinfold's legs gave way.

The flashlight popped, again and again on motor drive as the man fell writhing to the pavement, blood streaming from his broken nose. He glared up at her and spat out a piece of broken front tooth as Henwick rushed to help him to his feet.

Lomax and Littlechild burst out laughing and even Millman smiled. 'You going to arrest me, Chief Inspector?' Browne asked.

The detective could hardly keep a straight face. 'Do you want to press charges, Mr Pinfold?'

But there was no answer as Henwick led him away.

'Did you say Pinfold?' the photographer asked.

'Roger Pinfold,' Browne said. 'You'll have no trouble selling his picture.'

Lomax dragged her away and the defence team began walking across the road to the Magpie and Stump where Tristram Meyrick and Ronnie Rock were already setting up the first round of celebration drinks.

'God,' she said, nursing her hand, 'I think I've broken a bone. But, oh boy, was it worth it just to see the look on his face!'

'I love you when you're angry,' Lomax laughed.

She smiled. 'Which seems to be most of the time.'

'Just as well then.' And they both knew what he meant.

They barely noticed the busker outside the pub as they passed, sitting with his guitar and up-turned hat. Only Rodney Littlechild paused for a moment, listening to the haunting melody as the young man sang.

'Red is the colour of anger – And black is the colour of hate . . .'

Terence Strong's latest thriller, *Deadwater Deep*, is also available in Arrow. Read the first explosive chapter overleaf . . .

Prologue

The sonar operator's hunched shoulders stiffened suddenly.

'I've got somethin'.' Thumb and forefinger played deftly with the tuning dial. 'Yeah. Faint, but definitely somethin'.'

His laconic Tennessee drawl belied the surge of adrenalin he felt; this was not a man to break sweat easily.

The officer of the watch moved through the air-conditioned red twilight of the ops centre, deep in the bowels of the anti-submarine frigate *USS Knox* and peered at the console display. 'You sure, Crosby?'

'Only that it's *somethin'*, Sir.'

Crosby was good. Crosby had bat's ears, they all knew that. But even Crosby could be wrong. They were running on *USS Knox's* ED passive towed-array sonar, because the target was one hell of a mother. Her state-of-the-art stealth hull would simply absorb active sonar signals pinging out of the bow-mounted Western General Electric rig and give nothing away. So they were reduced to passive listening. Because, however dampened, you could never fully eliminate engine noise and, however slick the design, you could never stop water rushing over a submarine's bow.

USS Knox had only a bearing. You needed at least three bearings from separate ships to get a fix. And so far, they only had the one.

The officer of the watch made his decision, silently vowing to give Crosby a bad time he'd never forget if he'd screwed up on this one. 'Bearing?' he snapped.

'Oh-eight-five degrees, Sir,' Crosby snapped back.

'Get the wax out of your ears – track and report.'

'Sir.'

The officer turned to the communications suite. Time to stick his neck out, and pray he wouldn't be left with more egg on his face than on his cap. 'Signal Commander 7th Fleet. Unconfirmed contact, our bearing oh-eight-five.'

Forty-five seconds later Vice-Admiral Ross Harding was handed the message aboard the *USS Theodore Roosevelt*. Wearing tropical whites, he sat in a bridge high chair, which gave him a perfect view of the carrier's floodlit flight-deck below.

His was the appearance and build of a man who had not been born in the normal way, but hewn fully-grown out of limestone. Flinty eyes scrutinised the piece of paper in his huge fist.

After reading the signal, Harding took time to relight the well-chewed cigar butt before acknowledging the anxious faces of the small group of VIP visitors to the exercise. A bunch of grey suits. Politicians and spooks, he wasn't sure which he detested most. And he had them all here on the carrier's bridge, in equal measure. In Harding's strictly private view, each was as over-confident in his abilities and was untrustworthy as the next.

The Honorable Hal Katz, Deputy Assistant Secretary of Defense for Special Operations was one and Hank Aspen, CIA, Assistant Deputy Director of Operations, another. Both, he knew of old, had the smooth charm and all the backbone of a rattlesnake. Katz wouldn't agree to anything that meant he might have to explain away in bodybags, while Hank Aspen didn't mind any number of them as long as no one could pin the blame directly on him.

Obviously the vice-admiral wasn't familiar with his British visitors from across the pond, but he doubted they were much better. Their spook was Piers Lansdowne, a thirty something highflyer with a schoolboy's face and a pronounced Adam's apple. The trendy foppish cut of his blond hair and round-rimmed swot's spectacles were an anathema to Harding. But he had to admit the boy's mind seemed as sharp as the broken shards of his cut-glass accent. That told Harding everything: privileged background, English public school and now Far East Desk of the Foreign Office.

At least that was the fiction that the British junior defence minister insisted on maintaining.

But then Frank Hudd was new to high echelons of his government, the Armed Forces in general, and ships in particular. Even as Harding had received the signal from *USS Knox*, Frank Hudd was throwing up his guts into a plastic bucket out on the flying bridge. The sea was millpond calm.

Harding didn't bother hiding his irritation as he addressed Piers Lansdowne. 'You wanna see if your Minister is well enough to join us yet? I don't wanna go over all this again.'

Lansdowne had the grace to blush. 'I'll check on him, Admiral.'

The American grey suits and Harding shared expressions of silent exasperation: the entire US war machine held up for a bucket of British puke.

Moments later Lansdowne reappeared, helping Frank Hudd as he stumbled through the hatchway.

'Feeling better?' Hal Katz asked brusquely.

Hudd's watering eyes, set in a meaty bloodhound face, couldn't disguise the embarrassment he felt for displaying such feebleness before these men of iron. He smiled weakly, 'Thanks. Better out than in, eh?'

That drew no response, so he tried to look business-like, straightening his back and hiking up his crumpled off-the-peg suit to cover his beer belly. 'Piers says something's happened?'

Vice Admiral Harding nodded. 'One of our destroyers picked up an unconfirmed passive sonar contact two minutes ago.' He strode across to the wall chart that showed the small island off Saipan. The surrounding area of the Pacific showed the island ringed by ships of the Carrier Task Force. Harding jabbed a finger at one of these. FFT. '*Knox* puts the contact bearing at oh-eight-five. That's a bearing but no fix. Any number of miles along that trajectory. So it could still be outside *or* inside our protective ring.'

Frank Hudd looked concerned. 'Surely that couldn't be *Manta*. All this stealth technology stuff, it's supposed to be foolproof.'

'That's what we're here to find out, Frank,' Hall Katz reminded patiently. 'To see if it's all the boffins crack it up to be –'

Vice Admiral Harding cut in: 'We're ordering up three Sea Kings – they're anti-submarine helicopters with dunking sonars. We'll attempt to get a confirmation and triangulated fix on the contact.' Behind him, through the bridge windscreen, the three sea-grey shapes could be seen lifting off into the clear night sky. 'Now we're finally all together, let me bring you up to speed.'

He tapped again on the map of the island. 'Tim-wan is an island some two miles in diameter. It is deserted except for a small detachment of electronic engineers and US marines who maintain and guard a small listening-station. The destruction of its antennae is the ultimate objective to this technological exercise.

'The exercise is to evaluate the technical abilities of an experimental submarine and the efficiency of the crew and on-board assault team which combine to make up Project Deadwater.

'As you will be aware, the sub began development in Britain as a joint private and Royal Navy venture in the last few years of the Cold War. Under the designation SCUBA – Secure Clandestine Underwater Basing Apparatus – the sub employs state-of-the-art stealth technology to allow it to operate close to shore in enemy waters and remain undetected. Its function is to provide an operational base for clandestine activity – from the launch of commando raids to supporting agent networks – for up to a month's duration.'

Frank Hudd still felt queasy, but forced his mind to concentrate. 'Er, Admiral, since Project Deadwater became a joint British-American development after our Options for Change cutbacks at the end of the Cold War, we've had little detail of progress. What we have had, I'm afraid, is pretty incomprehensible.'

Hal Katz frowned. 'You have a Royal Navy liaison officer assigned?'

Hudd smiled sheepishly. 'Oh yes. I'm afraid it's me who's the problem. I used to be a coal miner. Don't know one end of a gun from the other.'

'New Labour,' Piers explained kindly.

'All that technical jargon is gobbledegook to me,' the British defence minister added. 'And I've had no sight of naval architects' plans, or even a snap.'

'Snap?' Vice Admiral Harding queried.

'Snapshot, photograph. I've begun to wonder if Britain *really* still owns the half it pays for.'

The CIA man, Hank Aspen, spoke in his usual flat and deadly serious tone. 'That's down to my department, Minister, we tend to be a little over-zealous on the secrecy front. Especially where new technology's concerned.'

'But we do have an artist's impression here,' Katz added. 'Don't we, Admiral.'

'Sure do,' Harding moved to the flip chart next to the map and threw back the cover.

'This is the *Manta*,' Hank Aspen said. 'And I hope this is something no one outside naval operations will *ever* see.'

Hudd fumbled for his spectacles and, as he focused on the drawing, his mouth dropped. It was like no submarine he had ever seen before. His first impression was of a sort of black underwater flying-saucer. But rather than being perfectly symmetrical, it was a teardrop-shape which tapered towards the stern. And he could see now where the name had come from. The wide stabilising 'wings' running the full length of each side of the craft gave it an uncanny resemblance to a manta ray. There was no conning-tower, or 'fin' as Lansdowne had taught him to call it, just a four feet smooth hump amidships from which twin masts protruded.

'The hull shape's been streamlined considerably since the original conception,' Aspen explained. 'She may look like something out of *Star Wars*, but inside she's still a one sixty tonne cigar tube carrying a four man crew and sixteen combat swimmers.' He grinned. 'Maybe a few more if they all breathe in. As you see, the outer is covered with sonar-absorbent panels. In layman's terms, they prevent any hostile sonar signals pinging back to give away the sub's location.' He pointed to the X-configured rudder and hydroplane control fins at the stern. 'Has fly-by-wire ailerons, so it operates more like an aircraft than a conventional sub. Plus port and starboard thrusters, so she can turn in her own length. GPS navigation and communications via satellite. All run by computer, of course.'

The junior British defence minister was lost. 'Of course.'

'Silicon Valley's best,' Aspen continued proudly. 'But when it comes to putting an assault team ashore, we embrace *appropriate* technology. High tech stealth sub, but the men go ashore by good old tried and tested means as required.'

'Quite incredible,' Hudd murmured.

'It will need to be,' Piers Lansdowne observed, 'if the project is to fulfil the role we have in mind.'

Vice-Admiral Harding's face remained inscrutable, only the fractional narrowing of his eyes indicating that his analytical mind was humming like a computer. Piecing together fragments of knowledge, linking them with threads of logic. Specialist submarine, special forces, intelligence experts on China, joint-American-British interests . . .

But when he spoke there was no curiosity in his voice. It was typically matter-of-fact. 'Whatever you have in mind, gentlemen, this exercise should tell you whether the sub and the Project Deadwater team is up to it.

'We have the island of Tim-Wan surrounded by a ring of ships from the 7th Fleet, deploying the most efficient anti-submarine technology in the world, including ASW aircraft from our Rota base. *Manta* will have to penetrate that ring undetected, their assault team destroy the dummy aerial, return to the mother ship and escape the ring of ships again –'

Hudd was enthralled, not conscious that he was chewing his thumbnail. 'And do *you* think they can do it, Admiral?'

Harding's back stiffened. 'A personal view, Minister?'

'Of course.'

'Not a snowballs –' He ignored Hank Aspen's withering glare. 'Looks like *Knox* is already on to them.'

The signals officer approached the vice-admiral. 'Sorry, sir. *Knox* reports it's lost the contact.'

'Thank you.' Harding did not bother hiding his annoyance. Fleet reputation was on the line here. 'When are our AS helos due on station?' he checked with the carrier's captain.

'A couple of minutes, Admiral.'

'Then it won't have gone far. I've every confidence.'

But Harding's confidence was apparently misplaced. After fifteen minutes of hovering while they lowered their sonar buoys into the water, the flight commander reported negative to contact.

Hudd felt a small rush of pride. After all, the initial concept of the SCUBA had been British, even if the Yanks had tinkered with it. 'If it's slipped through the net, Admiral, when might we expect them to reach the target?'

'At least another hour.' Harding indicated the CCTV monitor installed above the control console. It showed a hazy green monochrome picture of a patch of land and the base of the dummy radio mast on Tim-wan. 'That's being relayed direct from the target. Low-level light camera, so we'll be able to see when the assault team get there.'

'*If*,' reminded Hal Katz. 'And there are a dozen Marines on patrol.'

'Maybe it's time to take a break instead of hangin' round waiting for nothing to happen,' Hank Aspen suggested.

'The wardroom's at your disposal,' Harding said.

Hudd looked relieved. 'I could do with a stiff drink. Might settle the old tum.'

Harding gave the British minister a curious look as he showed the way.

Piers Lansdowne explained quietly. 'Sorry, Frank. It's a dry Navy.'

'Oh, God, I was forgetting.'

'No problem.' He held something concealed in his hand. 'Take this.'

'What is it?'

'My hip flask.'

Coke, Fanta and coffee were on offer in the wardroom and a range of snacks was spread on the gleaming table.

'A pot of tea would be nice.'

The steward smiled stiffly, sure he would find an old box of teabags hidden *somewhere* in the galley.

They had barely settled in their seats when the officer of the watch put his head around the door. 'Admiral Harding, Sir, message from the captain. Thought you'd want to know, one of the Hawkeyes has picked up a naval vessel fifteen miles to the north. Been identified as destroyer *Luhu*.'

Harding's left eyebrow lifted a fraction. 'Makin' this way?'

'No, Sir,' the officer replied. 'She's moved in to get an eyeball on *Knox* and is remaining on station. *Luhu*'s put up two Harbin helos to see what's going on, but her stance is non-aggressive.'

'And what's our counter-action?'

The officer smiled tightly. 'Two F18s are buzzing the helos to warn them off, and we've signalled *Luhu* this is a private party, invitation only.'

Harding nodded. 'Keep me posted. We don't want an international incident by accident.'

'Sir.'

As the officer withdrew, Hudd looked across the table at vice-Admiral Harding. 'What does all that mean?'

Harding offered one of his rare bleak smiles. 'It means the Chinese Navy is monitoring the exercise and it's playing a long way from home.'

'It's what we in the CIA have been warning,' Hank Aspen added darkly. 'We've had evidence for a long time that China has serious territorial ambitions. It's the only major power in the world that doesn't accept the geographical status quo and it's got major territorial disputes with all its neighbours. That's why Beijing is determined to project its influence with a modern blue water navy.'

Hal Katz swallowed the remains of his first sandwich. 'I've seen those reports, Hank. The assessment is it'll be at least fifteen years before the Chinese have an operational navy good enough to allow them to cause real trouble. And, anyway, that assumes causing trouble would be *in* their interest. To my mind they're too far down the capitalist road for that.'

'Sorry, Sir,' Admiral Harding interrupted, 'but that's not what I'm seeing. Since the French sold them the old *Clemenceau* carrier, they've been flexing their muscles. Two years ago you'd never have seen *Luhu* out here, nearly two thousand miles off-shore and aggressively poking its nose into an American exercise.'

Katz shrugged dismissively but Piers Lansdowne, from the British Foreign Office, added: 'Things have changed since the Hong Kong handover. It restored national pride and went to the heads of the leadership. Since President Deng Xiaoping's death, there's been an ongoing power-struggle and at the moment the hard men are holding sway. Two hundred years ago China was the most powerful nation on earth, and now they see the economic miracle as the key to restoring them to their former position in the world.'

'Nothing wrong in that,' Katz said defensively. 'Every nation has its aspirations.'

'Nothing wrong,' the admiral agreed, 'as long as we in the West don't help them there by selling them all our latest weapons technology.'

'That's not how State or the White House sees it,' Katz snapped back. 'They see it as the greatest investment opportunity for America that the world will ever see. A fifth of mankind and the second largest economy on earth.'

Admiral Harding did not respond. No point in reminding the senator that far from being a great market opportunity, China had actually become the largest source of trade deficit to both the USA and Europe. He just wouldn't listen, because the President wouldn't listen and Hal Katz was the President's man. If the President said jump, he'd ask how high. So Harding would save his breath to cool his porridge. Besides, as the old saying went, it wasn't his job to ask how or why.

The boy Lansdowne accepted a coffee cup from the steward, little finger crooked like the well-brought up kid he obviously was. 'Have you noticed how the slogans have changed?' he asked absently, his cultured English accent sounding oddly out of place.

'What?' Katz asked, bewildered.

A politely patronising English smile. 'If you read the Chinese newspapers, you'll notice the old 'To Get Rich is Glorious' slogans have gone. No more stories of businessmen successfully risking all to turn round ailing factories. The new slogans are full of reference to hostile forces abroad. Accusing them of using economics to democratise China in order to divide and control it.'

Hal Katz looked blank. 'I don't read Chinese.'

Piers Lansdowne sipped delicately at his coffee. 'Perhaps you should learn, Sir.'

Frank Hudd nearly choked on his tea. Beautiful! A stiletto straight between the shoulder blades. Young Piers was everything the ex-Nottingham miner thought he hated about the old establishment right-wing, but he'd warmed to the young man quickly during the long flight out from

Heathrow in the civilian airliner. He wasn't in the least bit patronising as the newly-appointed minister struggled to absorb the complexities of the briefing. Piers was friendly and witty, explaining that the main obstacle of their secret mission was the President of the United States himself.

Hudd noticed that, across the table, Admiral Harding and Hank Aspen of the CIA were looking at Piers Lansdowne with undisguised admiration. Then Hudd's eyes met theirs and the Americans' expression said it all. The boy from the British Secret Intelligence Service – sorry, Foreign Office – had put into words exactly what they thought.

For the first time since being flown aboard the carrier *USS Theodore Roosevelt*, Frank Hudd felt that he was among allies, if not yet friends.

An hour later, they returned to the bridge. Hudd was feeling much better, fortified by the tea he had surreptitiously laced with whisky from Piers' flask.

The carrier's captain informed them that nothing had happened during their absence. It was good from one point of view, thought Hudd. The stealth submarine was *still* undetected. But, as he could see from the CCTV monitor, there wasn't much point in that if the mission itself was unaccomplished. And no sign of life had yet been seen at the island aerial site so far.

Meanwhile the Chinese destroyer *Luhu* remained watching and listening on station, its helicopters now returned to the aft deck to refuel.

When thirty minutes had passed, Admiral Harding cleared his throat. 'Well, gentlemen, I have to tell you that it looks as though we are faced with mission failure. The US Marine detachment report no sign of activity on Tim-Wan and *Manta* has only thirty minutes left to return undetected to the outside of the cordon.'

'But the sub hasn't been found . . .' Hudd began.

Harding couldn't conceal his disappointment. 'That is

true, Minister, and I'm sorry my boys haven't located it yet. That may be because of some technical failure. If the sub is lying doggo on the bottom, it would explain why the AS sonars haven't picked her up.'

'And why they haven't reached their target,' Hank Aspen added.

Concern clouded Hudd's face. 'They're not in any danger, are they?'

'Highly unlikely,' Harding replied. 'In about thirty minutes they'll make themselves known to us, wherever they are.'

Hal Katz said: 'I expect it's the new computer software. They've been having trouble with that.'

'You're probably right.'

Hudd felt suddenly depressed. It just underlined what the military sceptics back at the Ministry of Defence in London had told him. The concept was fatally flawed. And if it was, so was the entire mission that Piers Lansdowne and Hank Aspen had set themselves. To set free the largest nation on earth. A thousand million people.

Piers sensed his disappointment, and placed a reassuring hand on his shoulder.

'Sir!' It was the communications officer. 'Signal from *Knox* again. Contact bearing oh-eight-one.'

'Inside the cordon,' Piers advised instantly.

Shit, Hudd mouthed.

'Picked up on active this time,' the officer added. 'Strong signal and they have a fix.' He rattled off the reference. It was barely a mile off *Theodore Roosevelt's* bow.

'Odd,' Harding thought aloud as the CTFC scrambled the anti-submarine Sea Kings again. 'Active sonar's usually hopeless against *Manta*.'

Hank Aspen from Langley said: 'Maybe she's lost some of her panels. That happened in earlier trials.'

'The panels absorb sonar signals,' Piers explained to Hudd. 'If some panels are lost, then an active sonar signal will hit the bare surface and bounce back to give a contact and approximate position.'

'So what happens next?'

Harding answered. 'We're dropping dummy depth-charges. If they go off close enough, *Manta* will surface. That will represent a kill or SD. Severe damage.' He turned towards the bridge windscreen and vast flight deck beyond, crammed with rows of naval fighters. 'If you look off our starboard bow, you should be able to watch the floorshow.'

The group craned forward to watch the helicopters speed across the sluggish swell of the Pacific, the surface glistening like hammered silver under the full moon.

Suddenly the bridge was filled with the squawk and static hiss and rapid radiospeak of radio traffic as the pilots assessed and confirmed their positions above the submarine.

'*Fired one, fired two*,' intoned the first helicopter.

He was joined by the second, forming a pattern. '*Fired one, fired two.*'

Hudd saw the dark shape of the charges falling like bird-shit from the helicopter pods. He held his breath, expecting an almighty roar and the great geyser of displaced water he'd seen on war movies.

Stupid, of course, because these were only dummies. So the small fountains of spray were a bit of a disappointment and they couldn't even hear the detonations at that distance.

A tense silence followed, Hudd aware of his heart's slow and steady thud from somewhere deep within his crumpled shirt.

'*We got somethin'*,' broke in one of the helicopter pilots, followed by a hiss and crackle. '*Standby, standby. Contact about to surface.*'

Hudd's spirits sank and he tuned to Piers in search of consolation, but the eyes behind the glasses were fixed and concentrated, showing no emotion. A cold fish and no mistake.

Off the starboard bow, where the Sea Kings circled like vultures waiting to feast on their prey, the sea began to ferment and bubble. Suddenly the frothing surface was illuminated by two fierce blades of light from the Nitesun lamps.

On the carrier's bridge, each VIP leaned forward hoping for a clearer view and their first sight of the mysterious craft. Hudd tried to focus the binoculars with which he'd been issued.

'Holy cow,' Aspen murmured. The slippery grey, blue hull was breaking through the cauldron of disturbed water.

'What the hell . . . ?' Hudd began.

'*Negative, negative,*' crackled the nearest pilot. '*False contact. Repeat false contact. Anyone fancy a fish-supper?*'

'A bloody sperm whale,' Vice-Admiral Harding growled.

Hudd breathed again, looking at Piers and this time seeing the big wide grin that made him look more like a schoolboy than ever.

'Sir, Sir!' It was one of the duty watch officers who constantly scanned from the carrier with night-vision aids. 'Unidentified contact bearing one-eight-one. Repeat one-eight-one.'

'What?' Hudd was totally bewildered.

'Aft,' Piers translated. 'Behind us.'

Outside the cordon, Hudd told himself, as Harding led the group across the bridge for a better view over the aft end.

Scarcely a half-mile off the stern a white froth was forming on the blue-black surface of the ocean swells. Piers helped his minister focus the binoculars.

It was bizarre, like something out of science fiction. The strangely globular monster rose from the deep, seawater spilling from her sides.

'USS *Manta,*' Aspen murmured in awe.

Then, barely without hesitation, it began gliding into the night. A fine wall of spray burst from the water jets around the hull's winged edge. They created an envelope of wet mist that broke up the craft's shape and merged it into the surrounding sea. Even as Hudd watched, it melted away before his eyes like an illusionist's trick.

'Cocky bastards,' the admiral growled, but there was no mistaking the admiration in his voice.

The Honorable Hal Katz grunted. 'They've no grounds for being cocky. They failed to reach the . . .'

The end of his sentence was drowned out in the noise of the explosion relayed from the island over the loudspeaker. Everyone turned as the TV monitor pulsed momentarily with white light. As the picture settled and the smoke cleared, they could all see the collapsed wreckage of the dummy mast and bewildered US Marines running in all directions.

'They can't have done,' murmured the officer charged with watching the monitor. 'I didn't see a thing.'

'We'll re-run the tapes later,' Harding said dismissively. 'See if we can spot when they planted the delayed charge.'

But Frank Hudd was no longer listening. They'd done it and that was all that mattered. A British concept backed with Yank know-how had managed to defeat the technology of the world's finest anti-submarine force. Then put a joint assault group of American SEALs and British Special Boat Service troops ashore, succeeding in planting the explosives even while being watched by CCTV cameras.

And they said it would never work. Well it had. And now Frank Hudd, ex-Nottingham miner and one-time CND protester, was going to claim his place in history. Ironically by freeing a fifth of humanity still yoked and shackled by the political philosophy he had once himself espoused.

Out there, unseen and silent, the Chinese frigate *Luhu* rose and fell gently between the long Pacific swells.

OTHER TITLES AVAILABLE